SABER'S GUARD

SABER'S GUARD

LAURA NAPOLI

Saber's Guard

CONTENTS

As promised, this book is dedicated to my aunt, one of my biggest champions. Thank you for all of your support, encouragement, and feedback. And, in case you're wondering, no, I still have no shame.

I know you were only teasing following the read-through of that first iteration, but it does bring up a topic that we, as a society, should discuss. Shame implies that I'm writing something wrong, something problematic, but what is right and wrong changes daily, even in the same society. Relationships that were taboo a few decades ago are normal now, and what is normal now will inevitably change tomorrow.

To the reader, Science Fiction has always pushed the boundaries of society and norms. It is inherently political. What is unacceptable in our society can be safely explored as part of another. I expect many will find issues with the relationships forming in this book because they believe differently than I do. What was important to me was to show happy, healthy, consenting individuals in loving and supportive relationships. May you all be so lucky and happy in yours.

There will come a day when another bears my name, long after most of us have forgotten the horrors of war. Thee will know it is her because she will do what no other has done before.

Protect her as best ye can, but do not test her or bring her into the guard until thee are sure she has transitioned on her own, or she asks thee for thy help. Thy oath is to thy people and she is the only one who can save them from the horrors to come.

Her journey will not be easy but it is necessary if she is to see as I do. In all things follow her lead. If you are not sure of the path to take, do as she would do, and always honor thy oath.

GENERAL MARSEE EZABET CHENZIRA

CHAPTER 1

Kendra: Challenged

Tail lashing behind her, Senior Honor Guard Kendra Hunt slammed open the doors of her guard station and scowled at the nearly empty room she found. Instead of her nephew and the squad of guards that should have been there, only a single guard remained to monitor the bank of feeds.

"Where is that fur-brained, incompetent nephew of mine?" she hissed. If he wasn't already dead, she was one whisker's width away from killing him.

Gretta startled slightly at her arrival but put Avery's position on the main monitor. "Trauma Center. East Wing, Level Four." Avery's dot highlighted in blue, while several squads lit up yellow around him, scattered throughout the Trauma Center. "The Seniors were worried that someone might try to take advantage of the prisoner transfer to...get rid of evidence. Marsee's watch is running dark. Senior's orders. You'll have to get the security codes from one of them. Avery doesn't even have them."

She smoothed her fur, realizing Avery hadn't abandoned his post or, worse, slept during a high-risk prisoner transfer, but her calm only lasted a moment as the feed switched to a view of Senior Councilor Surellis's balcony.

"Aris called in an alert about half an hour ago," Gretta explained before she could ask. "Surellis witnessed Marsee swipe at her mother upon waking. Then Marsee made the mistake of stating that she didn't feel it was safe for Little Flower to sleep with her anymore. The rest of the night watch left to provide backup. Nothing happened in the Trauma center, but Surellis has been pacing on his balcony since escorting the others back to their rooms."

That's not like him at all, she thought. "Pull up the recording. I want to see what happened." She scowled as she watched. There was nothing on the feed but a brief startle and frown during the initial swipe before Surellis locked his expression behind his mask, which meant Aris had alerted based on a waiver of his soul boundary and scent.

Even without her senses, there was no doubt in her mind that he would have put Marsee down if there had been any chance of making it to her side. If the entire night watch was still on him, then there was a very high chance he was on the verge of losing control, but it was the sight of Marsee in a muzzle that made her growl. She'd seen far too many children muzzled in her day, and she'd hoped, with the advent of sign language, even though she knew it was wishful thinking, never to see it again.

Her low growl was cut short by a snort of astonishment when Little Flower ordered everyone out. "I see she hasn't lost any of her audacity."

"She is fierce for one so small, but then that does appear to be a common trait among the Earth creatures." Gretta's tail curled slightly with amusement. "In case you're wondering. The current score is one to five, with George and Matilda in the lead. Quinn can't even get within sight of the Barn anymore without the whole flock making a racket loud enough to wake the entire compound."

She growled, not in the least bit amused by the reminder of her Second's failure to escape the flock of tiny cobra chickens unharmed. Between that and Avery's dereliction of duty, her reputation, along with the reputation of her entire guard, was severely tarnished. Her growling only increased the humor she sensed from Gretta. "Inform me if Surellis leaves his suite."

"Yes, ma'am," Gretta replied, tail spiraling now.

"And straighten that tail before I straighten it for you," Kendra snapped. "It's unbecoming of a guard on duty."

"Yes, ma'am," Gretta replied, not even remotely chastised. She did straighten her tail as ordered, although the very tip remained curled.

Impudent guard, Kendra thought but she chose to ignore it and made her way to her office instead. She had far bigger issues to worry about. Once inside, she shut her door and activated her privacy screen, then called the squad senior outside of Surellis's suite. He answered immediately.

"Report."

"Twanging hard and highly conflicted, but no signs of loss of control. He stops his pacing only long enough to look at something on his tablet before continuing to pace or glance between the Trauma Center and the Council Building. His primary emotion is worry."

She frowned as she considered everything she knew about her Senior Councilor. He had one of the calmest soul boundaries she knew, and even in moments of extreme stress, like the end of Little Flower's trial, he'd remained calm. If he was this conflicted, it was because he was trying to force himself to make a decision he really didn't want to make.

"Continue watching," she ordered and disconnected from the call. Then, with a heavy sigh, she started digging through her backlog which was several leagues long from four days out of communication with the universe.

Hours later, she growled as she finished reading the report Avery had sent shortly after she'd jumped, which detailed Marsee's suicide attempt and the injuries he and Tamarin had both sustained in trying to stop her. She signed off on the report and checked for an update.

"Nothing," she muttered, wondering if Avery had neglected his reports on top of everything else or if they were still bouncing between planets. It had been hours since she'd arrived, and the servers should have caught up, but the tech on the Water World was abysmal, a decade out of date due to the complexity of converting everything to work underwater, and council meetings always put a strain on the networks.

She still hadn't decided what she was going to do with Avery for leaving the Senior Councilors' children unprotected, but for starters, she swore at him in three different languages. Then, for good measure, she cursed him with a year-long infestation of Digger sand fleas, one of the itchiest crawlies in the known universe.

A faint sound of high-pitched laughter, barely audible to her heightened senses, seemed to echo off the wall behind her. Something about it made her fur stand on edge, and she spun in her seat to peer out the window, feeling like she was being watched, but no one was there. Only a few small fish swam nearby, and the closest building was well out of earshot, not that she could hear anything through the thick window.

Wondering if it had been a trick of acoustics, she turned back around to peer out into the outer office. She'd set the screen so she could see out and monitor the comms but prevent the reverse. She listened for a moment to the normal banter of the shift change, status reports, and the like, pleased at the efficiency and discipline she heard, but their voices were all deeper.

Little Flower, perhaps? She scanned the bank of monitors until she found the feed. Little Flower was awake now, wrapped protectively in Marsee's arms, but it appeared Marsee and Hope were still asleep.

She scanned the rest of the outer office, looking for anything to account for the sound she'd heard. Clear Seas had reconfigured the guard station since the last time she'd been on the planet to allow for the addition of a Hue-man guard, moving members of his own council to a newly built annex. The outer office was more than twice the size of the one she'd had before, and a portion of the dividing wall had been temporarily removed to better support the number of guards she had on the planet. Avery had been given the office reserved for the Hue-mans on the far side of the shared space, an office, she noticed, that was still dark.

In addition to the guards she'd brought with her, she'd sent a full contingent of guards to assist with arresting Clear Seas and aid in the search for Marsee. Once cleared of charges, Clear Seas had commandeered those guards upon arrival, not trusting his own, for good reason, and placed them in charge of Council Security for the upcoming meeting, not Stinger or any of the Water Sprite guards, which had never happened before. The Home Guard was always in charge of securing the meeting, just as the Home Senior would run the meeting. It was an unbroken tradition that went all the way back to the founding of the Consortium.

That put her in the awkward position of being higher rank than the Water World's own Senior Honor Guard, which would indicate the Seniors believed he'd been involved with Rip's coup attempt, yet she hadn't been called in to arrest him. That, added to the radiating waves of mistrust she'd sensed earlier, that hadn't been entirely directed at the prisoner she'd been transporting, made her wonder what other information they'd found in Rip's secret room, or if they were only angry at her for Avery's failure to protect their children. As if that wasn't enough.

They'd surprisingly said nothing to her about that incident, and Chenzira had dismissed her after the prisoner transfer was complete. She had a security update scheduled with Surellis later that day, but she'd been surprised that Jeran hadn't spoken to her, and she still couldn't believe they'd left Avery in charge after what he'd done.

If his incompetence is the best option they have... That thought downright terrified her.

Unable to find anything wrong, her gaze drifted back to the monitors as Marsee woke. An ancient Digger appeared a moment later, carrying a tray that appeared to be breakfast.

Rowena's here? That might complicate things. Has she told anyone yet, or is she still keeping our secret? It would have been so much easier if Marsee had died, she thought, then chided herself. *That was unkind. It's not the child's fault she's been kidnapped and tortured, and if she is the General, something like this was bound to happen.*

She'd prayed a thousand times that Marsee's name was a coincidence, even though she knew it wasn't. She'd been worried since the day Jeran had partnered with Myra and changed his family name, and every guard on the planet had wondered since Marsee's name day when Councilor

Tabor had taken a moment during a council meeting to officially offer her condolences to Jeran on the passing of Myra's parents and congratulations on their new cub, but she'd known for sure the day Marsee had protected her classmate.

Everyone else, including Marsee's father and uncle, had been terrified that day, although they'd done an admirable job of hiding it. She tended to have that effect on people, and it was rare for her to be called in for a cub's squabble, even if that cub was the daughter of a councilor. Rather than cower in fear, Marsee had crossed her arms and glared up at her, absolutely unrepentant in her belligerent defense of her classmate. It had amused her to no end, even though it had horrified everyone else.

She'd gone against all her training, multiple times in the years since, to follow the General's orders not to test Marsee or bring her in for training, and she was glad she had. So much good had come from following those ancient orders. They'd learned about the benefits of sign language and had uncovered Rip's plot, hopefully stopping the war before it even started, although she sincerely doubted they were that lucky.

That didn't make her current decision any easier: tell the child and the Senior Councilors what was really going on with Marsee, or let her continue to suffer through what she clearly thought was a death sentence until she was ultimately successful in taking her own life, or Councilor Surellis did when her senses started to return. It didn't help matters any that Marsee's mother was showing the early signs of psychosis, too.

She was honestly surprised that Damon had been captured unharmed when she'd heard that Myra had gone out after them, and that was the only reason she'd allowed Myra to travel. She knew Myra needed to see that her daughter was safe if she was to have any chance of recovering, but if Myra lost control during the council meeting, it would be bad, *very, very* bad. Granted, that might be the least of their problems if Surellis was starting to lose control. Thankfully, she hadn't seen any issues with Jeran. *I might have to look into their training methods more.*

Half lost in thought, she watched Avery and Tamarin enter. Avery glanced towards her office, saw that her privacy screen was on, and followed Tamarin over to the guard she'd spoken to earlier.

Kendra stood and walked over to her window to glare at him, tail lashing with annoyance, even though she knew he couldn't see her, and considered how she wanted to handle this as she listened to his conversation. *Public tail lashing,* she decided. Purposely standing on two feet to make herself appear larger, she waited until his back was to her and his attention firmly fixed on the monitors before hitting the switch to open her door.

He didn't notice over the din of the office, but others did, and the room quieted until her low growl could be heard above the chatter of the comms, now the only other sound in the room.

Tamarin gave him a nudge, and Avery took a deep breath before turning to face her and snapping to attention.

She said nothing, knowing he could sense her rage, even if her growl and lashing tail weren't evidence enough. She waited until he swallowed hard with growing fear before dropping down to all fours and stalking forward, radiating threat and intent to kill with every purposeful step, knowing he could sense that, too.

The other guards quickly backed away from him, leaving him alone in the middle of a semi-circle. His fear filled the room, but he didn't move or brace himself to fight back as she approached. He knew better. If he had, she would have killed him on the spot.

"I should claw you to shreds for leaving the Councilor's children unprotected," she hissed as she circled around him. His ears followed her, but he otherwise remained a statue, facing forward. "I gave a life oath that you could be trusted, and you *abandoned* your post."

"Yes, ma'am," he replied, his voice barely above a whisper, but instead of fear, guilt radiated off of him now.

"Do you have anything to say for yourself?"

"No, ma'am."

She growled and continued to stalk around him until she was right in his face. "No?! What possessed you to leave them unguarded?" She had his report, but she needed to hear it directly from him to see if he was lying.

Avery swallowed hard but didn't answer.

"If you don't answer me in five seconds, nephew or not, I *will* kill you. One...*Two*..."

"I left on her orders to find a rope. We needed to know what was so important in that canyon that people were willing to..."

She growled, and he swallowed hard as the room filled again with the scent of his fear. "Orders?!" she spat at him. "She doesn't have the authority to order you around. She's a *child*."

To her surprise, he clamped down on his fear and squared his shoulders. "No. She's not. She's an adult, and at the time, she was the Acting Senior Guild Master investigating a crime that happened on a Guild site, and backed by the Senior Council, which gave her authority. Besides, the Senior Council has already started to follow her lead. If they won't tell her what to do, who am I to do so?"

She snorted in absolute disbelief. "In a criminal investigation, you outrank any Guild Master, acting or otherwise, and she was on a watch that *you* put her on only hours before. Regardless of her *supposed* rank at the time, she had absolutely no authority to order you away. Even if Rip hadn't been around, someone or something could have easily attacked them, or Marsee could have lost control and killed Stormy and everyone on that build site. I know for a fact that I taught you better than that. How could you have possibly justified leaving two defenseless children alone in the middle of the ocean?"

He swallowed hard again but squared his shoulders. "I felt the few minutes necessary to find a rope were worth the risk to find the others and figure out what Rip was up to. I fully admit I made a mistake, but if she had come with me, she and Stormy would both be dead. Rip could have easily killed us before we even knew he was there. I honestly have no idea why he didn't kill me when he had the chance. I had no idea that he'd even escaped. The local guard had been compromised, and my gear disabled."

"If you think highlighting the rest of your failures is going to endear me to your cause, you're sadly mistaken. Even if you might not have been able to stop Rip on your own, you should have been able to spot him before he attacked." Waves of guilt radiated off of him. She leaned in, grabbed him by his harness, and snarled in his face. "Unless you *purposely* left them alone so they *could* be attacked?"

"Of course not!" he exclaimed. "I made a stupid mistake. Several, in fact, and I fully accept whatever the consequences are."

She stared at him, bringing all of her senses to the foreground, then lifted him off his feet by his harness. "Swear it. Swear that you are not involved in this mess."

"I, Avery Kassandra Hunt, swear on my oath, my life, and my honor that I had nothing to do with Rip and that I intended no ill will towards Marsee or Stormy when I left their side. I take full responsibility for the harm that was done on my watch, even if that means my death. I *am* sorry they were hurt and that I let you down. The last thing I want is for you to be killed because of my fur-brained stupidity."

There wasn't even the slightest waiver to indicate he was lying, although he still reeked of guilt. She let him go but continued to glare at him, trying to determine if that guilt was because he was lying or because he felt guilty that Marsee had been hurt.

"Ma'am, we're closer to war than we've ever been. *Please,*" he begged. "She needs our help and training. Let me mentor her before it's too late."

She snorted at him, surprised by the change in subject. "After you failed her so miserably? Why should I let *you* have the honor of mentoring her?"

"Because I owe her, and no one will be more dedicated. The only way I could ever make up for what I did is to help her to survive what's to come."

She flicked an ear back dismissively, knowing Avery didn't know the half of it, but then leaned in, nose wide as she sniffed him. "No. You're thinking that if she agrees to it, it's less likely her father and uncle will kill you."

"Or you."

She pinned her ears back in disbelief. "You honestly think that would stop me from executing you if I found out your negligence was anything more than a stupid mistake?"

"That's not what I meant. I think it might stop Jeran and Marcus from executing *you*. For some reason, Marsee still trusts me. I think that's the only reason I haven't been executed or, for that matter, dragged off by the mob. It's time we tell them. They've all willingly offered up their lives to save others. They'll protect us to protect Marsee. Surellis is ready for a change. He's the first person to even question the need for the test in ten thousand years, but he's already regretting that decision. We need to tell them now, or we'll lose both Marsee and her mother."

She glared at Avery, even more furious with him now than she had been a moment before. He'd said far too much in a recorded room. If the Seniors were watching or the feeds compromised, they would already know they were hiding something. She could deflect and claim that there were others with injuries or defects similar to Marsee's in the Guard. It had never worked in the past, but it might now. But what Avery was suggesting was that they inform the Council about the Transition, and that went against ten thousand years of brutal secrecy and everything she'd been taught.

Coincidence, ancient prophecy, orders, or otherwise, Avery was right about one thing. Marsee needed to be trained before her senses returned and overwhelmed her. But if she was wrong about her assessment of Marsee and her family, she could be exposing her people to a resurgence in psychosis and a rekindling of the Psychosis Wars that had destroyed their former world.

What would happen if the other species found out the truth about psychosis, that it was more than a term given to an uncivilized moment from their ancient history? Or worse, if her population found out that people could survive psychosis and started using their instincts again? No. She couldn't do it. The risk was just too high, and their history was rife with examples to prove it.

Avery's expression changed as he sniffed out her response. His body language hardened with determination. "If you won't tell them. I will."

She pinned her ears back, barely able to believe what she'd heard. "You would disobey my orders? That's bordering on treason. You know what happened the last time we tried. You would honestly risk that again for *one* child?"

"Not just any child. I'm risking it for Marsee and for every other *person* that follows her. This is the best and only chance we'll ever have to change the policy. We need to take it. What happens when Surellis kills Marsee because she has one too many night terrors? What will the population here do when their beloved Translator is executed for an illness they have medical proof she no longer has? If you can't see the risk, then it's time you step down."

"Are you challenging me?" she asked.

"If I need to," he replied.

To her further surprise, Tamarin stepped forward to stand next to Avery. "I agree with Avery," she said. "We need to tell them. I'm beyond sick of letting the Council kill those we could save if given half a chance. The other Seniors know about psychosis now, but Surellis came far too close to killing Marsee anyway last night, over a *night* terror. Mistakes may have been made in protecting Marsee, but she nearly died a few days ago because of *your* orders to keep quiet. I can understand waiting to see if she would survive her injuries, but now that she has, Marcus and Jeran need to know what's really going on with her, and she needs our help before she tries to take her life again."

The other guards in the room stepped forward to stand behind Avery and Tamarin, and she knew she was badly outnumbered. Individually, she could easily handle any of them, but as a group, she would be hard-pressed. The guards here were the ones most often called in for a test or to deal with those lost to psychosis. They had the most experience fighting, which is why she picked them for this mission in the first place, but they also knew the potential consequences better than anyone. If they weren't willing to go along with the Council's test or her orders to keep quiet anymore, then there was little she could do to stop them from exposing everything. Not legally, anyway.

Ancient Gods protect us, she prayed. With a heavy sigh, she nodded.

The tension left Avery's body, and he sighed with relief.

She refocused her glare on him and snarled. "*This* conversation is not over. It may be time to bring Marsee into the Guard, but I still haven't decided what I'm going to do with you. You abandoned your post after I put my life up as collateral that you could be trusted, and both Marsee and Stormy were hurt because of *your* incompetence. You will pay dearly for that, even if they haven't pressed charges against you."

"Yes, ma'am," he replied, swallowing hard at her anger and threat. "I really am sorry I put your life at risk."

"You didn't just put my life at risk, you put *everyone's* life at risk."

Faster than he could block, she swung, claws outstretched, and hit him hard enough to knock him to the ground but intentionally not hard enough to knock him out.

He lay there, stunned and blinking up at her as blood began to drip down his face. One paw slowly raised to the side of his head where she'd struck, but the only emotion she sniffed was surprise. She'd either caught him completely off-guard, or he didn't believe she would really hurt him. Her claws had purposely landed within a whisker width of being a kill shot, and he knew it.

"Get up," she demanded.

He tried, but she'd obviously hurt him enough that he stumbled and fell again.

She pinned her ears and snarled at him. "If you think for a moment that you're even remotely ready to challenge me for this position, you're sadly mistaken. I would wipe the floor with you and not even break a sweat. Consider this your *only* warning. I will not hold back the next time."

She glared at the others in the room. "And that goes for the rest of you. I understand and respect you for speaking up, but if you think you're ready to challenge me for this position, step forward, and we'll settle it now."

No one moved. She didn't expect them to. Avery was one of her best fighters, and she'd disabled him with a single blow.

She snorted her disgust at the group.

"Ma'am," Gretta called out hesitantly into the silence.

"What?" she hissed.

"You wanted to know when Surellis left his suite…"

She glanced up at the main monitor, which now showed him activating his drone. She nodded to Gretta, impressed and pleased that at least one guard had remained focused on their duties, and made a mental note to review Gretta's record for a possible promotion.

She returned her attention back to her nephew and pinned her ears at him, then reached down and picked Avery up by his harness again. He didn't resist, but she could smell his fear as he dangled in front of her. She glared at him for a moment, making sure he sniffed her rage and disgust with him, and then, after confirming there weren't any life-threatening injuries, tossed him at Tamarin, who staggered under his weight, trying to catch him. "Clean up this mess and get back to work."

"Yes, ma'am," Tamarin replied.

Turning, she stormed out of the station.

The other guards scampered to clear a path as they flinched away from the rage she did nothing to control. Rage was better than admitting to the cold nugget of fear lodged in her throat at what she was about to do.

CHAPTER 2

Marcus: Betrayals

Marcus yawned as he left his suite, knowing it was going to be another grueling slog of a day. He hadn't been able to sleep, far too worried about his family and the reality of what he'd seen the night before, a reality he could no longer deny.

Rowena had insisted that Marsee could no longer use her instinct, and he'd been cautiously optimistic, but now he knew it would only be a matter of time before someone got hurt and he would be forced to put his niece down. He was terrified that someone would be Little Flower or Hope.

He might have been able to dismiss her swipe upon waking as a trauma response, but then she'd admitted that she didn't feel safe around her sister. He now knew, beyond the darkest moon's shadow of a doubt, that her instinct wasn't gone. It had only been dormant because of her injuries, and it was now recovering. And she knew it, too.

Not only that, but Myra had nearly lost control at the first sight of his brother. He'd seen the flash of claws and the changing reflection of her eyes. She'd recovered quickly enough, but he knew it would only take a single incident to push her over the edge. But it was his brother that he was the most worried about.

He knew he should have put Jer down days before, but he hadn't been able to. He still couldn't. The very thought of it made his own instinct growl, but the guard's reaction to Jer's admission that he heard his instinct was terrifying. He had no idea what that meant or how close

Jer was to losing control. Would he even make it through the meeting? Would any of them? Even after hours of pacing, he still had no answers. His paws were tied. If he took action against any of them, the entire world would know about psychosis, and Wind Rider and Clear Seas had both threatened war if he hurt Marsee. There was nothing he could do but wait and pray that no one got hurt because he couldn't act.

He frowned as he approached the Council Building. Kendra was waiting by the entrance and watching him approach. He knew her well enough to know something was bothering her. They hadn't found anything on her or Avery that he didn't already know, but he still didn't trust either of them, not completely.

"What is it?" he asked but didn't stop his drone, figuring she'd follow him back to his office.

"I want to talk to you about your niece," she said.

That stopped him. He turned to face her, and a frown escaped his mask. "Did something happen last night?"

"No," she replied. "I intend to examine her this morning. I figured you might want to be present."

He stared at her for several moments, surprised that she even asked him, and considered the optics if they both showed up. Wind Rider and Clear Seas could very well take that as a threat of his intent to kill Marsee and act accordingly. He couldn't take that risk. Not yet, anyway. He shook his head. "I have a meeting I need to attend, but I thank you for the courtesy of informing me. Perform whatever evaluation you deem necessary, with medical restrictions, but otherwise, do not take action." He raised a paw to stop her from objecting. He knew she had the right to kill Marsee if she determined his niece was a threat, and he honestly had no idea what she would do. "I am not hiding anything or trying to overstep your authority. There's information you need that I can't share here. We'll discuss it during our scheduled meeting."

She pursed her lips as if trying to figure out how to respond but then nodded and swam off.

He watched her head out across the park for a moment, highly conflicted, wondering if he'd made the right decision. He didn't know if she would follow his orders, and he hated the part of himself that wished she wouldn't.

With a heavy sigh, he turned to continue on his way but found himself facing Avery and Tamarin as they popped up one of the vertical shafts. They both frowned when they saw him, and he wondered what that was about, but outside of a nod, they didn't stop. He watched as they zoomed past him to catch up with Kendra and chuckled when Kendra pinned her ears and lashed her tail in Avery's direction.

In an instant, Avery shifted from looking like a fierce guard to a naughty cub with his tail tucked tightly between his legs. *Someone got a tail-lashing this morning,* he thought, honestly surprised Avery wasn't being carried out on a stretcher or in a body bag. After what he did, Kendra had the right to kill him, even if they hadn't found any evidence that it had been malicious.

The other Seniors were already in the conference room when he arrived, digging through their latest files, even though they weren't actually scheduled to meet for another hour. Jer looked thoroughly dejected as he stared at his file, head leaning against one paw and fiddling with the edge of a piece of paper with the other. He was fairly sure his brother wasn't seeing any of it, seeing as he didn't even notice him enter.

"How did it go last night?" Marcus asked, but his brother didn't reply. He swam over and touched him lightly on the shoulder, concerned that his brother was going non-verbal again.

Jer startled slightly. "Oh hey. I didn't hear you come in."

"Obviously. How did it go last night?" he asked again, relieved to hear Jer speak. "I expected you to call."

Jer shrugged. "Sorry, I figured you were asleep by the time we finished. The prisoner transfer went smoothly. Damon refused an advocate when I offered again, but outside of that, he refused to talk."

"What's your impression of him?" he asked. "Do you think he's protecting someone?"

"Honestly, I think he's just given up. He knows he's going to die and has made peace with it."

"So why the long face?" he asked.

Jer let out a heavy sigh before answering. "Because I failed him. I failed to see the harm I was causing him, and I failed to see what my entire council was doing to him and the rest of the males. I should have given him his adulthood and let him go."

"He was on a watch," Clear Seas said. "It would have been irresponsible to let him go, especially if his own people didn't trust him."

"A watch I agreed to without proof of any crime," Jer replied. "I am as responsible for his actions as any parent, and he claimed that I and my entire council abused him. The only reason he's not pressing charges is because he wants to die rather than live in our society."

"What you did was not abuse by any legal statute," Marcus said. "If it was, then every parent who has ever told their child 'no' should be arrested."

Wind Rider snorted. "I'd be the first in line. Children push every button you have and then find those you didn't even know you had. He might have been an adult on his world, but that doesn't make him an adult on ours. If you had felt he could be trusted, you would have given him his adulthood, but you didn't, and you had good reason not to. The least of which was the harm done to Little Flower at the Agency. That was proof enough that the males couldn't be trusted, but then every female member of your council, and even some of the males, stated under oath that they had been sexually assaulted or raped during their time on Earth."

"If he were truly an adult, he could have come forward when Rip contacted him or even waited another week," Sammianna added. "His item was on the agenda for the meeting. Instead of diplomacy, he chose violence. I honestly don't understand why you're advocating for him. He nearly killed you and multiple members of your family."

"Do you honestly think the Council would have voted in his favor?" Jer asked. "We pushed off the item last time because there wasn't enough buy-in from the guilds. The only person I could convince to mentor any of the males was Nazari, and the only reason I managed that was because I told her it would help her appeal if she showed she was vested in the long-term care of a Hue-man. I had hoped that would convince others to do the same, but no one did."

Marcus pursed his lips as he grabbed the next folder from the box and took his seat, but before he could figure out what to say, there was a loud knock on the door.

Clear Seas swam over and flashed a hint of worry. "What's wrong?" he asked as Senior Honor Guard Stinger swam in and shut the door behind him.

Stinger turned to face Apakna. "Councilor. I regret to inform you that we lost contact with the council ships from your planet about two hours ago."

She frowned with worry. "More comms issues?"

"It's possible, but it seems highly suspicious that both ships are not responding. Even if their comms are out, they should have triggered at least three relays with their passing in that time."

"Could there be a problem with the relays?" Sammianna asked.

"That was our first thought, but everything appears to be in order. We've sent ships to both their last known location and the relays, but it'll be a few hours before they arrive, and if they're not there, then they could be anywhere."

Apakna frowned. "They're due in this afternoon. Have emergency crews on standby, and if you can, get visuals on the pilots before they land. Assuming anyone is still alive, they should be able to communicate with sign language. I want to make sure there's not a hostage situation before they get anywhere close to the platform."

"Yes, ma'am," Stinger replied and started to leave, but Apakna stopped him.

"If there is, take them down by whatever means necessary."

Stinger flashed his surprise, and everyone turned to look at her, equally surprised.

"Don't look at me like that. If it's a choice between my council and the innocent people of this planet, I will choose the people every time, and I will not negotiate with terrorists. Do what you need to in order to keep the population safe."

Stinger looked at Clear Seas and then the rest of them for confirmation. Clear Seas sighed and flashed his agreement, and the others all nodded.

Marcus nodded his agreement, too. Although he was praying hard that it was nothing more than an issue with the relays. "I want extra guards and techs checking over every ship and passenger before it departs. Let's make sure there isn't a bigger issue. Oh, and stop all outgoing flights to the Ice Planet until we can confirm the route is safe."

Stinger flashed his understanding and swam out.

Apakna waited for the door to shut before slamming her fist on the table. The motion lifted her out of her seat and sent glitters of frost into the water, but she didn't seem to notice or care. Instead, she turned away, fists tightly curled as she muttered quietly under her breath.

He wasn't sure if she was swearing or praying. "It could be nothing more than the relays," he said softly.

"Both ships, Temperate's, *and* mine?" she hissed, turning back to face him. "I seriously doubt it. I thank you for your optimism, Marcus, but you know as well as I do that they are as good as dead."

"You don't know that, and neither do I," he replied. "We found no sign that Rip was targeting your council as a whole. It's far more likely a technical issue. The Council Pilots are some of the..."

"Rip might not have targeted them, but someone else could have, including their pilots and everyone we've already found that was working with him." She waved her paw at the Pile in disgust. "For all we know, they could have taken over and disabled their communications because they have plans to attack when they arrive."

"Or they're making a run for it," Sammianna added. "But it's no different now than it was a few minutes ago, and there's nothing we can do about it until they arrive or we find the wreckage. Come. We have work to do."

Apakna made a noise halfway between a growl and a cry. "There are days I hate how...how *pragmatic* your species is. We might be made of ice, but I think your heart is frozen to the core. My uncle is on that ship, and I may have just ordered his death along with the rest of my council. Excuse me for needing a moment to compose myself."

Sammie pursed her lips. "Forgive me. I know I do not experience the strength of emotions your species feels, but I do understand grief and the pain of the decision we've all just made. They are my friends and colleagues, too. But whether they die today or not, far too many of them were already slated to die. For what it's worth, I believe you did the right thing. If your uncle is involved, then he deserves to die, too, and if he's not, then he would understand your decision." Sammie motioned to Apakna's seat. "Please, we have work to do and far too little time to do it in."

Apakna hissed at Sammie, and for a moment, Marcus wondered if she would attack, but instead, she stormed out of the conference room, slamming the door shut behind her.

In the silence that followed, Sammie watched her leave with a frown. "What did I do wrong?"

"Nothing, Sammie," Wind Rider said quietly. "She just needs time to grieve. She'll be back when she's ready."

"Ah," Sammie said and returned to her investigation as if nothing had happened.

He sighed, deciding it wasn't worth correcting Wind Rider, and returned to work himself. He flipped open his folder and swallowed hard when he saw who it was. He ran a paw gently across the image that stared back at him. *Ancient Gods, please not her,* he prayed and began reading.

It wasn't long before he realized his prayers would go unanswered. Only his decades of practice allowed him to keep from growling at what he read, but as he continued his investigation, what he found was too much, even for him. Closing the folder with a snarl, he swam out of the room and down to his office. He shut the door, hit the privacy screen, and then, and only then, let his mask fully drop. He cried and swore and yelled at the Ancient Gods for all of the friends and colleagues he would have to execute, but mostly, he wept for the one unrequited love of his youth. She had not only chosen another but, a century and a half later, had betrayed both him and his family.

There was evidence she had committed crimes that, on their own, would have been a death sentence. That alone was enough to make his heart twist with the weight of what he had to do, but to see the words of her betrayal tore his heart out. He had never stopped loving her and had no idea what he had done to cause her to hate him and his family so much. He pulled up her picture, one he had kept for nearly two centuries, and stared at it as tears streamed down his face.

"Why, Trisha? What did I ever do to you?"

Her beautiful, laughing face stared back at him. Once joyous, it now seemed to mock him.

Has she always hated me? he wondered.

He'd gone out to dinner with her only a few weeks before and had sensed nothing out of place. Their meal had been friendly and full of laughter. They'd focused on her district's needs and spoke of their families and the latest books they'd read. There had been no hint that she intended his family harm or that she had any animosity towards him. Even though she'd chosen to mate and partner with another, they'd remained friends throughout the years, and she was or had been one of his most trusted peers. Only now, he knew that every moment of that conversation, every detail he'd given about Marsee and the rest of his family, had been shared with Rip and used against them.

How could I have been so blind?

He went to delete the picture, but his paw hovered over the button and shook, and he couldn't make himself press it.

How can I execute her when I can't even delete her picture? he wondered bitterly and turned his tablet off instead.

His heart might be broken into a million pieces, but every tiny broken shard still loved her, even if those broken shards sliced at his soul and tore it to shreds. He walked over to the window and stared out, not seeing anything of the vibrant world in front of him, trying to find a way out of this mess, out of his duty and the oath he had sworn to his people.

An oath she broke, and people died because of it, he reminded himself. *Several members of my family nearly died because of it, and still might.*

Twenty minutes later, he was still trying to pull himself back together when there was a light knock on the door. He took a deep breath and wrapped the broken shards of his heart in the thick binds of his honor and duty, knowing what he had to do, even though he knew it would probably destroy him.

When he was sure his emotions were back under his mask, he turned off his privacy screen. "Enter," he called out.

Jer swam in. "Are you all right?"

"No, but I will be. Did you need something?"

Jer nodded. "Myra sent me a message. She wants to meet with us in private to discuss Marsee."

"Did she find something?"

Jer shook his head. "She sent it to the queue last night. I just noticed."

He glanced over at the clock. It was still early. "Have her come to my suite after she's had a chance to check on Marsee, say, around eight? That should give her enough time. I'll meet you in your office in a bit, and we'll swim over together."

Jer looked like he was going to say something but nodded and swam out.

He turned away from the door and stared out the window again. *Before yourself and family,* he reminded himself. Then, nearly buckling under the weight of his oath, he sent a message to Kendra for backup and left to find Jer, praying he wasn't swimming to his family's execution.

CHAPTER 3

Marsee: Proposals

arsee Bet Chenzira, will you Marry me?"

Marsee stared at her sister, so completely overwhelmed that she couldn't find the words to speak. *Marry? She wants to share her cub with me?! I'm nothing but a broken, fur-less in-betweener with life-threatening medical issues. Why would she possibly want me for her partner?*

She loved her sister and absolutely adored Hope, but Little Flower wasn't her litter-mate. She wasn't even the same species, and Marsee had never even considered the possibility that her adopted sister would propose to her over one of her own kind or that Hope could really be her child, not just her niece. She'd wanted to offer partnership since the moment Little Flower had woken from her coma, but her mother had advised against it for fear that her sister would give up without the responsibility of caring for her child.

Is that what this is? Marsee wondered.

Fear that her sister was giving up made her heart hitch, but before she could find the words to answer, her sister spoke. "I know that you're really young for someone of your species to consider a partnership, so I don't want you to feel pressured or feel like this is the only chance you have, but if you want to become Hope's father, then I want to share her with you. If it's too much to think about right now, and you just want to be the best Auntie a cub could ever have, that's fine, too. It won't change how I feel about you, but I really could use your help, and I don't ever want you to think you're not good enough or capable enough to be a parent, even if you can't ever have a child of your own."

Marsee blinked out of her shock and worry and carefully hugged Hope, who was snuggling in her arms. "Nothing in the universe would make me happier," she replied. "I just can't believe it. You *really* want me to be your partner? Injured, fur-less, me?! I can barely walk across the room, much less protect her, and I might die tomorrow from sneezing too hard or something equally ridiculous."

Her sister's face lit up at her answer. "I really do. I don't mind your lack of fur if you don't mind mine, and none of us knows how long we'll live, but if you do die, I hope it *is* from something ridiculous. That way, I can snicker every time I visit your grave. I'll commission a monument that reads something like, 'Here lies Chenzie Butt Chenzira, the first and only Saber to die by rocking chair.' And under that, 'I warned her to watch her tail. - Ellie.'"

Marsee snorted with surprised laughter, and her tail spiraled with an unbridled joy that began filling the hollow gaping wound in her soul. That is until another thought occurred, and her ears and tail drooped again. "I want to. More than anything, I want to say yes, but I can't go home. It's not safe for me there, and I can't take you and Hope away from your people."

"I knew that when I asked, and while I'll miss my grandfather, you're the one I need. *You're* my family. We'll go where you go until it's safe for you to go home, even if that never happens. We're staying here until you're recovered enough to jump anyway. I'm not going back without you."

"Are you sure?" Marsee asked, her ears perking up slightly.

"I am. The moment you left, I fell apart. I need you to hold me together, and I need your help. Part of the vow my culture makes when we partner says for better or worse and in sickness and in health. We've been through sickness and the absolute worst. Everything else just has to be better. I can't imagine anything worse except losing you entirely. As for protecting Hope, even as weak as you are from your injuries, you're still far more capable of protecting her than I am. You'll recover, but until you do, we've got a dozen scowling guards to protect us. You managed to defeat and kill someone more than twice your size, who was capable of killing you with nothing more than a touch. I know you'll be able to do it again."

Her ears drooped as fear started to claw her back down into that dark void she'd been lost to. "But I was only able to do that because of my instinct, and that's gone now. I don't know how to fight."

"Pah! If you can do it with your instinct, then you're physically capable of learning how to do it without it, and who knows, once you recover from your injuries, you might even be better since you won't be limited by pain."

"I doubt that," Marsee muttered, although Stormy had said much the same. "I broke my tail doing nothing more strenuous than swimming up and down the hall."

"Are you sure? Maybe Rip broke it, and they just found it because they were looking for it. If you didn't know it was broken, and it wasn't bothering you or limiting you in any way, did it really matter?"

"But how would I even learn something like that?"

Her sister snorted. "The same way every other species does: practice. I'd like to learn how to defend myself better, too. I've been attacked twice by members of my species in the last year, and even your crawlies are bigger than I am."

Could I learn how to fight without my instinct? Who would even be able to teach us? She'd never thought about learning how to fight, not until she'd been forced to. There was little need to learn, or there hadn't been until recently.

Motion outside her door caught her attention, and she looked over to see her guards changing shifts as Avery appeared at the entrance. *The guards! They must learn how to fight. I don't want to join the Guard, but maybe they would be willing to teach us something.*

She was about to call out to Avery but froze, instantly terrified, as he entered the room, followed by a guard she'd only met a few times but that everyone knew. *Kendra! Ancient Gods!* There was only one reason she would be there. They were coming to test her. She would fail, and Kendra would order her execution or kill her on the spot.

Not now, she thought. *Not when I've only just found a reason to live again. No. I'm not going down without a fight.*

You'll never win, you fur-brained bumble crawler. You can't even walk across the room without panting.

Maybe I can fake the test? How though? How do you make your eyes dilate on purpose, or will that just make her think I'm lying?

Little Flower saw her expression and spun to look at the two guards and then back again. "Marsee, what's going on?"

"I see you remember me, Marsee," Kendra signed. "Councilor Chenzira, it's good to see you again and see that you're recovering from your injuries."

Marsee relaxed slightly, but Little Flower frowned.

"Do I know you?" Little Flower asked.

"We've only met once, briefly. I'm Senior Honor Guard Kendra Hunt."

Little Flower's eyes widened. "Is this in response to me kicking your guards out of the room last night?"

Kendra gave a half snort. "While I did find that rather amusing, no. I'm here to talk with Marsee. May I have some privacy?"

"Marsee's under my protection. Whatever you need to say to her can be said in front of me," Little Flower replied with a glare that seemed to amuse Kendra, although there was only the slightest change to her expression.

"I see you haven't lost any of your bravery or audacity," Kendra replied, "but there's absolutely nothing you could do to stop me from taking action, legally or otherwise. Marsee is a member of *my* species, and if I determine she's a threat, I have the legal authority to execute her on the spot, regardless of Council approval."

Avery frowned, and his hand shifted to his stunner.

Little Flower unclipped something on her belt loop, and a moment later, a small knife appeared. "I don't care who you are. Hurt her, and I will see you brought before the Full Council for murder," she said in Hue-man. "She is under *my* protection!"

Marsee immediately translated. It was second nature for her now, but she set Hope down on the bed in case she had to protect her sister, not really sure what to do. Attacking or even threatening a guard could be a death sentence, but Kendra had worded it such that it could be considered self-defense, especially if Avery was reacting, too."

Kendra slowly raised her paws. "If I intended either of you harm, you'd already be dead. I was merely stating the law and the authority it gives me. It is my responsibility to evaluate and ensure that the people are safe from those like your sister. If she is truly safe, then you have nothing to fear."

Avery visibly relaxed, but her sister didn't and continued to glare up at Kendra.

"Why should I trust you?" Little Flower asked in Hue-man, not lowering her knife.

Kendra didn't seem surprised at all by the question. "You have absolutely no reason to trust me, but I was prepared to commit treason in order to save your life and the lives of your people during your trial. I would hope that would count for something."

Little Flower considered for a moment and then put the knife away. As she did, Kendra reached back and shut the door before activating the privacy screen.

Marsee looked between the two Honor Guards. "We were just talking about how neither of us has the ability to defend ourselves anymore. What kind of training do you have in the Guard? Do you practice fighting, or do you rely on your instinct?"

Avery visibly flinched as if she'd hit him and drooped in front of her, tail dragging on the floor. "I am so very sorry about what happened to you. I left you alone when I knew I shouldn't have, and I willingly accept whatever you want for reparations. If you'd rather another guard be posted, I'll have one sent over immediately."

Kendra raised a brow but was otherwise silent, watching the exchange.

Marsee sighed at the misunderstanding and shook her head. "I'm not questioning your ability to protect me or blaming you for what happened. I ordered you away after all. I'm sorry for putting you in that position and for not listening to you. That was my mistake. I'm asking because I, we, want to learn how to fight. My sister has been attacked twice now by members of her species, and I don't have my instinct to fall back on if someone else should try to hurt us."

"Oh," he replied and glanced at Kendra.

Marsee followed his gaze and swallowed hard. Kendra was staring at her with a look so intense that it felt like she was examining the depths of her very soul.

"*That* remains to be seen," Kendra replied, her entire body language turning threatening in an instant.

Marsee froze in panic again, but forced herself to speak, terrified Kendra would think she was non-verbal. "I swear I can't use my instinct. That part of my brain is gone. Please! I tried. I *really* tried. I know you have no reason to believe me, but..."

Kendra raised a paw to silence her and, to her relief, began pulling up scans on the monitor above the bed.

Marsee shifted so she could see what Kendra was looking at.

A few minutes later, Kendra refocused on her, and before Marsee realized what the Senior Honor Guard intended, Kendra had her head firmly grasped in her massive paws and forced her to look up.

"Turn it on," Kendra ordered.

"I can't!" To her own surprise, her words came out far more forceful than she expected or intended. She had no idea how to defend herself from the guard who now held her very life in her paws, but she glared up at Kendra, refusing to look away. She might have tried taking her own life before, but she had a reason to live now, and she was furious that they still didn't believe her, even after allowing Rowena to poke and prod at her for days.

Out of nowhere, a pillow hit Kendra squarely in the back of the head.

"No!" Little Flower screamed in Saber.

Kendra gave a slight snort of disbelief and slowly shifted her head to glare at Little Flower.

Her sister refused to back down and returned the glare just as fiercely, arm poised to throw her knife.

Practically before Marsee realized that Little Flower had taken her knife out again, Kendra let go of her and snatched the knife from her sister's paws.

"I believe you, Marsee," Kendra said as she examined the mechanism on the knife, closed it, and tossed it back to Little Flower, who was now rubbing at her wrist, although her sister hadn't stopped glaring. "Your training is the whole reason I'm here."

It was Marsee's turn to be surprised, but before she could say anything, Kendra continued in sign so they could both understand. "What I'm about to tell you is confidential. We never discuss our training unless you're in the Guard because most people wouldn't understand. We don't even let the Council know what we really do. To answer your question, yes. We train to fight, as do the other species, but we also train our instinct until, well, it either kills us or we kill it. You don't become an Honor Guard until you've passed the Transition, as you have now done."

Marsee stared at the Senior Honor Guard, barely able to believe what she'd seen. "Are you telling me you have the same limitations that I do?"

"Limitations? No. I have fully recovered. However, I did not have to deal with the same injuries you've sustained, and I am not sure how much that will affect your overall recovery."

Marsee frowned. "Recovery? Rowena said I might regain my senses, but the control hub was missing and that I wouldn't ever be able to use my instinct again."

Kendra nodded. "That much is true. It varies per person, but based on what I saw on your scans, I expect you'll probably start to notice your senses returning in a few days, assuming they aren't already. You won't have the control issues you had before, or at least not the same issues. Once fully recovered, your senses will be as strong as they were when your instinct was on, if not more so. The voice you heard will be gone forever, as will your ability to just know how to fight or hunt, but you'll be able to train to improve upon the skills you've already learned."

"Why didn't you say anything sooner?" Marsee asked Avery.

He didn't answer but instead glanced at Kendra.

"He had orders not to," Kendra replied. "We didn't know if you would survive your other injuries, and I needed to see for myself that you had transitioned. I'll be honest. I've been debating what to tell you because of how close you are to the Council. I'm putting the lives of my entire Guard at risk by telling you, but we owe you. You took an immense risk by sharing your experiences with us, and you've saved a lot of lives with that information. Nor do we want you to lose your chance at cubs because the healers are guessing at how to treat you."

"You know about that?"

Kendra nodded. "Aris informed me when she heard what Ammond intended. Now, as for your training, Avery has already offered to mentor you, although if you'd prefer another guard, that can be arranged. As for you, Little Flower, while I commend your bravery in attempting to defend your sister, there is very little you would be able to do to harm one of the other species with your natural abilities or even that tiny knife, but we could teach you how to use a stunner. It's the device that was used to sedate you during the rescue."

"A stunner would be perfect," Little Flower replied. "You've made it perfectly clear that I'm not strong enough or fast enough to defend myself from anyone right now, although my aim with a pillow still appears to be good, so I imagine my aim with the knife is, too. I might be a bit rusty and need a crash course on vital areas for the other species, but I'm well-trained on how to use it, both held and thrown. My father was a guard, and he made sure of it."

Kendra's tail curled slightly, although her expression didn't change. "You seriously consider that tiny thing a weapon?"

"Used in the right location, it's deadly," Little Flower replied with ferocity. "How well would you be able to fight if this was sticking out of your eye?"

Kendra's eyes narrowed with the threat.

"I'm fine with Avery being my mentor," Marsee said, hoping to defuse the tension as the two continued to glare at each other.

It worked. Kendra snorted slightly at her sister and refocused on her.

"Are you sure?" Avery asked, still looking fairly upset about having failed her before.

"Completely," Marsee replied. She knew Avery would do everything in his power to make up for what he perceived as his failure, even though she blamed herself for being stupid enough to order him away.

Kendra gave a single nod of approval. "I'm going to talk to your mother and see if we can figure out a way to keep everyone else from knowing what's really going on with you." Then, without another word, she turned and left.

"Thank you for trusting me," Avery said. I promise. By the time I'm done with you, no one will ever be able to harm you again."

"I fully intend to hold you to that promise," she replied.

He nodded and left, taking up guard outside her door with Tamarin, who had already relieved Aris.

"Well, that's exciting news," Little Flower said once the door was shut, but Marsee picked up a hint of sadness behind her words.

"It's a relief, for sure," Marsee replied, confused by her sister's body language. "I just can't believe you challenged Kendra. She could have easily killed you for that."

"Unlikely, she doesn't see me as a real threat, and she would have been hard-pressed to justify executing me for hitting her with a pillow. As for my knife, even after what Damon did, she still doesn't see it as dangerous. I'm just glad she didn't ask me to prove my aim. I honestly have no idea if I can still hit a target."

"You were serious?"

"Of course I was. If I'd had a proper weapon either time I was attacked, it would have been a very different story. I didn't have anything I could use for a weapon in the Agency, and I didn't dare throw my dinner knife at Damon for fear I'd miss and hurt Hope or my grandfather. A stunner will be perfect. I'd much rather have a non-lethal option and one that doesn't require physical strength or coordination to use."

Marsee nodded her agreement. A stunner would be perfect. "Now, back to your offer of partnership, I wholeheartedly accept. I'll send Papa a message to prepare the paperwork." Marsee reached for her tablet but stopped when she saw her sister's expression. "What's wrong?"

"I thought, for sure, once you found out you could have cubs, you'd want to partner with someone else," Little Flower replied.

"Why would you think that? Unless you don't want to raise my cubs when it's time? They could still be born with my issues, but that won't be for another twenty years, which I know is a long time for you, so I'd understand." She drooped as she said it, crushed at the very idea.

In response, her sister practically knocked her over with a hug. "Nothing would make me happier than to raise *our* cubs. I don't care what issues they might have. We'll work through them together."

Marsee hugged her back just as fiercely. "Good, because I want *lots* of them. Cubs, that is, not issues. I already have enough of those."

Little Flower snorted and pulled away. "You said it, Chenzie Butt. Not me."

Laughing, Marsee sent her father a message, sharing the good news about her partnership and expected recovery. Although, she was careful not to say too much. Kendra had said it was confidential, and she still didn't know if her account was secure. The last she knew, Lowell was still working on it.

"So, what kind of ceremony do you have?" her sister asked when she set her tablet aside. "Is there a party or any sort of religious observance around it, and when do you want to do it?"

"Ceremony?" Marsee asked, confused. "It's pretty much the same as the adoption oath our parents took for you. Sometimes there's a party, but that's often because there are brand new cubs that everyone wants to meet or if people haven't met your partner. As for religion, what would that have to do with forming a partnership? The ancient religions are just that, ancient. We still pray to the Ancient Gods when we're scared or need help, but we don't have any sort of ceremony or practice around it. Not like before the Great Awakening, anyway. I'm not sure if the other species do, but I'm not aware of any. As for when, now or as soon as Papa has the paperwork ready and can swim over."

Her sister frowned, which confused Marsee again.

"Don't you want to do it now?" she asked. "The sooner we do, the sooner I can legally protect Hope if something happens to you. If we don't, Hope will go to Mama."

Her sister thought for a moment before responding, and it was all she could do to wait.

"I don't have a problem with doing it now," her sister finally said. "It's just...well, for our species, partnership was a major life event. I never expected to be able to afford a big wedding, but I always pictured at least having one and not just going to our equivalent of a junior advocate for the legal bits. We called that eloping. I remember when my grandfather got married, it was like I'd been transported into a fairy tale. It was magical. After the ceremony, there was a party with dancing, music, and cake, and then, they left for their honeymoon. I can't remember where they went, but I was ecstatic as we stayed at the farm and took care of the animals while they were gone. It was one of the best weeks of my childhood."

"Liquid sugar moon?" Marsee asked, confused by the sign Little Flower had made up.

Little Flower spelled out a word in the Hue-man language: "H. O. N. E. Y. I have no idea where the phrase comes from. Honey was a sugar produced by one of our flying crawlies and was also a term of endearment. A honeymoon is a special kind of vacation, a trip to someplace exotic, just the two of you, where you'd spend a lot of time mating or getting to know each other better."

Marsee tilted her head, once again confused. "Why would you leave your cubs behind or partner with someone you didn't know?"

Her sister laughed at the question and shrugged. "I suppose because you would usually get married before you had children or when you found out you were pregnant. In some cultures, parents or elders would arrange partnerships based on economics or for political or religious reasons. That's what happened with my mother in her first marriage."

"You didn't even get to pick who you were partnered with?" Marsee asked in ears back disbelief. Her sister had said once that in some cultures, they would force the mother to partner with her rapist, but she'd always thought that was the exception.

"My mother didn't. She was raised in a religion where her partner was chosen for her. He was abusive, and she ran away from home a few months later after being badly beaten. My father met her that day. They were both waiting for the same public ground crawler. He was on his way home from the war and heard her crying in the public waste room. When he realized she had nowhere to go and no money for medical care, he brought her home with him and protected her when her husband eventually tracked her down. Her family and community shunned her when she refused to go back."

"Shunned?" Marsee asked, not familiar with that word either.

"They turned their backs on her and refused to have anything to do with her. It's an extreme form of peer pressure. In their eyes, she had committed the worst crime imaginable. She'd broken an oath given before her god."

"They would really force her to remain in an abusive relationship?"

Little Flower nodded. "They felt it was his right to treat her however he wanted. That's why GrandFather and I were so adamant about adding that clause to our charter to make ending a partnership with an unfit parent a protected right for either partner, even if it is already protected by the Consortium's charter. She told me it was hard, impossible at times, to cut off all ties with her family, but worth it in the long run. She met my father, had me and a new family, and was leading the life she wanted, not one dictated to her. I just hope, in the end, her god understood."

Marsee's ears drooped at the sorrow she saw in her sister's eyes. "If her gods didn't understand, then they weren't worth worshiping."

Her sister grunted but didn't reply, lost in some internal thought.

She waited until her sister's eyes refocused on her. "So, what do you say we do the legal stuff now and then have your ceremony later? Maybe after my watch is up, when it'll be safe for me to go home? We'll do every last little custom or thing you've ever wanted to do. I don't care how extravagant."

Her sister tilted her head in confusion. "How? I don't have any artwork to trade anymore. Everything we had was destroyed."

"You don't need to worry about what it'll cost. I can afford it. I'm probably the wealthiest person on all five planets right now. Neither of us will have to work a day in our lives if we don't want to." Marsee grinned, tail curled at the very idea of giving her sister a fairy tale wedding. Fairy tales were her favorite kind of stories.

"What?!" her sister squeaked. "When and how did *that* happen?"

Marsee flipped open her tablet and brought up her Guild account. "I've had so many gifts from the Water Sprites after what happened to me that I could buy my own private ship and not put a dent in it. Trust me, I've already looked." She handed the tablet over to her sister so she could see.

It was her sister's turn to look at her in shock. "I knew you'd been given gifts to help repair your room as several Guild Masters came and found me, but I had no idea it was this much. I swear."

Marsee frowned at the concern and worry she saw in her sister's expression. "How could you know? Only Ellie and Papa knew since they were here when I found out. Why would that even matter? Even if we weren't partners, you know I'd give you anything you ever needed if it was mine to give. You're my sister, and I will always take care of you."

Little Flower looked down at her hands before replying. "I didn't want you to think I only asked you to partner with me because of your resources."

Marsee's ears pinned back in surprise. "The thought never even crossed my mind. I honestly don't know what to make of it. Even before this, I barely touched my guild balance. At least not since you went into your coma. I was saving everything for when I had my own place I needed to furnish. I don't even have a clue what's been sent, and I've got so many messages from people to go through that it'll probably take the rest of my life to thank everyone. What do you think we should do with it all? I've been thinking about sharing a lot of it with the other victims."

"I don't know, but I like your ideas, especially the private ship part. I would love to explore all of the planets. Sharing with everyone else harmed by that bottom-dwelling scum-sucker seems fair, too, and likely far more than they'd be able to get for reparations since he's already dead, unless the Council makes up for it. Do you intend to continue training with the Guild?"

Marsee shrugged. "Up until a few minutes ago, I didn't think there was a point. I wasn't going to live long enough to replace Ellie or even earn my master's. I really liked collaborating with everyone on their projects, but I *loathed* the requisition meeting we attended. It was all I could do to stay awake. Even my instinct yawned. I'm not even sure Ellie would let me quit if I wanted to. I've tried at least a dozen times this past week. Then again, I probably own half the Guild at this point, so who knows if I'd even be able to quit without completely breaking it? I really need to talk to her. Honestly, it's been all I could do just to make it from one day to the next."

"I know that feeling. Let me guess. They've been working you so hard during your pickle torture that you fall asleep the moment you return to your room, only to have them rudely wake you up and start all over again?"

"I'm lucky if I make it back to my room. They've been pushing me until I pass out from exhaustion, not that it takes much. Only sleep is just as exhausting. I'm honestly afraid to go to sleep now because of the night terrors. What about you? Do you still intend to continue apprenticing with Ammond now that you know you won't have to chase around after me with a bone knitter and bandage putty?"

"I think so. For now, anyway. I'm enjoying it, and if we're going to have lots of cubs, and you're going to start training with the Guard, then there's still going to be a lot of work for me to do with that bone knitter and bandage putty. Besides, I really want to improve how they handle treating the mental health side of trauma."

"Yeah, that could use a major overhaul. I found out the reason I couldn't find anything when I was trying to help you before was because it's all council-protected information. They don't want anyone to get ahold of that information because it 'might be used against them.' Look how well that turned out." Marsee scrunched her nose and flattened her ears in disgust.

Little Flower snorted at her expression. "They really don't have a clue, do they?"

"No, but you do, and I think you'll make a phenomenal healer. Just don't give up on your drawing."

"I can't. Ammond made me promise not to before he agreed to take me on as an apprentice."

"Ha! He would!" She transferred Hope from where she was now snuggled in against her side back over to her sister's lap. Her tablet had gone off with another alarm to use the waste room, and she knew Rowena would be there at any moment to begin another grueling session of pickle torture. She wasn't wrong. When she returned, Rowena was waiting for her, although her attention was firmly affixed on Hope, who seemed just as intrigued by the ancient Digger.

Rowena looked over as she walked up. "You look like you're in a better mood."

"I am. Little Flower asked me to partner with her. I'm going to be a father!"

"Congratulations, Papa!" Rowena's face split with a matching grin for all of about two seconds. "But if you think you're going to get out of your pickle torture, you're sadly mistaken. You have work to do. You too, Little Flower."

"Me?!" Little Flower squeaked. "Ammond's in charge of my care."

After Marsee translated, Rowena glared at her sister with a look that could have easily rivaled the Senior Honor Guard's. "That old coot is far too busy playing with his *toys* right now to be bothered. But I do have it on good authority that you do well with positive motivation. There's a cookie waiting in Ammond's office for whoever makes it there first."

Marsee didn't wait for her sister. The moment she finished translating, she grabbed her mask and took off at a run, well, very slow trot, and dove out the door, swimming as hard as she could down the hall. She had no idea where Ammond's office was, not that it mattered. She knew they'd take the longest way possible to get there.

"Hey! That's not fair! I have to put my flippers on!" Little Flower yelled out after her.

"I don't care," Marsee replied. "I *want* that cookie!"

The guards immediately started placing bets, and to her ears-pinned annoyance, they both bet on her sister.

CHAPTER 4

GrandFather: Memories of Home

James woke as the first beams of sunlight filtered through the window of his underwater suite and decorated the room with a rainbow of dancing light. He hadn't seen the effect since his honeymoon, and he smiled wistfully at the memory of the family he'd lost. He'd been one of the lucky ones, though, one of the few that still had someone from before.

He yawned, still tired as it had been well after midnight by the time he'd returned to the suite from visiting with Marsee. He'd expected his granddaughter to insist on staying the night, although he'd also expected to end up on babysitting duty.

While he enjoyed every minute he got to spend with Hope, the last six months had been exhausting, as every free moment had been spent caring for the both of them and trying to learn enough to help find a cure for his granddaughter. He was astounded at how much Jessica had improved in the last standard week, even though it was nearly a month back on Earth, and he knew that if they'd still been on Earth, she would have died or been permanently disabled for the rest of her life, or saddled with crippling debt to pay for her medical care. She still had challenges to overcome, but he had a feeling Myra would stop at nothing to fix those, too.

The sounds of soft snoring caught his attention. Grinning, he carefully rolled over to watch Henry sleep. Their unexpected relationship had bloomed practically overnight, and he was still astounded that Henry was interested in him. He'd been attracted to Henry for months, but Henry had never given him any indication that he'd felt the same way. He'd never pushed the issue, knowing a good friend was far more valuable than a failed relationship.

He owed Henry everything for saving his family, but even without that, he was quickly falling in love with the man beside him. Henry refused to talk about his life before, and he was sure someone had hurt him badly, as every act of tenderness on his part seemed to surprise his quiet friend. But then, everyone rescued seemed to have their own horror story of their lives on Earth, those that shared anyway.

There were parts of his own life that he hadn't told anyone, not even his former husband or his granddaughter. When he was a teenager, he'd spent several years on active duty and saw horrors he never hoped to see again, yet they'd followed him to this new world where crime and war weren't supposed to exist. He'd hoped he'd never have to talk about those horrible days, much less instruct others on what he'd learned.

His conversation with Quinn had been almost more than he could bear. He'd excused himself, claiming exhaustion from his own injuries, and returned to his empty suite and shook for hours from fear and long-repressed memories, but every day after had been worse. It had taken every ounce of self-control he had to board the council ships, as they had no idea what they were flying into. He prayed that the worst was over now that Rip was dead, but he knew that people like Rip always left a vacuum that pulled in others even worse to fill the void.

Shaking himself out of those horrible thoughts and memories, he refocused on the man sleeping next to him. The night before, he'd returned to his suite to find Henry waiting up for him. Henry had struggled with the effects of exiting jump and had still been queasy when he'd left to visit with Marsee. They'd left the shared door between their suites open so that he could check on Henry when he returned, but his lack of babysitting duty and Henry's unexpected recovery meant they'd been up far later than James had intended, and he smiled at that far more enjoyable memory. In his opinion, their relationship was the best thing to come out of that horrible day.

Carefully rolling out of bed, trying not to wake Henry, he walked over to the window. It had been dark when they arrived, and while the swim lanes had been lit up and their drones had lights to allow them to see in the dark, he'd not been able to see much of their surroundings the night before.

What he saw now stunned him. His room overlooked a massive park where Water Sprites of all sizes were swimming and playing. Oddly shaped multi-storied buildings that seemed to defy gravity surrounded the park while shuttles traveled above them in what appeared to be well-established travel lanes. Everything was camouflaged by vibrant sea grasses and flowers, and a multitude of strange and impossible-looking creatures swam alongside the Sprites, who glowed and flashed a rainbow of vibrant neon colors as they spoke in their visual language.

It was as alien of a landscape as he could have imagined, and he itched to explore it all. Thankfully, they had the time to do so. They'd purposely scheduled their council's arrival early to have time to get to know the people here, although that had been scheduled before everything had happened. He knew the best way to save his people was to expand on the goodwill and friendships they'd made during the Halloween Festival.

Being so far underwater, he hadn't expected anything to be so well-lit, but he could see as clearly as if he were on the surface and with far less distortion than he was used to seeing whenever he'd gone snorkeling in the lake. Then again, the water was significantly cleaner here than his lake had been back home. He knew the building he was in was shielded, much like New Hope was, to protect from predators, so he wondered if that had anything to do with it or if maybe there was something different about their sun.

In the distance, he could see the Trauma Center, and he wondered how his granddaughters had fared the night. He was worried about both of them. While Jessica was so much better than she'd been the week before, she refused to talk about what had happened to her, both at the Agency and this past week with Damon, outside of giving her statement, and both Myra and Quinn had come to him to express their concerns about her ability to care for Hope and the comments that she'd made to her mother.

He'd always known that continuing the pregnancy would be difficult for her and had honestly been surprised that she'd chosen to continue with the pregnancy. The complications from Hope's birth had been as traumatic as Hope's conception, and he'd seen the looks she'd given Hope a time or two when she thought no one was looking. He didn't know how to help her, but he was glad she was at least trying to live again.

He heard Henry shift and glanced back to see him watching him from the bed. "You should come see this view."

"Got a pretty good view from here," Henry replied, with a smile that made him blush, but Henry climbed out of bed, dressed only in his birthday suit, and walked over to join him.

He blushed even more at Henry's handsome and well-endowed physique and turned away, which made Henry chuckle softly.

Henry came up behind him and gave him a hug as he peered over his shoulder to look out the window. "Well, I wasn't expecting to see that, but then again, I'm not sure what I was expecting."

He leaned back against Henry with a happy sigh, and they stood there looking out at the view in companionable silence.

"You're quiet this morning," Henry said.

"I'm worried about my grandchildren," he replied. "I can't get the image of the two of them last night out of my head. The looks on their faces as they held each other…" He shook his head. "I've seen that look far too often, and I prayed I'd never see it again." He shivered from his own repressed memories. "God, I don't know if I can do it."

"Do what?" Henry asked, hugging him tightly.

"Go to war. The people here don't have a clue what's at stake or even understand that the rules have changed, and I'm not just a soldier like I was then. The decisions I make now will affect everyone. I don't know if I'm strong enough for that."

"You are," Henry said. "You wouldn't be here if you weren't."

He sighed again, and Henry leaned down and kissed him on the neck. It did all sorts of things to his insides and distracted him from his thoughts. "If you keep doing that, we're never going to leave the room to explore."

"It'll still be there," Henry mumbled and kissed him again.

CHAPTER 5

Myra: Senior Honor Guard

Myra dragged a storage case through the static shield and into the dry room that Ammond had commandeered to set up his specialized equipment. Ammond was tinkering with the mesh hat for his brain scanner at his desk. "I found it," she said. "It was still on the ship."

"It's about time you're back. What took you so long?" Ammond handed her the hat and took the box from her.

"Sorry. It took me forever to get through security. I'm not sure what's going on, but there were guards everywhere, and I was stopped and questioned at least half a dozen times. You'd think they'd know who I was by now."

"That's probably why you were stopped so often. You *are* on a watch, after all." He scowled as he opened the box to find a tangle of cables inside. "What did you do, toss the box off the platform and then kick it the rest of the way here?"

She snorted. "You can thank the guards for that. Getting off the platform was even worse. They tore the case apart three times. Seriously, I think something's going on."

He grunted in reply but continued to mutter at the cables rather than respond to her concerns.

"You know, you should make a wireless version," she said after he let out a string of curses at one particularly bad tangle.

He pinned his ears and lashed his tail at her. "Impudent cub. Don't you think I haven't thought of that? Wireless wouldn't be nearly fast enough for the amount of data I gather with this scanner. What I need to do is figure out a better way to organize these cables. They were all nice and neat when we packed them. Now look at them." He held up the ball of wires. To be fair, she was rather impressed at how badly tangled they were.

"That's one of the laws of the universe. If it can be tangled, it will. Then again, one of the guards was a Flyer, so I wouldn't put it past him to have tangled those wires on purpose. It's something Bresdone would have done."

He continued to growl at the mess, but the tip of his tail curled.

"Now, if you want really tangled, you should have seen Marsee when she was first learning how to weave."

He snorted, and his tail spiraled. "I remember the picture you sent me. I'm surprised you managed to keep your hands still long enough to take the picture. I laughed for a week."

"It took me a few tries," she admitted, "and about an hour to cut her out of it. I still don't know how she managed to weave her tail into that rug. I should probably dig that picture up and send it to Ellie. She could use a laugh."

When Ammond finally wrangled the mass of wires into some semblance of order, he stood up, grunting with the effort. Four days of ship travel and the damp ocean were not doing well with his old bones, and she frowned at the sight.

"I can set this up for you if you'd like."

His growl intensified, and his tail gave another lash. "I may be ancient, but I'm not feeble, and I will claw you if you keep saying stupid things. The last thing we need is for you to hook something up the wrong way and break it. You know we don't have replacement parts."

She scowled at him in mock outrage. "I only did that once, and that was a century ago. Are you ever going to let it go?"

"And risk you doing it a second time? Not a chance." After a lengthy stretch, he made his way over to the pile of cases delivered by the platform staff earlier and started digging through them. "We need to label these cases better for the return trip," he grumbled. "Ah, here it is." He pulled out the stand for the mesh hat and started putting it together.

"Myra?"

She turned at the sound of her name and froze, swallowing hard, as the Senior Honor Guard stepped inside. It was all she could to keep her tail from poofing.

This can't be good, she thought.

"I'm guessing from your expression that you remember me."

Is she here for me, or is this about Marsee? she wondered. Myra swallowed hard again and felt her instinct stir with her fear. She shoved it down hard and glanced at Ammond, wondering if he'd reported the issue she'd had with her instinct after capturing Damon.

Ammond set the stand down and carefully removed the mesh hat from her grip. It was all she could do to keep her paws from shaking and her mask in place as she tried to figure out what to say or even what to do with her hands after letting go of the hat. She normally crossed her arms, but she was afraid Kendra might think she was hiding her claws.

When she looked back at the Honor Guard, Kendra was watching her with a raised brow.

"I...How can I help you?" Myra finally managed to stammer out.

"I'm here to talk to you about your daughter," Kendra replied.

Myra's fear ratcheted up several levels at the confirmation. *Ancient Gods. She's here for Marsee!* She felt her instinct growl in response to that thought and squashed it down hard again.

"Marsee is fully in control of her instinct, Ma'am," she said. "In as much as she doesn't have any left. Those parts of her brain were damaged. Please believe me. She's not a danger to anyone. She's completely incapable of turning it on anymore."

"I am fully aware of her injuries," Kendra said, then made a pointed look in Ammond's direction. "If we could have some privacy, please."

"Ammond is my mentor and is fully aware of everything that has happened to Marsee. Whatever you have to say to me can be said in front of him," she replied, honestly not wanting to be alone with Kendra.

Kendra frowned for several moments before nodding and shutting the door but then frowned again at the lack of a privacy screen before turning back to them. "What I'm about to tell you cannot leave this office," she stated.

Both Myra and Ammond raised their brows but nodded.

"Marsee is not the first person to survive the advanced stages of psychosis," Kendra said. "She is not broken or damaged. Her brain will heal for the most part. She won't ever lose control again, but she will need training to help manage her senses as they recover, as they'll be as strong as they were when her instinct was on."

Myra crossed her arms and glared at the guard. "I have read every last published article on psychosis for the last several thousand years to try and help my daughter. Not one of them has ever mentioned what my daughter is going through. What makes you so sure about this? You're a Guard, not a Healer."

Kendra snorted and looked thoroughly amused, enough that her tail curled briefly.

Myra frowned with confusion, not expecting that reaction.

"Technically, I am. I earned my Masters with the Healer's Guild over a century ago. But more importantly, I'm an Honor Guard, and I've survived it myself, as has every other Honor Guard of our species since before the Great Awakening."

"What?!" both Myra and Ammond exclaimed in slack-jawed astonishment and disbelief.

"Nearly half of the Guard comes from people on the watch list. When we have the chance, we recruit those who are posted and try to save those we can, although not everyone makes it through the Transition like your daughter did."

"You're serious about this?" Myra asked, still not believing it but wanting desperately to believe her daughter would recover.

"I am. I would never lie to you, especially not about something this serious. Scan my brain if you need proof. From what I saw a few minutes ago, Marsee is already showing signs of improvement. Although, I don't know how much the rest of her injuries will affect her overall recovery. Many of the symptoms she's reported, from not feeling pain to the changes in taste, smell, and her other senses, are all the same symptoms we deal with in the initial phases of the transition. Her extreme physical weakness and difficulty swallowing are not. Even when her sense of pain returns, she'll still have to deal with the long-term issues from her other injuries and trauma, but we can help her there, too."

She was going to object, but Kendra raised a paw.

"I mean no disrespect, but for both your sakes, this is the kind of thing that is often better handled by an impartial person. As much as I hate to admit it, we're used to dealing with the kinds of trauma your daughter has experienced, and we find that there are often things a person cannot tell their parents, no matter how good their relationship is. What matters is that Marsee gets the best care available."

She sighed but nodded. She had nearly lost control watching Marsee's statement, and that had been a recording, and it was more than obvious that she'd failed to help Little Flower deal with her own trauma and had actually made things worse.

Ammond pulled out his hand scanner and aimed it at the Senior Honor Guard. His eyebrows lifted, and his ears shot straight back with astonishment. "I think she's telling the truth, Myra," he said and handed her the scanner so she could see for herself.

She sighed with relief when she saw the scans. There were signs of injury similar to Marsee's, but it was clear Kendra's brain had recovered, too. Only one small section was still dark. "Thank the blessed moons!" she whispered.

"For Marsee's sake, yes, but it presents *us* with a problem. Marsee's popularity, as well as all of the healers you've wrangled into helping you treat her, means that it will soon become public knowledge that psychosis is now somewhat treatable, and we can't have that."

"Why not?" Myra asked.

"Because we'd be right back where we were before the Great Awakening. Imagine the chaos that would occur if people knew that you had a fifty-fifty chance of gaining the Hue-man equivalent of superpowers by training your instinct rather than shutting it down. How many cubs would we lose because they wanted to be like Crawly Man? On top of that, people would fear the Guard even more than they do now. We rarely tell our own families. Time and again, when we've tried, they end up wanting nothing to do with us because they don't believe we can control it. Instead, they think that we've become a monster instead of defeating one. If people knew about Marsee, they would turn on her out of fear, just as they would if they found out she'd lost control. Her returning senses could be explained away as her injuries recovering over time, but the scans you take must not become Guild knowledge, or at least not lower-level Guild knowledge. There are things that are not taught until a certain rank. This is one of them, and the Council can't know. Nerissa already knows to some extent, as do my healers and...Rowena."

Myra blinked at this. She'd been actively working with both Nerissa and Rowena, and they'd said nothing.

"Jeran and Marcus would never do anything to harm Marsee," Ammond said before she could reply.

Myra chose not to correct him since Jer *had* harmed her daughter. She was still furious with him about that, but in this, Ammond was right. Jer would do everything he could to protect Marsee's reputation, if for no other reason than it would protect his own.

Kendra raised a brow. "You both know they will kill her if they even suspect she's losing control, but they are both Senior Council and far too close to Marsee for them not to figure out what's going on or for her to eventually slip and discuss it with them, assuming she hasn't already informed them, but I don't recommend it be shared with the rest of the Council. Please believe me. People don't do well with this information. We have ten thousand years of history to prove that."

"I don't understand why. It's not like it's anything we can't do anyway. I would think it would be more of a problem not being able to shut it off," Myra said.

Kendra nodded. "True, but most people don't know what we're capable of doing, and for good reason. We don't want anyone to try to train on their own. Even though Marsee was able to do so safely, it's far too dangerous for most people and everyone around them. There just aren't enough guards to watch everyone. It's better if people think it's nothing more than a cub's instinct to pounce on every tail that wiggles. I know what kind of training you go through as a Healer to learn to deal with being around blood, and I know you took the survival course during your training. You have more training than most, but most of your training is in learning to shut it off, not actively use it, which brings me to the next reason I'm here. It's my understanding that you tracked Damon Minor for hours. How much of that time did you use your instinct?"

"Pretty much the entire time," Myra replied, instantly on edge again. "But I'm fully in control of my instinct. I didn't harm Damon, and Councilor Paxton, Quinn, and Ammond have all tested me."

"I am fully aware that Damon was unharmed. That's the only reason you were allowed to travel. As for whether you're still fully in control, that remains to be seen. I know about the incident with Healer Samin."

"I was angry, honestly more at Jer than her, but I wasn't out of control, at least I don't think so."

"Did your instinct talk to you, either during your hunt or after?"

"Sure, but isn't it like that for everyone?" Myra asked.

Worry crossed Kendra's face, and her body tensed. "No. How long has it been speaking to you?" she demanded.

"My whole life, or as long as I can remember anyway." She shrugged, honestly confused as to why Kendra was so tense. She was in full control of her instinct, always had been, well, except for that one odd incident.

Kendra's ears flicked back, and she sniffed deeply. "You're telling the truth. Astounding!"

It was Myra's turn to flick her ears back. "You can tell if I'm lying?!"

Kendra didn't answer her. Instead, she continued to question her. "Has it been harder for you to control lately, or different in any way?"

Myra looked over at Ammond, who looked at her and then motioned with his eyes to tell the guard.

Kendra frowned and tensed even more at their nonverbal exchange and focused hard on her.

It made the hair on the back of Myra's neck spike. She shrunk under the glare, instinctively recognizing the power and authority that the Senior Honor Guard had over her and if she could somehow tell when she was lying...

She sighed. "Different, yes. Harder, no. The other day, Ammond and I were trying to explain to Little Flower about her sister's injuries, and in the process, she described something similar that they have. As she was describing it, I was remembering how it felt right before I captured Damon, when my instinct was the most on I've ever had it. The descriptions were remarkably similar, and I had all of the normal physical reactions to turning on my instinct, but it wasn't actually on. My claws were out, my eyes dilated, and my reaction speed increased, but I was wholly me. I was never out of control or had any difficulty speaking. Ammond scanned my brain at that time and found that the same areas that were damaged in Marsee were active in mine. I wasn't able to turn off those physical reactions until Little Flower, of all things, made me try turning it on. It wasn't actually on. She thought I was having what their species call a panic attack or what we would call a trauma response. She's routinely caught in them from the trauma she's experienced and has even broken her grandfather's nose thinking she was being attacked by her rapist again when he was only trying to care for her."

Kendra looked astonished at her ramblings, and Myra wondered if she'd said too much.

"I spoke to your daughters a few minutes ago, and they both requested training on how to protect themselves," Kendra said after a moment of thought. "I only intended to train Little Flower in the use of a stunner, but I may have been wrong. If they have a form of instinct like us, then we should learn all we can about it. As for you, turn it on."

Myra wasn't surprised by this request and had expected it the moment Kendra walked in the door. She was on the watch list, and while she'd been tested multiple times already, the Honor Guard had the authority to kill her if she so much as hesitated in turning it on or off.

She was expecting the same on/off test Kendra had used before, but the moment it was on, Kendra attacked faster than Myra could even think to respond. Her instinct didn't hesitate, and both blocked the attack and prepared for a second one. She clamped down hard on her reaction and didn't retaliate. Attacking a Guard, even in self-defense, could be seen as being out of control. That would be a death sentence, and she knew it.

"Can you still understand me?"

"Yes, ma'am," Myra replied.

"Turn it off now," Kendra ordered.

Myra did so immediately, although her heart was still pumping hard from the surprise of the attack.

Kendra examined her closely for several moments before nodding. "You do appear to be in control, but I am concerned. That you're hearing your instinct means you're dangerously close to being in the same situation as your daughter. Most people only make it a few days before losing control once they hear theirs. The only reason I am not bringing you in for closer observation now is because it's apparently not a new occurrence for you. My understanding is that your daughter started hearing hers the day she hunted Little Flower. I'm assuming that you taught Marsee what you learned as a healer? Did she ever mention it before that?"

Myra shook her head at the last question. "We all worked with her from the moment we realized she was having difficulty as a cub, although it never really helped. She never mentioned hearing her instinct, just that it pressured her to act, and that only started the day Little Flower arrived. She was so much better these past eight months, calmer.

I never saw any issues, but I know she went out a few times with Jer for a run when she was feeling stressed. Motion always calmed her. The only time she acted out of the norm was after Jer tested her and she left with Ellie. I thought she was just overwhelmed with caring for Little Flower and figured the break and opportunity would be good for her. If I had known what he had done then, I don't know what I would have done. I'm still angry, but she's apparently forgiven him and I'm trying hard to respect that, for her sake."

Kendra nodded. "I understand your anger. Any parent would be livid, but what he did is consistent with the Council's methods for training, testing, and containment. I am honestly surprised that she didn't kill him. Alone, he would have had little chance to defend himself if she were truly out of control. Whether she would have eventually lost control if it hadn't been for Rip is anyone's guess. What Rip did to her would have pushed any of us over the edge, even if we weren't struggling before."

"The Council does that to everyone?" Myra asked.

Kendra pursed her lips. "The Council has their own training methods to ensure that they can kill without losing control, and those are far more violent than what your daughter went through with Jeran. As for the test, it depends on need. For most, what I did here today is enough. Your daughter *was* showing signs of losing control, including spraying and marking, which I verified myself. Whether you admit it or not, your partner did the only thing he could to save your daughter's life. If he had called in the Guard or even his brother, she would be dead now, and not just because we would have had no choice but to put her down. What she learned in that fight gave her the skills and training she needed to survive what Rip did to her. She said as much to Clear Seas the day after she was rescued from the cave."

"I thought she didn't tell anyone what happened until the day she threw her father out of her room. Was she trying to have Jer arrested?"

"Quite the contrary. My understanding is that she was trying to help Clear Seas, who was worried about how his son, Stormy, was taking the news of Deep Current's death. He was apparently blaming himself for not being fast enough to save them both, and Marsee was trying to explain how she'd felt much the same after her sister ended up in the coma. It was that guilt that caused her to run from her father that day, or part of the reason anyway. She was also feeling overwhelmed by the massive influx of people in New Hope and the loss of her territory."

Myra sighed and looked away as her own guilt clawed at her. She'd been so focused on Little Flower that she'd neglected Marsee.

"For what it's worth," Kendra continued. "Your training may very well have been what allowed her to regain control, although from what you've just told me, it could be hereditary. I'm not aware of anyone who has been able to talk with their instinct for as long as you, but then perhaps that means their control was always so good that they never had reason to come before the Guard. She was mentally strong, even as a child."

Myra frowned. "What do you mean? She struggled as a child. You saw that. You were there for both incidents."

Kendra shook her head. "I'm honestly not sure that she did. She was in full control during the first incident, even after tasting blood, and she remained verbal and in control during the second incident, where her friend did not. Even with Little Flower, her ability to stop on her own during that first hunt, is unheard of, and to last as long as she did before losing control in the garden, astounding." Kendra shrugged. "Either way, it's you I'm worried about now. I am giving you the option to join the Guard, which I would *prefer*, or never use your instinct again. If you do have the need to use it or have even the slightest issue with your control, I want to be notified immediately. If you do not and I find out about it, I will assume that you are out of control and...*take* the appropriate measures. Is that understood?"

She swallowed hard at the implied threat. "Yes, ma'am."

Kendra turned and left without another word.

Myra's legs buckled, and she sat down hard where she was. "Ancient Gods."

Ammond walked over and wrapped her in a hug. She leaned into him, taking comfort from his show of affection, as her entire body started shaking from the adrenaline crash. Moments like this were rare, and she treasured them, but it wasn't long before he returned to his normally grumpy self and slapped her hard across the back of her head. "I always knew you were thick-headed and stubborn, Myra. Why didn't you ever tell me your instinct talked to you?"

She chuckled as she rubbed at her head, honestly glad for the distraction from her thoughts. "Because I didn't know that wasn't normal or any different from talking to yourself when you think about a problem," she replied. "I'm serious. I've been able to do this my whole life."

Ammond snorted and walked away. "I would end up with the most stubborn pair of proteges in the universe. Between you and Little Flower..." he trailed off, rolling his eyes and shaking his head at the ceiling.

"I prefer to think of it as strong-willed," Myra replied with a snort. "Just like my old coot of a mentor."

"Impudent cub. Now get over here and help me finish setting up this equipment. They'll be here any minute."

She did as ordered, but her thoughts were a tangled mess, even more so than the wires, and Ammond had to thwack her with his tail on more than one occasion to snap her out of it.

CHAPTER 6

Myra: Scans

By the time high-pitched Hue-man laughter sounded outside her door, Ammond had finished setting up his scanner, and Myra had mostly pulled herself together.

Little Flower appeared first, followed by a large female Saber Guard who was struggling to hold onto Little Flower's wiggly cub. Little Flower carefully stepped through the static shield, wobbling slightly as she adjusted for gravity and the awkwardness of her artificial fins. "Cookie?" Little Flower asked in Saber as she wobbled and reached for the guard's leg to steady herself.

Myra's tail curled from both amusement that 'cookie' was one of the first words Little Flower had learned in Saber, and the proof that while Rowena would never admit it, she did listen to Ammond on occasion. "On the counter," she replied in Saber and pointed.

Ammond walked over and took Hope from the guard while Little Flower started making her slow way across the room, her fins flapping on the floor with each step. Suddenly, Ammond shifted out of the way as Marsee launched herself through the entrance, stumbling slightly as she skidded to a stop and scanned the room with a nearly feral expression on her face.

A moment later, she locked in on the direction Little Flower was heading, found the cookie on the counter, and took off at a slow trot, far faster than Myra expected, easily making it to the counter before Little

Flower did. Marsee swiped it off and started unwrapping the protective covering.

"Hey, that's mine!" Little Flower signed and tried grabbing Marsee's arm for it. "I made it here first."

Marsee easily kept it out of her sister's reach and popped the entire thing in her mouth with a wicked grin, then moaned with delight as her ears drooped with evident satisfaction.

Her sense of taste must be returning, Myra thought.

The cookie was gone in two bites. Marsee tossed the wrapper in the nearby recycler and sniffed deeply as she scanned the room for more.

"What happened to sharing everything with me?" Little Flower asked.

"I said I would gladly give you anything you *needed*. *You* didn't need the cookie. *I* did. That was the first bite of real food I've had in a week," Marsee signed, then purposely licked her claws as if to remove the last bit of crumbs, not that there were any.

Little Flower crossed her arms and scowled up at her sister, but Myra had learned her Hue-man child's moods and knew she was only teasing. Mostly.

"You know the food here is atrocious," Marsee signed when she was done licking her claws. "Besides, there are more in that drawer over there."

Myra chuckled as Little Flower dove into the drawer and pulled out the stash Ammond had hidden. She was surprised that Marsee had been able to sniff it out. She couldn't even smell it. That gave her hope that Kendra had been telling the truth, although she wondered what that would mean for her daughter and what it would be like to always have those senses available without the risk of becoming feral herself.

As Little Flower munched, Marsee flopped down, now panting hard from the effort of her swim. "Did you hear the good news, Mama?"

"Kendra just left," Myra replied. "I'll admit I'm relieved to know you'll recover if still thoroughly flabbergast as to how you managed to kill off your instinct in the first place."

"Relief doesn't even begin to cover it," Marsee said. "But there's more good news."

"More?"

"Little Flower asked me to be her partner!"

She blinked several times, not even remotely expecting that news, and frowned with worry. Little Flower had been so depressed these past few months and had expressed concerns about her ability to parent because of her past trauma. "Partner? Little Flower, I would have thought you'd want to partner with one of your own species."

"I don't know any of them well enough even to consider it," Little Flower replied. "And besides, Marsee's been caring for Hope since the day she was born. I'm just making it official. You're not upset I didn't ask you, are you?"

"No, of course not. I'm worried about the suddenness of it, especially considering our past conversations."

Marsee frowned at that response and turned to face Little Flower. "What conversations?"

"I was really depressed after you left," Little Flower replied. "It's the whole reason Ammond did the surgery, but I'm better now. Not perfect, but at least I'm not a useless lump anymore. I know I still need help, but I want that help to be on my own terms and with someone who loves Hope as much, if not more than I do."

Marsee leaned her head against Little Flower's side, purring, as Little Flower draped an arm over her head and scratched absently at one of Marsee's ears.

Myra's face split with a grin at the look of love that passed between the two of them. "Well, in that case, congratulations!"

Rowena appeared at that moment and carefully stepped through the door with the assistance of Marsee's guard and shuffled her way over to Ammond's equipment with a look of greed and excitement on her face that nearly matched Marsee's the moment before.

Ammond grabbed his brain scanner with his free hand, tucked it behind him, and pinned his ears back with a growl. "If you think I'm going to let you put your grubby paws all over my brain scanner after failing to let us know that Marsee would recover, you're sadly mistaken."

"You knew?!" Marsee asked Rowena, after she finished translating for Little Flower.

"Of course, I knew, child," Rowena replied. "I was a healer in your guard for decades, and I lost my best friend to this illness. I've made it my life's mission to find a cure, which hasn't exactly been easy since Kendra took office."

"Kendra's stopped you from researching?" Myra asked.

"No. She cut my funding, stating that it was better used elsewhere. She's of the belief that surviving the Transition is a sign of a person's honor, and I suppose, in a way, she's right. Those without honor don't survive. How or why, I still have no idea."

"But we're family," Myra said. "Why wouldn't you tell us? We'd have kept it secret."

"I gave an oath a long time ago that I would never talk about it with anyone outside of your guard, and I knew Kendra would eventually cave and tell you. She's stubborn but not stupid. Between sign language and Jer and Marcus's willingness to give Marsee a chance, it's the first opportunity her guard has had in ten thousand years to make a change in the policy around psychosis. I've seen what knowledge of this does to people who find out. It never goes well. Rather than believing that the person has recovered, they believe they've succumbed to it. You know as well as I do that people are going to be nervous around Marsee for months simply because of what happened to her. Imagine how they would react if they found out she lost control, or worse, if your council found out. When the Council gets involved, it never goes well. I did my best to make sure Jer and Marcus fully understood that Marsee wouldn't ever be able to use her instinct again, or at least not in the same way, and that she might experience strange side effects as she recovered. It was the best I could do to protect her and honor my oath, and I know Marsee's guards have been doing what they can as well."

"Speaking of protection. Avery's going to teach us how to fight and use a stunner," Marsee said.

Myra frowned at her daughter. "Kendra told me. I'm glad you'll learn how to use a stunner, but you'll need to be careful. Your replacement heart isn't strong enough yet to handle being stunned and it'll be several months before you're healed enough to fight. Speaking of which, let's see how you're doing. Come on." She tapped the side of the exam chair.

Marsee groaned and crawled her way over to the seat, not even bothering to stand up on four feet, much less two, and they'd purposely turned the gravity down in the room.

"What happened to that burst of energy you had a moment ago?" Ammond asked.

"That was all I had left," Marsee replied. "And I *really* wanted that cookie. I'm also fairly certain you've turned up the gravity since I entered the room. It feels about three times stronger than it did a minute ago."

They hadn't, which worried Myra as she was afraid Marsee had hurt herself. She helped Marsee onto the seat, focusing hard on her mask. The light in Marsee's room had been dimmed the night before, and she hadn't gotten a good look at all of Marsee's scars, although she'd been staring at the scans of them for days. Seeing them in person was far worse.

Her instinct growled at the harm that had been done to her children.

They both survived, and Marsee ripped him to shreds, she reminded herself and felt it settle back down with pride at how fierce their children were.

Once Marsee was comfortably settled and Myra confirmed that there weren't any new injuries, Ammond plunked the hat on her head and started the scan. Rowena shuffled up close to the monitor, squinting at it. "Impressive. You've improved the resolution since the last scan I saw."

Ammond grabbed at his chest. "Myra, I think I'm dying. Rowena just gave me a compliment."

Myra's tail curled, and Rowena chuckled briefly.

"Don't get used to it, you old coot," Rowena said. "That's the only compliment you're getting from me until your memorial service. It's about time you did something useful with your life."

"And there's the snark I remember," Ammond added, although his tail curled.

Rowena ignored him and zoomed in on the scan.

"Forgive my curiosity," Little Flower signed. "I don't want to come across as rude, but I noticed that you're squinting. I haven't met many Diggers yet. Are your vision challenges normal for your species, or is that just you?"

Rowena turned to Little Flower with a half-scowl. "My vision is perfect for my species. I'll admit that as we primarily live underground, our long-range vision isn't as good as the other species, or yours, from my understanding, but our ability to see in dark environments is unparalleled. With our hearing and sense of smell and touch, we can easily navigate in complete darkness. I'm only squinting because the monitor is too bright. If I turn the brightness down to where it's comfortable for me, no one else would be able to see."

Little Flower nodded her understanding. "The screens are rather bright. Have you thought about wearing sunglasses like we do?"

Rowena tilted her head. "That's not a bad idea. However, I haven't been off of Digger in close to fifty years, so it hasn't been an issue, and squinting for a few days won't hurt me. It's perfectly normal for my species. Now, let's talk about Marsee. That's a far more interesting topic than my old eyes."

The next half hour was informative, to say the least, although she could tell there was quite a bit that Rowena wasn't saying in Marsee's presence. It wasn't until her children left with their guards in tow to return to Marsee's room that Rowena shut the door and turned to face them with a far more serious expression.

"What's wrong with Marsee?"

"Nothing that you're not already aware of. What I want to know is how you're doing?"

"Me?!"

"Yes, you. I know that look. I've seen it often enough. You're frazzled. Psychosis is often hereditary, and you know it. If you're having problems, you should deal with it now before it gets worse."

"I'm fine. Kendra just tested me, and she didn't drag me in."

"That's because she can't. Not here, anyway. And don't lie to me. I know all about the incidents with Little Flower and Healer Samin."

She frowned and looked at Ammond. "You told her?"

"Of course I did," he replied. "I know you say you're in control, but that incident with Little Flower scared me."

She pursed her lips, not sure whether to be annoyed that they didn't believe her or touched to know he cared about her so much to reach out to Rowena for help rather than reporting her.

"Have you scanned her, Ammond?"

"No," he replied. "We've been focusing on Marsee, and I wasn't sure how to broach the subject without making things worse."

"Well, what are you waiting for?"

When neither she or Ammond moved, Rowena growled at them. "I'm not getting any younger. Get in that chair now before I take Ammond's scanner and hit you over the head with it."

"Yes, ma'am," Myra replied with a curled tail as Ammond moved the scanner away from Rowena and growled. Rowena ignored him. The moment she was in the chair, Ammond gave Rowena another scowl but put the hat on, and the monitor lit up.

Rowena squinted at it for some time, blocking the monitor so she couldn't see. "Hmm. Are you hearing your instinct?"

"I have since I was a child," Myra replied. "You know that. At least, I'm pretty sure I told you when you scanned me a century ago."

"You did, but I didn't know if you'd ever told Ammond or not, and you asked me not to tell anyone."

Ammond pinned his ears at her. "You told her, but you didn't tell me?"

"Just because I thought it was normal doesn't mean I was going to go around telling everyone I was hearing voices. Besides, you'd only been my mentor for about a month, and the last thing I wanted was for you to decide I wasn't worth the risk."

He grunted. "I suppose I can understand that. I was a bit of a grump back then."

"Back then?!" Rowena scoffed. "If you were a grump then, what does that make you now?"

Ammond scowled at Rowena. "A curmudgeonly old coot, and proud of it, but at least I'm not the one keeping secrets."

Rowena snorted at Ammond and turned back to her. "Are you hearing it more, or is it harder to control?"

"No, and no," Myra replied. "And before you ask, yes, Kendra knows about everything."

"You're serious? And she didn't kill you on the spot?"

"I'm still here, aren't I? She ordered me to either join the Guard or avoid using my instinct again. I chose the latter."

Rowena let out a sigh and turned around to face her completely. "While it pains me to admit it, she's right. You can't ever use your instinct again. You are dangerously close to losing control if my research is accurate. You know that the more you use it, the bigger and stronger it gets, and if you keep using it, it will try to take control the next time it perceives that your life is at risk. Yours isn't as big as Marsee's was, but it's far bigger than normal and far bigger than it was a century ago. Don't use it again. *Ever.*"

She nodded. "I have no intentions of using it, but for some reason, people keep trying to kill members of my family. If protecting them means losing myself to psychosis, so be it. If Marsee can survive, so can I."

"I suppose I can't fault that reasoning, but please be careful. I've seen people transition on more than one occasion, and far too often, others get hurt or killed. I know you would feel awful if that happened."

She nodded again, and Rowena seemed to accept it.

"Why don't you go check on Marsee and make sure she makes it back to her room in one piece? As hard as she pushed herself on the way over, I'll be surprised if she makes it halfway back before passing out. As interesting as your brain is, I want to tinker with Ammond's toys for a bit."

"Who says I'm going to let you?" Ammond growled.

"And pass up the opportunity to gloat about what you've accomplished before I return home? I seriously doubt it."

Ammond's ears drooped. "You're leaving already?"

Myra's heart hitched at the disappointment in Ammond's voice, and she understood why. It had been decades since they'd seen each other in person, and it would likely be the last time. It didn't take a healer to see how little time Rowena had left.

"Marsee doesn't need me anymore," Rowena said. "You're here now, and I have several experiments running back home. I'll be leaving first thing tomorrow morning once my klutz of a nephew gets everything packed up. Until then, gimmie." Rowena wiggled her fingers in a greedy motion and grinned wickedly. It was such a strange expression to see on a Digger, but somehow, it fit the Ancient Healer who had defied all expectations and stereotypes for most of her life.

Ammond growled and hid the scanner behind him again.

Myra smiled at the two. She knew how much they cared for each other, even if they both denied it. They squabbled as much as her first litter of cubs did. "I'll leave you two to fight it out. I'm late for a meeting with Jer anyway. Rowena, please try not to take the scanner apart. We really do need it."

"I'm greedy, not stupid," Rowena muttered. "Now get! I don't want any witnesses if I have to claw your mentor to get at that scanner."

Laughing, she left, only half sure Rowena was joking.

CHAPTER 7

Ammond: No Time to Waste

Ammond frowned as he watched Myra swim out of his office and frowned even more when Rowena's expression turned serious again. "I know you too well. You saw something on the scans."

"I did. You can't let Myra transition. She won't survive."

"Why not? Her instinct is smaller than Marsee's. You said so yourself."

"That's true, but I honestly have no idea how Marsee survived. Perhaps it was the addition of sign language or the nanos that were still active in her system, but I can't be sure. Whatever the reason, we can't assume that Myra will survive simply because Marsee did. And now that Myra knows about it, Kendra will push her to transition at the slightest sign of an issue, so you'll have to do everything you can to keep Myra calm and, above all else, avoid using her instinct." Rowena turned and looked at the scan that was still displaying on the monitor. "I'm honestly surprised she hasn't lost control already."

He sighed and sat down. "I honestly can't believe they didn't kill her when she went after Samin, or that Kendra didn't today. I've never seen Myra so...so not herself." He sighed again, at a complete loss for words to describe what he had just seen.

"Has she been non-verbal?"

He shrugged. "All morning, but I can't tell if she's just distracted or if it's more than that. It took her far too long to answer when Kendra first appeared, and her paws were shaking when I took the scanner from her. Fear or psychosis, I don't know, but there was a moment when Kendra did the swipe test…" He shook his head and looked at his paws. "I've seen Myra livid, distraught, and terrified, but for a brief moment, I saw something I've never seen before. There was something so…so feral about her. I thought for sure she was going to retaliate, and I'm pretty sure Kendra did, too." He forced himself to look up at Rowena. "I'm going to lose her, aren't I?"

"Not if I have anything to say about it. I've never lost a patient, and I don't intend to ruin my record now."

He smiled sadly at Rowena for the familiar lie. "Thanks. So why do you think Myra won't survive the Transition?"

"I'm surprised you didn't see it, although it has been over a century, and I know you don't have an eidetic memory like I do. Myra's brain looks almost identical to Arianna's, bigger, although in every other way, identical. Arianna survived the transition but died a few hours later. It happens. People forget how to breathe, or their heart stops, and we've tried it all: transplants, months of life support, you name it. It's the whole reason I invented nanotech. Marsee's recovering at a phenomenal rate. Most people take months or years to have the kinds of improvements we're already seeing. But if she hadn't recovered as quickly as she did, she would have died too, and she came far too close on several occasions."

"Do you think it was the nano bath? Hyacinth completely flooded her system."

"It certainly didn't hurt, but for all I know, it could have been nothing more than sheer stubbornness on Marsee's part. It does tend to run in your family."

He snorted. "So why didn't you tell Myra not to transition?"

"Because she can't know. If she's to have any chance at surviving, she has to believe with her entire being that she's in control and can beat it. If she doubts it for even a second, it'll take advantage and win. And you can't let Kendra get ahold of these scans either. If she sees them, she won't bother risking her guards to give Myra the chance. I'll send you everything I have. Perhaps you'll have the time I don't or see what I've been missing for the last century. While I hate to admit it, I'm losing pieces of my shell every day. I've got three, maybe four months left before it's critical, but I'll do everything I can to help."

Ammond swallowed hard at the thought of losing both Myra and Rowena. He'd already lost so many. Myra was his first protege, and he had known Rowena since he was a cub. "You're not allowed to die before me. You've been telling me that for over a century."

"Believe me. I'm just as annoyed by the thought. Now, enough moping, or I'll make that a reality. We don't have time to waste. Not if we're going to save your protege."

GrandFather: Market Square

Two hours later, clothed in their newly re-invented wet suits and carrying their flippers and masks, James and Henry made their way down to the exit and out. They'd all been provided with a map of interesting sites to visit, including several museums, the Arboretum, and a local market.

It was still quite early, so they decided to make for the market first and see what they could find for breakfast rather than eat what had been provided for them in the suite or the restaurants in Council Platform that focused on off-world cuisine for guests staying in the Platform.

Most of their protein sources came from here, and out of all the planets, this world was actually the most comparable to Earth, even though there was little in the way of land above water. It had been proposed that they take over one of the larger uninhabited islands as their own, but there was no infrastructure there. It was still on the list for a possible colony when their numbers increased enough to sustain it.

James fully expected they would be inundated with curious Sprites wanting to meet their first human, but surprisingly, while it was obvious they had been noticed, no one approached them as they traveled.

It didn't take them long to find the market. They stopped on the edge to take it all in. It was far bigger than he'd expected, with what looked like several hundred booths with vendors trading just about everything imaginable and thousands of people shopping and milling about.

He watched as their presence was noted, but again, they all kept their distance.

"Well, it looks like we've been spotted," Henry chuckled beside him. "Might as well mingle with locals."

"Shall we hit up a food vendor first and then wander the rest of the market?" he asked.

Henry nodded, so they directed their drone up to the nearest food vendor and browsed the offerings.

The Sprite smiled at them. "Good morning, Councilors. Welcome to our world. My name is Opal. I made sure that everything I brought was on the list of safe foods and will do so for as long as you're here, but I won't take offense if you want to confirm it. I don't know your species preferences. If you don't like something, please let me know, and I will freely exchange it until you find something you do, or if there's something you know you like but I don't have, let me know, and I'll make sure to have it tomorrow."

"Thank you for your consideration, Opal. You've gone above and beyond my expectations. I'll be sure to let the others know. I'm GrandFather, and this is Henry Curtis."

Opal's expression changed to wonder. "Henry Curtis! The Translator told us of your bravery. It's an honor to meet you and have you at my booth," she signed. Then, she surprised them both by flashing a purple and silver pattern on her skin and bowing low to Henry.

They both turned as Opal's words traveled through the market, and every Sprite turned and did the same.

Henry bowed back, clearly embarrassed, and turned back to Opal. "What does the purple and silver mean?"

Opal made a sign that he didn't recognize and then considered for a moment to try and explain. "Are you familiar with the creature that Stormy faced down to find the Translator?"

They both nodded.

"It is our most dangerous predator," she replied. "And before we joined the Consortium and had ships capable of keeping the beast away from our communities, many died every year protecting us from that creature. We called them Leviathan Slayers. That ancient term has fallen out of use, but in this context, it is a sign of great respect for the immense risk you took to save GrandFather, Little Flower, and Hope."

"Thank you," Henry replied, although clearly surprised and overwhelmed by the display.

"Look at that, Henry. You're famous, and all you had to do was ride fifty leagues to save my sorry butt."

Henry chuckled but didn't reply.

"What do you suggest we try?" James asked, changing the subject. "I don't recognize anything, but our tastes appear to be fairly similar to that of the Sabers."

"If that's the case, then I recommend you try these. They're the Translator's favorite." Opal handed them each a stick, which they dutifully tried. The first few bites were fairly savory, but the third one nearly knocked him over with an inferno of heat.

Henry whistled. "These have some real kick to them. What do you call them?"

"It's a mix of yellow tail, fire fruit, and jelly eggs," Opal explained, pointing out each item. "The Translator calls them fire sticks."

"That's an appropriate name for sure," James said, then tried the jelly eggs, which helped to cut some of the pain in his mouth.

"Do you like them?" she asked.

James nodded as he finished his stick. "I do. However, the fire fruit is very hot. Many of our people might not like them because of it. I recommend warning them first."

"That's good to know. If you like the other parts, then you'll probably like these. They're called brenna berry sticks.

James took the offered stick and tried it a little more tentatively but nearly cried at the flavor that burst in his mouth.

"It can't be!" Henry exclaimed as he stared at his own stick. "Strawberry?!"

Opal looked worried. "Forgive me. Is everything alright?"

"Better than alright," James said. "It tastes exactly like a very popular fruit we lost. We called them Strawberries. It even has the same color, although the shape and texture are a little different. I'll let the others know. I hope you have a lot more available because you're going to be very popular with my species once they find out. I expect Jordan will want to talk to you about setting up shipments to New Hope, too. I've heard her lamenting its loss on several occasions."

Opal lit up a neon blue, so bright it made him blink, which he took to mean she was happy. "Would you like to try anything else?"

The sticks had been quite large, designed for the bigger species, and he considered. "Honestly, I'm quite full, but we're planning to visit with Marsee after we've explored the market. If these are her favorites, would you mind setting aside some for her that I could pick up when we're done?"

"Gladly!" Opal said and began wrapping up a selection. "How is she doing? Please let her know I'm thinking of her."

"I will. I only saw her briefly after we landed last night. She's still very weak and struggling to come to terms with her injuries. There's one in particular that might still prove fatal in the long run. We'll know more later today."

Opal's skin darkened until it was nearly black at this news.

"If I know Myra, she'll stop at nothing until she finds a cure," he said.

His tablet dinged with the sound he'd configured for Little Flower. "Forgive me. It sounds like I have a message from my granddaughter."

Opal nodded as she continued wrapping up their order.

He unclipped his tablet and whooped as he read the message.

"What is it?" Henry asked.

"Very good news! That issue I just mentioned might not be an issue after all," he replied.

Opal lit up even brighter than before.

"And it looks like I'm going to need those sticks now. Henry, we're going to have to postpone our exploration of the market. We have a wedding to attend. Little Flower finally popped the question."

"It's about time," Henry replied. "She's been moping since Marsee left."

"Forgive my curiosity. I don't know the sign 'wedding.' What question did Little Flower ask?" Opal signed after handing over a bag with the food for Marsee.

Henry took the bag and hooked it on the front of his drone while James answered. "Little Flower asked Marsee to be her partner and adopt Hope, and Marsee accepted. Wedding is the Hue-man term for the partnership ceremony. How much do I owe you for the food?"

Opal flashed a rainbow of brilliant colors before settling on that neon blue again. "That's wonderful news! I'm so very happy for them. There's no charge. It's my gift on this happy occasion. Please pass along my congratulations. I pray they have a long and happy life and that the bountiful seas bless them with as many children as they want."

"I will. Thank you." James put his tablet away, grabbed his drone, and with a nod towards Opal, they took off back towards the Trauma Center.

CHAPTER 9

Jer: Second Chances

Jer paced, unable to remain still as he waited for Myra to arrive. He'd been so afraid she'd lose control and attack the moment she saw him on the platform. Thankfully, she hadn't, but he had never seen such controlled fury on her face before, and he couldn't figure out why she wanted to talk with him now. It wasn't necessary to end their partnership, as she was Marcus's citizen.

"Jer, sit down. You're wearing a hole in the carpet with your pacing."

Jer pinned his ears and growled at his brother but sat down anyway and tried to focus on the latest findings from his investigation. Five minutes later, he was back up and pacing. Myra was late, and he was worried that something had happened.

Marcus sighed and set his tablet down. "If you start clawing the furniture, I'm going to call a guard in here."

"Ha, ha," Jer replied, but he stopped his pacing and looked out the window, trying to spot Myra leaving the Trauma Center, and then returned to his chair and flipped open his tablet, looking for a message from her. He didn't find one from her, but he did find a message from Marsee that he'd missed. He opened it and then had to read it three more times before he believed it.

"What's wrong now, cub?" Marcus asked with a weary sigh.

Jer looked up at him and back at his tablet, reading it yet again. He opened his mouth to tell Marcus but changed his mind and forwarded the message instead, knowing his brother needed to read it for himself.

Marcus's tablet dinged, and he peered at it with trepidation before gingerly picking it up, nose scrunched, as if it was one of the Hue-man's stinky poop sacks that they used for their cubs. He started reading, and Jer watched as his brother's expression turned to one of surprise followed by happiness, then astonishment, and finally consternation.

"Well. It's nice to have some good news for a change, but it looks like we need to have a little chat with Kendra."

Jer snorted at the understatement, but before he could reply, there was a knock at the door. He bolted for the door, confirmed it was Myra, and hit the switch to let her in.

Myra swam into the small water foyer, shut the door behind her, and stepped through the static shield keeping the water out of the suite. Her face was a blank mask, but he knew her too well. The very tip of her tail shivered with repressed emotion when she saw him. "I take it from your expressions that you've heard the news?" she asked.

"I just received Marsee's message," he replied. "I'm not sure what I find harder to believe, that Little Flower asked her to be her partner or that the Honor Guard has managed to hide people like her from the Council for thousands of years."

"You always were oblivious to what was right under your nose, especially when it came to Marsee, but then relationships were never your strong suit, were they?"

He wilted under Myra's glare and accusations. He knew she was never going to forgive him for what he'd done to Marsee, even if she did recover like the Senior Honor Guard said she would. "I'm sorry, Myra. I know you'll never believe me, but I was only doing what I needed to do to keep everyone else safe. I truly thought she was losing control again. On my oath as a Senior Councilor, I promise I wouldn't have done it if I didn't think it was absolutely necessary."

"You thought pushing her until she was completely out of control was the way to fix her?" Myra snapped.

"Myra, she was marking trees and spraying," Marcus interrupted. "Had I witnessed it, I wouldn't have taken the chance that I could contain her on my own and would have killed her if I'd been able to get close enough or, more likely, called in the Guard and let them handle it. Jer gave her a chance to prove herself, and she passed."

"I didn't know what was going on with her," Jer added. "She was not acting the way psychosis normally presents. You know as well as I do that people lost to psychosis go non-verbal. She was talking clearly to me but referring to herself in plural. I didn't know if that meant she was losing control or fully in control, so I tested her the same way the Council always does. You should know I wouldn't do anything to Marsee that I haven't been through myself."

Myra scowled at him. "Kendra mentioned that the Council has their own methods for testing. What exactly does that entail?"

Jer looked over at his brother, not sure what he could say.

Marcus let out a sigh. "Myra, none of this leaves this room, understood?"

Myra nodded.

"Your oath," he repeated.

"I, Myra Beth Chenzira, promise not to tell anyone what you're about to tell me," she replied, although her ears flicked back in surprise that Marcus had required it of her.

"If you had not volunteered to execute Little Flower's rapist, it would have been Jer's responsibility. To ensure that a councilor remains in control during that process, we require every junior councilor to fully embrace their instinct and hunt and kill some random animal out in the wild. The moment they're successful and have the first taste of their kill, we chase them off to see if they can regain control. There are other reasons why we do this, but that's the main one. Most have no problems in regaining their control that first time. The problem comes later when it's their turn to do the same for their proteges. They've now had a taste for meat and have used their instinct to hunt. Our instincts sometimes get confused, and we end up hunting our proteges instead. All new councilors are watched carefully during this process to ensure their proteges are not harmed. Those who lose control are usually put down."

"Usually?" she asked.

"If the person struggles with their instinct during their Junior Advocates test, we'll either fail them or put them on the watch list, or both," Marcus replied. "Depending on how bad it is, we'll often recommend that they don't run for councilor for several terms while we work with them on their control. Of those who do lose control when testing their proteges, only one in a hundred manage to regain control before we have to kill them. When that happens, we spend months working with that person, testing them by doing what Jer did to Marsee, but far worse, to ensure that they have full control over their instinct before they're allowed to return home. Most mentors aren't willing to even try due to the risk and time involved. What Jer did to Marsee was a fraction of what I did to him. Only he knew what I was attempting to do. Jer didn't have time to explain that to Marsee, and for better or worse, Marsee beat him. I'm not aware of that ever happening before, at least not where the mentor survived and the protege didn't succumb to psychosis."

Jer watched as the implications of what his brother had just said dawned on Myra's face.

"You lost control?" Myra asked him, and he could see her doing the math. "Wait, is that why you were gone for months that one year?"

"I did, and yes. I nearly killed Samantha and would have if Marcus hadn't stopped me. I couldn't tell you, but I wanted to so much it hurt. I didn't dare leave the remote location we were in to get close enough for a signal to send a message. I was terrified I'd lose control and hurt you or someone else, and I was in a bad state. Not just because of my instinct but over the guilt I felt for hurting Sam. I almost lost you then because of my silence. Part of me wants you to walk away now so that you and the rest of our family will be safer, but the moment I saw you walk off that ship last night, I knew I couldn't live without you. You're the very air I need to breathe, my reason for living, for not giving up all those years ago, and the source of every joy in my life. Please don't walk away from me now. I love you, Myra. Please forgive me. I hated to do what I did, but I saw no other way to save her and protect the people of New Hope."

Myra frowned at him, and his heart sank as he waited for her to speak.

"Both Marsee and Kendra have told me that they believe she wouldn't have survived her kidnapping if it weren't for the lessons she learned during that...incident...and I suppose if Marsee can forgive you, I can too."

"Thank you!" He ran over and hugged her tightly.

She let him hug her for a few moments before pushing him away. "I am still furious with you, but I will retract the papers. You should have at least seen that she was properly checked over by a healer. She had a broken shoulder!" Myra hit him hard in his shoulder, hard enough to make him stumble, although not nearly as hard as he was expecting or deserved, and her claws remained sheathed.

"I tried," he replied. "She said she was fine. I didn't know her shoulder was broken until the next day, and I used all the nano cream I had on my ship to treat her cuts. Myra, if she injured her shoulder when I think she did, she ran at least a league with that broken shoulder and still managed to pin me to the ground by the neck. I thought for sure I was dead. I've never seen anyone move like she did, and I've seen Kendra fight those lost to psychosis on more than one occasion."

Myra glared at him. "It would have served you right if she had killed you."

"You're not wrong there," he replied.

"Speaking of Kendra, I am assuming you've been able to corroborate her claims?" Marcus asked, changing the subject.

Myra glared at him for a moment longer before refocusing her attention on Marcus. "We have. Ammond scanned Kendra and found similar changes in her brain. All but the control hub appears to have recovered."

He was surprised to hear Kendra had the same issues, but that did help to explain how she remained in control all these years. He wondered how many there were like Marsee.

His brother was quiet for a moment, frowning at some internal thought. "And Marsee?"

"She's showing signs of recovery. Based on anecdotal evidence, her sense of smell is stronger than mine, and her sense of taste has returned, as she was able to sniff out the location of a cookie I hid and seemed to enjoy it. Her hearing is no different than it was before, but she still has no sense of pain. I've also spoken to the Senior Healer here and sent a message to Nerissa. This information is being restricted to Level Four Masters only. Little Flower knows, as she was there when Kendra arrived, and I expect Marsee will tell Ellie. Kendra didn't want this information widely known and was not particularly comfortable with me talking with the two of you, although she fully expected you'd find out from Marsee. She would rather it not be shared with the rest of the Council."

"She's right," Marcus replied. "It would not be good if anyone else found out about this, both for them and for Marsee."

"Why not?" Jer asked. "Wouldn't it be good for the population to know that psychosis isn't always fatal?"

"No. Far from it. I've read enough from before the Great Awakening to know just how bad of a problem it was. Even if it is survivable, you saw how close Marsee was to losing control. At a minimum, we'll need to wait until Marsee's watch is over. If we say anything now, the Council will likely think we're trying to hide her issues, and the more information we have on how successful sign language is at helping people recover, the better. In the meantime, Jer, I believe you have some paperwork to fill out and an oath to administer."

"I thought for sure you were going to fight me for that," Jer said with a grin.

"Nothing to fight over. They're your daughters. Even if Marsee is under my jurisdiction, I wouldn't dream of taking that away from you, but I am claiming the right to officiate over the Hue-man ceremony that Little Flower wants. From my understanding, you'll have your own part in that to play anyway."

Jer flicked an ear back, wondering what he would need to do, but decided he didn't care. Whatever made his daughters happy, he would gladly do. "Deal."

Marcus stood up and motioned them towards the door. "I'm ordering you both to take the rest of the day off."

Jer frowned. Senior Councilors didn't get days off, certainly not when an entire council was missing, but before he could object, Marcus raised a paw.

"I'll let you know if there's an issue. Go on. You need to spend time with your family. It'll be good for all of you."

He nodded and turned back to Myra, unsure what to say. "Myra..."

She, too, raised a paw to stop him. "Let's not keep Marsee and Little Flower waiting. We can talk after, and since I'm apparently not going to be sequestered for the rest of the day trying to fix her, why don't you show me around? I hear there's a garden I should check out, one that apparently makes mine look like a root-bound potted plant."

Jer beamed at his partner. "I thought you'd never ask!"

She snorted at him and shook her head. "All these years, and you still haven't learned."

He frowned, as that had been their saying since the day she'd asked him to partner.

"Jeran Frederick Chenzira, I was waiting for *you* to ask me." She rolled her eyes and shook her head as she strode out, and he was pretty sure he heard her mutter 'clueless,' as the door slid shut behind her.

He stared at the door as his entire worldview shifted.

"You really are a fur-brained cub," Marcus said. "What are you waiting for? Go after her!"

He didn't need to be told a second time.

CHAPTER 10

GrandFather: A Family Worthy Dying For

James waited for the guards to authorize Henry's access to enter the ward. Even though the Water Sprite guard had clearly recognized Henry and flashed the silver and purple the moment they entered the Trauma Center, they still weren't letting Henry through. And even though he was Jeran's Acting Senior, that apparently didn't give him the authorization to grant access either.

"I don't want to be a bother," Henry said. "I can wait out here."

"Nonsense. Little Flower invited you, too. It'll only take a minute."

As he expected, a minute or two later, they were waved through. They still had to verify who they were at the next set of doors, but that went quicker.

"They aren't messing around with her safety, are they?" Henry said to him after they were stopped by a third set of guards.

"I should hope not," James replied. "She's been kidnapped and attacked twice on their watch, and just because we think we've caught everyone involved doesn't mean we have."

James rounded the corner and stopped as he realized that there weren't any guards on Marsee's door, but before he could start to worry, Marsee rounded the far corner with Jessica, Hope, and two patient guards in tow. Marsee looked about ready to pass out. For all that Hope was only a toddler and had little experience with swimming, it appeared like she was easily beating Marsee in a race.

"Gampa!" Hope squealed as she caught sight of him and started paddling faster.

Marsee lifted her drooping head to see him.

"Come on, Marsee!" he signed. "You're not going to let Hope beat you, are you?"

Marsee's ears flattened with annoyance. I didn't take a healer to see how little she had left, but the tails of the two guards curled, and they said something that made Marsee growl.

"Winner gets a bag of fire sticks courtesy of Opal!" he added, holding the bag up. Her ears flicked forward, and she put some effort into her swim again.

"That's it, Marsee!" Henry called out.

Jessica kept pace with Hope but called out encouragement to Marsee. Marsee pulled ahead, but about halfway down the hall, she had to stop and rest, panting and breathing hard, long enough for Hope to catch up and pass her.

"There are brenna berry sticks, too!" he signed. "At least, I think that's what Opal called them."

She let out a huge sigh and started trudging her way forward again.

In the end, it was a tie, but Hope wasn't interested in the bag at all.

James caught his great-granddaughter in a hug as Marsee swiped the bag from him and started pawing through it, but before she managed to pull anything out, the female guard took it from her. "No fire sticks. Your system isn't healed up enough for it."

Marsee let out a ferocious ears-pinned snarl that Hope imitated, and then she swiped the bag back, claws fully extended.

"You'll be sick," the guard warned with a scowl.

"I honestly don't care," Marsee signed. "They're mine. Try to take them from me again, and I'll have you arrested for theft." With another glare at the guard, she turned back towards her room. After awkwardly trying to swim with three paws, she stuck the handle of the bag in her mouth and continued on.

"I see Marsee's feeling better," James signed, which caused the others to chuckle.

Marsee turned her head back to glare at everyone before refocusing on her room, which made everyone laugh even harder. Her ears pinned, but she didn't look back again.

They easily caught up with her but waited until she stumbled her way into her room and practically crawled onto her bed.

He flicked off his flippers and tossed them to the side, where Jessica tossed hers. As his hands were full of a squirming and giggling toddler, Henry was the one to help Jessica up onto Marsee's over-sized bed before climbing into one of the chairs himself. James placed Hope on the bed and then climbed up in the chair next to Henry.

Marsee hid the bag and pinned her ears in warning as the guard approached.

The guard completely ignored Marsee's low growls as she examined the monitor over the bed. "Congratulations. It would appear you managed not to break or pull anything this time. We'll try for five laps this afternoon."

Marsee slumped in her bed. "Five?! I barely managed one!"

"Well, if you think you're recovered enough to eat fire sticks, then you're clearly recovered enough to manage a few extra laps," the guard replied.

Marsee growled something, and he heard the rumble of the guard chuckling out in the hall.

"So be it. If you get sick from those sticks, I don't want to hear about it, and I'm not cleaning up the mess," the guard replied and stormed out to take up position outside the door.

Marsee glared at the door for a few moments, then pulled out the bag from where she'd hidden it and reverently unwrapped one of the packages inside, which turned out to be the fire sticks. He expected her to dig in, but she just stared at them.

"Is there something wrong?" he asked, wondering if she was having second thoughts.

"I'm honestly afraid they won't taste the same," she signed. "And that would be a real tragedy."

"You didn't seem to have any problems with the cookie," Little Flower replied.

Marsee flicked an ear back in the Saber's equivalent to a shrug but then picked one up and handed it to Jessica before she picked up another and sniffed at it. Clearly, she was able to smell something as her ears flicked forward. She took a tentative bite and let out a relieved sigh. "Thank the blessed moons! The flavors aren't as strong as I remember, but it's still *so* much better than what they've been feeding me."

He was surprised that Marsee didn't eat more of them but instead wrapped it up, opened the other package, and devoured two of those sticks instead.

Jessica's reaction to the fire sticks didn't disappoint. Within moments, she was gasping and wheezing, which had them all laughing hysterically. "You could have warned me!" she signed at him, unable to speak through her gasps.

"What, and spoil all my fun? Besides, I seem to remember something about bandala chips. Eat the rest. It kills some of the fire. The brenna berry sticks aren't hot. You'll like them."

His granddaughter looked at him suspiciously but took one of the other sticks and sighed with happiness. "So I take it you got my message?" she mumbled through another bite, then took a piece off and handed it to Hope.

"I did. Congratulations! Opal sends hers as well. So when's the ceremony?"

"As soon as Papa gets here with the paperwork," Marsee replied. "But we're going to have another one when we get home so Little Flower can have the big wedding she's always dreamed of." Marsee handed a piece of her own stick to Hope, before devouring the rest. She was finishing up the last stick when she stopped mid-bite and frowned, then suddenly bolted off the bed to the bathroom, slamming the door shut behind her. Several minutes later, she returned, moving far slower.

"Are you alright?" James asked.

"No one says anything to Tamarin. It was worth every bite."

They all roared with laughter.

"What's so funny?" Jer signed as he and Myra swam into the room.

"Let's just say I've found a way to know when I need to use the waste room and leave it at that," Marsee signed to everyone's further laughter and her parents' utter confusion.

That is until Jer saw the remains of their meal. "You're on a very strict diet. Did you make someone pick you up some fire sticks?" he asked.

"No," Marsee said innocently. "They were gifted, and it was worth every bite. They weren't as good as before, but they were far better than everything else I've had to eat around here. The stuff Rowena brought us this morning was barely edible."

"I'll vouch for that," Jessica signed. "Horrible-tasting hospital food must be a constant in the universe."

"Was it really that bad?" Myra asked.

"I had better at the Agency," Jessica replied, which caused Myra's ears to flick back. He had since learned that even the healers had been disgusted by what they'd been sent to care for them.

"So, how long does Marsee have to stay here?" Jessica asked.

"I suppose that depends on how many fire sticks she keeps eating," Myra said and turned to Marsee. "But if you promise to stick to the meal plan and the pickle torture, I'll see about having you released today. You won't be able to jump home for another few weeks. Your new organs won't be able to handle it, but I can care for you as easily in the suite."

Marsee brightened. "That works for me. I'm getting sick of these walls."

"Are you ready to give your oath?" Jer asked.

"No, we're still waiting for Ellie and Ammond," Marsee replied.

"Ah, well, while we wait, we can get the boring paperwork out of the way. There are some added challenges and nuances since this is a cross-species partnership. The first thing I'll need you to do is to sign this intent-to-partner form. This releases all medical, legal, and financial records to the other person. You'll need to review that information and then attest that you've reviewed it." Jer handed his tablet over to each of them to sign. Once they did, Jer signed it as well, and a moment later, both of their tablets dinged. "The information is now in your account."

They both pulled up their tablets and reviewed. "Marsee's still on the watch list?" Jessica asked a moment later. "Why?"

"Legally, it's required for our species since she executed Rip," Jer replied. "We know she's not a risk, but she will have to be tested each month for six months before she can be officially removed. It's not a disciplinary watch, so there won't be any restrictions on the transfer of custody if something happens to you. It's merely a precaution."

"Ahh," Jessica said and kept reading, but Marsee frowned at her father.

"You didn't let me have custody of Hope until I was off the watch before, and that was informal. Why is this different?"

Jer paused as if considering his words, and Marsee's frown deepened. Jer glanced back towards him and Henry and then said something to Marsee in Saber.

Marsee frowned and looked at them, too.

"You're welcome to speak in Saber," Henry said. "Or if you'd like me to leave, I will. I won't take it personally. If you're worried I'll tell someone anything you say here, I won't. I give you my word. I already know about psychosis and your injuries. I witnessed the Senior Honor Guard test Nazari after we tracked down Damon, and I had a long conversation with her about it later."

Marsee's frown deepened. "How many people know?"

"I haven't told anyone," Henry replied.

"I've only spoken to people in Healers," Myra said. "And I trust all of them."

"Outside of your uncle, the Senior Council knows about your injuries but not your most recent update," Jer added. "Unless your uncle has informed them, and your uncle has locked your medical record so no one outside the Senior Council or those responsible for your immediate care or protection can access it. I know you might not believe us, but we are trying to protect your reputation."

Marsee nodded. "I believe you. I know I haven't made your job any easier, and I trust Henry. He can stay."

Jer tilted his head in acknowledgment. "To answer your question, by your own admission, you hunted Little Flower. While she was thankfully not hurt, it elevated the severity of your first watch along with the consequences, even if it was...informal. We had no idea how effective sign language would be long term, and handing custody of Hope over to you when you'd already seen a member of her species as prey would have been irresponsible."

Marsee stared at her father for a long moment and looked like she was going to say something, but instead went back to reading.

Jessica snorted a few minutes later. "Am I reading this right? You bit your classmate's tail?"

"That's in there?" Marsee leaned back against her pillow and groaned with embarrassment. "Well, to be fair, he deserved it. He wouldn't leave my classmate alone, and I warned him I would if he didn't stop picking on her."

Jessica snickered.

"What? You never got in trouble in school?" Marsee asked.

"Well, I never bit anyone," she replied.

James coughed. "Jessica, I seem to recall your parents telling us about how you were suspended for three days in kindergarten for dumping a gallon of paint on your classmate."

His granddaughter glared at him. "That may be, but I never *bit* anyone, and it was second grade. Besides, they deserved it."

"What did they do to deserve that?" Marsee asked.

"They laughed at my painting. I was only, what, two of your years old at the time? They said it needed more red paint, so I picked up the paint and dumped it on them instead. I'm pretty sure it was one of my best paintings that year."

The room roared with laughter.

"I'm thinking maybe Little Flower should have been Ellie's protege," Myra said just as Ellie swam in.

"Why's that?" Ellie asked. She chuckled after they explained.

"Oh, that reminds me," Marsee said. "Ellie, Agate has a picture of you when you dumped green stain all over Uncle Ammond."

"She does?" Ellie asked.

"Yeah, it's hanging on her wall in her office," Marsee replied.

"I had no idea a picture even existed. I need to have a little talk with her. I've been in that office hundreds of times, and I've never seen it. She's been holding out on me. Don't you dare tell Ammond, either. I want to surprise him." Ellie glared at them until they all agreed.

Ammond appeared a few minutes later and scowled at the grins everyone directed his way. "You all look like a group of Flyer weyrlings. What are you up to?"

The room burst out laughing, but regardless of Ammond's further growls and glares, no one said anything.

"Why do I have a feeling you're behind this," Ammond growled at Ellie.

"I have absolutely no idea what you're talking about. However, I did just learn that Little Flower takes after me far more than I thought. She apparently dumped paint all over one of her classmates as a child."

Ammond turned to Jessica. "Don't get any ideas, or I will have you scrubbing the surgery floors for a month."

Jessica grinned and looked up as if considering. "It might be worth it..." she replied a moment later, to further laughter.

"I would end up with the universe's two most impudent apprentices," Ammond muttered in reply.

The room roared with laughter again, all except for Ellie, who frowned with confusion. "What do you mean by that?"

"Oh? Haven't you heard?" Ammond replied sweetly. "Little Flower joined the Healer's Guild as *my* Apprentice."

"You did not!" Ellie replied, shifting her glare to Jessica. "You're pulling my tail."

"Nope. I joined on the way here," Jessica replied.

Ellie didn't believe her, of course, not until she pulled up the information to verify for herself.

He wasn't sure, but it looked like she was going to cry. She settled on a scowl, which made everyone laugh again.

When the laughter finally died down, Jessica and Marsee went back to reading their information. Marsee was done reviewing Jessica's file much sooner than Jessica was, but then they only had a little over a year of history on Jessica, and Marsee knew most of it already. Plus, Jessica had to ask for translations on dozens of words she didn't know. When they were done, they signed the attestation.

"Now as you're different species, your partnership would normally allow you the option to switch species legally without the normal waiting period or council approval, but there's a caveat with regards to switching to Little Flower's. In order to protect her species' right to vote and the council positions, we've placed a temporary ban on all transfers to the Hue-man species until after the first vote, or unless you're voted in by the Council. Little Flower, since you would have to give up your council position to transfer to Saber, I wouldn't recommend it, and Marsee, it would be up to you if you wanted to petition the Council to transfer, but with the current political climate, even if you turned down the council position, it could...cause unforeseen consequences. At the very least, I recommend waiting until the end of your watch."

"That works for me," Jessica said, and after some thought, Marsee agreed.

Jer nodded and tapped something on his tablet. "Do you have any questions before I administer the oath?"

They both shook their heads.

"Then please stand."

Marsee slid off the bed and helped Jessica down, then handed Hope over to her. Hope immediately started wiggling to get back over to Marsee, but Jessica held onto her.

"Little Flower Chenzira, do you wish for Marsee Bet Chenzira to be your partner in life, to adopt and raise Hope Chenzira as if Hope were her own, with all of the rights and responsibilities that come with being Hope's father and your partner?"

"I do," she signed awkwardly around her wiggling toddler.

"Marsee Bet Chenzira, do you wish for Little Flower to be your partner in life, to adopt and raise Hope Chenzira as if Hope were your own, with all of the rights and responsibilities that come with being Hope's father and Little Flower's partner?"

"With every fiber of my being, I do," Marsee replied.

"Then it is my final decision as representative of the Senior Council that Marsee Bet Chenzira is now recognized as Hope Chenzira's legal guardian and father and that Little Flower and Marsee Bet Chenzira are recognized as legal partners with all the rights and responsibilities that come with that partnership."

Marsee scooped Jessica and Hope up into a hug while everyone else cheered.

He plastered a smile on his face as he didn't want to ruin the special occasion, but he was hit hard by a wave of grief and conflicting emotions. More than anything, he wished the rest of his family could be here to witness this happy occasion. The last time everyone had been together was at his own wedding. When everyone was looking away, he wiped the tears off his face, hoping that no one saw him crying, but Henry did. He looked over as Henry wrapped an arm around him and squeezed. All he saw was compassion and understanding on his friend's face.

"They're here, too," Henry whispered softly in his ear. "Those we love are always with us."

That did nothing to stop his tears, but they turned to laughter moments later as Jessica scrunched her nose and held Hope out to Marsee.

"Congratulations, Papa. It's a girl, and from the smell of things, she needs changing!"

Marsee's tail spiraled as everyone laughed. "Hope, do you need to use the bathroom?"

"No. I pooped!" Hope signed back.

"My beautiful, silly daughter, you're supposed to use the hole. Come on. Let's get you cleaned up," Marsee said, then carried her over to the bathroom as everyone continued to laugh.

By the time Jessica turned to face him, he'd pulled himself back under control and grinned at the happiness that he saw on his granddaughter's face. The universe may have taken one family from him, but it had brought him another, one he knew was worth fighting for and, if necessary, one worth dying for, too.

CHAPTER 11

Little Flower: Her Sleeping Saber

Little Flower watched Marsee carry Hope across the room. She was exhausted from their pickle torture, and Marsee had pushed herself hard to keep up with her and the unexpected advantage her fins gave. It had felt good to win their race earlier, knowing she was improving, but she hated seeing Marsee so weak. Hope might weigh next to nothing compared to the normal strength and size of a Saber, but walking on two feet while carrying something was hard for them, and Marsee was focusing hard on every step and doing her best to hide it.

Hope ran back out a few minutes later, but Marsee slumped, leaning heavily against the doorway. "I hate to cut the celebration short," Marsee said. "But I think I'm going to pass out now."

Her father bolted to Marsee's side, catching her just as she started to wobble. He scooped her up and gently carried her back over to the bed. Before he even made it back, her mother had her scanner out and was checking her over.

"I'm just tired from my race with Hope," Marsee signed weakly. "Tamarin already checked."

"I know she did, but I'd rather be safe," her mother replied.

Ammond wasn't taking any chances either and was reviewing the scans on the monitor above the bed.

She tried to find a position where she could see the monitor, but there were too many furry heads in the way. A few minutes later, they parted, and what she understood and could see was all good.

"She's fine," her mother said. "But I think we should let her rest." Her mother turned back to Marsee. "When you wake up from your nap, let me know, and if everything still looks good, we'll help you back to the suites."

"Okay, Mama," Marsee mumbled through a massive yawn that showed her razor-sharp teeth, teeth that had defeated the villain that had hurt them all.

She smiled at her new partner and how much everything had changed since the day she first met Marsee. She had once feared those teeth, but now she was very thankful for their existence and felt comforted to know she was so well protected.

Ellie walked over and hugged Marsee and then turned to face her with a scowl and lashing tail.

"What? I don't get a hug, too?" Little Flower asked while making her most angelic expression, knowing full well why she wasn't getting one.

Ellie snorted at her. "I still can't believe you joined the Healer's Guild and not mine."

She grinned up at Ellie. "I had to. I needed to learn how to help care for Marsee, and Ammond wouldn't agree to teach me unless I joined. But don't worry. I have no intentions of giving up on my artwork. Ammond made me promise not to."

Ellie huffed at her. "If it were for any other reason besides helping Marsee, I would thwhack you with my tail. Still, I suppose, if anyone can knock some sense into you, it's that old coot."

Ammond scowled at her. "Old coot?! You need to learn to show some respect for your elders, cub."

Ellie looked affronted. "Is your hearing going, too, you ancient furball? I just complimented you. You're probably one of the only people stubborn enough to mentor Little Flower. It's not everyone that can make Tabor run out of the council chamber with her tail tucked between her legs. I can't wait to see what she does with you, but then again, you managed with Myra, so I suppose you'll be able to manage her daughter. If I can't have her, at least it'll be entertaining watching you splutter on a regular basis."

Everyone laughed except for Ammond, who scowled at Ellie.

Ellie turned back to face her. "If you change your mind, let me know. I could use a protege capable of keeping the Council in line. This one," she said, tilting her head towards Marsee, "has potential, but she keeps quitting on me."

She was surprised at the offer, although she wasn't sure if it was a joke or not. Based on the reactions of the others in the room, she decided it was serious. "Thank you. Your offer means a lot to me, and while I can't even believe I'm saying this, I have to decline. My artwork brings me joy, and I love bringing joy to others through my work. It's a need much like breathing, but I realized this week that it's not my purpose. We've all been through trauma that I don't think your world understands. The healers here are phenomenal when it comes to finding cures for physical problems, but there's a gap in treating the emotional and mental side of trauma. How do you make a person want to live with the memories of what they've been through or the challenges they'll have to face in the future? I want to fix that. I want to make it easier for the next person. Being a healer may have started as a necessity to help Marsee, and I'm guessing Ammond didn't expect me to agree to his demands, but I'm honestly really enjoying my studies. I was horrible in school and barely passed most of my classes. I never even considered the possibility of becoming a healer before. With my grades and learning disabilities, I would have never qualified for the education, much less been able to afford it back on Earth, and I've never had a teacher like Ammond before either, one who sees me as capable of learning anything and is patient enough to knock that knowledge into my brain in a way that both makes sense and makes the smallest details seem...monumental. He's showing me a universe I never knew existed, and I can't wait to see what's around the corner."

"Ellie, I think you should be asking Little Flower to be *your* mentor," Ammond said into the stunned silence that followed. "*That's* how you give a compliment."

The room roared with laughter. Ellie scowled at Ammond, huffed at her, and stormed out, tail lashing behind her.

Little Flower frowned. "Did I say something wrong? I didn't mean to insult her."

"No child," Ammond said. "You said everything right. She's not really mad, either. That was all for show. Ellie is about as high ranking as it gets, perhaps even more powerful than the Senior Council in her own way. She's used to getting what she wants, and she wanted and expected to get her paws on you, but you surprised her. I don't think anyone in the universe would have turned down her offer of mentorship, and the fact that you chose me, of all people, is a thorn in her tail. She'll get over it and respect you far more because of it."

Ammond picked her up and set her on the bed after giving her a hug, then tossed Hope on his shoulder before his expression turned from smugness back to scowl. "But, if you think I'm going to let you get out of completing your homework just because you went and got yourself partnered, you're sadly mistaken. I'll take care of this little ball of wiggles while you get to work. However, since you said such nice things about me, I'll be kind and let you stay here while you work on it."

She chuckled as Ammond didn't wait for a reply and walked off with her child. If it was anyone but him and for any other reason, she would have complained, but Marsee needed her sleep, and Hope was not the least bit tired.

The others trickled out after Ammond.

The moment they were alone, Marsee yawned again and grabbed her protective gear. "I know you've got work to do, but will you snuggle with me until I fall asleep?"

"That depends. Will you protect me from Ammond when *I* fall asleep and don't get my homework done?"

Marsee's tail curled as she pretended to consider it. "I hear Ammond hits hard, but what's a few more scars? It'll be worth it if it keeps the nightmares at bay like it did last night."

She scooted her way into the middle of the bed, and they curled up in their usual position. Once situated, she propped her tablet against Marsee's arm and started to study. Marsee fell asleep with an exhausted groan within seconds of settling down, but an hour or so later, she started to twitch and mutter in her sleep.

"Marsee," she called out quietly.

Marsee didn't wake.

"Marsee, wake up," she called out a little louder. "It's okay, you're just dreaming." When that failed, she started gently stroking Marsee's arm.

Marsee still didn't wake up and instead started growling and twitching as her dream turned into a nightmare. The guards outside turned to look in. She shook her head at them and started singing quietly. She knew she needed to figure out how to calm Marsee's nightmares and wake her safely. Marsee's ears twitched, and then she sighed. She kept singing and gently stroking Marsee's arm until she fully calmed and relaxed into a deeper sleep. She trusted Marsee, but that didn't mean she wasn't fully aware of the risk she was taking, even with the protective gear.

When Avery saw that Marsee had settled, he turned back around, but the other guard remained, watching both Marsee and the monitor. "What is it you were singing?" the guard asked. "I really liked the tune, and you seemed amused."

She grinned and signed the slightly modified translation of 'The Lion Sleeps Tonight' while trying not to wake Marsee with her movement.

The guard's tail spiraled. "How appropriate! Your Saber is sleeping better than I've seen her all week. You're good for her."

She sighed with contentment and snuggled in. "She's good for me, too. I feel safe and protected in her arms."

"I promise. No harm will come to you on our watch," the guard said.

"Don't make promises you can't keep," Little Flower replied. The guard honestly seemed upset, so she explained, not wanting to insult her. "I'm not questioning your dedication, but I'm realistic. I know there's only so much you can do, only so many you'd be able to fight off."

The guard frowned. "Your concerns are valid, and while I can't speak for anyone else, I promise, whatever happens, I will fight to protect you with my last breath."

She raised a brow at that. "Why? You don't even know me."

"Because to do otherwise would be to let them win, and I don't want anyone to ever go through what the two of you have been through. That kind of evil cannot be allowed to exist in this universe."

She snorted. "If only it were that easy. That kind of evil will always exist."

"Then there will always be guards like me, with sharpened claws ready to fight back." The guard flicked her claws out briefly to emphasize the point.

She nodded, and the guard resumed her position.

Little Flower watched both guards through the mirror outside the door. They were calm statues of feline grace and power, save for constantly moving ears and gently shifting fur, and she wondered if she could trust them the way Marsee seemed to. Avery had left Marsee alone, but Marsee had been the one to order him away, and he seemed genuinely sorry for the harm his absence had caused.

Before she could come to any sort of decision, Marsee groaned in her sleep and pulled her in tight. Little Flower sighed with contentment and closed her eyes as she snuggled in, held in the strong, protective arms of her sleeping Saber. Within moments, she, too, was fast asleep.

CHAPTER 12

Little Flower: Tips and Triggers

Little Flower woke with a surprised yelp as Marsee rolled over and stretched, dumping her on her back.

"Sorry," Marsee said, scooping her back up and snuggling in so that Marsee's head was now resting across her belly.

Little Flower unpinned an arm to reach up and unhook the muzzle, then started stroking the back of Marsee's head as she often did. It felt weird without Marsee's fur, but Marsee closed her eyes, leaned in, and purred with contentment, so she kept doing it.

"That feels nice," Marsee said eventually, her deep voice rumbling in Little Flower's belly. "Different, but nice."

"I gathered that from the purring, Chenzie Butt," Little Flower said with a chuckle. "But you're going to have to move. I need to pee."

"You always need to pee," Marsee grumbled.

"When you have cubs of your own, you'll understand," Little Flower replied but didn't stop patting, and Marsee didn't move.

A moment later, Marsee lifted her head and scowled down at her. "Out of all the words to learn in Saber, you learned Chenzie Butt first?"

She grinned up at her sister. "Of course. I focused on the important things: how to swear, how to ask for a cookie, and how to say your name." She ticked off the items on her fingers.

Marsee snorted at her and rolled her eyes. "Fish Breath."

Laughing, she sat up, and Marsee slid off the bed to help her down. After they were both done using the facilities, Marsee texted her mother and started pulling artwork off the walls.

"Who are those from?" Little Flower asked.

"Stormy," Marsee replied. "He brought a drawing or two every time he came to visit."

"I take it he's a fan of the comics?"

"He's my biggest fan," Marsee replied. "And I his. He saved my life." Marsee stared at one of the pictures for a moment, sighed at some internal thought, and shoved it in the bag.

She walked over and wrapped an arm around Marsee's shoulder. "Are you okay?"

Marsee's tail wrapped around her. "I am now that you're here." They leaned against each other for a few moments before Marsee grabbed another painting.

Their mother arrived a few minutes later with Hope. "Your father is moving your things to Little Flower's suite."

"I'm mostly packed up," Marsee said, pointing to the pile of bags by the door as she scanned the room, checking to make sure she hadn't missed anything. Then, sighing, she limped over to her cloak and threw it on.

Marsee had told her all about it the night before. It seemed strange to see the Sabers wearing clothing, but it fit Marsee like it had been tailored for her, not for someone of an entirely different species. It had been damaged during her fight with Rip, but Ellie had lovingly repaired it as part of her own physical therapy.

"Why are you limping?" her mother asked, pulling out her scanner. "You weren't earlier."

"My paw feels weird." Marsee flexed her paw to show it still worked, but their mother didn't take her word for it. Marsee scowled as her mother tried to scan her and moved away. "I'm fine, Mama. I've been scanned a half a dozen times already today. It just feels weird to walk on because it's all numb and tingly."

"You can tell me you're fine when your sense of pain is back. Until then, we scan regularly, especially if something feels off. Now, hold still so I can get a good scan."

Marsee sighed again, tail thwapping against the floor in annoyance, but held out her paw.

Little Flower rolled her eyes at her mother, and Marsee snorted, which caused her mother to look back with a scowl. Little Flower pretended to look innocent, which caused her mother to make essentially the same expression she'd made them moment before.

Once her mother was finally satisfied that Marsee's paw was uninjured, or at least no worse than it had been before, they made their way out. By the time they'd made it to the entrance of the Trauma Center, they had a dozen guards surrounding them, both Water Sprite and Saber. Along the way, Sprites who saw them flashed blue as they recognized Marsee or a checkered purple and silver pattern, and bowed low as they passed. Whether Marsee saw them or not, she couldn't tell. She didn't stop or acknowledge them, and the guards scowled fiercely enough that no one approached. It wasn't far to the other building, but even with the help of her drone, Marsee looked exhausted by the time they arrived.

Dropping off their drones and leaving the Water Sprite guards behind, they entered the dry area of Council Platform. Marsee grunted the moment they stepped inside and dropped down onto all four feet. By the time they made it to the lift, she was panting hard, and her legs were shaking, even with one of the guards helping by grabbing the back of her carry harness.

Marsee's head practically dragged on the floor as they made their way down their hall, and she had to stop halfway to rest. "I thought I....was doing better...than this," she huffed out, too tired to even sign. One of the guards translated for her.

"You are doing better," Avery replied. "You couldn't even walk three steps in this gravity a few days ago."

"We're in a Flyer section?" Marsee asked.

"Hue-man," Avery replied. "You're not ready for Flyer gravity yet."

"No wonder it feels right," Little Flower said.

"You can adjust the gravity in your suite, but I wouldn't recommend lowering it," Avery continued. "You both need to build up your strength."

When they finally made it to their room, Little Flower hit the lock, but the guards stopped them from entering until two of them had checked out the suite, along with their mother's adjoining suite, where they found her father waiting for them. Deeming it safe, they finally let them enter.

Marsee crawled over to the bed with the guard's help and collapsed on it in an undignified sprawl, not even bothering to take her stuff off. The bed, as with the rest of the suite, had been designed with humans in mind, not Sabers, but Marsee was much closer to her size than the adults, and it would fit her reasonably well. The lower bed would be far easier for both of them to crawl into than the one in the Trauma Center. None of the furniture was big enough for her parents, but there were several pillows scattered about for them to use if they desired.

Little Flower watched, surprised by the tenderness the guard showed Marsee as she helped her out of her gear and hung it up. She had been gruff with Marsee over the fire sticks, but the compassion Little Flower saw now, added to the comments from earlier, belied that gruffness. Something told her the guard actually cared for Marsee, that she was more than just an assignment.

"What's your name, again?" Little Flower asked when she turned around.

"Tamarin Fields, ma'am." The guard spelled it, used a name sign, and spoke it.

She couldn't quite hear it. "Can you say it higher?"

Marsee beat the guard to it. "Tamarin is the name of a plant. It blooms with sweet-smelling multi-colored blossoms in the spring."

"Most of our species are highly allergic to them," Tamarin added. "Touching them causes our skin to form blisters, and the seeds are deadly if inhaled or ingested and not treated in time. However, Diggers love them sprinkled on their food. I'm told Raja is very spicy. It's highly regulated for obvious reasons."

"You were named after a deadly flower?" she asked.

"No. I chose it on my name day," the guard replied.

"Why?" Little Flower asked, curious.

Tamarin grinned. "Perhaps someday I'll tell you the story, but today is not that day."

"Does this have anything to do with your tail and why Kendra is afraid of Rowena?" Marsee asked.

Tamarin's tail corkscrewed with laughter, but she walked out without answering.

"I honestly think they're making it up," Marsee muttered after the guard shut the door. "I've been trying to get her to tell me for days."

"Good luck with that," her mother said as she scanned Marsee again. "Assuming it's the same story, I've been trying to get Rowena to tell me for over a century. Now, get some rest. Your father and I are going to explore the Arboretum. If you need me, call. I'll be back this evening for your pickle torture. We'll try for three laps up and down the hall."

"Yippie," Marsee muttered in English.

Little Flower had said it enough during her own pickle torture that she snorted with surprised laughter.

Her mother rolled her eyes and shook her head at the two of them but left without another word.

Still laughing, Little Flower peeled out of her wet suit and dug through the bags she'd brought with her for a change of clothes that were more comfortable.

"Are you thirsty?" she asked after she finished changing.

"No. Maybe? My mouth is dry from panting, but I don't feel thirsty."

She dug around in the small kitchen and found what looked and smelled like star fruit juice and poured them all drinks. She carefully brought a large glass over to Marsee, who drank the whole thing in one large gulp.

"I guess I must have been," Marsee said, handing the empty glass back.

Little Flower chuckled and poured her another.

Hope ignored her drink and set her glass down on the floor and started digging through one of the bags that had already been in the room when they'd returned.

Little Flower scooped up her daughter, making her squeal with laughter. "What are you doing, you little imp?"

"Want play," she signed.

Marsee crawled off the bed with a groan and padded over to one of the bags. "I picked her up a bunch of new toys the other day," she said and then moved over to another bag. "Here they are." Marsee pulled them out and set them on the floor, so she set Hope down next to them. Marsee curled up on the floor next to her daughter and began playing, looking exceedingly happy but with very little enthusiasm, clearly fighting her fatigue.

"I picked you up some new art supplies, too. They're in the first bag. They work underwater," Marsee said, followed by a massive yawn.

"Really? How?" Little Flower dragged the bag over, seeing that there was more than just art supplies in there, and handed it to Marsee.

Marsee dug through the bag. "The artist I bought the supplies from was still learning to sign, so I'm not entirely sure how they work. I think he was trying to say the pens change the paper rather than leaving any ink or pigment behind, and you can reuse the paper. There should be an eraser in here somewhere, too." Marsee kept digging through the bag until she found it and handed it over.

Little Flower carried the supplies to the small table. Small was relative. It was bigger than the formal dining table they'd had back on Earth, but the height and chairs were all designed for her species. It felt strange to actually have furniture her own size. For the last several months, aside from the rocking chair, everything in her room had been sized for those caring for her, not for her convenience and comfort. It made the entire room feel cozy.

She watched as Marsee laid her head on one of her paws and used the other paw to continue playing with Hope. Her fingers itched to draw the scene, but she hadn't drawn anything since she'd woken from her coma, and she was terrified she wouldn't do it justice. She picked up one of the pens and tested it against the paper, getting a feel for how it worked. She tried out each of the colors before taking a deep breath, clearing the page, and starting.

She looked up at one point to find that Marsee had fallen asleep. She smiled but kept drawing. Her lines were nowhere as straight and controlled as she was used to, and she erased often, but as she drew, she figured out ways to make that work with her sketch, and when she was done, she had a drawing that she actually felt reasonably proud of. It was nothing like her normal style, and it took her significantly longer to draw, but it still captured the essence of the scene.

When Marsee started twitching and growling in her sleep again, Little Flower walked over and picked up Hope. Marsee hadn't put her gear on, and Hope had no way of knowing that her Papa might not be safe when she slept. As she did, she started singing again, but unlike before, Marsee didn't calm down. Instead, she continued to mutter and growl in her sleep.

"Marsee, wake up," Little Flower called out. "Marsee, you need to wake up!"

Marsee's eyes opened, and Little Flower breathed a sigh of relief, but then Marsee stood and started pacing, showing no signs of the fatigue from earlier.

"Marsee, wake up. You're safe!" she called out louder.

Marsee's head turned in her direction, and she crouched low as if stalking her.

She swore and moved to the other side of the table. "Marsee, stop!" she yelled.

Marsee growled instead.

Picking up the eraser from the table, she threw it at Marsee, hitting her in the side of the head, but rather than waking her, Marsee roared and poised to leap.

The noise startled Hope, and she started crying. The next thing she knew, the guards were swarming in the door. "She's sleepwalking!" Little Flower signed.

Tamarin ran over to protect her while Avery called out something in Saber.

Marsee turned to face Avery and growled something at him, which made him frown with confusion. He said something in reply, but whatever it was, it made her angry, and she leapt at him with a vicious snarl. He twisted faster than she could see, grabbed Marsee out of the air, and pinned her to the ground, grabbing her by the scruff.

Marsee instantly relaxed and then woke with a jolt, but then started panicking and trying to get away from the guard that had her pinned, not realizing what was going on or who had her.

"Marsee, you're okay. You were sleepwalking," she called out. "It's just Avery,"

Marsee stopped fighting and relaxed with a heavy pant, and Avery cautiously relaxed his grip and backed off. Marsee sat up and looked around, seeing her protected by Tamarin, and then noticed Hope crying. Marsee's ears drooped with horror. "Did I hurt her?"

"No, she's just scared," Little Flower replied.

"What happened?" Marsee asked, walking slowly over to Hope, who was hiding her head in Little Flower's arms. Marsee took Hope from her, but Hope started screaming louder. "Shhh. It's okay, little one. I won't hurt you." Marsee started purring, and Hope eventually calmed.

Little Flower turned to the guards. "Thank you. We're good now."

The guards didn't look convinced and a look passed between the two of them. Avery pursed his lips as if he was going to say something, then raised his arms to sign instead. "What were you dreaming?"

"It doesn't matter. It was just a dream," Marsee replied.

"Dreams have a way of surfacing things that our brains try to keep hidden. You said something to me, and I need to understand what it meant."

"I don't remember saying anything," Marsee said.

"Yes, you do. Tell me," he demanded.

Marsee sighed. "I was trapped in the cave again, but it wasn't the cave. It was a ship, I think, a hall anyway. I was trying to find my way out, but everything was a mess. It was cold, and dark, and I couldn't breathe, and then Rip was there, and he was going after Stormy, but I couldn't get to him. Then, an escape hatch opened, and Stormy was being sucked out. Somehow, I knew that was the only way out and told Stormy to let go. I leapt, not to catch Stormy, but to stop Rip from going after him. What did I say?"

"Go for the hatch," Avery replied. "I wasn't expecting that, but it makes sense now."

"You were thinking about Stormy earlier and buying a ship," Little Flower said. "I bet that just mixed with your memories of being trapped in the cave and needing to find a way out. Brains are weird."

Avery nodded his agreement and motioned for Tamarin to follow him back out.

"What did I do?" Marsee asked after the door was shut.

"You were twitching and muttering in your sleep. I tried to wake you, but you started sleepwalking. When you started heading towards us, muttering and growling, I threw an eraser at you, but that just made you mad. The guards entered, and you attacked Avery. He caught and pinned you to the ground, and you woke up."

Marsee's legs wobbled, and she sat down hard. "I attacked Avery! Dark moons! They could have arrested or killed me for that!"

Hope wiggled and signed that she wanted down. Marsee set her down, barely noticing as Hope toddled her way back to her toys. Her entire focus shifted to her paws, claws now outstretched.

"I doubt they will," Little Flower replied. "If they were going to, they would have done so already."

"Moons. I'm so sorry. I could have hurt you. I really don't think it's safe for you to be around me when I'm sleeping." Her whiskers and tail shivered with emotion, and it looked like she was on the verge of tears.

"Nonsense. It'll just take time for you to process what happened to you, and besides, you calmed earlier when I was next to you. If anything, being closer seems to help, and now I know never to throw anything at you to wake you up."

Marsee shivered hard. "That's how he woke me up."

"Noted, and I'm sorry. I wouldn't have done that if I'd known. No throwing things ever. Is there a scent, sound, or action that makes you feel calm and secure? Singing seemed to help earlier."

"Yeah, music has always calmed me in the past," Marsee said, considering.

"Good. Send me some of your favorite songs, and I'll try that next time."

Marsee nodded but didn't look convinced and continued to stare at her claws, and then began to rub at her hands.

"Marsee, I'm going to have to learn your triggers, just like you had to learn mine, but we'll get through this. If I have to order armor for you to feel safe around me, I will, but I know you won't hurt us."

"I don't understand how you can feel safe around me. I hurt Papa and I could easily kill you." Marsee's voice wavered, and tears broke through her control.

Little Flower stroked the side of her face, and Marsee leaned into it. "I feel safe because I love every bit of you, even these wonderfully sharp fangs of yours." She grabbed one of them and gave it a little tug. "Do I need to stick my head in your mouth to prove it?"

Marsee let out a depressed snort.

"Marsee, I want you to have sharp fangs and claws and learn to protect us with everything you have. I need your protection. I need to feel safe from those who want to harm us. I couldn't protect my daughter or my grandfather. I need a partner who can. I'm not worried that you'll hurt me in your sleep. You didn't last night or this morning, and you won't in the future. Now, how are you feeling? Is everything working okay, or should I dig out my scanner? Avery threw you pretty hard."

"You'd better check me over or have Mama check," Marsee said, then tilted her head. "How much have you learned from Ammond anyway?"

"Enough to identify a broken bone and provide minor first aid. We've been focusing on what we expected would be common injuries for you." She walked over to the first aid kit that Ammond had made up for her on the ship and pulled out the scanner. "I'll do the scans and send them over to Ammond for review. I'm not allowed to do anything more than emergency first aid until I earn my journeyman's rank without a master healer present, but neither of us wanted you to have to go to a healer every time you bumped into something."

Marsee nodded, and Little Flower began scanning.

"It looks like you might have a bruise forming on your hip, but there's so much interference from the scars from your burns that I'm not sure, although your hand looks a little swollen, too." She sent the scans off to Ammond, along with what she thought she found.

A few minutes later, Ammond replied and identified another smaller bruise that she'd missed.

"Well, I found two out of three. That's not bad, right?" she asked, as she dug the nano cream out of the kit and began rubbing it into the bruised and swollen spots and then carefully into Marsee's still-healing paw.

She was putting everything away when Marsee's tablet dinged. Marsee grumbled something in Saber that Little Flower was sure was one of the swears Ammond had been teaching her. She climbed to her feet with a groan, shut off her tablet and dragged herself into the bathroom, then swore again.

"What's wrong?" Little Flower asked.

"There's no hole, just the seat for you," Marsee called back.

"So sit on it or use Mama's."

"This is so weird. How do you do this?"

"Easily. What's hard is learning how to use the hole of muck without getting everything all over you."

"Hue-mans are weird," Marsee teased.

"Sabers are weirder," Little Flower teased back. "Oh, I drew something for you while you slept. I hope you like it. It's on the table."

"You did?!" Marsee hurried over to check it out after she was done in the bathroom. "Oh, Little Flower. This is fantastic! I love it!"

"Really? It's nothing like I could do before."

"It's a totally different style, and I can see how you worked around your shakiness, but I probably wouldn't have noticed if I didn't know what your style was like before. It still has your eye for capturing the essence of a scene and, in a lot of ways, actually highlights it better. I'm just so happy that you're drawing again. We should go pick up a frame for it. I used the last of the ones Ellie brought over yesterday."

"What? Now?" Little Flower asked.

"Sure. Why not?"

"Are you up to it? You were exhausted from the trip over here," she asked.

"Once we get outside, I'll be fine. Using the drone wasn't hard, and I really want to show you the market. The vendors are incredible, and I need to thank Opal for the meal and get something for dinner."

"There's stuff in the fridge."

"Meh," Marsee said, making a disgusted face. "I *want* Opals."

"Alright. If you're sure that you're up to it."

"I'm sure. Besides, I'd rather do that than walk up and down the hallway."

She chuckled. "That I agree with, but you let me know if you start to feel even the slightest bit tired, and we'll head back."

"Deal."

After a trip to the hole of muck herself, they made their way out. The two guards on the door followed behind, but she was surprised not to see any of the others. "Is it just the two of you now?"

"No, there are others scattered about," Avery replied. "They're in less conspicuous places now that Marsee is out of the Trauma Center. I assure you, you're protected."

As before, the people they passed all flashed purple and silver, although this time, Marsee clearly noticed. Every time it happened, the tip of Marsee's tail shivered with annoyance, although she did her best to ignore it. It would have taken them hours to make it to the market if she hadn't. When they finally arrived, everyone turned and bowed when they realized Marsee was there. Marsee sighed and bowed back.

The market was packed, but thankfully, people seemed to give them space. She wasn't sure if it was because of their respect for Marsee or the two menacing guards that flanked them. Either way, she was glad. Marsee was on edge, and even she found the sheer number of people to be overwhelming, especially since most of them were so much bigger than she was. A few made the adult female Sabers look small and had to be nearly twice as long when fully stretched out.

Only one person tried to approach them, and Marsee scowled when she saw them. The guards somehow managed to appear even more threatening, and whoever they were suddenly found someplace else to be. It was rather impressive to watch.

"Who was that?" she asked in English to give Marsee some privacy.

"The Press," Marsee replied. "I really don't want to give an interview, but I imagine I'm going to have to eventually."

"Well, our pair of fuzzy shadows seem to be decent anti-press repellent. One scowl from them, and they bolted. If they had tails, they'd be tucked between their tentacles."

Marsee snorted. Tail curled, she led them directly to a food vendor.

Little Flower noticed with some amusement that the guards shifted to take up positions around the booth, where they could still watch them but keep the crowd at bay, while everyone who had been in line at the booth shifted to let Marsee cut. *There are some serious benefits to Marsee's popularity,* she thought.

Marsee, however, frowned at the sight. "It's not necessary. We can wait our turn. Please."

No one listened to her, and they, too, suddenly found someplace else to be.

Marsee sighed and swam up. "I'm sorry for scaring your customers away, Opal."

"Nonsense," the vendor signed. "They'll be back once you're done. They're just giving you some privacy. It's wonderful to see you again. I heard you finally left the Trauma Center, but I didn't expect to see you today. I hope that means you're feeling better?"

"I tire very easily, but I am a little better every day. Opal, I'd like you to meet my partner, Little Flower, and our daughter, Hope." Marsee's face positively radiated her joy at being able to sign those words, and her tail spiraled with happiness.

She grinned at her partner, thrilled to see Marsee smiling again.

Opal glowed her own happiness. "I heard you were getting married today from your grandfather. He was here when he received your message. Congratulations! It's an honor to meet you, Little Flower, and I can't think of anyone better suited for partnership than the two of you. I've watched the end of your trial many times, and I cheer every time. I've never seen anything like it, the way you managed to save your family and the look on Councilor Tabor's face as she stormed off. Absolute perfection!"

Little Flower chuckled at the expression on the Sprite's face. "Thank you. I've heard rave reviews about you and your food as well, and what I've tried so far has been wonderful, although those fire sticks should come with a warning label and a side of the fire brigade."

Opal's skin bubbled with what she'd been taught was laughter. "Councilor GrandFather did say that they tasted exceptionally hot to him, and I have been warning the others of your species. The reaction from those who have tried them has been very entertaining. I hope you're not upset."

"Not at all. It's a running prank between us. We had something as hot on Earth called a ghost pepper. I'm not sure if it had that name because it was so hot it could kill you or because it was so hot it could wake the dead. You wouldn't happen to have anything else I could use to get even with him later?"

More laughter bubbled across her skin. "I heard you Hue-man's have the soul of a Flyer, and I can see that it's true. Sadly, I don't have anything else hot with me today, but I do have something that tastes sour to us, if you like that kind of thing."

"Perfect," she signed. "He wouldn't expect that at all."

Opal handed her a stick full of bright orange fruit.

She took a cautious bite, and her mouth and face instantly puckered. "Oh, these will do nicely, although I think I'm going to need something sweet to stop my eyes from twitching." Opal and Marsee both laughed.

Hope reached for the stick, and Little Flower moved it away. "Want!" Hope signed.

"You won't like it," she signed back.

"I want!" Hope signed again and started to fuss, so she carefully removed a small piece and handed it to her. Hope took it and stuck it in her mouth, and they all laughed as Hope's face puckered and contorted. To their surprise, Hope ate it and reached for another bite. "Want more." This was in Saber.

Giving her another piece, she looked up in time to see a slight shift in Opal's expression.

Marsee must have noticed it, too. "Hope has only just started eating solid foods and has not yet learned to use the Hue-mans utensils or your sticks for eating. I don't know the sign for them. I apologize for any rudeness."

Opal smiled and showed them the signs. "There's nothing to apologize for. It takes our small fry time to learn as well. Please forgive me if I showed confusion. She spoke in Saber. I thought you couldn't hear each other speak?"

"Not entirely," Marsee replied. "The biggest problem was the damage to their hearing from the Cataclysm, which my uncle has had some success in fixing."

"Ammond restored about half of my hearing this past week. I can hear Marsee just fine now," Little Flower said. "But the bigger adults have to raise the pitch of their voices, and I have to lower mine."

"The cubs are far more adaptive than we realized," Marsee continued. "Hope learned within a few weeks that my parents couldn't hear her unless she used a deeper voice, and she has quite a talent for mimicry and language. She's been speaking in all of the languages since she was about two months old. There are cubs of all of the species in New Hope, and she plays with them regularly. I am quite convinced she can understand far more than she speaks."

"All the languages? Even Flyer? Our children don't start vocalizing until they're almost two years old, and very few of us can speak Flyer even as adults."

"She has difficulty making some sounds in all the languages, but she's rapidly improving." Marsee made a whistling noise, which Hope replied to.

Little Flower hadn't even realized that her daughter could speak in the other languages outside of Saber. Granted, for the past two months, she'd either been sleeping or swearing her way through pickle torture.

"GrandFather says Hue-man children are quite skilled at learning languages, which would make sense since they had hundreds of them and a much shorter time in which to learn them. On Earth, they only lived about twenty-five or thirty standard years, although my mother says we should be able to extend their lifespan to closer to a hundred with our technology. Hope will likely be an adult by the time she's three or four. Little Flower is only six."

"I'm almost seven," she replied, annoyed at feeling like a child again, although neither Marsee or Opal seemed to catch her annoyance.

Opal instead flashed her surprise, if Little Flower had her color meanings right. "Seriously?! I knew you matured young, but I had no idea your lifespan was so short. How horrible. I am glad to hear we'll be able to correct it." She paused as if she were considering something. "I understand better now why your time in quarantine was so hard. That was something I hadn't quite understood. Certainly, months of isolation would be hard on anyone, but that would have been about the equivalent of around eight of our years, which I can't even imagine. I am sorry. I must say, though, if you can manage to take on the Senior Council at six, I can't wait to see what you accomplish in the coming years. It certainly has been interesting since you Hue-mans were rescued."

She relaxed, realizing that Opal didn't hold her youth against her, and chuckled. "Thank you. My people had a curse disguised as a blessing, 'May you live in interesting times.' I've personally had my fair share of interesting times and could do with some normalcy."

"I completely agree. So, what can I get for you today? Would you like more fire sticks?"

Marsee sighed. "More than anything in the universe, but sadly, my stomach is apparently not ready for them yet."

"I warned you," Tamarin signed.

Marsee pinned her ears at the guard. "But the...discomfort was worth every bite," she continued. "I can't even begin to describe how revolting the nano drink I had to take was. I'm still convinced it was part Leviathan poop, and frankly, the food in the Trauma Center doesn't even qualify as food when compared to yours. Do you have any more of the brenna berry sticks?"

"I do," Opal said, flashing a beautiful blue/green at the compliment laced with hints of bubbling laughter. She handed Marsee several and gave one to her as well.

"Thank you," Marsee said, but her expression turned serious. "Now. Before you say otherwise, I am paying for these, and I don't want any arguments about it."

"But I can't charge you on your wedding day," Opal signed, equally adamant.

"You can, and you will. I have been given so much by your people. Let me give some of it back. Please."

Opal glared at Marsee for several moments, but Marsee glared right back. Opal broke first. "Fine, but you're taking another package with you, and those *are* a wedding present."

"Deal," Marsee said and pulled off her tablet. Opal quickly wrapped up the packages, entered the purchases, and touched Marsee's tablet with her own. Marsee typed something into her tablet and confirmed the purchase.

"Thank you for your purchase, Trans…" Opal started, did a double take, and froze, staring at her tablet. "Translator…This is far too much!"

Marsee gave Opal a smug grin. "Buy that restaurant you've always wanted, Opal. I expect an invite to your opening day, and your fire sticks had better be on the menu."

Opal floated there, speechless as they swam away. Marsee's tail spiraled with happiness, making Little Flower wonder just how much Marsee had tipped the vendor.

CHAPTER 13

Carrie: Emancipation

Carrie devoured the plate of food the healers had left her in a matter of minutes but she was still so very hungry. It was never enough. Her body craved food, but the healers were worried she'd eat too much too quickly and get sick, and they were probably right. When every last crumb was gone, she grabbed the special nutrient-dense drink they gave her and tried to nurse it to make it last until her next meal, but it never did. A minute later, it, too, was gone.

She sighed and set it aside, then picked up the tiny stone figurine in the shape of a Flyer that sat on the table beside her hanging net. It was simple, crude even, by Guild standards, but to her, it was priceless. It was the one thing that had been specifically left for her at the vigil. There was no name attached, so she didn't know who to thank, but it was good to know that at least one person still cared for her.

Her tablet rang, and she checked to see who the caller was, then ignored it. It was her father. He called at the same time every day, and she hadn't been able to answer. There were only a few days before the council meeting. She knew she should say goodbye, but she didn't know how. Nor did she know what was going to happen with her life after he was dead.

She was finally free from the cage she'd been held in for over six months but she was no more free than she had been before. Aside from regaining her weight, she was as recovered as she was going to be, yet she couldn't leave the Trauma Center. She had no next of kin or guardian to sign her out, and a pair of bored guards followed her everywhere.

Her father had given a list of people he recommended for her care, but none of them had agreed. When that had failed, a public notice had been sent out to everyone who had registered to be notified of such an event, but no one had come forward. She knew they wouldn't, but she had hoped that maybe if someone had cared enough to petition the gods for her soul, they might come forward. Granted, they could very well be a child themselves based on the crudeness of the carving.

What do I need them for, anyway? I managed on my own for months. I could easily take care of myself if they let me. Tilting her head at that thought, she grabbed her tablet and did some research but frowned at what she read. There weren't a lot of options available to her until she was physically mature, and she didn't like any of them.

She sighed and stared at the open door, then decided she'd had enough of waiting for others to save her. Grabbing her things, which amounted to nothing more than her tablet and figurine, she swam out of the room. The guards followed silently behind as they normally did when she went anywhere, which typically amounted to nothing more than swimming around the halls to relieve her boredom, and to her surprise, they didn't say anything until she tried to go through the main door.

"Where are you going?" the Senior of the two asked.

"To take control of my life," she replied. "You can follow me or not, but I'm leaving."

She honestly expected them to stop her, but they didn't. There were guards outside the Council building, but they didn't stop her either. Inside, signs pointed the way to various locations, and she followed the ones she wanted, eventually swimming inside the public-facing guard station. The two that had followed her swam off the moment she entered and began talking with someone else.

A bored-looking guard sat at a desk near the door and looked up when she approached. "Name?" he flashed.

"I'm Carrie, Snapper Fish's daughter."

That caught the guard's attention, and he straightened. "Are you here to see your father?"

"No. I'd like to speak with Honor Guard Red Fin," she replied.

The guard shrugged and nodded towards a row of nets along the wall. "Have a seat. I'll see if he's available."

She flashed her thanks and swam over. A few minutes later, Red Fin swam into the office and over to her. "You wanted to see me?"

She nodded. "Can we talk in private?"

"Of course," he replied and led her over to a small conference room. Once inside, he turned on the privacy screen and sat across from her. "What can I do for you?"

"I'd like to ask a favor. It's a lot, but I don't know what else to do."

He frowned. "Are you in trouble?"

"I suppose that depends on how you define trouble. No one has come forward to claim guardianship for me when my father is executed, and I'm not physically mature enough to claim adulthood on my own. I don't want to spend the next several years of my life in the Trauma Center or be followed around by guards who won't even speak to me. I'm certainly not an expert on the law, but as far as I can tell, there aren't many options left to me, and none of them are particularly good. Before you say anything. I'm not asking you to be my guardian. I was hoping you'd be my witness."

"You intend to petition the Council for your adulthood?" he asked.

"No. I don't want the universe to know that no one wanted me. I intend to claim the right of emancipation. No one will think twice about me wanting to separate myself from my father after what he did."

"Emancipation? He abused you?"

She snorted. "He left me alone with Rip for over six months and never went for help. That sounds an awful lot like abuse to me."

Red Fin tilted his head. "There is certainly a case to be made for that, but I witnessed you advocate for him to the Senior Council. To emancipate yourself might hurt his chances at leniency. Do you really want to do that?"

"Do you honestly think there's a chance they won't kill him after what he did?"

"No. Not really. I'm honestly surprised that they haven't already."

"Then one more strike to his record won't matter, not to him, but it'll matter to me. I have been held in a cage for months. I might be out of that cage now, but I am no less free than I was before, and I don't really trust anyone enough to be my guardian. I may be young, but I'm two months older than Stormy, and it's all over the news that he was granted his adulthood. If he's old enough to be an adult, then I am, too."

"I can't fault that logic or your ability to care for yourself and others, but you don't need to emancipate yourself if your father brings you forward for adulthood."

"I thought he couldn't do that anymore," she replied.

"He's charged with a crime but hasn't officially been found guilty yet, and as you've pointed out, you haven't been assigned a new guardian, so he still has that right. You should talk with him. If he doesn't agree, then I will gladly witness for you."

She flashed her thanks, but it was tinged with hesitation. "I don't know if I can talk to him. He calls every day, but I haven't been able to answer."

"I know. He's worried about you. Why don't you want to talk to him?"

She fiddled with the figurine while she tried to figure out how to explain her conflicting feelings, but her skin must have said enough as he nodded.

"You have every right to be conflicted," he said in Saber. "What you went through was horrible, and I imagine it was far more than you put on your statement."

She looked up to see compassion on his face, not an accusation.

"Do you want my advice?"

She shrugged.

"Talk to your father. Let it all out. Let him know what really happened to you. Whatever his intentions, he will likely die because he chose not to risk your life by going for help. Whether that was because he loved you too much or not enough, I don't know, and that's not my decision to make. But I believe he should know the full extent of the harm his decision caused you before he dies. You won't get another chance to condemn him, or forgive him, or even just say goodbye."

"So many others didn't get a chance to say goodbye to their families."

He tilted his head to acknowledge the point but didn't say anything else, leaving it entirely up to her.

Eventually, she gave a small nod. "Will you go with me?"

He smiled kindly at her. "Of course."

He led her down another floor, then stopped and had her press her hand to a panel on the wall. A small compartment slid open. "Please place your belongings inside."

She placed her tablet in but hesitated to put the figurine in. It was the one thing giving her strength right now.

"I promise it will be safe. Once locked, only you or a member of the Senior Council can open this box."

She sighed heavily but still couldn't make herself put it inside.

He held out his hand. "May I see it?"

She handed it over, and he examined it closely.

"Do you promise not to throw it at him?"

"No," she replied. "How could I possibly make a promise when I don't know if I could keep it."

"I suppose that's fair," he said, flickering with humor. "Did he make this for you?"

"I don't know who it's from. Someone left it for me at the vigil. It was the only thing left specifically for me. It's nice to know that at least someone still cares for me."

He frowned. "This is all you got?"

She nodded. "That's all they brought me."

"That's not right. I left something for you, and I know my mother did, too. I'll look into it. Perhaps it's being held somewhere while you recover."

"You did?" She flashed her surprise and nearly cried to know someone still cared for her.

"Of course we did. You saved my life and Petra's and all the other people in that cage. How could we not?"

"Thank you."

He handed her back the figurine and shut the door, then led her down the hall. Guards were outside several doors, but he stopped outside the first one. "Carrie is here to see her father."

"There's someone in with him at the moment. You'll have to wait." One of the guards said, then unclipped her tablet and typed at it for a moment. "Please press your thumb here for verification."

She did.

The guard reviewed something for a moment but looked up as the door opened and a Saber swam out. Carrie blinked in surprise when she recognized them, not expecting to see them here, and certainly not in her father's cell, but they simply nodded and swam off. She shrugged and looked back at the cell.

Her father lay sprawled in a sleeping net, facing away from the door. A tray of untouched food sat on a table beside him. She stared at the dark blue of his back for several long moments before swimming inside.

Red Fin followed after, and the door slid shut behind them as he shifted over so that he could observe their conversation.

She opened her mouth several times to let him know she was there but couldn't form the words.

"You have a visitor," Red Fin finally said for her.

Her father turned his head to look back and gasped, flashing bright blue with joy. "Carrie!"

He rolled over so quickly that he ended up rolling the net and getting tangled in it. When he finally untangled himself, he started to swim towards her again but stopped, realizing she hadn't come to him. His eyes scanned her, and the light of his skin dimmed until it was nearly black. "Oh gods, Carrie. What did he do to you? He promised me he wouldn't hurt you."

Her anger bubbled to the surface, lighting the room a pulsing red. "And you honestly believed him?"

Guilt flashed across his skin now.

"He locked me in a cage where the only source of food was whatever tiny fish swam inside. Just about every other day, he would appear and shock someone to hear them scream until they passed out. If they refused to scream for him, he found other ways to break them until, eventually, they never woke up again. He saved me for special occasions when he wanted something from someone, like he did with Petra. Sometimes, he would show up with others and let them pick someone to do with as they wanted. They always picked me because I was too young to get pregnant. His only stipulation was that they couldn't kill me or leave a mark where *you* might see it."

Horror flashed across her father's skin, and she turned so he could see the scars that covered her back.

Red Fin interrupted at that point. "Who else was involved?"

"I don't know," she replied. "He never said who they were, and it doesn't matter. Like Leaf and Willow, they're all dead." Turning back to her father, she scowled. "Why didn't you tell anyone?"

"I wanted to," he replied. "But I didn't know who I could trust. Rip said..."

"I don't care what he said! I've heard more than enough of his lies to last me seven lifetimes. You should have killed him the first moment you had a chance and then gone straight to Clear Seas or one of the other Senior Councilors. Starving to death would have been preferable, and so many others would still be alive now."

"I know. But I couldn't lose you, too. You're all I have left."

"Left?!" she yelled. "That's all I am to you, isn't it? Mama's leftovers."

He frowned and shook his head. "No, of course not. I..."

"Isn't it, though? Ever since Mama died, you changed. You stopped seeing me. I was just a reminder of what you lost. You were never home, always taking extra shifts. How long was it before you realized I was missing? An hour? A day? Two? Do you even know when he took me?"

The guilt on his skin told her everything, and her anger turned to disgust. "I should have known. Honor Guard Red Fin, I claim the right of emancipation on the grounds that my father's neglect led to my captivity and torture, and due to the fact that no one has come forward to offer guardianship due to my father's crimes, I request to be granted adulthood. As evidence, I put forth the six months that I kept myself and the others, who were also harmed by my father's negligence and cowardice, alive for that time. I also put forth my injuries as evidence that others saw me as physically mature and used me in that way."

Red Fin nodded. "I accept and stand as witness to your evidence and grant you the right of emancipation. Do you understand and promise to uphold the laws of our people from this day forth?"

"I do," she replied.

"Do you promise to care for and take responsibility for your offspring, should you choose to have them, to the best of your ability, until such time as they themselves reach adulthood?"

"I can certainly do better than my father," she replied.

A slight flicker of amusement crossed Red Fin's skin as her father hung his head in shame. "Please, just say I do."

"I do."

"Then it is my decision as granted to me as a senior member of the Honor Guard that you are now recognized as an emancipated adult with all of the rights and responsibilities that come with that designation, from this day forth."

She glared at her father for a moment, then turned to swim out.

"Carrie, please wait," her father called out.

She paused but didn't turn around, hands clenched tightly at her side to keep from turning around and shocking him like she wanted to.

"For what it's worth, I do love you," he said in Saber. "I have always loved you, and I am truly sorry for the harm I caused you."

She felt something snap and looked down to find her figurine was broken, the wings snapped off, just like Petra's had been. *How appropriate,* she thought bitterly. She turned and swam back over to him, dropping the figurine in his hands.

He examined the pieces briefly before looking back up at her in confusion.

"You didn't just hurt me. You hurt a lot of people. Petra claimed responsibility for your crimes to save my life, and Rip practically tore her wings off anyway. Even broken and dying, she was more of a parent than you've been since Mama died. I curse you to spend the rest of eternity wandering the abyss alone and suffering the same torment you caused me and everyone else you harmed. And I hope you spend every moment of that eternity knowing that you will never see Mama or me again."

With that, she turned and swam out, her father's anguished cry of pain the last thing she heard as the door slid shut behind her.

CHAPTER 14

Kendra: Alert

Kendra felt like a massive weight had been lifted from her shoulders as she swam back to her office. The morning had gone far better than she'd expected. She was still concerned about Myra, but the fact that she'd met with Jeran without losing control boded well for her chances of survival. The following conversation she'd had with Marcus in his suite had been far less contentious than she'd expected. There had been no accusations, simply relief and surprise as she filled in the details that Marsee hadn't shared, followed by concern as they discussed how to protect her and others like her in the future. That didn't solve all of her problems, but there was a path forward, and she would take it.

As she entered the outer office, the guards inside all looked up and sighed with relief, picking up on her emotions. She scowled at them anyway for their mutiny that morning. "By Surellis's orders, Marsee's status is not to be shared with anyone, not even other members of the Council or Guard outside of those here. If anyone asks, state that she is doing well and that any further questions should be directed to him. His prior orders regarding testing and training stand while we...gather further information on the effectiveness of sign language. Are there any questions?"

"Is Marsee joining the Guard?"

"Officially, no. As far as the public is concerned, we are simply helping Marsee and her sister recover from their respective traumas and teaching them the use of a stunner. As they have been attacked twice, we feel that no one will question it."

"Unofficially?" another person asked.

She grinned. "Marsee's *honor* is not in question. Treat them both as you would any new trainee in the same situation."

That ended the questions, so she returned to her office. By mid-afternoon, she had finally caught up with the urgent messages from her backlog and was making use of the facilities before leaving for Command to monitor the situation with the Ice Giant Council when the comms blared with an alert. She swore at the Ancient Gods, convinced for the past two centuries that they were Flyers, as they had a knack for calling in alerts when she was similarly occupied. The moment she was done, she bolted out of her office just in time to see Marsee attack Avery.

"What happened?" she bellowed, wondering how her fur-brained nephew had managed to lie to her.

"She's sleepwalking," a guard said, "and she was going after Little Flower and Hope."

The office went silent as they watched Avery control the situation, and then she swallowed hard as Marsee told of her dream. That she would be dreaming about a ship when the Ice Giant Council ships were still missing set her fur on edge. There was no indication that Marsee knew about it, or Little Flower would have said something.

Is it related, or is something else going to happen?

"Where's Stormy now?" she demanded.

"He's outside the primary school," the guard replied.

"Squad Two, go," she ordered, and the squad bolted out of the office at full speed.

"Ma'am, do you think..." the guard started to ask.

"I have no idea. It could be nothing more than a dream, but if there is something nefarious going on with the Ice Giant ships, I wouldn't put it past whomever's behind it to make another attempt at harming the Senior Council or their families while we're all distracted. I'd rather be safe than sorry."

CHAPTER 15

Quinn: Red Sky

His shift over for the day, Quinn signed out and turned off his camera. With the suns setting with spectacular beauty on the horizon, he made his way into the Barn and up to the second floor, following the sounds of high-pitched childish laughter and an amber scent he'd come to know well. His walks with Nazari around New Hope were quickly becoming the favorite part of his day.

He had few friends outside of the Guard and knew he was pushing every boundary by not keeping his emotional distance from her. While she had improved significantly since gaining custody of Sari, there was still the chance that he would be forced to put her down, but he also knew friendship was the best way to save her. The more she trusted and cared about him, the better chance he would have of bringing her safely through the Transition, if that became necessary. He found her and her new cub in the puppy pens. His tail curled at the sight of Sari practically swarmed with happy, wiggling puppies that climbed all over his lap and licked at his face. The joy the tiny Hue-man cub radiated was just as pure and innocent as the puppies.

"One cub wasn't enough?" he teased Nazari. "You needed another twenty?"

She glanced in his direction and then grinned, delighted to see him. "It makes him happy. He doesn't interact with the Hue-man cubs at all, but he's fascinated by all the creatures in the barn."

"So I see. Has he spoken anything yet?"

"No. He hasn't spoken a single word in Saber or Hue-man, and I have no idea if he understands Sign. Occasionally, he'll come when I motion, but that's about it. He can hear, according to the scan Ammond did a few months ago, and he does react to unexpected or loud noises, but I don't think he understands that language has any meaning."

He sniffed hints of worry and sadness, although her outward expression didn't change. "I'm sure with your love and compassion, he will have a wonderful life, even if he never learns to speak, but perhaps you could use the same methods Henry Curtis and GrandFather use with Buster."

"I spoke to GrandFather about it before he left. I'm not sure how I feel about treating a sentient creature like an animal, not after what happened at the Agency."

He tilted his head. "I suppose I see your point, but perhaps language of any form is better than none?"

"He communicates in his own way," Nazari said. "He's happy, and for now, that's all that matters."

Nazari reached over, grabbed a small, well-chewed, and slightly slobbery ball, then tapped her son on the shoulder to get his attention.

Sari looked up at her and grinned. There was no doubt in Quinn's mind that Sari recognized and loved his mother.

She held out the ball, made the sign for it with her other hand, and tossed it gently across the pen. The swarm of puppies took off after it. There was a scuffle, and one of the puppies returned victorious with its prize, tail wiggling furiously, which he had come to learn meant it was happy, not angry. She took the ball from the puppy and did it again.

This time, Sari chased after the ball along with the others, although he was nowhere near as fast as the puppies. Based on his infectious laughter, it didn't seem to bother the cub that he was the slowest.

Nazari repeated the process a third time, then held the ball out to Sari, curious what he would do. Sari took it and stared at it for a moment before throwing it and then ran after it along with the puppies.

The puppy who caught the ball this time didn't run back to Nazari but instead ran off across the pen, and a mad chase ensued.

"He's capable of learning," Quinn said as they watched. "but you're right. I don't think he understands that the motion you're making is language."

"He is smart. The first night, I woke and found him in the refrigeration unit with food spilled everywhere. I still don't know how he managed to open it, much less the bedroom door."

He chuckled. "The Hue-mans have quite the natural ability when it comes to climbing things. I had to drag Ben down out of the tree this morning. It's rather impressive how well they can climb without claws."

"Ben was in the tree again? Did something happen? He only goes up there when he's upset."

"He didn't say, although he was rather annoyed I made him come down."

She frowned. "He won't talk about his life before. I think something happened, something other than the Cataclysm. He's very protective of the other children, but he's angry all the time, too. GrandFather said mood swings are normal for his age, but if he were one of our cubs, I'd be worried."

He sighed. "That's my observation, too. If the Hue-man's had a guard, I'd recommend him for training. I've seen him watching our squad on several occasions."

One of the puppies yipped, followed by a growl, and it snapped at Sari. Faster than he could react, Nazari scooped up her son. Rather than wanting comfort, he started screaming and wiggling to get down. This set off all the puppies as they started reacting to his screams, and then the older dogs in the other pens started howling, too.

He pinned his ears back at the high-pitched noise and watched as Sari covered his own ears with his paws. The anger the cub had been radiating a moment before changed to fear, and his screams changed to cries.

"Shh. It's alright," Nazari said, frowning with worry as she tried to comfort her cub and pull her scanner off at the same time.

"He's unhurt," Quinn said. "He was angry about being picked up, but now the noise is scaring him. Come on. Why don't we go for our walk."

Nazari frowned at him but followed his orders. As soon as they made their way down to the first level, Sari calmed, although there were still a few hiccups and whimpers, nearly covered by the volume of Nazari's purr and gentle reassurances. "You're alright, my little one. I know it was scary. They can be quite loud when they want to be."

By the time they made it outside, Sari had forgotten his fear and was wiggling to get down again. Instead, Nazari dropped down onto all fours and tossed the cub on her back. Once he was situated, she proceeded to bounce lightly in her step. Sari started laughing immediately.

"That's effective," Quinn said with a surprised chuckle.

"It's easier than carrying him everywhere, and as you can see, he likes it. I used to do the same with my first litter."

She said nothing else until they reached the small scrub tree, where they regularly sat to talk. As she sat down, she used her tail to pull the cub off her back. Once he was comfortably situated in her lap, she took out her scanner to confirm he was unhurt. She frowned with confusion as she examined the scans.

"Is everything alright?" he asked. He hadn't sensed any injuries, so he wondered what she was seeing.

"Yes. How did you know he wasn't hurt and only angry?"

"I watched it happen. Sari stepped on the puppy's tail by accident. The puppy only snapped a warning. It was close but it didn't make contact, and as you said, he communicates in his own way."

She clipped her tablet back to her harness and used her tail to tickle and distract the cub, but she was otherwise silent. "I think you're lying," she said several minutes later.

"That's quite the accusation," he replied. "But, I would not lie about someone's safety, and certainly not about your cub."

"I believe that. What I don't believe is your comments about his emotions. Several times now, you've said things you couldn't possibly know. How are you doing that?"

He shrugged, trying to deflect. "We are trained in the Guard to observe everything, especially a person's body language. It can mean the difference between life and death. I could be wrong about his emotions, as my experience with Hue-mans is limited, but if he had been hurt, he would have been going to you for comfort, not trying to get away."

She grunted, but he could tell she wasn't convinced. "I think there's more than that going on."

"What makes you say that?"

"Well, in the past, when I asked for clarification on how you knew something, you stated that you couldn't tell me unless I joined the Guard."

"I am sure there are things that you can't tell others unless they're in the Healer's Guild."

She squinted at him, not a glare, but as if she'd caught him in a trap. "Indeed. Speaking of which, we were all waiting for Marsee's scans to arrive this morning, but they didn't, and when we went to check to make sure there wasn't a missed notification, we found our access to her account had been revoked, not by Marsee or Myra, or the Senior Council who had locked it down before, but by Kendra. When we asked Nerissa, she stated Marsee's medical status was being restricted to level three masters and up, and Myra's not responding to my messages. What's going on? Are they alright?"

"I've not heard anything to say otherwise," he replied. "In fact, I saw a press report earlier stating Marsee had been released from the trauma center. Myra was with her."

"I saw the same report. They were surrounded by an entire squad of guards. It looked more like Marsee was being arrested, not released. One of the guards was even dragging her by her harness."

"That was an Honor Guard formation, not an arrest. They were delivering her home with honors. It signaled the end of her official Honor

Guard, although she's still being guarded. If she were being arrested, they would have loaded her onto a ship on the roof of the Trauma Center rather than parading her through the park. The guard you saw helping Marsee was Tamarin."

"The Journeyman that took over her care after she moved to the dry room?"

He nodded. "Tamarin has been in the Guard for almost two hundred years. She's not highly ranked in the Healer's Guild, but she would easily qualify for her masters if she wanted it, level two or three at least. She's one of the best we have and she's seen and treated just about everything. She'll be able to help Marsee recover better than anyone. We all go to her for help when we're injured or need someone to talk to."

"Why her and not one of the Guard Healers?"

He grinned and made a decision, hoping she might be one of the few who would understand. "Can I trust you with a secret?"

"Of course," she replied. "I am a Healer, after all."

"Tamarin is the best because she was taught by the best. She's Rowena's daughter and protege."

"I didn't know Rowena had any children."

"Nearly a dozen, I think. Most of her children are in the Guard on Digger. Her extended family is nearly big enough to form several contingents on their own."

"How did she end up adopting a Saber child? Cross-species adoptions are rare, according to my research."

"Tamarin was brought in as a small cub with her litter mate. Her father lost control of his instinct and killed her mother and two of her other litter mates. She and her sister survived by hiding in a field of Tamarin, in full bloom, hence the reason for her name. The guards who responded all thought the cubs were long dead, as was their father, who died from inhaling the spice when he went in after them. They called in Rowena to retrieve the bodies, but she found them very much alive even though they were absolutely covered in raja. It turns out that Tamarin and her sister have a genetic mutation that makes them immune. It's that immunity that helped Rowena find a treatment. As you can imagine, both cubs were terrified and non-verbal, but Rowena refused to allow Senior Councilor Edent to go anywhere near them until their injuries were treated."

"That takes some nerve to stand up to a Senior Councilor."

He grinned. "Rowena's nerve is harder than her shell, and she's fierce when she needs to be. As he didn't want to go anywhere near the spice, he allowed it. Rowena brought the cubs in for treatment, and she took Tamarin's sister, who was far more injured, while Kendra treated Tamarin."

"Kendra?! I didn't realize she was ever in the Healer's Guild."

"She's earned her master's, although she rarely practices anymore, mostly just enough to maintain her certification. Back then, Kendra had only just earned her journeyman's. My understanding is it was her very first solo operation. While she was wearing a static shield to protect her from any spice that the shower hadn't remove, her own instinct took over, from a combination of fear of the spice and the smell of blood, at *exactly* the wrong moment. Rather than suturing the cut on Tamarin's tail, her hand shook, and she ended up cutting Tamarin's tail clean off."

"Ouch! That must have hurt," Nazari replied.

"That it did. From what I've heard, Tamarin screamed bloody murder. Rowena turned to find Kendra holding Tamarin's tail and staring at it, her own tail fully poofed. Tamarin dove into Rowena's pouch to hide before Rowena even fully realized what was going on. When Rowena demanded to know what had happened, Kendra couldn't get two words out."

"Are you saying Kendra went non-verbal, too?"

He nodded. "Rowena realized what was going on, picked Kendra up by the scruff, took Tamarin's tail from her, and quite literally threw her out of the clinic, a good fifty feet at least, and right into the arms of the guards stationed outside. Rowena followed after and told Kendra to 'deal with her issues,' or she would remove her tail, one bone at a time. Kendra was so terrified that Rowena would follow through on that threat, that she wiggled out of the guards' hold and took off down the hall at a run, fully poofed and tail tucked between her legs."

"She ran?! And they didn't kill her right then and there?"

"No. Obviously."

"So what happened?" Nazari asked when he didn't offer further information.

"She did exactly as ordered. She ran right to the arena, and *dealt* with it, although not before injuring several guards and her father."

Nazari frowned at his implied wording, and then her eyes widened. He would have been concerned that she was losing control of her own instinct, but there was no twang, just shock as she put the pieces together.

"Are you saying Kendra's like Marsee?"

He nodded. "We *all* are. You can't tell anyone. I wouldn't tell you now, but I imagine Myra will when she returns. Marsee went through what we call the Transition. You can't train to fight without eventually losing control, and like Marsee, if we're lucky, we kill it before we lose ourselves to it. Marsee will recover her senses as strong as they are when they're on, but there won't be any chance of a future loss of control. That part of us is gone forever, along with the instinctive knowledge that comes with it. The reason I could tell what your son was thinking was because people's scent changes with their emotions. You're worried now. I didn't mean to scare you. I assure you, we're safe, as is Marsee."

"I believe you. That's not what I'm worried about. You're going to make me go through this Transition, aren't you?"

"No," he said quickly, seeing the first hint of a twang. "Only if you lose control. You've been significantly calmer since you regained your cub, so I don't think that will be necessary."

The twang vanished. *Did it really understand?* he wondered. He hadn't spoken to Kendra about the odd conversation he'd had with Nazari yet, although she had observed Nazari briefly before leaving on the council ships.

"You can really sniff my emotions?" Nazari asked.

He nodded. "When you used your instinct to track Damon, could you see his scent at all?"

She frowned. "That was real? I thought I was imagining things. I only saw it briefly right at the very end when we were sneaking up on Damon. It was dark, but they seemed to have a glow about them."

"Very much so. With practice, our brains get better at seeing scent in color, not just smelling it. Your base color appears a rich amber to me right now. The shape and color change with your mood. The happier you are, the brighter it gets."

"Really? As the Hue-mans say, that's seriously cool. What color is Sari's?"

"His scent is changing. It was a dark brown, almost the same color as Henry's skin the day he became your son, but it's been getting lighter every day, and there are thick streaks of your amber in it now. It's quite common for children to take after their mothers, although some gravitate more towards their father's color, depending on how close their connection is."

Nazari's tail spiraled, and she purred with happiness as she picked Sari up to hug him. Sari looked up at his mother and smiled back. "So what happened after, with Tamarin and her sister?"

He was surprised she didn't ask more questions about the Transition or what he could do. He shrugged. "Pretty much what you'd expect. Rowena reattached Tamarin's tail once she was able to convince Tamarin to come out of her pouch again. As far as the Council was concerned, they both died. They were given new identities, and she unofficially adopted them. Councilor Edent was one of the most brutal Senior Councilors we've ever had, and Rowena knew it. He never let anyone with even the slightest hint of an issue survive. He didn't think anyone could. Rowena saved their lives and is the only person who, to this day, still intimidates Kendra. Tamarin's sister is a Healer in the Guard, but she now lives in the East River District to be closer to her cubs and grandcubs."

"I can't imagine Kendra being intimidated by anyone, much less a Digger Healer."

He grinned. "Rowena was an Honor Guard before switching over to Healers, and they're an entirely different species. Most join the Guard because they don't fit the standard Digger mold. They're misfits, much like we are, although, in Rowena's case, she grew up in the Guard. Her father was their Senior Honor Guard for about three decades before he died."

She raised a brow. "I wouldn't exactly call you a misfit."

"Thank you. I think."

"It was a compliment," she replied. "You've done well for yourself in the Guard."

"It was exactly what I needed, even if I was angry about it for years. I couldn't read, and instead of admitting it, I caused problems, a lot of them. I was kicked out of school by the age of ten for multiple fights with a classmate. My mother was so mad that she dragged me by my scruff all the way to Kendra's office and stated that if I wanted to fight so much, Kendra could have me."

"That's a bit harsh," she said. "At ten?"

"So I thought at the time. My mother thought I was on the verge of losing control, so I don't blame her now."

"Does she know about the Transition?"

"I tried to tell her once. She didn't believe me and nearly killed me to get me out of her house. Kendra warned me not to tell anyone. We all are, but I missed my family, and I wanted her to trust me. I wanted her to see I had changed for the better." He sighed. It was one of his few regrets in life. "It doesn't really matter. The Guard is my family now."

"Do you have any children?"

He grinned at her. He'd wondered when this particular conversation would come up. It always did. "Genetic offspring, yes, but I've never met them. Cubs of my own, no. We lose far too many of our cubs in the Guard, and while several have offered, I couldn't put myself in that position."

"What about outside the Guard?"

"Relationships outside the Guard rarely work. Most people don't understand why we're never home. I have no idea how long I'll be stationed here, for example. It could be a week or months. And before you ask, no. I will help you with him however I can, but I cannot enter into a partnership with you."

She blinked. "How did you know I was going to ask?"

"I can smell your desire. Please don't misunderstand. I'm honored that you think that highly of me. I like you quite a bit, actually, and if the situation were different, I might take you up on that offer, but I legally can't enter into a partnership with you. It would be a conflict of interest."

"My watch?" she asked.

He nodded. "That's part of it, but mostly because I'm Kendra's Second and the District Senior for Council City, and there's a very good chance I'll be the Senior Honor Guard in a few days. Council City is my home, and you wouldn't be able to join me there for very long. Sari needs to be with his people."

She frowned. "Why do you expect to become Senior? Is something wrong with Kendra?"

"No," he replied and let out a heavy sigh laced with worry for his mentor. "She gave a life oath that her nephew could be trusted, and he left Marsee and Stormy alone. We both fully expected them to execute her or the very least arrest her the moment she arrived on the Water World. That they haven't either means they're waiting for the meeting to charge her officially or haven't finished their investigation. On top of that, we're fully expecting something else will happen, either before or during the meeting. The life of a guard is dangerous in the best of circumstances. You never know when a cobra chicken is going to sneak up and bite your tail."

She snorted with surprised laughter, as he'd intended, and her tail spiraled. "I did warn you," she said.

"So you did."

They were silent for a long time as they watched the suns continue to set in the distance. There were colors he'd never seen in a sunset before. He mentioned it.

"There's a storm coming," Nazari replied. "It'll be here by tomorrow."

He raised a brow. "The weather report said nothing about a storm."

"Those reports are always wrong, but the sky never is." She sniffed deeply. "There's rain coming, perhaps the last we'll see for months. It's going to be hot and dry until spring, and the conditions are ripe for a brush fire."

"Did you use your instinct to figure that out?"

"No. It's something you learn when you grow up in this part of the world. The weather can change in an instant, and if you're not prepared, it can kill you. Do you see that haze over there? That's smoke. Something's already on fire, but the wind is currently going in the other direction, so we should be safe."

She examined the ground for a moment, then picked a blade of grass next to her and rolled it between her thumb and index finger before handing the remains to him. "We call this fireweed. If you roll it and still feel moisture, then fire is not as much of a risk, but it's bone dry and crumbling, which means there's no surface moisture left. This will all be sand in a few weeks, if not sooner. Everything smells dusty like this plant. It's a bad sign. It's going to be a hard summer. That storm will be a big one. I just hope it brings rain and that the wind doesn't change. If it keeps blowing to the east, that fire will miss us and most of the homes in the area. If it starts blowing south, we're in trouble. The shields should protect us, but the smoke can cause problems, and we can't afford to lose any of the crops. For several of the species, there's no replacement."

"But how do you know there's going to be a storm?"

"You don't get these colors unless it's going to be brutally hot and there's sand or smoke in the air, and the more particulate matter, the more likely there will be a thunderstorm. I expect we'll see heat lightning tonight, too."

"Good to know. I'll inform my guards and put an alert out."

"No need. The alert will go out shortly."

Just as she said it, both of their tablets dinged. He glanced at his and scowled as he read the message. "You accused me of knowing things I couldn't possibly know. How did you know an alert would be going out?"

She grinned. "And you said you were trained to be observant." She pointed off to the side. "Illana's got the fire brigade out, and I'm guessing she's giving them the exact same lecture, and once she's done, they'll be heading out to dig a fire break. That's what those two machines are over there. At least they don't have to do it by hand like I did when I was a cub."

He snorted. He hadn't noticed. "Why did you do it by hand? You didn't have a machine?"

"We did, but my mother never let me use it. She insisted it built character, and usually, it was punishment for my snark. My mouth got me into a lot of trouble as a cub."

"I see some things never change."

She snorted and rolled her eyes at him, but then they sat in silence again for a while.

"Can we still be friends, or is that a conflict of interest, too?" she asked.

His tail spiraled with relief that she hadn't rejected him, and he grinned. "That I can do, and gladly."

She smiled back at him and then down at Sari. He'd fallen asleep in her arms.

"Thank you," he said.

She frowned at him. "For what?"

"For believing me and not turning away from me like my family did," he replied.

"You're welcome. Consider us even. Thank you for not turning away from me or killing me half a dozen times this past week."

"Only five," he replied. "There was your night walking, the twang in the cat pen, the conversation we had after, and after you got the letter from the Senior Council."

"That's only four. What's the fifth?"

"When you didn't open the goose pen that first time," he replied with a wicked grin. "I was a bit annoyed."

She snorted and thwacked him with her tail.

His own tail spiraled in response. He more than deserved it. Nothing more was said, and they stayed there in companionable silence until the suns finally set. He guarded her back and nodded a goodnight outside the Trauma Center where their suites were located, but he didn't follow her in.

He watched her leave, then turned, intending to go for a run, when Lark jumped down from the wall next to him.

"I can't believe you told her," she said.

"She would have found out anyway when Myra returned."

"I know, but the risk..."

He grinned. "A good friend is always worth the risk."

She raised a brow and smiled wickedly. "Are you sure it's not more than that?"

"I'm sure. In six months, if she still feels the same way, and I'm not stuck in Council City, I might consider it. Besides, you know it's not her talking right now anyway. It's her instinct."

"You say that, but you've turned everyone down. Is there anyone you care about enough to consider a partnership with?"

He shrugged. "You heard what I told Nazari. I can't bring myself to partner with anyone in the Guard. It's bad enough when I lose a protege, and you know how rarely relationships work outside the Guard."

"But is there even anyone you're interested in?" she pressed.

He gave her a knowing smile and walked away.

"There is!" She trotted after him. "Who is it?"

"It doesn't matter," he replied. "And you need to get back to work."

"You're deflecting. I've never seen that color on you. Who is it? Please. You have to tell me."

"I do not have to tell you anything." He glared at her for not obeying orders, but she didn't care. This was a juicy bit of gossip, and she'd sunk her claw into it. He knew if he didn't do something, the betting pool would start the moment he was out of sight. Although, he was fairly certain there was already one.

"Yes, there's someone I care a great deal for, but it doesn't matter. There won't be cubs. She's already had her second heat."

"But there could be a relationship."

He shook his head. "No. It wouldn't work. We're both far too busy. Now, enough gossiping. Get back to work before I demote you."

"Yes, sir," she replied and took off, but her tail was curled tightly, and her step was nearly as bouncy as Nazari's had been earlier.

He groaned, knowing he would never hear the end of it until he confessed, but there was no way he would ever tell anyone. Not now. And if he became Senior, then it could never happen.

CHAPTER 16

Temperate: Flight Plans

Temperate floated on a rock outside the Primary School, reading through his messages while he waited for his brother. Technically, he didn't have to wait, as Stormy had his own personal guard now, but he was enjoying spending time with his little brother while he was still on leave. He looked up as a swarm of children flooded out of the school, but he didn't see his brother. Stormy was usually one of the first out as he didn't want to waste a second of his time with Marsee.

He was still scanning the crowd when there was a sudden sharp pain in the middle of his back. He yelped and spun, ready to defend himself, only to find his brother a few feet away and pretending to look innocent. "You are a snot-nosed blubber fish," he flashed at his brother.

Stormy bubbled with laughter and puffed his lungs and cheeks out, making a fairly decent impression of said blubber fish. "That may be, but you left your guard down and your back exposed. I've been behind you for the last several minutes. What was that odd-looking blob you were so fixated on?"

Temperate rolled his eyes and started swimming away from the school. He switched to Hue-man for privacy. They took every moment they could to practice, and while not anywhere near fluent yet, they were good enough to converse, albeit roughly. "That blob you niece."

Stormy stopped and stared at him. "She say yes to partner?"

It took Temperate a moment to find the words in Hue-man. "She say after...meeting. Say yes no."

"Maybe? That better. She say no before."

Temperate grinned and flashed his happiness. "When safe she say yes. She..." He couldn't remember the word, so he flashed "Scared."

Stormy nodded his understanding and kept swimming, but Temperate stopped him.

"No visit Marsee. She move Platform."

Stormy flashed both happiness and disappointment. "I hope meet Little Flower."

"I hope, too. Papa say we eat Little Flower."

"Eat Little Flower?" Stormy flashed, laughing. "Somehow, I don't think that's what you meant to say."

Temperate laughed and switched to Sign. He needed to practice that, too. "No. He says we'll invite them over for dinner when Marsee's feeling up to it. Maybe after the meeting. It'll be a while before she's recovered enough to fly home."

Stormy nodded and continued in Hue-man. "Marsee no go home. No safe uncle."

Temperate frowned at his little brother. "What mean? No safe uncle? What know?"

"I no say," Stormy replied.

Temperate scowled at his brother. "What's going on? If you know something..." he flashed.

"I can't tell you. It's confidential, but I promise, Papa already knows."

He squinted at his brother. If it was council business, he had no authority to pressure his brother for that information. He decided to drop it and switched back to Hue-man. "More news. Little Flower and Marsee partner today."

Stormy flashed his surprise, but flickers of worry soon took over.

"What wrong?" he asked.

"Make things worse? They family but now partner. People like Rip get more mad...maddest?"

He paused to consider and then shook his head. "Madder. No. Sibling partner normal. Marsee Papa for Hope long time. This make...make real." He made a note to look up the words official and legal, but Stormy understood.

"Good. What we do? Go fly?"

Before the accident, Temperate had often taken his brother flying, but ever since, he'd been finding it ever more impossible to fly each day. He shook his head and kept swimming. Stormy picked up on his mood, and they swam the rest of the way home in silence.

"What's wrong?" Stormy asked, switching back to Water Sprite when they were alone.

He sighed. "I can't do it anymore," he flashed, feeling dejected.

"Do what?"

"Fly. I spent all day checking everything over on my new ship, but I couldn't make myself leave the bay."

"You're worried someone might tamper with it again?"

He nodded. "That's part of it. I don't know how to explain. I used to love flying, but now there's just fear."

Stormy looked at him and nodded. "I understand. I look at everything and everyone differently now. It's hard to leave the house sometimes, even knowing there's a squad of guards following me everywhere. I may be an adult now, but all I want to do is hide under Mama's tentacles."

"I'm sorry, Little Brother. It's all my fault you got hurt. I should have gone with you."

Stormy snorted at him. "What happened is not your fault. You were injured and needed to rest. I'm the one that left Marsee alone."

Temperate sighed. "My arm was just an excuse. I was too scared to leave the ship unattended. I had a feeling something was wrong when they wouldn't let Papa off, but I didn't say anything because I've never felt like that, and I didn't want to scare you, and it just got worse after. I haven't flown since I flew Papa's ship back. I just sit there and can't make myself take off. I don't know if Papa told you, but I've asked for a position in Command."

"He did." Stormy took a deep breath and squared his shoulders. "But, as your future Senior Councilor, I'm not allowing you to take it."

Temperate snorted with surprise. "You can't do that, little brother. You don't have that kind of authority yet."

"In this I do," he replied. "You are not going to allow that bottom-feeding trench-dweller to take your joy of flying away from you. I order you to get back on that ship and fly until the fear goes away."

"I wish it were that easy."

"It *is* that easy. I understand why you're worried, but you can't let fear ruin your life. If you do, he wins." Stormy turned and swam away without another word.

Temperate watched him go and sighed. Part of him was amused by his brother and how innocent he was. Even if he was now legally an adult and making adult decisions, those decisions were still influenced by the naivety of youth. But another part cried to see him forced to grow up so soon, knowing that, too, was his fault. Stormy would be Senior Councilor someday because he wasn't strong enough to take on the mantle himself. Just like that day in the canyon, Stormy had stepped up while he had remained behind and hid.

That future Senior Councilor just gave you an order, he thought to himself, but he didn't move towards the shuttle bay where his new ship was parked. Fear froze him solid.

The Senior Commander herself had delivered his new ship. She'd claimed that she'd checked everything over personally but hadn't insisted he take it out for a spin, knowing he would need to run his own maintenance first. She'd refused to discuss his request to move to Command both times he'd asked, stating that it was under review. As of that morning, he was officially cleared to return to duty, but he hadn't been sent his orders or schedule yet.

He was still sitting there when he heard the sounds of the shuttle bay doors opening and the whine of the engines. "What does that little blubber fish think he's doing?" He bolted for the shuttle bay just in time to watch as Stormy took off in *his* ship. He knew Stormy knew how to fly as he'd been teaching his brother for years, even if it wasn't technically legal, but he was the only one who had authorization to access, much less fly his ship. He'd locked it down the moment it had arrived. Only the Senior Council could override it. He followed through the shuttle bay doors just before they slid shut, and Stormy turned the ship around to face him.

"What are you doing?" he flashed.

"If you don't feel comfortable testing it out, I'll do it for you," Stormy replied. He then rolled the ship over until it was hovering upside down. "Oops. I did not mean to do that."

He snorted at his brother. "Liar."

"Are you impinging on the honor of a future Senior Councilor?" Stormy asked after turning the ship back over. "It looks like I could use another lesson. I have little arms, and this board is configured differently, although I suppose I could figure it out. I wonder what this button does."

A second later, a stunner bolt fired, just barely missing him.

"Knock it off!" he yelped, flashing both his annoyance and concern as he bolted away from the beam. "How are you even doing that? I locked the ship down myself."

"Papa had me take my pilot's test this morning before school, and, when I passed with flying colors, gave me clearance to use any ship, including yours," Stormy explained and then opened the door to the ship. "Are you going to get on, or am I going to have to stun you and drag you on."

"You wouldn't dare!" Temperate replied, flashing bright orange with outrage, although secretly, he was proud of his brother for passing his test. The pilot's license was not easy. Few people ever earned more than a shuttle license. It had taken him three tries just to pass the written test alone.

Stormy just grinned and fired again. This time, it was close enough that it made his scales tingle.

"Stop it!" Temperate flashed, bright red with anger now. "That stunner is strong enough to kill a juvenile Leviathan. It's not to be played with."

Stormy just grinned and stared him down. "Your choice, Master Pilot. I won't miss next time."

He glared at his annoying little brother, then shifted his attention when he saw someone come up behind the ship. He realized it was one of the Saber guards, likely trying to protect him. "You are the world's most annoying little brother," he said and swam towards the ship, waiving the guard off once he was out of Stormy's sight. "I've got this."

"Are you sure, sir?"

"Yes, he's just being a snot-nosed little brat. He knows perfectly well how to aim that stunner."

The guard's tail curled. "My little sister can be just as annoying," he replied and backed off.

He swam onto the ship and closed the door behind him, but then he swam up behind Stormy and purposely shocked him hard enough to make his skin ripple.

Stormy grunted but didn't seem surprised, and he didn't move out of the primary pilot's net either.

Temperate glared down at his brother. "I'm not sure I like this new side of you."

"Get used to it," Stormy replied, "And get in your net. You have ten seconds before I take off. 10...9..."

"You're lucky. You almost got taken out by a guard."

"I saw him and the rest of the squad the moment I left the bay, and you're running out of time. Where was I? 5...4..."

Temperate growled and climbed into his safety harness. The moment it clicked, Stormy took off. Only his brother did not go in a straight line. He punched the engines and took the ship into a very tight barrel roll, just barely missing the top of the ridge their home was built into.

"You're going to lose your license if you keep flying like that."

"Unlikely," Stormy replied. "I logged that I was intending a training maneuver flight. I do have to learn how this ship handles. It's far more responsive than your last one." Once they were out of the city, Stormy dipped and rolled until even he was slightly dizzy.

"Alright, that's enough," Temperate said with a laugh. "Or I'm going to be too sick to fly."

Stormy grinned and brought the ship around to hover. "Of course, if you don't want the ship, I might ask to see if I could keep it."

"Be careful what you ask for. The Senior Commander might put you to work. You really passed your pilot's test?"

Stormy grinned. "The proctor said I was in the top one percent on the written and even beat your score on the practical."

"Not possible. I had a perfect score."

"You might have had a perfect score," Stormy replied. "But I am officially the youngest pilot of our species to ever pass, which puts me higher on the rankings."

"Snot-nosed blubber-fish," Temperate teased.

"That's Future Senior Councilor Snot-nosed blubber-fish to you."

"You do realize I'm going to call you that for the rest of your life?"

"I wouldn't expect it any other way. Now, are you going to fly this ship, or do I need to chase down that old Leviathan, upside down and backwards?"

"I'm beginning to think Rip zapped a few brain cells loose in that empty head of yours."

"Probably, but you're the one who's procrastinating."

Temperate glared at his brother because he was right. He was procrastinating.

Stormy's skin rippled with amusement, but he otherwise said nothing as he waited for Temperate to take over.

He took a deep breath and another, trying to get past the sudden burst of fear in his chest, and he nearly jumped out of his safety harness when the comms blared to life at the exact same moment his hands touched the controls.

"Warning! Alert level five! All available sea-patrol pilots to Sector 1.43.2."

"Sheet," Temperate swore.

"I think the word is 'Shit,'" Stormy replied. "What's wrong?"

"Level five is as bad as it gets, and I don't have time to bring you home." Temperate reached for the comms. "Command, this Temperate Seas. In case you haven't received my clearance, I'm reporting for duty." As he did, Stormy grabbed the controls, flipped the ship around, and took off.

The monitor flicked to life, transparently showing Command overlaying the view outside, and to his further surprise, all of the Seniors, save for Senior Councilor Chenzira, were in attendance. *Then again, with an alert that high, I shouldn't be surprised. I wonder where Jeran is, though.*

His father blinked to see Stormy but immediately started explaining. "Temperate, I'm glad you called in. I need your eyes on this. We lost communication with the Ice Giant Council ships early this morning. They're scheduled to come out of jump in a few minutes. I need you to establish visual communication with the pilots and determine if their ship has been compromised. If you have any indication that they've been hijacked or they open fire, I want you to take them out. Do *not* wait for clearance."

"Out, sir?" he asked.

"You heard me correctly. By unanimous decision of the Senior Council, you take them down by whatever means necessary, but if possible, in an uninhabited area. We are not negotiating with terrorists."

"Yes, sir," he replied, although he swallowed hard at the decision his father had placed on him. It was one thing to chase off a Leviathan or two, but these were people, many of whom he knew personally. Still, this was the kind of decision he would have to make if he moved to Command.

"I'm sending you the pilot roster now," Senior Honor Guard Stinger said.

Temperate scanned the roster as it scrolled past. Being a pilot for the Council was a coveted position that required the highest clearances due to the secure information they might be exposed to. He knew most of them as he often provided an escort as his father's representative.

"Received. There are only two on here I haven't met personally," he replied. "Haldak and Eesarka."

"What's your impression of the others?" his father asked.

"Until this past week, I would have said they could be trusted. Now, I have no idea. I would have said the same about Leaf and Willow, and I knew them far better."

His father pursed his lips.

"ETA to estimated arrival ten minutes," someone in Command called out.

Temperate checked his flight plan and took over the controls, punching the speed even faster. A moment later, they exited the atmosphere. Adjusting his course to take the rotation of the planet into consideration, he soon hovered at the designated coordinates. Other ships appeared and spread out around him in formation by squad.

His board lit up with their designations, squads, and positions as one ship pulled up right next to him. He glanced over, and the Senior Commander flashed a greeting that indicated she understood he had seniority on this mission. A moment later, a trauma ship pulled up on the other side, and he blinked when he realized who was on board: Senior Honor Kendra Hunt. She glanced in his direction and also saluted.

That felt entirely too uncomfortable. She outranked both him and the Senior Commander. He took a deep breath to try and calm his nerves as they waited.

"ETA two minutes."

He tightened his harness, even though it was already far tighter than normal, and noticed Stormy did the same. He counted down in his head with the guard in Command and tried not to hold his breath. *Please let them be safe,* he prayed to the Gods of the Deep. "5...4...3...2...1..."

...

"Nothing," he muttered and scanned the sky around him, looking for the wink of a ship coming out of jump. "Where are they?"

Designated jump points were carefully coordinated. A delay of even a few seconds was highly problematic as it increased the risk of impact with other incoming ships and put the planet further away. There were protocols if arrival had to be adjusted mid-flight, and certain coordinates were reserved for emergencies. "Squads three through seven, Emergency Protocol one."

The indicated squads bolted to their new locations, each a designated emergency jump spot, but he remained where he was.

With only a few seconds remaining in the window of viability, a single ship appeared and tumbled erratically towards them.

"Sheet," he swore again, and this time Stormy didn't bother to correct him.

CHAPTER 17

Temperate: Warble Greep

"Command, I'm seeing major signs of damage on the ship, and only one of them arrived," Temperate called out.

"Confirmed. Approach with caution and see if you can get a visual on the pilots. Trauma Center One, prepare for incoming casualties."

The ship spiraled as the planet's gravity took hold. Only a few of the maneuvering thrusters fired, not enough to stop the rotation or bring the ship into a stable orbit. Someone inside flashed the landing lights in an emergency alert designed for just this situation. It was a basic pattern that simply said they needed help. That much was obvious.

He flashed the expected reply and then dove and spun to match the rotation of the other ship. It made what Stormy had done seem tame.

"The pilots appear to be Haldak and Eesarka," he said once he got a good look. "Stormy, I'll keep us in position. See if they understand Sign."

"Are you able to understand me?" Stormy asked immediately.

"Yes," the lead pilot replied. "The comms and thrusters are out. I can't stabilize her."

"What happened, and where's the other ship?"

"They alerted to an engine problem between relays. We exited with them, but their engine exploded upon exit and took out our transponders. There were injuries, most thankfully minor, but several people are in stasis. The other ship was too damaged to jump, but as no one knew where we were, we decided to move our passengers off and take the chance."

He considered the reply. It would take weeks to locate ships that came out of jump mid-flight without active comms, if even possible, and depending on how badly their ship was damaged, they might not have weeks. "Ask for the coordinates for the other ship," he told Stormy.

The pilots signed the lengthy interstellar coordinates, and he spoke them aloud in Saber in case the visuals weren't good enough.

"Command, can you confirm those coordinates are on route?"

"Confirming now," someone called out. "Confirmed, and it's only a parsec before we lost contact."

"Trauma Ships 2 through 5, proceed to those coordinates. Squadron 2 provide backup," he ordered.

"Yes, sir," came the replies, and ships around him winked out of existence.

He considered the rotating ship. Without thrusters, it would lose orbit quickly. "Squad one, initiate tether maneuver three. I'll take point. Stormy, tell them we're going to try to stabilize their orbit and dock. They should be prepared to exit quickly."

"Yes, sir," came the various replies. The two other ships in his squad, plus his commander, positioned themselves around the transport ship and fired their tethers, which were basically nothing more than a large electromagnet attached to a strong cable.

"Tethers attached," the pilots each called out in turn.

"Begin counter rotation in 3, 2, 1." He watched as they slowly adjusted their thrusters and the tethers tightened. Too fast, and the tethers would come loose, potentially causing damage to the other ships, but this was a maneuver they practiced often, and ever so slowly, the council ship stopped tumbling. Inside the view port, the pilots disconnected from their safety harnesses and disappeared inside the ship.

"Hunt, you should be clear to approach."

The Trauma Ship pulled up, and he watched it dock. A few minutes later, Hunt came on the line. "The pilots are on board," she replied.

"However, they're saying one of the Councilors came with them, but he wasn't in his jump seat."

"How confident are you that they're telling the truth?"

"Enough that I'm going to check it out. They seemed quite concerned and didn't want to get on the ship, even though one appears to have a broken arm."

"Copy. Have your pilot disconnect and take the other two to the Trauma Center. I'll scan and then dock and provide backup and a cart."

"Yes, sir," she replied.

"Did they say which Councilor?" Apakna asked.

There was a brief pause. "Garaptk, Ma'am," Hunt replied.

His father looked over at Apakna, and the look he gave her said far too much, although her face only hardened further behind the mask of Senior Councilor.

"Should I be concerned, Councilors?" he asked.

"If it is actually him, that's my Uncle," Apakna replied.

"Understood." It was either a trap or her uncle was at risk. He started scanning and found several heat signatures, but only one big enough to be a male Ice Giant. "Cargo bay," he told Hunt as the Trauma Ship flew off. "I'm not detecting any movement. There are two smaller signatures near the front, but they aren't big enough to be him. One is moving in a way that it might be a small fire. I would say the fire suppression systems are offline, so keep your mask on and be careful."

"Copy," she replied, and his scans showed her bolting off in the direction of the cargo bay before he shifted out of his current position to dock. His ship locked on with a jarring clang, and his monitor flashed with a blue warning light a moment later. They had a seal, but not a tight one. He unclipped from his restraints and grabbed the backup comms unit, clipping it to his harness.

"Stormy, if you lose contact with me, disconnect and leave. Do not come after me or the others. Is that understood?"

His brother swallowed hard but nodded. He flashed his pride and love and turned towards the door. The ship on the other side wouldn't have water for him to swim through, but this was something they trained for, too. He swam over and hit a switch on the wall, and a compartment slid open. He grabbed the water breather, clipped it on his harness, and activated it. It suctioned on to ensure a tight seal over his gills. It gave him an hour of breathable water, assuming there was oxygen on the other side, and twenty minutes if not. The tech was expensive, so typically, only emergency crews had access, but there were emergency breathers on every ship, just like there were masks.

That made him pause briefly. *I wonder why Rip didn't use a breather?*

Shrugging as it didn't particularly matter, he checked that the breather was secure and hit the switch that opened both doors. The static shield between the two ships hissed as frost formed from the cold of space and the other ship. The Ice Planet's gravity was nearly twice his own, but he was used to the immense pressure of the oceans. The cold would be a bigger issue. He unhooked the emergency cart. It was basically nothing more than an anti-grav board that they used for moving patients, but for him, it was also mobility. He'd be able to move significantly faster, and if the Councilor was hurt, they'd need it.

"Command, confirm you can access my cam."

"Confirmed," his father replied. "Be careful."

"Yes, sir," he replied and slid himself through the door. There was a slight jarring as the cart adjusted to the gravity. Using his hands, he pulled himself down the short hallway and turned onto the main one that ran the length of the ship. Grabbing one of the railings, he pulled hard, and the cart shot forward. Using the railing and his tentacles to steer the cart, he quickly caught up to Hunt, who had pulled a panel off the wall and was digging through the wires.

"Jammed or disabled?" he asked.

"Not sure. The powers out, and I couldn't budge the override."

He crawled off the cart and over to the wall. Wrapping several of his tentacles around the railing for leverage, he grabbed the override lever and pulled. There was a loud screech and the clunk of the locks disengaging. Then, grabbing the wheel that manually pulled open the doors, he started turning it. Something was definitely jammed, but the door still slid open, albeit slowly.

Kendra stopped what she was doing and stood. "If I ever needed evidence of how strong your species is, this would do it." Kendra grabbed ahold of the door and started pulling. It helped, but not very much. She ducked inside once it was open enough for her to squeeze through. He kept at it, though. Garaptk would need more room to get through, and so would he with the cart.

"Command, I've found him. He's unconscious. It looks like a container fell and hit him. Injuries appear to be minor. A concussion and a broken leg, but it's a clean break."

"Copy."

The moment the door was open enough, he crawled back over to the cart and climbed on. The cargo bay was a mess. Containers had fallen everywhere.

"Where are you?" he called out.

"Here! Right far quadrant," Kendra replied.

He directed the cart in that direction, throwing containers out of the way to clear a path. By the time he arrived, Kendra had wrapped an emergency brace around Garaptk's broken leg, and he was starting to wake, mumbling and moving weakly. He slid off the cart and positioned it next to Garaptk, then helped Kendra to shift him on the board.

Garaptk's eyes flickered open, and they tried to focus on him. "Sprite? We made it?"

"You did," Kendra replied as she activated the restraints that would secure him to the board. "But we need to get you off quickly. What were you doing back here?"

"Transport," he whispered and tried to roll off the cart, even though he was held tight. "Endangered...Only four females left...Oh, my head hurts."

"Don't move," Temperate said, or hoped he said. Ice Giant wasn't his best language, and the breather made it difficult to speak. "I'll find. Where?"

"Should be here, but everything shifted. Red stasis pod."

"Get him to the ship," he told Kendra. "I'll find the container and follow."

Kendra frowned but nodded and took off, leaving him alone in a massive cargo bay full of containers.

A stasis pod would have to be near the wall where there was power and well-labeled for just this purpose. He started shifting containers aside, worried about how long he had when he finally came across it. A quick scan of the display said it was undamaged, and thankfully, it had a grav-pad, too. It was too small for him to use as a cart, so he pushed it in front of him and started crawling his way out.

He was halfway back when the ship rocked hard, and an alarm sounded in Ice Giant. "Warning! Decompression in forward compartments. Abandon Ship. Warning…"

"Get out of there!" his father yelled. "Leave it!"

Kendra appeared around the corner ahead of him, and he made a split decision. He shoved the container as hard as he possibly could in Kendra's direction. "Take it and get out of here! The pod's closer!"

Kendra didn't argue. She grabbed the case and bolted back to his ship. He heard her yell at Stormy. "Disconnect and go."

"But Temperate's…," he heard Stormy say.

"Now!" both she and his father yelled.

"Stormy, you promised! Get out of here," he called on his comms and turned around to head back for the nearest escape pod. He heard the clank of the ship disconnecting and sighed with relief, but his relief didn't last long. When he arrived at the escape pod hatch, it was empty.

"Sheet," he swore. "Command, I have a small problem. Papa, tell Melody I…"

An explosion rocked the ship just as the gravity systems fluctuated, throwing him hard against the ceiling. His lungs burned as his breather shifted out of place, and he screamed in fear and pain, but he started grabbing for handles to make his way back to the cargo bay door, hoping he could make it in time. He'd only made it a short distance before the gravity fluctuated again, sending him back to the floor, where he hit hard again before it disengaged completely.

"Go for the hatch," he heard Kendra yell. "It's closer."

"Yes, ma'am," he replied and spun back around to head in the direction where the hatch was located. With the gravity off, he was able to pull himself along far faster than he could crawl.

He was in sight of the hatch when a third explosion went off. This time behind him. A burst of pressure and flame sent him flying. Pain and darkness engulfed him, and he was only dimly aware as he was yanked back in the other direction as decompression pulled the air out of the ship. He curled himself into a tight ball to protect himself, and the last thing he knew was the pain of slamming into another wall and the sound of metal crunching as the weight of gravity reactivating again tossed him hard against another wall.

CHAPTER 18

Temperate: Escape Hatch

Temperate, answer me!" The voice was distant, and he could barely focus on it through the stabbing pain in his lungs. "Please, gods. Answer me! Temperate!"

"Papa?" he mumbled and opened his eyes, but he couldn't see anything.

"Thank the gods! Are you alright?"

He groaned. Everything hurt, and it was darker than he'd ever experienced, although he was thoroughly surprised to be waking up at all. "Not sure. Hurt. Can't breathe. S'dark."

"The lights are out," his commander replied. "Light up your skin."

He did. "Oh yeah. That works. Silly me."

"Check your breather," she ordered, but the words barely made any sense. The hall he was in was now a tangled mess of wires, beams, and assorted shrapnel that came in and out of focus. The heat of the flames from before was gone, and it was quickly growing colder than he'd ever experienced before, yet his lungs burned, and he gasped for air.

"Temperate, check your breather now!"

He glanced down. His breather had shifted completely off, and a slight crack was letting water drip out. A thin film of ice was forming around it. He adjusted the breather back in place, and his vision and thoughts cleared almost immediately, although his lungs still burned.

"You need to make it to the hatch. You're not that far. You can do it. I'm directly across, and I'm not leaving without you."

"Ma'am," he replied, but he blinked as the voice came from behind him. He looked down and realized his comms unit was no longer attached to his harness. "Stormy? The others?" he asked.

"I'm okay," Stormy replied, using one of the few spoken phrases in their language.

He shifted a piece of debris aside and found the comms unit. "Oh, good. I hope you didn't scratch the paint on my new ship."

"Um..." There was a definite pause.

He clipped the comms unit back onto his harness and started looking for a way through the rubble. "How bad?"

"Nothing we can't fix," his commander replied. "I'm actually quite impressed with your brother's flying. I'm not sure you would have been able to do any better. I might have to recruit him to fill your seat if you don't get your tentacles moving."

"Yes, ma'am," he replied with a half-chuckle. "I am trying. They left a bit of a mess in here."

"So I see. I'll be sure to mention it to them later."

He examined the space around him, trying to gain his bearings, astonished that nothing had impaled him as he was completely surrounded by debris, and he realized if he had gone in the direction of the cargo bay, he'd be dead, as the force of compression had completely collapsed the hall behind him. The only thing stopping it from continuing further was a large beam that had missed him by only a few inches.

"To your right. If you can get around that beam, it looks like it might give you a clear path."

He looked over and examined the beam and the space beyond. It would be a tight fit, but his commander was right. It was a clear shot on the other side. He reached over to test whether he could move the beam and yelped. It burned with cold, telling him whatever was on the other side was exposed to the cold vacuum of space. "Note to self. Do not touch the metal."

"Behind you. I think I saw a piece of fabric."

He spun far too quickly, and his vision swam. "Ooh. I shouldn't have done that. Command, be aware. I might have a few parts loose in my head."

He heard the sounds of several people chuckling.

"Only a few?" his father teased. "I could have sworn there were more than that missing this morning."

"It's a good day," he replied. When his vision cleared, he found the cloth and grabbed it. It was caught on something, and he yanked, tearing it free. Wrapping it around his good hand, he turned back around, slower this time, and gingerly touched the metal with the protective covering. It was cold, but it didn't burn like before. Stringing himself out as much as possible in the confined space to make himself as narrow as his body allowed, he pulled hard and slid through with a scrape. The medal burned as it slid down his stomach, but he made it through. He looked down and saw a large welt forming. "That's going to leave a mark."

"You won't have to worry about it if you don't get those tentacles moving," his Commander replied. "You're low on air, and it's getting dangerously cold. Your thoughts are going to get even groggier the longer you wait. Move!"

"Yes, ma'am," he replied and did as ordered. It didn't take him long to make it to the hatch, and he peered through the slightly cracked window. The cold that seeped through made him shiver, but he barely noticed as fear turned his skin solid white. His Commander's ship was floating outside but nowhere close to the ship. There was debris everywhere.

As he watched, her ship pivoted, and the door slid open. The static shield rippled with frost as moisture from the water inside froze on its surface.

"I can't dock, so you're going to have to make it to me. Hit the emergency release. The remaining air should shove you right over."

He swallowed hard and looked back at the wall of shrapnel behind him. "And everything else," he replied.

"You'll be fine. We've practiced this. The shields will protect you and it'll only be a second. I'll catch you. I promise."

The odds of her actually catching him were slim to none. Even the slightest shift in trajectory would knock him off path, but it was the only chance he had. He activated the emergency shielding on the breather. It was much like the masks the other species wore, but there was very little charge left. Still, if it lasted, it would give him some protection from the vacuum of space and smaller debris.

The moment he turned it on, the breather began beeping a warning.

After taking a deep breath to calm his nerves and racing heart, he grabbed the emergency switch tightly with both hands and pulled.

Nothing happened.

He flashed several swears in rapid succession, not wanting to waste precious oxygen on speaking them aloud, then slammed his body against the door.

Whatever held it in place gave way, and he was yanked out so much faster than he expected. He didn't think there was that much air left on the ship, but it caught the door and yanked it from his grasp. He slammed into it hard a fraction of a second later as it hit the shield of his commander's ship.

His aim was good, but he was on the wrong side of the door. He rolled and reached for the side of the ship to pull himself in as pieces of shrapnel broke free and started heading right for him. He screamed and froze in fear, but his commander was right. The shield stopped the sharp pieces. One large and very pointy-looking piece stopped only a breath from his eyes.

The next thing he knew, he was being yanked back into the ship hard enough that he banged against the far side.

He floated there, shaking and pure white with fear.

"Breath, Pilot. You're safe," his commander said.

He looked down and wiggled his tentacles, counting them to ensure all five were still attached, and then promptly passed out.

CHAPTER 19

Clear Seas: On His Orders

Clear Seas swam hard out of Command the moment the Senior Commander confirmed Temperate was still breathing, followed close behind by Apakna. They were waiting on the roof of the Trauma Center with half a dozen healers when the squadron appeared, but only one of the ships landed. After a short pause, the rest took off away from the Trauma Center.

The healers swarmed the ship that landed the moment the door opened, and a minute later, they swam off, carrying Temperate on a stretcher. To his relief, his son was awake.

"I'm okay, Papa," Temperate signed on his way by. Cuts, burns, and bruises covered his son, but they appeared to be minor. They might leave some scarring, but the fact that he was alive was nothing short of a miracle.

The Commander followed everyone off the ship and swam up next to him.

"Stormy and the others?" Clear Seas asked.

She pointed in the direction the other ships had gone. "They're fine, but the door is jammed, and as you probably saw, there's no landing gear. We'll need to cut them out, but I'd rather not do it here in case there's more damage than we realize. I'll keep watch and escort him back to your office *after* giving him a lecture about disobeying orders." She turned to Apakna. "Councilor, if you want to fly back with me, I'll be glad to give you a lift."

Apakna shook her head. "Thank you, but I need to have a conversation with the other pilots first. Please keep me informed."

He watched Apakna swim into the Trauma Center, and only then did he let his mask drop a little.

"I am quite impressed with Stormy," the Commander said quietly. "He flew exceptionally well for someone so young. It could have been a lot worse."

"His brother has been taking him out flying for years."

"I'm well aware of that."

He looked hard at the Commander, demanding an explanation.

She bubbled with amusement. "That level of skill does not develop in the few days he's been listed as an adult, even if his big brother has supposedly taken him out flying every day since. Which I know he hasn't. I've been monitoring Temperate's flight log. Did you know he's afraid to fly?"

He sighed. "We've talked about it a few times. I understand. I haven't wanted to board a ship either since the report came in."

She nodded. "I've taken my ship apart twice. We'll see how this incident affects things. I know he put in for Command, but I've not approved it on purpose. I don't want him to lose his joy of flying. I've seen it happen far too often after someone gets hurt. It's natural to be scared, but he's too good of a pilot to let that happen. Oh, and just so you know, I am alerted whenever anyone fires the stunner on one of my ships. When you get a chance, there's a rather amusing recording of your sons in your inbox."

He snorted. "I've already seen it. They were playing it on repeat when I swam into Command. Stinger wanted to know if I wanted to arrest Stormy or recommend him for the Sea Patrol."

She grinned. "I would take him in a heartbeat, but he's not destined for the Sea Patrol. Is he?"

"What makes you say that?" he asked.

"He may have his brother's skill at flying, but he has your attitude, Senior Councilor."

He frowned, trying to determine if that was an insult. The Commander had known him since he was a child and knew the trouble he'd gotten into, as she was usually the one his father had sent after him.

She grinned at him. "No insult intended. Stormy knows his future place in the universe and is testing the waters to see what that means. That's why he didn't immediately follow orders today. He had to believe they were the right ones. Thankfully, his heart is in the right place, unlike someone I know who took a few years to figure that out."

He snorted. "A few years? Try a decade. I'm still surprised you didn't shock me that last time."

"I thought about it, but that wouldn't have stopped you. Dragging you before your father worked far better, and I needed a new ship anyway." She glanced in the direction Temperate's ship had flown. The damage had been minor in the grand scheme of things, although it had come far too close for his liking. "Your family has a way of running through them. I'll send you the bill."

"And I'll pay it every time. Thank you for saving my son today."

She shrugged. "I was just there to give him a ride." She tilted her head at him and swam back onto her ship.

He watched her fly off, briefly lost in memory of the dozen or more times she'd told his father the very same thing. He was grateful they hadn't found anything on her, although Rip had been looking. The last thing he wanted to do was execute the person who had saved his life so many times he'd lost count and who had just saved his son.

Sighing, he turned and swam into the Trauma Center to find Temperate.

CHAPTER 20

Stormy: Gen Eral

Engine warning lights flashed on every dashboard, and Stormy was nearly pure white with fear as he followed the other ships from his brother's squadron to a remote location outside of the Sea Patrol. His brother had taught him how to land the ship in an emergency, but this was far outside of his training. The autopilot was gone, the landing gear didn't work, and the door was wedged shut. He'd expected Kendra to take over from him, but she was busy treating the Councilor's injuries and had ordered him to keep flying.

The ship had fought him the entire way down and now drifted hard with the currents. It was all he could do not to run into the other ships flanking him, even though they were keeping their distance. Thankfully, the shield was still working, or they would have burned up on re-entry.

"Alright, Stormy. Set her down nice and easy. Without landing gear, you'll hit first on the front of the ship and then tip back and to one side once you turn the engines off."

"Yes, sir," he replied, pivoting the engines for a decent. More alarms blared, and the ship started to spiral almost immediately as one of the engines started to cut out. "Sheet," he swore under his breath and fought the controls to compensate.

"Your left engine isn't fully down. Adjust the right by twenty degrees forward. That should compensate."

"Yes, sir," he replied. "Struggling not to say the ten snarky things he really wanted to say, as he'd already figured that out. The right engine refused to adjust that far, but he did manage to slow the spiral. "I think that's as good as I'm going to get," he flashed.

More lights flashed and shifted from warning colors to failure.

"Alright. You're going to hit hard, and there's a good chance you're going to flip the ship. On my command, cut the engines and hold on."

"Yes, sir," Stormy replied, not entirely sure how he was going to do that and keep his hands on the controls. He lifted a tentacle, but it didn't quite reach. *Of course not,* he thought.

"Now!"

Out of ideas, Stormy let go of the controls and slammed the engines off. In the brief moment it took, the ship spun hard to the side, and he screamed with fear as the ship hit and started to roll. Emergency shielding enveloped him. There was nothing he could do now but wait for the ship to settle and pray it didn't blow up.

For a moment, it felt like the ship was going to flip, but it teetered and rolled back the other way.

He held his breath as it rocked several more times before coming to a stop.

"You alright in there?"

Kendra yelled out, "Garaptk and I are good. Stormy?"

It took him a moment to remember how to breathe and squeak out a "Good."

"Well done! I thought for sure it was going to flip."

He reached for the controls to disengage the shielding, but his tiny arms were too short to reach. Sighing, he stayed where he was. A moment later, he heard a clank and high-pitched whine as someone started to cut them out. A few moments later, Kendra appeared and disconnected his shielding.

"Not bad at all, Pilot," she said to him as she began scanning him for injuries.

"I'm okay," he signed.

She didn't listen and kept scanning. "Stay in your harness until they have the door open," she ordered when she was done and returned to treating the Councilor.

"Yes, ma'am," he replied but turned his seat to look back at their passengers. The Councilor was still strapped to the board and appeared to be unconscious. He'd been awake, if delirious, when Kendra had brought him on board. "Is he alright?"

"He'll be fine," she replied and began treating his head injury.

His eyes drifted to the stasis unit she'd shoved inside the ship moments before the other ship had decompressed. He wondered what they were. All he could see were several little brown fluffs of fur. His brother had nearly died for those little brown fluffs. *He* had nearly died for those little brown fluffs. He had nearly died. Again. The reality of the situation hit, and he began shaking. His skin must have flickered as Kendra looked up from what she was doing.

"Breathe, Pilot. You're alive, and you're safe. They'll cut us out of here soon."

He was breathing, he thought, but he didn't feel so good.

"You're having an adrenaline crash," Kendra said and went back to treating the Councilor. "It's quite normal following a traumatic event. Slow your breathing. It'll pass quickly." She was right. By the time she'd finished treating the concussion and glanced back at him, he'd stopped shaking.

"Better?" she asked.

He nodded, and she began repairing the Councilor's leg. She was nearly done when he started waking. She stopped, unclipped a hypo, and injected him, knocking him out again. She was done repairing the leg long before the door was cut away, but she didn't wake the Councilor. Instead, she swam over to scan the creatures in the stasis unit. "Fuzzy little things. Aren't they?" she muttered, then shifted to scanning the stasis unit.

"Is there a problem with the unit?" he flashed.

She looked up, and he repeated the question in sign, not sure if she knew his visual language. "Not that I can tell, but I'm more concerned about something hidden inside."

He frowned and glanced at the Councilor. "Do you have reason to believe he's involved?" He remembered the looks the Seniors had given when they'd learned who it was.

"No, but these are unusual times, and I'd rather be safe than sorry." He watched as she opened various maintenance panels, scanned them again, and eventually clipped her scanner back on her harness before returning to the Councilor and waking him.

Garaptk's eyes blinked open, focused on Kendra, and then shifted down to her badge before glancing around the rest of the ship and stopping on him. "The Sprite, I remember, was a lot bigger than you. You seem quite young for a Pilot." The words were Ice Giant. He understood the language but couldn't speak it.

"That was my brother," Stormy signed. "I was with him when the call came in."

"Ah." Mystery solved, the Giant ignored him and looked back at Kendra. "Is everyone alright?"

She nodded. "Assuming there wasn't anyone else on your ship besides the two pilots and you."

"The warble greeps?" he asked.

"They appear uninjured, but I know nothing about that species. Where was their intended destination?"

"The Habitat." He frowned. "I know this will only add suspicion, but Rip organized the transfer for me. The Warble Greeps' habitat is mostly gone, but a thermal vent near the Habitat on an otherwise uninhabited island is perfect for them. They should be expecting them. I sent food samples a couple of months ago so that they could prepare the environment."

Kendra frowned and unclipped her tablet to place a call. A moment later, someone answered. "I want to speak to the Senior Healer."

"You're speaking to her," the Sprite said back. "How can I be of service, Honor Guard."

"Were you expecting a delivery from the Ice Planet?"

"Yes," the healer replied. "An endangered species. They're called warble greeps. Why?"

"Just checking. We'll be sending a ship with the creatures in the next hour or so."

"We'll be ready. Thank you."

Kendra disconnected and looked down at the Councilor.

"Thank you," he said and tried to sit up, but the restraints held him in place. "Why am I still restrained?"

"For your protection. I've treated your concussion and broken leg, but it's been decades since I've had the opportunity to treat one of your species, and I would prefer that someone with more experience confirm there aren't any other injuries before you move. The concussion was severe enough that I imagine they'll keep you for a few hours of observation."

"Ah," he replied and laid back down.

There was a loud clang and screech from the Techs cutting them out. "The ship?"

"Your ship imploded. Ours was damaged before we could get away. They should have us out soon."

Garaptk frowned. "The other Sprite?"

"He was injured in the implosion, but we were able to rescue him. He's at the Trauma Center now."

"Who was it? I want to make sure to thank him."

Kendra hesitated a moment before answering. "Master Pilot Temperate Seas."

"Clear Seas' son?!" He exclaimed and then glanced over at him. "You're Stormy?"

"Yes, sir," he replied.

"Huh," Garaptk said, laying back down and staring at the ceiling. Kendra stiffened beside him. Eventually, Garaptk refocused on him. "Rip really attacked you and Marsee?"

Stormy nodded and raised his arm, the white scar still visible. He darkened his skin to make it even more so. That part of his arm no longer changed color. "I followed him from my house after he expressed glee at my father's arrest. I watched him dump his nephew in the Trench, and we found Marsee bleeding and nearly frozen to death. Deep Current died trying to keep her warm. She lost all her fur from being shocked so much, but she went out less than a day after being released from the Trauma Center to find all the other missing people. She ordered our guard away to find a light in the canyon, and while we waited, we looked for another entrance. I found a small tunnel, took off to explore it, against her orders, and found the others. When I returned, I told her to follow me, but I didn't realize she didn't until it was too late. When I returned, Rip already had her and was trying to kill her. I tried to stop him, but I wasn't big enough to kill him. He tried to kill me, but she recovered and killed him instead."

"It looks like I owe you not only my thanks but an apology. I honestly didn't believe it. I thought your father was the one behind Marsee's kidnapping. That didn't seem like the kind of thing Rip would do."

"I don't blame you for that," he said. "You weren't the only one tricked into believing the evidence Rip fabricated. I accept your apology."

"Were you involved in his coup attempt?" Kendra asked.

"No. He told me he had evidence he wanted to share with me when I arrived that proved Jer and Marcus were complicit in a crime and that he was going to present it before the Council. I honestly don't believe either of them deserves their position, but they were legally elected, so I have no grounds to fight it. I certainly wouldn't resort to torture and kidnapping."

"What crime did he accuse the Seniors of?" Kendra pressed.

"He didn't say. I can show you the conversation if you'd like."

Kendra nodded, and he reached for his tablet, but when he tried to turn it on, it didn't work. Kendra took the tablet from him, examined it, and handed it back to him before opening her own and eventually handing it over to him. He scrolled and frowned. "It was here. I promise."

"More tampering?" Stormy asked.

Kendra grunted and flicked an ear back as she took the tablet from him. There was another loud bang before she could say anything else.

"Move away from the door," someone yelled.

"Clear!" Kendra yelled back. A moment later, the door burst inward, followed by four Sprites with Healer's badges.

"He's been treated but should be reevaluated to make sure I didn't miss anything," Kendra told the pair of Healers that swam to the Councilor's side. "And Stormy and I are both uninjured."

The other two Healers ignored Kendra and began scanning them both anyway. Kendra huffed and flattened her ears in annoyance, but they ignored that, too. It was all he could do to keep the humor off of his skin at her expression. He was pretty sure his own had matched a few minutes before, but he must not have kept his expression as blank as his skin as Kendra rolled her eyes at him. It was too much. A bubble of humor rippled across his skin, and then fully-bodied laughter that he tried to control but couldn't.

Kendra's tail curled as she waited out the Healer scanning her.

When his own deemed him uninjured, he unclipped his harness and followed Garaptk out. A mix of patrol and guards of both Sprite and Saber were floating outside, along with several ships floating a safe distance away. Kendra motioned to a pair of her guards.

"Take the stasis unit inside to the Habitat. Wait for the creatures to be unloaded and place the stasis unit in evidence."

"Yes, ma'am," they replied and swam onto the ship.

He expected to fly back on the trauma ship, but halfway there, a Sprite he knew well swam up.

"Commander Hybodi," he flashed in greeting. "How's my brother?"

"He was awake when I dropped him off at the Trauma Center, and I expect he'll make a full recovery," Hybodi replied. "You?"

"We're all uninjured," Kendra said before he could reply. He hadn't realized she'd followed him. "Thanks to Stormy's quick reflexes."

The Commander grunted, not looking relieved at all. If anything, she looked annoyed as she glanced towards his brother's ship. "You're lucky it wasn't far worse," Hybodi stated, glaring at him. "You disobeyed direct orders from not one but three individuals, including a member of the Senior Council, and, in doing so, nearly got everyone killed, including members of an endangered species, which your brother and a member of the Council risked their lives to save, and in the process you destroyed a brand new state-of-the-art ship, one that took several years to design and build and far more of my budget than I care to admit."

The humor and relief he'd been feeling a moment before vanished as the Commander continued to lecture him.

"You might be Senior Councilor someday, but you aren't one now, nor were you in charge of the mission. You need to learn to work as a team and learn to follow the orders of those higher ranked than you. You've been lucky this past week, but that luck won't beat hard training and centuries of experience. There's a time and a place to question orders or offer your own ideas. The middle of a crisis when every second counts is not it. Do I make myself clear, *Pilot*?"

"Yes, ma'am," he replied. He still felt guilty about leaving Marsee behind and not following her orders, but he had followed orders. Leaving his brother behind had torn his heart out. Shutting the door had felt like he had killed his brother with his own hands. He admitted that he'd hesitated, but he *had* followed orders. She seemed to understand where his thoughts were going.

"I understand how difficult that moment must have been for you, but that's what it's going to take to be a Senior Councilor someday. It's one thing to risk your own life, but it's an entirely different thing to risk the lives of others. Your people will have to come before everything else.

In a split second, you'll have to decide who lives and who dies. You may have to order your family into a situation that will mean their deaths. You may have to kill a friend with your own hands or leave your child in the hands of a terrorist to keep that terrorist from gaining power. Can you do that? Can you make that kind of decision? Can you weigh the value of one life against another without letting your own personal feelings for them weigh the scales down?"

He squared his shoulders and flashed a yes. That much he knew. It was all he'd been thinking about since his father had asked him if he had any interest in being Senior some day.

The Commander raised a brow at his simple reply. "Yes? That's all you have to say?"

"What more is there to say? I may be young, but I understand the oath I will have to take and the target it will place on my family. I closed the door on my brother today and left him behind because of that oath."

"But you hesitated *and* questioned your orders."

He nodded. "Yes. I did, but perhaps not for the reasons you might think. My brother was placed in charge of that mission, not Senior Honor Guard Hunt, which tells me that the Senior Council doesn't trust her or you. I needed my brother's orders to leave because I didn't know if she was intentionally leaving him behind to get rid of a member of my family. I may be a Senior Councilor someday, and I know I will make mistakes and people will die because of it, but I did follow orders. I wonder, though. If something happens to my father and I'm sworn in, will you be willing to follow *my* orders in a crisis, even if you believe they're the wrong ones?"

Surprise flickered across her skin. "I have never disobeyed an order, and assuming you don't order me to break the law, I see no reason why I wouldn't follow yours, but you are not Senior Councilor now, and you may never be. Until then, you do not have the authority to act as if you are. Part of being a Councilor, Senior or otherwise, is learning to work with people you don't trust, people who might even be trying to kill you. You have valid reasons not to trust us, but until we are stripped of our rank or you are promoted, we outrank you, and that means following our orders. You may not be a member of our guilds, but if we tell you to duck or move, you'd better duck and move like your life depends on it, because it does."

"Is that a threat?" he asked.

She snorted at him. "It's a warning, Pilot. I'm trying to save your life and as many lives as I can in the process. If I'm telling you to duck or to move, it's because *not* doing so *will* kill you. Every second matters. If you hadn't hesitated, you would have had time to get away without damage, just as the rest of us did. How do you think your brother would have felt if he'd sacrificed his life to save you and everyone else, only for you to die and kill those he was trying to save? Your hesitation put everyone at risk. You need to trust us to do our jobs, to fill in the gaps in your knowledge because it's impossible for you to know everything or every order that has been given to those in charge above you."

He nodded. "Yes, ma'am."

She glared at him, obviously not satisfied with his response. "Go wait in my ship while I deal with your mess. I told your father I would escort you back. If you're not there when I return, I will personally hunt you down, collar you, and drag you back to your father by your tentacles."

He snorted at what he perceived to be an absent threat, and she flashed orange.

"Don't think I won't, and if you don't believe me, ask your father. I dragged him before your grandfather when he was twice your age and size, and I'm more than willing to do it again if you keep it up with that attitude. Don't tempt me."

"Yes, ma'am," he replied and started swimming off in the direction of the other ships. To his surprise, Kendra followed him. He glanced back at her.

"I swear on my oath I am not going to hurt you, but I am not leaving you unprotected either. If you don't trust me, you're welcome to pick another guard."

He flashed a shrug and kept swimming. The Commander's ship was well-marked, but Kendra wouldn't let him enter before checking it over herself and scanning for potential damage. When he was finally allowed inside, he slumped in a seat to wait and watched as the Trauma Ship flew off and salvage crews began to descend on his brother's ship. His thoughts were heavy as he contemplated the lecture from the Commander and wondered if he was going to get a lecture from his father, too.

Is she right? he wondered. *Am I acting too independently? I had to go out alone after Rip. No one would have believed me, but I did leave Marsee alone, thinking I knew better. I nearly got her killed, and I nearly got everyone else killed today because I hesitated.*

He glanced back at Kendra, who was floating outside the door, wondering if he could trust her. He knew she was hiding something. He'd spied on her that morning, but he hadn't been able to hear everything that had happened in the other room, even with the new hearing aids he'd picked up the day before that allowed him to hear the higher-pitched voices of the Hue-mans.

As he was watching, another one of her guards swam up to her and began talking to her in a whisper he could barely hear, but when he heard Marsee's name, he quickly flipped the hearing aids out of their case, put them in his ears and turned up the volume.

"...Gen Eral is coming?"

Kendra let out a low growl and slapped the guard hard, knocking them back several feet in the water. "Now is not the time for idle gossip," she hissed at him, fully loud enough for him to hear without the hearing aids. "I expected far better than that from you. Get back to work before I demote you."

The guard bolted away as fast as he could swim without so much as a reply.

Kendra continued to growl after the guard and then glanced back towards him.

"Is everything alright?" he asked.

"It's nothing you need to worry about," she replied as calmly as if she hadn't just attacked one of her guards. He decided not to press it but wondered who Gen Eral was. It wasn't a name he'd ever heard before, and he wondered what they had to do with Marsee. He took the hearing aids out and stowed them the moment her back was turned again, although they were quite hidden behind his ear fins. Before he could make up his mind if he should question her further, the Commander returned. He decided he would do some research and further investigation first. It could be nothing, and he'd only heard a small portion of the conversation.

"So you can follow orders," the Commander flashed. "I wondered if I'd have to chase you down."

He rolled his eyes and clipped his harness in place as she took her own seat and continued to lecture him the entire way back to the Council Building. By the time he arrived, he wondered if he was going to be arrested. Kendra said nothing to defend him or counter the lecture the entire way back, and when they landed, she escorted them to his father's suite and checked it over before leaving him and the Commander alone in the suite.

As much as he didn't trust Kendra, her absence was even worse. He watched her swim out, then turned back to the Commander, who was still scowling at him. "Thank you for seeing me safely back. You don't need to stay."

She snorted at him. "Nice try, Pilot. I'm staying until your father gets here. Maybe by then, I'll decide if I want to press charges for the destruction of Sea Patrol property and disobeying orders."

He sighed and slumped into his favorite chair to wait, wondering if she would effectively end his future career over a few seconds of hesitation.

CHAPTER 21

Clear Seas: Tempting the Gods

To Clear Seas' utter annoyance, the healers wouldn't take him back to Temperate, so he cooled his tentacles in the waiting room and scowled impatiently at the Healer watching the desk. Sadly, she was one of the more senior healers and wasn't intimidated in the slightest by his mood. If anything, she seemed amused, knowing he wouldn't pull rank in this situation, not that he expected them to give in even if he did.

He'd joked with his partner on a number of occasions that he fully believed they were keeping score of the number of times they got to tell him no and make him wait. The amused smirk on the healer who had seen their conversation proved it. If they hadn't then, they did now.

He scowled at the Healer again at that thought. "What's your score, Healer?"

"My score, sir?" she asked, flashing confusion.

"How many times you've made a member of the Council cool their tentacles in the waiting room?"

Humor bubbled across her skin. "That's a Guild secret," she replied. "I'm bound by oath and patient confidentiality not to tell you."

"Uh, huh," he replied.

"I can tell you, I am slightly behind the lead for inventive new swears yelled at me. If you come up with something, I would greatly appreciate it."

He snorted. "Would it get me back to my son any quicker?"

"No, but it could help pass the time."

"Would that count though?"

She shrugged. "I don't see why not as long as you're yelling at me."

Surprisingly, half an hour later, he hadn't come up with anything new when Temperate swam out, but he felt surprisingly better, even if keeping the laughter off his skin was proving to be painful. His humor vanished, replaced by worry that seeped out at the sight of his son. Several large bandages were wrapped around his midsection, two of his tentacles, and one across his right hand.

"I'm fine, Papa," Temperate signed. "It looks worse than it is. Where's Stormy? Is he alright?"

"He's fine. He should be cooling his tentacles in my office, assuming the Squadron Commander is done lighting them on fire for disobeying orders."

Temperate groaned. "How bad was the damage?"

"Let's just say your brother was fortunate it wasn't worse and leave it at that, but if you keep blowing up your ships, I'm going to make you start paying for them."

"To be fair, *I* didn't blow it up this time, and someone had to go on board to help Kendra. I certainly wasn't going to let anyone else take that risk."

"I know, and I'm proud of you. Now, the real question is whether I need to press charges against your brother for using you for target practice?"

Temperate's skin, what was still visible anyway, tinged with embarrassment. "You know about that?"

"Of course I do. I would be surprised if the press hasn't gotten their fangs on it by now. They were playing it on repeat in Command when I arrived. You've done well in training him, but his aim could use a little work if he's going to make it believable."

"It was more than close enough, if you ask me," Temperate muttered.

He chuckled and turned to the Healer. "Thank you for keeping me entertained. I haven't had such a hard time keeping the laughter off my skin in years, and I needed that distraction more than you might realize."

"We aim to heal," she replied.

Temperate raised a brow questioningly, and he explained as they swam out.

His son snorted. "You honesty didn't come up with anything new? I would think you had people swearing at you all the time."

"Trust me. No one is more surprised than I am." He didn't say anything else as they entered the Council Building, although several people flashed their concern when they saw Temperate's injuries.

The door to his office was open, and both Stormy and the Senior Commander were there. Stormy slumped dejectedly in his net, although he thankfully appeared to be uninjured, while the Commander scowled down at him, arms crossed as she waited.

"Thank you, Commander," he said as they swam in.

She nodded and examined Temperate. "How long are you out this time?"

"Only a day. The bandages come off tomorrow. The only concern is a mild concussion, which they want to check tomorrow morning. I'll know for sure then."

She grunted. "I'll bring a ship over, but if you think you're getting a new one this time, you're sadly mistaken. As for the old one..."

"Ma'am, about my request for a Command position..." Temperate interrupted.

"I already told you it was under consideration. I'll let you know when I've decided."

"I know." Temperate glanced at Stormy. "But my brother believes I shouldn't take it, and he's right. If I let my fear take over, then Rip wins, and I realized today that I couldn't ask anyone else to do what I'm not willing to do myself. I'd like to withdraw my request."

She grinned. "Granted. Welcome back, Master Pilot. Now, if you could, please avoid destroying your next ship. I'm running a little low on them for some reason."

He grinned. "I'll see what I can do."

She nodded at him, glared at Stormy for a moment, and started to swim out, then turned back around. "Oh, and I expect you to teach your brother how to aim that stunner better. He missed every shot."

Temperate groaned dramatically, although his skin bubbled with humor. "Yes, ma'am."

She swam out, and Clear Seas shut the door behind her and turned to face Stormy with his own glare.

Stormy somehow managed to look even more dejected. "I'm sorry I disobeyed your orders, Papa."

He scowled at his son. "No, you're not. I understand why you hesitated, and while I commend you for your bravery, you did put the others at risk and damaged property in the process. I expect you to help pay for the damages to Temperate's ship."

Stormy sighed. "I don't have that kind of credit."

"I'm well aware of that. You'll work it off. I am ordering you to work with your brother to give whatever junker the Senior Commander delivers a complete overhaul, and as you disobeyed your brother's orders, until such time as he is cleared to return to duty, you will do whatever he needs or wants you to do." He glared at Temperate, whose eyes gleamed with mischief. "Within legal boundaries."

"Yes, sir," Temperate replied, although the mischief didn't vanish.

"Am I being charged with a crime, then?" Stormy asked. "The Commander threatened to press charges about the damages to the ship."

"No. No one is going to arrest you for hesitating over leaving your brother behind and if they do, I'll shock them myself. Frankly, I'm proud of you. That was some fantastic flying, and while you hesitated, you ultimately made the right decision, as impossible as it was, but there are always unforeseen consequences, as Little Flower said, to every decision we make. Consider this a learning experience."

Stormy straightened and brightened, clearly pleased to know he wasn't being arrested or stripped of his future position.

His tablet rang, interrupting their conversation. He answered it, recognizing the tone, and threw the call up on his monitor. It was Stinger.

"We've heard back from the trauma ships. Everyone on the passenger manifest is accounted for, and their story matches. The first group of Councilors with the worst injuries will arrive in about an hour via emergency jump. Three councilors are in stasis, but their condition is stable. Two of the pilots are critical, but they believe they should make it. We've already sent additional transports to retrieve the rest and salvage the ship if we can."

"I want a full report on both ships," he ordered and disconnected before Stinger could reply. "All right, you two. Get out of here before my patience and relief wears off."

"Yes, sir," they both said and bolted out of his office with a speed that told him they were both truly okay.

He waited until the door slid shut behind them and began to shake with repressed fear. He had come so close to losing both his sons again, this time on his orders. "Gods of the Deep," he prayed. "Please, no matter how you feel about me, please keep protecting them. Keep them safe. Please."

He was still praying when there was a knock on his door. He took a deep breath, then two, before opening it.

Apakna swam in. "How are they?"

"You just missed them. They're both fine. Temperate's ship, however..."

Apakna surprised him as she awkwardly attempted to kneel, or as best she could underwater, in her people's sign of respect. "On behalf of my Council, I wish to formally thank you, your sons, and your people for the risk they took in trying to ensure my uncle was safe."

He nodded. "No thanks are necessary. You would do the same for us."

"I'm not sure I would be strong enough to put my own children in danger, as you just did. It's the whole reason I haven't had any yet."

He flashed his understanding. "There are days I wish I had that luxury, but I'm glad I didn't. They are the joys of my life and my moral compass. Temperate is a Master Pilot. It's his choice to put himself in danger to save others, and Stormy will most likely be my heir. They both know the risks, especially Stormy, perhaps more than any of us going into this profession, but he has his brother's bravery, his sister's compassion, his mother's brains, and, for better or worse, my attitude. As you saw, I have little control over him. The only person he has ever listened to is his brother, and that dynamic is quickly changing."

She grinned. "Well, it could be worse. He could have gotten your brains *and* your attitude."

He pretended to scowl at her, but he wasn't upset by the teasing. "How's your uncle?"

"Kendra had him patched up before they even got the door off the ship. Thankfully, she had all the right equipment on her. Did you know she's a Master Healer? I didn't. Anyway, they're observing him for a few hours because of the severity of the concussion he had, but he'll make a full recovery. If it wasn't for your children, he'd be dead. There's nothing left to that cargo bay."

"The endangered species?"

Apakna's expression changed to a scowl. "Warble greeps. It's one of the few plant-eating species we have left. I didn't realize they were transporting them. Apparently, my uncle made arrangements with Rip to have them transferred to the Habitat before everything happened. Kendra verified with the Senior Healer that she was expecting them."

"Well, that's good, at least. I didn't realize you had endangered species."

"Councilor, everything on my planet is endangered. It's something we need to talk about, but that can wait. We have more important issues to deal with right now. I just can't believe my uncle risked his life for a warble greep. They're...endangered for a reason. Just about everything else on our planet is carnivorous. Their only natural defense is the ability to bury themselves in mud and scream to warn others. It's the most annoying high-pitched noise I've ever heard. Our people have considered them pests for just about forever. Apparently, an island near the Habitat has an above-ground spring that is almost perfect for them. Because of their tendency to hide at the slightest sign of danger, they're seen as cowardly, and it's considered a rather rude insult to call someone a Warble Greep. My uncle is probably one of the only people on our planet who even cares about them, and frankly, if our people found out he was injured trying to rescue them, he'd probably be laughed out of the Council."

"I'll keep it quiet if you want, but I can't guarantee I won't pick on him about it."

She grinned back at him. "Well, you've earned that right. Your children are worth far more. Anyway, I wanted to let you know that I'll meet the incoming ships. I think it best if you monitor from Command."

"Are you sure? I don't want anyone to take offense."

"Most of the people on the first transports are injured and will be going directly to the Trauma Center. If they don't understand, I'll claw them myself. These are unusual days, and that calls for caution. There's still the chance the healers were forced to say what they did."

He flashed a hint of worry before controlling it. "I pray not, but we'll know for sure soon enough. Until then, I suppose we should go read the Charter or do something productive to earn our keep around here."

"You're starting to sound like Marcus," she teased.

"Oh, gods. Can this day get any worse?" He swam towards the door but stopped as Apakna growled at him. "What?"

"Did you seriously just ask the Gods *that* question? After the day we just had? I should put forth a vote of no confidence for that statement alone."

He snorted. "By all means, please do. I could use a vacation." He knew she was mostly teasing, but the superstitious part of him shuddered, and he offered another silent prayer as he made his way out.

CHAPTER 22

Temperate: Junker

Temperate bolted out of the rear of the Council Building with Stormy right beside him. Guards appeared the moment they did, but they ignored them and remained quiet on the way home. They avoided the most populated areas and made it home with only a few people seeing them.

Once safely inside, he turned and crushed his brother in a hug. "Are you sure you're okay?"

"The only thing that was damaged was my ego," Stormy replied. "You're the one that was injured. How bad is it, really?"

"I was a mangled mess, and I'm not going to be able to do *anything* for the next twenty-four hours," he replied and pretended to limp over to the nearest seating net. "Will you get me something to eat? I don't think I can make it that far."

Stormy rolled his eyes at his act but swam off and returned with a bowl of fruit.

He was only a bite into it when there was a frantic knock on their door.

Stormy swam over to answer it but frowned. "I don't recognize her," Stormy said but cautiously opened the door.

"Can I…"

"Is he okay?" a frantic voice asked, interrupting Stormy.

"Melody?" Temperate asked, recognizing her voice.

She pushed her way inside past Stormy and gasped, flashing bright with concern when she saw his bandages. "Bottomless Depths! What happened?"

"I'm fine," he said and swam over to hug her. She barely knew where to hold him, terrified she would hurt him, and eventually just leaned against him as he held her. "This looks worse than it is. How did you find out?"

"My mentor saw you and called me. What happened?"

"I'm not sure I can give any details yet, but I was called to a rescue, and their ship imploded. Thankfully, everyone got out alive."

She flashed bright white with fear and hugged him tighter. "I wish they'd hurry up and move you to Command."

"About that," he began and glanced at Stormy. "I withdrew my request to move to Command."

"Why?" she asked, pulling away. "I thought you wanted to switch."

"So did I. Melody, I love you more than words can explain, and I do want to be a father, but I realized something today. This is who I am, who I've always been. I'm a Master Pilot for the Sea Patrol. I go into burning ships to pull people out, and I can't ask someone to do that and sit back and watch."

She sighed heavily as flickers of dark blue and white crossed her skin.

"I'll understand if that means you don't want to partner with me."

"I just...I don't know if I can handle worrying about whether you're going to come home every time you go out. The fear I felt when Sea Turtle called me to say you were injured again..."

"I know," he replied. "But this is who I am, and unless something happens to my father and I find myself on the Council, this is who I want to be. I don't want to sit behind a desk in Command or even sit on the Council. I can't make decisions for other people. I can't order them to die and sit back and watch that happen. Someone has to go onto those ships. Someone has to chase off the Leviathans, and that someone is me. If you can't handle that, then as much as I love you, we're not right for each other."

She nodded, although her skin was nearly black with grief. "I love you, too, but the thought of losing you...I...I just...I just don't know." She turned and swam out.

He sighed and watched her leave, then glanced at his brother.

"I'm sorry," Stormy flashed.

He sighed again. "I'll be in my room." He felt nearly as black as he flopped into his hanging net, wondering if she would decide to stay with him or if the risk was too much for her. He flipped open his tablet and stared at the picture she'd sent that morning of the child he already loved. *Perhaps it's better this way. She won't be a target because of me.*

He was still staring at that picture when there was a knock on the door. He looked up as Stormy peered inside. "The Senior Commander is here with your junker."

"How bad is it?"

His brother shrugged and swam off.

He followed him out to find the Commander waiting in their living room. "I wasn't expecting you until tomorrow."

She shrugged. "I figured you might need or want time to give it a full servicing before you take it out."

"That bad, huh?"

Humor escaped her control. "It'll do, but it does need a bit of a paint job."

He followed her out and had to blink in surprise at the ship that sat out in front of his home. "Yours?! But you love this ship."

She smiled at him. "I do, but you need it more than I do. Destroy this one, and I'll reassign you to Big Bertha. I've been over the ship twice since your accident, but you'll want to make sure there isn't any damage from today's little adventure."

He chuckled. Big Bertha was their fleet's biggest but slowest ship and one of their oldest, reserved for transport, not chasing Leviathans. "Yes, ma'am. Thank you."

She nodded. "Thank *you*. Now *I* can put in for that upgrade I've been wanting." She ran a hand along the nearest engine nacelle. "Take good care of her. She's been a very good ship for me."

"I promise," he replied.

He watched her swim off before swimming up to the ship. While the one he'd had before had been brand new and a state-of-the-art ship, it was nothing like the Commanders. He'd been drooling over it for the past year, ever since the moment it arrived. This ship was bigger, far more powerful, and maneuverable and designed for interstellar travel, unlike the one he'd had before, which, while it could technically fly between the planets, would be an uncomfortable trip, if for no other reason than the lack of onboard waste room facilities.

One hand lovingly caressing the side, he slowly swam around the ship that the Senior Commander had risked to save his life. There wasn't a scratch or dent anywhere that he could see, and if he knew her, she'd already given it a thorough scan before bringing it over, even if she expected him to do the same. The only thing out of place was a temporary covering that hid her designation until he could bring it in for that paint job she'd mentioned.

When he finished his circuit, he smiled at Stormy. "Come on, Little Brother. Let's take her out for a spin and see just what she can do."

CHAPTER 23

Carrie: Packing

Carrie left her father's cell bright red with anger, but by the time she reached the end of the hall where her tablet was stored, she had regained most of her composure, and guilt now clawed at her.

"I'm sorry," Red Fin said softly. "I know this is a difficult time, but I will need you to fill out some paperwork for me."

She nodded and followed him into an empty conference room.

He tapped away at his tablet for several moments. "Please sign here that your statement earlier is the truth."

She did, although a mix of grief and rage flickered on her skin. He said nothing about her loss of control.

"Thank you. Your account has been credited with the standard allocation for newly emancipated individuals. This will come directly out of your father's account, but I don't think he's going to need it."

He frowned a moment later as he scrolled through something. "You currently don't have a residence, and your father's residence has been impounded for evidence by the Senior Council, but it looks like your former home hasn't been reassigned. Do you want to go back there or be reassigned someplace else?"

"I don't know. For so long, I just wanted to go home, but I don't know if I can return there. Will I be able to get my stuff?"

He frowned again as he checked on several things. "Yes. I see here that Clear Seas has granted you authorization to remove personal belongings with supervision. He frowned again. It looks like we'll need Kendra to supervise."

"Kendra? The Saber's Senior Honor Guard? Why her and not Stinger?" she asked.

"Stinger is under investigation for possible involvement with Rip and your father. He hasn't been stripped of duty yet, but his authorization has been severely restricted."

"He was involved, too?" she asked.

"I honestly don't know," Red Fin replied. "None of us do. The Guard has been compromised. The feeds were tampered with, and one guard was arrested for helping Rip escape. Nearly half my squad is still missing and presumed dead. I don't think they were involved, but I don't have any proof to say otherwise. We were all watching Marsee. I was knocked out and never saw who did it, but your father admits to having done so. He claims he left everyone where he knocked them out and that Rip must have gone back and taken them, or perhaps some creature got them while they were incapacitated."

"I'm sorry," she replied and looked away, wondering if her father *could* have gone to anyone for help if the Senior Honor Guard was involved.

"Is there somewhere you'd like to stay?" he asked in Saber.

"Somewhere here in Council Platform, for now, I suppose. I've already received orders to attend the Trial in case I'm called as a witness. I don't have any other family and..."

"No friends?"

She shrugged. "No one has reached out to me, and..."

He nodded his understanding and showed her a map with several available houses for her to choose from. She picked one close to the school, figuring she might as well continue her education until she figured out what she wanted to do with her life. It was also the only one listed as fully furnished, which would save her the effort of doing so herself, and she would only have to pack up those things she wanted to keep. She didn't want to stay in her father's house any longer than she had to.

Once that was done, at her request, he helped her to enroll in classes. That was when she found out that Rip had placed her on medical leave, which is why the schools had never escalated her absence to the Council. She then followed him out and up a level to Saber's guard station. He had her wait outside while he swam inside, but a minute later, he returned and led her back down again, but to a different door, this one marked "Evidence Locker. Authorized Personnel Only."Once again, he had her wait outside, and a moment later, both he and Kendra swam back out.

"Hello, Carrie," Kendra signed. "Do you know how much you have to move?"

She shook her head. "I've never been to my father's current home before. I don't know what he brought with him."

Kendra nodded, ducked back into the room, and returned carrying a large stack of collapsible boxes. On the side was written. "Property of the Guard. Authorized access only."

"If we need more, I send for them," Kendra said after Red Fin took the boxes from her.

Carry followed both guards out of the building and onto a guard ship, where they met up with another half-squad waiting for them. A few minutes later, they landed in the middle of a street, but she couldn't see much from where she was sitting. To her surprise, Kendra frowned at whatever she saw from the pilot's net, and the squad of guards, save for Red Fin, all bolted off of the ship at a sign from her.

Kendra turned back to face her. "I want to make sure the property is secure before you enter."

She nodded and waited. There was little she could do anyway. A few minutes later, the all-clear came in, and she swam off the ship after Kendra but stopped in surprise at what she saw as she rounded the front of the ship.

"No wonder you were worried," she signed.

The home was a disaster. It had been painted in hate-filled graffiti, and the windows had all been smashed out. A pair of bored-looking Water Sprite guards floated outside, seemingly not caring in the least about the destruction of the property.

Kendra, however, was livid, and she lit into those guards with a lecture that almost negated the pain of the words she read. Not all of them were targeted at her father. People had written awful things about her, too. She didn't blame them. She deserved their hate. People had died because of her.

The guards seemed ambivalent to Kendra's lecture, which seemed to infuriate Kendra even more. "Do you have anything to say for yourself?" she hissed.

The senior of the two guards looked at Kendra with what could only be described as apathy. "My orders were to prevent anyone from entering the dwelling, which I have followed. No one has said anything about not allowing people to express their feelings, and in case you're wondering, the Seniors have been here several times. The damage inside was all their doing, and they said nothing about the...artwork. Besides, the building is scheduled to be demolished after the trial, and he'll never even see it."

Kendra growled. "He might not, but this is hate speech, and it's directed at more than just him. His daughter is here to gather her belongings. How do you think she feels?"

Only then did the guards glance at her and then back to Kendra, but their expressions didn't change. A flicker of a shrug crossed his skin. "I didn't write it, and I wasn't here when it happened, but people are dead because of her. I consider this reparations."

Kendra's scowl deepened. "Get out of here. You're both relieved of duty."

The guards shrugged and swam off.

Kendra motioned to two of her guards to take their place, then took a deep breath and turned to her. "I'm sorry you had to see this. I should have verified that the property was secure before bringing you here."

"It's alright," she replied. "I understand. People did die because of me, and their families are angry and grieving. If this gives them even a little closure, then I accept my reparations."

"You were a victim," Kendra said. "You should not be treated like this."

She shrugged. "Can I get my stuff now?"

Kendra nodded and unlocked the door.

Inside was even worse. Every wall had been stripped down to the studs, and debris floated everywhere. She sighed and looked around the room at the handful of items she could see under the debris while Red Fin started putting a box together. She swam over to the window, where a flash of color caught her attention, and found a broken plant, barely alive. A large rock had landed on it. She carefully uncovered it.

"Do you have any tape or something that could be used to support this stem?" Carrie asked.

Kendra didn't even question her desire to rescue the nearly dead plant. Kendra nodded, pulled out a small bandage from her medical kit, and wrapped the plant while she held it in place. Once it was stabilized, she carefully placed it in the box Red Fin held. The other guards Kendra had brought started digging through the debris, looking for anything personal in nature. They found a few pictures in broken frames, a broken monitor, and a pair of torn hanging nets. She kept the pictures and moved on to the next room.

It was a waste room. It was in better condition, likely only because the guards outside would have needed to use it. In a small cabinet, she found her tooth cleaner, scale polisher, and ear fin brush, but left her father's there. The small kitchen contained nothing but a container of rotting food and a set of utensils. She didn't bother with most of those, as they had been listed in the furnishings that were included in her new home. The only thing she kept there was her favorite pair of sticks and the ones her mother had used.

Her father's room was next, and it was as much of a disaster as the main room had been, although several boxes remained seemingly untouched in the closet. She pulled out the first one and found her mother's belongings. Kendra went through it before handing it off to a guard to load onto the ship while she dug through the other boxes. The other guards dug through the remaining rubble but didn't find anything that she wanted.

A small closet in the hall held a few random items, which she ignored and moved onto the last room, but she didn't enter.

"Are you alright?" Kendra asked, peering over her shoulder at the untouched room.

"It's set up exactly like my room was before," she replied. "Even down to the book on the desk that I was reading at the time." She forced herself to swim in and picked up the book, flipping it open to the page she'd last read, but she couldn't even see the page. Memories flashed in her brain, scenes she had relived thousands of times over the past several months and then tried everything she could to forget.

Kendra reached out and touched her shoulder. Startled, Carrie reacted without thinking. She spun, grabbed Kendra's arm, and released a shock as strong as she could make before bolting out of the room. She was out of the apartment and halfway down the street before she realized what she'd done.

"Bottomless depths. I've killed her!" She swore and spun, fully panicked now, seeing several guards chasing after her. Pure white with fear, she swam with everything she had.

"Carrie, wait!" Red Fin called behind her, but she didn't stop. All she knew was that she had to get away and find a place to hide. She was dead if she didn't.

CHAPTER 24

Kendra: Shocked

Kendra swore under her breath as she woke and rubbed at her throbbing arm.

"I didn't quite catch that," Red Fin said, although humor bubbled on his skin.

"You heard me perfectly," Kendra replied with a scowl at his teasing. "Where's Carrie?"

"She took off, fully terrified. The others went after her. Are you alright? A trauma ship is on the way."

"I'm fine. It's not like it's the first time I've been shocked, and it was entirely my fault for startling her. Call off the Trauma Ship. I'll go after her and send the others back to help pack up this room. I don't think she should come back here."

While Red Fin did as ordered, she pulled up the squad's position on her tablet. Deciding it was far enough away that swimming would take too long, she grabbed a drone from the ship and took off after them. Carrie's fear scent was easy to follow. A few minutes later, she found the others.

"Are you alright?" the nearest guard asked as he swam over to her.

"Fine. Where is she?" Carrie's scent was overpowered by large flowering bushes surrounding a small park, making it difficult to pinpoint her location in the shifting current.

The guard pointed to a rock formation in the center, surrounded by more flowering plants, where another guard was peering through the bushes. "She swam inside the rock formation and won't come out."

"Take your squad back to the house and finish packing up Carrie's room. I'll handle this."

"Yes, ma'am," he replied and whistled. The other guards swam over immediately and took off following his command.

She watched from a distance for a moment, curious if Carrie would exit and take off with the other guard's departure. She didn't. Kendra slowly swam up. Fear and guilt radiated out of a small crack in the stone structure. Even though she knew how flexible the Sprites were, it still surprised her how small of a space they could fit into. She slowly sat down and leaned back against another section of the sculpture where she could still see the small hole but not close enough to be threatening.

"I am sorry that I scared you. I am unhurt, and you are not in trouble."

There was no sound of movement, but the scent changed to include disbelief.

"I know you have no reason to trust me, but I am not going to hurt or arrest you. I promise. I only want to make sure you're okay. It can't be comfortable in there. Why don't you come out so we can talk? I promise I won't come any closer, and I've ordered everyone else back to your father's home to pack your belongings, so you don't have to go back there if you don't want to."

She waited patiently, giving Carrie time to decide what to do. A minute or two later, Kendra blinked as a section of the rock started to move, ever so slowly, away from her. It was only then that she realized that Carrie wasn't in the hole. She *was* the hole. "I'm impressed! That's some of the most detailed camouflage I've seen a member of your species perform. You had me completely fooled, but when you move, it gives you away."

The hole let out an audible sigh, and a moment later, eyes and ear fins appeared in the rock formation as Carrie uncovered the parts of her body that couldn't change color.

"Is that how you hid from Rip in the cave?" Kendra asked.

Carrie stared at her for a moment, then uncurled and shifted her skin back into the normal blue-grey color of their unlit skin, but she kept her distance, and based on her scent, Kendra was quite sure she was ready to bolt at the slightest movement on her part.

"He liked to wander the cave and pick a target at random," Carrie flashed after another long moment. "Unless he was specifically looking for me, it was safer to hide. I'm sorry I shocked you."

"I know, and I forgive you. It was my fault for scaring you. You seemed like you needed a hug, but I forgot your culture does not touch each other unless you're close friends. I apologize for overstepping my bounds."

"It wasn't that," Carrie replied. "It was seeing the room exactly the way I left it. I was home alone, waiting for my father to return from work and reading when it happened."

"When Rip kidnapped you?"

Carrie nodded. "I never heard him approach. I had my favorite music playing loudly in the background, and I was so engrossed in that book that I didn't know he was there until he touched me on the shoulder, just like you did."

Carrie was silent for a long time as both fear and anger flickered on her skin.

"He shocked you?" Kendra prompted.

"No," Carrie flashed. "He told me my father had been injured at work and that he was going to care for me while my father was in surgery and recovering. I wanted to go to the Trauma Center, but he said my father wouldn't be out of surgery for hours, so there was no point in waiting there. I didn't even question it. He brought me to his house, gathered up a meal for me, then showed me to my room. It was nicer than any room I had ever seen. He left, and I pulled out my tablet to see if I could find anything about my father's accident, but my tablet didn't work. When I tried to leave the room to tell Rip, I couldn't. The door was locked. He didn't return for hours. When he did, I tried to shock him, but I was too small, and he... I spent the next six months wishing I had shocked him when he first appeared when I still had a chance to get away."

Kendra wondered if others had been taken the same way and made a point to investigate other missing children in his district. "You had no reason to believe he couldn't be trusted," she replied. "Don't blame yourself for his actions or yours today. Give yourself time to heal and re-cover."

"I know, but..."

"It's impossible not to. I know. If it makes you feel any better, you did the right thing today. You had no idea what my intentions were, and I had no right to touch you, even to get your attention."

"You're really not mad?"

"I'm really not," Kendra replied. "The only thing I'm mad about is my own stupidity and the teasing I'll get from my guards later. I'm sure the footage is all the way back to Saber by now if not already playing on the news. I can just see it. 'Breaking News: Senior Honor Guard de-feated in a fierce battle by a tiny Water Sprite,'" she said, making several silly faces and pretending to be shocked.

Humor bubbled across Carrie's skin briefly, but it didn't last long, replaced by guilt and grief.

Kendra was quite sure that it had nothing to do with her. "What happened that has you feeling so guilty right now?"

Carrie didn't answer.

"Did Rip make you do something?"

Carrie still didn't answer, but her guilt and grief grew stronger.

"Tell me what happened. I promise you're not in trouble. You had no choice but to do what he ordered."

Carrie sighed and looked in the direction of the house. "It's all the people that were hurt because of me."

"That's not your fault. That blame lies entirely on Rip's shredded carcass and your father's."

"Is it, though? I blamed my father for not going for help, but I'm just as much to blame. Petra was forced to make a false statement to stop Rip from hurting me, but she wasn't the first. I learned very quickly to do what he wanted, whether that was to scream for him or sing for the others he brought to the cave. The better I performed, the sooner it would end or the sooner they would break and give him what he wanted. I knew they'd die anyway. He never let them live once he got what he wanted from them. Doesn't that make me complicit?"

"No," Kendra replied, although her heart broke for what the child had endured. "What you did was self-defense. You had no way to stop what was happening to you or the others. You aren't big enough to kill someone Rip's size yet. If you were, I have a feeling I'd be dead right now."

"I could have at least resisted like Red Fin did to save Wind Rider."

"Red Fin is an Honor Guard. You can't hold yourself to his century or more of training. You did what you had to do to survive, and you kept the others alive."

Carrie shrugged. "It would have been kinder if I had just let them die. Most refused to eat after the first day or two anyway. How many other people were harmed by my father, like the Translator, because of me?"

"I don't know, but I doubt Petra and Red Fin feel that way. They're alive and recovering because of you, and your testimony kept Wind Rider and Petra from being executed."

"That doesn't seem like enough."

"Carrie, by keeping Petra alive, you saved the entire Consortium. It is more than enough. You kept him from putting others in power."

Carrie frowned. "There are other Councilors involved?"

"I can't say for sure, as I haven't seen all the evidence, but I believe so. If that doesn't feel like enough, find a way to give back to those who were harmed."

"How?"

"I don't know. I suppose that's up to you and what your skills are. You could join the Guard and stop others like Rip. We could certainly use someone with your skills, or perhaps you could become a healer and help care for others injured like you. Most importantly, what you need to do is live your life to its fullest to show the universe that Rip failed and that you were stronger. You survived. He didn't."

A depressed sigh rippled across Carrie's skin as the ship they'd flown in flew over them and settled in an open space on the other side of the rock sculpture.

"I understand your feelings. Give yourself time to heal. Now, come on. It looks like they have everything packed up. Let's get you settled in your new home."

Carrie sighed but turned and swam towards the ship. A few minutes later, they were outside Carrie's new home. A pair of her own guards floated outside, sent ahead to prepare the place. It was a traditional Water Sprite home, built into the side of a hill, but the prior owner had clearly spent a great deal of time on the landscaping out front. It was wild, having been untended for a time, but still quite beautiful.

Inside, the place was well-maintained and fully furnished. Carrie explored the place with interest and picked the smaller interior room for her bedroom. Kendra approved of her choice as it was the most secure. The guards had everything unloaded and unpacked in a matter of minutes, and when they were done, they exited and returned to the ship, leaving only her, Red Fin, and Carrie inside.

Carrie glanced out the window at the two guards still floating outside the home. "Are they staying?"

"Until after the trial, at the very least. Senior Council's orders. All of Rip's victims are being guarded. If you would prefer, I can order them to remain hidden."

"Do you trust them?"

"They would be dead if I didn't," Kendra replied. "I know you have no reason to believe that after what was done to your father's home, but the guards I brought with me are some of my best, and they will do everything they can to protect you."

Carrie didn't seem convinced but sighed. "Hidden, I think. Thank you for your help today."

"You're very welcome," she replied. "And if you need someone to talk to, my door is always open. If you need anything, just swim outside and ask."

Carrie thanked her again, and Kendra swam out, followed by Red Fin. She ordered the two guards outside to remain and watch discreetly and then swam onto the ship. As she clipped into her harness, Carrie watched them from the front window of her new home.

Kendra's heart broke at the sight. Leaving the child alone, even if she was legally an adult and being guarded, seemed wrong, but there was nothing else she could do, and she had far more important things she needed to attend to.

"I'll check in on her tomorrow," Red Fin said, perhaps picking up on her mood or feeling the same.

She nodded her approval. Red Fin was one of the few Water Sprite guards she currently trusted. She had known him since he was born as she was good friends with his mother, but more importantly, Carrie seemed to trust him, and right now, that was all that mattered.

CHAPTER 25

Little Flower: Gift of Music

After purchasing the most exquisite set of chopsticks Little Flower had ever seen and a game designed to help teach Hope how to use them, they wandered the market at random. Marsee bought everything that she or Hope expressed even the slightest interest in and had to glare down the first several vendors into letting her pay. After that, word must have spread as the vendors stopped arguing.

They'd only hit a small fraction of the booths before Marsee started yawning.

"Time to head back," she told Marsee.

Marsee didn't argue, which told her that she'd overextended herself. By the time they made it back to their floor, Marsee was struggling hard, even with Avery's help, and flopped down on the other side of the elevator, not even trying to make her way back to the room.

"Are you alright, or should I go find Mama?" she asked.

"I'm okay. I just need to rest for a few minutes."

While Marsee recovered, she took Hope and returned to the room with Tamarin, who checked everything out and helped to carry the packages back. Once the room was cleared of monsters and villains and everything dropped off, she returned to with Marsee until she was ready to make her way down the long hallway. Tamarin remained behind to watch Hope, who had dug into the bags to get at her new toys the moment the were set down. Once in the room, Marsee used the hole of muck, grabbed her safety gear, and crawled onto the bed. She was asleep before Little Flower had even started changing out of her wet suit.

In an attempt to help Marsee stay relaxed, she downloaded one of Marsee's older siblings' albums, as Marsee hadn't shared anything with her yet. The translation program failed entirely on the title, but the cover had a picture of her mother's garden on the front, complete with several flicker flyers, so she guessed it was intended to be relaxing. It was different from anything she'd ever heard before, but then she figured most of it was likely out of her range of hearing. Even still, what she could hear was soothing.

Marsee slept soundly and without incident and didn't wake until nearly dinner time when there was a knock on the door. Marsee looked up but didn't climb off the bed.

Once she was sure Marsee was fully awake and had taken her gear off, Little Flower walked over to the door and found her grandfather and Henry waiting outside. She let them in and shut the door. GrandFather scooped up Hope, who was still playing with some of her new toys, and walked over to the couch to sit down with her. Henry followed, silent as ever, but he nodded at them.

"How was your day?" she asked them.

"Fantastic," her grandfather replied. "We checked out two museums and the Arboretum and plan to check out the market tomorrow. You should check out the children's museum. It's all interactive. Hope would love it. There are plenty of places where you can rest if you're not up for a lot of swimming yet, as they don't allow the drones inside."

"That's good to know," Marsee said, "and I'm glad you're here. I have something for both of you."

Marsee crawled off the bed, shook and flexed her injured paw, and then padded slowly over to the bags with her gifts.

"Is your paw still bothering you?" Little Flower asked.

"No more than when Mama fussed over it this morning," Marsee replied. "It just feels weird. It's all numb and tingly." She dug through one bag, then shifted to another before bringing it over to GrandFather. "I saw these and thought they would go well with your collection."

He reached in and pulled out a series of articulating sea-creature sculptures, setting each down on the small table in front of the couch. "Oh, these are fantastic!" He examined them closely while trying to keep Hope's pudgy hands away. They were far too delicate for her to play with.

"There's a book inside, too, which explains more about their habitats. They're all endangered species, and the credits I spent on them are going to conservation efforts."

"That makes me love them even more. Thank you!"

When Hope kept struggling to get out of her grandfather's hands to play with the sculptures, Little Flower moved them to the counter near the kitchenette, where Hope couldn't get at them. Hope was annoyed and started crying, but her grandfather started tickling her, and she quickly forgot about them.

"I'm glad you like them," Marsee said, walking over to a much larger bag. She didn't even try to lift it but instead carefully dragged it over. "Henry, this is to thank you for saving my family's life. I wasn't sure what you were interested in outside of animals and music, so I hope you like it."

Henry carefully lifted out the large object inside. It was wrapped in the most beautiful shimmering fabric Little Flower had ever seen, but they all gasped as he unwrapped it. She had no idea what it was, but it was covered in a fortune of jewels depicting various sea creatures in motion. It was a stunning work of art and craftsmanship. If it existed back on Earth, it would have made the crown jewels look ordinary and fake.

"Oh wow!" Henry exclaimed. "Thank you. I've never seen anything like this before. It's absolutely stunning."

"It's a drum. There should be mallets in the bag as well. I have instructions for you, and Sea Turtle, he's the master musician who gave the drum to me to give to you, said he would gladly mentor you if you wanted to learn how to play. He said it belonged to his grandfather and was awarded for a similar deed. If nothing else, you should bring this down and hear him play it. Underwater, the sound makes the water ripple, and the animals dance and flash. Sea Turtle is so good he can make the creatures talk in their visual language."

Henry gently tapped the marked top. It let off a beautiful, if muted, tone. He looked into the bag, pulled out a set of ornate wrapped mallets, and gently hit it with one. This time, it let out a gloriously pure tone. He smiled and then proceeded to tap methodically on the various markings, each letting off a separate tone. When he was done, he surprised everyone by starting to play, and then he began to sing.

They all sat there in stunned amazement at the performance.

"That was beautiful!" Marsee exclaimed.

"I had no idea you played," GrandFather said. "How come you've never joined in back in New Hope?"

Henry shrugged. "I never played for anyone before. My father always thought music was a waste of time. I had a small hand drum that I bought after I...moved away from home. I saw someone play once and loved how it sounded, but that was nothing like the quality of this masterpiece, and I never thought I was that good. I could never figure out how to read music, so I just played what I remembered and only for myself. Thank you very much, Marsee. It's by far the most beautiful thing anyone has ever given me, and I will enjoy it greatly."

Marsee looked at him with ears-back, wide-eyed astonishment. "You did that without training?! Henry, you *have* to show Sea Turtle what you can do."

Henry ducked his head and rubbed at the back of his neck. "I don't know how I feel about playing for a stranger. I'm not that good."

"Not that good?!" Marsee exclaimed. "Henry, you're amazing! My siblings are all master musicians, so I know. None of them would ever be able to pick up an instrument they've never played before and do what you just did." She grabbed her tablet. "You know what, I'm asking Sea Turtle to come over now. He needs to hear you play."

"Marsee, you don't need..."

"Done," she said. Her tablet dinged almost immediately. "He's going to meet us down in the Arboretum in fifteen minutes."

Henry groaned. "*Marsee...*"

"Henry, I won't hear another word out of you. You're far too talented to let this go to waste." She walked over and yanked the mallets out of his hands, then began wrapping them up.

Little Flower chuckled. "You'd better listen to her, Henry. She's practically the head of the Guild."

Henry sighed and leaned back on the couch, clearly outmaneuvered as Marsee began wrapping up the drum. "Do you really think I'm that good?"

"I really do," Marsee said.

Little Flower changed back into her wet suit, starting to think she might need to keep wearing it. It was quite comfortable anyway, even if it was a bit of a pain to get on and off. *Maybe I can get some alterations made.*

While she did, Marsee changed Hope, and they took off. On their way out, they met their parents, who were just returning, and told them what was going on. To Henry's utter embarrassment, they followed back out with them to hear.

They swam out of the building and then down and around to the Arboretum's entrance, where they found a Sprite waiting for them. Marsee introduced them all.

"It is an honor to meet all of you," he signed. "What can I do for you, Translator?"

"Master Sea Turtle, I just gave Henry the drum, and he started playing almost immediately. I didn't even have a chance to send him the instructions. He says he's self-taught on a similar instrument. You simply *have* to hear him play!"

"Marsee, I'm not that good."

"Enough," she growled at Henry. "You're better than good, and you need to stop doubting yourself."

Henry just sighed in defeat.

"Well then, I'm intrigued and very excited to hear you play," Sea Turtle said. "Shall we find a comfortable place to float?"

Marsee nodded and swam inside.

Henry groaned again but followed, and they followed after him.

She noticed that Marsee hesitated slightly as they passed a section and then turned in another direction. *That area must be where she was when she was kidnapped,* Little Flower thought and glanced up at her mother. Her mother had caught the hesitation, too, and frowned. So, too, did the guards as they somehow went from invisible to menacing in a heartbeat.

The Arboretum itself was stunning, and she fully intended to return here to explore if Marsee was up to it. *Perhaps as long as they avoid that one section?*

Marsee swam until she found a small protected area that was unoccupied. Everyone arranged themselves comfortably on the netted seats that surrounded the area. The guards took up positions on either side of the path, and anyone who had been swimming in their direction suddenly decided they had somewhere else to be. She was really starting to like that benefit from having their fuzzy shadows follow them everywhere.

There were several low tables near the seats. Henry carefully removed the drum and set it on the table where it stayed. It was heavy enough not to float away. Then he pulled out the mallets, sighed, and stared at the drum.

"What's the matter, Henry Curtis?" Sea Turtle asked.

"Henry, please, and I'm not used to playing in front of others. My father didn't approve of me playing, so I've always hidden it. I wouldn't even sing in front of anyone until GrandFather caught me singing one day and said how much he enjoyed it."

A look passed between her grandfather and Henry, and she smirked at them. *Love at first sight? eh?*

Her grandfather rolled his eyes at her.

Sea Turtle nodded, seemingly oblivious to the interaction. "Try to forget we're here. You're among friends, and there's no judgment. I only wish to help you learn if you're interested in improving your skills, although I do admit I am curious to hear what has impressed the Translator so much."

Henry nodded, took a deep breath, and hit the drum a few times, trying to get used to the motion in the water. The water rippled with each note. He frowned and hit it again, then started running through the various notes as he had before, but after only a few, he floated off as his body reacted to the motion.

"Well, that makes things a bit more challenging," he said as he readjusted and scratched his head, trying to figure out what to do. The table was too far away for him to sit and play, and there was nothing for him to grab onto with his feet.

Her mother shifted over as she was closest, reached out, and grabbed him gently by the belt around his waist, holding him in place as she dug her claws into the dirt floor for added traction.

Henry nodded his thanks and tried again. This time, he didn't float away, and after a few times through the notes, he started playing and singing. It was the same song he'd played earlier, but it sounded completely different underwater, right, in a way she couldn't explain. The jewels sparkled with the vibration, giving the animals the appearance of movement, as Marsee said they would. It was fascinating to watch.

Henry was completely absorbed in his playing.

After a few moments, she looked over to see Sea Turtle's reaction. He kept his skin blank, clearly trying not to distract Henry, but his reaction was still quite obvious. *Add slack-jawed with astonishment to the list of universal constants,* she thought, highly amused.

When Henry finished playing, he looked up to see what Sea Turtle thought.

It took Sea Turtle several moments to blink out of his astonishment and flash a blue so brilliant that it made her blink. "You've seriously had no training?"

"Nothing formal," Henry replied. "I had a small drum once, but nothing like this. I just played whatever I heard. I can't read music. I tried teaching myself once, but it didn't make sense."

"What do you mean you played what you heard?" Sea Turtle asked.

Henry shrugged. "Just that. I'd hear a song I liked and played it."

Sea Turtle swam over and held his webbed hand out for the mallets. Henry handed them over.

"I'm going to play something. I want you to repeat it if you can."

Henry nodded, so Sea Turtle played a simple tune and handed the mallets back.

Henry repeated it exactly, at least as far as she could tell.

Sea Turtle took the mallets back and played a far more complex and beautiful piece. The creatures on the drum danced and swirled in his skilled hands and she wondered what it meant.

"Can you play it again?" Henry asked when he was done.

Sea Turtle did, and then Henry took the mallets back and started playing. As far as she could tell, it was no different than what Sea Turtle played, maybe a little hesitation in a few spots, as if he wasn't sure he remembered it correctly.

Sea Turtle's tentacles went slack. "How...How did you do that?!" he flashed, too astonished to even remember to sign. Marsee translated. "That was a master-level piece, and you played it flawlessly. There's no way you could have heard it before, either. I just finished composing it."

Henry shrugged. "I don't know. I just can."

"Is this normal for your species?"

"We had very talented musicians on our world," GrandFather answered. "I've heard of a few people who can do what Henry just did, but it was very rare."

"Incredible! Do you compose your own music?"

"No, I tried a few times, but it always ends up being bits and pieces of other songs or embellishments. That's why I always got in trouble as a kid. My Papa said I was copying other people, that it was stealing, and that music was for girls anyway. He wouldn't let me play after that."

Sea Turtle flashed several colors that Marsee translated as surprise, astonishment, and disbelief, with a touch of anger on Henry's behalf. "Can you embellish the piece you just played for me? Perhaps add the first song to the second?"

"I can try. I don't want to steal your work, though," Henry replied.

"It's not stealing if I ask you to. Go on. Give it a try," Sea Turtle said.

Henry shrugged, thought for a moment, and began playing. The two melodies wove in and out of each other to form an entirely new piece and then changed keys which completely changed the mood and tone. Henry lost himself in the music as he became comfortable with the drum but then suddenly stopped, as if he became aware of himself and his audience again.

Little Flower had never heard anything like it before, and it almost made her cry. To hear something so beautiful and unexpected come out of what had happened to her and her family helped to soothe some of the anxiety and rage that had consumed her most days since. And for that to be one of the first pieces of music she'd heard since regaining her hearing, far more priceless than the jewels that decorated the drum.

Sea Turtle didn't speak or move.

Henry slumped. "Was it that bad?"

Sea Turtle's skin flashed with astonishment at the question. "Bad?! Henry, the only bad thing I've heard tonight was that your Papa stopped you from playing. He was a fool, bordering on abusive. That piece was exceptional! When it comes to this instrument, you are far better than I will ever be, and I've been playing for over two hundred standard years. I learned tonight that you're a very short-lived species. If I might ask, how old are you in standard?"

"About seventeen," Henry replied.

"Seventeen!" Sea Turtle exclaimed. "When I was your age, I could barely play the first piece I had you try, and badly at that! Henry, there is no doubt in my mind that you are a master musician and one of the most gifted I've ever had the pleasure of hearing. Have you played anything else besides the drum?"

Henry shook his head, stunned and overwhelmed with the praise. "Not really. I didn't have my own drum until after I moved away from home, but my older sister had a toy piano. It could play maybe twenty-four notes. I only got to play with it a few times before my father stopped me."

"Hmm. I wonder if your skills transfer to other instruments. Either way, you have a perfect ear for music. Between your singing and the drum, you never hit a bad note. I can teach you how to read music and the theory around what you just did without trying. I can also teach you to play the drum in such a way that it speaks our visual language and how to harmonize and play with others if you're interested."

Henry blinked with surprise but nodded, a grin slowly creeping across his face. "I would really like that."

Sea Turtle smiled and flashed his happiness. "Good. I know you have much to do to prepare for the council meeting, but when you have time, come find me in the market or send me a message."

"Did your piece have meaning?" Little Flower asked.

Sea Turtle nodded. "Very much so, Councilor. It started as a prayer to our gods of the deep to find you all safe and unharmed but has since changed with the events that unfolded and now begs for your full recovery and removal of the darkness that infects our people. It has felt...unfinished until today, but I now know I was not the one destined to finish it. I was not worthy or skilled enough."

He then turned to Marsee. "Translator, I know your people are not religious, but I believe I have witnessed what can only be described as a miracle. Like the cloak you wear, this drum sat in a place of honor in our family, in this case, since before our people joined the Consortium. I don't know how much of our history you're aware of, as we rarely share it with off-worlders, but the heroic deeds of my grandfather are what ultimately brought our world peace following our last war."

"I only learned of that war recently, but I don't know much of anything about it," she replied. "Not even the cause."

"The specifics don't particularly matter. The society we had then no longer exists, but the animosity is still there, whispered in the dark. People who once had the power to do as they pleased are now constrained by the rules and laws of the Consortium, and overall, I think we're a better people for it. Perhaps something like what happened to you was always bound to happen, a test of that peace, of our honor. The vigil was as much an affirmation of the people's desire for peace as it was a prayer for your recovery."

He looked down at the drum and ran a hand lightly over it, making it sing a beautiful, if muted, chord. "My grandfather never had the chance to play this drum as he died from his injuries shortly after it was presented to him by Clear Seas' grandfather in honor of his actions. Until the other day when I played for you, outside of ensuring that it was maintained and tuned, it has only ever been played once, at my grandfather's funeral by his mentor, a master musician unparalleled by any our world has ever known. That is until today. I have a recording of that performance that I will share with you. It was the last public performance his mentor ever gave and one of such unparalleled grief and love, for it was his mentor's daughter that he saved, my grandmother, who he loved enough to face an entire army to free."

"That's the story you played for me the other day in the market?" Marsee asked, gasping with realization.

He nodded. "I fell in love with music the first time I watched that recording and have worked my entire life to feel skilled enough to play that drum. That you found joy in my unworthy performance means more to me than you'll ever know. I have wondered and prayed for years for guidance on what to do with this drum and knew the moment you swam up to my humble booth and asked that you were meant to have it. When I think about all that you have all survived to make this moment happen, it can only be the will of the gods for my grandfather's drum to end up here where it was always meant to be, with someone who exceeds the skills of my great grandmother, and who has given me an answer to my prayers with his masterful performance. I think perhaps because this world needs the joy and light that music can provide in our times of darkness, just as much it needs its Leviathan Slayers and heros. Thank you both for all you have done to protect our worlds. May the gods protect you in return."

Sea Turtle bowed and flashed the silver and purple to Marsee before doing the same to Henry. "Until later?" he asked Henry.

Henry replied with a nod and finally managed to remember his manners and blink his way out of his shock to sign a 'thank you' before Sea Turtle turned and swam off.

Little Flower looked over to Marsee, who looked smug, exhausted but smug.

CHAPTER 26

Marcus: Blubber Fish

Marcus rubbed at the headache forming behind his eyes and shut the folder he was investigating. He didn't have the energy to deal with yet another person involved in this moons' forsaken coup and the day had been one extreme after another. He rubbed at his eyes and then checked the time. The others, save for Clear Seas, had called it quits shortly after the final transport of councilors from the Ice Planet had arrived.

Preliminary evidence showed it was nothing more than an accident, and he prayed that would remain the case. They purposely kept the accident quiet, as they didn't want to scare the population any more than they already were. A few on the Council had chosen to take their own ships, as happened with every meeting, and those were all scheduled to arrive periodically throughout the next day. Concerningly, most of those councilors were all on the pile, and he wondered if they would even show up.

The ships with most of his own Council were scheduled to arrive within the next half hour. Communication had been established, and there appeared to be no issues with those ships. Protocol stated he should be there to greet his Council along with Clear Seas, but he wasn't sure he could do it, not and keep his mask in place, especially if he saw Trisha. He glanced at the pile where he had placed her file earlier, his investigation complete, and her fate sealed.

"I think maybe protocol can be dropped this one time," Clear Seas stated, seeing his expression. "We've had quite the day and you look like you could use a break."

"Wouldn't that just give away that something was up?"

"Marcus, my old friend. Your mask is good, but it's not that good. I know there's someone you don't want to see. Who is it?"

"Trisha Westrose," he replied with a heartbroken sigh. "I asked her to be my partner once, a very long time ago. She turned me down. She had four cubs in her first litter and two in a second litter about twelve years ago. I know the whole family. I've known her my whole life. We remained friends, or I thought we did. I never once thought she felt any animosity towards me or my family, but she sent Rip everything I told her about my brother and his family the last time we went out for lunch. I don't know how to handle that level of betrayal or how I'm going to bring myself to kill her."

Clear Seas flashed his sympathy and understanding. "When I figure that out for myself, I'll let you know. Why don't you go hide in the Archives or something? If anyone asks where you are, I'll say you probably lost track of time with your nose stuck in a book. No one would find that the least bit suspicious."

Marcus rubbed at his eyes again and nodded, not even bothering to acknowledge the teasing. A few minutes in the Archives would do his soul good.

"Now, if you don't show up tomorrow morning, I'm sending the guards in after you," Clear Seas continued.

"Then I clearly need to find a new place to hide. I wonder how difficult it would be to renovate Marsee's cave," he mused. "Getting bookshelves down there might be a challenge."

Humor bubbled on Clear Seas' skin as it was becoming a common joke among all of them. "I've considered it myself. The renovation would be easy enough. It's the neighbors you have to worry about. They screech at all hours of the day and night."

Chuckling, he swam over to the door to head out with Clear Seas and found himself face-to-face with Kendra, her paw raised to knock on the door. He stepped back to let her in.

"What's wrong?"

"Per your orders, I've finished interrogating each member of the Ice Giant Council. Councilor Breydhik is missing. If you're not aware, he has two sons, Brack and Enowk. Per the manifest, he was originally on the ship that arrived this afternoon."

"Is there any sign of a body in the wreckage?" Clear Seas asked.

"No, sir. We did find his tablet, though."

He frowned. "The missing escape pod?" he asked, looking at Clear Seas.

Clear Seas shrugged. "I figured it had been used to evacuate everyone to the other ship. Send someone back to the crash site and have them check for a damaged or drifting pod."

"Yes, sir," she replied and started to leave but he stopped her.

"I want visual confirmation of every member of the Council by to-morrow afternoon at the latest and confirm everyone on the council ships landing tonight before they leave. That includes pilots and staff."

"Yes, sir. Is there anything else?"

He shook his head, and she left. He turned to Clear Seas with a sigh and found him shaking his head and humor bubbling on his skin, It was not what he expected at all.

"I suppose this is my fault," Clear Seas explained. "I might as well hand in my resignation once Apakna finds out."

He raised a brow. "How is this *your* fault?"

Clear Seas explained the conversation he'd had with Apakna earlier in the day, his skin shifting to flickers of embarrassment.

He chuckled and shook his head. "You *should* know better than that. I'm not religious, and even I'm not stupid enough to challenge the gods." He paused for a moment and then pulled out his tablet. "I'm go-ing to have Lowell see if she can track down Breydhik and inform us if anyone on the Council meets in groups of greater than four outside of the Council Building. It might not mean anything, but if anyone is planning something, it might give us a warning."

Clear Seas nodded and waited while he sent the message and swam out with him.

He left Clear Seas at the platform and continued on to the Archives. Hanging up his drone at the entrance, he made his way in and immediately felt himself relax. The Archives looked and smelled completely different from the ones back on Saber, but surrounded by books, whatever their shape and form, it still felt like home.

As he often did when he didn't have a project in mind, he swam at random until a book or two caught his attention and then made his way to his favorite reading nook. Setting his stack on the table and clamping them down so they wouldn't float away, he grabbed the first one, climbed into the lounging net, and wiggled until he found a comfortable position to read. Within moments, he was lost in the book.

"Some things never change. Do they?" a voice chuckled, and he looked up to see Trisha peering down at him.

His heart fluttered as it always did when she was around, but he quickly reminded himself of what she'd done. "Can you blame me? I needed to forget the horrors of this past week for a few minutes."

Sadness briefly coated her eyes, but then her tail curled as her expression drifted to his book. "I had no idea you were interested in the life cycle of the blubber fish."

He shrugged. "I wanted something as far away from politics as I could find."

"That would certainly do it," she replied. "So, how's your niece?"

"They're *both* recovering, thankfully."

"Did Marsee...?" She stopped and looked around. "You know?"

He frowned, wondering why she was digging. "She had some minor issues when she first woke after being rescued, but the guards were with her, and she responded to sign language once she realized she was safe. She was severely hypothermic, so we're not even sure if it was truly an issue or not. Outside of night terrors, we haven't seen any problems, and I was there when she woke after the second attack. There wasn't even the slightest issue."

Trisha's ears flicked back in surprise. "I saw the guards outside her suite. They're not letting anyone down that hall, not even members of the Council."

He glared at her in warning, wondering what her intentions of even trying to approach Marsee were. "They're for her protection, not anyone else's. Both Kendra and I have tested her. She's on a watch, of course, but I have a feeling she'll manage."

"I'm not questioning you, just surprised. I can't imagine anyone going through what she did and not having issues. Do you think there are others involved? Is that why the Council has been restricted from accessing her account?"

He pursed his lips at the implied mistrust as he tried to figure out what to say without giving away that he knew of her involvement.

"You do, don't you?"

"My family has been attacked several times now. I'm not taking any chances with their safety or the safety of those we rescued. Marsee's account was compromised by a member of the Council and used to track her down and hurt her. Until we have worked out a solution to protect her, it will remain off-limits to all but the Senior Council. I assure you the important information has been shared."

She nodded and looked away, and an unreadable expression crossed her face. "I know Rip didn't like your family, but I never thought he was capable of something like this."

He'd been a councilor long enough to know that people were capable of anything, although it was rarely premeditated, at least amongst his own species, or so he'd once thought. But she had intentionally shared information that Rip had then used to harm his family. He wondered if this was an apology or an attempt to deflect him from finding the truth. "So, were you looking for me for a reason?" he asked instead.

She gave a half smile. "Mostly, I wanted to check in on your family, but I did want to give you a little grief for pushing off those projects we talked about before you go and sequester yourself again."

He snorted, pretending to be amused. "I'm sorry, Trisha. I wasn't exactly planning on a member of the Council kidnapping my family and attempting a coup when we first put them on the docket. If we have time, we'll bring them back on."

"I know," she replied. "I'm still going to give you grief about it."

He plastered a fake smile on his face. "You wouldn't be the Trisha I know and love if you didn't."

"Ruffling your fur has been a constant joy in my life. Why do you think I finally joined the Council?"

"You mean it wasn't because of my wit and loving renditions of the Charter?"

She snorted, and her tail spiraled with humor. "Oh, my dear, Marcus. Only you would put 'loving' and 'charter' in the same sentence. Well, I'll leave you to your enthralling study on the life cycles of the blubber fish. Try not to stay up too late. You have a planet to run in the morning."

"Please don't remind me," he said with a shudder, only half faked.

She grinned at him and swam off.

He watched her until she was out of sight, wondering just why she'd searched him out, and prayed it was nothing more than pretend concern for his family, although his gut said far more was involved. It was a long time before he looked down at his book, and with a heartbroken sigh, he set it aside, no longer in the mood to read.

CHAPTER 27

Marsee: The Moons are Made of Honey

Marsee's tail curled with happiness as Sea Turtle swam off, relieved that he was truly happy about the gift of his grandfather's drum. She'd struggled hard with accepting it in the first place, although it did remind her that she needed to finish the translation of the Night Flyer and send him a copy as she'd promised. It was the first time since killing Rip that she even felt good enough to try.

She'd known Henry was exceptional the moment he started playing, but she'd been blown away by the full extent of his talent. The piece he'd created was one she would never forget. When he'd been able to recreate Sea Turtle's piece, she'd pulled out her tablet and recorded his next performance, knowing it would be phenomenal, but it had exceeded every expectation she'd had. She sent it off to Ellie and her siblings, knowing they would appreciate it. If her books had been popular and needed additional servers to handle the load, Henry's music would break them.

It would need a professional recording, of course, far better than her current tablet could handle, but she could just imagine a duet with Sea Turtle. *It would be glorious!* she thought, her tail spiraling at the very idea. Part of her also hoped that this might distract Ellie from her threats about having her record with Henry. That thought still made her shudder. *Sing for the public? Never.*

Henry shook his head, still shocked by the praise he'd received.

After he wrapped up the drum and put it back in the bag, they made their way back to their suites at Little Flower's slower pace. Everyone was talking excitedly, to Henry's obvious embarrassment, but she wasn't paying much attention to the banter. Her brain was still wrapped in the music. She didn't even notice the long walk back to her room.

The music had somehow soothed the sharp and broken edges of her missing instinct, and for a brief moment, the ever-present feeling of hollowness had gone away. She hadn't been positioned well enough to see the prayer Sea Turtle had claimed the piece had spoken, but as she walked, she imagined his song being a thread made of rainbow light, sewing the shards of her broken soul back together again. She chuckled at the silliness of that idea, but it didn't stop the notes from dancing in her brain.

She blinked in surprise when they arrived back at their room, as she had little memory of the return trip. After the guards finished checking for monsters and villains, GrandFather entered with them, long enough to retrieve his gift and give them all hugs goodnight, but Henry thanked her again for the drum and left without entering. A few minutes later, she heard the sounds of him playing across the hall and sighed with happiness as she listened. It was by far one of the best things to have come out of her ordeal, second only to her partnership with Little Flower.

Her parents stayed to visit through the evening meal. Thankfully, her mother decided that her swim to the market earlier qualified for most of her pickle torture. To be fair, she had completed two of her three laps, although they did work on some exercises for her paw, which was still stiff and numb. She was glad to see that her parents had made amends and let out a huge sigh of relief when her mother informed them that she'd officially retracted the paperwork to end their partnership.

After they left, Marsee helped her new partner get her daughter ready for bed and set Hope down in the small crib that had been provided for the room. *Her partner! Her daughter!* Her tail spiraled tightly at that thought. They were such beautiful words and something she'd never thought she'd be able to say. She'd been so sure she'd lost all chance of that ever happening.

What an incredible and unexpected day, she thought. A partnership, finding out she wasn't doomed to suffer her injuries forever and had a long life ahead of her, cookies *and* fire sticks, (even if the fire sticks did burn their way out, leaving the Trauma Center), her sister drawing again and managing so much better than she'd been the last time she'd seen her, exploring the market and being able to pamper her new daughter and partner with everything they wanted, her parents back together, and all of it wrapped up with such glorious music. She knew this would probably go down as one of the best days of her life.

She purred and gently stroked the soft fur on Hope's head as her daughter snuggled in with Fuzzy. Little Flower leaned up against her, and Marsee wrapped her tail around her sister's side as they watched their daughter fall asleep. When Marsee was sure Hope was out, she turned and rubbed her face against Little Flower's in a show of affection and then padded her way over to the waste room to get ready for bed herself.

"I think my sense of pain must be returning. My skin is all tingly now, not just my paw. It doesn't hurt, but it feels weird." Marsee rubbed up against the sill, trying to stop the sensation, then stood up on two feet to get at a spot in the middle of her back. She had to press really hard to make it stop. Groaning in relief, she flopped back down to all fours and made use of the incredibly awkward raised waste hole the Huemans used and then rubbed against the door again as that feeling was already back.

"Maybe it's the salt from the seawater on your skin. Try taking a shower," Little Flower suggested.

Shrugging, figuring it was worth a try, she jumped in the sonic shower and giggled at the feeling. "Nah, somethings different. The shower tickles!"

When she made her way out of the waste room, Little Flower had stripped out of her clothing and climbed onto the bed. Marsee froze.

Her sister's face said she was happy, but her body language and scent said she was anxious and nervous. She was sitting on the bed with her knees tucked up and her arms wrapped around them, with her head resting on top. She frowned, wondering what her sister was nervous about, but then saw her safety equipment on the bedside table.

The day hadn't been entirely good, she realized. She'd nearly attacked Little Flower and Hope and had actually attacked an honor guard in her sleep. No wonder her sister was nervous.

For Marsee, that was honestly far more terrifying than losing control of her instinct. She'd been able to fight that. There hadn't been anything she could do while she was asleep. She hadn't even known what she was doing or had done until she'd woken up, and she was terrified it would happen again. She didn't understand how Little Flower could be so calm about it. It was one thing for her sister to suffer night terrors as there was little she could do to hurt Marsee. Marsee, on the other claw, could easily kill both of them without even trying.

She walked over and picked up the safety equipment but just stared at it.

"What's wrong?" Little Flower asked her.

"I'm worried. What if I try to attack you again?"

"You won't."

"You don't know that. How many night terrors have you had, and it's been months since you were first attacked."

"Because you didn't even twitch this afternoon while you slept or last night. Music has calmed you twice now, and I know what not to do. Mama is right next door if something happens, and the guards are outside."

"What if I..."

"You won't. But, if it makes you feel better, I'll take Hope and lock ourselves in the waste room until you wake up if you start sleepwalking again."

Marsee nodded, still not entirely convinced, but she desperately needed her life to return to normal, and she slept so much better when Little Flower was beside her.

Little Flower shifted to sit on the edge of the bed and caressed the side of her face, which felt so good she instantly started purring. It felt so different without her fur.

"I trust you, Marsee. Now get into bed. I'm cold, and I need my not-so-furry blanket."

Marsee grinned at her sister's show of confidence and put her protective gloves on. She climbed onto the bed and shifted so Little Flower could snuggle in next to her. She wasn't quite ready for the muzzle. It was a little uncomfortable, and surprisingly enough, for the first time, she didn't feel like falling asleep. She curled around her new partner and rested her head on Little Flower's side as she often did and breathed deeply. "Mmm, you smell really good tonight. My sense of smell must be returning, too."

"It looks like your fur is starting to grow back in, too. That's probably why you're so itchy."

Marsee peered closely at her arm and sighed with relief to see a hint of fuzz. "Oh, good. I was worried it was never going to grow back."

Little Flower started tracing one of the scars on her arm, and it sent shivers through her body.

"Did that hurt?" Little Flower asked.

"No. Not at all, but I could feel what you're doing all the way down to my tail. It feels good to finally feel something again, even if it feels different."

Little Flower kept absently swirling, still deep in thought, even though the smell of anxiety had vanished.

She purred in contentment as she enjoyed the novel sensation. Her sister fiddled with her fur often, and while she'd always enjoyed the attention, it had never felt like this. It made her wonder if it was her new senses or just the really short fur. Either way, she didn't want Little Flower to stop. Her sister had once said that she needed physical contact to counteract the isolation of her time in the Agency. She'd accepted that without question but hadn't really understood. Now she did. She never wanted to leave her sister's embrace again. Ellie and her father had both tried to hold her together, but it wasn't the same. They weren't the missing piece to her soul.

Eventually, her sister shifted so she was lying on her back. Her head now rested on Little Flower's stomach and her sister shifted to patting the back of Marsee's head like she had earlier.

Marsee groaned. "Oh, that feels so good."

Little Flower stopped and smelled of embarrassment.

Marsee frowned and looked down at her. "Why did you stop?"

Little Flower didn't answer right away, and her sister's skin flushed with color. "I never expected I would need to give the talk to my partner," she mumbled. "I'm not sure how to explain."

"The talk?" Marsee asked, confused. "So, there is something bothering you?"

Little Flower's skin blushed even more. "Do you remember the conversation we had that day in the garden after reviewing the footage from the Agency?"

Marsee thought back. They'd discussed a lot of things that day.

When she didn't reply, Little Flower sighed again. "You mentioned to me that when you mate, touch feels really good. Touch is a big part of our mating process, too, when done right, or so I'm told.

Marsee's head snapped up, and she sniffed again, now thoroughly concerned. "Are you in heat? Is that why you smell so good? I thought Mama had you on hormone blockers. Do you need to go home and find a mate? There's only GrandFather and Henry here. Maybe Mama could..."

"I'm fine!" Little Flower replied quickly, smelling even more embarrassed. "I don't need to find a mate, and I have no idea if I'm on hormone blockers or not. I thought I wasn't having a cycle because I was nursing Hope, but that doesn't matter. My species doesn't have to be in heat to enjoy the act of mating, remember? We can mate at any time we want, even if we're not fertile. I'm worried because you told me that your mating is pheromone-based, and you've been rubbing against everything tonight, including me, and just told me I smelled really good. I stopped because I don't want to cause any complications, if that's what's going on or...if you didn't want to do that."

"I'm far too young to be in heat," Marsee said dismissively. "I won't be fertile for another twenty years, at least, and you heard Ammond this morning. He said in-betweeners rarely react to pheromones, but you *do* smell really good, like better than chocolate chip cookies right out of the oven good, and I really liked how that felt. I liked how it felt this morning, too. It's probably just my fur growing back or the changes in my senses. If you don't mind, I'd really like you to keep doing what you were doing. I've felt so alone and scared and...numb. I've been rubbing up against you because I need to keep reminding myself that you're here and safe, and really my partner, and that I'm not alone and stuck in that horrible cave."

Little Flower nodded and hugged her but seemed lost in thought.

"If you don't want me to rub up against you, I'll stop," Marsee said, trying to figure out what was bothering her partner.

Her sister didn't answer for a while. "No. I like how it feels, too. I feel safe when I'm in your arms."

"So what's bothering you? Wait...you said '*want* to do that.' You *want* to mate with me?" She was sure she was misunderstanding. That wasn't physically possible. They were two different species.

Little Flower sighed and tried several times to explain before the words would form. "No, it's...well...maybe? Partnerships for my species typically include mating, but I know that's not the case for you, and I don't want you to think that I had any expectations of that with our partnership. It's just...I...I don't think I'll ever feel comfortable mating after he..."

Her sister started shaking, and Marsee hugged her tightly, understanding immediately.

Little Flower leaned into her for several long moments before calming and pulling away. "But I'm also curious to know what it's supposed to feel like when done with someone who isn't trying to hurt you."

Marsee nodded. "Why wouldn't you be curious? All you've known is pain. I've wondered what it's like, too, ever since Mama told me. We obviously can't mate and have cubs together, but if you want me to touch you, I can. I don't know what your species likes. I don't even know what *my* species likes. I just want you to be happy, but I don't want to hurt you, either. I know how hard it is for you when someone touches you there."

Little Flower's scent changed from embarrassment to anger rather than the fear that she expected. "That's just it. He's dead, yet he keeps hurting me. I don't want him to have any control over me, but I'm scared. I'm not attracted to anyone, but what if I did find someone I wanted to mate with? I don't want to end up punching him in the nose the first time he touches me."

Marsee chuckled. "Yeah, I imagine that wouldn't go over well."

Her sister smiled but didn't laugh.

Marsee reached over and caressed the side of her sister's face. "You deserve a mate, preferably one who loves you as much as I do, who treats you with kindness and understanding, and you deserve to enjoy your matings. If there's anything I can do to help you get over that fear, I want to try. I want you to be happy in every aspect of your life."

Little Flower leaned into her paw, closed her eyes, sighed, then took a deep breath, opened them again, and nodded. "Just not down there. I...I don't think I'm ready for that."

Marsee looked at her gloves and considered. The material was fairly rough, and her sister's skin was delicate. She took the gloves off and set them aside. She didn't have any fur on her paws right now, but the pads of her paws, normally rough and calloused, were soft and smooth from all her time in the water and the nano wash she'd been treated in. Carefully keeping her claws sheathed, she traced one of the swirling lines on her sister's arm.

Her sister closed her eyes and sighed.

Marsee's nose flared as her sister's scent intensified, and she felt weird sensations in her own body. *She must be in heat,* Marsee thought, wondering why she was reacting to it, but she didn't stop. She was curious, too, and the amount of trust Little Flower was showing her right now made her heart ache with love.

Little Flower reached up and caressed the side of her face again, and Marsee felt it through her whole body.

"That feels good," she said, tracing another line that traveled down her sister's side. "How does this feel?" Marsee asked when Little Flower shivered.

Little Flower just murmured and laid back on the bed, lifting her arms to make it easier for Marsee to access that area.

I'll take that as a yes, she thought, paying some attention to the spot that had made her partner shiver. Then Marsee continued on down the outside of Little Flower's leg to her foot, circled the base of the paw and the spot that she knew was sensitive. Rather than being ticklish, it made her partner flex her feet and breathe harder.

How very strange, she thought. She continued up the inside of the leg but switched to the other side after circling her knee, avoiding the area that she knew her sister didn't like to be touched and had asked her not to. She was watching closely for any signs of nervousness or fear.

She followed the other leg and made the same circle pattern on the other foot before returning up the side of her body, tracing her arm and then along her neck and around her ear. Little Flower seemed to really enjoy that area, so she focused on it for a bit until she suddenly found herself fighting the urge to bite. She stopped immediately and scrambled back, nearly falling off the bed in her fear and haste to get away.

Little Flower sat up. "What's wrong?"

"I don't know," Marsee replied and swallowed hard. She would have been fully poofed with fear if she had any fur left. "I had this sudden urge to bite you, but... I don't understand. Kendra said it was gone and wouldn't ever take control again, but it felt just like before. Oh Gods. No. I thought it was gone! You'd better leave before I hurt you."

"I'm not leaving," Little Flower said and scooted closer. "You didn't bite me, so it obviously didn't take control. Maybe this is part of how your species mates. That would be consistent with lions from Earth. I don't know if you're the same, but you did seem to have more of a reaction when I rubbed at the back of your neck earlier. If you're worried, try turning your instinct on and see if anything happens."

"But what if I…"

"You're not going to hurt me. I trust you."

Marsee swallowed hard and cautiously tried, but nothing happened. "Nothing. The only thing that ever changes is a feeling of hollowness where my instinct used to be. Rowena says that's phantom pain."

"Well, there you go. It's probably normal, but we can stop if you want. Your safety is far more important to me."

"*My* safety?!" Marsee exclaimed. "You're the one that could get hurt. I nearly bit you!"

"You are not going to hurt me. You've never hurt me." Little Flower scooted even closer and turned around so her back was facing her. "Go on. Bite me."

Marsee stared, absolutely convinced her sister had lost her mind. "You *want* me to bite you?!"

"You need to prove to yourself that you can control your instinct, and I trust you not to hurt me."

"You've lost your moons' forsaken mind."

Little Flower chuckled. "Probably. Ammond has been mucking around in there quite a bit lately. Go on. Show me just how much I can trust you not to hurt me. It felt good when you touched me there, too."

"You're sure about this?"

Rather than answering, Little Flower spun around, grabbed her by the head, and then touched her on the lips with her own.

It made Marsee's own lips tingle. She rubbed at the strange feeling after Little Flower pulled away.

"We call that a kiss. When we mate, we do that all over each other's bodies, and according to the book I just read, sometimes we even bite. Not enough to break the skin. Go on." Little Flower shifted her head back, exposing her throat. Only instead of seeing Little Flower, she remembered holding Rip by his neck in her jaws.

"No," Marsee said, nearly panicking again. "I can't. Not there. That's how I killed him. I don't want to hurt you, even accidentally, and..."

Little Flower nodded and caressed the side of her face again. "I understand. I won't have you do anything you're not comfortable with, but if you ever want to face that fear, I trust you won't hurt me."

She purred and calmed with the sensation that washed over her and the complete lack of fear she smelled. Her sister truly did trust her. "I thought this was about facing *your* fears?"

"I want you to be happy in all aspects of your life, too," Little Flower replied, repeating her words back to her. "And I imagine your future mate would appreciate you not uh...not doing what you did to Rip. That would be a very short mating."

Marsee chuckled and considered. She didn't want Rip to have control over her either. She wasn't confident enough to try biting her sister, but if this was part of her partner's mating practices, she wanted Little Flower to feel comfortable with the contact, and if it was part of hers...

Curiosity won. Slowly, carefully, she leaned in and pressed her lips against Little Flower's neck in a kiss.

Little Flower tilted her head, exposing her neck, but otherwise didn't move. They stayed there as she breathed in and out, savoring the smell but worried that she'd get that urge to bite again. Suddenly, Little Flower shivered.

She pulled back immediately. "Are you scared?"

"No, your warm breath on my neck did all sorts of things to my insides. It felt good."

Marsee smiled at her sister and kissed her on another spot, a little lower on her neck. Then, she began traveling around her sister's body, paying extra attention to anywhere Little Flower reacted, especially whenever her scent increased, until she was almost back where she'd started.

Little Flower lifted her head, exposing her throat, and Marsee felt that urge to bite again. She didn't move away this time but instead allowed herself to feel it, to try and understand it. It wasn't quite as strong as it had been before or even the same as it had been with Rip, yet her sister's scent was just as delectable, and it made her feel things she'd never felt before. She pulled back and looked down at her sister, seeing only trust in her eyes. Marsee caressed the side of her face with her palm.

Little Flower leaned into it for a moment, then turned and then kissed the base of it. "Try rubbing at my breasts. He hurt me there, but it's supposed to feel good."

Marsee rubbed her thumb gently across her sister's lips in response and then made her way down to her sister's breasts and gently circled them for a while, watching as the nipples tightened to form a little button like they did when she'd nursed. She rubbed at them. Her sister's breathing picked up, and she started to squirm. More of that delicious scent wafted through the air, and Marsee's purring intensified.

She was going to repeat the process, but Little Flower surprised her by grabbing her paw and moving it down to the area she'd avoided.

"Are you sure?" Marsee asked as she smelled hesitation.

Her sister nodded and shifted, spreading her legs apart.

Marsee gently circled the area, going closer and watching and sniffing for any sign of the panic her sister normally showed when she'd had to be touched there to clean her during her convalescence.

The hesitation vanished, and her sister groaned and grasped at the sheets on the bed.

"Do you want me to stop?" Marsee asked. Her scent said no, but she wasn't taking any chances.

Little Flower shook her head, arched her hips, and pushed against Marsee's paw. Marsee traced up and down, and every time she came near the tiny bump of skin at the top, Little Flower jerked.

"Does that hurt?" Marsee asked.

"Moons, no. That's where it feels the best."

Taking that cue, She focused her attention on that area. Little Flower's breathing increased, as did her scent. She had never smelled anything so intoxicating in her life, and it made her skin shiver. The scent wound around her like the music had, so thick she could almost see it. Suddenly, Little Flower's muscles all tensed.

She stopped immediately. "Are you okay? Do I need to get Mama?" Marsee asked, both surprised and concerned at the reaction. *Is she having some sort of seizure?*

"Better than okay. I think that's what's supposed to happen, at least from any description I've ever read," her sister said after a moment. "Don't stop."

Marsee stroked that spot again, and soon, her sister was groaning with the strain of her tense muscles and whatever sensation she was feeling. Her sister had said it felt good and not to stop, so she didn't until her sister collapsed to the bed, gasping for air.

"Did you enjoy that?" Marsee asked.

"Mmm hmm," Little Flower replied with a happy smile.

The scent faded, but Marsee wanted more. She didn't know what else she wanted, but her insides squirmed with the need for more of that delicious, intoxicating scent, and she was tired of fighting it. She leaned down close and sniffed, then moaned as her sister's scent nearly overwhelmed her. "Bright moons, you smell incredible. I've never smelled anything like it." She rubbed the side of her face along her sister's lower belly and groaned, wanting to rub harder, but she didn't want to hurt her sister either.

Her sister reached up and started stroking the back of her neck and along her ears.

Marsee's groin spasmed and twitched, which surprised her, but she didn't pull away. If anything, it intensified the need for something she didn't understand. She knew she could stop if she wanted to. She just didn't want to.

"If I smell good to you, I wonder what I taste like." Little Flower reached down and stuck her paw between her legs and then brought it back up and ran it under Marsee's nose and then across her lips.

Marsee half purred, half growled with need, and opened her mouth, panting hard. She didn't understand why she was reacting this way, or even reacting to her sister, but she didn't want the feelings to stop. It felt so incredibly good, especially against the days of pain she'd endured and the past week of absolute nothingness. Little Flower stuck her paw right in her mouth, and the sweet aroma bloomed. It was better than fire sticks, better than chocolate chip cookies and fried star fruit combined, but there wasn't enough on her sister's paw.

She shifted on the bed until she was below Little Flower, laid her nose right between her sister's legs, and slowly licked at the strongest source of the smell.

Little Flower moaned and grabbed at the sheets again.

Marsee had never tasted anything so delicious before and she wanted, needed more. She licked again, and Little Flower's back arched, and Marsee's lower region spasmed again.

"A little lower," her sister said.

She adjusted and found a small opening, and her sister gasped. More of the sweat liquid pulsed, and it was all Marsee could do not to bite. She licked again and again and again, delirious with the smell and taste.

Her sister's muscles spasmed again as she grabbed the sheets on the bed and then collapsed with a gasp.

She didn't stop, wanting more and feeling like she was on the edge of something herself, but Little Flower shifted her body slightly away from her attention. She stopped immediately, worried she'd gone too far, and lifted her head. "I'm sorry. Are you okay? Did you like that?" Marsee asked.

"Oh wow, did I ever. It just gets better and better. Thank you."

"Of course. I want you to be happy. Whatever you need, if I can give it, is yours," Marsee said.

"Good, but it's my turn now."

Marsee's ears flicked back. "But I'm not in heat."

"So. You seem to be enjoying yourself. Let's see what you like."

Marsee nodded, curious to see what else there was to experience. She was not even remotely ready for it to end if Little Flower was still interested.

Little Flower sat up and started tracing her fingers along Marsee's face again, then along her sensitive ears and the back of her head and neck. As she ran her soft fingers along Marsee's scruff, tingles shot down to her toes, making her claws curl.

"Ooh, right there," she said, leaning into it. It was too soft, though. "Harder."

Little Flower increased pressure, but it still wasn't enough.

"More," she growled and arched her back to press against it.

Little Flower thought for a second and then shifted and leaned over and bit her.

Marsee groaned as warm sparks sent shivers down her spine, and her paws twitched.

"Well, I guess that answers that question," Little Flower mumbled through her mouthful.

"It feels incredible, but somehow it's still not enough."

Little Flower considered and grabbed her scruff with both hands and bit harder.

Marsee whimpered to keep from roaring like she wanted to and risk calling the guards in.

Her sister stopped immediately.

"Moons, no. Don't stop. That felt...I don't know how that felt. I don't have the words to describe it, but I don't want you to stop. Please!"

Her sister bit her hard again, then shifted, biting lower, sending a whole new wave of feeling through her.

She started kneading the bed as her sister shifted lower along her spine. Each nip sent tiny bolts of electricity down to her toes and groin, but unlike what Rip had done to her, this felt so incredibly good, and she never wanted it to end. She flipped over to lay on her back, slowly kneading the air as her sister shifted to run her paws along her belly and up and down her arms as she'd done to her and then circled each of the dozen tiny nipples that had been uncovered by her lack of fur.

She gasped when Little Flower leaned over and licked one and then sucked. *Would cubs feel like that?* she wondered briefly, but then Little Flower gently bit it, and she moaned. *Why does that feel so good?*

"Do you like that?" Little Flower asked.

"Mmm hmmm," Marsee rumbled in reply.

Little Flower did the same with each nipple, and as she did, her lower region started to ache but not in a painful way, more of a wanting, needing feeling. Little Flower moved her paw lower, rubbing them along the insides of her back leg, and the ache grew until she squirmed with need.

"What is it?" Little Flower asked.

"I don't know. I feel like I need something. My groin aches but in a good way. It feels so good to feel anything, and this is so outside of anything I've ever felt before."

Little Flower shifted so she could reach lower and around to her backside.

Marsee's paws flexed and kneaded the air, and she felt her lower region spasm hard.

Her sister ran her fingers along the underside of her tail.

She had an uncontrollable urge to roll over and stick her haunches up in the air, with her tail to the side, so she did. Little Flower shifted onto her knees and started running her fingers up and down the area that she'd only ever thought was meant to remove waste until her mother had explained that's where her cubs would be born and how they used to mate naturally when they had males. The area was spasming hard now. Her sister reached back and grabbed her hard by the scruff and then stuck a finger inside her.

It was all Marsee could do to keep from roaring out how good that felt. The last thing she wanted was to wake Hope or have the guards storm inside to see what was going on. She knew she would die from embarrassment if that happened, so she grabbed a pillow and bit it, trying to keep from making a sound.

Little Flower moved her fingers in and out and around until she could barely stand it anymore and then her muscles started spasming like her sisters had, and a wave of feeling washed over so intense it made her gasp. Her sister kept going, and wave after wave after wave crashed over her until her legs gave out, and she sprawled on the bed.

"By all that is holy under the brightest moons in the universe. I had no idea anything could feel that good," she said when she could finally talk again.

"The feeling's mutual," her sister said.

Marsee lay there panting hard, more winded than if she'd walked the hallway several dozen times but feeling far better than she'd ever felt in her entire life. "Mama said touch felt good, but I had no idea that's what she meant. I don't understand, though. I shouldn't be able to do that. I've always been told I won't have the parts to mate until I go through my growth spurt, and if I were in heat or reacting to someone in heat, I shouldn't be able to stop either, not without pheromone blockers anyway."

"Ammond said in-betweeners sometimes reacted. How often can the males mate?" Little Flower asked.

"As often as they want, I'm told," Marsee said. "As long as there's a female in heat."

"Well, there's your answer," Little Flower said.

"So you are in heat?"

"No idea, but if I am, then we'll know for sure when my period starts. I'll check with Mama on the hormone blockers in the morning."

"Moons, I hope we don't have to wait for you to come off the hormone blockers to do that again. That's assuming you want to," Marsee said.

"I do, but if that ends up being the case for you, then we'd better take advantage of it. It's still early." Little Flower reached down and fondled herself briefly before running it along Marsee's nose again, and all thoughts of exhaustion vanished.

After another repeat of the experience on both their parts, Marsee had to call it quits. "I'm exhausted, and if we do any more, I think my new heart might explode." She was honestly surprised it hadn't.

"Well, we can't have that, but I think we're going to have to order some new pillows. There isn't much left of this one," Little Flower teased, holding up the punctured and soggy pillow Marsee had used to muffle her growls and tossed it to the floor.

Marsee chuckled and closed her eyes as Little Flower snuggled in beside her, and was asleep before she remembered to put her protective gear back on.

CHAPTER 28

Quinn: Fire Brigade

By the time Quinn returned to his own suite, the heat lightning Nazari had mentioned was flickering on the horizon, and he slept fitfully. Nightmares plagued his sleep and left him feeling unsettled when he suddenly woke several hours before his alarm was scheduled to go off. The suns weren't up yet, but there was a glow on the horizon out his window, signaling their approach.

He listened, hackles raised to the world around him, and frowned when he heard footsteps on the roof above him.

Grabbing his harness, he gave a low whistle to alert Lark, who was still on duty in the outer room, listening for potential problems with Nazari. She quickly joined him, and he pointed to the roof, where he could now hear the murmur of voices.

He quietly slid open his balcony door to better hear what they were saying. The air hit him, dry and hotter than he'd ever experienced this late at night and thick with smoke. He frowned as he scanned the area, but he didn't hear sirens and couldn't tell where the smoke was coming from as it seemed to be everywhere.

Was the building on fire? he wondered.

"We're going to have a very bad day," a voice said above him, and he recognized Healer Morningstar's voice.

"That's for sure," another voice said. He didn't recognize that one.

Relieved it was someone authorized to be on the roof but worried about the situation, he quickly scampered up the side of the building to join them, rather than taking the stairwell, as it was quicker, and found Brice and Illana staring off in the distance with their backs to him.

"What's going on?" he called out.

They started slightly and turned in his direction.

"Sorry, I didn't mean to scare you."

"Fire," Illana replied and pointed in the direction they'd been looking. "A really big one."

He swallowed hard as he trotted up and realized the glow he'd thought was the sun wasn't. A line of fire burned along the entire horizon.

"The wind shifted, and it's picking up," Illana stated. "We've got maybe two hours before it gets here."

"What do you need?" In this situation, she was in charge. He'd worked with the fire brigade in Council City before on many occasions, but he'd never dealt with a brush fire and certainly not anything this big.

Illana frowned as she stared at the horizon, then opened her tablet to show satellite footage of the area. The fire was even bigger than he realized. Hundreds, if not thousands of leagues had already burned. "I've got New Hope under control. The shields and fire break we dug last night should protect the compound, although smaller fires, heat exhaustion, and smoke inhalation are still a risk. Additional resources are standing by in Sand Dune, but there are at least a dozen homes between the current front and New Hope."

"You can't put it out?" he asked.

"A fire this big? No. The best we can do is try to keep it away and put out any small fires that get too close. Most homes will keep all vegetation away from their compounds for just this reason. Fire is a common occurrence this time of year. That's why everything is built with stone or other fire-retardant materials. "

"The families have all been sent warnings and instructions to evacuate, but the people here are stubborn," Brice stated. "Most will stay to try and save their homes and livelihoods. This family here has a herd of chenzies. They won't be able to evacuate without leaving them behind, and they won't leave without them, no matter how bad it is. They're family."

"Understood. We'll get them out."

He turned to leave, but Illana stopped him. "Honor Guard, wait."

He turned back around.

"Something's not right about this fire."

"Explain," he demanded. "Nazari said the conditions were ripe for a brush fire."

"It is, but I'd bet my tail fur, this fire isn't natural." She held up her tablet again. "The burn pattern is all wrong. Most fires start from a single point, with lightning being the most common cause." She pointed to another location. "This is where that ship went down. See how it fans out from that point?"

He nodded. "Is that what started the fire?"

"No. But that's what bothers me."

She zoomed out so he could see the entire path. "That fire was out days ago, stopped by this stream and access road here."

She shifted the map slightly. "This is where the current fire started. I've checked that area twice with aerial scans to confirm there wasn't a rekindle. That fire was cold."

He frowned, trying to understand what he was seeing. There were several fan-like spots starting on the other side of the stream. "Multiple lightning strikes?

"Possibly," she replied. "But when have you ever known lighting to travel in a straight line and start next to an old access road, one that I happen to know hasn't been used in years? The family that used to live out that way moved to Sand Dune a few years back when their aquifer failed. I think someone used the other fire to hide what they were doing. Most wouldn't question a rekindle, but I've been fighting fires for two and a half centuries out here. I know how they work, and I don't take chances with people's safety."

"Arson," he growled and stared out at the fire as his hackles raised. "This is a trap."

"Quite likely," Illana replied and zoomed out again. "There are three other smaller fires around New Hope, all currently going away from populated areas, but based on where the wind was coming from last night, at least one of them would have hit us. Those are far more random and could have been caused by lightning, but my gut says otherwise."

He felt instantly torn. If he went to help evacuate the others, he would be leaving New Hope unprotected from a potential attack, and with a fire that big, they might need everyone's help to save the compound.

"Prepare the compound, then evacuate everyone to the tunnels. It'll be safest there, and the air is filtered. I'll leave half a squad with you and take the rest to check on those homes."

He didn't wait for their reply but turned and ran for the side of the building where he'd climbed up. Grabbing the edge of the roof, he flipped around and landed neatly back on his balcony, where Lark was waiting for him.

"You heard?" he asked.

She nodded. "I take it my squad is staying?"

"It is. You're in charge until I get back. We'll be running dark. Whoever set this is most likely listening to the comms to see if we head out."

"They'll see the ships."

"True, but we're not taking the guard ships, and they won't know who's onboard." He unclipped his tablet and sent urgent orders to the rest of the guards stationed in New Hope. Once sent, he ran to the waste room, knowing he wouldn't have time later.

Three...two...one..., he thought to himself as he squat down over the waste hole, waiting for the fire warning to go off. He scowled and shrugged when nothing happened, but the gods, as always, had a sense of humor. The moment his thoughts shifted, it went off. Even though he'd been expecting it, the blare made him startle and pin his ears as it went off on every tablet in the building.

"Gods, I hate that noise," Lark muttered.

He snorted. There wasn't a sound he hated more. It was the bane of every guard's existence. Other sounds were louder or more painful. Thunder was the worst, but this one was dissonant, designed to get people's attention and wake them from the dead of sleep. But for him, it meant people were going to die if he failed.

Business done, he grabbed the emergency kit out of his pack and bolted out the door with Lark, who had done the same, only to practically run into Nazari, who had her paw up to knock on his door, and a still-sleeping cub in her other arm.

"I heard your conversation. I'm coming with you," she said before he recovered from his surprise.

"You have a cub and the creatures here to take care of," he said and started to push past her.

To his surprise, she physically stopped him. No one did that. Interfering with a guard on duty was a serious offense. He raised a brow and scowled as he waited for an explanation. Friend or not, she had better have a good excuse.

"The animals are all in the barn at this time. They'll be fine, but you'll need help with the chenzies. They'll be nearly uncontrollable without my help, and the people won't leave them behind even if you order them. Please, you have to trust me. You need me."

He pursed his lips, considering, then took Sari from Nazari and handed him to Lark. The cub started crying immediately. Nazari pinned her ears, but her focus hardened. That convinced him. He knew she wouldn't leave Sari behind if she didn't believe this was the right thing to do, and he had to admit he had almost no experience with chenzies. They didn't live in his district.

He bolted down the hall with Nazari right beside him. When they hit the bottom, Nazari bolted into the Trauma Center rather than following him out. He skidded to a stop and followed after her to the supply closet, where she tossed several more emergency kits at him and then started pulling other items down off the shelves and clipping them to her harness. The moment she was done, she grabbed two more emergency kits, clipped those to her harness as he had done, and nodded for him to lead the way.

He bolted out of the Trauma Center at a full run with her right beside him and people dodging out of the way. When they arrived at the shuttle bay, the rest of the guards were there, waiting as ordered.

Nazari didn't stop but bolted for the biggest of the ships. With a flash of sign, he split his guards into four teams, tossed them his emergency kits, and followed Nazari onto her ship. Nazari already had the map up and engines on, and a moment later, they were in the air. She punched the ship as fast as it would go to the home Brice had mentioned had the herd of chenzies. "Have your other guards hit the homes closest to the fire first. They all have shields now. That was a condition Little Flower insisted on with the transfer of property to New Earth, but they might need help getting ready. We'll take Serin's compound."

He relayed the information, and the other three ships veered off toward their destinations.

"Serin's family?" he asked.

"She has a partner, Pep, and five cubs. Rowin, Jowin, Sowin, and Dowin are nearing adulthood. Seventeen or eighteen, I think. Peep is an only cub. He's four. They have eleven chenzies, one of which is less than a year old."

"Is this the one mentioned at Little Flower's trial that GrandFather saved?"

She nodded and a few minutes later, they were landing outside a compound. There was no shimmer of a shield yet, nor was there any sign of activity around the compound preparing. Nazari tried calling them from the ship, but no one answered. His hackles rose. Something was wrong. He just knew it.

The moment they landed, a small cub bolted out of the compound and ran right into Nazari's arms, fully poofed and crying hysterically.

"What's wrong, Peep?" Nazari asked, "Where's everyone else?"

The cub tried to speak but failed, too scared to form legible words around his hiccuping sobs, although he was trying.

He squatted down next to them. "Do you know sign language?" he asked.

Peep nodded and raised his hands to speak. "Mama didn't come home last night with the herd and Papa's in Council City. We tried calling for help, but we couldn't get ahold of anyone. The others went out looking for them when we got the alert about the fire. I told them not to, but they wouldn't listen to me." Peep turned and looked back at the fire that was clearly visible from here, and he started to shake with fear.

"You did the right thing in staying here," Quinn said. "You're safe, and we'll find the others. Which way did they go?"

Peep pointed in the direction of the fire. "Mama went that way, but everyone spread out. They were worried she missed the compound in the dark." Peep pointed out the other directions.

"Go inside, turn the shield on, and stay there until we get back," Quinn said.

Peep grabbed Nazari tightly and buried his head in her fur.

"I know you want to come with us," Nazari said, hugging the cub. "But it's safer for you here right now. Besides, they might come back while we're looking and need you to let them in."

Peep let go with a sob and ran back into the compound, but Quinn wasn't watching the cub. He was staring at the fire, trying to decide which way to go.

"The herd can travel fifty leagues in a day in search of food," Nazari said. "There's another compound in that direction. Serin might have decided to hole up there instead of trying to make it back with the herd, but she would have contacted her children if that was the case."

"Peep said their comms are out. I don't like it." Quinn hit the one on his harness. "Squad Two, report."

Nothing.

"Command, report."

The silence was defining. Even if the Mana's comms were out, he should still have access anywhere on the planet through the ship's comms. He unclipped his tablet and confirmed he had a signal, but calls to both New Hope and Command failed, too.

He growled. There were only four of them on the ship, and five missing people, along with a herd of chenzies and this was looking more and more like a trap.

He motioned to one of the guards. "Stay here with Peep."

The guard bolted for the compound.

He turned to the last remaining guard. "Take the ship and see if you can find the cubs from the air. Nazari and I will track the herd on foot.

"Sir," the other guard replied, and he and Nazari took off as the ship rose behind him. The smell of smoke was so thick he was having a hard time filtering it out, but he locked on to the smell of the herd. It wasn't hard once they left the immediate area around the compound. Grasses taller than Nazari on all fours surrounded them, but a clear path had been eaten, showing the way.

"Keep your instinct off," he told Nazari.

"Not going to happen," she replied, easily matching his pace. "If I lose control, so be it, but there are people out there that need my help and someone apparently trying to hurt them. I won't be able to live with myself knowing I could have given more if they died."

He looked over and grinned at her. Her eyes glowed red from the light of the fire, showing her instinct was on, but she was still speaking, which was good enough for him. "You start having any problems, shut it off and keep it off, understood?"

She nodded, but her focus was entirely on where she was running.

They'd been running for a good five minutes when she suddenly veered into the grasses around them.

"Where are you going?" he asked. "The chenzies went this way."

"Yes, but Rowan went this way, and someone or something is following her."

He sneezed several times to clear the smoke from his nose and immediately recognized what she was smelling. He swore, honestly surprised he hadn't picked it up before as the scent was strong. "Ice Giant," he muttered.

She pinned her ears and growled but kept running. She put on a speed that he was hard-pressed to keep up with until she suddenly stopped and backtracked, circling. "If they've hurt her, I will tear them to shreds."

"We'll need them alive for questioning," Quinn replied.

"Oh, they'll live long enough for that," she promised but sighed with frustration a moment later. "I can't smell the trail anymore. Can you?"

"No. The smoke is too thick. Someone must have picked them up. The Giant wouldn't be able to survive long in this heat."

She growled again and took off back the way they came.

They were nearly back to the chenzie's trail when he came to a sudden stop and face-planted into the dirt as something caught his foot and pain exploded in his back leg. He screamed and rolled into the grass just as a stunner shot nearly hit him.

"Trap!" he yelled. "Stunner!" He tried to back away, but his leg was caught, and whatever held him burned with every movement. He unclipped his own stunner and waited for them to appear.

"I was hoping it would be you," a deep male voice said, hidden by the grass and smoke, but his ears fixed on the location.

"Why me?" Quinn asked, hoping to distract them from Nazari and get a clear shot.

"Revenge, of course," he replied. "You killed my boys."

A shot fired, hitting him in the hand that held the stunner, knocking it from his hand and turning it numb.

Quinn hissed, shaking his hand. "You won't get away with this."

"Probably not, but at least I'll know you'll be dead."

He tried to grab the stunner with his other hand, but another shot fired, just missing him.

The Ice Giant stood up, stunner pointed towards him, along with the cub they'd been following, held tightly by the scruff in his other hand. She hung limp and unmoving in his grasp. "Move, and I'll kill her."

He stopped moving, hands raised. "I'll do what you want. Just let her go."

"You'll do what I want anyway," he said and fired at him again. This time, hitting him in the other leg.

"What have you done with the others?" he asked through gritted teeth until the pain subsided as his leg went numb and useless.

"They're probably extra crispy by now, just like you did to my boys and just like you will be when the fire gets here." The giant raised his stunner to fire again.

He braced himself for the shot, but just as the Giant fired, Nazari pounced on the Giant's back, and the shot went wide, just barely missing him as he rolled out of the way. Hissing with the pain of whatever was wrapped around his back foot, he scrambled awkwardly to his feet to try to help Nazari subdue the giant that was a good five feet bigger than she was. Before he could, there was a loud snap, and the giant hung limp in her mouth.

"Stop. He's dead!" Quinn called out.

Nazari looked up with a growl, eyes wide and feral. "Leave him," he signed. "He's dead. The others need our help. So do I. I'm hurt."

To his utter astonishment, she turned off her instinct and immediately focused on the cub curled up in a tiny ball at her feet. "Rowin, are you alright?" Nazari asked.

Rowin looked up, recognized Nazari, and bolted into her arms, instantly sobbing.

"Shhh. You're safe. He's dead," Nazari said. "Are you alright?"

"Yeah," the cub said through a hiccup. "But Mama's missing."

"I know," Nazari said and unclipped her scanner. "Are you sure you're not hurt?"

"My back is sore where he held me, but I'm okay."

Nazari scanned Rowin anyway, found the cub unharmed, and then came over to check out his trapped leg and growled at what she saw. "This is a nasty piece of work."

It took them a minute to figure out how the trap worked. He hissed with pain as it disconnected, and his leg started bleeding heavily. She scanned his leg. "You're lucky. Nothing's broken, but it will need suturing. Several of these cuts are pretty deep."

"No time for that now," he said. "Slap a bandage on it, and we'll go. My hand is still numb from the stunner. I won't be able to open the package."

While Nazari patched him up, he turned to the cub. "Rowin, is it?"

She nodded. "Yes, sir." Outside of the occasional hiccup, she'd regained her composure.

"Were there any others with him?"

"I didn't see anyone," she replied. "But I didn't even get a good look at him until after he caught me."

"What about a ship?"

She shook her head. "I saw some fly over a few minutes ago, but they didn't stop. They were heading towards the fire."

"Those were probably ours," he replied and stood the moment the bandage was on, testing his weight on his injured leg. It hurt, but it was manageable. The stunned limbs he could handle. They trained for that, but Nazari hit him with several hypo shots before he could move, and both the pain and numbness receded.

"I've given you a general antibiotic as well. Who knows what kind of nastiness was on that trap."

He limped over to the corpse and rolled it over before pulling out his own scanner. "Councilor Breydhik."

"Why would a councilor do this?" Rowin asked.

"Because I killed his children a few days ago. They were working with Rip and were part of the kidnapping attempt on Little Flower."

"If they were working with him, why wasn't he arrested?" the child asked.

Quinn sighed. "Because all we had were their names. They're fairly common on the Ice Planet, and we weren't even sure they were their names. They could have been trying to incriminate him. Come on. We don't have time to waste." He picked up the cub and carried her, worried that there were other traps.

The sun was up on the horizon now, but it was hidden by the thick black smoke. The only real light came from the fire, giving everything an eerie red tinge.

They made their way carefully back to the main trail, checking for further traps, and found two more. How they had missed them on the way in was anyone's guess unless they'd been laid after they'd run through. Once they were back at the trail, he stopped them. "Rowin, I want you to head back to your compound as quickly as possible. Tell the guard there what happened and follow her orders."

"Yes, sir," the child replied and took off running without hesitation.

He watched her for a moment and then took off in the other direction, pushing the pain of his injury to the background. "How are you doing?" he asked Nazari.

"Livid, but I'll manage," she replied. "Sorry about not keeping him alive for questioning. When I saw him with Rowin, I..."

"It's alright. You did the right thing in that situation, and we're alive because of it. I would have done the same. He was bigger than both of us combined, and in a fight, he could have easily overpowered us."

She grunted but said nothing as she kept running. They hadn't gone more than a quarter league when she suddenly grabbed him hard by his harness and yanked him back. "Watch it!" she hissed as she continued to drag him back.

"What is it?" he asked. He couldn't see anything.

She pinned her ears and stared at him. "You weren't lying, were you? You don't know?"

"I know quite a bit, but not about whatever it is that's got you so scared."

"Get your stunner out," she ordered, then, once he had, she tossed something ahead of them right where he was about to step.

The sand exploded, and several enormous twelve-legged crawlies appeared.

He blinked in surprise and felt his fur stand straight up. He had no idea what it was, but he had a feeling it was quite deadly.

"What are you waiting for? Shoot them!"

He blinked out of his surprise and did as ordered.

"Those ugly little things are sand spinners. If it stings you, you've got maybe five minutes to make it to help before you're unconscious. Within 30 minutes, your insides will start to turn to mush, and if you're lucky enough to survive, you'll likely lose a limb or be stuck with permanent neurological issues, including seizures, memory loss, and more. Sniff it, commit that smell to memory, and avoid it like an outbreak of spotted fur. Avoid anything that looks like a stick lying on the ground, especially where there aren't any trees. That's its nose, the only thing it keeps above ground." She unclipped something from her harness and handed it to him. It was bright orange. "If someone gets stung, inject them with the entire vial and get them to help quickly."

He did as ordered but then allowed her to pick their way through the nest. He made sure to step only where she did.

Once they were through, they ran for a good half hour or more before a ship flew over and landed next to them. "We found the other cubs. They're all back at their ompound. One of them said you were attacked?"

"Councilor Breydhik," Quinn replied. "Keep searching in the air for the herd. We'll continue on foot."

They ran for another fifteen minutes as the ship began a search pattern in the air above them before Nazari skidded to a stop again, sniffing hard, ears forward.

"More..."

She gasped and pulled him off the path, covering his mouth with her paw.

A moment later, he swallowed hard as a massive Heela Monster lumbered past. It was the biggest creature on the planet at more than five times the size of an adult female Saber, and while not fast, it was known to attack everything with a spit that burned like acid. Stunners didn't phase it, and it was nearly impossible to kill. To his surprise, the moment it was past, Nazari took off in the other direction.

He pulled out his stunner, expecting it to attack her, but it kept lumbering along. He reclipped his stunner and followed after her. "That was stupid," he whispered when he caught up.

"It's more worried about escaping the fire than hunting," she replied. "But I wasn't taking any chances. We're going to see more creatures fleeing the closer we get." She wasn't wrong. Dozens of creatures crossed their path or ran past them, many of which could have easily attacked, but they all completely ignored them, terrified by the fire.

Five minutes later, the trail veered, heading away from the fire. He sighed with relief as they were already far too close as it was. He could easily hear the crackle of fire behind him. The ship above them noticed and adjusted their search pattern to follow. A minute later, they began flashing their lights to get his attention and circled for a moment before landing. Nazari noticed and pushed the pace even harder. His injured leg screamed, but he ignored it as he did his best to keep up.

The ship was further away than he thought, but they eventually crested the top of a hill. Below them, he could see the faint outline of the ship through the smoke and hear the low bleating of the chenzies.

The herd was milling under a bandala tree that had been badly trampled, leaving a muddy pit around it that they had used to cover themselves. The guard on the ship approached them as they arrived. "If there's anyone here, they didn't answer my call, and I can't get close to the herd."

"They're terrified," Nazari said. "Let me handle it. See if you can find signs of Serin. She has mostly white fur, with a patch of black over one eye."

Quinn nodded and took off, leaving the other guard to help Nazari.

"Drop the cargo hatch. I'll get them onboard," he heard her say as he made his way around the tree, giving some distance to keep from spooking them.

"Hey, there. Remember me? I'm here to take your family to safety. That's it. I know it's scary. I'm not going to hurt you. I bet you're hungry. You've eaten everything around here and made quite the mess. It was very smart of you to cover yourself in mud, but I wonder why you haven't run back to your home."

That thought made him frown. Had Breydhik done something to the herd to keep them there?

Nazari kept up a gentle commentary as she continued her approach. "That's it. You're so brave to let me approach. Are you hurt?"

He made a full sweep around the tree but couldn't pick up anything over the smoke and smell of the chenzie's fear. As he came back around, he saw that Nazari had attached a rope to the harness around the head of one of the creatures, and he wondered where she'd kept that, as he hadn't seen it before.

"That's it. I bet you're feeling sleepy now. Come on. You can sleep safely on the ship."

The creature's head hung lower than the others, and he realized she must have given it a sedative. To his surprise, the rest of the herd followed behind, and she had no problems loading them on the ship. He stayed back, not wanting to scare them, and watched as she sedated all of them. One by one, their knees buckled, and they lay down until their massive horns rested on the floor of the ship and their eyes closed.

"Well, that was surprisingly easier than I thought," he said to her when she was done.

"Like I said. You needed me. This will keep them sedated for a good hour. Fluffers, the matriarch, is missing, along with her new cub. They can't be far, or the rest of the herd would have returned to the compound rather than waiting. Did you find anything?"

"The smoke is too strong," he said, "All I could smell was chenzie."

She nodded and turned to the other guard. "Get them and the children back to New Hope. Brice and the older cubs will know how to handle them. I'm not going back without Serin."

Quinn nodded his approval, and the other guard ran for the ship while Nazari turned and began examining the area around the tree. Suddenly, she bolted off into the grass. He couldn't smell anything over the smoke, but he followed her without question. She knew Serin, which was a major advantage, but her instinct gave her an even bigger one. There were things it could do that he no longer could, and while he'd worked hard to make up the difference, he had never felt more unprepared for a mission than he did now. She'd been right. He'd needed her. If anything, he'd been more of a hindrance than a help.

"Serin!" she yelled over and over again as the fire crept closer. They didn't have much time left before it would be too dangerous to remain. It was already far closer than he liked.

"Wait!" he called out. "I think I heard something.

"Serin!" Nazari bellowed.

"Help!" came a faint reply, and they both bolted in that direction.

They found Fluffers first. She bellowed and reared on her four back feet at their approach.

Nazari waived him back. "Let me go first."

"Hey, Fluffers," she said calmly. "We're here to help. Remember me? I helped you give birth."

Fluffers snorted and waved her massive trunk as she swung her head from side to side.

"That's it. I'm a friend. I'm here to help. Where's your baby?"

Fluffers screamed again, and he heard the sound of a higher-pitched reply off to the side. He started to move in that direction, but Fluffers screamed and charged towards him.

"Raise your hands to appear bigger, and don't move or look away," Nazari yelled.

He did as ordered, but his tail was fully poofed as the massive creature, with very sharp-looking tusks, barreled towards him. Every fiber of his being said to run or move, but he held his ground, and to his relief, the beast stopped charging a few feet from him and reared again. "I'm not going to hurt you or child," he said. "I'm here to help."

When he didn't move, Fluffers snorted again and then reached out with her trunk and sniffed all over him. Her massive ears flopped forward, but then she turned and lumbered away in the direction he'd heard her cub.

Nazari walked up to him. "I'm impressed, Honor Guard. I'd thought for sure you'd pee yourself."

He chuckled as he started breathing again. "Let's just say it was a good thing I went before we left."

She grinned at him and trotted off after the chenzie, who led them, not to the cub as he'd expected, but to Serin, who lay in the grass with blood dripping down her head. The chenzie nuzzled Serin, who groaned up at them.

"Nazari?" Serin asked weakly. "What are you doing here?"

"Looking for you, obviously."

"I was attacked."

"I know," Nazari said. "I killed him."

"There were two..."

He swore and stood up on two feet to scan the area, but just as he did, a sharp pain hit him squarely in the middle of his back.

CHAPTER 29

Nazari: Sand Dune

Nazari's instinct forced her to duck as Quinn collapsed next to her. A second stunner bolt flew overhead, just missing her. Before she could even process what was happening, her instinct had her running into the tall grass to escape.

"Here, kitty kitty," someone called out in rough Saber.

No! she thought with a growl and fought her instinct for control. *I'm not leaving them.*

We make them follow us away from the others. Then we kill them.

She considered and agreed. *They won't last long in this heat.* She was honestly surprised that they were still conscious. She was having a hard time with the heat and smoke, and the Ice Giants couldn't handle the temperatures of her world for very long, even on a cool day.

Fluffers bellowed with rage behind her, followed by a loud scream. She couldn't tell who it was coming from, but she gave up on running away and circled back around, worried that the giant had attacked Serin or Quinn rather than chasing her.

She slunk as quietly as she could through the grasses until she could see into the small clearing that Fluffers had made around Serin and grinned when she saw that Fluffers had already taken care of the situation.

Relaxing slightly but still cautious, she approached. "Good girl, Fluffers."

The giant matriarch seemed quite pleased with herself. On the end of her sharp tusks was an impaled Ice Giant female, slumped over and unmoving. If the female wasn't already dead, she would be shortly.

Fluffers groaned, and her knees buckled, whether from the weight of the giant or an injury Nazari couldn't tell.

Cautious about a trap, she gave the Giant a sedative before scanning her. She wasn't quite dead, but there was no way she was making it back to New Hope for treatment, not without a stasis tube, and even then, survival was unlikely. With a yank, she pulled the female off of Fluffer's tusk and tossed her to the ground, fighting hard with her instinct that roared up again at the smell of blood.

Kill it! her instinct demanded.

She'll be dead in a minute, she thought, but her instinct was stronger than her control. A second later, she had the Ice Giant in her mouth, and with a vicious shake, her neck was snapped. She had to fight hard to regain control and not tear her prey to shreds like her instinct wanted.

She's dead. The others need our help, she thought, and it finally shut off. She didn't move for several moments, breathing hard through her fear and the dizziness of the adrenaline crash that followed.

"That can't be good," she muttered but dismissed her worry. She didn't have time for that, and instead scanned Fluffers, as that didn't require moving. Deciding that the chenzie must have been shot with the stunner, she gave the creature an anti-sedative and went to check on Quinn. He was sleeping soundly but was otherwise unhurt. She gave him a dose of the anti-sedative, too, and moved on to Serin, who was injured but not critically. A bad concussion that could easily be treated appeared to be the worst of her injuries. She blessed the gods that she'd grabbed the right equipment before heading out.

Quinn groaned and sat up as the stunner wore off.

She glanced back to find him rubbing at his head.

"Gods, I hate being shot. What happened?" he asked.

"Fluffers took care of things. The body, what's left of it, is over there."

Still rubbing at his head, Quinn walked over to examine the body while she treated Serin and explained what had happened so far. Serin sighed with relief to find out her cubs and the rest of the herd were safe.

Quinn returned a few minutes later, just as she was finishing treating Serin. "That was Breydhik's partner."

"I figured as much. Did you find the cub?"

"Yes. We have a bit of a problem there."

She helped Serin up and then followed Quinn. "Dark moons. How did he get down there?"

"Cubs have a way of finding trouble," Serin replied. "And so do I. He was running around without a care in the world when the ground gave out under him. I was trying to figure out how to get him out when their ship flew over. I waved them down, hoping, if nothing else, that they could fly for help. The next thing I knew, I was knocked over the head and shoved down in with him. When I woke, it was night, and they were gone, but it took me forever to climb out. I kept passing out. I got as far as you saw before passing out again."

She stood on two feet and looked back at the fire, which was nearly upon them. Even at a full run, they would be hard-pressed to escape, and the cub wouldn't be able to keep up for long. "There's got to be a ship around here. The Ice Giant would have passed out a long time ago from the heat if there wasn't and there was no sign of heat exhaustion when I scanned her. Quinn, see if you can find it. I'll try to get the cub out."

He nodded and took off as she examined the large hole and cautiously flicked her instinct back on to get its perspective. The world brightened around her again. The smell of smoke was nearly overpowering, but she was glad as it covered the smell of blood. Then, picking out a path, she cautiously started making her way down the loose sand of the sinkhole. Her footing slipped halfway down, and she skidded the rest of the way as more sand caved in around her.

"Are you alright?" Serin called when she came to a stop.

"Fine," she hollered back. "But I can see why it took you so long to get out."

The cub bleated as she approached but didn't seem scared. If anything, it was happy to see her and started rooting around for a nipple to nurse, even though she was a separate species. *It must be starving,* she thought. "Not now, little one. Your momma is waiting up above for you."

She grabbed the cub by its scruff with her teeth, knowing she would need all four paws to climb back up, but it bleated again, this time in fear, and wiggled hard to get away. Her teeth punctured the skin, and she tasted blood.

Mmmm, her instinct purred at the taste.

Not prey! she growled back. *Focus on climbing!*

Thankfully, it did. It was a grueling slog. Every foot placement was treacherous and brought more sand down on her. She was nearly halfway out when her footing slipped, and she growled with frustration at the lost ground. She was running out of time. Serin kept glancing behind her at the wall of fire quickly approaching and her fur was fully poofed.

We should kill it and go before the fire kills us all.

No, she growled, horrified by the very thought. *Either we all survive, or we all die. Fluffers won't leave without her cub, and Serin won't leave without Fluffers or the cub, and if we kill the cub, Quinn will kill us.* Her instinct thankfully backed off some, and she kept climbing.

She was almost to the top when she heard the sound of a ship landing nearby, and a moment later, Quinn appeared.

"I found the ship, but you need to hurry. The fire's almost here."

She rolled her eyes at him as her mouth was too full to speak, but the loss of focus was enough, and she slipped back several feet again. Growling in frustration, she dug her paws deep into the sand and leapt with everything she had. She almost made the ridge but started sliding back again.

Quinn lunged for her and grabbed her by her harness, stopping her descent, then dragged her and the cub back over the edge. She was seriously impressed by his strength. She doubted she could have done the same, and she was significantly bigger than he was.

The moment she let go of the cub, he ran straight to his mother, bleating the whole way.

"Thanks," she said, gasping for air.

He lifted her to her feet and pulled. "No time for rest. We need to go now."

That much was obvious. The fire was nearly on them. She was amazed that the chenzies weren't running off, but they had been hand-raised and trusted Serin, who was already leading them onto the ship, and Fluffers had more than proven her intelligence. She followed after and quickly sedated the two so they wouldn't get scared on the trip back.

Quinn took off the moment he was in the pilot's seat, but he frowned at her as she collapsed into the seat next to him, still breathing hard. She didn't dare treat the cub. Even though they were safe, her instinct wasn't shutting off.

"How are you doing?" he asked.

"I'll manage," she replied as she strapped herself in tightly.

He frowned at her again but said nothing the rest of the way back to New Hope. For that, she was grateful. She needed the quiet to focus.

They were halfway back when the other ship returned and circled around them. Quinn tried to contact them through the ship's communications, but nothing happened, so he flashed the landing lights and then made a sign to the other guard that she didn't recognize. She barely noticed. A few minutes later, they landed outside the barn.

Serin's family, a squad of guards, and several healers were waiting for them. She watched as the healers woke them and led them off the ship, but she didn't move. The smells of the barn and all the creatures inside had her instinct purring again.

Quinn frowned at her and hit a switch once everyone else was off. She heard the door shut behind her but didn't turn to look. "You're not okay, are you?" he signed.

She opened her mouth to speak, but no words came out, and he swore.

She half smiled at the inventiveness of it, but she wasn't really paying attention. Everything felt distant and strange. She was having a hard time remembering what she was supposed to be doing, although she had a feeling it was important.

"Fight your instinct, Nazari. You can beat it. I trust you. Everyone is safe. You were incredible today. If you can do all that, you can regain your control."

That's right. My instinct, she remembered and tried to turn it off, but she couldn't remember how. "Go," she signed, breathing hard as it felt like her instinct was scratching at the back of her mind. "I don't want to hurt you."

He didn't leave. Instead, he swiveled in his seat and took off.

She wondered where he was taking her, but she didn't care as long as it was far away from anyone she might hurt. Terrified she would slip further, she pushed hard at her instinct, using her feelings for Quinn as leverage, and regained a bit of control, just long enough to unclip her hypo and sedate herself.

What felt like a moment later, she found herself lying on her side in a building that looked like the Arena but was filled with strange objects. Quinn sat next to her, and as the grogginess of the sedative wore off, she realized they were surrounded by guards.

"Where am I?" she asked, glad to see she could speak again and honestly surprised that he'd even bothered to wake her up.

Quinn was just as relieved, and he relaxed slightly. "Sand Dune," he replied. "And thank you."

"For what?" she asked as she sat up and rubbed at her eyes, which refused to focus.

"For saving my life at least six times today."

"Six?" she asked. "I only counted five."

He lifted his paw to count, sticking out a claw with each example. "When Breydhik attacked, from the Sand Spinners and Heela Monster, from Fluffers, from Breydhik's partner, and from you."

"Ah. Fluffers killed Breydhik's partner, not me. Technically, I guess I did, but she was mostly dead before I finished her."

He grinned. "Well, whatever the number, I still thank you. That being said, we have a bit of a predicament."

She rolled her eyes. "That tends to be the case when you find yourself surrounded by a contingent of guards. Since you haven't killed me, I'm assuming I still have a chance?"

He nodded. "You have a choice. We can try to work with you, but you won't be able to return home for at least six months, and there's a very good chance you'll lose custody of your child. It's not safe for you to be around him anymore. The alternative is to join the Guard, transition, and go home if you survive."

She sighed, although she'd half expected it. "I'm not really interested in being a guard. I'm an animal healer, and New Hope needs me."

"I know. What's important is not what you do in the Guard. It's your oath. We can always use healers like you, especially ones as fearless and intelligent as you are."

"Why, though? Why do I have to join?" she asked.

"You'll be able to do what you did today without the risk of losing control and, quite likely, more. Those abilities could be used to take advantage of others."

"I would never do that," she replied. "Unless there's a bet with you involving a cobra chicken."

Several around the arena chuckled, and Quinn's tail curled. "I know. That's why I'm giving you this choice and why I didn't just kill you when I had the chance."

She smiled briefly in thanks but felt her instinct stirring as the effects of the sedative wore off. *Give up her child or her instinct?* Neither seemed like a particularly good option, but only one gave her a chance at keeping her cub. She nodded and opened her mouth to make her choice, but the words she wanted to say wouldn't form.

Her instinct growled and took control of her voice instead. ***"How dare you threaten to take our child from us!"***

Quinn stiffened, as did the guards around her, and she had a feeling there really wasn't a choice any longer. She wasn't leaving this room alive if she didn't figure out how to defeat her instinct.

Quinn stood and quickly backed up. "Fight it. Kill it before it kills you."

How do I do that? she wondered.

No! He said he wouldn't separate us if we remained in control. He lies.

But we're not in control. You forced me to kill that giant and tried to make me kill the cub.

I only did that to save our lives, just like I'm doing now. Separating us will kill us. We need to kill him before it's too late.

No, she thought. She didn't want to kill Quinn. He was her friend, and she wanted more than that. She wanted to partner with him.

Not anymore, her instinct growled. Any desire she had once felt vanished, and rage replaced it. Her instinct's desire to kill was so strong that she growled and rose to her feet, preparing to attack.

She fought back, and her body stumbled before she could leap.

"That's it, keep fighting. The sooner you kill it, the sooner you can go home to Sari."

"Sari," she whispered. That was her choice. That was what mattered most to her. She shoved hard at her instinct, trying to force it off.

It retaliated harder than she'd ever experienced. In an instant, it felt like she was shoved so hard that she was shoved entirely out of her body. Her vision swam, and instead of the arena, she found herself sliding down the bank of the sand dune again, only it was far bigger. It seemed to tower infinitely high above her.

It was the strangest experience. Even though she couldn't see anything but sand, she could still somehow see Quinn and a strange, ethereal, glowing version of herself circling each other on what was both the grasslands she'd been on earlier and the floor of the arena. Flames in the shape of the guards surrounded them, licking at their feet.

Confused but not sure what else to do, she dug her claws into the sand and started climbing back. Only peripherally did she feel her actual body as it launched toward Quinn with a feral snarl.

"No!" she growled and leapt with everything she had towards the bank. The distance seemed to shrink, far more than it felt like she'd jumped, but she still had a long way to go.

Pain wracked her as Quinn tossed her aside, knocking the wind out of her.

Her instinct roared with fury, and the sands shifted beneath her paws, making her slide back down the dune. She scrabbled hard, trying to slow her descent, and suddenly jarred to a stop as her claws found purchase on something under the sand.

Pain flared as she dug her claws in and kept crawling, one slow, painful step at a time. She didn't know why it hurt so much, but she ignored it. All she knew was that she needed to make it to the top of the dune, or she would die.

"That's it," Quinn signed. "Keep fighting. You can do this."

Her instinct leapt again.

Quinn shifted aside at the last second and sent her body flying through the air, only to land with another painful thud.

Gritting against the pain, she looked up to see her body sprawled, teetering on the edge of the cliff. She leapt again, but once again, she jumped short. Not wanting to lose her chance, she scrambled hard.

Her instinct turned to face her with a snarl and swiped sand at her. She turned her head to block, but the sand still got in her eyes and stung, and she slid back down the dune as she tried to wipe the sand away.

Nearly blind, she gave up on clearing her vision, ignored the pain, dug her claws back in, and kept climbing until she felt the top of the cliff under her feet and heaved herself back over. She wiped the tears away to see Quinn and the glowing version of herself circling each other again.

"Fight it," Quinn signed. "Remember Sari. He's waiting for his mother. Don't make him an orphan again."

Her instinct roared. **"You're the one taking him from us!"**

"No," Quinn replied. "I'm protecting him from you. You can't be trusted not to hurt him. Your instinct is too strong. It needs to die so you can be safe around Sari."

"I would never hurt him!" Furious, her instinct leapt at Quinn, catching him this time, and he screamed with pain as he writhed to get out of her grip. Other guards closed in, and she felt the fire burn at her feet as they tried to find a way to pull her off him as they rolled over and over again in the sand.

She knew that she was out of time. If she didn't act now, they were both dead.

She leapt on her instinct's back while it was distracted and bit hard and twisted, just as she had done twice that day. Pain erupted in her own mind, greater than anything she'd ever experienced before, but she didn't stop. She shook it hard until she felt its neck snap in her mouth and then, with a mighty heave, pulled it hard off of Quinn and threw it over the embankment. She watched it fly through the air and then felt herself fall back into her own body, where she still had hold of Quinn.

She let go immediately and backed away, horrified by the blood she saw on him and the taste of it in her mouth.

He lay unmoving on the ground. A pair of guards grabbed her and pulled her further away as a healer bolted forward to check on him.

"Oh, gods, no! Quinn!"

CHAPTER 30

Nazari: Oath Bound

Nazari waited in silence along with the rest of the guards as the healer checked on Quinn.

The healer injected him with something, and he gasped in a ragged breath, then another before turning his head to face her. Blood dripped down his neck and sides where she had hurt him.

She sighed with relief that she hadn't killed him, but the world spun hard on her, and she felt her legs give out. The guards laid her down on the sand, and another healer approached, scanner in hand.

"She's transitioning," the Healer said, but she barely heard them as her hearing and vision were fading rapidly. She wondered briefly if Quinn had been lying about the Transition and if she was dying, but she didn't care. Quinn and her cub were safe, and that was all that mattered.

"Quinn?" she whispered

"Yeah?" he croaked back.

"That's...six."

The last thing she heard as the world faded to blackness was the laughter of the guards around her.

She had no recollection of the passage of time, but when she woke, Quinn was sitting beside her, and everyone else had left.

"Welcome back," he said with a rather smug look plastered on his face.

Her relief from earlier was gone, replaced immediately by annoyance. She glared up at him. "That was some choice you gave me. Why do I have a feeling there really wasn't one?"

His grin widened. "There was, but you made the right decision."

"And if I had chosen to stay and train?"

He shrugged. "Then you'd be dead."

She frowned and carefully sat up. "You'd really have killed me if I'd chosen more training?"

"No. Of course not. The guards here would have worked with you, but I don't think you would have survived. You would have lost control the moment you lost Sari, and without him, you wouldn't have found your way back."

She paused to consider his words and rubbed at her head. She felt so different now, a shell of the person she'd been before, and it was so hard to think. Sari had been her choice, but she'd clawed her way back to save him, only she didn't feel the same way about him now. She still liked him, but the intense attraction she'd felt before was no longer there. She wasn't sure what she felt about anything anymore, much less him.

"That hollow feeling will ease eventually," he said. "It won't go away entirely, but you will learn to forget about it. Pain meds help."

She grunted and looked down at her harness to grab some but realized her harness was missing, then remembered he'd been hurt. "How bad did I hurt you?"

"I'll manage," he replied with another shrug. "My injuries were mostly superficial. They patched me up while we waited for you to wake. I am impressed. It's been a while since anyone has managed to land a strike, much less choke me out."

"Well, you were injured and stunned today. I'm sure that didn't help."

"Thank you for soothing my bruised ego, even if I will be teased about it for months."

"Serves you right. So, how long have I been out?"

"A few hours."

"Hours?!" she exclaimed. "New Hope?"

"They're perfectly fine. Shortly after we arrived in New Hope, the storm you predicted arrived and put out most of the fire. The fire brigade is dealing with the rest, but there's no longer a threat to New Hope."

She sighed with relief, but her relief only lasted a moment as his expression hardened.

"I know you probably want to return, but there's one more thing you need to do before I can let you leave."

"Join the Guard?" she guessed.

He nodded. "Do you, Nazari Jabri, swear that you will defend and guard the freedoms, rights, and lives of the people against all enemies and threats, before your family, the Guard, and the Council?"

That oath wasn't difficult to make. Her oath as a healer was similar, but she still wasn't sure about being in the Guard. It was better than dead, though, and she knew he would kill her if she said no. "I do."

He smiled briefly and continued. "Do you also understand that your life will be forfeit should you be found guilty of any crime, no matter how small?"

She blinked. There was a similar clause in her healer's oath about harming a patient, but this was so much more. "*Any* crime? What if I hurt someone by accident?"

"Accidents are just that, and if the other person agrees to reparations, it is not considered a crime. You also have the right, as any citizen, to plead your case before the Council, but if you should lose, the consequences are typically far more severe. I have rarely seen the Council give leniency, but it does happen. We'll teach you all the nuances, but you should know we can also tell when you're lying."

She pinned her ears and glared at him. "You're joking."

He shook his head. "No. I'm not. You'll learn how to do it yourself eventually. Guilt is a very ugly color, and your soul will twang as much as it did when you fought your instinct."

She squinted at him. "If that's the case, how did you fall for the bet with the cobra chicken?"

A wry grin escaped. "I didn't. I knew you were telling the truth about being bitten. I underestimated your abilities. It's rare that anyone can beat me, but you have, multiple times, in fact, and I'd be dead if you hadn't."

She sniffed, curious, and realized she couldn't smell anything. She frowned and rubbed at her nose.

"That will start to return in a few weeks."

"You can really tell when I'm lying?" she asked.

"Try me. Tell me several things I couldn't possibly know and throw in a lie or two."

She thought for a minute. "When I was an in-betweener, I found an injured baby doba. It's what got me interested in healing."

"True," he replied.

"I have a tiny black spot in the shape of a crescent moon at the base of my tail under my fur."

"Also true," he said.

"I feel like I'm going to throw up."

"False. You're slightly dizzy, but your stomach isn't upset. And yes, there's medical training that I think you'll find very useful in your line of work."

She raised a brow, intrigued. "You snored after you were knocked out."

"False," he replied with a grin.

"It's your word against mine," she said with a wicked smile.

"Libel is a crime," he replied, his face now serious, but his tail spiraled, recognizing that she was only teasing.

She glared at him, but he only raised a brow.

"I can tell that you believe me," he said eventually. "You're stalling. Do you understand the conditions?"

She sighed. "I do, although I'm rather terrified I'll make a mistake."

He smiled kindly. "We all make mistakes, but I have a feeling you'll be fine. You've more than proven yourself to me today, Honor Guard Jabri."

"Ugh," she replied. "Honor Guard Jabri. I can just imagine what my mother would say if she knew I was an Honor Guard now. She probably wouldn't stop laughing for a month and tell me it served me right for all the times I got in trouble as a cub."

He laughed and helped her up. The world spun, and he caught her before she could fall. "That will take some getting used to. Go slow and try not to move your head too quickly."

She grunted and took the anti-nausea tablet he handed her once she was steady. She frowned as it tasted off. Not that it ever tasted good, to begin with.

"That will return, too, along with your sense of pain and your re-flexes. You'll need to be careful for the next week or two, as you could easily hurt yourself."

"Now he tells me," she muttered and started carefully walking to-wards the door. "I feel like I've had one too many Fuzzle Knockers."

He chuckled. "After the day you've had, no one would blame you if you did. It might be a good excuse if anyone asks why you're walking funny."

That brought up a good point. "So what do I tell people now?"

He considered her point. "The Seniors will have to know, but it might be best if you moved to Sand Dune or Council City for training. After a second incident involving the death of two people, even in self-defense, our people will be nervous around you whether you join or not."

"Do I really have to move? I want to keep Sari near his people."

"No. Not unless there's a problem. Your classwork can be done re-motely, and I, or one of my guards, can work with you as long as we're here. Technically, you have six months of maternity leave you can use be-fore your official training. Even as a guard, that still stands, so you could travel for training and tell people you're visiting with family, but whatever you decide, you will need help as your senses return."

"New Hope is my home. It's the first place I've ever felt like I fit, and I have my own proteges to train and creatures to care for. Plus, with the Council gone, we're short-staffed. I'd like to stay if I can."

He nodded. "Then we'll figure out a way to make it work."

She wobbled and nearly fell again as she started climbing up the ramp out of the arena, but again, he caught her and, this time, didn't let go. "So, now that I'm in the Guard, does that change anything about us?"

"Technically, I suppose it does. I'm now your Mentor and superior officer unless you want someone else to mentor you, and any orders I give will need to be followed as long as they don't break any laws, and I could punish you for your attitude and snark."

"Great. You might as well kill me now. I'll be in trouble before the end of the week."

He laughed. "I give you a day at best, but I said I could, not that I would. I know this isn't what you wanted, and I don't want you to have to change. I like the snarky side of you. It's refreshing. Your primary rank and guild affiliation will remain with Healers. There won't be any expectation that you train to become a guard and take on those responsibilities unless you want to. You will need to take courses in the Charter, and I expect you'll want training on how to use your senses to triage a patient. What you learn can't be shared with anyone outside of the Guard or perhaps Myra since she already knows. I wasn't lying when I said we could use healers like you in the Guard. Animal Healers are few and far between and your knowledge and skills saved my life today and could save a lot of others in the future. A big part of our job is relocating or dealing with various predators. You're a phenomenal instructor, better than any I had in school, and we could use your training."

She grinned. "If you think being a guard is hard, just wait until you take one of my classes."

He grinned back. "I'm sure I'll manage."

"Care to place a bet on it?" she asked.

"Oh, no. I think I've learned my lesson there."

She grinned and wobbled again, but he still had a firm grip on her. "Don't think I'm letting you get out of the last bet, though," she said once the world stopped spinning on her. "As unstable as I am right now, there's no way I'm going after those eggs."

"I wouldn't expect you to, on either point. For better or worse, you're one of us misfits now and the Guard takes care of its own. We'll help you with whatever you need, whether that's chasing after cobra chickens or tiny Hue-man cubs."

"How about mucking horse stalls?"

"I thought that was Henry's job," he replied.

"It is, but he's off playing Councilor for the next week or two."

"Fair point. Whatever you need, including mucking horse stalls, my help is freely and happily given. You saved my life. I owe you."

She found her harness hanging on a rack and gave herself a shot of pain medicine. The hollow feeling dulled, but it didn't go away entirely. It was better than nothing, though.

Taking a deep breath, she turned to face him. "Quinn, about that tiny Hue-man cub and our conversation yesterday."

He smiled knowingly at her. "That was your instinct talking?"

"I think so. I don't feel the same way I did about you anymore. Are you upset?"

"No, not at all. I knew it wasn't really you offering. It happens more often than you might think. We save someone or their child, and suddenly, their instincts decide we would make a worthy mate, and I know how people look at me. I am a prime specimen of masculine beauty." He flexed a muscle and preened.

"I'm surprised an ego that big can fit inside your tiny head," she teased.

He grinned. "It gets knocked down to size on a regular basis. Today, it's quite bruised. I hope we can still be friends, even if your instinct is no longer dreaming about biting me?"

She snorted and nodded but instantly regretted it as the world spun on her again. "That was a mistake," she muttered as he kept her from falling again.

"What, being friends with me or nodding your head?" he teased.

She thwacked him with her tail. "Nodding, you fur-brained oaf, but I am starting to question the other decisions."

Grinning, he helped her back to the ship and gave her a run-down of what she should expect over the next few weeks, and it floored her to learn what she would be able to do if she chose to train. She blinked in surprise when he led her, not to the Ice Giant ship they'd arrived in, but one very clearly marked. "Are you the Senior Honor Guard now?"

"No," he replied. "But I am Acting Senior, and one of the benefits is the use of the ship while she's away. The other ship has been sent back to Council City with some of the guards I called in for backup."

"There weren't enough guards here in Sand Dune to subdue one Animal Healer?"

He chuckled. "Not when most of those guards are all out helping to put out several other fires. I am curious, though. How did you manage to sedate yourself? Most people wouldn't be able to move for fear I would kill you the moment you were out."

She grinned, but her embarrassment must have given her away.

"Ah. You convinced it you wanted to *bite* me, not bite me," he said with a knowing smile.

"Something like that," she replied. "Sorry if that makes you uncomfortable."

"If it works, it works. We're both alive, and that's all that matters."

He hit the switch to open the door, and she stepped inside with his help. "This is...not what I was expecting."

"Kendra thinks the interior is atrocious, but she got the ship in a bet with Oscar."

"Oscar? The head of the Ship's Guild Oscar?"

"The one and only. They regularly play Rando Tat. He hasn't won a single game. There's a massive betting pool on the date he actually does win one. I doubt he ever will."

She glared at him. "What were you saying about using your abilities against other people? Wouldn't that be cheating at the very least?"

He nodded. "Very much so. It's one of the reasons we rarely bet outside of the Guard unless we're putting our physical skills to the test. Oscar used to be in the Guard, although he shifted over to the Ship's Guild before he transitioned. I honestly don't know if he knows, but he has a guard's soul when it comes to bets."

He helped her over to her seat as he continued to explain. "This particular bet is legendary. She had been playing with Oscar for years at that point and refusing to bet every time, stating that she would never take advantage of someone so horrible at the game. Finally, he came up with a bet that she was willing to agree to. She'd been due for an upgrade for decades but refused it and put the credit to other uses, so he bet her that she couldn't beat him in six moves."

"Six?! Even if you can tell when someone is lying, six moves seems impossible. That's barely enough time to get across the board."

"That's why she agreed to the bet. She honestly didn't think she could win."

Once seated, he started to strap her in. She would have insisted on doing it herself but was feeling a bit queasy now and didn't want to throw up on such a nice ship.

"I take it she did?"

"No. She won the game, but it took her seven moves."

She frowned at him. "But you said she won it in a bet."

"I said she got it, not won it. The bet was that if she lost, she had to take whatever ship Oscar provided, with stipulations that it would still be good enough to do her job. If she won, she got to pick the ship and the interior." He motioned with his arm. "This was all Oscar's doing. He sent her the fastest ship in the fleet, knowing she would put it to good use and likely not upgrade for decades, but made the interior so...so..."

"Ostentatious?"

He grinned. "Exactly. Oscar knew how much it would annoy her. She might be a Senior, but she loathes this kind of luxury. She doesn't think it's appropriate for a guard. She chooses to live in the same housing as the rest of us, although she does have her own suite. From what I understand, most of her spare credit is donated to various organizations and causes. She's been due for another upgrade for half a century now, but she says she's grown used to this ship, and it does what she needs. If she needs something faster, she takes one of the fleet ships or, more often than not, ends up traveling with the Senior Councilor. If you ask me, she keeps it just because Oscar's the one that gave it to her."

"She has feelings for him?"

"She says otherwise, but our noses say differently. They both care a great deal about each other."

"Doesn't she already have a partner?"

He nodded. "They've been separated since Kendra's daughter died. He'll show up for functions and play the part. It's too difficult to stay together, but neither wants to end the partnership."

"I can understand that. It would make her death final."

He grunted and pulled a throw-up bag out of a hidden compartment, then handed it to her. "I suppose. There's a bet in the Guard as to when she finally moves in with Oscar. I don't think she will, not as long as she's Senior. Conflict of interest and all that."

"You bet on everything, don't you?"

He laughed and took his seat. "That we do. There's an entire guard app dedicated to keeping track of our bets. It should be on your account now."

Curious, she pulled off her tablet to check it out while he focused on leaving the shuttle bay. It was a mistake. Within moments, she was sick. Thankfully, there wasn't much there to begin with, as she hadn't had breakfast that morning.

He said nothing, but once she was done heaving, he took the bag from her, disposed of it, and handed her another.

She leaned her head against the window and watched the world below her but frowned when the grasses suddenly disappeared, replaced with the harsh scars of fire. He circled for a bit, and she figured he was checking out the damage, but to her surprise, he landed.

"What are you doing?" she asked.

"There's something I need to check. You can stay on the ship if you want. I won't be long."

"Not a chance. You have a bad habit of getting yourself in trouble out here."

He snorted, and his tail curled, but he didn't argue.

With his help, she carefully stepped off the ship and dropped down onto all fours, as it was easier for her to keep her balance. The air was dry and dusty and smelled of smoke, even through her numb nose. There was no sign of rain, and the dirt under her feet was bone dry. *The storm must not have hit here,* she decided.

Quinn sniffed deeply, sneezed several times, and then sniffed again before trotting off. She followed more slowly, but thankfully, the world wasn't spinning nearly as much as it had been earlier. By the time she caught up with him, he was squatting down, looking at something, and taking pictures with his tablet.

"You found something?" she asked.

He sighed but didn't answer, so she peered over his shoulder.

Her ears pinned back when she saw what it was. "You really do have a knack for finding trouble, don't you?"

He grunted at her teasing, but there was no humor in his tone, and she understood why. There in the sand, as plain as could be, was a Hueman footprint.

"Can you tell who it is?" she asked.

He nodded. "Paul Markson, if my memory is correct." He stood and scanned the area. "The Ice Giant ship went down over there. We found the shuttle about a league off in that direction. It's possible this is nothing more than a coincidence. This is an access road, and he could have gotten out of his shuttle to look around."

"Are there signs of anyone else?"

"Not that I can pick up," he replied. "But any sign of that could have easily been burned away."

"You should be able to confirm if the shuttle tread matches, at the very least," she said and motioned him over. "See this pattern? There are different treads for different environments. This one is better suited for rocky terrain, not sand. With sand you want a wider tread that will spread out the weight of the crawler. This one would get stuck pretty easily in terrain like this, which would tell me it doesn't belong to someone from around here. This time of year, we'd never pick a tread like this."

"Once again, your help has been invaluable." He took a picture of the tread mark and continued on down the road.

They checked several other locations, but Quinn couldn't pick up any other scents, and they didn't find any other footprints. By the time they returned to the ship after their last stop, she felt almost normal again, outside of that hollow feeling. When she declined Quinn's help getting in the ship, he raised a brow and looked at her with an expression she couldn't quite decipher.

"What?" she asked.

"You recovered your balance remarkably quickly. It took me nearly a week before I could walk straight."

She shrugged. "What can I say, except that we have already determined that I am better than you in just about everything."

He snorted. "You know most guards would take that as a rank challenge and demand you put your claws where your mouth is, but then most guards didn't just have their tails handed to them either." He looked down at his tail to make sure it was still attached.

"So, does that make me second in command now?" she asked with a wicked grin.

He laughed. "No, there's a bit more involved than that, and I *was* trying not to hurt you. It would be a different story if we truly fought. That being said, I have no doubt you'd be capable of accomplishing anything you desired. You're quite special. I've never met anyone quite like you."

She frowned at him, not used to compliments or praise. "Quinn. I don't know what you expected of me before or expect of me now, but I'm not special. I'm just an animal healer and no different from anyone else who grows up in this part of the South District. I'm independent and tough because I have to be. Life is hard. Everything is dangerous, and what you don't know will kill you. We can be cut off from help leagues away from anyone else. Only the strongest and smartest survive. You survived today because you listened and learned. You didn't let your ego get the best of you. You might just make it out here if you ever decided Council City wasn't for you, but you and your guards have got a lot to learn and even more to unlearn if you want to survive for any length of time out here." She reached out and tapped him on the nose. "This will help, but it won't save you from Heela Monsters and Sand Spinners if you're not paying attention, or the five thousand other creatures that will kill you out here."

"Yes, ma'am," he replied and looked back out at the burnt landscape. "That point has been made more than clear to me today. Let's get you home and back to your cub. Then, if you're feeling up to it, I'd like you to work with our guards this evening and give us all a crash course on how to survive out here. I have a feeling we're all going to need it."

She nodded. "Gladly. On one condition, though."

He glared at her. "What?"

"You muck the horse pens first."

He snorted and thwacked her with his tail as he turned to make his way to his seat.

Grinning, she strapped into her own, and he took off again.

"Quinn?"

"Yeah?"

"Thank you for not giving up on me."

He turned his head and smiled at her. "A good friend is always worth the risk, and besides, if I'd let you die, I'd have never won my credits back."

She laughed. *"That* is *never* going to happen."

"Care to make a bet on it?"

"Gladly."

When they landed back in New Hope, she had to smile. They'd barely made it out of the shuttle bay when Serin came running around the corner and skidded to a stop.

"Thank the moons!" she cried and bolted forward. The next thing she knew, she was being crushed in a hug. "I was so scared when you didn't get off the ship. Are you alright?"

"I'm fine," she said.

"It was merely a precaution," Quinn stated. "While she'll be on a watch for the next six months, I believe she's fully in control. How are your children?"

"They're currently in the pool with the other cubs, including yours, Nazari. Honor Guard Lark, along with several other guards, are attempting, rather unsuccessfully, to keep them corralled. We'd all be dead if it weren't for you, Honor Guard. Thank you."

He shook his head. "We'd all be dead if it weren't for Nazari, and that includes me. Save your praise and thanks for her. And you? How are you doing?"

"Much better now," Serin replied. "Now that I know everyone is safe."

He smiled. "Well, I have work to catch up on. Then I believe there's a horse stall I need to muck."

"They're all set," Serin said, frowning with confusion as to why a guard would be mucking the stalls. "My cubs and I already took care of them."

"You didn't have to do that," Nazari said.

"I know, but I wanted to. It helped keep me from worrying about you."

She hugged Serin again. "Well, in that case, I'm starving. I haven't had anything to eat today. Care to join me?" She wasn't actually hungry, but she wanted to distract Serin.

"Gladly, if only to hear how you managed to trick Kendra's Second into mucking stalls."

Before she could answer, Quinn spoke.

"I owe her. She saved my life today, six times at least," he replied and nodded to them both before walking away.

Serin watched him walk away until he was out of sight and then turned back to her. "How are you, really? And don't lie to me. I saw how much you struggled."

"I'm fine. Really. Quinn wouldn't have let me back here if I wasn't. I just needed some time to recover my balance and process what I had done."

"Rowin said you killed a Councilor, too?"

She nodded. "He was going after Quinn and using Rowin as bait. It was revenge. Quinn killed his sons. They were the ones waiting for Little Flower and Damon."

Serin sighed. "How many more are involved?"

"I have no idea," she replied and straightened as she made a split-second decision. "But if anyone else comes after the people of Little Earth again, they'll suffer the same fate. I'll make sure of it."

"You?" Serin asked.

She nodded. "That's partly what took so long. Quinn was so impressed that I didn't lose control after everything that's happened that he offered to mentor me, and I accepted. I gave my oath about an hour ago, and we've been checking out the fire since."

"You?!" Serin asked again. "An Honor Guard?"

"Don't act so surprised," she replied, rolling her eyes at the teasing. "Someone has to keep him out of trouble. On top of everything else, he nearly ran into a nest of Sand Spinners and face-first into a Heela Beast."

Serin snorted. "Typical city boy. They don't have a clue how to survive out here."

"That's for sure. I don't know how long they're sticking around, but I'm staying. This is my home, and it needs protectors. Even if the Huemans don't want a formal guard, they've got one now. I don't want what happened today publicized, though. I'm worried about what people will think, and I don't want to let our enemies know I'm here."

"Well, I, for one, am glad you were around today. Now, let's get you fed and go rescue a few of your fellow guards before our children drown them in the pool."

"Let's do both. I'll grab something from the kitchenette by the pool."

Once there, she grabbed one of the pre-made fruit dishes and something to drink before searching for an empty table near where the cubs were playing. Lark noticed her immediately and went to gather Sari, but she shook her head. He was actually playing with Peep, and she didn't want to interrupt him. It was the first time she'd seen him play with anyone besides the puppies.

Lark walked over to her instead.

"Sorry about taking so much longer than I expected. Thank you for watching him. I hope he didn't cause too much of a problem."

"Not at all. Outside of being scared when Quinn woke him, he's been fine. He's a very happy cub and easily entertained."

"I see he's made a friend."

"Sari's been taking good care of Peep," Lark replied.

"Sari?"

"Peep was still non-verbal when they arrived, fully poofed and shaking, but thankfully able to sign. I set Sari down next to Peep so I could help unload the chenzies, who were not doing well with all of the strangers. Fluffers charged one of the visiting Ice Giant Healers and knocked down two stalls to try to get to him."

"Understandable after what happened," Nazari said.

"Indeed. Anyway, I told Sari that Peep was scared and needed a friend and asked if he could help protect him for me while I dealt with Fluffers. I figured the joke might help Peep calm down a bit, and it seemed to. After corralling Fluffers, I turned back around and both were nowhere to be found. Figuring they'd been scared by the commotion, I followed their scent and found them in the puppy pens where Sari was showing Peep how to play fetch with them."

"My Sari did that?"

Lark nodded. "So Peep said. Sari apparently ran off the moment my back was turned, but Peep couldn't get his voice to work or get anyone's attention, so he followed. They were both laughing when I found them and Peep had found his voice again. Sari might not speak, but he understood exactly what Peep needed."

"Huh. I'm sad I missed it."

"I'll send you the recording," Lark said. "Do you need anything else?"

"No. Thank you."

Lark nodded and left, but the other guards remained, still playing some sort of game with the older cubs that involved throwing a ball into a hoop that hung over the side of the pool.

She watched them play as she ate. The food tasted bland, but she'd had far worse, and she was far more interested in watching her son. "So, how long are you sticking around?" she asked Serin.

"Honestly, I was thinking about moving here if Councilor Chenzira will allow it. I don't feel comfortable leaving my cubs alone when I go out with the herd anymore and they're over here all the time anyway for school and guild classes. Pep's been talking about transferring here, too."

"I don't think Jer would have a problem with you staying. I think the issue is space. There's a waiting list several years long at this point."

"I know," Serin replied, looking rather dejected.

"Do you really want to give up your home and all that land and space?"

"You did."

"Yeah, but I was never home anyway. Most of the time, I slept in my shuttle. At least here, I don't have to search fifty leagues to find my patients."

"That's part of it. I used to love being out with the herd, but last night, I was so alone and scared. I think if it hadn't been for Fluffers, I would have lost it completely. Every time I woke up, she was there. I honestly don't know if I can go back out."

She nodded. "I understand completely, but it might be even more dangerous here."

"Trouble found me in the middle of nowhere. At least here, there would be others looking for me if I didn't come back in."

"True. Well, if you don't mind getting woken up in the middle of the night or sharing a room with your cubs, you're welcome to stay with me until a suite opens up."

"You?!" Serin asked.

Nazari snorted. "Well, I don't know anyone else with the name of 'me' that lives around here."

Serin rolled her eyes. "Yeah, but...five cubs?"

"They're good cubs, hard-working and mature for their age, even Peep, as young as he is. Besides, look at him play with Sari. If you really want to stay, I'd like you to stay with us. They're good for each other. Sari won't interact with the Hue-man cubs at all. It's like they don't even exist, and Peep could use others closer to his own age right now. I know I could use the help, and you wouldn't have to worry so much about your cubs when you go out with the herd."

Serin blinked at her. "I don't really know anything about raising a Hue-man cub."

"Neither do I, but if you ignore the lack of a tail and fur, they're not all that different, and you've done a fine job with your two litters."

"I want to say yes, more than anything, but I'll have to talk with Pep and see what everyone else thinks. He's not scheduled to return until after the council meeting, but I'll give him a call this afternoon."

"Of course. Even if you just want to stay for a few days and get your feet back under you, that's fine, too. You shouldn't be alone after what happened today."

"Thanks. I really appreciate that."

She nodded, and they were silent for several minutes. The sounds of laughter cooled her burnt soul as she watched her son play and reflected on everything that had happened that day. Becoming an Honor Guard was the last thing she expected, and she was worried she couldn't live up to that oath, but as she reflected, she realized that was what she was, what she had always been.

She had chosen a profession where she was one of the few. She was a Healer, but she had chosen animal healing because they didn't have anyone protecting them, even though she told most people it was because they didn't complain about her attitude and snark. Most of her species avoided Animal Healing due to the risk. Treating a person was one thing, but treating an animal meant fighting her instinct to hunt with every patient. She had been one of the first to sign up to care for the Earth creatures and had risked her own execution for going against the Council's orders to stay away from Sari. She had gone out after Henry and Buster, tracked them for leagues, knowing she might lose any chance for custody of her son. She had killed two people today to save others and had faced down Heela Monsters and a raging wildfire to save neighbors that she barely knew. She knew the chenzies better than she did Serin and her family. She had defeated a part of herself to keep from killing Quinn. She had spent her entire life protecting others who had no one else to protect them.

Honor Guard Nazari Jabri, she thought. *What do you think, Mama?*

Her eyes watered with the pain she always felt when she thought of her mother. She had joked with Quinn that her mother would have laughed, but she had a feeling her mother would have been proud of her, too.

Thanks, Mama.

Sari looked up, and a huge smile lit his face as he noticed her. He dropped the toy he was playing with and took off running towards her.

She scooped him up and hugged him tightly, purring with everything she had. He might not be able to speak or even say 'mama,' but she was his choice, just as he was hers. He was her reason for living and for fighting to ensure that he would be safe from people like Rip, and Breydhik, and even her own instinct. The tears began to fall, and she hiccuped with a sob, not at how close she'd come to losing everything, but because of everything she had gained: family, friends, and a purpose that was bigger than her.

"Are you okay?" Serin asked.

"Yeah. Yeah, I think, for the first time in my life, I really am."

CHAPTER 31

Marsee: Pain

The cave was cold and so dark that Marsee couldn't see anything around her, not even her paw held in front of her face. Everything ached, and the water was starting to lap at her feet again. Fear rose as she tried to climb the wall at her back, but it was damp and slick, and her aching claws found no purchase on the smooth rock. She was trapped, and she was going to drown if she didn't find a way out, but she was exhausted and collapsed with a groan that turned into a whimper as the cold of the stone seeped painfully into her stomach.

Marsee, you need to wake up, her instinct called to her.

She looked up to see it standing in front of her.

You need to keep moving. You need to stay warm and be ready for when he returns.

She struggled to her feet and started limping through water that was ankle-deep now, her paw broken and useless. She felt something touch her foot, and she flicked it away, yelping in fear.

Marsee, you're safe. You need to wake up, she heard her instinct say again.

"But I am awake," she replied. "And I am far from safe."

She felt the touch again and yelped, flicking it off her. Suddenly, she heard music, and the cavern lit up around her. There was a shape in the distance, but she couldn't make out who it was. *He's back,* she thought and growled as she prepared to attack.

"Marsee, you're safe. Sniff, it's just me," the voice in the distance said.

She took a deep breath and smelled her sister instead of him. *What is she doing here? Has he caught her, too?* The thought made her heart hitch with worry, but suddenly, her sister was there beside her and rubbing her face, her scent strong and comforting, and she started purring. Oh, how she'd missed her sister!

"That's it. I'm here. You're safe. You're not in the cave. You're just dreaming, and you need to wake up," her sister said and caressed the side of her face again.

She closed her eyes and leaned into the touch. It took her a while to realize that she was no longer dreaming and that her sister was, in fact, caressing her face. She snapped her head up in panic when she realized that her sister was able to touch her face. *I didn't put my gear back on!*

"It's okay. You're safe," Little Flower said and continued to stroke her. "You need to wake up."

"I am awake, and I don't have my gear on. Did I hurt you?" she asked, nearly frozen with panic.

"No, of course not," her sister said, "Now come back down here so I can reach you better."

Marsee lowered her head and allowed herself to be calmed by the gentle caresses. "I could have hurt you," she whimpered.

"But you didn't," her sister said gently, "and you stopped twitching as soon as you smelled me. Now I know how to break through your nightmares, so you don't have to worry about it anymore. Do you want to talk about it?"

"I was back in the cave with the water rising around me," she said. "And I was cold, and I hurt, and the sea creatures were starting to nip at my injured paw again. I can still feel the ache in my paw." Marsee flexed her broken hand. The ache increased, and she flicked her head back up and stared at it.

"What is it?" Little Flower asked.

"My paw! It hurts!" Marsee took a claw and carefully pressed it into her other palm, and it hurt. "I can feel it!" She sat up quickly and groaned. "Moons, I can feel that, too. Oh, oh, that doesn't feel good.

You'd better get Mama." She carefully laid back down as the ache radiated and spread through her body. She groaned and curled into a tiny ball, wrapped around the pain.

Little Flower scrambled out of bed, ran over to the shared door, and knocked loudly. "Mama!" she yelled out and then opened the door.

"What's wrong?" she heard her mother say before waking enough to realize that Little Flower wouldn't understand the Saber speech, and then the light flicked on.

"Marsee's in pain," Little Flower signed from the door.

Moments later, her mother was up and in the room, scanner in hand. "Where do you hurt?"

"Everywhere, but my hand and stomach are the worst," she said, trying to breathe through the pain that kept growing.

Her mother scanned her and then frowned and scanned her again.

"What's wrong? Did I injure something?" she asked. They'd been fairly active, so she was worried she'd injured herself again without knowing it.

"No, it's not that." Her mother sniffed deeply, and her ears flipped back in surprise. She turned and started scanning Little Flower. Marsee watched as her mother's normally calm expression, hidden by over a century of medical training, flicked through half a dozen different emotions, ending with a sigh. "I'm so sorry, Little Flower. We had to take your hormone blocker out when you had the seizure after your brain surgery. It conflicted with the medication we needed to give you, and I completely forgot about putting it back in. You're in heat."

"Yeah, we kind of figured that out already," Marsee said, and Little Flower's face blushed a bright red.

Her mother looked back and forth between them and then looked horrified as she realized the implications. "You..."

Marsee nodded.

"Dark moons! I'm so sorry! Little Flower, I had no idea this could even happen."

"It's alright, as long as Marsee's not harmed by it. It was consensual," Little Flower replied, but if anything, her sister's blush deepened.

She looked up as her father entered the room. "Is everything okay?" he asked. Then his nose flared, and he started to purr.

Her mother's head whipped around at the sound, and she bolted for the door. "Out!" she yelled and shoved him hard in the direction of the door.

Her father was so surprised by her mother's actions that he stumbled and fell. The look on his face made her snicker and curl her tail. He was belly up, purring, and looking at her mother like she was a god, not someone who had just knocked him over.

"Is everything alright?" Aris called from the hall.

"We're fine," her mother replied, but she didn't waste any time waiting for her father to regain his feet. Instead, she grabbed him by his scruff and physically dragged him through the door. She returned, slamming the door shut behind her and locking it.

Her mother took a deep breath to regain her composure, plastered her healer's mask back on, and turned to face her. "You'll need to remain in the room until Little Flower's heat passes. I have no idea why you're responding to Little Flower, but your father clearly just reacted to you, and every fully grown male is going to react the same way, as strong as you smell right now."

"Am I in heat, too?" Marsee asked, worried. She knew she was far too small to have a litter of cubs and nowhere near recovered enough. Although if she hadn't found out that morning that she would recover from her injuries, she would have gladly walked out into the hallway. Even still, she was considering it.

Her mother scanned her again. "No...I'm not seeing any hormonal changes that would be consistent with a heat, but your pheromone levels are off the chart."

"So I'm reacting like a male?" Marsee asked, confused.

"Possibly. You don't have a male implant, so you're still releasing female pheromones, but I don't know why you reacted to Little Flower in the first place. Every female in the agency went into heat at the same time when we took them off their hormone blockers, and there were no issues with either sex. I'm certainly not responding to it," her mother said, frowning at her scanner. "And you're not reacting like a female in heat either. If you were, you would be clawing at the door to get to your father or another male, not laying here calmly talking to me. I suppose that could be your age."

"She smells really good, though. I mean, *really* good. I can practically see it," Marsee said.

Her mother's ears flicked back at that, and then she looked towards the door, clearly considering something. "I suppose that could do it," her mother mumbled and took another deep breath. Marsee noticed that her mother's eyes dilated briefly before her mother shook her head at some internal thought.

"What?" Marsee signed, reminding her mother that Little Flower couldn't understand her.

"Kendra said your senses would return, but back to where they were when your instinct is on. It's possible that's what's happening now. I'll talk to Kendra in the morning about it. At the very least, she should know that her guards could be affected by a Hue-man female in heat. If you want, I can pick up some pheromone blockers from the Trauma Center. I know they have those, but I don't know if they have any of the hormone blockers Little Flower would need. I don't think we brought any with us."

"It's up to Little Flower," Marsee said. "I don't mind staying here for a day or two if that's what it takes. It's a very enjoyable experience."

Her sister blushed again. "If it's not going to hurt Marsee, it's alright by me. If you don't have an implant, I'll need supplies for later. I didn't bring anything with me."

Her mother nodded. "You should have a dozen local days or so before you start shedding the lining unless you want to be pregnant again. I wouldn't recommend it right now. You're still far too underweight to carry a cub to term safely, and the only two males on the planet are your

GrandFather and Henry, so I'd have to talk to them to make a donation if you insisted on it. They're not genetically related, so it should be…"

"No, I'm not ready for another cub yet," Little Flower signed, with far more urgency and embarrassment than Marsee expected. "It's hard enough caring for Hope with my injuries," Little Flower explained. "I want to be fully recovered before having another one."

Her mother looked relieved. "Now, as for you, Marsee, back to the original reason I came in here. The good news is it would appear your sense of pain has returned, as Kendra said it would, and thankfully, nothing new appears to be wrong. The bad news is that you can now feel your injuries." Her mother grabbed the small jar of nanos on the bedside table and frowned when she realized it was mostly empty. "I'll swim over to the Trauma Center to pick you up something stronger."

Marsee nodded, and her mother left after double-checking that the door to the other suite was locked. She heard her mother talking to the guards and groaned with embarrassment, although she couldn't make out what her mother was saying.

Little Flower started snickering.

"What's so funny?" Marsee asked as she opened the jar and started rubbing it into her hand.

"This whole situation. Here I was, worried I was never going to be able to experience mating since I wasn't attracted to anyone left of my species, and I somehow ended up in a partnership with the only cat in the universe that's physically attracted to us."

"Well, the other guards could be attracted to you, too. We don't know that," Marsee said, although her tail curled since she'd been worried about much the same for herself.

"True, but if they've got a super sniffer like you do, then they've probably known I've been in heat all day, and they've been swimming around with us everywhere and haven't reacted or said anything. Of course, they could have learned how to deal with it, or perhaps they weren't close enough like you were."

"You mean like here?" Marsee stuck her face right in her sister's groin and sniffed.

"Hey! Not yet. Mama will be back soon," her sister said, pushing her away with a laugh.

Marsee chuckled and held up the jar of nanos. "Fine, you can help slather me in this. Everything hurts."

Little Flower grabbed a scoop of the cream and started rubbing it in.

She sighed with relief as it kicked in. There wasn't nearly enough to go around, so she focused on those areas that hurt the most, but it didn't even touch the ache in her belly. "I can see why the healers were so worried when I said I wasn't in pain before. If I still hurt like this, I can just imagine what it would have felt like when I first woke up."

When the jar was empty, she curled up in a ball around the ache in her stomach. Little Flower leaned up against her and began stroking the back of her neck again. She purred with the feeling that washed over her. It helped, even if it didn't stop the pain. But her pain turned to fear as she remembered her dream and how she'd been hurt. She flipped around, grabbed her sister in a fierce hug, and wrapped herself protectively around her sister as she shook with how close she'd come to losing those she loved.

"Is the pain that bad?" her sister asked.

"It hurts, but the thought of how close I came to losing you is so much worse," she whispered.

Her sister buried her face into the embrace and said nothing as they held each other together and waited for their mother to return.

CHAPTER 32

Myra: Implant

The guards turned and peered in the suite, nose flaring as Myra exited. Thankfully, both guards were female, having swapped out at some point during the evening, as she had not been looking forward to restraining an honor guard, especially Kendra's nephew. She recognized the two from the night before and relaxed slightly.

"I take it her treatment failed?" Aris asked quietly once the door was shut. It was more of a statement than a question and laced with sadness.

Myra opened her mouth to speak and couldn't even begin to find the words to explain. She eventually settled on simplicity. "They...both are."

"Both?!" Aris asked.

After what had happened to Little Flower at the Agency and her subsequent conviction, she knew she was treading a fine line. "And for some reason, Marsee's reacting to her sister. They apparently figured it out on their own and appeared to be...enjoying themselves. I...we had to remove Little Flower's hormone blocker to treat a seizure she had after her surgery. With everything that happened after, I completely forgot, and apparently, so did Ammond. Marsee doesn't realize she's in heat, too. I couldn't bring myself to tell her."

The guards' eyes softened with understanding and, thankfully, not recrimination and arrest.

"What do you intend to say?" Aris asked.

"I honestly don't know, but I'm half a mind to let her think it's just a reaction to her sister's heat. You should probably also know, if you haven't figured it out, that Jer reacted to Marsee before I realized what was going on. I got him out of the room before any harm was done. He's currently locked in my suite. He should be good until I get back with the pheromone blocker, but keep an ear out, just in case. Oh, and Marsee's sense of pain has returned."

"Already?" the other guard asked.

Aris scowled at Thatcher, and Myra frowned at the interaction, but Aris continued without responding. "With the door shut, I couldn't smell anything, so the filtration systems appear to be working. I'll let Avery know our watch got a little more interesting, and we'll keep everyone away, just in case."

Myra glanced at the door, sighed, and trotted away, focusing hard on presenting a calm mask, but inside, she was shaking. *What is wrong with me? Why do I keep making stupid mistakes? How could I have forgotten to put Little Flower's implant back in? Is it just exhaustion and stress, or is something else going on? Gods. Am I losing control? I don't feel like it, but I didn't even make it a day without talking to my instinct. How am I going to explain this to Kendra? I don't want to Transition, but if it's that or execution, do I have any choice?*

A pair of Water Sprite guards appeared the moment she exited the platform, but she ignored them. Guards following her around for the next six months would be the norm, and she was honestly glad for their protection, even if she didn't fully trust them after what had happened to Marsee.

She punched the drone as fast as it would go and was soon at the Trauma Center, where the guards left her. The healer at the triage desk flashed a greeting but didn't stop her. This late at night, the halls were empty as she made her way back to the supply closet and started scanning the shelves for what she needed, but she frowned when she realized that everything was labeled in Water Sprite. She was passable in the written language and could manage the basics of their visual language, but she was not fluent by any means.

It was the last straw, and a sob broke loose from her control. Her mask crumbled away as she could no longer deny what had been done to her daughter.

"I thought I saw you swim in. What happened?"

Myra looked over to see Rowena in the doorway, surprised to see the old healer awake, and forced her emotions back behind her mask. She wouldn't be the first healer to lose control in the privacy of the supply closet. Even with all their training, sometimes it was just too much. No one would blame her, least of all Rowena, but she knew Diggers didn't like large displays of emotion. Rowena was far more expressive than most Diggers and used to witnessing them, but she still tried for Rowena's sake.

"A mess," she replied when she was sure her voice wouldn't break. "Marsee's sense of pain has returned, and both she and Little Flower are in heat and have mated with each other."

"Both?!" Rowena asked.

She snorted at the unintentional duplicate response, but rather than trying to explain, as she had no words left, she handed over her scanner and returned to digging through the shelves for what she was looking for. It gave her the time she needed to finish pulling herself together. Finding the pain meds she was looking for, she pulled off her tablet to confirm her translation was accurate and moved on to the next. "Where is that stupid pheromone blocker?" she muttered. "I know we brought some."

"Third shelf, fourth column over," Rowena replied. "I didn't realize the Hue-man's mating was pheromone based."

She pulled several vials out. "I wasn't either. None of the Hue-mans have mentioned anything about it, but Little Flower's scent has changed and I've noticed a change in GrandFather's scent when Henry is around." After clipping the vials to her harness, she asked Rowena if she knew where the hormone's she needed were located as she started scanning the shelves, but Rowena didn't respond. She looked up and over at Rowena and found the old healer looking at her with compassion.

"Myra it's too late for that to work. These levels are too high."

"I know but I have to try," she said. "Maybe with the pheromone blocker."

"Myra…"

"Little Flower's scent *has* changed and she smells better than it normally does, but I didn't react to it, and no one else has ever reacted to a Hue-man female in heat, but that's the only thing that makes sense."

"Myra…"

"Thankfully, no harm was done. They figured out Little Flower was in heat and stated their mating was consensual, and I let them continue to believe that's all it was. I suppose it's no different from what we can manage outside of a heat."

"Myra…"

"And if Marsee is reacting like a male to Little Flower, then the pheromone blocker should stop it."

"Myra stop! Look at me!"

She turned and looked at Rowena, head tilted questioningly.

"You need to listen to me. The hormone treatment was barely working before and it's too late now. A pheromone blocker won't work. Her hormone levels are too high. You've got a day, maybe two before it'll be too dangerous to stop and she's not strong enough to survive a failed heat. You have to give her an implant."

"She doesn't want to be male. She wants cubs and if I give her an implant now, she'll never grow up. I have to try."

"Myra, you know as well as I do, even with her sense of pain returned, letting her go through her growth spurt will be far too dangerous. Whether you give her the implant now or in a few years, you will have to give her the implant."

She shook her head. "Kendra said she could help her with that. The guards must deal with far more scarring."

"Scarring yes, but not four replacement organs. She'll bleed to death before you could even get her in a stasis unit, just like she nearly did this week when she tore out her sutures. The only reason she's alive is because a healer was with her when it happened."

Her jaw shook with grief as she struggled to shove it behind her mask. "Ancient gods, how do I tell her? After everything she's been through? To take that hope away from her now would kill her."

"Don't tell her. Let her continue to believe that she's reacting to Little Flower, and give her the implant tomorrow morning when you treat her for her pain. That should be safe enough and she could certainly use a few hours of joy. Besides, if you tell her, she's more than likely to deny the implant and take a chance at a cub. As injured as she is right now, she wouldn't survive long enough to bring even a single cub to term."

"Don't you think I know that?!" Myra yelled and then took a deep breath to calm herself again. "Rowena, what you're suggesting is illegal. I have no grounds to give her an implant without her knowledge."

"Jer and Marcus already gave us permission, and if you want, you could always blame me. Frankly, I think it would be best if you did. You've been in enough trouble this year and I'll be long dead before she figures it out. Tell her it was given to her when I ran all those tests the day I arrived and made her itchy. Or don't tell her anything at all and blame her lack of growth on her other injuries. "

"Long dead? She'll figure it out in a couple of weeks when Little Flower goes into heat again."

"That's only if you can't replace Little Flower's implant by then. You could always claim it had more to do with the timing of her returning senses."

"I was wondering about that. Could that have been what triggered Marsee's heat?"

Rowena looked at her with pity. "Myra. I know you want to believe otherwise, but you know as well as I do what happened to her, and it had nothing to do with Little Flower, her injuries, or the Transition. Even if what is going on with her now is entirely unrelated, your daughter *was* raped."

Her instinct growled and demanded action for the harm that was done to Marsee, but there was nothing for them to do. Rip was already dead. After a long moment, she squashed her rage back down. When she refocused, Rowena had shut the door and swum up to her. She hadn't even noticed.

"How long has that been happening," Rowena demanded, staring hard into her eyes.

"What?" Myra asked, confused.

"Don't pretend you don't know what I'm talking about. You were non-verbal for several minutes."

Myra shook her head. "Minutes?! No. I..." She was going to deny it as it had only felt like a few seconds to her, but then Rowena's expression changed, harden, and she remembered that Rowena was still an Honor Guard and could legally execute her. "I don't know. Ever since this all started, I suppose. My instinct is demanding revenge, but there's nothing for us to act on. Rip is already dead, and the others will be soon. I am so angry about what has happened to my family and scared something will happen again. I'll admit it's taking longer for me to get it to settle because I have to control my anger and fear first, but I'm still able to do so, and I'll be fine once this is all over. I really don't want to Transition unless it's absolutely necessary."

"Then you need to focus even harder on controlling your emotions and triggers. Keep your mask up at all times. This a major trauma situation. There are lives at risk if you don't gain control and gain it quickly. You need to accept what has happened and focus on saving those you can, and above all, do everything in your power to remain calm, for their sakes, not yours. They can't see that you're scared. They need to believe that you know what you're doing and will protect and save them so that their own instincts don't take control. If they doubt you for even a second, you'll lose them, and others will get hurt. What do you tell them if they ask if they're going to die?"

The lecture Rowena gave her was word for word what Ammond had told her during her first major trauma event, and like back then, it settled and focused her. She grinned at Rowena. "I haven't lost a patient yet, and I don't intend to ruin my record now. Thank you. I needed that reminder."

Rowena stared at her for a moment and then nodded. "You're stubborn enough to beat this. Don't let Rip further harm your family by his actions. You can't control what he did, but you can control how you react to it. Now go on. Your daughter is in pain, and she needs you." Rowena unclipped a vial from her harness and handed it to her.

Myra looked down at it and then frowned. "A female implant?"

"She's stated she doesn't want to be male, and I see no reason why she has to be, even if your species believes otherwise. When she's ready, then you can tell her. If she decides later to be male, you can always swap the implants."

"You can't swap out an implant. It doesn't work like that."

"Are you sure? Or is that what you were taught, and you never questioned it? Your species likes to keep secrets, and when it comes to your instincts, there are a lot of them. This is one of them. I'm surprised you haven't figured it out. It was obvious to me the moment I started looking into psychosis."

"You're serious?" Myra asked, but her brain had already started making connections.

Rowena nodded. "The implants are essentially identical. The only difference is how it affects the pheromones a person releases. They could be swapped at any time. You just choose not to. Ethically, I can't say whether it's right, but it's been your specie's practice since you...*lost* your biological males, so it's ancient history at this point."

"Lost?" Myra asked, picking up on the insinuation.

"Like I said. Secrets. Anyway, that's not important now. What's important is caring for your daughter and giving her the best possible care and chance of survival. Give her the implant, and don't record it."

Myra blinked. It was one thing to give her the treatment if Jer and Marcus had already approved it, but not marking it on her record was a major crime. "I could be executed for doing that."

"No, you won't. You'd be doing it to protect her. If you record it, her legal gender will go on her public record, and the press will get their hands all over it. She doesn't need to find out that way, and neither do they. In a few years, you can break it gently to her that she is never going to be able to have cubs of her own, that it's too dangerous for her to go through her growth spurt, and that she would be better off male. She'll make the right decision, but she needs time to recover from her trauma first."

Rowena paused, tilted her head at some internal thought, and grinned. "I'll write up the report to Kendra and copy you and Ammond on it. I should be able to send both of them on a wild cobra chicken chase that'll keep them scratching at their whiskers for a few decades."

Myra grinned at Rowena's use of the Hue-man slang and the wicked expression on her face. "One last prank? I'm beginning to think you're a Flyer, not a Digger."

"I'm an Honor Guard. We're a different species altogether."

"Will you ever tell me what you did to Kendra?"

"Perhaps someday, but today is not that day," Rowena replied with a grin.

She scowled at Rowena, which made the old healer cackle with laughter.

"If I don't see you before you leave," Myra said, "Thank you. For everything."

"If you really want to thank me, you'll sneak that scanner of Ammond's onto Ellie's ship before I leave. The old coot took it back to his room with him, stating he was worried I would steal it. He's probably not wrong there."

Myra snorted with laughter. "I'm not stupid enough to even try, but I'll send you the specs."

"I suppose that'll have to do. Now go on. Your daughter's in pain, and I imagine Jer's not too comfortable either."

"He can wait. I'm still annoyed with him." But she hugged Rowena and took off. Her escort was waiting for her outside the Trauma Center, but she ignored them, far more lost in thought about how to break the news gently to Marsee. By the time she made it back to the suite, she decided she wasn't going to let anyone know about the implant. It would be too easy for someone to slip up, and when Marsee eventually found out, she would take credit for it, even though Rowena had offered. It was the least she could do to protect the legacy of the person who helped her so much this past year.

Regardless of her comments, she stopped first to give Jer the pheromone blocker.

He was pacing, tail held to the side, when she entered, and rubbed up against her, purring. "Do you think you could wait a little before giving me that? I haven't felt this good in years."

"I honestly wish I could," she said as she injected him. "You smell good, too, but now is not the time."

He sat and rubbed at his nose before sneezing hard several times, and she scanned him to make sure he was coming out of it. Her nose detected the change long before her scanner did. His ears drooped with disappointment as the reaction ebbed.

"There. You should be safe around Marsee now, but you'll need another shot every twelve hours."

He opened his mouth to ask a question, and she raised her paw. "Let me treat Marsee first, then we can talk."

She left the suite again, gave the guards a hypo, preloaded with another dose in the event they needed it, and entered her daughters' room through the outer door to find Marsee curled up so tightly around Little Flower that she could barely see her Hue-man daughter. She knew she'd never forget the sight. It was exactly what she wanted to do, but that wasn't what her daughters needed right now.

Marsee's ears perked up as she entered, but neither moved as she walked over and sat down next to the bed.

She injected the implant first before she could change her mind, hiding it in the worst of the scar tissue in her daughter's arm. It wasn't the normal place for an implant for her species, which would make it less likely for another healer to find it and slip up. Her heart broke into a million pieces as she did it, but there was really no other choice. Besides the medical risk of a failed heat, if she waited too long, Marsee could lose control as her mating instinct grew stronger and more insistent, and Little Flower could easily get hurt. A moment later, Marsee started to squirm and let go of her sister to roll on her back.

"Are you alright?" Myra asked.

"Something's not right, Mama. The pain is still there, but now I'm really itchy."

She frowned and pulled out her scanner, although she already knew why Marsee was itchy. It was in response to the hormones that were now flooding her system. "I've never used this particular pain medicine with you before," she lied. "It looks like you're having a mild allergic reaction. I can give you something for that, but it may stop your reaction to Little Flower. The anti-histamine can dampen your sense of smell."

Marsee sighed with disappointment, but she was still writhing on the bed. "I'm not exactly going to be able to pay attention to Little Flower as itchy as I am right now. Gah!"

Myra pulled out the actual pain medication, which would also stop the itching, and injected her daughter. A minute later, Marsee sighed with relief as it took effect.

"Better?"

"Much. I still hurt, but it's manageable now, and the itchiness is gone." Marsee rolled over and sniffed her sister deeply, then began to purr, and her toes curled. "She still smells *really* good," Marsee said. "And I can feel it in my toes. Is it always like this?"

Little Flower's face turned bright red, which she had learned was a sign of embarrassment, and she grinned at her daughters. She was truly glad that Marsee was still able to react to her sister, even if she herself was no longer in heat. She supposed it was no different than what they could manage outside of heat, and it got her thinking about what Rowena had said, but she refocused on the question her daughter had asked.

"In a true heat, it's even stronger. Most people can't talk or stop mating when they're in heat. Since you can, I expect what you're experiencing is more in line with what we can manage outside of a heat. It takes a great deal of effort to counteract our implants to release the right pheromones to make the act enjoyable. Why you're reacting to Little Flower, I still don't know, but as long as it remains consensual, I don't see any problems with it. Little Flower, I'm going to leave you with a hypo, preloaded with a pheromone blocker. If Marsee's reaction gets to be too much, that should stop it cold in a few seconds."

Marsee flicked her ears back. "I would never do anything against her will."

"I know that, but this is an unusual situation, and I would feel better if we took precautions. Our mating instincts can have a mind of their own. It's why there are guards stationed at the mating clinics, and I have no idea how much of yours remains."

Marsee pinned her ears straight back in horror. "If that's even a possibility, give me the pheromone blocker now."

"It's alright, Marsee," Little Flower said, although her face was still bright red with embarrassment. "I know you won't hurt me. If it was going to be an issue, it would have been already. You've been perfect. I couldn't ask for better. You never went any further than I allowed and checked in often to make sure I was still okay. It was exactly what I needed. Plus, you stopped immediately when I said no a few minutes ago. I don't want you to miss out on enjoying it, too."

Little Flower reached up and caressed the side of Marsee's face. Marsee started purring again and leaned into it.

"Good," Myra said, honestly impressed that Marsee had been able to stop. "The meds I gave you should last until morning at the very least. Let me know when you need more." She stood and started walking back to her room, then stopped and picked up Hope, who woke just enough to snuggle into her fur. "You two have fun. If you need something, send me a message, and if you wouldn't mind, please try to go a day without another medical mystery."

The moment she shut the door behind her, she heard the sounds of their laughter, followed by the muffled sounds of giggles and something far more enjoyable.

"I don't think we'll be getting much out of them for a few days," Myra said as she walked over to the bed and carefully handed Hope over to Jer, trying not to wake her.

"So the treatment failed? She's in heat?"

Myra unclipped her harness and tossed it on the back of a chair. "No. The treatment was successful. Little Flower's in heat, and Marsee's responding to it. In all the chaos, I forgot to put Little Flower's implant back in. We had to remove it as it was incompatible with one of the medications we needed to use to treat her seizures after her surgery."

The look of both surprise and horror on Jer's face made her chuckle. "Luckily, it appears they both figured it out. And that…" She nodded in the direction of the sounds in the other room. "is consensual. I've confirmed it twice. At the moment, Marsee is just releasing pheromones, much like males do. My scanner would have already alerted me to it if it had been more than that. We've been monitoring her closely. If Little Flower's heat is the same length as the others, they should be safe to play. If necessary, I'll give Marsee a dose of the pheromone blockers before it becomes an issue. That should stop it. I did leave one with Little Flower and the guards, just in case."

Jer seemed to accept her lies without question. "As depressed as they've both been, I'm happy they'll have this," he said. "A tad jealous, but happy."

"I am, too," she replied. "Although I could do without another medical mystery."

Jer didn't reply. Instead, he curled around Hope, much the same way Marsee had curled around Little Flower. She was still furious with him, but they'd spoken for hours, and their decades of partnership and love for each other were slowly chipping away at that anger. Sighing, she climbed on the bed and curled around him as they usually slept.

He let out a purr of happiness, but it didn't last long before he let out a heavy sigh at some internal thought. "Myra. I think Marsee's heat was...my fault."

She lifted her head and clamped down hard on the growl that wanted to escape. The last thing she needed was for the guards outside to hear. "What have you done to her?"

"Not what you're thinking. I promise. When she was losing control in the canyon, I bit her scruff to try and snap her out of it. It sometimes works. It worked with me when I lost control. Marcus and Clear Seas were both there, so they can confirm nothing else happened. It worked. Her body relaxed, at least, but it still took her several minutes to regain control, and I had her wrapped tightly in my arms the whole time. If she wasn't raped or medically induced, it seems the most likely cause."

Her anger evaporated instantly. It was common knowledge that a bite or grab to the scruff could sometimes snap someone out of the early stages of psychosis, especially with young cubs who easily and often lost control if something scared them. She shook her head before laying down across his shoulder again. "Unlikely. It doesn't work that way, at least not that I've been taught. Granted, it's been thousands of years since that happened."

"Are you sure?" he asked, lifting his head to look back at her.

"We may never know what really caused it, but there's no sign of forced entry, and she hasn't come forth to say he raped her. After Little Flower's rape, I made her promise to tell a healer if anyone touched her there, even if she didn't feel comfortable telling me. If she were medically induced, we'd know. There's a bio-marker that stays in the system for weeks. It's an intentional safety measure. It's far more likely it was caused by the electrocution or lack of oxygen from her failing mask, but even if her instinct got confused, it doesn't matter. He's already dead, and I don't want to cause her any more pain than she's already been through by even letting her know of the possibility."

She felt Jer relax as if a weight had been lifted. She fully understood, even if she could no longer deny what had really happened.

"Why would she be reacting to Little Flower?" he asked a few minutes later.

"That I don't know. My guess is that it's a combination of her senses returning, Little Flower's change in scent, and perhaps close proximity. Or perhaps it's nothing more than her love for Little Flower. I suppose it's no different than when we mate outside of a heat and how we eventually react to the other person's desire and change in scent. She's certainly not acting like she's in a true heat. She was able to stop for one."

He nodded slightly and then scrunched his nose. "Ugh. Hope messed her poop sack again."

"You smelled it first," she replied with a chuckle and shifted off him so he could clean the cub. "Although I'm surprised you could with the pheromone blockers."

"It's not difficult when her butt is only a few inches from my face," he replied. "I don't know what they fed her today, but I'm surprised you didn't sniff it out, too."

"Oh, I did. I was curious how long it would take you to say something."

He squinted back at her with suspicion.

She chuckled at the look. "I needed to know how well the pheromone blocker was working, but a deal's a deal, Councilor. It's not my fault the Hue-mans invented poop sacks, making it unnecessary to change the sheets."

"Fair point, well made, " he replied and climbed off the bed, holding Hope as far away from him as he could get her.

Her tail curled tightly in amusement at the expression on his face. Hope truly did smell awful.

"Hold still! Ugh! What did you go and do that for? Now it's all over my fur! That's it. You're going in the shower."

She was still laughing when Hope ran out, fully naked. She heard the sounds of the shower running a second time, then a third. "Hope, did you mess all over your Grampa?" she asked as Hope climbed up on the bed.

Hope nodded. "I pooped."

"Well, it serves him right. He's been a stinky poop sack lately," she replied and then looked up as he exited the waste room with the cleaned poop sack in hand, and her chuckles turned into hysterical laughter.

"I think there's a problem with the static shower," he said.

"You think?" she signed, laughing too hard to get the words out. Jer's fur was sticking straight out with static electricity that sparked with the slightest movement, all except for the large smear of poop on his midsection. He looked absolutely ridiculous and stunk horribly. "Don't move. I need to get a picture of this."

"Blackmail?" he asked with a frown.

"Oh no. Far worse than that. Reparations. I'm sending it to your mother."

CHAPTER 33

Jer: Blanket Bumbler

Jer scowled as Myra took his picture, but it was all for show. It was so wonderful to see her laughing again, even if it was at his expense. He rolled his eyes as she deliberately sent the message, and his tablet dinged a moment later.

"I'll be back in a few minutes," he said, tossing her the cleaned poop sack, and left to find another shower.

The two guards on duty outside his daughters' room looked over at him and tensed as they saw him but then snorted with barely controlled laughter as their tails both spiraled.

"That's a...rather unique pheromone blocker, Senior Councilor," Aris said, "but I admit it's highly effective. *I* certainly wouldn't go anywhere near you."

He snorted as he walked across the hall and knocked on GrandFather's door.

A minute later, the door opened, and GrandFather appeared, half-clothed, took one look at him, and started snickering. "I take it you made Myra angry again?"

"Ha ha," he replied. "May I use your shower? Mine appears to be broken."

GrandFather grinned but stepped aside and motioned dramatically in the direction of his waste room. "By all means. It might be a tight fit, but you're more than welcome to use it."

Henry was there, sitting on the bed with a blanket across his lap and scratching at the back of his head. He couldn't tell if Henry was embarrassed or trying not to laugh. It was so hard sometimes without the movable ears and tail to tell what the Hue-mans were really thinking, but it was good to see proof of their growing relationship.

He nodded to Henry. "Sorry to wake you. I'll be quick."

The shower was a tight fit, but he did manage to squeeze inside. A minute later, he let off a litany of swears and stepped back out into the main room. "Yours isn't working either."

"It worked earlier for me," GrandFather said.

"You can try my suite," Henry offered.

He did and had the same results. If anything, it was worse. Growling with frustration, he returned to GrandFather's room. Henry was now up, dressed in loose-fitting grey sweatpants, getting something to drink, and nearly snorted his drink out at his appearance. His fur was somehow even more poofed up than it had been before, and the smear had doubled in size.

"I don't know what's going on. Henry's shower isn't working either."

"Maybe they're programmed for our species, not yours," Grandfather suggested. "Looks like you're going to have to do it the old-fashioned way. Assuming you don't groom yourself the way our felines do, there's soap in the waste room and towels underneath the sink, although I suppose you could jump in the ocean and wash it there."

He shuddered at all three suggestions, but the soap and water option was by far the least embarrassing and disgusting. "Unless it's an emergency, we don't groom ourselves. Our saliva does have a clotting agent, but the very idea of grooming this is revolting."

"I can't imagine why," GrandFather teased.

It took him a good twenty minutes to get most of his fur clean and somewhat settled, but even with the pheromone blockers, he could still smell it. When he exited, Henry offered him a drink, but he declined.

"So, how did you end up in the waste hole?" GrandFather asked.

He sighed, not sure how to explain or how the Hue-mans would take the news. "We have a bit of a situation. Little Flower started her heat this evening, and Marsee is reacting to her."

Both Hue-mans looked at each other and burst out laughing, which was not what he was expecting at all.

"And they think we're the pranksters," Henry said to GrandFather.

"This is not a prank," Jer replied, although the irony that they didn't believe him wasn't lost on him. He hadn't believed Rowena when she first told him that Marsee was starting her heat. "Myra had to take Little Flower's implant out to treat her seizures after her surgery and, in the chaos, forgot to put it back in. We have no idea why Marsee is reacting, but apparently, Little Flower's scent has changed enough to trigger her, and they've mated. Myra says their mating is consensual, and she left a pheromone blocker with Little Flower in case she changes her mind. As for my appearance, Myra and I are on cub-sitting duty, and Hope flung her dirty poop sack at me when I was trying to change her. The shower did the rest."

To his further surprise, both laughed even harder.

He frowned at them in confusion. "This is a serious situation."

"I take it you've never encountered a flying poop sack before?" GrandFather asked. "I recommend dodging next time."

Henry snickered.

Jer rolled his eyes. "I'm talking about Little Flower and Marsee," he explained.

GrandFather's expression changed enough that he realized they were being purposely obtuse to tease him. "I don't see what you're so concerned about," GrandFather signed. "If it's consensual, there's no crime." Grandfather stopped laughing as a thought occurred to him. "Are you worried because Myra removed the implant? I won't press charges, and I doubt either of them will. It's not like any of us had any idea your species could react to us, and this week has been impossible. If mistakes were made, I doubt they were intentional."

"You're not upset or concerned about them mating?"

"Far from it," GrandFather replied. "Unique circumstances aside, I'm honestly relieved that Little Flower is able to be intimate with anyone after what happened to her. She's expressed both her concerns and curiosity in that regard. She's not attracted to any of our species, male or female, and it's quite obvious to both Henry and I that she cares a great deal about Marsee. We both expected her to follow your traditions around partnership, but I did discuss the possibility of a more intimate relationship if that's what they wanted, as that's part of ours."

"You did?" The idea of intentionally mating with a member of another species had never even crossed his mind. Until Rip, he didn't even think it was possible. "She's been wanting to mate with Marsee? Could this be a result of her removed implant?"

"The Implant?" GrandFather shook his head. "Unlikely. As for wanting to, I don't know. She seemed surprised at the idea, or perhaps that I would suggest it. We don't partner or mate with our siblings. It's considered taboo."

"Taboo?!" That further surprised him. "Why would you not want your closest family members to help care for your children? Partnering with our siblings or other members of our family is one of our most common forms of partnerships."

"We know that. The difference is that your partnerships don't imply a physical relationship. They're all about caring for a child. Ours do. For us a marriage not only implies that we'll care for each other and our offspring but also implies an exclusive mating relationship. Mating outside of that relationship is grounds for ending a partnership, primarily because of broken trust and the increased risk of sexually transmitted diseases. Siblings would not be allowed to legally partner because of the risk of inbreeding."

It took him a moment to understand what GrandFather meant by the sign he made up. "A lack of genetic diversity?" he guessed.

GrandFather nodded.

"Ah. My species doesn't have legal restrictions like that. Our mating instinct picks whomever it deems is the strongest and most powerful mate available when we go into heat. We have little choice in that matter once our heat starts and there are no sexually transmitted diseases that we can't cure. If we're choosing a mate ahead of time, we'll usually get genetic testing done to determine the risk of producing a failed embryo, even if we're not related. There's far too much risk to the mother with a failed heat not to. Even those allowed at an open mating are carefully chosen for the best outcome."

"We know that, too. We didn't have those capabilities. Obviously, there's no risk of that here, but some of our people might deem their physical relationship as wrong, just as they might my relationship with Henry."

"If that's the case, why did you mention the possibility to Little Flower," Jer asked.

"Because, from my perspective, it was obvious how much Little Flower loves Marsee. I want her to be happy and know that I support her in whoever she chooses, regardless of gender, species, or tradition, as long as they treat her right. For most of my life, I could have been arrested for who I loved. I don't care who a person mates with. What's important to me is that all parties are legal adults and capable of giving their consent when they do."

Jer nodded. "As is mine. Myra confirmed it twice, and from what I heard coming from their room, I have no grounds to believe otherwise." He was silent for a few moments, considering several thoughts that ran through his mind. "Our laws don't cover cross-species matings. As far as I know, it's never happened before. If Marsee reacted, it's possible others will, too, and that could be an even bigger problem. Our cubs and in-betweeners don't have hormone blockers like the adults do or training even to know what might be happening to them. The only reason Marsee does is because Myra taught her after finding out about Little Flower's rape, but I'm not sure how much detail Myra went into because of her age. That's something we explore as part of our growth year as we're trying to decide which sex we want to be. We're taught almost everything by healers, not by our parents."

GrandFather nodded. He was quiet for a moment and then glanced at Henry. "If that's the case, then we should inform the Council of the possibility, but I don't know if the males of our species should be informed. At least not right away. There are more men than women, and if Damon was willing to do what he did because of a lack of intimacy, I wouldn't put it past someone to try and figure out a way to get the same reaction out of one of your children. I wouldn't be surprised if many of the men haven't already considered it."

Henry frowned, then nodded. "I've had enough conversations to know that many of the men are...sexually frustrated. There are ways to relieve symptoms, but it's not the same. With the current laws in place, we've all been effectively castrated. I can't say that we don't deserve it. Everything the women have said about us is true, and then some. But that doesn't change the fact that we're all lonely and missing any sort of physical connection."

Henry glanced at GrandFather before continuing. "I've been interested in a relationship with James for some time now, but I didn't even dare mention it until after he told me he would sponsor me for adulthood, and not just because I wanted to mate with him. I can't explain what it's like to go home to an empty apartment every night or to wake to an empty bed. The ghosts of everyone I lost fill that space. It's enough that I've slept in the barn on more than one occasion rather than go home. At least there, I'm surrounded by the other creatures. I'd have adopted a puppy to fill that void if I'd been allowed to, but even that was denied to us because we're not legal adults. We're social creatures. We need the physical touch of others. We need families. We need something or someone to love and to love us back."

Jer considered how he'd felt for the half hour or so he'd been waiting for Myra to return and how disappointed he'd been that she hadn't waited to give him the pheromone blocker, but more than that, how much he'd hated the idea of sleeping alone for the rest of his life. "Do you think adopting one of the puppies would really help?"

To his surprise, they both nodded.

"Raising pets as a child is a part of our culture," GrandFather replied. "It's one of the ways we teach our children how to care for their future children. Cats, dogs, and horses especially, but just about every creature has been kept as a pet at one point or another, regardless of how dangerous they might be. I even remember seeing a news report on an experimental program in our local prison where inmates who showed good behavior were allowed to keep pets during their incarceration. They had a significantly higher reform rate, and it helped find homes for those pets who didn't have one."

Jer flicked his ears back in surprise. "If that's the case, why then did your council vote against it when it was first brought up?"

"Because animals were...abused, too," GrandFather replied. "We couldn't afford to lose any of the creatures rescued."

Jer nodded his understanding of the reasoning, but then paused at the hesitation. "Abused? You're implying more than physical violence aren't you?"

GrandFather sighed but nodded. "Men have been known to stick it just about anywhere. It was very much a Taboo, but it didn't stop people. Why, they did it, I couldn't tell you. Mental illness, curiosity, or some sort of genetic predisposition, I don't know. I do know that cross-species matings and births commonly happened with many species in nature, usually within similar families that were genetically close. Some of those pairings were even domesticated and desired for their physical traits."

"You're serious?" Jer asked, ears pinned back in surprise. "I'm not aware of that happening anywhere on any of the planets."

GrandFather surprised him by actually laughing. "I will forgive you as you're not a Healer, but it happens all the time, even on your world. How do you think we're saving those species where you didn't rescue a female representative? We're using the same techniques that your healer's used to save many of your own species from extinction."

His stunned silence caused both GrandFather and Henry to chuckle and GrandFather said something to Henry in Hue-man.

"I'm sorry, I didn't catch that entirely. I don't have my hearing aids in. Broken brain? You believe this is a mental illness? Could this be a result of Little Flower's brain surgery?"

GrandFather chuckled nervously and rubbed the back of his neck. "Please don't take it the wrong way, but we've noticed that we have a habit of breaking your species' brains with new ideas."

Jer snorted. "That you do. I have a headache after every council meeting. I can't understand your species at all. You never react the way I expect you to and when I think I'm finally starting to understand you, you go and do something like ride a horse."

"Poor cowboy. It was bad enough when we had to compete with Horses. Now we have to compete with Sabers," Henry signed and whistled a tune.

GrandFather burst out laughing and was unable to stop laughing for several minutes. He tried unsuccessfully to explain, but after the third attempted, he just shrugged and gave up.

Realizing this was another situation where he was never going to know what he had said that was so funny, Jer for GrandFather to regain his composure, and grab a drink from the refrigeration unit before continuing.

"My last report says that several species are now recovered enough to move them off the endangered species list?" Jer asked for confirmation.

GrandFather nodded. "As long as the breeding programs continue, yes."

"Then I am not even bringing this before the Council for a revote. I would like the two of you to put together an adoption program for those creatures that are ready to come off the endangered species list. To start, the program will be open to *any* member of your species over the age of two standard years or to any permanent resident caring for one of your cubs younger than that. I want training to occur in the proper care of those creatures before they leave the Barn and regular wellness checks to ensure that they are not being abused."

GrandFather nodded and Henry grinned at GrandFather.

"Before you even ask, no, you can't have my horse," GrandFather replied, with a scowl.

Henry sighed dramatically. "Oh well. I suppose it's a good thing I get the friends and family discount."

GrandFather snorted, and Jer found himself just as confused as he'd been before.

"Discount?"

Both males burst out laughing again.

"You're not going to explain, are you?" Jer asked.

Further laughter was his only response.

Jer shook his head at the two of them. "As far as the laws go for cross-species matings and partnerships, I'll discuss it with the Senior Council to see if we need to make adjustments to the Charter."

They both nodded, and he bid them a good night, but the moment the door was shut, they both burst out laughing again. The guards outside were professional when he reappeared in the hallway, but both tails were still curled. He rolled his eyes at the teasing, wondering how long it would take the press to get ahold of that image from their cams or the one Myra had taken, but then shuddered at the thought of Layton getting his paws on it.

When he entered his room, Myra was attempting to get Hope to settle again by reading her a book, but Hope wasn't really paying attention, and he had a feeling the cub would be awake for hours as the Hue-man's slept for a fraction of the time they did.

Myra sniffed deeply when he entered. "You still stink."

"GrandFather and Henry's showers didn't work either. I have no idea what's going on. I tried to clean it up as best I could."

She snorted and returned to reading the book.

Yawning, he sat down in the chair closest to the bed to get some work done. Scanning the list of messages, he opened the one from Myra and grinned at the picture before moving on to a message that had come in from Quinn while he'd been asleep. The humor he felt vanished as he read.

"What's wrong?" Myra asked.

"Nothing you need to worry about," he replied and kept reading.

"Jeran Frederick, don't make me use all three names. I know that look. What happened?"

He sighed and looked up to find Myra frowning at him. Before he could figure out what to say, Hope climbed down off the bed and into one of the storage cupboards. He snorted at the cub and turned back to Myra, who was now glaring at him. He really didn't want to scare Myra any more than she already was, but he supposed she should know as it involved family. "There was another attack, but everyone is okay, and the people behind it are dead."

"Were they targeting our family again?"

"Not directly. They were going after Quinn this time. The parents of the two Ice Giants that were waiting for Damon and Little Flower set a fire and used the Mana's for bait. The Mana's are okay, and the fire's out. According to Quinn, Nazari is the hero of the day. She's the one who killed the Ice Giants."

"Nazari?" She frowned with worry. "Is she alright? She was struggling with her instinct before."

He shrugged. "I don't know. Quinn says she joined the Guard and that he's mentoring her."

She frowned again. "She transitioned?"

"He doesn't say, but I think so. Her watch has been upgraded for killing two people in self-defense, but the chenzie herd was brought in without issue, only a slight puncture wound from having to carry Fluffer's cub up out of a sinkhole. He also said that he brought Nazari to Sand Dune for several hours of observation and that he wasn't concerned about further issues. I'm assuming that means she transitioned. I don't think he would have let her return to New Hope otherwise. Assuming he returns to Council City after the meeting, she'll be going with him for a few months for additional training under the guise of her maternity leave and will return once her training is complete."

Myra sighed with relief. "I was so worried about her. I think she'll make an excellent guard, and it'll be good to have at least one guard there permanently."

"I couldn't agree with you more. The Council still won't authorize a permanent guard presence, even after everything that happened. I'm seriously considering overriding it."

"You should. How are the Manas?"

"Scared but managing. Peep was terrified and non-verbal for about an hour, but he was able to sign and he's since regained his voice. They're most concerned about Serin and Rowin, as they were the two targeted, but both were in control when tested by Lark."

"They should stay in New Hope," Myra said. "It'll be better if they're around people."

"That's what Quinn thought. Nazari has already offered to share her suite, at least until after the meeting when Pep can return."

"That was kind of her."

He nodded and yawned, then set his tablet down and walked over to the cupboard where Hope had disappeared. He smiled at what he saw and motioned Myra over. Hope had found one of the spare blankets and covered her head with it. A small lump, one foot, and tiny giggles were all that gave her away.

"I wonder where Hope ran off to," he said.

More giggles.

Myra grinned and opened another cupboard. "She's not over here. Maybe she grew wings and flew away."

More giggles.

He opened a third one. This one up high. "Nope. She's not up here either." He sighed dramatically. "Now, where should I look? Under the bed, maybe?"

He crouched down low and pretended to look under but watched through his periphery as the lump crawled out of the cupboard and pretended to sneak up behind him.

"Rawr!" she yelled, in her tiny little voice, and landed on his tail.

He jumped dramatically and spun in the air, landing on the bed on all fours, and poofed up all his fur, pretending to be scared. "Oh no! It's a blanket bumbler!"

More giggles followed.

Myra went to scoop her up, but Hope ran under the bed, leaving Myra with nothing but the blanket. She chased her around to the other side. Hope saw her and ducked back under the bed.

He tried to scoop her up as she ran out the other side, but she weaved around his paw and ran back under. She was surprisingly fast for her tiny size.

He leaned down over the side of the bed, purposely letting his tail hang down over the other side, and wiggled it.

Hope took the bait as well as any of his cubs ever had, and yanked hard on his tail.

"Yeouch!" he yelped and spun around, but Hope ran out the other side, climbed up on the bed, and pounced on him. He flattened down as if thoroughly caught. "Help! It's got me, Myra!"

"Sorry, Jer. There's no saving you from this particular crawly. It's been nice knowing you."

He snorted and glared at her as Hope climbed up his side and sat on top of him. "You're not even going to try?"

"Nah," she replied and curled up on a cushion, kneading it several times. "You're a lost cause, and I'm going back to bed. I'm exhausted."

He sighed dramatically as Hope growled and pulled at his fur. "Well, at least I'll get out of requisition meetings. It's hard to take those from the belly of a blanket bumbler."

Myra chuckled, closed her eyes, and was instantly asleep, showing just how tired she really was.

Several hours later, he woke Myra. "I need to go. She's been fed and changed."

Myra nodded and took Hope from him. "Thank you for letting me sleep. Ship's lag."

He smiled, knowing she'd been running on fumes. She always pushed herself to exhaustion when others needed her help. Hope had not been quiet, and Myra had slept through it all. "No worries. I'll catch a nap in my meeting later when Marcus starts quoting the Charter as he inevitably does." He nodded his head in the direction of the other room. "They've been quiet for about an hour or so."

She nodded and stretched before glancing at the clock. "I suppose I should probably go talk with Kendra while they're sleeping. Give me a minute, and I'll swim over with you?"

He nodded and waited for her to use the waste room, but when she returned, she frowned at Hope.

"I'll be right back. Keep your nose shut." She cautiously ducked into Marsee's room and returned a moment later with Hope's water clothing, mask, and some sort of strapping. "They're both snoring," Myra said as she gently closed the door behind her.

Hope refused to put on the water clothing, and after a minute or two, Myra gave up and put on her own harness instead. Then, after some fiddling, clipped the strapping onto it. He didn't recognize it until she put Hope in it.

He raised a brow. He understood Little Flower's need for the attachment. She wasn't strong enough yet to carry Hope otherwise, but Myra had never used anything like it.

"This will keep her from swimming off. I have no idea how to swim or use the drone and carry her at the same time. I can barely paddle around the pool back home."

He grunted. "I've never even considered that. There's a hook on the front of the drones for carrying objects. I suppose you could put her in that bag Marsee gave you."

Myra rolled her eyes at him. "I am not putting a child in a bag, even if she does pretend to be a blanket bumbler. She'd swim out of that in five seconds. Come on. I am not looking forward to this conversation."

"Are you worried?" he asked.

"No. Not really. I expect she probably already knows by now, but it's still going to be an awkward conversation."

"Do you want me to come with you?"

"No. You have your own meetings to attend. I'll handle this catastrophe and give you an update tonight."

He nodded and followed her out. Along the way, he told Myra what he had learned about Hue-man partnerships and his decision to allow the males to adopt a pet. A pair of Water Sprite guards appeared the moment they exited the platform and followed them to the Council Building, so he stopped talking and did his best to ignore them as he led Myra to Kendra's office. He knew she could find her way, but he felt better knowing she made it safely.

He stared at the door that closed behind her for a moment before leaving. He ducked into his office and attempted to use the shower there, but it, too, malfunctioned. Giving up, he made his way to the Senior's conference room, hoping that the water and his mask had done a good enough job cleaning him. There was no one in the conference room yet, so after putting in a work order to fix the showers, he curled up in his seating net and closed his eyes. Moments later, he was asleep.

He didn't wake until Marcus gently shook his shoulder. Everyone else was there, but he hadn't noticed them enter.

"Sleeping here? Did you have another fight with Myra?" Marcus asked.

"No, but it was a long night." He filled them in on everything that happened and had to chuckle at his brother's expression on several occasions. It was rare that he surprised his brother. The room was silent when he was done, but it was Sammianna who was the first to speak.

"What is it with your family?" she asked. "Do you like causing problems?"

He snorted, as did everyone else. Poor Sammie didn't seem to understand why they were all laughing. "No," he said, at her confusion, "but they have a way of finding me. I'm beginning to think that prankster god of the Hue-mans is behind all of this."

Wind Rider chuckled. "I've heard from several of the Hue-mans that they did have a god that looked much like us. We don't have any gods, but I wouldn't put it past one of our ancestors to have found their planet and caused chaos just because they were bored. It is the kind of thing we would do."

"I'll keep that in mind," Apakna said. "Never let a Flyer get bored."

"It's a very dangerous state to be in," Wind Rider replied. "Second only to a bored Digger."

Sammie frowned at Wind Rider. "What is *that* supposed to mean? We don't get bored. It's a pointless state to be in. There's always something to learn or do."

More laughter followed her statement.

Wind Rider grinned at Sammie's further confusion. "Exactly. The last time my Senior Staffer got bored, they reorganized our entire Council Building. It was complete chaos for weeks."

Sammie frowned again. "I am aware of that reorganization effort. It was a massive undertaking. The case study that came out of it was quite interesting. Your Council was horribly disorganized when we took over staffing it. No one who worked together had offices nearby, and your filing system was ridiculously out of date. You were still using paper copies. Who does that? I don't know how you managed to get anything done before. Efficiency is up ninety-three percent, and everything is now digitized and accessible immediately."

Wind Rider tilted her head, acknowledging the point, and it was all he could do not to laugh. "Quite true," she replied. "And I fully appreciate that effort. However, the only reason I authorized that effort in the first place was that I found Faden organizing my clutch by hue and size. He had finished the project I had given him and got bored waiting for me to finish clutching. I believe my exact words were. 'Don't you have something better you could be doing? It was my mistake, really. He took it quite literally.'"

Sammie raised a brow. "Why would that be a problem? I would think having your eggs organized would make it easier for prospective parents to find a weyrling that matches their scale color."

Wind Rider chuckled. "That was his assumption, too, but that's just not how it works. Some do pick an egg that matches, but for most, it's a feeling. Prospective parents will wander the hatchery until they're quite literally drawn to an egg. I love watching it. It's pure magic and has absolutely nothing to do with logic and numbers."

"That seems like a highly inefficient way to reproduce."

More chuckles followed.

"Perhaps, but then, is yours any better? You lay eggs and then carry your pups in your pouch for more than a year. That seems both unwieldy and exhausting to me. The few weeks I carry mine are uncomfortable, to say the least."

"My sister didn't seem to think so. She was quite sad when their shell hardened and they left the pouch. She was far more exhausted trying to corral them once they learned to roll."

"At least none of you have to deal with cubs who throw their dirty poop sacks at you," Jer muttered.

Marcus grinned. "Mama sent me the picture this morning. In case you're wondering, she sent it to *everyone* in the family."

He groaned. "Why am I not surprised." He slid further in his seat as his brother pulled it up on the monitor, and everyone chuckled, even Sammianna. "In case you're wondering. Every shower I've tried this morning is broken." He glared at Wind Rider. "Somehow, I have a feeling *you're* behind it."

"Me?!" Wind Rider squeaked. "I don't know a thing about showers."

"Uh, huh," he muttered. "One shower I could understand, but both Henry's and GrandFather's, *and* the one in my office? That's highly suspicious."

"Perhaps it was confused by the species using the shower?" Sammianna suggested.

"That was my first thought," Jer said, "But I know that expression. Wind Rider is acting far too innocent. She knows something."

"I swear on my oath, I had nothing to do with it," Wind Rider replied. "But if it was a prank, I'll admit I'm rather impressed. It's not one I've seen before."

"What I don't understand," Marcus said. "Is how Breydhik knew Quinn was the one who killed his sons. That information was locked down. Only a handful of people knew that information."

Everyone turned and scowled at his brother.

"There you go, Marcus, spoiling all our fun by bringing up work again," Wind Rider muttered. "And here I thought for a moment you were finally developing a sense of humor."

"It does appear more likely that Kendra's our mystery guard," Apakna said after the laughter at his brother's expense died down.

"Why would she go after Quinn, though?" Jer asked. "She's his mentor and raised him since he was a cub."

"Fair point," Apakna said. "Still, we know everyone who was there. We can focus on them and see if there's any correlation with the people we've found already."

He yawned and grabbed another folder. "I'll add it to the list, but at least we don't have to worry about Breydhik anymore."

"Darn. One less person for me to kill," Apakna muttered with dripping sarcasm. "What will I ever do?"

"I have a few extra I could trade with you if you don't have enough," Clear Seas replied.

"You're so kind," Apakna said. "What would you like in exchange?"

Clear Seas shrugged. "Got any more of those warble greeps? I called the Habitat to check on them last night. They're quite adorable. I don't know why you don't like them."

She snorted. "Did you even listen to them? Their screech is painful."

"I asked about that. They're outside of our range of hearing."

"Well, in that case, you can have the whole lot free of charge," she replied. "As for the councilors, you can keep those, too. I wouldn't dare to spoil your fun."

"You're so kind," Clear Seas replied. "Are you sure?"

"Quite."

Jer snorted at the exchange and flipped open his folder.

"How about you, Jer?" Clear Seas asked. "You seem to be low on people to shred."

"One is enough for me, thank you. With the showers not working, the last thing I want to do is get my fur dirty again. Sammie can have my share."

CHAPTER 34

Myra: Lies and Goodbyes

Myra took a deep breath, locked everything tightly behind her mask, and knocked on Kendra's door. Her other paw was wrapped protectively around Hope.

Kendra looked up from her tablet, raised a brow to see her, and motioned her in. Once she was inside and the door shut, Kendra activated her privacy screen and motioned to the chair across from her. "I wasn't expecting to see you this early. Is everything alright?"

"I take it you haven't heard?" Myra asked as she took the proffered seat.

Kendra leaned back in her chair. "That depends on what you think I should have heard about."

Myra scratched at the back of her head for a moment, trying to figure out how to explain without lying, if Kendra could, in fact, sniff out the truth. "Marsee and Little Flower are...they..." She sighed. "I had to take Little Flower's implant out to treat a seizure she had after her surgery. She's in heat now, and Marsee is responding to her."

Kendra actually snorted and shook her head. "Is Little Flower all right?"

"Yes. They both claim that it was consensual. I confirmed it twice and left Little Flower with a pheromone blocker. I'm here because I was concerned that Little Flower's scent might affect your guards, as I have no idea why Marsee is responding to Little Flower. I briefly turned on my instinct to see if there was any sort of reaction. There wasn't."

Kendra nodded. "That's a fair concern, but we purposely train all of our guards to recognize and avoid reacting to pheromones, so it shouldn't be a problem."

"They can do that without a pheromone blocker?"

"They're not always successful, but they eventually learn, and every guard is equipped with a dose in the event of an emergency."

"Good to know. I provided additional doses for the guards on Marsee's door. I...Prior to our arrival, Marsee's hormones were elevated and, as of yesterday morning, had mostly returned to normal. While there's no physical proof, it's Rowena's belief that Marsee was raped."

Kendra nodded again. "Quite likely, unless Rip found a way to medically induce her without leaving a bio-marker. Is there any indication that Rowena's treatment failed and this is nothing more than a coincidence?"

She sighed. "I honestly don't know. Her levels were still slightly elevated yesterday morning but returning to normal. I wouldn't have let her leave the Trauma Center if they weren't. Unfortunately, I slept through the alert on my scanner. I didn't know what was happening until Little Flower woke me, several hours later, to inform me that Marsee's sense of pain had returned. Marsee's the first in-betweener to have any contact with a Hue-man in heat. I don't know how likely it will be that anyone else will, as the other females are all on hormone blockers or pregnant, but they can mate outside of their heat, and I've noticed a scent change whenever Henry is around GrandFather. I don't know if that will affect anyone, either."

Kendra was silent for several minutes, then turned her head to look at something in the outer office before hitting the privacy switch. "Avery! My office!"

"Ma'am!" he replied and trotted over.

Once inside, Kendra hit the privacy screen again. "Have you had an update from Aris yet?"

He nodded. "Yes, ma'am."

"Have you or any of your guards noticed a scent change on Little Flower or GrandFather?"

Avery nodded. "I did, but didn't think much of it. I don't have a lot of experience with Hue-mans to know what's normal for them. I didn't react if that's what you're asking."

Kendra nodded and turned back to her. "How long do you expect Little Flower's heat to last?"

"Based on where she is in her cycle, she should be done before the meeting. Two, maybe three local days."

Kendra made a dismissive motion to Avery, and he immediately left, but she didn't say anything for several more minutes. "When you have another female wanting to get pregnant, let me know, and I'll send a few of my younger guards over with their mentors to see if there's going to be an issue or not. Everyone here is past their growth spurt. It's quite likely that our hormone blockers are strong enough to prevent a reaction."

Myra nodded and started to stand, but Kendra raised a paw to stop her and leaned in.

"How long have you been going non-verbal?" Kendra asked.

She just stared at Kendra, surprised by the change in topic and not sure what to say. *Did Rowena say something to Kendra or had someone overheard their conversation? If so, why hadn't Kendra known about what had happened?*

"I...don't know how to answer that question," she finally said. "I wasn't aware that I was even giving that impression until last night. I've been flustered, distracted, and at a loss for words, certainly, but I didn't think I was non-verbal."

Kendra pursed her lips and scowled. "What happened last night?"

That answered her question, but she still wondered why Kendra had thought she'd gone non-verbal. "I...had a bit of an emotional breakdown in the supply closet, and Rowena saw me."

"A breakdown?" Kendra asked, and her scowl deepened. Clearly, she didn't believe her.

"Ma'am, with all due respect. My children have been kidnapped, tortured, and quite likely raped. My nearest neighbor was attacked only hours ago, her children kidnapped, and I nearly lost one of my mentors and my home last night because a member of the Council decided to get revenge on your Second for stopping them from hurting my children in the first place. I'm angry, scared, and holding it together, even if everyone seems to think otherwise. I should be allowed to scream my fury at the people who continue to hurt my family or to break down in a supply closet and cry when I can no longer deny that my daughter was raped, but I don't have that luxury. I know what people will think if I do. I am doing my best to remain calm, and I believe I am still in control. My instinct is as furious as I am, but there's no pressure to act because there's nothing we can do. I don't have the right to go after those who have been arrested, and I don't know who else is involved. So, all I can do is wait and try to pick up the pieces, and sometimes, turn into a complete mess in the supply closet when it gets to be too much. I'm not the first healer to do so, and I won't be the last."

Kendra softened. "What has happened to your family is horrible, but I honestly don't understand *how* you're remaining in control. I've seen parents lose it completely at far less, and you were struggling to speak when you first arrived."

She snorted at Kendra. "By that definition, I imagine every single person you talk to has gone non-verbal. No offense, ma'am, but you are rather terrifying, and I had no idea how you would handle the situation with my daughters, especially considering my past history. I honestly didn't know if I was going to be arrested or executed on the spot. So excuse me for taking a moment to figure out what to say."

Kendra tilted her head. "I suppose you have a point there. I spend most of my day scowling at guards. My bedside manner could use some work. As for your other points, I have ordered additional guards to New Hope, all of which I thoroughly trust and we are doing everything we can to ensure the safety of your friends and family. That being said,

Quinn would be dead if it weren't for your mentor. Nazari has *joined* the Guard, in case you haven't heard."

Myra raised a brow at the emphasis that Kendra used. "Jer told me."

"Quinn has offered to mentor her, and with Avery unofficially mentoring your daughter, that makes us family. I don't want you to be scared of me. I want to help you. Tell me what I can do to make things easier for you. What do you need?"

She raised her other brow, not expecting that at all. "Well, you can start trusting me, for one."

"I do trust you. I don't trust your instinct. You are an anomaly, just as your daughter was. I gave her a chance, and I'm giving you one, too." Kendra stood and walked over to her kitchenette. She opened a cupboard and pawed through it. "Ah, good. They did stock it." Kendra handed her a canister. "Managing stress is a major challenge in my profession, as you might imagine. This tastes atrocious, but I find it helps. Mix one scoop with water or juice and drink it an hour or so before bed."

"What is it?" Myra asked. The label was written in Digger, and she didn't recognize the words.

"I have absolutely no idea and I'm not sure I want to know. My father used to drink it. I always knew he had a bad day when the canister came out. All I know is it's one of the few things from Digger we can consume. He called it Bottled Digger. They drink it when they don't want to have to deal with 'pesky emotions.' It'll help calm your thoughts enough to sleep without any side effects."

"Thank you." Myra tucked the canister in one of her pockets to keep Hope away from it. "Leave it to a Digger to find a way to lessen their emotions. How *effective* is it in the long run?"

Kendra shrugged. "Historically, no. By the time people are brought to us, nothing seems to help, but perhaps it might help you remain calm. Would you like to talk about what's happened to your family?"

"Not really," she replied. "Thinking about it makes it harder to stay calm. I'd prefer to stay focused on the immediate problems and...deal with it later when the crisis is over."

"I can understand and respect that. If you change your mind, my door is always open, or perhaps if it would make you feel more comfortable, you could talk with Tamarin. She's quite skilled as a trauma healer, even if her rank says otherwise. Now, as far as the immediate issues are concerned, what do you intend to tell Marsee about what happened to her?"

"Nothing," Myra said. "At least not until she's had time to recover. I don't see as it will do any good, and she'll be occupied for a few days anyway."

Kendra gave a slight grin. "Well, if nothing else, it does make our job of guarding them both a bit easier. Keep me informed if there's any change."

"Yes, ma'am." She stood and started to walk out.

"Myra," Kendra said, stopping her again.

She turned back around.

"*One* chance. If there's even a hint of you going non-verbal again, we'll bring you in for observation."

"Yes, ma'am," she replied and left, honestly surprised she was being allowed to leave.

As she left the Council Building, she saw Ammond, Rowena, and Rowena's nephew heading across the park to the platform. Punching her drone so she could say goodbye, she caught up with them just as they entered the platform.

Hope squealed with happiness when she saw Ammond. "Uncle Ammy!"

Ammond pulled Hope out of the carrier the. moment she arrived. "What happened to your clothes?"

"That little Blanket Bumbler wouldn't hold still long enough to put them on," Myra explained. "I gave up trying after a while. It's cool enough here for her anyway."

"Blanket Bumbler?" Rowena asked, squinting at Hope, who Ammond had thrown up on his shoulder as he often did.

"It's a very deadly crawly," she explained as they started walking with Rowena at her slow pace, "Able to defeat Senior Councilors in a single pounce. In case you're wondering, the Hue-man cubs are just as attracted to tails as our cubs. If not more so."

Rowena chuckled. "I am quite thankful I don't have a tail. It doesn't seem to have any purpose besides getting it stuck in things or pounced on."

"Or rolled over by a rocking chair."

They turned to find Ellie behind them and Myra gave her a hug.

"Coming to make sure I don't break your ship?" Rowena asked Ellie.

Ellie chuckled. "It would be worth every credit. Thank you for coming. I know how difficult this trip has been for you."

Rowena scowled. "What's difficult is completing my experiments without that nano-particle accelerator."

"I am sorry about that mixup. Nardal is looking into what happened with your order. Let me know if you haven't heard anything by the end of the week."

"I could be dead in a week," Rowena huffed, "but I suppose it'll have to do."

Ellie reached over to pick up Hope, but Hope hid her face in Ammond's fur.

"Hey there, Hope, I know I look a little different, but it's just me," Ellie said and reached out to pat her.

Hope shied away even further.

"Hope, don't you want to see your Auntie Ellie?" Myra asked.

"No!" Hope yelled. "Want Uncle Ammy!"

Ellie's ears drooped, Ammond preened, and Rowena cackled, which caused Ellie to scowl at her.

Still laughing, Rowena turned and kept shuffling towards the ship. They were stopped twice on their way but were soon outside the docking port. Rowena sent her nephew onboard to stow the last of the equipment she'd brought with her and turned to face them.

"Thank you, for everything," Myra said.

Rowena grunted. "You're very welcome. It was good to meet Marsee and Little Flower in person and especially this little ball of wiggles who has somehow managed to soften the heart of your mentor. If you have the opportunity, stop in on the way home. I'd love for you to meet the rest of my family."

"I would like that. Thank you. I do have a question for you before you leave. I was just talking with Kendra and she gave me something to help me sleep. I don't recognize the words on the label. What is it?" She pulled out the canister and showed it to Rowena.

Rowena actually burst out laughing. "Bottled Digger? I haven't seen this since before my father died. I thought they stopped making it years ago."

"Is that what it's really called?"

"That's your species name for it, and yes, it does have a mild calming effect on your species that should help you sleep, although not nearly as much as it does for ours. It tastes atrocious though, even for us. I recommend mixing it with a strong fruit juice. It will still taste atrocious, but it's better than on it's own." Rowena opened the canister and breathed deeply as a grin crossed her face. "The smell reminds me of my father. He used to make some every night before bed and always offered, even though I always turned it down. I never saw the point of hiding my emotions, even as a child. They are as much a part of me as my shell and it's far more fun to growl at people. They never expect it from a Digger."

Myra grinned at Rowena. "I wouldn't want you any other way. So, why did you think they stopped making it?"

"Because we found alternatives that taste far better. Sadly, you'd be allergic to those, as it's made from a derivative of Raja Spice."

Rowena took another nostalgic sniff before handing the canister back and turned her gaze on Ellie, and her expression shifted to a glare that made Ellie cower slightly. Myra was honestly impressed. It had been decades since she'd seen Ellie buckle under anyone's glare.

"You take good care of that protege of yours. The next six months are not going to be easy for any of you, especially her. If you need to, bring her to Digger. My family will protect her. I give you my word, but it'll be up to you to get her there before the Council gets their claws on her."

"Do you think that's still a concern?" Ellie asked.

Rowena snorted. "How someone as soft-shelled as you ever made it to Senior Guild Master is beyond me. The only thing standing between Marsee and your Council right now is Marcus, and the sands are shifting against him. If he's voted out or killed, Marsee is as good as dead. No Senior that replaces him will take the same chance on her that he is, medical proof or not. At the first sign of a problem, get her out and bring her to me, and don't go back to Saber until your watch is up. That goes for all of you. You're all far safer here."

Ellie frowned but nodded. "Thank you."

Rowena turned to Ammond and actually smiled at him. Ammond now had a deep scowl on his face that Myra was sure was hiding his grief. "Well, you old coot, it might have taken you two and a half centuries, but I think Master Bresdone might have actually been impressed with what you've done with that brain scanner of yours and your work with repairing the Hue-mans, but you might need a new name sign. Ear Healer is far too small of a designation for you. I think Uncle Ammy suits you far better."

Without waiting for a response from Ammond, who stood there slack-jawed in astonishment, Rowena turned and walked onto the ship, closing the door behind her.

"Myra," Ammond finally managed to splutter out.

"Hmm?" she asked.

"You'd better scan me. I'm pretty sure I'm dead."

Myra snorted. "Well, if you are, so am I. I heard the same thing, Uncle Ammy."

They waited there in silence until the ship pulled away, and they could no longer see it through the docking port, although at one point, the ship came so close to Sammianna's ship that it made them all gasp. Through the port of the window they could see Rowena cackling with laughter before it pulled away.

"Wait till I get my hands on those pilots," Ellie scowled. "Flyers! Now, do you know if Marsee is up? I need to talk to her."

"No, and she's going to be occupied for a few days," Myra said.

Ellie frowned. "Days? Doing what?"

"It's a long story, and I don't want to talk about it here. Why don't you come back to my suite, and we can talk about it there. Ammond, did Rowena fill you in?"

"She did," Ammond replied. "I'll meet you in my office later."

Myra reached over to take Hope from him, but Hope started screaming immediately and grabbed tightly onto Ammond's ears causing him to wince. "Hey now. Not so hard, you're hurting Uncle Ammy."

Ammond rolled his eyes. "She's not hurting me," he lied. "Hope obviously likes me better. I'll take care of her while you two get caught up." He turned and walked off before she could say no, bouncing slightly to make Hope laugh.

She watched him walk away, knowing that he needed a distraction from his grief, as even though he was being silly for Hope, his tail drooped behind him. She wrapped her own tail around Ellie. "Come on. We have a lot to talk about."

"That we do," Ellie replied. "I want to hear all about that picture you sent me last night. I didn't stop laughing for an hour and I'm sorely tempted to send it to Layton."

"Oh, that's just cruel, but please let me know when you do, so I can record the broadcast."

A few minutes later, they were back in the room. Myra grabbed breakfast for both of them and hadn't even sat down, when there was a knock on the door. She set the food down and opened it to find a Flyer who, according to the badge on his harness, was the Senior Platform Tech waiting outside with Tamarin guarding from behind him.

"I'm here to fix the shower," he said. As a wicked grin on his face, he lifted his tablet and tapped it once.

"Thank you Timothy," Ellie said from behind her. "Your work, as always, is perfection. I'll be sure to put in a recommendation for you."

"Same time tomorrow?" he asked.

Ellie chuckled. "I can't say as I'll be here, but I expect you'll get another call. Thank you in advance."

"The pleasure is all mine," Timothy replied and bowed dramatically before walking off, whistling a happy tune.

Myra watched him leave and then both she and Tamarin turned back to Ellie. "*You're* behind the shower?" Myra asked.

Ellie grinned and peered at her claws. "I might have something to do with it, but in my defense, I was following the orders of the Senior Council to check that the security flaw Snapper Fish made use of was no longer an issue. I informed Timothy that he might get a maintenance request or two while we worked through it. Sadly, it would appear that there's more work to be done. It only took me ten minutes to break in and reprogram the showers yesterday. I must admit the results were far better than I expected. How long do you think it will take before Jer figures it out?"

She chuckled and Tamarin snorted behind her. "Pay up, Aris. I told you Ellie was behind this." She then turned to Ellie. "I give him three days"

"Four!" Aris called out.

"I'll give him two before he decides Wind Rider's behind it," Myra said. "So what exactly did you do to the shower?"

"I programmed it to look at Jer's official species designation rather than his biological one. Consider this my gift to you for what he did to Marsee. She might have forgiven him, but I haven't."

Myra grinned. "He should have known better than to mess with your protege."

"You'd think, but you and I both know, he's a bit fur-brained at times. Now, what's going on with Marsee?"

She sighed, and thanked Tamarin before shutting the door and turning back to Ellie. "We have another medical mystery, because the Ancient Gods have clearly decided we haven't had enough."

CHAPTER 35

Marcus: Guilded Cage

Marcus had been staring at his latest folder for some time, lost in thought about everything Jer had told them and all the possible ramifications, but he looked up as Clear Seas swam over to the Pile, his skin radiating grief and anger.

"Who is it this time?" Marcus asked.

"Snapping Turtle," Clear Seas replied.

Marcus sighed heavily, numb with grief. He knew Snapping Turtle well and had worked with the Sprite for decades, as he was more often than not Clear Seas' Acting Senior when he was off-world. "What did he do?"

"Treason and child abuse," Clear Seas muttered, staring at the growing pile of crimes that were all serious enough to warrant execution.

"Seriously?" Apakna asked. "Well, that would explain why Blue has always been so quiet at functions."

"Multiple flags from the healers for injuries Blue sustained. Out of everyone, why did it have to be him?" His anger shifted to the dark blues and black of grief and mourning, and the conflicting colors pulsed off the walls and the stack. "We're supposed to be better than this. We're supposed to be protecting our people, not hurting them."

"Sometimes, even when we're trying to protect them, we end up hurting them," Jer said quietly.

Marcus glanced at his brother and saw guilt on his face. Marsee and Myra may have forgiven him, but it was clear Jer hadn't forgiven himself.

"The people are never going to trust us again once this information gets out," Clear Seas muttered. "I don't even know who to trust anymore."

"They'd be right not to," Wind Rider replied.

"So what are we going to do about it?" Apakna asked. "Besides prosecute? Every offense in that accursed pile is a death sentence. All jokes aside, I honestly don't know how I'm going to do it. Those are our friends."

"And family," Clear Sea whispered, running a hand over Snapping Turtle's folder.

"I fully intend to have the Guard do it," Marcus said. "This is the whole reason I never wanted the job in the first place."

Jer snorted. "We can't even trust the Guard at this point."

Before anyone could answer, there was a knock on the door. Clear Seas brought his skin back under control and swam over to open it. "Ellie, what brings you here this early in the morning?"

"I have a little problem I need to talk to you all about," she replied.

Clear Seas motioned her in and shut the door behind her.

"Sorry, Ellie," Marcus replied dryly. "We're full up on problems. You'll have to take a number."

"How does two hundred and fifty-one billion sound?" Ellie asked. "Give or take a few hundred million."

Marcus raised a brow. "That depends on what that number represents."

"That would be Marsee's current guild balance," Ellie replied.

"*What?!*" They all exclaimed at the same time.

"It was only a few million when she showed it to us the other day," Jer replied. "What happened?"

"Clear Sea's people happened. That doesn't even include the physical donations that are being gifted to her. I'm pretty sure just about everyone on this planet has sent her something at this point."

Clear Seas swam over and sat down, looking defeated, but then, to his surprise, started laughing.

"I don't see what's so funny," Marcus growled. "This is going to cripple our economy."

"*My* economy. My people did this. We'll suffer the consequences. But that's just it. Rip was so convinced that your family was trying to take over, yet by his own actions, he essentially made Marsee the most powerful person in the universe. I might as well step down so my people can vote her in. I wouldn't be surprised if they write her in at the next election anyway, even if she's not a citizen."

"She'll decline," Ellie replied. "She loathes requisition meetings."

"Who doesn't?" Apakna asked.

Sammie started to raise her hand, but she stopped and looked at them all, utterly confused, when they burst out laughing again.

"I suppose we could use that as leverage," Marcus said, not bothering to explain to Sammie why they were laughing.

"Leverage to do what?" Apakna asked. "Keep her from buying a fleet of ships? For that amount, she could buy them all."

"She does want her own ship," Ellie said. "But from what I can tell, she's still only looking at the smaller ones. I've had Nardal monitor her browsing history and what she's purchasing. And before you say anything, yes, I know that's not entirely legal. That's partly why I'm here."

"I propose we give Ellie permission to continue monitoring Marsee's purchases and to inform the Senior Council if there's any purchase exceeding a thousand credits," he proposed.

"Granted," the others all replied.

"I'm hoping you came here with a few ideas," Wind Rider said.

"A few, but that all depends on whether or not we can get her back into the Guild. She's tried to quit several dozen times in the last week, but I've flat-out denied it. She thinks it's a joke, but if she were to quit, she'd bankrupt the Guild."

"Has she bought anything yet?" Sammie asked.

"Some, although nothing particularly substantial. She raided the market yesterday and made one large donation to Opal. According to the scuttle I heard, she told Opal to open the restaurant that she's always wanted. I've also been charging her premium rates for the repairs to her room, although I doubt she's even noticed."

"Marsee has good taste," Clear Seas said. "If I didn't have to avoid the appearance of favoritism, I'd eat at Opal's every day. Maybe it won't be a problem if that's the kind of investments she's making."

"She wants to have a large partnership ceremony for Little Flower when they return home," Marcus said.

"That'll hardly touch that amount," Jer replied. "She could literally pay for every Hallowed Eve Festival for the next several thousand years with that budget."

"So what did you have in mind?" Apakna asked Ellie.

"Honestly, the best we've been able to come up with was to suggest other ways she could donate the credit back, like she did with Opal. From the Guild's perspective, I was thinking of suggesting the Research Fund. Agate said she seemed to enjoy meeting with all the masters and discussing their projects. I might be able to convince her to come back and run the fund, especially if she gets to pick the projects she wants to work on. I figured I could offer a percentage of whatever benefit came out of those projects. You know, as well as I do, most of the time, they're complete flops, but Marsee has a unique way of looking at the universe. She salvaged at least three projects in that hour alone, and I don't even think she realizes what she did."

"Do you honestly think she'd give up that kind of credit?" Apakna asked.

"What else is she going to do with it?" Ellie replied. "She's a good cub. If we explain what keeping all of it would do, I think she'd do the right thing."

"Or she could use it to leverage us to make us do what she wanted," Apakna said. "That's the annual budget for half my planet."

Marcus glared at Apakna. "She's nothing like Rip. Don't even suggest it. She wouldn't do that. If she loathes requisition meetings as much as we all do, we could threaten to make her contribute as if she *were* five districts."

"How would that even work?" Clear Seas asked. "You can't exactly ask one person to perform five districts worth of labor."

"No, but we could require her to fund various projects," he replied. "The Hue-mans did something like that. I think they called it a tax."

"Require? I don't like the sound of that at all," Wind Rider said. "That sets a dangerous precedent and feels an awful lot like theft. We can't require a person to work or contribute more than the maximum number of hours just because someone gave them a gift, regardless of how large it is. Even in reparations, the number of hours a person can work is capped per day as a guaranteed right."

"We could give her some added incentive to donate," Jer suggested. "The Research Fund is a good idea, but it's not going to solve the immediate budget shortfall we're going to have. Even if the Sprites take the brunt of it, it'll eventually affect all of our planets. Marcus's idea has potential merit, but she would need to get something out of it in exchange to keep it from being theft, as Wind Rider stated. The Hue-mans credit system was fundamentally broken due to systemic deregulation and corruption, but they did have exceptionally wealthy people. GrandFather might have some ideas. Shall we see if he's available to discuss?"

The others agreed, and a few moments later, Jer flung the call up on the main monitor and filled GrandFather in on the situation.

GrandFather blinked at them for several moments and scratched the back of his head. "I take it you've never had this problem before?" he finally asked.

"No, our system doesn't normally work like this," Clear Seas explained. "People gift of their time. A few hours here or there doesn't matter as long as both people are happy with the trade, but never anything to this scale."

"There was a fairly significant gifting to New Hope, but that all went into the community for us to use as we saw fit, not to a single person," Jer added. "It basically reduces the funding available for projects in that person's own community. It's not an issue because every person is allowed to indicate where they want their credits to go. The challenge comes in ensuring that it remains in balance. We were gifted more credit than we could use in a single quarter because we don't have the resources to build all of the structures at once or even know what we're going to need, so those donations have been earmarked for future quarters to lessen the burden elsewhere, and there are skills that we don't need that were traded for ones that we do. A large portion of the council meetings are to trade credit and determine which projects actually get built and when."

GrandFather nodded. "I understand that. What I don't understand is why it's a problem that she's been gifted so much."

"For one," Clear Seas said. "If she called it all in, we'd have no choice but to build whatever she wanted. We could certainly advise her not to, but even if she did nothing, my people would struggle from the lack of available credit. We'd have to put a lot of critical projects on hold."

"There's also the added challenge of her being a resident of New Hope," Marcus said. "It skews the numbers in New Hope's balance substantially, which was already badly skewed from previous gifting. If people like Rip are willing to do what he did because they thought our family already had too much power, I can just imagine what they'll do when they find out how much power Marsee has over the Consortium now. She'd be dead in a week, as would the rest of our family, and it would quite likely put the rest of New Hope at risk, too."

Jer swallowed hard. Clearly, that thought hadn't occurred to him, but GrandFather nodded.

"We had a saying that money, our word for credit, is the root of all evil. It breeds corruption, jealousy, and greed. As far as what to do, we had a few ways we handled situations like this. One was taxes, where the government took a percentage of our credit to pay for programs once we reached a certain income level. I don't recommend that route. It's a slippery slope that ends in resentment. Your approach is fairer, at least from what I've learned so far, and gives people a sense of pride in what they build and accomplish in their communities. A loan could work. It's a fairly basic math problem. She would give you credits, which you would pay back with interest over time. She'd make more in the long run. How much depends on what percentage you paid back, how frequently you made payments, how frequently the interest compounded, and how long you took out the loan. Usually, the bigger the loan, the better the rates for the lender...which I can see Councilor Sammianna is already working on."

They all turned to Sammie, who was furiously scribbling away on her tablet. "You had me at 'math problem,'" Sammie said, and the others all chuckled. A few minutes later, Sammie scratched her chin. "I suppose that could work." She shared her screen, and they all stared at the information.

"Do you think she'd agree to it?" Clear Seas asked. "It'd be tight for a few years, but we could make that work. It still leaves her with an obscene amount of credit, but she'd be handing over an enormous sum to us, and frankly, she has no reason to, not after what Rip did to her."

"That's just one option," Sammie replied and made some adjustments. "This would be far more lucrative for her in the long run and easier for us to offset, but we'd be paying back longer."

"That would be better for us for sure, although I'm going to have to bring this up with my Council," Clear Seas said. "I'll call an emergency meeting. Can you put together a few proposals?"

"I think I'd like in on that too," Ellie said. "What if we split it up between the Guild and Council? That way, I can approve the projects coming in from the other guilds that aren't Council expenditures."

"How much do you think you need, Ellie?" Sammie asked.

"What if we suggest a quarter to the Research Fund, a quarter to the Guild, and half to the Council?" Ellie suggested.

"I'd be good with that," Clear Seas replied. "It would certainly be much easier for our Council to absorb, and that significant of an investment in the Research Fund could benefit us all greatly."

"I propose the Full Council absorbs this, not just the Water World," Wind Rider said. "Rip was targeting all of us, and the Water World reacted with love and generosity. It's not exactly fair that their generosity has such a devastating effect on their world. If we react harshly, they might not gift with the next crisis."

"Agreed," the others said.

Marcus noticed that Apakna hesitated briefly, but she, too, nodded her agreement.

"The real question is whether or not she'll agree to this," Wind Rider stated.

"She will if we do this right," Ellie replied. "Once she's done with her candy moon..."

"Honeymoon," GrandFather corrected.

"Whatever it's called," Ellie said, waving dismissively. "I'll talk to her about her plans for the Guild. I need to convince her to stay and figure out what she wants to do anyway. I doubt she wants anything to do with being my replacement, not after what Rip did to her. She might have her own ideas that we should consider, too, but I think she'll go along with this, especially if she knows how devastating this would be if she didn't. Clear, draft up a list of all of the projects that would have to be put on hold if she didn't. If I were you, I'd focus on things like trauma centers, schools, and public infrastructure. Projects that would hurt people if they weren't approved. She might not care if a shipyard is delayed by a year or three. But put people's lives at risk, and she'll sign it all over. I'll get her thinking that way, and then Jer can swoop in with the Council's needs. Sammie, make it as complicated as you can so that she doesn't just agree to the first option. That way, she'll talk to her father about it before deciding. She's horrible at math, so that shouldn't be hard, but I'll be sure to suggest it as well."

"You picked a protege that was horrible at math?" Sammie asked, to further laughter, which she clearly didn't understand.

Ellie shrugged. "She's young. I figured I had a few years to knock it into her before it would matter. It was her character that impressed me."

Clear Seas nodded. "Her honor is not in question, but this is asking a great deal of even the most honorable, especially after what she's been through. If she doesn't, we'll take the brunt since we did this. My people will understand and see it as fair and just compensation for what happened to her. I won't put people in danger, but we can wait on many of the projects."

"I'll work with Nardal to draft up plans and the legal paperwork," Sammie said.

"Thanks, Sammie," Marcus replied. "GrandFather, thank you for your guidance."

"Any time," GrandFather replied and disconnected.

The moment the screen was off, Jer let out a massive yawn.

"Sorry to bore you with my little problem," Ellie teased.

Jer chuckled. "I am chronically sleep-deprived at this point. Do you have any interest in cub-sitting duty?"

"I've already been over to see Myra this morning. If you want a cub sitter, talk to Ammond. I couldn't even get Hope away from him. She's thoroughly attached to that old grump." Ellie sounded rather annoyed at the fact.

"Are you still mad that Little Flower chose Ammond to be her mentor?" Jer asked.

"No, of course not. That was all show, for Little Flower's sake. She needed to know I still valued her, even if she couldn't draw anymore. Besides, the Hue-mans bounce from one interest to another, just like Marsee. It's what makes them special. I'll get my claws in her again, eventually."

"That's assuming they don't spend the rest of their lives mating," Jer said. "Just so you know, Clear Seas. Those suites are *not* soundproof."

Everyone burst out laughing except Sammianna, who was thoroughly confused once again as to why they were laughing.

"I'll explain later," Wind Rider whispered to her.

"Well, if Ellie sent me that back-ordered shipment of privacy screens, you wouldn't have that problem," Clear Seas replied.

Ellie scowled at Clear Seas. "Don't blame that problem on me. That one is entirely your fault. You canceled the order. Twice."

Rather than reply, Clear Seas pursed his lips, considering. "Twice? I think I better add that to the list of things we have Lowell investigating. I know I'm useless when it comes to tech, so it didn't surprise me when it happened the first time, but I am quite certain I have not canceled it a second time."

"You did. Three weeks ago. I was surprised as I knew you wanted them for the new council suites. Jelly told me that you needed an emergency shipment of cooling units for the Giants suites as a batch was damaged in shipment. That was obviously a higher priority."

"Well, there's your problem," Marcus said.

Ellie frowned at them. "Jelly's involved?"

Clear Seas sighed. "You can't tell anyone. We haven't arrested her yet. We don't want anyone else to be forewarned until we finish our investigation." He pointed to the mountain of remaining evidence. "We still have all of *that* to go through."

"That's what all this is? Jer told me you found evidence in Rip's home, but I didn't realize it was this much." She let out a heavy sigh that he fully understood. "I'm not going to like this next meeting, am I?"

"No," Marcus replied and glanced in the direction of the Pile. "No, I don't think any of us will."

CHAPTER 36

Carrie: Primary School

Carrie floated behind a bush outside the market, her stomach rumbling. The food she'd ordered the night before had never arrived, and her complaint to the vendor had gone unanswered. She knew she could report it to the Council or the guards shadowing her, but she wouldn't. It wasn't worth the aggravation, but now she was starving, and fixing the issue meant facing the crowd. Her stomach rumbled again, but she still didn't move.

"I can get something for you," a quiet voice said behind her. She looked back to see one of the Saber Guards that was shadowing her. "Or go with you if you prefer to pick it out yourself."

Feeling instantly safer, figuring no one would give her a hard time if she had a guard with her, she nodded her thanks, took a deep breath, and swam out with the guard behind her. The market quieted and stilled as they caught sight of her. Flashes of "Isn't that *his* daughter?" and "I can't believe they didn't arrest her, too." caught her attention, and those were some of the nicer comments she saw.

"Ignore them," the guard behind her said. "Those scum suckers aren't worth your time or attention. You were a victim and kept Wind Rider's daughter and the others alive at your own expense. They should be treating you with respect for giving them the food you so clearly needed and still need." His voice was just loud enough to carry, and shock and disbelief flickered through the crowd at his insult, but she ignored that, too. She appreciated the guard's support. It was good to have someone on her side, but he didn't understand her people the way she did. She knew it would only make things worse.

She swam up to the nearest vendor and waited in line. The people in front of her ignored her, or appeared to at first, but then she realized they were all purposely taking a ridiculous amount of time to order their meal or chat with the vendor before making a decision. Checking the time, as she didn't want to be late for her first day of school, she looked around the market for a shorter line and decided to head there. Before she could arrive, a dozen people filled in before her. The guard behind her growled quietly, clearly recognizing what they were doing to her, but the people ignored him. They weren't technically doing anything illegal, so there was little he could do.

She did her best to wait patiently, but the line barely moved, and when she checked the time again, she sighed and started to swim away. She couldn't wait any longer or she'd be late for school.

"Carrie, wait!"

She turned to see a Sprite swimming hard towards them. The guard shifted in front of her protectively.

"I mean her no harm, Honor Guard," the Sprite flashed as she came to a quick stop. "My name is Opal." She raised a bag. "It's food. No charge. I had set this aside for the Translator in the event she came by this morning, but I just sold my booth and everything else in it to another vendor and I like you to have it."

The guard took the large bag, confirmed what was inside, and handed it to her.

"Thank you," Carrie flashed with relief as her stomach growled its impatience.

"You're very welcome," Opal replied. "I'm in the process of setting up a restaurant. When it's ready, you're welcome there anytime. Until then, my contact information is in the bag. Let me know what you'd like, and I'll personally deliver it." Without another word, Opal turned and swam away, scowling at everyone else in the market.

Carrie waited until she was out of sight of the market before her growling stomach overrode the last of her control, and she tore into one of several wrapped packages inside the bag, praying that Opal hadn't handed her rotten food. It smelled and looked good so she took a tentative bite and groaned with happiness. "Oh, this is good," she flashed.

"So, I've heard," the Guard replied. "I've yet to partake from her booth, but several of the other guards were raving about her last night. She is the Translator's favorite and from what I understand bought Opal her restaurant from some of the credits gifted to her."

Carrie held out one of the sticks to the guard, but he shook his head.

"You need it more," he replied, "and I'm on duty, but thank you."

She shrugged and, after another bite, took off for school. By the time she arrived, her stomach was visibly distended, and half the food was gone. For the first time in as long as she could remember, she actually felt full. It was such a wonderful feeling. She just hoped her nerves didn't make her throw it all back up.

You survived Rip. How hard can primary school be?

Taking a deep breath, she opened the door, and to her surprise, the guard followed her inside.

"Are you coming to class with me, too?" she asked. "Shall I enroll in Water Sprite 101?"

"No," he replied with a grin. "I am fully fluent in your visual language, but I do need to know which classroom you'll be in, and I want to make sure you don't have any further issues."

She nodded, grateful for his support, and swam into the clearly marked main office.

A female sprite at the front desk looked up. "Good morning. You must be Carrie."

She nodded.

"You'll be in pod c room 14 with Master Slate," the Sprite told her and handed her a small packet. "You'll find a map inside, along with your class schedule, upcoming activities, and after-school groups you can join if you're interested. We've placed you based on where you should be so that you're with your age group. A tutor has been assigned to help you get caught up. You have a session scheduled for an hour each day after your regular classes until you decide you no longer need it. If you find you're too far behind, let me know, and we can adjust."

Carrie nodded again, relieved. She'd been worried about that.

"I see you brought food with you. If it needs refrigeration, there's a small unit in each of the classrooms and a larger unit in the cafeteria. All three meals are included at no charge even on days school is not in session. The cafeteria schedule is included inside as well. I didn't see any food allergies listed on your registration, but if you do have any, please notify the Healer in the station just down the hall, and she'll inform the cafeteria staff. If you need anything else or anyone gives you any trouble, come find me, and I'll make sure it stops."

Carrie nodded yet again and followed the instructions the Sprite handed her to her classroom, ignoring everyone she passed, who all turned to stare at her and the guard following her. When she was outside the classroom, she turned to thank the guard for his assistance, but he had disappeared. She spun, looking for him, and then shrugged before facing the door, trying to build up the courage to swim in.

Several minutes later, she was still there. Others had passed her or gone inside. Most ignored her, but a few who recognized her flashed their disgust before swimming away.

"Hello," a quiet voice said behind her.

She spun again and found a Sprite about the same size as her floating there. She blinked in surprise when she recognized him.

"You're Carrie Fish, Snapper Fish's daughter, aren't you?" he asked.

She didn't know what to say. Technically, she wasn't anymore.

After an awkwardly long pause, he added. "I'm Stormy Seas, but I'm guessing by your expression that you already know that."

She nodded. "It's just Carrie now. I've emancipated myself. I know you probably won't believe me, but I am so very sorry for what my father did."

"I do believe you," he replied. "I've watched your statement along with all the others, and I don't blame *you* for what your *former* father did. I haven't seen you around before. I take it you're starting classes today? "

She nodded again, surprised by his generosity and the change in topic. "It's my first day. This is apparently my classroom, but I admit I'm a little nervous."

"Don't be," he replied. "You'll like Master Slate. He's one of my favorite teachers. He's got an incredible sense of humor and can make pond scum seem interesting. Come on, you can sit by me."

"Seriously? You want me to sit next to you?"

"Sure. Why not, unless you don't want to?" He lifted an arm and sniffed. "I don't think I stink."

"That's not what I meant," she said, flashing a nervous humor. "I'm just surprised you'd want anything to do with me after what my father did."

He raised his other arm, revealing a scar like hers. "I know what you went through, and I'm grateful for what you did for Petra. She and my brother are close friends, one of his few. I don't have many friends either, not real friends anyway. They all want to associate with us because of what we might do for them in the future."

"I would never do that," she said. "I don't want to be anything like Rip."

"And that's why I want to see if we can be friends. Come on, let's get in there before all the good seats are taken."

She grinned and followed him in, feeling hopeful for the first time in months. It was enough to know that he didn't blame her, and if he could forgive her, perhaps with time, others might, too.

They found a pair of seats in the back, near a window, and he flopped into his net. She stored her lunch inside the desk, like he did, rather than putting it in the refrigeration unit, and examined the room with curiosity as she waited, but she didn't have to wait long. Classes started almost immediately, and Stormy was right. Their teacher was quite entertaining, and even though the material was all new, she had no problems keeping up.

When they broke for lunch, she followed Stormy outside rather than to the cafeteria. He led her over to a seat along the wall surrounding it. "I hate the cafeteria. It's too loud and crowded," he explained. "and with everything going on, I'm bringing my own meals these days."

"Are you worried about the cafeteria workers?" she asked. She'd been hopeful about getting her meals there instead of the market.

"No, not really. They've always been polite, and most everything is pre-prepared for you to just pick up, but my mother insisted, and I suppose she's right. I had to argue for hours just to come back to classes in person after Marsee was kidnapped. I don't do well with online classes. I get too distracted."

She nodded her understanding. "I'm the same way. I thought about taking classes online instead, but I know I can't hide forever."

He frowned. "Are people mistreating you?"

She shrugged. "People are angry at my father and believe I was involved."

He flickered briefly with orange and red. "I'm sorry."

She shrugged again and opened her meal.

"Did you get the Flyer I carved for you?" he asked, changing the subject as he unwrapped his own lunch. "I know it wasn't the best. My carving skills are atrocious. My father is so much better than I am, but I wanted you to know how much I appreciated you keeping Petra alive."

"That was you?" she asked, nearly overcome with emotion.

"You didn't know?" he asked, frowning.

"No. There wasn't a note attached when they delivered it. I loved it. Thank you. I do have to apologize, though. I got mad visiting my father yesterday and broke it by accident."

Stormy shrugged. "No worries. I'll make you another."

"You don't have to."

"I know, but I want to. That carving really was atrocious. If it broke, it was probably my fault anyway."

"It wasn't *that* bad," she replied.

He snorted with humor. "I appreciate your kindness, but it really was."

"I'm serious. It might not have been Master level quality, but it was the most beautiful carving I've ever seen."

His skin flickered with disbelief.

"I'm serious. I can't even begin to explain how much it meant to know someone still cared for me. It got me through a lot of rough days and even harder nights. Thank you."

"You're welcome," he replied. "So, what do you have for lunch?"

Before she could answer, something plopped on her head, followed by the sounds of rude noises above her. She reached up and pulled some of it off and realized it was a ball of mud and seaweed. Practically before she realized what it was, Stormy flashed bright red and bolted up and over the wall.

She blinked out of her surprise and followed him, only to find a pair of female Sprites surrounded and held by half a dozen guards, both Water Sprite and Saber. The guards were scowling, and Stormy was fuming mad and yelling at the two. She sighed and wiped the rest of the mud and seaweed off of her head before swimming over.

"It's alright, Stormy. Let them go.

"It's not alright," Stormy flashed. "It was uncalled for, and they could have hurt you."

"But they didn't. It was just mud and seaweed. I'm not pressing charges unless it happens again."

The guards reluctantly let the pair go.

"I can't believe you're hanging out with *her*," the older of the two Sprites flashed, their words laced with disgust and derision.

"I'd rather hang out with her, someone who saved the life of my friend, than a bully like you," Stormy flashed back.

The Sprite huffed and swam off with her friend.

Stormy watched them leave, then turned back to her. "Are you sure you're unhurt?"

"I'm fine," she replied.

Stormy frowned at her and then turned to the guards. "I want their records and their parent's records checked for signs of abuse and involvement with Rip, and if either of them should come anywhere near us or anyone in my family, stop them. I'll send a message to my father letting him know what happened."

The senior guard nodded. "Yes, sir." The guard motioned to the others, and they disappeared again.

She was surprised at the level of authority Stormy projected and the deference the guards gave him. It made her wonder if Clear Seas had picked an heir. She hadn't heard anything, but that didn't mean he'd announced it yet, either.

He turned to look back at her and cocked his head. "What is it?"

"You're you're father's heir? Aren't you?"

Stormy shrugged. "Perhaps someday. I doubt people will vote for a seven-year-old as Senior Councilor over either of my siblings, but I am training for that possibility."

She nodded her understanding, and they returned to their spots, but she frowned when they arrived. Her lunch was missing.

Stormy flashed red with anger again.

"It's alright," she replied with a sigh.

"No, it's not. It's theft, and anyone who knows something about it and doesn't come forward is complicit. Come on. The school has cams, and we can get you another lunch from the cafeteria."

"No," she said. "It's alright. I'm honestly still full from breakfast."

He frowned but honored her request and sat back down, but then dug through his bag and handed her a small box. "Here. Try one of these."

She took the box and opened it but frowned, as she had never seen anything like it before. "What are they?"

"They're Hue-man. A gift from Councilor Ross to my father. She wants to set up a trade agreement. I believe they're called carah melts. At least, that's what I think they're called. Whatever they're called, they're delicious. You suck on them. They'll get stuck in your teeth if you try to chew."

She popped one in her mouth and groaned with delight as an explosion of flavor hit her starving taste buds. "I may have to take back my statement earlier," she flashed.

"Which one?" he asked.

"About not wanting to be your friend for what you can do for me. I will be your best friend for life if you convince your father to set up that trade agreement with Councilor Ross."

His skin bubbled with laughter. "Well, that's an easy bargain to make. My father has already agreed. I think he likes them even more than you do. You can have the rest if you want."

"You sure?"

"I have more at home, assuming my father didn't swim home and run off with the rest. You should have seen him last night. I caught him going back for more at least half a dozen times, and the container was half empty this morning when I packed my lunch."

She chuckled. "I don't blame him. They are good."

"Good? They're incredible. I can't wait to visit New Hope someday. I was supposed to go to the Hallowed Eve festival, but I was sick. Papa..."

The rest of their lunch period was spent discussing the Hue-mans and everything Stormy had learned about the Hue-mans. It was a fascinating topic, and before she knew it, the teachers were calling out the warning to return to class.

"What do you have for your creative elective?" Stormy asked.

"Music," she replied.

"Oh? What instrument do you play?"

"A variety, none of them well. I was still exploring the various instruments to find one I liked. You?"

"Art," he replied. "Woodworking right now. My class is in the same wing. I'll show you."

She followed him inside and through several twisting hallways before coming to the music room. People were already practicing inside, but she didn't swim in.

"Is there a problem?" he asked.

Once again, she found herself at a loss for words.

"He did more than shock you, didn't he?" Stormy asked.

She had once loved music, but now the sounds of the off-key playing inside reminded her of him, and she was sure she was going to be sick.

"Carrie?"

She blinked and refocused on Stormy. "Hmm?"

"Why don't you come to art class with me? I know my teacher won't mind. I think...I think you're not ready for this class yet. Or if you'd like to face whatever it is that's scaring you, I'll go with you."

Relief and gratitude washed over her. "Woodworking," she replied. "I thought I could..." she glanced in the direction of the music room, "but..."

"When you're ready, I'll be by your side."

"Why? Thank you, but why? You barely know me."

"Because I have no intentions of ever letting Rip or people like him win, and I don't want anyone to ever go through what you went through."

She smiled at him, full of gratitude and respect. "Somehow, I have a feeling you're going to be a very popular Senior Councilor. You've already won my vote. So, woodworking?"

Stormy grinned and led her down the hall.

The teacher inside looked up as they swam in. "You have a friend with you today, Stormy?"

Stormy nodded. "I do. This is Carrie. Carrie, this is Master Bramble."

Carrie flashed a greeting.

"Any friend of Stormy's is always welcome in my class. Do you have any experience with crafting?"

She shook her head. "I was going to take music, but..."

"She thought she'd try something different," Stormy finished for her.

Master Bramble nodded his understanding. "No worries. This is perfect timing. We're starting a new craft today. Basket weaving. There's an extra bundle of reeds in the cabinet over there. Grab one and find a seat."

She did as instructed, and by the end of the class, she had a slightly lopsided but usable basket. She was honestly quite proud of it, having never done anything like it before. She looked up from her work and over at Stormy. It was all she could do to keep from laughing.

"It's alright," he said. "Go ahead and laugh. Basket weaving is clearly *not* my gift."

"On the plus side, it does make your carving skills look significantly better," she replied.

He snorted and bubbled with laughter.

While her basket had been slightly lopsided, she wasn't sure his would hold anything, much less hold together if he picked it up. The teacher swam around, checking everyone's work, and eventually made it to their table.

"Well done, Carrie. This is solid work. You were only a little off here with this reed. Let me show you how to fix that." He made a small adjustment on one of the reeds, and suddenly, everything was level. Then, after handing the basket back, he shifted over to Stormy's and very gingerly picked it up. Even with the extra care he gave it, it fell apart. "Unfortunately, I think this basket is..."

"Unsalvageable?" Stormy asked. "Better used as a placemat?"

"An...opportunity for improvement," the teacher replied. "Take a fresh bundle home and keep trying. I expect a usable basket by our next session, or at the very least, one that holds together when you pick it up."

"Yes, sir," Stormy replied. "I'll see what I can do, but I'm not promising any miracles. Apparently, when it comes to underwater basket weaving, I am all tentacles."

The teacher chuckled. "Well, we can't all be perfect. Unless you want to show the Senior Guild Master your unusual interpretation of the lesson plan, I suggest you toss this...uh...*placemat* in the recycler on the way out."

"Yes, sir," Stormy replied, taking the mess back from the teacher. It fell apart even more in the process.

The teacher swam off to the next desk, and Stormy turned to look at her, hands full of broken reeds, and they both burst out laughing. It was the first time she'd really laughed since the day her ordeal started, and she knew that whatever came of their friendship, this moment would be one she would remember forever.

CHAPTER 37

Marsee: Moon's End

The next two days passed in bliss, at least from Marsee's perspective, even though, to her parents' utter confusion, it wasn't entirely spent mating. They had no problems stopping when either wanted or needed to, and as they were both still healing from their injuries, they slept often. She would have been more than willing to play the entire time, but there were times when her sister just wanted to be held, or they needed to work through some of their past traumas when something happened that triggered them.

Marsee's love for her sister grew with the trust her sister showed her in those moments and their matings after each episode were even more special to her because of it. More than anything, she wanted her sister to be able to mate with a male of her species without fear should she ever decide to do so, and as her sense of smell returned, Marsee learned to spot issues before her sister was even fully aware of them herself.

Their mother stopped in every eight hours to give her more pain medication and check for injuries, and they took the opportunity to play with Hope and get caught up on everything that was happening. Even though her father was on pheromone blockers, they were cautious and avoided entering her parents' room, but her mother said he was only there for a few hours each evening to sleep. The rest of the time, he was sequestered with the Seniors in preparation for the meeting.

Yawning, Marsee woke from a deep sleep, for once entirely nightmare-free, and smiled with love as she considered how she would wake her sister since Little Flower's shorter sleep cycle usually meant she woke first.

Deciding she was hungry, she went in for a taste but frowned a moment later. Her sister smelled different. She tasted anyway, but stopped after a single lick. Her sister tasted different, too, bitter, and Marsee's body didn't react to it at all. Groaning with disappointment, she realized her sister was no longer in heat.

"Why'd you stop?" Little Flower asked.

"You're not in heat anymore," she said sadly, laying her head on her sister's stomach. Little Flower reached up and patted her head, and while it felt good, it didn't send sparks down her insides like before, and she let out a disappointed sigh.

"Honeymoon's over?" her sister asked.

"Looks that way. You don't smell or taste the same, and I'm not reacting to your touch like before. I could grab a wand if you're still feeling in the mood."

At some point during the first day, GrandFather had snuck in a large package of what he called adult toys while they were sleeping. Little Flower had been embarrassed when they woke to find it, but it had made for an entertaining couple of days as they explored.

"It would be worth a try to see how you react, at least," Little Flower said, so she grabbed her sister's favorite wand. Little Flower climaxed quickly, but it did nothing for her outside of the joy of being able to make her sister feel good.

Little Flower tried the wand on her, but rather than feeling good, it hurt, and she had to tell her to stop.

"Well, that's a bummer," her sister said with a matching sigh.

"Quite literally," Marsee agreed, but then she supposed she couldn't spend her whole life doing that. Well, technically, she could. She didn't have to work another day in her life if she didn't want to, but she should spend time with her daughter.

"Now the question is, do I go back on the hormone blockers, or do we lock ourselves in our room for several days at a time?" Little Flower asked. "I know what I'd prefer, but we might have to move out if that's the case."

Marsee purred. "I know what I'd prefer too, but I think Mama would get annoyed if we did that too often since we'd need a cub sitter. Then again, Mama's had Hope to herself for the past several days, and I haven't heard a complaint from her yet. Knowing her, I wouldn't put it past her to purposely stop the hormone blockers so she could have an excuse to spend quality time with her granddaughter."

Little Flower laughed. "You're probably not wrong there. I don't know about you, but I'm hungry. Shall we find our wayward child and perhaps check out that children's museum GrandFather was talking about after we raid Opal's booth?

"That sounds like a wonderful plan." Marsee slunk off the bed and padded over to the waste room as she realized that she needed to pee. That feeling was thankfully starting to return. Having to set an alarm was embarrassing. She used the sonic shower to clean off the rest of her sister's scent and then moved out of the way so her sister could do the same.

"How's your pain level today?" Little Flower asked.

"Not too bad, actually. Still a little achy but manageable. I don't think I'll need another treatment from Mama."

While her sister changed into her special water clothing, she knocked on her mother's door, but there was no answer. Opening it, she checked. The room was empty. She pulled out her tablet and checked there. Sure enough, there was a message. "They're over at the Trauma Center." She clipped the tablet to her harness, threw on her cloak, and sighed with the added warmth. Her fur was growing back, but it wasn't even remotely thick enough to keep her warm in the water yet or the cooler temperatures her sister preferred, and she pulled it in close.

"Cold?" her sister asked.

"A little, but the cloak helps," she replied, and then opened the door and stepped out.

The two female guards waiting outside looked down as she opened the door and grinned at them. If Marsee could have blushed, she would have. Her sister did.

"Not a word," Marsee growled at them, not remotely caring that she didn't have the rank or authority to order them to do anything.

They both chuckled but wisely kept their mouths shut.

As they walked down the hall, Marsee realized that she no longer had a problem with the walk but that it was far brighter than she remembered. She caught whorls of different scents in her vision. Each of them had subtly different colors, and it made her brain itch in much the way the lights had back home. She rubbed at her nose and eyes as they waited for the lift to take them down to the exit.

"Everything okay?" Little Flower asked.

"It's a little overwhelming out here," she said. "But I'll manage."

"Are your senses returning?" Aris asked.

She nodded. "And then some. The lights are really bright, and I'm seeing dozens of different scents, all slightly different colors. It makes my brain itch."

"Try focusing on a single scent," Aris suggested. "That will push the others to the background. Eventually, you'll learn to identify them and dismiss them if you're not interested. The stronger or brighter the color is, the fresher it is. As for the lights, you'll just have to put up with it. You'll adjust fairly quickly."

Marsee nodded and tried to focus on Hope's scent since that's where they were heading anyway. As she did, the others faded, and Hope's pinker scent bloomed, leaving a trail for her to follow. She struggled to maintain that trail as the lift opened and they entered the common area of the platform. It was strong enough that it made her stumble as she exited the lift, although part of that was due to the stronger gravity of the common area.

Aris reached out a paw to catch her. "Careful. The gravity is stronger here. Do you need help?"

"No," Marsee said and sat down off to the side of the lift so she wouldn't block others from using it. "I can do it. Just give me a minute."

The others accepted her lie, and she used that time to refocus on Hope's scent. Little Flower wandered over to the railing and examined the platform, just as she had done on the first day. Aris followed Little Flower while Tamarin kept her company. Once she was sure she could see properly, she walked over on all fours and joined Little Flower.

"It's quite impressive, isn't it?" Marsee asked. "I've never seen a building this big."

"I have. Our cities were full of buildings like this, but they were nowhere as beautiful, at least not the ones I ever saw." She ran her hand along the railing and it left a faint indigo trail on the polished wood. "Everything you do is a work of art, even this railing. How many hours were spent carving this railing alone, and has anyone besides me even noticed?"

She examined the railing, trying to see it from her sister's perspective. She hadn't paid any attention to it before. It was carved, but it was a fairly simple and repetitive pattern. "It probably didn't take very long," she replied. "It might look ornate, but this is a fairly basic pattern, and this wood, although expensive, is easy to carve with the right tools. There are enough minor defects that it was probably carved by a Journeyman. A Master wouldn't waste their talent on a railing, even one in a focal point like this. It would bore them to tears."

Her sister snorted and turned away, but Marsee had a feeling her sister's thoughts had nothing to do with the railing. "Are you alright?" she asked.

Her sister nodded and then shook her head. "I just don't get it. Your society's baseline is something only the most wealthy of our species could have ever afforded, yet we were nearly killed because that was seen as too much. I wonder how many others resent resources going to what they see as nothing more than a hairless rodent?" Little Flower turned and walked off, effectively ending the conversation.

Marsee sighed at the anger and grief she saw in her sister but said nothing. She knew exactly how her sister felt.

She waited while her sister put on her artificial fins. Hope's scent vanished the moment she stepped through the shield to the outside, covered by the scent of the ocean and other strange creatures. It was even more overwhelming than the common area, as she didn't know what any of the scents were. She did her best to ignore them as they started across the square, but it was so thick that it was hard to see through them. The colors were all so vibrant. Shaking her head, she stopped her drone and rubbed at her face again, but it didn't help, and she growled in frustration.

Tamarin swam up in front of her. "Focus on my scent, Marsee."

She did, and Tamarin's light lavender scent bloomed while the others faded away.

"Better?" Tamarin asked.

She nodded.

"Good, now keep your focus on me as I move behind you.

Marsee did, and she had the sense that it was still there but she couldn't 'see' it anymore, and everything else faded away. "That's an odd sensation for sure, but so much better. Thank you," Marsee said and started her drone again.

The light was muted in the water, but the moment she entered the Trauma Center, she was overwhelmed again and blinked furiously. A horrible tang filtering through her mask made her sneeze several times. She realized it must be what the Sprites used to sanitize the water. She'd barely noticed it before. She focused hard on her sister's scent, and the tang faded into the background.

"Are you feeling sick, Translator?" the healer at the triage desk asked as she pulled out her scanner.

"No, I'm fine. I'm here to see my mother," she replied and floated through the door, making her way towards the office Ammond had set up, deciding to check there first. It was a good guess and turned out to be the right one. Her mother, Ammond, and Hope were all there. Hope was currently curled up in one of Uncle Ammy's arms, sucking on her thumb.

Marsee floated through the shield first, and Hope saw her.

"Marsee!" Hope squealed and then 'Mama!" as Little Flower floated through behind her.

"Well, look who finally decided to join us," Ammond signed with a grin.

Marsee walked over, took Hope from Ammond's arms, and gave her a big hug while Little Flower thwapped her way over to a chair, not bothering to take her flippers off.

She needs flippers that can flip up out of the way when she's not using them. That way, she won't have to take them off all the time. Marsee decided to put in a sketch to the local guild to see what they could craft.

Hope squirmed to see Little Flower, so Marsee handed her off.

"How are you feeling?" her mother asked.

"Much better. My senses are back, or appear to be, but they're pretty intense right now. My stomach still aches, but not as bad."

"Have a seat," Ammond said. "Let's see how you're doing,"

Marsee sighed at yet another scan but sat down in the chair anyway. She'd expected it.

Ammond ran the scanner over her body and then gave her a repeat of the physical exam he'd given her a few days before.

"Your reflexes are still not where I'd like them, but you're at least reacting again. I'd recommend continuing to wear your static shield or face protection if you're crafting or in an area that's sandy or dusty. If you do get something in your eye, you should be able to feel it, but you might not react quickly enough to prevent something from getting in there in the first place."

Marsee nodded. Many of her crafts required eye protection, so she was used to that, but she was very grateful she wouldn't have to wear one all the time like she'd been afraid was going to happen.

"Your pheromone levels appear to be back to normal. I'm assuming Little Flower's no longer in heat?" Ammond asked.

"Yeah, Little Flower's scent changed this morning. I'm not reacting to her at all anymore," she grumbled. "We tried, and it was painful, which was very disappointing."

"Well, I'm honestly a little jealous since you'll be able to have the experience more than twice in your life," her mother muttered back, "but there are things you can still do. It just takes some assistance. You'd have learned all about that during your growth year. I sent you the information, but from the sounds of things, I'm assuming you never looked at your tablet."

Little Flower blushed furiously, and Marsee squirmed with embarrassment. "No, we were a little busy," she replied.

Her mother chuckled. "There's nothing to be embarrassed about, even if the timing and circumstances were unusual. This is a normal and natural biological function. Just so you know, I did speak to Kendra while you two were having fun. Avery and the other guards were completely unaffected by Little Flower's scent and haven't had any issues while in New Hope either. However, none of the in-betweeners in the Guard have had any significant interactions with Hue-mans yet, so it's unclear if this is related to your current medical condition and age or if it has more to do with being in close physical contact with your sister, both, or neither."

"I still don't understand why I reacted at all, species differences aside. I'm female. Why would I react to another female in heat? Does that happen?"

"That's what we've been researching, and we haven't found anything in modern history, but that may very well be because mating is such a closely monitored practice," Ammond replied. "We know when someone is going to go into heat, either because they're ending their growth spurt or because they've stopped the hormone blockers, and females typically move to one of the clinics with their chosen partner if they have one. We have few medical documents prior to the Great Awakening and only anecdotal evidence from legends and stories passed down from that time, so who knows what happened before."

"One possible hypothesis is that having the scent of more than one female in heat in an area might help to attract more males to choose from," her mother continued. "Additionally, being in heat when there aren't males around could be quite frustrating, so being able to respond might have helped to relieve those symptoms until a mate could be found. It could also help to build a closer bond with your chosen group. Of course, this is all conjecture."

"Those all seem like perfectly reasonable ideas," Marsee replied.

"For now, though, you shouldn't have to worry about it with any of the other Hue-man females since they're all currently pregnant or on hormone blockers," Ammond continued. "As for your other injuries, you're recovering nicely, and there's still no sign of rejection from your new organs, so I think we're clear there. There's still some internal swelling and bruising, but that's normal and should mostly go away in a few days. You should expect swelling and pain for several weeks, especially if you're active. Our internal organs don't heal the same way our muscles and skin do and printed organs take even longer to fully integrate into your system. Until then, you're stuck here. They can't handle the stress of jump the way more solid structures like your new claws or even Little Flower's new rib bone can. You'll need to be very careful to avoid serious injury for the next several months, at least, because they can't handle stasis either. Guards, did you hear that?"

"Yes, sir," came Tamarin and Aris's reply from the door.

Ammond nodded, seemingly pleased they were paying attention. "Most of your electrical burns appear to have healed, although I don't think you'll lose the scarring."

He pointed to a section of the fine, jagged lines where she'd been shocked. While they were no longer the angry red they'd been before, they were still quite visible. "Your fur appears to be regrowing, so that should eventually hide it. How's your hand feeling? I'm still seeing significant inflammation around that nerve."

"These two fingers still feel stiff and numb," Marsee replied, flexing it to show it worked.

"Keep applying the nanos twice a day or after any significant use. Until the swelling goes down, we won't know if there's further damage that needs repairing."

Marsee nodded.

"Now, let's take a better look at that lovely brain of yours." Ammond put the stretchy hat on and threw the live images up on the monitor, and for a moment, his mask dropped, and he stared at the scans with what could only be astonishment.

"Is everything alright?" she asked.

"Better than alright," he replied. "You're looking remarkably better than the last time I scanned you. If I hadn't personally scanned your brain a few days ago, I wouldn't believe they were the same brains. I'm seeing much of the same rewiring that I saw in the scan I took of Kendra's brain the other day, here, here, and here, but based on hers, you're still not even close to half of the way through with those changes. I've never seen a brain repair itself like this, certainly not as quickly. What sort of changes are you experiencing?"

"The biggest change is that I'm actively seeing scents in color again, like when my instinct was on before. Yours is mostly green with a hint of gray around it, especially near your knees and fingers." She sniffed deeply, focusing on Ammond. The colors sharpened, and a sickly yellow spot appeared. "And there's something here. It's not right. It smells icky to me." She reached out and touched the spot on Ammond's arm.

Ammond's ears flicked back, but then he scanned his own arm, his ears flicking forward as he focused on the results, and then flicked back again. "Astounding!"

"What is it?" her mother asked.

"A small collection of precancerous cells. If I wasn't looking at that exact area, I'd have missed it. It's easily treatable at this stage," Ammond said, noticing her look of concern. He handed the scanner off to her mother to see. "But I probably wouldn't have noticed for months or years, and at that point, it would have been much harder to treat, if not fatal at my age. Thank you, Marsee. I had no idea we could sniff out illness like that."

"We used to train dogs to do that. Their noses are really sensitive, too," her sister said.

Ammond's eyebrow raised at that. "How did you manage to do that?"

Her sister shrugged. "Probably the same way we taught them everything else. I just remember reading about it."

Ammond snorted and looked back at Marsee. "Overall, you're recovering nicely. Little Flower, your turn."

Tamarin leaned in through the door. "Is Marsee cleared to begin training?"

"That depends on what you mean by training," Ammond replied with a frown. "If you're talking about fighting, no, not even close. Just like ship travel and stasis, her new organs are not even remotely ready for something like that and won't be for at least a month or two. No impact whatsoever to her midsection. Anything else, yes, within reason." He turned to look at her, "If you're tired or your stomach hurts at all, stop and have someone check you over."

Marsee nodded, climbed out of the chair to swap places with Little Flower, and took Hope from her.

Little Flower thwapped her way over to the seat, awkwardly climbed in, and wiggled her flippers as they stuck up in the air.

Marsee's tail curled at how ridiculous her sister looked.

Ammond snorted, clearly just as amused, and plunked the stretchy hat on her sister. "I'm only seeing minor changes since last time, so I think the nanos are done. There are still several smaller areas we could treat in another session, but I imagine you aren't going to leave here until Marsee does, and I'm not willing to do that procedure here. This Trauma Center isn't outfitted for your species. For now, let's keep focusing on your pickle torture. You're walking much better, even with those ridiculous fins of yours. How's your manual dexterity? Have you been keeping up with the coloring?" He scowled down at her before she could answer. "I know for a fact you haven't done *any* of your homework for the past several days."

"I haven't colored, but I did draw something the other day," Little Flower replied.

Ammond's ears flicked forward, and his scowl changed instantly to a grin. "Really? How did it go?"

"Difficult. It took longer than before, and I had to erase constantly. My hands are still shaky, but I made it work."

"I have a picture of it," Marsee said. She unhooked her tablet and scrolled through until she found it and handed it over. Little Flower looked surprised. *She must not have seen me take the picture before I framed it,* Marsee thought.

Ammond took the tablet, and a moment later, a smile lit up his old face. "I want a copy of this, framed, for my office back home."

"Really?" her sister asked.

"Really. I've seen much of your other work. Your drawing of Marsee and the chenzie is one of my absolute favorites, but I personally think this one is far better. More importantly, I'm proud of you for trying."

Little Flower smiled at the praise but then frowned when Ammond's expression turned back to a scowl. "But I expect your homework to be done on time from now on, and I expect you here at seven tomorrow morning for your lessons."

Little Flower groaned. "Seven?"

His scowl deepened, and he let out a slight growl. "Impudent cub. I'm letting you sleep in. Keep complaining, and I'll change it to six."

Marsee wasn't sure if he was teasing or not.

Little Flower sighed. "Yes, sir."

"Good, now get out of here. I have work to do." He waved his paws in a shooing motion.

Her sister didn't hesitate and scrambled for the door as fast as her flippered feet would go.

Laughing, Marsee followed behind.

CHAPTER 38

Marsee: Sensory Overload

The trip down to the market was an experience. Every tiny detail exploded in Marsee's brain, and she struggled to maintain her focus on where they were heading. Neither of her guards nor Little Flower said anything as she stopped, again and again, to check something out, distracted by the beauty of some creature or object. Even the smallest of details seemed like a work of art, and the joy of knowing she hadn't lost this part of her after all made her practically giddy with excitement.

Her guards seemed amused and perhaps a bit nostalgic. She looked up at them questioningly after pulling her attention away from a flower.

"You get used to it after a while, but I remember those first few days," Aris replied. "I was a belligerent and angry cub, so I didn't appreciate it as much as I should have, but I remember being just as overwhelmed with every tiny detail. It took me a long time to find the beauty of our gifts or even feel like it wasn't a curse. I'm happy you're able to find joy again. It's a very beautiful color on you."

She smiled at the guard, although slightly embarrassed that her emotions were so evident.

"We'll teach you how to control that, too," Aris replied. Now, come on. Your partner is hungry, and that's making her grumpy. The Ancient Gods know we don't want her in a bad mood."

That made everyone chuckle, even her sister. "We Hue-man's call that emotion 'hangry.' It's a very dangerous state to be in and has been known to start more than a few wars."

"Well, we certainly can't have that," Marsee said and refocused her attention on where they were heading.

It wasn't long before they arrived at the market, but to her utter disappointment, Opal's booth was staffed by someone she didn't know.

"Is Opal alright?" Marsee asked the vendor.

"Very much so, Translator. She's setting up her new restaurant. Word in the market is that she's hoping to have it ready to open before the meeting starts."

Marsee beamed with happiness for Opal and bought a wide variety of items from the other vendor, who assured her that they were safe for both of their species.

Little Flower barely waited for them to sit down at one of the tables before digging into her package with a vengeance. While they ate, she observed her sister's scent and watched as it changed both color and shape.

"Interplanetary war averted?" Marsee asked her sister when she slowed down some.

"Mostly, although a small skirmish is still possible. Hand me that other package."

Marsee did as ordered, but her tail curled with amusement, as did their guards'.

Little Flower tore it open and tried a bite but immediately spit it out. "It may be safe to eat, but that doesn't mean it tastes good."

Marsee handed her another package to try and took a piece for herself, curious. "It's not that bad. Better than what they served in the Trauma Center."

"Hope's dirty poop sack would be better than what they served in the Trauma Center," Little Flower grumbled.

Marsee chuckled. "When I complained that Leviathan poop would taste better than the nano drink they made me take, the Senior Healer offered to send out for some. Perhaps we can set up a trade agreement."

Her sister snorted and tentatively tried the next item. Apparently, it passed inspection as she kept eating.

After they'd finished their meal, they made their way down to the Children's Museum and spent several enjoyable hours exploring before she began to tire, and they returned to the suite. Her sister wasn't tired, so she caught up on her homework and prep for the council meeting while Marsee curled around her daughter and quickly fell asleep.

She woke long before Hope did, but rather than trying to extricate herself, she grabbed her tablet and started digging through her backlog of messages and wondered if she'd ever get to the bottom. She did the math and realized there was literally no way she'd ever be able to read and reply to every message individually, even if that's all she did for the rest of her life, so she crafted a message and put it on her public page thanking everyone, and then fired off a message to get a quote on hiring the Guild's staffers to help respond. She instantly approved the quote when it arrived, as it was far less than expected.

When she was done, she checked her Guild balance. Even between that purchase and her gift to Opal she'd barely touched it. So she went back to looking at ship manifests, trying to decide what she wanted.

Most of the ships were geared towards a specific species, size, or purpose. Few people owned their own ship. Ellie and the Senior Council had smaller personal ships on permanent loan that they could use since they had to travel between worlds so often, and there was a fleet of smaller ships that could be borrowed by guild masters and councilors when there was a need. Everyone else had to take the public transport ships, and that was expensive. She had the credit to buy one of the Earth delegation ships if she wanted, but it was so large it was impractical. She wanted something as comfortable and fast but smaller. Something more like Ellie's ship but better designed to fit Little Flower.

"What do you want on our ship?" she asked her sister, after staring at the options for some time.

Little Flower set her tablet down and looked up. "I don't even know what's possible, but something better suited for our size would be nice. Everything was too big on the council ship, but if we have guests, then we'd need to have at least some accommodations for them. Maybe with adjustable furniture like the council chamber in New Hope? Our own room, at least. I had to share with GrandFather, Henry, and Mama. More storage. Maybe something similar in size to Papa's? I don't think we need anything bigger than that. What can we afford?"

"Anything we want. Each class of ship has its own rate based on cargo and passenger space. To have our own ship available whenever we want to use it, we're basically paying that rate and reserving the pilot's time even if they aren't flying it. While I could easily afford to buy a ship like Ellie's, reserving one from the Ship's Guild is far more economical. They'll handle any maintenance it needs and ensure it's stocked with food for the trip, within reason. Anything extra is up to us to provide, and we'd have to pay for any major retrofit."

"Can we trade up or retrofit later?" her sister asked.

"I don't see why not," she replied.

"Well, we're not going to be able to jump for several weeks. Why don't we tour the shipyard and see what's available? Maybe just rent a shuttle for use while we're here? I want to see the Habitat. Can we borrow Ellie's for the day?"

"No. She doesn't have a wet dock. I'll make sure that's on our list. We'd have to borrow a Water Sprite shuttle. I'm not sure I feel comfortable flying one right now with my paw still numb, so I'll requisition a pilot, too."

"Don't forget about our guards. Maybe they fly. We're going to have to drag them along anyway. How long do they intend to follow around after us?"

"I'm guessing until we tell them we don't need or want them anymore. I don't particularly feel safe not having them around. Who knows if we've caught everyone?"

She carefully climbed out of the bed, trying not to wake Hope, and padded over to the door. The guards had changed while they slept. Avery was now back at his post, and Aris had left. "Hey, I have a question for you. We're thinking of renting a shuttle, but I've only just earned my shuttle license, and I'm not sure how well I'll be able to fly with my paw still numb. Would you be able to pilot it, or should we hire someone?"

"We're all trained pilots. I would personally feel much better if we flew you. However, you don't need to pay for a shuttle. As Little Flower is on the Council, she has access to make use of any available ship or shuttle in the fleet for any length of time she needs one. There's an app on her account for just that purpose."

"Oh, I didn't realize that benefit extended to off-world travel, too."

Avery nodded but then motioned towards the suite, indicating there was something he wanted to talk about, but not out in a hallway, even if no one appeared to be around.

Marsee returned to the room and sat on the edge of the bed.

Avery entered, shut the door behind him, and asked for permission to turn off his camera.

"What is it?" she asked after giving it.

"Aris said you're starting to have issues with your senses returning," he signed.

"Some, but I'm good now."

He flicked an ear back, almost as if he didn't believe her. "What are you experiencing so far?"

"Well, everything is brighter and more colorful. I'm seeing scents in color again, and in the dark or with my eyes closed, I can almost see with my ears. It's not as clear as it was in the cave, but then it's not as dark as it was in the cave, either. My sense of taste and pain are back, although my injured paw is still numb. Ammond says my reflexes are back some, but they're still sluggish. I only had problems this morning because the scents were too thick to see through. Tamarin taught me how to manage that, so I'm good now."

"No increase in your hearing outside of being able to echo-locate?" he asked, sounding a bit surprised.

"Not that I've noticed. Everything is quieter here anyway. I've not had any problems with the electronics, not like I do back home."

He flicked an ear back at that. "What kind of problems did you have before?"

"Everything buzzed. I've always been able to hear them, but no one believed me until Ammond tested my hearing. My range of hearing is better than everyone else's. Mama's is almost as good, but she didn't have issues like I did. On the plus side, I can fully hear the Hue-mans. Ammond gave me some hearing aids so I can block it out when it gets overwhelming."

He snorted at that last bit. "Your family is a fountain of surprises. Well, that's one less thing you'll have to learn to deal with, and it's often the most problematic for new guards. May I try these hearing aids?"

"Sure," she said and reached over for the case that sat on her bedside table. She tipped them out and then opened the other compartment where she kept the different-sized sleeves Ammond had given her. "You'll probably need a different sleeve since these are fit for me.

Avery took one of the hearing aids, placed it in his ear, and then took it out, grabbed one of the bigger sleeves, and swapped it out with her instructions. He put it back in his ear, then did the same with the other.

When they were both in, they automatically turned on to her favorite preset, good enough to hear Little Flower but enough to block out the electronics. The look of absolute relief on Avery's face was one she knew well. After a few moments, he popped them out, turned back to the door, and physically dragged Tamarin inside.

"What is it?" Tamarin asked as Avery motioned for her to turn off her camera.

"Put these in your ears," he ordered after.

She looked at him with a raised brow but did as ordered and nearly wept with relief. "By the brightest moons in all the heavens! Where did you get these?"

"Apparently, our newest honor guard has had a full range of hearing her entire life. Healer Greyfoot gave her a set of these to help tune out the electronics."

"How much do you want for them?" Tamarin begged.

"Wait, what?" Marsee asked, but that was in response to Avery's comments, not Tamarin's.

"Please, I'm serious. I'll give you a year's worth of credit for these," Tamarin replied.

Marsee blinked. "You don't need to do that. They're covered under medical equipment. Just order a set from the Healer's Guild. Ammond might even have a few sets with him since he invented them. I don't know what he brought with him, though. I think he just brought what he thought I might need to be scanned and treated. If not, you can borrow these until yours are shipped in. I don't have nearly the same issues here as I do back home, and I mostly use them to listen to music. I'm sure he has more back in New Hope."

"Ammond gets an Honor Guard," Tamarin told Avery.

"Agreed," Avery replied.

"What are you talking about?" Little Flower asked. "Why does Ammond need to be guarded?"

"Not a guard, an Honor Guard, for when he passes away. It's how we show respect for those who have done something exceptional with their lives. Typically, it's reserved for those who have already died, or in Marsee's case, when we thought we were going to lose her to her injuries. Had she died, we would have escorted her body home."

"What?!" Marsee squeaked and then switched back to sign. "This is an Honor Guard? I thought you were just protecting me from whoever else might be involved in Rip Current's plot."

"It's both," Avery replied. "The Guard failed you twice. We will not fail you a third time. You'll be guarded until you're fully recovered and are capable of defending yourself again, or you tell us you've had enough of us following you around."

If she hadn't already been sitting down, her legs would have probably given out on her. "Is that why you called me an Honor Guard? I know you offered to mentor me to learn how to fight, but I didn't realize I was *joining* the Guard."

"No. You are not *in* the Honor Guard. You *are* an Honor Guard." At her look of confusion, he continued. "There's no expectation that you will become a guard and perform the work that we do, although you'd be welcomed if you decided you wanted to. But you can't be in the Honor Guard without being an Honor Guard, and you've met all of the qualifications of that. You survived the Transition, and you've fought and killed to protect others."

"*What?!*" Marsee yelped. "*That's* a requirement?! Just how many people have the Guard killed?"

"Far too many," Tamarin muttered.

"This is why the Council doesn't know what we do with our training," Avery continued. "Not all of it. You can't tell anyone, not even your father. Nearly half of those we bring in from the watch list don't survive their psychosis, and they have to be put down. It requires all of the guards training, and usually many guards to do so. Even the stunners don't reliably work on someone fully lost to psychosis. Untrained and only half grown, you were able to beat someone more than twice your size, who could immobilize you with a touch. Imagine how challenging it is to bring someone down who's fully grown and trained, which happens far more often than we care to admit. It's often someone we know and many times have trained with for years. If they haven't already been pushed over the edge by training how to fight or by being brought in too late, having to kill someone almost always does it, as it did with you."

Marsee looked down at her claws and flexed them. She could still remember exactly how it felt to dig those claws into Rip and how much she'd enjoyed it. "I wanted to kill Rip. We both did. That isn't what made me lose control," she signed and then stopped.

The guards waited for her to explain. She looked up at them and saw no judgment from them, only patience and understanding.

"I lost control because my father tried to make me stop. My instinct thought he was trying to steal our prey or get close enough to kill us. Between the test he did several months ago and everything Rip did to twist my brain all up, we didn't trust him. I think if I'd been given time to work through my fury at Rip, I would have been fine, but it turned on the people I cared about."

She let out a heavy sigh. "It's still there in my dreams. I hurt Papa, stalked Little Flower and Hope in my sleep, and for dark moons' sake, I even attacked you. I'm so sorry about that. Little Flower has been helping to calm my night terrors, but I'm terrified I'm going to hurt someone I care about. If even a part of me was capable of hurting someone I love, what's to stop the rest of me? My instinct, I could fight. How do I fight my night terrors?"

Avery knelt down in front of her and grabbed her still-flexing claws. "Marsee, our instinct *always* turns on someone we love or care for. Every time. It's the excuse it makes for taking control. It takes our insecurities, heightens them, and uses them against us. I attacked Kendra several times before I was able to defeat mine. Even though she was my mentor and cared for me after my mother died when I was a cub, it saw every swipe she landed on me, every taunt or jibe to make me lose focus in my training as a personal attack, and it blocked my memory of why she'd been doing that. I had to push back against my instinct to keep it from hurting her, to save her. It's like that for all of us."

"Really?"

"Really. The ones we lose are those who don't have honor in their soul. Without it, it makes everyone seem like strangers. It's why you were able to stop the first time. Even if it had been less than a day, you already cared deeply for Little Flower."

"But that was my instinct, not my night terrors. How do I control *them*?" Marsee asked.

"With time and patience and the love and support of your family. I had night terrors, too. We all do. It's the same with sleepwalking. Your brain is going through a major transformation, and you still have a lot to process. You might have another episode of sleepwalking, but I doubt it since you've gone without doing so for several days now. It almost always happens when your brain first starts hooking your senses back up, and none of the night guards have reported you waking up screaming from night terrors either, not like you did in the Trauma Center. It takes time, but you're healing, and you will heal. You'll be stronger than you ever were before. I promise."

Marsee sighed, doubting that she would ever recover from the terror of what had happened to her, but it helped that she wasn't alone.

"Now, I want to start working with you on learning how to control and manage your senses before they're fully activated again. We should spend several hours each day between now and the meeting working on them. You won't want to be trying to deal with them in the middle of the Council. Trust me."

"This isn't fully activated?" Marsee asked.

"Not even close. Not if you're still able to manage them," he replied.

Marsee's ears drooped in dismay. She was already far exceeding what she'd been able to do with scents, and while her hearing wasn't back to the brain-scratching itchiness of her childhood, she was still able to use it to sense her surroundings in the dark. Her sense of taste was as good as it had ever been. The experiences of the past few days had shown her what was possible there. Her sense of pain was back, and she wondered if she would experience pain stronger or, like when she'd given herself over to her instinct, if her pain would recede. She'd not felt the pain from her injuries until after she'd killed off her instinct, but what else was there?

She nodded her agreement. "When do you want to start? Hope is still sleeping, so I don't want to go anywhere until she's awake. I'm not leaving my family unprotected."

"Of course," he replied. "We can start your training here, and I heard that Little Flower has lessons with her mentor in the morning. We can meet then, and Tamarin can watch Hope while you train."

She looked over at Little Flower.

"Works for me," Little Flower said.

Marsee nodded her agreement to Avery.

Avery turned back to Tamarin and tilted his head in the direction of the door.

Tamarin sighed, took the hearing aids out, handed them back to Marsee almost regretfully, and left to return to her post.

"Let's start with your sense of smell since that was the one you were having issues with earlier."

"Aris and Tamarin showed me how to push the scents to the background this morning," Marsee said.

"They told me, and I know that you're able to isolate them individually, as you did with Ammond, which is a fantastic start. We'll build on that. I want you to close your eyes and bring everything to the foreground."

She did, and he switched to speaking in Saber. Colors swirled in her brain like an abstract painting, with bright, beautiful globs of color for Little Flower, Avery, and Hope. But with her eyes closed, she could now 'see' in all directions, even behind her, which was more than a little disorienting.

"You should be able to see the scents in the room."

It wasn't a question, but she nodded.

"Good. Pick whichever scent is the strongest. For me, it would be your scent, but I'm guessing Little Flower's is brighter for you."

She nodded again and brought her sister's beautiful indigo scent to the foreground.

"Now try to dismiss just the portion of the scent that's surrounding her right now. You should start to see a trail of scent around the room, on the floor where she's walked, or on objects she's touched."

It was a lot harder to dismiss just a portion of the scent than the entire scent, but eventually, she managed and nodded. "Okay, got it."

"Excellent! Now tell me where the next brightest spot of her scent is."

"The bed," she said immediately.

"Next?"

She considered it for a moment. There were several that were about equal in strength. "Her water clothes," she decided.

"Very good. Continue."

She named off several additional bright spots in the room and dismissed those but was then left with a trail of footprints all over the room. "There's a lot of footprints and scents that are all fairly equal in strength left."

"One footprint to the next is almost impossible to distinguish, so you'll need to try to find an endpoint and compare it to the other tracks. If it gets gradually brighter or dimmer, it will tell you which way they're going. Start by the door and see if you can track where Little Flower went when she first came in."

"She came in, walked over to the table, then the bed, then over to the drawer with Hope's clothing, returned back to the bed, walked over and dropped Hope's water clothing off, then went over to the fridge before sitting down at the table," she replied. "But I knew that already."

He chuckled. "You can open your eyes now."

She did and noticed that Little Flower had gone back to her studying since she wasn't able to understand them speaking in Saber.

Avery looked at her for several moments.

She had the sense that he was surprised to have made it this far with her, and she wondered why. She tilted her head at him in curiosity, and he smiled at her but didn't explain.

"I want you to go out in the hallway for a few minutes," he said.

She shrugged and walked out. Tamarin seemed amused but said nothing.

A few minutes later, he came out and brought her back in but made her stop by the door. "I've hidden something somewhere in the suite. I want you to tell me what it was and then find it."

She closed her eyes and focused on his scent. His was more of a yellow-green scent, and in the few minutes she'd been in the hallway, he'd walked everywhere in the room, even over the bed. She tried following the trail, but it crisscrossed so many times she couldn't keep track of it, so she filtered out everything at floor level. That left several spots around the room. She opened her eyes to see where they were. One was on the table.

"It was one of Little Flower's pens," she guessed.

He flicked his whiskers forward in a yes and raised a brow, waiting for the rest.

She found three spots on various drawer handles and went to each in turn but found nothing inside. Frowning, she thought and then had an idea. She brought up Little Flower's scent and looked for places where they both existed, but they were everywhere, so she dismissed that idea. She pulled up his steps again and realized that there was one area where it was slightly stronger, so she walked over to that area, sniffed again, and dismissed his footsteps. A tiny fourth spot appeared, and she walked over to the bed, lifted a pillow, and found the missing pen.

Avery grinned at her success. "Now that you can reasonably track strong scents let's see what else you can identify in the room. Dismiss my scent, Little Flower's, Hope's, and Tamarin's. What remains?"

She closed her eyes again and did as asked. "There are several scents that all do the same thing: enter the door, walk over to the waste room, and then over to Mama's door and back out. One belongs to Aris, so I'm assuming the others are the other guards." She dismissed them. "Mama and Papa have both been in here, as have GrandFather and Henry. Uncle Marcus was in here as well. He came in, walked over to the wall controls, and left. I don't recognize anyone else's scent, but they're a lot older. Maybe the people stocking the room before Little Flower arrived?"

"Good, now dismiss those scents. What remains?"

In her mind's eye, there was nothing left. "Nothing?" she said tentatively. "It's all just the normal sparkles I always see when my eyes are closed."

"Our brains naturally filter out what it considers unimportant in our surroundings, but that doesn't mean you can't sense it. Right now, you're at the normal background level. You'll eventually learn how to automatically bring everything down to this level, but it will take practice. Aris said you sniffed out some bad cells on Ammond's arm. Focus on the table like you did with Ammond."

She took several deep breaths and focused on the spot where she remembered the table to be, and suddenly, the table bloomed in her vision as the tan sparkles all brightened in contrast to the other sparkles. She could almost taste the wood it was made of.

"Now expand your senses out to reveal the items on the table."

She did. The pens each had their own distinctive tang to them. *The chemicals in the pigments?* she wondered. She watched as one of the pens seemed to float in the air and move.

"I've just asked Little Flower to move one of the pens away from the others. Did you see that?"

She nodded.

"Good. Now expand to the rest of the room."

It was hard, but as she kept focusing on an area, that part of the mental picture came into focus, and she was eventually looking at an image of the room that swirled and shifted in colors. It looked nothing like her vision, but she could tell where everything was now.

"Keeping your eyes closed, I want you to walk over to the table and pick up the pen I had your sister move."

She took a step forward, but the scents swirled and shifted on her as her steps caused the air to move. She stopped as it made her queasy. Refocusing, she took slower steps until she made it to the table, then reached down and picked up the pen.

"Fantastic! Now I'm going to move somewhere in the room. Bring the pen over to me, but follow the path I take."

She heard him moving, but focusing on that made her lose focus on the scent, so she layered his scent back into the picture and watched him walk into the waste room and back out, around the table twice, and then back over to the door.

"Okay," he said when he was done.

She slowly followed his path, wobbling as the swirling eddies of his scent shifted. She walked into the waste room but paused as she made her way back out. He'd moved over by Hope's crib. She walked around the table twice and over to the door and then layered in his steps, looking for the brightest leading away from where she was. She found it. He'd walked back over to the bed and past the kitchenette, but there was something odd about part of the path as the scent was swirled and distorted. She focused on that part and realized that he'd pulled a chair out behind him. She walked over, pushed the chair out of the way, walked up to him, and handed him the pen.

"Now, bring everything back into focus."

She did and nearly fell over with the overwhelming amount of information pouring into her brain. She felt Avery reach out and steady her as she tried to make sense of the swirling tapestry of color, smells, and taste.

When she steadied, he continued. "Now, for the hard part. Keep it on and open your eyes."

If Avery hadn't been holding her, she would have fallen over. Her sense of vision and smell overlapped and vied for dominance. It was like that morning but a hundred times worse. It took her nearly fifteen minutes to stop feeling like she was going to throw up. She nearly did several times as the room bent and warped as every breath they took swirled the air around them.

He waited and held her while she recovered. Eventually, her brain figured out how to layer the scent on top of what she was seeing, and the world stabilized again.

When she nodded, he smiled. "Impressive. Now dismiss everything back down to that baseline sparkle."

It took her a minute to work her way back down to that, but when she was done, she was left with a slightly sparklier version of her vision. She nodded when she was back down to that level.

"Good. Now, you should only notice new scents." He took that moment to pass gas, and it wafted around him.

Little Flower groaned and faked passing out as she smelled it, which made both of them laugh.

"Identify it and add it to the baseline."

She did, and the smell and sight of it vanished. *That's a useful trick,* she thought and nodded again.

He grinned, and she could tell he was impressed. "That's enough for now. You'll want to practice that until it becomes second nature to smell something and bring it back down to your baseline. The more familiar you are with a scent, the easier it will be to learn to ignore it. I highly recommend practicing in the Arboretum or the Market every time you're there. As this sense progresses, you'll be able to smell and identify smaller scents, tell if someone is getting sick before they feel sick, or tell where they're bruised and injured. You'll be able to sniff out people's moods and emotions, and eventually, you'll even be able to tell if someone is lying."

"So with all of this, how is it that Rip Current was able to sneak up behind you?" she asked.

He frowned, and she noticed his scent change. "Partly because your nose can only detect the scents that make it to it. Rip approached from down current, so I didn't smell him until it was too late. The ocean currents mess everything up, just like the wind does. You can smell things that originated thousands of leagues away one minute and not smell something right in front of you the next."

"That makes sense," she said and then wrinkled her nose. Hope had pooped in her sleep. "Hope needs changing," she signed to Little Flower.

"You smelled it first, Papa," Little Flower replied with a grin. "It's not my fault you have a super sniffer now."

Marsee's tail curled in amusement at the reference to her parent's deal, but she quickly changed Hope's poop sack, far too happy about the use of 'Papa' to care. Hope woke in the process, so Marsee picked her up after. Hope curled up in her arms and started sucking her thumb.

"I can't get over how tiny she is," Avery said.

"She was even smaller when she was born. Curled up, she could easily fit in my paw."

He smiled, patted Hope's tiny head, and left to resume his station.

After he left, Little Flower turned to her. "So you'll be able to sniff out my mood, eh? I guess I won't be able to hide anything from you anymore."

"I always could with you, but I don't need my nose for that. I can tell just from your body language," she replied.

"Oh really? So what's my mood right now?" Little Flower asked with a glare.

"I believe the word you Hue-mans use is hangry."

Her sister's scowl turned to laughter. "You're not wrong there. I was wondering if Hope was ever going to wake up from her nap. Shall we rectify the problem?"

CHAPTER 39

Apakna: Rock Fish

Apakna stared at the folder in front of her, not wanting to open it. Far too many of her council, her lifelong friends, and colleagues were already on the Pile, but this was the last file from her Council and the one she'd purposely set aside and left for last.

Everyone had left the room at some point, angry, frustrated, and grief-stricken, even Sammianna. Which, for a Digger, was saying something. She had apologized to Sammie after her outburst before, but as expected, Sammie hadn't even taken offense.

Her people were very much the opposite of Diggers. They were an angry lot, quick to take offense and even quicker to act, so she honestly wasn't surprised that so much had been covered up or that Breydhik and his partner had gone after Quinn in revenge. She'd dealt with her fair share of crime over her career and had even kicked a few of her Council out for minor offenses, and more than a few had been kicked out over the millennia for fighting during council meetings, but what they were finding now was anything but minor.

Taking a deep breath, she forced herself to open her uncle's file and began reading through it. Like all the others, there was information on family and cases highlighted, each of which would need to be investigated to determine if something illegal occurred. One caught her attention, as the number on the ticket referred to their old systems, one that hadn't been used in over a century. Curious, she put in the request, knowing it would take hours for the information to return, as those servers were back home.

Several hours later, she'd made her way through the other cases but hadn't found anything obvious. There were a number of decisions that were different than what she would have decided but well within the scope of his power and authority, more often than not leaning towards leniency, especially when minors and new adults were concerned. That didn't surprise her, as it was completely in line with the person she knew.

The next section in the file was a log of her uncle's purchases. The only thing highlighted was a payment made to the same person once a year on the same date and for the same amount. It was a large transaction, but not ridiculously so. She pulled up the name of the person it was transferred to and began reading through their information. Nothing seemed out of the ordinary, a master scientist on the climate project.

A personal donation to the research? she wondered. She knew her uncle was passionate about that issue, and rightly so, as her planet was dying, but the payments went all the way back to her uncle's youth.

There wasn't anything else in the folder, and she was about to set it aside when her tablet dinged with the notification that the records she'd requested were available. She opened them up, and it was all she could do to keep from gasping as she read the statement from the Senior Honor Guard at the time.

Ruled an accident, she sighed with relief. *No reparations. So why the payment, Uncle? A memorial or a bribe?*

She switched to her uncle's account, applied the filter they now all knew about for retrieving deleted messages, and looked for anything between her uncle and Rip. They'd long since learned that it was the easiest way to find what they were hiding. She frowned when a number of deleted messages were highlighted and began reading.

When she was done, she tapped her claws on the table. *Not enough to prove guilt. Could Rip have been setting him up, too?*

She pulled up the scanned copy of Rip's journal and searched for any mention of her uncle. Sammianna was the one who figured out that the numbering system on the files was the key to the journal but found little there that was incriminating. If anything, Rip seemed to enjoy working with her uncle. They had fairly strong economic ties between their districts, but that wasn't a crime. Most of the journal entries detailed fishing trips they'd taken.

Were they actual trips, or is this code for something else? She looked up the locations for the trips, mostly to the poles, which would make sense, as her species couldn't handle being out in the warmer water for very long, even with modified shields. *I need more information,* she decided. She sent a message to her uncle inviting him to an early dinner, then leaned back, trying to decide how to approach it without giving away too much.

Her uncle responded with a yes almost immediately.

"I'm taking a break," she told the others, shutting off the shield and current that cooled the water for her seat. I'll be back after dinner."

She didn't get more than a grunt of acknowledgment from the others, heads buried in their own work.

Her uncle was already waiting for her outside her office. "I thought you were in meetings all day."

"I needed a break," she replied. "Shall we hit Ice Waters?" It was one of her favorite restaurants, as it specialized in cuisine for her species, and it was one of the few places on this planet cold enough to be comfortable.

"Sounds perfect," he said, and they started swimming towards the entrance.

"How are you feeling?" she asked.

"Fully recovered," he replied. "I saw the Senior Healer this morning. In case you haven't heard, the last of the injured were released today."

"I hadn't. That's good to hear."

"Any word on the cause of the accident?"

"Possibly. There wasn't much left of the engine that blew, but they found a stress fracture in one of the other engines. They're still trying to determine if that was the cause or caused by the explosion. In the meantime, we've grounded all of the same model of ships until they can be serviced. It's a limited supply, so it shouldn't have a major impact, but the return trip home won't be quite as comfortable for our council."

He shrugged. "As long as this one doesn't blow up, I don't really care if I have to take public transport back."

She grinned. "Well, you're in luck. It's not quite as bad as public transport. Our Earth Delegation ship will be here in time to take everyone back, but you'll probably have to share a berth." That last bit was a bit of a lie. By the time they were done executing everyone, there would be berths left over.

He grinned for good reason. The Earth Delegation ships were the best in the fleet. They'd spared no expense, knowing the people on those ships would be living on them for a long time, possibly years. "I think I can manage. How's the rest of your investigation going?"

"Slowly. You worked with Rip pretty regularly. Did you have any sense he was up to anything like this?"

"No. I do know he was angry at the Senior Council for the decisions at Little Flower's trial, especially Jer's promotion. We often vented with each other. I considered him a friend, and he took me hunting rock fish a few times in the northern seas. The last time I had a message from him, he said he had evidence to bring up against Jer and Marcus, but he didn't tell me what it was and said he would show it when I arrived for the meeting. He wanted my support in forcing an investigation if they didn't agree to step down. I agreed. I figured he wouldn't bring something up if there wasn't definitive proof of a problem."

She frowned. It matched what she read. "So you have no idea what Rip had on them?"

"Api, if I had any sort of information like that, I would have brought it up with you immediately. I honestly have no idea if it was legitimate or not after what he did. If he fabricated evidence against Clear Seas, it wouldn't surprise me if he was planting evidence against the others, too."

"Have you looked into it?"

He shook his head. "No, I was waiting for his information to determine if it was warranted. You know as well as I do that if I looked into their accounts, they'd be notified, or at least that was my understanding."

She nodded. "I imagine it comes as no surprise that we're looking into everything and everyone who was working with him."

"I would expect no less, and you're obviously hunting for information. What is it you really want to know?"

She chuckled at his astuteness. "It's probably nothing, but I came across a payment in your account made to the same person on the same date, going back decades. Master Scientist Treadak?"

He sighed. "You've found more than that. Haven't you?"

"What really happened, Uncle."

"It was an accident. I swear on my oath. Ippak was my best friend. We grew up together. I was about a month younger than him and we had been planning for years to go on an extended hunting trip after we both earned our adulthood. He was so excited for the trip. We both were. It took nearly a week to hike up into the mountains and another week before we found suitable prey. We were attempting to retrieve the carcass when a crevasse opened under him. We had safety lines on, of course, but I was nearly pulled in before I managed to drop an anchor, but not before dislocating my shoulder. The gear mechanism on the safety line jammed, and I couldn't pull him up. He was badly hurt and unconscious. I called for help, but he died of his injuries on the way to the trauma center. That was long before we had stasis or grav belts. He wanted to be a scientist. He had a feeling our planet was dying and wanted to find out why. That was part of the reason for the location of our trip. We were setting up sensors to monitor the ice pack in that area. His father took up that research after, and I've been funding it ever since, in his memory."

"I'm sorry. That must have been a horrible experience."

He nodded, his expression wistful. "You know, I didn't go hunting again until Rip asked if I was interested. I turned him down at first and told him why. Rip's words, if I remember correctly, were, 'Your friend was lucky. He died doing something he loved and with his best friend by his side. I envy him.'"

"He envied him?"

"He was lonely. I'm not sure he had many close friends." He stopped and faced her. "I know this may put me at risk, but he *was* my friend. I don't know how to justify what he did with the person I knew. I knew him long before he became a councilor. We met at a function on Digger a few months before his father died. I stepped out to a cooling room and found him there. I was surprised because the other species rarely make use of them, especially the Sprites, and he said he'd been looking for a place to hide from his father. When I asked why, he told me his father had just tested him, and he wasn't sure how he felt about it or about his father, or about the fact that he would one day have to do the same to his own children."

"He seemed to have no problem hurting other people's children."

Her uncle sighed but said nothing in reply and took off again.

They were both panting hard by the time they made into the platform and over to Ice Waters. The cold water was a welcome relief as they entered, not nearly cold enough, but any colder would be too cold for the other species

"Welcome back, Councilors. Will it just be the two of you?" the attendant asked.

Apakna nodded and followed her back to one of the dry booths. She hit the temperature control on the booth, pre-programmed for her species, and sighed with relief as the frigid air blasted her the moment she stepped through the shield.

"Will it be the usual?"

"Yes, please," Apakna replied.

"I think I'll have the rock fish today," her uncle said.

She raised a brow at him after the attendant left and adjusted the shield to give them privacy.

"I don't deny what he did, but I intend to remember the good. I may be the only person in the known universe to think that way about him, but he was my friend, and I mourn his loss, not just for his death, but for the person he could have been."

Apakna nodded. She could respect that.

Her uncle raised a brow at her. "So, tell me, when are you and Maki going to have pups?"

She snorted at the unexpected change of topic. "We don't have any plans to. Maki and I are far too busy for that, and I'm pretty sure she's decided never to have pups after the last time my sister visited."

Her uncle laughed. "Yes, those two are quite the handful. I don't know how the Sabers do it with litters of five or six at a time."

"I don't know how Raki does it with two," Apakna replied. "The last time they visited, we ended up with a year's worth of credit in damages. I came back from a meeting, and they were bouncing on the couch and had already broken the thing beyond repair."

"Where were their parents?"

"Passed out from ship's lag in the other room. Raki tried to pay us back, but Makenta wouldn't allow it, stating it was ancient anyway, and she'd been looking at replacing it. That was a complete lie, of course, but she did enjoy herself for the next two months as she decided what to re-place it with. I'm surprised she even lets me sit on it. She growls at me if I even think of bringing food or drink over."

"Well, for that price, I'm not surprised. The cost of imports has gone up another seven percent in my district this past quarter, and what we're getting is backordered for months."

"I'm well aware of that, Uncle. It's on the agenda."

"It's been on the agenda for the last year," he grumbled.

She said nothing as there was little she could say. Every council meet-ing was a losing battle for her species, and she knew her people didn't like that New Hope got so much of the funding when they were struggling, too, but a gradual increase was hard to justify prioritizing against a species that had just lost everything.

"Have you had a reply from Marsee yet?" he asked.

She shook her head. "No. I don't think it's even been proposed yet."

"Why not?" he asked with a frown.

She pursed her lips, trying to figure out how to explain without giving away what was really going on. "I'm assuming you've heard that Marsee and Little Flower have partnered?"

He snorted. "How could I not? It's been on all the news channels for days, although no one has seen them since the day she was released from the Trauma Center."

"They're spending a few days to themselves. It's apparently a Hueman partnership tradition. Plus they might be out of the Trauma Center but they're still recovering from their injures. Jer says they've both been sleeping every time he's gone over to talk with them."

"There's not much time left before the meeting," her uncle replied.

"I know, but it's worth every second we wait. The more time Marsee has to heal and process her trauma, the more likely she will be to decide in our favor."

"Do you think she actually will?"

She leaned back in her seat to consider. She had the same worry, and if Marsee didn't, her people would struggle even more than the Water Sprites as most of the projects on the chopping block heavily relied on exports from the Ice Planet. "The others seem to think so," she finally said.

"But you don't?" he pressed.

She sighed. "I honestly don't know. After what she's been through? I stopped in to visit with her once while she was still in the trauma center. She was polite, but..." She shrugged, not sure how to explain what she had seen. "We're all fairly certain far more happened to her than what she put on her statement. Whatever it was, it was bad enough that she tried to take her own life a few days ago."

Her uncle looked away with a frown and then deactivated the privacy shield as their meal arrived. The attendant waited to make sure everything met their satisfaction.

Her uncle groaned with contentment with his first bite, causing the Sprite who delivered the food to flash bright blue with her happiness.

"Have you ever had rock fish?" her uncle asked.

"I can't say as I have," she replied.

"Try some," he said, shifting his plate towards her.

She took a bite. "Oh, wow. This is fantastic. I wonder why this isn't on our imports?"

The Sprite flashed blue and then explained. "The adult rock fish only exists in the polar regions, which makes it hard for us to hunt, and it's not something we find particularly enjoyable. To be honest, we loathe it and would rather eat rocks, hence the name, but once we found out it was popular with your species, we made sure to have some available for every council meeting."

"I appreciate the courtesy. I have a feeling this is going to be a new favorite of mine," she replied.

"Would you like me to change your meal out?"

"Thank you but no, I won't waste food, but I would like an order sent to my suite."

"Gladly!" the Sprite replied and swam off.

She looked back at her uncle as he reactivated the privacy screen. "Do you think hunting trips to the poles would be popular?"

"Very much so, if people could afford to visit and there was housing nearby," he replied. "It'd be seasonal, but the adult rock fish are quite large, and two or three could easily feed a family for a year. The difficult part would be getting it home. It certainly wouldn't fit in a public transport berth."

"I'll talk to Clear Seas and see if we can't figure something out. From what I understand, many of the Earth creatures rescued prefer colder temperatures, too, and they spend a lot of energy keeping the tanks cool enough. Perhaps a small habitat in that area could serve both purposes."

"Speaking of the Earth creatures, did you try any of the fried fish they had at the Hallowed Eve's festival?" he asked.

"I did," she replied, "That was incredible. I've already ordered one of the heating units, but it'll be half a year at least before the Hue-mans get their factory up and running."

He grunted acknowledgment and resumed eating.

She dug into her own meal, which was far less appetizing now but still good. They never wasted food or any part of the creatures they hunted. It was far too valuable of a resource and one that was getting scarcer every year.

After their meal, she returned to the conference room. The others had left, presumably for their own meals. She pulled up her uncle's medical record and confirmed he had dislocated his shoulder, along with other injuries that were common for that type of accident.

Leaning back in her chair, she considered the evidence. *There's nothing to indicate it was anything but an accident or proof that he knew anything about what Rip intended. So why did he delete the messages?*

She pulled up the messages again and flipped over to the code that Marcus had shown them, code that Marsee had taught him about. None of them had known that was even possible. Somewhere along the way, someone had neglected to inform them about that ability, and she wondered if it was intentional. Ellie stated that that particular code had existed long before she took control of the Tech Guild.

She didn't have a clue what most of the code meant, but once she found the message again, the information she needed was obvious. She sighed with relief. Rip had deleted the message, not her uncle. There was still a risk that her uncle was lying about not knowing more, but she had nothing to charge him with. She certainly couldn't kill her uncle just because he was Rip's friend when far too many of those she would have to kill were her own friends.

She quickly scanned everything in, marked the file as reviewed, and, with a prayer that she was making the right decision, she closed the case.

CHAPTER 40

Marsee: Gift of Silence

Marsee jerked awake as Little Flower's high-pitched alarm blared the next morning, far too early for her own preference. She was still not used to the shorter days and nights on the Water World.

Her sister crawled out of bed and yawned her way over to use the waste room, but Marsee closed her eyes, trying to catch a few more minutes of sleep. She'd nearly drifted off when Little Flower started chopping up some of the fruit they'd picked up from the market the night before. The noise of it cut through Marsee's brain like it was her that was being chopped instead of the fruit.

"Ugh, do you have to do that so loudly?" she grumbled. Then, realizing she'd spoken in Saber, she repeated it in Hue-man.

"Do what?" Little Flower yelled back.

"Ha. Ha. No need to yell. If you want me to get up, I'll get up," she replied.

"I'm not yelling, Marsee."

"Yes, you are."

"No, I'm not," her sister said, this time raising her voice to a volume that made her cringe and whimper.

"Sounds like I'm going to be working with Marsee on her hearing today," she heard Avery say from the hallway.

"Sounds that way," Tamarin replied. "Marsee, put your hearing aids in for now."

She whimpered again when she realized how much louder every-thing would be for the rest of her life. It had been almost more than she could take before. With a half sob, she buried her head under a pillow instead.

"Trust me, the pillow won't help," Tamarin said.

"You can hear that?!" Marsee squeaked. "Moons! You heard every-thing, didn't you?"

The guards chuckled, and she groaned and shuddered with embar-rassment.

"If you're done muttering to yourself, breakfast is ready," her sister said and started chewing.

The sound made what little fur she had stick straight up on her spine, and not in a good way. Growling, she rolled over, grabbed her hearing aids, and put them in. It was better, but not nearly good enough. She flipped open her tablet and made some adjustments until the sound of her sister's chewing was somewhat tolerable again and sighed with relief.

"Better?" Avery asked.

"Much," she replied and then fired off a message to Ammond asking if the hearing aids were waterproof. She nearly wept with joy when he said they were.

"I take it your hearing is back?" her sister asked.

"And then some, and I wasn't talking to myself. I was talking to the guards outside."

Her sister looked at the door, back at her, back to the door, and blushed. "They heard everything, didn't they?" she signed.

Marsee nodded.

Little Flower blushed harder and then swore in Saber.

"Your privacy is safe with us," Avery said with a slight chuckle.

"It had better be. You do not want Little Flower after you when she's angry," Marsee replied.

The guards howled with laughter, which apparently even Little Flower could hear because she frowned.

"If you think I'm joking, remember what she did to Senior Councilor Tabor," Marsee reminded them. "And she wasn't hangry at the time."

Their laughter stopped instantly.

Her sister looked at her, brow raised in a question.

"I reminded them of the consequences of crossing you," Marsee said with a grin. "Especially when you're hangry."

Her sister smiled wickedly in response and handed her a plate of fruit. "I may be tiny, but I bite."

Marsee curled her tail in humor and purposely barred her fangs as she ate a piece of fruit. "Yes, you do, and I enjoyed *every* second of it," Marsee signed back.

Her sister grinned and blushed but grabbed another bite of food.

Once everyone was done eating and the dishes cleaned, they made their way out. The guards' faces were blank masks as Little Flower glared up at them, although Tamarin's tail curled ever so slightly. Marsee blinked in surprise, but not at the curled tail. She'd expected them to be amused, but Tamarin's scent made her head tilt as she examined it.

"Is there a problem, Translator?" Tamarin asked.

"Your scent is all...bubbly."

"She's amused," Avery said. "And doing a very poor job of hiding it behind her mask."

Tamarin rolled her eyes in Avery's direction, which made Marsee chuckle, but the bubbles vanished from her sight.

"How did you do that?" Marsee asked.

"Practice," Tamarin replied. "Lots and lots of practice. You'll learn eventually."

Marsee shrugged and kept walking. The static shield of her mask made the hearing aids buzz as it activated, sending shivers down her spine. Thankfully, the noise stopped once the shield was fully in place.

They made their way to the Trauma Center with several minutes to spare, even arriving before her mother.

"I'm impressed. You made it on time," Ammond teased when they swam through his office door.

Surprising her, Tamarin swam in as well.

"What can I do for you, Honor Guard?" Ammond asked, raising an eyebrow in her direction.

"Marsee said you invented her hearing aids," Tamarin began and paused.

Ammond nodded.

"Would you happen to have another set with you?"

"So that's what that message was about." He stood and walked over to a stack of equipment cases in the corner. "You're in luck, Honor Guard. I do have an extra set with me. I wasn't sure if Marsee lost hers or not, what with everything that happened."

Ammond motioned Tamarin over and had her lift the stack so he could pull out the case on the very bottom, which he then set on the chair and flipped open. He pulled out a small case that matched the one she had and a package of the fitting sleeves before walking back over to his desk and fiddling with his tablet.

"Your name date, Honor Guard?"

She provided the information, and a moment later, Tamarin's tablet dinged.

"I've sent you the app for configuring them. Please go ahead and install it."

Tamarin whipped out her tablet, practically dropping it in her haste. Once she finished, Ammond reached a paw out for the tablet. Tamarin handed it over and then watched as Ammond paired the hearing aids and checked the fit.

Once they were both in and turned on, Tamarin let out a huge sigh of relief.

Marsee frowned as she watched Ammond explain how the app worked. *Am I going to have to wear them all the time now, or like my sense of smell, will I be able to tone it down or get used to it?*

Tamarin's expression as she learned what else they could do was entertaining to watch, at least. When Ammond put it on silent mode, Tamarin's knees actually buckled and she sat down hard.

"By all that is holy under the three full moons, you may have just saved me from going mad," Tamarin said after a few moments of stunned silence. "Avery snores. I haven't had a peaceful night's sleep since the day I joined his squad."

Avery chuckled from the doorway. "No wearing them on duty."

"Yes, sir," Tamarin replied, and almost reverently stored them back in their case. After she clipped the case onto her carry harness she checked three times to ensure they were secure. "From the very depths of my soul, I thank you," she said to Ammond.

Ammond grinned. "Am I correct in assuming the rest of the Honor Guard would appreciate a set?"

Tamarin nodded. "Yes, sir. Our hearing takes the longest to learn to control, and it wears on you after a while."

"I imagine so. Well, come on then," he said and swam out. "You too, Apprentice."

They followed Ammond back out after waiting for Little Flower to put her artificial fins back on, and he led them over to the Guild. When they arrived, he informed the Sprite floating by the main desk that he was there to pick up his order. The Sprite left, and they waited.

"Giving up on teaching Little Flower already?" a voice called out from behind them, and they turned to see Ellie and Agate swim down the hall. "Because I'll take her back if you don't want her."

"Ha! Not a chance. She picked me. That must really ruffle your fur," Ammond said with a grin as he gave Agate a hug.

"What fur?" Ellie replied with a laugh. "Little Flower, I'd like to introduce you to Guild Master Agate, one of my dearest friends and an incredible painter in her own right."

"It's nice to meet you," Little Flower signed and held out her hand.

Agate looked at her hand in confusion, so Little Flower explained. "Hue-mans from my part of Earth shook hands as a greeting."

"I thought shaking hands was how you formalized a deal," Ammond said with a scowl.

"It's both. It's a show of trust."

Agate flashed her surprise. "We do not touch or hug anyone we do not consider close friends or family, for obvious reasons, certainly not someone we've just met. You would trust me after what happened to you and your family?"

"I figured if you intended any ill will towards us, our fuzzy shadows would have been a bit more growly and pokey the moment you approached, and Ammond trusts you, which is good enough for me."

"Growly and pokey?" Agate's skin bubbled with laughter, and the effect continued on with her scent. It was rather distracting but beautiful at the same time. "That's an apt description of Saber's guards."

Little Flower held her hand out again, and this time, Agate carefully took it and shook it. "It is a pleasure and honor to meet you in person, Councilor, and I am quite relieved to see you in such good health."

Little Flower grinned. "There might be a few parts still out of place, but Ammond did a fairly decent job of putting me back together again."

Ammond grinned at the praise, but Ellie scowled.

"He could have clearly done a better job. If he'd put you back together right, you'd have picked my guild over his." Ellie kept her glare up long enough for Ammond to scowl, "But that being said, please believe me when I say I am not really upset. I fully approve and understand your reasons for doing so. Please just promise me you'll give him a hard time."

Little Flower plastered on her most innocent of expressions, which made everyone howl with laughter, except for Ammond, who scowled at Little Flower, although his tail was curled tightly.

"While there are still some improvements to be made, I suppose you'll be happy to know I did a good enough job that she's drawing again," Ammond replied.

"You are?" Ellie asked. "That's wonderful news!"

Marsee pulled up the image and handed it over.

"Oh, Little Flower, this is simply fantastic! May I have a copy?" Ellie asked.

Agate peered over Ellie's shoulder and flashed blue with happiness.

"Not before I get mine," Ammond replied before Little Flower even had a chance to respond.

"This style of drawing would be perfect for a children's book," Agate said. "You and Marsee should collaborate and write one. It would be an instant hit."

Little Flower beamed. "Do you think so?"

"I really do," Agate replied. "The one you did on the extinct Earth creatures is very popular here. I know many are wondering if you'll do the same for the creatures that were rescued."

"That's what I wanted to do before, write children's books, but my father didn't think I would be able to earn a living off of doing that," her sister said.

Ellie rolled her eyes. "No offense, but your father was blind not to see how talented you are. It seems to be a real failing among your species to let talent go to waste. Between you and Henry Curtis... Oh well, their loss is our gain. Henry's album is going to break the servers."

"Henry recorded an album?" Marsee asked. "They didn't say anything last night when we saw them."

"They're finishing it now. It should be ready to post by this evening," Agate replied.

"I can't wait to download it!" Marsee said. "Please let me know when it's up."

Just then, the Sprite who left to retrieve Ammond's order returned with several large bags and one wrapped object tucked under her arm. "Senior Guild Master, your order is ready, too." The Sprite shifted things around and handed the wrapped package to Ellie first.

"Thank you, Iruki. Ammond, this is actually for you," Ellie said, handing it over to him. "Although I should probably keep it for stealing Little Flower out from under me."

Ammond flicked his ears back in surprise as he took the package and unwrapped it, revealing an upside-down picture frame. He flipped it over and started laughing so hard that if he'd been standing, Marsee was sure he would have fallen down but then crushed Ellie in a hug. "Oh, child, thank you! You've made this old coot very happy!"

Only Ammond could get away with calling The Senior Guild Master 'child,' Marsee thought.

He flipped it up to show them, and Marsee smiled when she confirmed that it was the picture of him covered in green stain that had been hung in Agate's office.

"Who took the picture?" he asked.

"Master Bresdone," Agate replied.

Ammond's ears drooped. "Not a day goes by that I don't miss him. Thank you. This means even more to me now," he said, hugging the picture close to his heart as his voice broke with emotion.

Agate flashed her grief and sorrow briefly, and even Ellie looked sad.

"Who was Master Bresdone?" Iruki asked.

"He was my mentor," Ammond replied sadly. "He died, what? Nearly fifty years ago now. He was a consummate prankster, which isn't surprising since he was a Flyer. When I was still an apprentice, he rigged up the cadaver dummy we used to practice operating on with a speaker and had it start screaming in the middle of surgery. Scared the whiskers off me so much I sliced the nose clean off the cadaver." He turned to Ellie and glared. "He didn't put you up to this, did he?"

"I tripped. It's the moons' honest truth," Ellie said with far too straight of a face and a tightly curled tail. Marsee caught a hint of a change in her scent, but it was too quick to decipher.

He continued to glare at her. "If I find out you're lying to me when I die, I'm going to come back and haunt you. You'll never be able to sit in another rocking chair again."

Ellie burst out laughing, although she did wrap her tail in close to her side, which caused everyone to laugh even more.

Ammond slid the picture through straps in his harness and then took the bags from Iruki and hung them on his drone. "Well, as much as I'd like to float around and reminisce all day, *I* have an apprentice to train," he said after, with an exaggerated air of smugness.

Ellie rolled her eyes again, but otherwise ignored the barb. "Marsee, when you're done with whatever it is you're up to with this old coot, swim back down here. We have a lot to talk about."

Marsee snorted at the understatement, said her goodbyes to Agate, and swam out after Ammond, who asked Avery to lead them to Kendra. They swam back towards the council building. Honor guards were out in front, which usually meant the Local Council was in session. Others were being stopped and searched at the entrance, but they were allowed in without so much as a challenge.

Avery led them down several floors, not quite as deep as where the prisoners were being held, and down a long hall before turning off his camera and entering a large room full of guards and monitors. They were noticed immediately, and the room quieted. Her gaze fixed not on the people but on everything that could be seen on the monitors. *Were they watching her all the time? How much have they heard, and who has access to that information?*

"Stop your gawking and get back to work," Kendra bellowed from her office, "before I find you all something far less enjoyable to do."

The guards snapped to action, and she pulled her attention away from the monitors and followed Avery into Kendra's office, which was far more opulent than she expected. She'd been to the guard station in Sand Dune as a child, and it had been very utilitarian, just as the area outside was, but everything in this room spoke of richness and luxury.

Kendra's desk was clearly built and carved by a master or several masters. It looked nothing like any desk she'd ever seen. Beautiful swirly burls had been carved to look like waves, while small sea creatures danced among them, their eyes decorated with sparkling jewels, and it must have been freshly stained, as the smell wrapped around her, almost like her sister's scent had, and pulled her in. The rest of the furnishings were designed for the comfort of the various species, and a medium-sized window looked out over another complex of buildings. There was a beautiful mural on the ceiling, but none of that captured her attention the way the desk did.

She walked over and ran her paw over the surface, completely forgetting about the others, even Kendra, as she examined it. It appeared to be carved of a single piece, as she couldn't find any signs of joints, although it was a material she had never seen before. She didn't remember where she was until Kendra spoke.

"Is there a problem with my desk, Honor Guard?"

"No," Marsee said absently as she continued to rub her paw along one of the carvings. "This desk is a work of art. Do you know who made it?"

"I do not," Kendra replied. "And as...artistic as it might be, I'm assuming there are other reasons you're all here."

Marsee looked up to find Kendra's arms crossed and a single brow raised as she watched her. She swallowed hard with embarrassment as she realized what she was doing and hastily pulled her paw back.

Avery broke the awkward silence. "Healer Greyfoot has developed a solution to one of our more...aggravating problems."

Kendra's other eyebrow raised at this, but she motioned for Ammond to have a seat, then hit a button on her desk before taking her own seat. The large window and door to the outer office turned opaque.

"It turns out that Marsee has had a full range of hearing for her whole life, although perhaps not full volume. Master Greyfoot has invented hearing aids to help tune out the more annoying frequencies," Avery explained.

Kendra leaned forward with excitement at this. "Really?"

"They were originally built to help remove background noises for the hearing impaired," Ammond said as Tamarin unclipped hers and handed them over.

Kendra took them out of the case, popped them in her ears, and gasped before closing her eyes and sighing in what appeared to be pure bliss. It was not an expression she ever expected to see on an Honor Guard and most certainly not this particular guard. Eventually, Kendra opened her eyes and looked at Ammond. "Please tell me you have more of these," she said after taking the hearing aids out and handing them back to Tamarin.

Ammond lifted the bags he'd brought in with him and set them on the desk. "There should be two hundred pairs here. These, in particular, were adapted to shift Hue-man speaking voices into the ranges the rest of the species can hear and vice versa. I'm guessing you could easily justify the expenditure. If not, send me a list of the numbers you need, and I'll authorize more. I marked Tamarin down as a beta tester rather than medical necessity, figuring you might want to hide the real reason your guards need them and will do the same for these."

"You can even turn the sound off altogether," Tamarin said.

"And use them as private speakers to listen to music or other audio on your tablets," Marsee added.

Kendra raised her eyebrow again and then refocused on Ammond. "Why exactly do you have so many? Here?"

"They were originally supposed to be shipped back to New Hope as part of a larger shipment, but since I was coming here anyway, I told them to hold a portion of the order. I was planning to bring these over to Jeran to give to the Hue-man Council, but I think your need is greater. It's not like the Hue-mans will be able to learn our languages in a few days, even if my Apprentice has quite the aptitude for learning how to swear."

Her sister snorted. "Excuse me for focusing on the most important phrases first."

Ammond rolled his eyes. "Hue-mans. Remind me again why I agreed to be your mentor?"

"Because I give the best compliments," Little Flower replied with a grin, "and because I'm adorable, and you knew how much it would annoy Ellie."

Kendra snorted at the exchange, then pulled one of the cases out of the bag, handed it over to Avery, and took out another for herself. "Send me the app," she ordered Tamarin, who did so immediately.

To everyone's surprise, Kendra then walked around her desk and knelt down in front of Ammond. "Master Healer, I cannot even begin to express my gratitude for this. If you need anything, and I mean *anything*, the Honor Guard is at your service."

Ammond flicked his ears back in astonishment and smiled. "There's no need. I'm honestly glad that they'll go to good use. Let me know if you need any adjustments. Now, I need to get back to my research. Come on, Apprentice," he signed and stood, looking uncomfortable and embarrassed by the praise.

"When will you be done with Little Flower?" Avery asked.

"Her brain should be sufficiently mushified by the noon meal."

"Good, we'll swing by to pick her up then," Avery replied.

"Mushified? Is that a medical term?" Little Flower teased at the newly made-up sign.

"It is. It means an Apprentice's brain that has either been stuffed full of information from their esteemed mentor or thwapped to a pulp with a tail for insubordination," he teased back, and they started to leave.

Kendra turned to Avery. "Are you planning to train Marsee this morning?"

"I am," he replied.

Kendra turned off the privacy screen. "Zatara! My office!" she called out. Aris showed up a moment later. "Escort the Master Healer and Little Flower back, and then return here when you're done," Kendra ordered.

"Yes, ma'am," Aris replied.

Surprisingly, Ammond didn't argue, or at least not until Little Flower went to take Hope out of the carrier and hand her over to Tamarin to watch.

"What are you doing?" he growled.

"Tamarin's going to watch Hope while Marsee trains," Little Flower signed back.

"What? You don't think I can cub-sit *and* thwack you with my tail?" he grumbled.

"No, we figured you'd want to be able to have both hands free, too," Marsee replied with a curl of her own tail.

"Ha! Well, you focus on your training. Uncle Ammy will take care of Hope. Besides, I have no desire to mess up all that hard work I did putting that brain of hers back together again." He motioned Little Flower out with a glare, and they left.

The moment Ammond was out of earshot, Kendra turned to Avery. "Ammond gets an Honor Guard."

Avery laughed. "Tamarin and I already agreed to it. I have a feeling that his will be the most honored funeral we've ever done once these are handed out."

"You're probably not wrong there," Kendra replied, but then turned and focused entirely back on her.

It was so intense that she wanted to squirm and look away, but instead, she squared her shoulders and stared right back. Kendra might be more than twice her size, but she had defeated and killed bigger. She might be injured and recovering now, but she was ready this time, and she fully intended to learn how to protect her family. No one was ever going to harm her or them again.

Kendra gave a slight nod as if pleased with her response and returned to her seat. "Training Hall C," she said to Avery.

He raised his brow.

"Ammond said no fighting or impact to her torso, but everything else is fair game. She wears the safety gear until she's cleared. I want a full assessment. Let's see what we're starting with."

"Yes, ma'am," Avery replied and swam out.

Marsee took one last look at Kendra, wondering just what she was getting herself into, and followed out after Avery.

CHAPTER 41

Kendra: Spy

Kendra watched until Marsee had left Command and then activated her privacy shield again. She tapped on the arm of her chair with her claws for a moment before walking around to the front of her desk. Marsee's scent was easily visible where she'd touched the desk. It was clearly a work of art that someone had spent a lot of time and effort on, but she personally hated everything about it and her office. It wasn't fitting for a guard.

She tried to look at it from Marsee's perspective. As a crafter, it was not surprising that Marsee would appreciate it, but it had gone far past appreciation. She'd been drawn to it, so much so that the embarrassment from the scene before had completely vanished, and she'd forgotten about everyone and everything else while she examined it.

New guard senses or something else, she wondered. It wasn't uncommon for new guards to get overwhelmed when their senses returned, but this felt like more. Sniffing deeply, she dismissed Marsee's scent and examined the desk closely. The smell of polish was nearly overwhelming, and she could certainly see how that might affect Marsee, but she dismissed that, too. She had no idea what material was used to make the desk, but it felt wrong to her senses somehow. She examined the structure closely, trying to figure out why, then gasped when she realized what it was. It wasn't wood. It was bone. *That's one heck of a large creature,* she thought.

Why would that matter, though?

She shifted closer, examining one of the carvings that Marsee had been so focused on, and frowned. One jeweled eye did not glimmer like the rest. She reached out with a claw and pried it off, then examined the tiny camera closely.

What are you doing here?

She knew that the room was recorded, per the law, but those cameras were purposely large and well-marked so that anyone entering would see them and know. She couldn't smell anything on it save for Marsee's scent, the sharp tang of electronics, and a hint of adhesive.

She growled and began examining the rest of her office for further signs of cameras. Finding nothing and no scents that she didn't recognize, she left her office and swam up to the Senior's Conference Room, deciding to start there first. They needed to know if someone was spying on them, and she needed permission to examine their offices. A pair of guards floated outside. They saluted but otherwise didn't stop her as she knocked, not that she expected them to. Based on the chatter she heard as she left her office, the local council meeting was over, so there was no reason to stop her.

Clear Seas opened the door and motioned her in. The others were all there and watching her. She waited until the door was shut and opened her paw to reveal the tiny camera. "A few minutes ago, I found a camera hidden in the jewels of my desk."

There was no reaction of surprise from anyone. If anything, they seemed pleased. She squinted at them. "You put it there?!"

"We did," Clear Seas replied. "Or, more specifically, I did."

"Why? My office is already recorded, and you have full access."

"And the comms system has been compromised," he replied. " Rip was able to disable cameras at will. Until such time as we're able to confirm it's secure again, the only people who have access to that camera are the six of us. It's a backup system. It should also come as no surprise that we don't fully trust you, although we are pleased that you informed us directly upon finding it."

She sighed. Her interactions with the Seniors had been far more cordial since she'd rescued Apakna's uncle, and she hadn't smelled mistrust from them in several days. She peeled the badge off her harness and held it out to Surellis. "If you don't trust me, then I have no right to be your Senior Guard."

He raised a single brow. "And who should I replace you with? Everyone is suspect at this point, including you. For better or worse, you are still my Senior Honor Guard. Return the camera to where you found it, and don't inform anyone else about it."

Kendra nodded and returned to her office. Activating her privacy screen again, she carefully replaced the camera, then sat in the chair opposite it and stared at it for a long time, wondering how long it had been there. She hadn't sniffed Clear Seas on it or even that he'd been in her office, and none of her guards had mentioned his presence. *Were they ordered not to, or did he get in here another way?*

She remembered the high-pitched laughter she'd heard and the feeling of being watched that first day. She stared out the window behind her desk for a moment before walking over and checking it for a possible entry point, but she found nothing. *He would need water, and that would wash away any scent.* But that gave her another idea. She hit the switch that started filling her office with water and watched where the water entered. Activating her shield, she swam over to investigate, but they were far too small for Clear Seas to use, even as flexible as his species was. Spinning, she examined everywhere she could now reach but again found nothing.

She spun slowly, examining the room, and was about to give up, deciding that perhaps her guards were ordered not to say anything, when she realized there was one area she hadn't checked: the waste room.

She swam inside, shut the door, and sniffed deeply. She didn't find anything until she glanced up, thinking. With her senses still activated, the hidden door was easily visible, and then some. She swam up and considered what she could see and then pressed a spot on the ceiling.

The door slid open, and for a brief moment, she was face to face with a tiny Sprite before he bolted.

Prepared for his escape, she swiped and managed to grab him by the end of one tentacle. She braced for the pain of a shock, but to her surprise, he didn't resist when she pulled him into the room.

Stormy flipped around to face her, floating upside down as she held him out in front of her.

"Hello," he signed. "Fancy meeting you here."

"Care to explain yourself?"

"No," he replied. "Not really."

She snorted at his audacity. "I could have you executed for spying on me."

"You have no proof I was spying. I have full authorization to use the tunnels and maintenance shafts, just like the guards do. If you don't believe me, ask my father."

That sniffed true.

"Why are you in the tunnels?" she asked.

"That's secure council business. I'm not authorized to tell you. You'll have to ask my father that, too."

That also sniffed true.

"Then why did you run from me?"

He wiggled his other tentacles. "In case you haven't noticed. I'm physically incapable of running anywhere. I don't have any legs."

She growled slightly, although she was rather amused by his snark and that he wasn't the slightest bit afraid of her. "Why then did you *swim* from me?"

"To avoid an awkward conversation and being held upside down by my tentacles, for one," he replied.

"And for another?" she demanded.

"I don't trust you. Now let me go." He moved one hand to his harness. "If you don't," he flashed, "I'll set off my emergency alert, which will notify my father of my location."

She did, and he flipped around. "Why don't you trust me? Is it because I made you leave your brother behind?"

"No. Those were my brother's orders, and I understand why you did it. I don't trust you because I know you're hiding something. Who is Gen Eral and what do they want with Marsee?"

It took her a moment to realize who Stormy was referring to, as his ability to speak was limited, and she wondered who had mentioned the name loud enough for Stormy to hear. She'd had several conversations following Marsee's dream, but those had been subvocalised, and she knew that was outside of the range of hearing that the Sprites or cameras should have been able to pick up. Then she remembered the guard she'd chastised outside the Squadron Commander's ship. *How had he heard them?*

After considering how to answer, she decided to be honest about it and gave a slight chuckle. That surprised him. "The General?" she asked. "Where did you hear about her?"

"Where I heard it doesn't matter. Who is she?"

She raised a brow at his refusal to answer. He wasn't Senior yet, which meant she technically had authority over him, and not answering a direct question given by a guard had serious consequences. But if he was acting under Council orders to spy on her, then her not answering could be seen as treason.

"Marsee Ezabet Chenzira was our very first Honor Guard long before the Great Awakening. General is the title she had at the time. It's our word for military commander. Legends state that she was instrumental in winning our last war and could somehow see the future. The legend also states that one day, she will return when we are on the verge of another war. The story is told to new recruits around campfires during wilderness training. My guards are a bit superstitious about the similarity in her name and current events. I don't hold with prophecy. It's far too easy to manipulate them to fit any situation."

Stormy stared at her for a long moment, clearly not expecting her response. "You're serious?"

She nodded and then shrugged. "I've never found anything in the Archives about her to corroborate the story. Personally, if there's any truth to that prophecy, I'm hoping she's already averted war by killing Rip. I know she's your friend, but I don't recommend you tell her or anyone else. It'll just make things far more awkward for her than they need to be." She glanced in the direction of the hidden door. "Now, Get out of here and stay away from my office. If I find you here again, council business or not, I won't be as lenient."

He tilted his head, accepting her warning, and swam off.

She stared at the door for a moment, giving him time to swim off, then swam up to examine it and the small tunnel. She followed the tunnel's direction back into her office and found the tiny spy hole in the ceiling disguised as the eyes of another sea creature. She considered her options and then decided to leave it. There was nothing that couldn't be accessed from the cameras anyway, and now that she knew about it, she could easily scan for potential spies, which could ultimately prove in her favor, and knowing about the hidden door could save her life.

The fur on the back of her scruff raised at that thought, and she knew, somehow, not only was that important in the way that Marsee's dream had been important, but that was why Marsee had been so fixated on the camera. If it hadn't been for that, she'd have never known about the door.

Why, though?

Her eyes shifted to the pair of hearing aids on her desk and a brow raised at all the possible implications and uses.

CHAPTER 42

Marsee: Training Hall C

Marsee followed Avery out the back door, which was close to Kendra's office and at ground level. She hadn't realized the building had been built on a hill. There was a large open space where dozens of small ships painted with the colors of the Guard and Sea Patrol were parked, along with one ship that she recognized as Clear Seas'. It was identical to her father's, save for the planetary logo. They swam past them and into the complex of buildings that she'd seen from Kendra's office.

"This is the Guard Complex," Avery explained. "While the public-facing offices and Command, which you just saw, are in the Council Building, this is where the guards live and train. Most cities only have a single building, which contains barracks, offices, and training arenas, but each of the council cities, save for New Hope, has a complex, not just for the guards stationed there, but designed to support two contingents of guards from each species, the maximum allowed by charter unless approved by the Senior Council."

She nodded. She was aware of that, having worked through the various charters with her sister.

"Right now, we're at maximum capacity. Something that, from my understanding, has never occurred."

She swallowed hard, wondering how many of those guards could be trusted, but nodded her understanding.

"Each species has its own building and guard post, designed to support their unique requirements. I noticed your discomfort earlier when you saw the monitors. Your privacy is safe, or as safe as we can make it. Only members of our guard can access our cams and positions unless that permission is granted to another Guard, and there are multiple layers of protocols to make that happen. We, the guards watching you, are all running dark. That means our feeds and locations are further restricted. Only Kendra, the Seniors, and those assigned to your personal protection have access. Additionally, our feeds will only display on the main monitor if one of us alerts to a problem or a guard specifically puts it up there. If, at any time, you want us to turn off or mute our cameras, we can, and for your protection and privacy, they were muted per your father's orders while you and your sister...enjoyed your honeymoon."

She was both relieved and embarrassed to hear that.

"For the most part, these buildings are completely off-limits to members of the other species. Outside of an emergency, anyone entering a building that does not belong to their species must be accompanied by a guard from that species. The Hue-mans don't have their own barracks yet, as they've chosen not to have their own guard, and we don't really know what they would need or want for their own training. The extra guards Kendra brought as part of their allotment are currently being housed in suites in the Platform."

He pointed to one building. "That building is a communal space which includes a cafeteria, recreational facility, reservable offices, conference rooms, and the armory." He then pointed out each of the species' individual barracks as they swam past. She expected to stop at Saber's barracks, but he kept going.

"In addition to the private training areas in each of the barracks, there are also communal training areas. Training Hall A is water-based, B is designed to be configurable to support both, and C is land and air based. D, which is the newest training hall, is the shooting gallery."

She looked at him. "If Training Hall C is land-based, why were you surprised Kendra said to go there? Because it's communal?"

He nodded. "That's one reason. It's also the largest of the land-based training halls, and much of it you'll probably not be capable of using because of your injuries. I had intended to start you in the smaller arena, but Kendra wants a full assessment."

"Do the other guards know of our...unique abilities?"

"They know we have a very strong sense of smell and hearing. Every species has its own unique advantages and disadvantages, along with tech to help mitigate them."

He swam up to the access pad by the door and palmed it open. "You and your sister have both been granted access to this hall and Saber's barracks, even if, for some unexpected reason, we aren't with you. Attempting to access the other halls will open a call to their Command, which they can open remotely if there's an emergency."

She swam inside the large water foyer, where they hung up their drones, and then stepped through the static shield onto a balcony that looked down into a space that reminded her of the arena in the barn, only this space was full of walls, ramps, bridges, rope nets, and dozens of other contraptions she wasn't familiar with and couldn't even tell what they were used for.

Looking up, she found even more obstacles on the ceiling for the Flyers, many of which moved. She watched in fascination as a blue Flyer dove and twisted as he flew through the course, avoiding some obstacles and striking out at others. A static shield caught objects before they could fall to the ground. After watching for a moment, she pulled her attention back to the arena below, trying to get a sense of what to expect, feeling rather intimidated by everything she saw.

Avery let her watch for a moment and then pointed to a wall of hooks where several harnesses and masks were hung up. She unhooked her cloak, hung that up, and started to unclip her harness, although the guards left theirs on.

"Leave your mask on, but take your hearing aids out," Avery ordered.

She sighed but took them out. The buzzing of the lights in the arena hit her immediately, making her skin crawl, and she flinched at the noise of the people training, but she did her best to ignore it.

Avery led her down the ramp and walked over to a wall where a number of strange objects were hung. He examined them and her for a moment and then pulled one down and put it on her, adjusting the straps so everything fit where he wanted it. By the time he was done, thick heavy pads wrapped around her midsection, held in place by far more straps than she was used to for her carry harness, including a section that wrapped uncomfortably around her tail.

"How are you supposed to move in this?" she asked once he was done fiddling with the straps. She shook to try and make it comfortable and winced as it rubbed against the sensitive skin under her tail.

He chuckled but didn't reply. Instead, he grabbed another padded object and ordered her to close her eyes. She did and felt him remove her mask, then plunked the other object on her head and buckled it under her chin. The moment the buckle was on, she heard the buzz of a static shield.

"You can open your eyes now. It's a solid shield," he said, tapping on the visor to show that nothing could get in. "The gear will protect you from an impact, and the weight will help build your muscles and endurance faster. Follow me and do your best to keep up."

Avery dropped down to four feet and took off at a jog around the outside of the arena.

Marsee sighed and followed after. She hadn't tried anything but a slow trot since leaving the Trauma Center, and the gravity here was significantly higher than her hall and room. The gear didn't help either. It rubbed uncomfortably with every step and she had a feeling her tail would be raw before she was done. She tried clamping down with her tail to keep it from shifting, but that messed up her balance, and she nearly fell on the first corner. She was breathing hard by the time they made it a single lap around the arena, but the other two didn't even look phased. It was all she could do to finish a second lap.

He gave her exactly two minutes to recover before leading her up, over, under, and around various obstacles. They crossed wobbly rope bridges, climbed walls, crawled under beams, and then turned around and leaped back over them. They walked along narrow platforms high above the ground, slid down some poles, climbed others, and leapt from the tops from one to another.

She fell once and screamed, but there was a shield under the poles that caught her and slowed her descent, so she landed safely. She managed it the second time.

The only thing she couldn't do was the rope climb. She couldn't curl her injured paw well enough to hold onto the rope, and it made her new claws hiss with pain. Avery didn't push her after the first attempt. When she said no, he marked it down on his tablet and moved on to another obstacle without comment.

A number of the obstacles took her several minutes to overcome her fear of even trying them, but the guards encouraged her, and eventually, she made it through. Eventually, Avery led her over to an area where several other guards were resting or stretching. She collapsed to the ground, panting with exhaustion, her tail held awkwardly away from the strap. Tamarin scanned her, checking for injuries, then pulled out a small tube of nano cream for her tail and handed it over.

"Not bad," Avery said as she squirmed, trying to reach the base of her tail, which was nearly impossible with the gear on. "Thirty-four and a half minutes with only one fall and the one obstacle you were unable to complete due to your injured paw."

She looked up, trying to decide if he was being serious or not. They'd barely touched a fraction of the equipment. Both guards had completed every obstacle as well, but they weren't even winded while she was gasping for breath. "You're serious?" she finally asked.

Avery nodded. "It's above average for the assessment course for our species. You'd be surprised how many people are afraid of heights, and I rarely see people manage the rope bridge on the first try, or even the seventh, without flipping it. Ladders are exceptionally difficult for our species, but you had no problems with that."

"I have to climb one up onto the roof of my tower to service the solar panels," she explained. "I love heights, as long as it's nice and solid underfoot. Little Flower once climbed all the way to the top of our Bandala tree. Several of the Hue-man cubs have as well. It's a constant battle to keep them out of it, and as one of the smallest Sabers in New Hope, I've been sent up after them a few times when there weren't any Flyers available. Granted, I had a grav belt. The branches aren't strong enough to hold my weight."

"Good to know," he replied with a wicked grin, and she had a horrible feeling she'd made a terrible mistake.

She let out a groan, and both guards chuckled, confirming her suspicions.

Exactly two minutes later, they had her stand and walk around the outside of the arena. Thankfully, the nano cream had done its job, and by the time she'd completed a lap, she'd regained her breathing, but she was still exhausted, and her stomach was starting to ache. She let Avery know.

He nodded, but rather than leaving, he led her over to the back half of the arena, which, from the balcony, had looked like a maze. There were two doors, one on either side. Avery whistled so loudly it made her ears ring. From around the arena, the others whistled back.

Avery motioned her in one of the doors. "This won't be physically demanding. All you need to do is find your way out," he said and slammed the door behind her.

She jumped from surprise but started making her way around the maze. A few moments later, she heard Avery whistle again, but this time, there were no responses. Before she could figure out what that meant, the lights went out. It was all she could do to keep from screaming as she was instantly transported back to the cave and the pitch-black darkness that she'd been trapped in for days.

Terrified, she scrambled back to find a wall and pressed herself against it. The warm, smooth surface was reassuring and snapped her out of her panic. It wasn't the cold, slippery rock wall, and there was dry sand beneath her feet, not wet stone.

She focused on her breathing and tried to calm her beating heart, which sounded like a drum in her ears. She heard something above her, but when she looked up, she couldn't make out anything but the darkness. However, that sound had briefly illuminated the space like it had in the cave. Reminded of that ability, she started tapping on the wall behind her. With each tap, the space around her came into focus.

Her breathing calmed, and she walked forward to the first intersection and tried to decide which way to go. Sniffing deeply, the scents of the arena came into focus as well. She eliminated all of the airborne scents, focused on the ground, and found a very clear trail to follow, so she did, tapping along the wall as she went. A few minutes later, she made her way out the other door, and the lights flicked back on to a large crowd of cheering guards.

One of the guards nudged the one next to her. "I told you she wouldn't scream."

"Two minutes and thirty-eight seconds, a new course record. Well done, Marsee!" Avery said as he jumped down from the building to land next to her.

She blinked in surprise. "Seriously? A record?"

"You'd be surprised how many people are terrified of the dark. Parker screamed for a good ten minutes," the other guard said.

"That may be, but at least *I* didn't pee myself," Parker replied with a lash of his tail.

The other guard scowled and leapt at Parker. The rest of the guards shifted out of the way as the two fought, fur flying everywhere, not even remotely concerned about the fight occurring. She noticed several making bets on who would win.

"Don't mind them," Avery said, shifting her aside just in time to avoid being landed on. "They're litter-mates and find something to fight about at least twice a day."

That honestly surprised her more. She couldn't imagine fighting like that with any of her siblings. It looked and sounded like they were killing each other, although they were moving so fast she could barely keep track of what was going on. Suddenly, they split apart. Parker looked smug, while the other guard looked thoroughly annoyed, as did several of the people who had apparently lost the bet. Outside of fur everywhere, there wasn't even the slightest sign that either of them was injured.

After a brief break to review the fight, Avery flashed some signs that she surprisingly didn't know, and guards bolted for the maze, with some going through the door and others climbing or flying over the walls. They all looked excited, even the Diggers.

Confused, She looked back at Avery and Tamarin, who were the only two who remained behind.

"Playtime," Tamarin explained, which left her even more confused.

Avery flipped open the lid on a box next to the wall and pulled out several strips of fabric, which he and Tamarin began tucking in and around her vest. "There are ten flags. Your job is simple: keep these away from the others. They'll be positioned throughout the maze but can't move their feet from wherever they've stationed themselves. For every flag you still have when you exit, they have to run laps. For every one you lose, you have to run. Now, tapping the walls was a great idea, but you won't always have a wall to tap. You can also flick a claw or cluck your tongue, but remember, they'll be able to use it, too. Ready?"

She nodded.

Avery whistled again, and everyone whistled back. He motioned her through the door and shut it, although he didn't slam it this time.

When his second whistle came, she was prepared, and the dark didn't scare her. Taking his warning to heart, she didn't click but instead brought her sense of smell fully forward and took her time to analyze before moving. The trail was even clearer now, although some had run off in different directions.

Trying to walk as quietly as possible, even though her own breathing sounded loud in her ears, she crept forward until she came to the first large wafting of scent that told her someone was waiting around the corner in the direction she needed to go.

She decided to risk a few flicks of her claws to get a better sense of her surroundings and stopped the moment she found a gap she could use to go around the guard. Carefully feeling her way, since there wasn't a trail to follow, she made her way through the gap and past the guard.

Picking up the trail again, she continued on until she came to another waft of scent. After clicking a few times, however, she still didn't see any way to work around them, and she knew they knew where she was. Deciding there was nothing for it but to make a run for it, she walked forward on two feet until she was only a few feet away and bolted forward, dropping down onto all fours and twisting to make it harder to grab the flags.

She felt a pull along her side, and then the guard whistled. He'd capture one of her flags. Swearing, she continued on. She heard his chuckle from behind her, but it also illuminated the way ahead of her.

The next guard she encountered was one of the Flyers hanging from the ceiling above her. Crawling down on all fours, she easily made it past them.

Around the next corner, she came across the scent of two Digger guards. She clicked and realized there was something above them. It took her several clicks to realize that there was a platform above each guard. She leapt up onto the closest one, slipping with her back feet as she nearly missed the ledge, and felt the guards paw feeling for one of the flags, but she scrambled up before they could grab one.

Clicking several times until she was sure of where the platform was, she leapt through the air, the world going dark as she did, to land safely on the other side. Panting hard to contain her fear, she clicked again and leapt down away from the second guard.

"Well done," she heard one of the guards say.

Continuing on, she rounded the next corner and froze. There were three male Ice Giant guards, at least, ahead of her, based on their size, taking up most of the path. Clicking, she tried to find her way around them and noticed an irregular pattern along the wall. Looking up, she realized that the roof above her was open. She climbed up but had barely stuck her head out when there was a tug at her back and another whistle from the Flyer that had been waiting for her. She hadn't sniffed him with the other guards there.

Swearing, she dropped back down. She couldn't go that way. Clicking again, she decided that she might be able to squeeze past on the far side of each of them. She'd have to switch sides, though, and she couldn't tell how far away from each other they were. Inching up against the wall, she kept clicking. She needed to be able to tell exactly where they were. The first guard swiped, trying to grab a flag, and she twisted out of the way only to feel another tug and a whistle from the second guard. Bolting at a run, she twisted and ran past the third, barely keeping her flags.

The next guard was hanging over a platform, so she crawled under them and avoided them with ease. Beyond the platform and around the next corner, the hallway had several guards as well, but there was a small ramp, barely a paw's width wide, leading to the open ceiling above it.

Remembering last time, she focused on the opening, trying to catch the scent of someone waiting, but she didn't find anything. Standing and putting her back to the wall, she inched her way up the ramp and sniffed again before exiting. Still nothing immediate, she climbed carefully up onto the wall. It, too, was barely a paw's width wide, and she clicked furiously. There were several guards on the walls around her, but none close.

Making her careful way across on all fours, she considered what to do next. There was a guard ahead of her and directly below her, and no good way to jump back down into the maze. She checked around her, looking for another way. There were guards behind her, too.

The only clear way to go was to leap across three walls to the exit. Clicking furiously, she awkwardly shifted around, muttering under her breath at how awkward the gear was, and judged the distances of all three. If she kept tapping her claws, she'd lose sight of the walls, and that was downright terrifying. It had been bad enough on platforms, but they'd been much lower to the ground. She switched to clicking her tongue, as Avery had mentioned, took a deep breath to calm her nerves, and bound nimbly across all three walls, then walked along the outer wall to the other door.

She checked the distance carefully before jumping down but still winced as it jarred her stomach.

Avery let out a long whistle, and the lights came back on. He let out a different whistle, and everyone came streaming out of the maze. Avery confirmed that she still had seven of her ten flags, and they started their laps. The other guards, even the Diggers, who were the slowest of the species, were all done theirs before she'd even finished her first lap, and she was barely above a walk by the time she finished her third. Avery and Tamarin stayed with her the entire way.

"Well done," he said as they took a cool-down lap. "Very few ever attempt that route on their first try, or tenth for that matter, and certainly not with your injuries."

"I may have overestimated my readiness for that last jump. I think I might avoid doing that for another day or three. That hurt a bit, but I'll admit, once I got over my panic at being in the dark again, this was actually a lot of fun, far more than the cave was."

"I should hope so," Avery said. "It will get harder, though. The guards will be allowed to move and fight, and we have several different drills that we do, both in the dark and with the lights on. Every planet has a different layout, and we change them regularly. Many of the walls are designed to move and shift easily. How are you feeling now?"

"Exhausted and like I've been run over by a herd of chenzies," she replied.

Avery chuckled. "Perfect. We'll do it again tomorrow. This afternoon, I'll teach you and your sister how to use the stunner and work with both of you on some basic self-defense that we can do without impact or added stress on your stomach."

She nodded wearily, not realizing they'd be coming back again in the afternoon, but she was determined to recover so she could defend her family as quickly as possible.

When they finished their cool-down lap, he led her over to a water station, where she took a long drink. Rather than heading out as she expected, he spent another hour working with her entirely on footwork until she could comfortably move out of the way of the swipe and grab that she'd failed so miserably at in the maze. By the time they left, her legs were wobbling as she walked up the ramp on all fours, too exhausted to even consider standing on two and unlike before, neither guard offered her assistance.

"I'm thinking I might need a nap before we come back and maybe a float in that nano bath in the Trauma Center," she muttered as she put her harness and cape back on. She left the hearing aids in the case, though, as she'd gotten used to the sounds in the arena, and she knew that it would be far quieter outside.

Both guards chuckled.

Avery looked at the clock on the wall. "You still have a few hours before we need to pick up your sister if you want to go back to your suite for a nap instead of meeting up with the Senior Guild Master. "

"Moons. I forgot about that. Suite first. If I went down there now, I'd fall asleep on her. Ellie hits hard, and I have enough bruises as it is."

She yawned the entire way back to the platform, and it was all she could do to drag herself down the hall to the suite. After it was checked for villains and monsters, she climbed into bed, thankful it wasn't any higher, and fell asleep before her head even hit her paws.

CHAPTER 43

Marsee: Negotiation

An hour later, which felt like mere minutes, Marsee swore as her alarm blared. She thwacked it with her tail to shut it off and immediately fell asleep again. Several snoozes later, she finally decided she'd better get her exhausted tail in motion before Ellie came looking for her. After making liberal use of the nano cream, she crawled off the bed and limped her way out.

"Better?" Avery asked.

"Honestly, no. But hopefully, I won't fall asleep on Ellie now. I'm pretty sure I overdid it. I ache everywhere, even after using the nano cream."

"Just wait until tomorrow," Tamarin said with a chuckle. "The day after is always worse."

She glared up at the honor guard. "Why do I have a feeling I'm going to regret ever asking you to teach me how to fight?"

They both laughed but said nothing else, once again confirming her suspicions. She glared at them for several moments but huffed and started walking, knowing if she didn't, she'd fall asleep again. Before long, they were swimming into the Guild.

"I'm looking for the Senior Guild Master," she told Iruki.

"Right this way, Translator," the Sprite said, and they followed after.

Even though she'd been given a tour of the facility, she still found it disorienting. Very much a Water Sprite building, it was carved into the side of a hill and followed a natural cave structure, twisting and turning and branching in every direction. She was lost almost immediately. They eventually made it to the main cavern, a large, well-lit open area with a massive skylight above. Workbenches and offices surrounded the perimeter of the cavern, with the highest-ranking desks and offices near the top, where the best natural light was located.

Naturally, Ellie's office was at the very top, where Agate's office was also located. When they arrived, the door was open, and Ellie sat floating behind a desk.

"Thank you," she told Iruki and knocked.

Ellie looked up and motioned her in as her guards took up station outside.

"Shut the door," Ellie said.

Marsee did, although she now knew that the Guards could easily hear their conversation and briefly wondered if they could hear through a privacy shield. She guessed not since Kendra had activated hers that morning. She floated over to one of the hanging nets the Sprites used for a chair and climbed in with a sigh of relief.

"You look like you've been run over by a chenzie."

"No, I'm pretty sure the whole herd got me. I had my first training season with the Guard this morning. This is me after a nap. You should have seen me before. They practically had to carry me back to my room." She let out a heavy sigh. "I still have a long way to go before I'm fully recovered. I could barely make three laps around the training arena without passing out. It's a far cry from the leagues I used to be able to run."

"You're training with them?" Ellie asked. "I thought they were just teaching you how to use a stunner."

"That too. I want to be able to defend myself and Little Flower if someone should try to hurt us again. My instinct won't be there to help next time. Avery agreed to mentor me."

"I pray there never is a next time," Ellie replied.

"You and me, both, but I'm not foolish enough to count on it. Rip claimed that there were others just as upset at my father and I for our 'little coup,' as he called it. I don't know if that's true or not, but I have to assume it is."

Ellie frowned. "So, am I losing you, too?"

"No, not to the Guard anyway. While I actually had a lot of fun today, even if it was exhausting, I have no desire to spend my days floating outside of a door. I'm stuck here for weeks until I'm cleared to jump home, and this is more fun than what the healers have been having me do. Consider this more like another special interest or advanced pickle torture."

Ellie nodded and then squinted her eyes at her. "If not to the Guard, then who *am* I losing you to? Please don't tell me you're joining the Healer's Guild."

Marsee laughed. "No. I have no interest in that either, but that's the question of the day, isn't it? I don't know what I want to do. With my Guild balance, I won't have to work another day in my life if I don't want to. The one thing I do know is that I have no desire to spend a single minute in another requisition meeting."

Ellie snorted. "Does anyone?"

"Master Nardal?" Marsee suggested.

Ellie considered and then nodded. "You're probably not wrong there. He was downright giddy the last time I sent him. However, you now essentially own a significant portion of the Guild. In all rights, the Council and I should be negotiating with you since what you now have is on par with the annual budget of a district or two. What do you intend to do with it all?"

"I have absolutely no idea. I used some to start digging my way out of the mountain of messages I received from the Water Sprites and I made a gift to Opal to help her start her restaurant. I'm planning to give a sizable amount to the other victims once they figure out who that is. I don't think it's fair that I've been given all of this when they haven't. They were hurt just as much, if not more, than I was. But even if I donated half of everything that was given to me, it's still more than I could use in my lifetime, or several lifetimes. We're planning a Hue-man partnership ceremony for Little Flower when it's safe for me to return home, and we've talked about requisitioning our own ship and traveling around the universe, but even with all of that, I would barely touch it. Do you have any ideas?"

Rather than answering, though, Ellie asked her another question. "Out of everything you've ever done in your life, what makes you the happiest?"

The first thought that came to mind would have made her blush if she could have.

"Outside of that," Ellie teased, clearly guessing where her mind had gone. "What makes you want to leap out of bed before your alarm goes off or keeps you up at night because you don't want to stop working on it? Or conversely, what makes you lose interest in something or makes you want to avoid it altogether?"

Marsee leaned back in the chair and thought hard about all of her favorite projects she'd worked on and the moments that stuck out in her brain as the happiest. She couldn't pick just one. *So what ties them all together?* she wondered.

"I guess if anything, it would be designing something new or learning a new skill to make something I want to build. I don't have the patience for the minutiae. Not very often, anyway. Most of the time, I'm happy with good enough unless I know you're going to be critiquing it. Then I want to crawl under my bed and hide."

Ellie chuckled at that comment. "I do tend to have that effect on people."

"I had a lot of fun the day I came here and wandered the Guild talking and collaborating with the other masters on their projects," she replied after further consideration. "There were a dozen projects or more that I wanted to stay and spend hours working on, but I needed to leave to meet with Clear Seas."

Ellie grinned. "Agate was very impressed, as were the other masters with your suggestions, although I heard you used *my* schtick for promoting that Journeyman." Ellie's grin turned into a glare in an instant, but she couldn't help but chuckle after a few moments.

"You aren't upset?" Marsee asked.

"Moons no. I've seen that drum. I had to see what impressed you so much to feel confident enough to promote her, even if you had that right at the time. She more than deserved it."

Ellie leaned back in her seat, quiet and thoughtful for a moment. "If you enjoyed collaborating with the masters, you should keep doing that. They have a list that would stretch from here to the moons and back of projects they want to work on but don't have the personal resources to accomplish. As much as I would like to give my crafters everything they need, to work on whatever they want, I have orders that need to be filled and limited resources to go around, but I do have a small budget that I use to fund several projects each year. The Guild ends up with the majority of the risk and the profit, but the lucky master gets to work on their dream and shares in the reward. Sometimes, they work out. Most of the time, they're a complete flop, but we learn a lot from those failures, too. You could do something similar, but if you didn't want to manage the financials on it, you could donate to the fund directly, and the Guild would pay you a percentage back on any profit. If you're concerned about what gets worked on, you could take over reviewing and picking what projects to invest in. I know I don't have nearly enough time to manage that, even if it is one of my favorite responsibilities."

She appeared lost in thought for a moment and then shrugged. "Don't bother wasting your resources on a ship, however. If you decided to take over the fund, then I could justify paying for it through the Guild. As far as donating to the other victims, I think that's a wonderful idea, and I'm really proud of you for even considering it. Figure out how much you want to give, and I can have Nardal put together a scholarship fund to manage it, with regular annual payouts to the victims. I can reinvest those funds into the Guild and make it a sustainable program that would ultimately pay out more than a one-time gift would.

You should talk to your father about it, too. He might have suggestions on other projects or funds you could contribute to."

Marsee nodded. "That sounds interesting. Have Nardal send me the information, and I'll take a look at it and discuss it with Little Flower. She has her own plans with Ammond that I don't want to interfere with, and I don't want to be away from her or Hope all the time, either. I hated being on separate planets from them."

Ellie nodded. "I understand completely, and if you want to take a few years off, that's fine too. I always expected to lose you for a few years to a litter or two of cubs, just not quite so soon. Still, I'm just relieved you're looking towards the future again."

"Well, it helps to have one," Marsee replied and then leaned forward with the same intense stare that Kendra had given her earlier. "Now, I think it's time we discuss my Guild rate, especially if you've been hiding that my books are on the top downloads."

Ellie burst out laughing. "I was wondering when you were going to bring that up."

Marsee kept the glare on Ellie, refusing to break under her laughter.

"Alright. For your original work on the Adventures of Super Stormy, I'm promoting you to Journeyman Writer Level Three. Poof and all the blah blah blah. I'll backdate your rate to that publication.

Marsee didn't stop her stare. "*Top* downloads and top print as well for *all* of them, not just Super Stormy. I've looked. You neglected to block Little Flower's tablet, and I believe you mentioned being able to fund New Hope for the past several months on *my* translations alone."

Ellie's eyebrow raised, and she returned the same glare.

Marsee refused to give in or look away.

"Fine, Journeyman Writer Level Four, but I'm not going any higher. You're too young to be promoted to Master."

Marsee snorted. "I was acting Senior Guild Master for a day, intentional or not, and if Little Flower can be a Master at six, so can I. Age has nothing to do with it, and don't try to change the subject. You hid that information from me for months, long before I was your protege. I get what you were trying to do, but I've spent my entire life thinking my work wasn't good enough, and you knew that. What right did you have to hide that success from me? If I had known how much those translations were benefiting New Hope, I would have spent far more time and effort on those projects. And you and I both know, if I hadn't already informed you that I wanted my share of the profit on those works to go to New Hope, you'd have been breaking the law for withholding information relating to due compensation."

They stared each other down for nearly five minutes before Ellie huffed. "Fine. I am not promoting you, but I will authorize the Master Level One rate for new original books and translations."

"You also created toys, capes, and other themed products based on my artwork," she continued. "Without my authorization or knowledge, which *is* against the law. I expect full compensation for that, with interest, in my account by the end of the day, or I'll go to my uncle."

Ellie's ears flicked back in astonishment and confusion. "You said you wanted the profit from your translations to go to New Hope."

"For the books, not for everything else. I've checked my contract. Nowhere on there does it say anything about giving up my rights to my artwork to be used in other products without my consent." She pulled up the contract on her tablet and handed it over to Ellie.

Ellie spent several minutes reading and then sighed, rubbing the back of her neck, and Marsee caught a hint of fear in Ellie's scent.

"You're right. It looks like I sent you the wrong contract. That's my fault, and I'll take full responsibility. That's what I get for not having Nardal handle the contracting, but you'll bankrupt New Hope with those demands. That's a significant portion of their annual budget and a capital offense on my part."

Ellie glanced towards the guards outside, and Marsee caught another hint of fear. "What if I backdate your rate across all disciplines to Master Level One for six months in exchange for updating the contract? I know it doesn't come close to what you're owed, but..."

"And you neglected to inform me about or send me the five hundred printed copies of my works given with every new publication."

"And unlimited copies, to be printed at your demand," Ellie said quickly.

"Deal," Marsee replied and smiled at Ellie's shocked expression.

"You're serious?" Ellie asked.

Marsee chuckled. "There's no way I would hurt New Hope or you like that, and you should know it. I sent the updated contract to Nardal back when I was Acting Senior. I certainly don't need the credits. I just wanted to see you squirm for a minute or two. I figure *that* makes up for feeling overwhelmed when I found out about what you'd hidden." She chuckled again at Ellie's expression. "That being said, Rip knew about it. I also informed my uncle so he and Lowell could look into everyone who had accessed that contract. It wouldn't necessarily indicate a crime, but I figured it might help tell us who was working with Rip. I also wanted confirmation that I was reading both contracts right. I'm surprised neither of them mentioned it to you."

"You just saved my life," Ellie finally stammered out, still staring at her, ears flattened in shock.

"I fully intend to rub that in for the next six months," Marsee replied with a wicked grin. "If not longer."

"You've been hanging around Little Flower for far too long." Ellie replied with a growl, but her expression changed to a grin moments later, "But it's about time you started acknowledging your worth, and thank you for fixing that before it became a real night terror for me. Now, get out of my office before I change my mind and demote you for nearly giving me a heart attack." Ellie picked up her tablet and began scrolling through it as her ears shifted to annoyance.

Marsee chuckled, knowing it was entirely an act and swam out, tail curled behind her. She sniffed amusement from both her guards, confirming they'd heard every word, but they said nothing.

CHAPTER 44

Ellie: Desperate Measures

The moment Marsee swam out, Ellie set her tablet down and stared after her, relieved at how well the meeting had gone and floored by the crisis Marsee had averted. She wondered if there were similar contracts but shook her head. It was unlikely. Very few people gave up their rights to their work like Marsee had, and even fewer people were as popular as she was.

Still, she sent off a message to Nardal asking him to audit similar contracts, if he hadn't already, and instructed him to send the prearranged plans in a few hours to avoid giving Marsee any hint that they'd already had everything ready. She then informed Jer that Marsee had nibbled on the bait.

Messages sent, she swam over to her window and watched Marsee and her shadows swim off, relieved to see her laughing and joking with them. That, more than anything, made her happy. She'd come far too close to losing her protege, and it was good to see her laughing again.

A few moments later, Agate swam in. "So, how did it go?"

"Even better than we hoped. She hasn't said yes yet, but she will." Ellie didn't turn to face Agate until Marsee was out of sight.

"How much did you have to give up to keep her in the Guild?" Agate asked.

"Far less than I was prepared to. Her own ship was a given. She's only mentioned that to me about a dozen times now, and she's been learning how to pilot one for months, but she thinks that'll be a perk for running the Research Division. She negotiated me out of a Journeyman Level Four rank and Master Level One rate, back-dated six months, and we'll need to send her those printings of her books we've been storing for her. Where did she get the idea that we only sent authors five hundred copies?"

Agate's skin bubbled with humor. "That's how many were in the first printing I sent to Stormy. Clear Seas contacted me before I brought them over, wanting to know how big of a bookcase he needed for them. We have the rest in storage."

Ellie grinned. "Why don't you throw in a selection of the other toys and merchandise for good measure? She'll enjoy giving those out to the cubs. That'll come off as an apology for hiding everything from her and put us in her good graces. Although I have a feeling that's impossible. She just informed me that I sent her the wrong contract, one that didn't include giving up merchandise rights to the artwork on her translations."

"Bottomless depths," Agate swore, "her skin rippling with emotion, immediately understanding the severity of the mistake."

"She made me squirm for several minutes, demanding instant repayment, before letting me know she'd already sent Nardal and her uncle the corrected contract. She said she considered that payment for hiding her popularity from her."

Agate snorted. "Well, you should have known better there. I believe I warned you that would come back to zap you."

"You did, but you should have seen her after I scanned her artwork and they became so popular. She was comatose for days. If she'd known how popular she was here, I'd have never gotten her off the ship, much less agree to the trip in the first place."

"Well, that does bode well for her accepting the plans Nardal and Sammianna drafted," Agate replied.

"That it does. As we expected, she'll probably take time off for paternity leave and finish recovering, but I have a feeling she'll be back sooner than we expect, especially if we drag Little Flower back into the Guild.

At least, I hope so. That's going to be the biggest challenge. Marsee doesn't want to leave Little Flower behind, and if Little Flower's training with Ammond, she might not want to travel. But she's drawing again, so I'll be able to sink my claws back into her, eventually."

Agate chuckled. "I'm beginning to see why Rip hated you so much. You're devious. I'm surprised Marsee didn't demand a master's rank. She certainly deserves one."

Ellie laughed. "She does, but she doesn't quite believe it yet, at least not about her own skill. She was pushing to see what she could get away with. I let her stare me down for a good five minutes before pretending to cave and bumping her rate, but she didn't even question that I wasn't going to promote her to master."

"I still find it hard to believe that someone as exceptional as she is can't see just how talented she is when she can clearly see that in others."

"She hasn't had a project big enough to really tax her abilities," Ellie replied.

"Managing the Research Fund should do that."

"We'll see."

"You're serious? You don't think an entire division will be big enough?" Agate asked.

"If I know her, the hardest part she'll have will be deciding who gets those funds. She didn't even hesitate to step in and take over for me while I was recovering, even knowing she was still at risk and that her promotion might not be legitimate, and that was with only a few days of training. She's been through more in the past few weeks than most people go through in their entire lives. Heck, she's been out of the Trauma Center for what? Five or six days now and won't be fully healed for weeks, and yet she's already training with the Honor Guard. Do you honestly think a little thing like the research fund will tax her? She'll eat it up and ask for more."

"You'll be out of a job at this rate," Agate said with a chuckle.

"That's always been the plan," Ellie replied, then turned back around to look out the window again. "Now the question is whether or not she'll be ready in time to take on that mantle permanently."

"Have you told anyone," Agate asked, swimming up next to her and wrapping an arm around her in comfort.

"No, just you," she replied, leaning into her friend.

"There's still a chance you'll survive," Agate said.

"One in a hundred," she replied. She watched absently as people swam by and rubbed at her injured paw to help control the instinctive urge to rub that was getting stronger every day.

"You should tell Myra and Ammond. If anyone can stop this, they can. Look what they've been able to do for Little Flower."

She turned to face Agate, "I don't want them to stop it."

Agate flashed her grief. "Are you really willing to take that risk?"

Ellie didn't answer, and Agate stared at her.

"You really are? Aren't you? You should tell Myra anyway. She'll honor your wishes, and you'll need someone to help you through this. You know I'd be there if I could."

Ellie sighed and nodded. "I know, and I thank you for that, but right now, I need you here. If things go badly, will you mentor Marsee?"

"Of course," Agate replied, although hints of black flickered on her skin.

"Thank you." She turned and faced out the window again with another sigh. "Well, you're right. I should tell Myra, and I better tell her now before I lose my nerve."

Grabbing her drone at the entrance, she looked down the street where the top of the Trauma Center could be seen and gave another silent prayer before setting off. She confirmed with the front desk that Myra was still there and made her way through the halls to the office she and Ammond had commandeered.

"Hey, Ellie," Myra said as she stepped through the shield and into their office. "We were about to head out to find something for lunch. Did you want to join us?"

"I would, but there's something I need to talk to you about first. If you have a few minutes?"

"For you, always. What's up?" Myra asked.

Ellie shut the door, walked over to one of the empty chairs, and sat down, but it was several moments before she could talk.

Myra frowned and sat down in front of her. "What's wrong, Ellie?"

"When Rip attacked me, he..." She paused, took a deep breath, and tried again. "There was an injury that I've asked the Senior Healer to keep from the Council," she said. "I didn't want it to become public knowledge, at least not yet anyway."

Myra looked concerned, and Ammond set down the equipment he was fiddling with to focus entirely on her.

"What did that monster do to you?" Myra growled.

"He took out my implant," she said finally. Ellie watched as her friends realized what she meant and the implications as they started doing the math.

Myra scrambled for the stack of cases in the corner. "Why didn't you say something sooner? I don't have a female implant, but I have a male one. You could swap it out later."

"Hyacinth already talked to me about it, and I refused it. Besides, it's too late now. I had confirmation this morning."

Myra looked back at her in horror. "But you've already had your second heat. A third will kill you. No, I refuse to allow it. I'm not losing you so soon after getting you back from the dead." Myra scrambled back to grab her scanner, the look of horror now replaced with panic.

"Myra, I don't want you to stop my heat."

Myra stopped and stared at her. "You want to die?" she asked, ears pinned back in disbelief.

"No, I want cubs. I've always wanted cubs and lots of them. You know that. The healers refused to even let me try a third time. I'm not wasting this chance."

"What chance?! You nearly died with the first two pregnancies and with your injuries carrying a cub to term will be nearly impossible. Please, let me try to stop it."

"No," Ellie said. "It might be nearly impossible but I'm taking this chance, however small it might be. I want cubs."

"No, I can't lose you again!" Mrya grabbed her tail and twisted it hard.

"Myra," Ammond growled. "She said no. You need to accept her decision in this. She knows the risk she's taking."

Myra glared at him, lashed her tail, and then stormed over to her desk, where she collapsed into her seat and buried her head in her paws. "Why, Ellie? Why didn't you leave when you had the chance?"

"Because I want this, Myra, more than I've ever wanted anything in my life, and I didn't leave because I needed to be here to protect Marsee."

Myra's head snapped up to look at her in confusion. "But..."

"She spiraled out of control into a deep depression the moment you jumped, and she tried to kill herself. It took me and both of her guards to stop her long enough for Tamarin to sedate her, injuring both guards in the process. As it was, she still needed surgery. She came very close to ripping her throat out. I found out the same day, but I wasn't leaving her alone for a second after that."

Myra growled. She'd seen Myra angry on more than one occasion, but Myra looked like she was ready to kill. Apparently, Ammond thought so, too, as he reached over from his seat and grabbed her by the scruff, pulling her in close. Myra sagged against him, and he held her as she cried. "Suicide?! Why didn't anyone tell me?"

"Marsee promised us that she wouldn't try again as long as we kept it from you, and after Little Flower proposed, there was no need. She can't know I told you or know that I had a chance to stop this but chose to stay and care for her instead, and there were other reasons I needed to stay. The least of which was because I didn't trust Jer or Marcus around her, Jer because of what he did, and Marcus for what I was afraid he was going to do."

Myra growled at that reminder but then froze. "You're not going to make it back before your heat starts, are you?"

"Like I said, it's already started, but you and I both know I can't miss the trial portion. For once, my disability is proving in my favor. Hyacinth thinks I should make it through the first few days before I start releasing pheromones if my prior two heats are any indication. It'll be four long days on my ship, but I'll manage. It's not like I haven't been through it before. Thankfully, my ship is back from Digger and my new pilots are all Flyers, so that won't be an issue."

"You're not going to stay here?" Ammond asked.

"You know there aren't exactly many of our species here. While I could saunter into the middle of the Council Meeting to find a mate, that would certainly cause a scandal, and Ammond, while I love you to pieces, you're too much of a father figure to me to ever consider mating with you."

Ammond chuckled. "That's quite alright, child. At my age, I'm pretty sure a mating would do my old heart in, although it would be a good way to die... Still, Theresa would haunt me for eternity if I did that to her."

Ellie grinned at Ammond's impression of his partner, and turned back to Myra. "Even if I don't make it out of here in time, Hyacinth says they're not equipped to handle an implantation here. I intend to hit up one of the mating clinics and see where my nose takes me. I'd like you to come back with me and perform the procedure. And, if you're willing, I'd like to move into Little Flower's room through the pregnancy unless you think it'll be safe to come back here. I don't want to be away from Marsee, but if anyone can keep me alive through this, it's the two of you. I've seen you pull off miracles before. The Ancient Gods know I need one right now."

"You know you're always welcome in my home, but are you really sure you want to take this risk?"

"Completely," she replied.

"Then you know I'll do everything in my power to keep you alive. And if I can't, I'll care for your cubs, should they survive."

"I'm counting on it."

"Are you letting anyone else know?" Ammond asked.

"Only a few people. Nardal will need to know. Agate already knows, and I imagine you'll need to tell Jer, but I don't want the rest of the Council to know. It won't change anything. I intend to wait until after to tell anyone, and that includes telling Marsee and Little Flower. They have enough to deal with right now. If I don't survive, I don't want the reason to be released. Just say it was a complication from jumping too soon or something like that."

Myra nodded sadly. "That's a risk too. We did bring all the equipment, just in case we couldn't stop Marsee's heat in time, but if you have recovered enough, it would be far safer for you to go back to Saber." She flipped out her scanner and nodded toward the exam chair. "Have a seat."

Ellie stood and gave her friend a fierce hug before sitting down and letting Myra and Ammond perform a full exam on her. While the healers here were good. They were not experts in her species care. It wasn't Ammond's specialty either, but it was Myra's and she had delivered hundreds, if not thousands, of cubs in her long career. What mattered most was that she knew they would stop at nothing to give her the best possible outcome, and, well, if she was going to die, she wanted a friend to be by her side.

Just one, she prayed to the Ancient Gods. *Please, just give me one beautiful, healthy cub. That's all I'm asking for. Just one.*

CHAPTER 45

Little Flower: Target Practice

"You should have pushed for Master," Little Flower told Marsee as they picked out their lunch.

"Nah, I thought about it, but I want her to do that on her own when she's good and ready. I don't want anyone to think I blackmailed her into it. Besides, she's right, I am young for my species. Jumping two ranks puts me back to where I should be for my age if I'd stuck with one discipline instead of jumping around everywhere."

"As long as you're happy about it," Little Flower replied.

"I am. I'm getting paid as if I am a Master, and my title as Translator has far more weight here than that, anyway. So what do you think about her suggestions?"

"I think they sound like great ideas, especially the scholarship. We may not know everyone Rip hurt for a while. This will give us a way to ensure that those people aren't left out, but I think we should go even bigger. Talk to Papa about having the Council redirect whatever reparations they decide on to the fund as well. Together, you'd be able to do even more."

"That's a fantastic idea! What about the research fund?"

"Seems like a win-win to me. We get a ship out of it without having to pay for it, and you get to pick the projects you're most interested in working on."

"I would be gone a lot, and I really don't like the idea of being on different planets," Marsee said.

"Then we'll go with you," Little Flower replied.

"But what about your mentorship with Ammond?" Marsee asked as she paid for their meal.

"What about it?" Little Flower asked after Marsee finished. "He can load me up with homework. I can work on it while you're at the Guild and spend time learning from local healers on their species care. I'm not in any rush. Don't get me wrong, I'm really enjoying it. Ammond is a fantastic instructor, but if it takes two years or ten, so be it. Plus, I have my responsibilities as a Councilor to consider. Jumping to the different planets and getting to know everyone and their cultures will mean I'll be able to do that better. Nothing says I can't be in more than one guild at the same time. That cub's book sounds like fun, and I can work on that while we jump and consider it part of my pickle torture."

"Are you sure? That's an awful lot," Marsee replied and scanned the crowd, looking for an open table where they could eat.

Avery tapped her on the shoulder and pointed to one out of the way, where they could easily guard them from. Marsee nodded to him, and they took off in that direction.

"And you being in the Guild, caring for me and Hope, and translating books at the same time, isn't? You're the one adding Honor Guard to the mix. No offense, but you look like a chenzie sat on you."

Marsee snorted and switched to sign after setting their meal down on the table. "You should have seen me this morning. I almost didn't make it to the suite for a nap, and I seriously considered asking Avery to carry me, but I figured he wouldn't."

"Not a chance," Avery replied. "If you can't make it back to your room, you can sleep in the hall. It doesn't bother me one bit where we stand to guard you."

Little Flower laughed. "That sounds like a challenge to me. Five credits says Marsee can find someplace to nap that *does* bother you."

Marsee rolled her eyes as the conversation devolved into the logistics of the bet, which Tamarin gladly took up, to Avery's utter annoyance.

"So, how much do you think I should put into each of the funds?" Marsee asked once they were settled on the bet.

"That's totally up to you. It's your credit," she told her sister.

"No, it's our credit," Marsee replied. "I want your input."

"As long as we have enough to live comfortably, I don't care all that much. I don't even know how much that needs to be. Check with Mama and Papa to see what we should reasonably expect for expenses. Set aside a bunch for the wedding and a rainy day fund. Maybe see how much the Halloween Festival cost as a guide there, and any other random gifts you want to make, and see what's left."

"Rainy day fund?" Marsee asked.

"Unexpected expenses, like fixing a leaky roof, or for doing something fun, like going on a vacation or picking up new craft supplies for a project you want to work on outside of the Guild," she explained.

While they ate, Marsee took notes as they brainstormed on projects they were interested in.

"Avery wants to teach us how to use the stunner unless you want to do something different this afternoon," Marsee said after they ran out of ideas.

"That sounds like fun, but we can't stay all day. I still need to prepare for the council meeting, and I'm woefully behind."

Marsee tossed the remains of their lunch, and they followed after Avery, who led them to a large, nondescript building with no windows.

A Water Sprite floating behind a counter was busy tapping away on a tablet, not particularly focused on them, or so it appeared at first, but she set the tablet down before they made it over and flashed the silver and purple briefly at Marsee. "Translator, Councilor. How can I be of service?"

Avery answered for them. "We're here to requisition two stunners on permanent loan."

The guard nodded and swam off through a locked door, returning a few moments later with two flattish and slightly curved objects, which she placed on the counter. She scanned one of them. "Translator, do you promise to only use this stunner for practice and self-defense of yourself and others?" the guard asked.

"I do," Marsee replied.

"Do you understand that this weapon, although designed to be non-lethal, does have the potential to kill, and if used outside of self-defense or training, or to intentionally harm or threaten another, can and will be grounds for execution if someone should die?"

"I do," Marsee replied.

"Please place your thumb here," the guard directed after handing over her tablet.

Marsee did as requested.

The guard repeated the same process with her. "Have you been trained in how to use them?"

"I'm here to do that now," Avery replied.

"Excellent. Have fun. Range's five and six are available," the guard said and handed the stunners over to Avery, who clipped them to his harness.

"I thought you said the armory was in a different building," Marsee asked.

"It is. You can get all the standard guard equipment there, including stunners, but a small supply is kept here for anyone new wanting to learn or borrow for practice," Avery explained.

"Is anyone able to requisition a stunner?" Little Flower asked Avery.

"No, only the Council and Guard are allowed. Anyone else would need permission from the Council. While the stunners are designed to be non-lethal, it's possible someone with a weak heart could be killed, and everyone is required to be trained on their usage before being allowed to take them out of the building."

"So Snapper Fish and Rip Current could have had one?" Marsee asked.

"Yes, and they both did," Avery replied and palmed his way into another room.

This was obviously a target range, and outside of the fact that it was underwater and the targets had non-humanoid shapes to them, it looked no different than any she'd ever been in. Quieter, though, since the stunners made very little noise when they fired, at least not that she could hear.

She handed Hope over to Tamarin as she didn't want Hope in where weapons were being fired, even if they were non-lethal, and at her orders, Tamarin remained outside.

Avery brought them to their appropriate lanes, although it was fairly obvious which ones were theirs as the others were all currently in use by guards of every species. Avery unclipped his own stunner from his harness and showed them how to hold and fire it.

"Each stunner is registered to one and only one person. No one else can use it. To activate it, you'll need to press your thumb anywhere along this surface. It'll light up blue to indicate it's active and ready to fire. To fire, you press here. Each stunner has three shots before it needs to recharge, which takes about five seconds. These two points here are used to sight in your target. Lift, line up the points, and shoot."

Avery aimed and fired, and a small blue ball of electricity shot out of the device and hit the target. He fired off two other shots and hit two additional targets. Shots fired, he hit a button on the counter in front of them, and the marks where the shots hit vanished.

"Is it electricity?" Little Flower asked. "How do you keep it from spreading out?"

"No. I don't know, and before you ask further questions on the tech, that information is classified. Only the Senior Council, Senior Honor Guards, and the techs who build them have clearance to know that information," he replied.

"So the water doesn't affect it?" Marsee asked.

"It does. The biggest challenge is visibility. The water can distort where a target is and make it difficult to judge distances. The maximum effective range is about a quarter league above water but half that under. Outside of the effective range, it will hurt but not stun. You need to hit the person's head or torso to effectively stun them. A limb shot will only stun that limb. Alright, Marsee, why don't you try first? Do you know which eye is your dominant eye?"

Marsee shook her head, so he helped her to figure it out and then handed over her stunner. She swam up to the spot where he'd shot from, raised her paw, adjusting to try and figure out where to aim, and shot. She completely missed the target.

Little Flower watched as Avery corrected her sister's position and told her a number of different things that she couldn't understand. *I really need to learn more Saber,* she thought, *but it doesn't appear to be different from any other weapon.*

Marsee tried again and hit the target this time, just barely. Her tail curled with excitement, and she tried again. This time, she hit the target closer to the center but down lower. Marsee's tail curled tighter, and from his tone, Little Flower assumed Avery congratulated Marsee. She cheered her sister's success as well. She also noticed that the others in the gallery were watching, although they were trying not to be obvious about it.

Marsee waited the five seconds needed for it to recharge and switch from yellow to blue, then tried again. This time, all three hit the target around the edges. Avery said something to her, and she nodded and swam out of the way.

"Alright, Little Flower, your turn," he said, handing over her stunner. "Do you know which eye is dominant?"

She nodded and took her place. It felt weird to be shooting while floating underwater, but she'd been to enough target ranges with her father and older cousins to know how to shoot and was reasonably good at it, or she had been before she'd been injured, enough that her cousin had wanted her to try competing, and she'd been considering it. She had no idea how good her aim was now or how much the water would affect it. Lifting the stunner, which felt no more substantial than a remote, she pointed it at the target, aimed, and fired.

"Bullseye," she whispered and fired twice more, both hitting in the same spot.

She hit the reset button before Avery could do it and decided to aim for the other targets. *Kapow, Kapow, Kapow,* she thought, to make up for the lack of noise. When she was done, she turned around and realized that the entire gallery was silent and watching her. Several of the Sprites flashed what she believed was surprise. Avery, however, looked like she'd hit him with the stunner instead of the targets, eyes wide and ears pinned flat.

"Have you fired a stunner before," he asked.

"A stunner, no. Similar weapons, yes. Do you have anything harder I could try?" She'd noticed that several of the other ranges had moving targets.

Avery flicked his ears and whiskers forward but said nothing as he hit another button. The targets reset and started moving.

She smiled at him and took her place. She knew everyone was watching, so she took several deep breaths to calm herself before firing and hitting them all. They weren't moving all that fast, and without any kickback to adjust for, it had been easy.

Avery walked up. "Hit the red ones only," he signed, and then hit the control board again.

Targets started popping up, and she began firing. She didn't miss a single one.

He reset them, and she fired. They did it again and again, and each time, they moved a little faster. She didn't miss a single shot and forgot about everything around her but those targets, taking out her rage and fear at being unable to protect her GrandFather and daughter. It was surprisingly cathartic to know she could defend herself again. Eventually, the targets stopped, and she looked up in surprise.

"That's as high as the simulator goes," Avery signed, looking surprisingly uncomfortable.

The rest of the room was silent, and then they started cheering her performance. She noticed several had apparently bet on her as people started transferring credit.

After a moment, Avery turned to the others and signed something she didn't recognize. They all immediately went back to what they were doing, but she noticed they all seemed far more focused than before.

He turned back to her and looked at her for a long time with an expression she couldn't quite place. "If you're this good with a weapon, why did you run and not fight back during the rescue?"

"I was unarmed. Weapons weren't allowed in my school," she replied. "Not even knives."

"It seems the Ancient Gods were looking out for me that day. These weapons were designed specifically in the event your species turned out to be violent. I'm beginning to think we were vastly unprepared."

"Yes, you were," she replied, looking him square in the face. "I imagine almost everyone from my district would have fired a weapon at least once in their lives, and most owned many. It was a highly controversial but protected right for citizens in my district to own them. My father was a guard, or the equivalent, when he was younger and deployed to active war zones multiple times before he retired. He made sure everyone in my family knew how to shoot to defend themselves and how to hunt and track. We practiced often, and I went hunting with him and other members of my family all the time. I think the only reason you didn't experience any resistance was because most of my people were already dead and the rest severely wounded. If you had, you would be dead. Most of our weapons were designed to kill."

She paused and frowned at him, reconsidering what he said. "You were there?"

He nodded wryly. "I was wondering if you'd recognize me. I'm the one that rescued you. Half of the crew on the ships were guards, there to protect the others. I was the Senior Guard for the mission. The guards watching you now were all there, too. We travel as a squad most of the time, although only half of our squad is here at the moment. Your father could only fit six of us on the ship he took to get here, and the rest of my squad remained behind to guard New Hope."

It was her turn to be surprised. "Well then, I guess owe you a debt of gratitude. Thank you for saving my life. I thought you looked familiar, but I couldn't figure out where. I figured I saw you when I was in Council City," she replied.

Avery looked at her for a long time before replying. "We were there, too. For a long time, I thought you were exaggerating the violence of your people in order to make your species appear stronger, seeing as you lack natural defenses and were surrounded by species that were so much larger than you. I don't believe that anymore."

"Avery, what I told the Council, at least in public, didn't even begin to scratch the surface of what my people were capable of and still are. But then again, my species is not the only one capable of such violence, are they?"

She tilted her head in Marsee's direction. "I'm guessing it happens far more often than people are told, or there wouldn't be a need for the Honor Guard in the first place. Would there?"

Avery frowned and didn't answer.

"That's what I thought. How much of this is kept from the Council?" she demanded.

Avery stared her down for several moments before whistling loudly. The firing stopped immediately. He made another sign she didn't know, and everyone instantly bolted out the door, leaving them alone. Avery was obviously of high rank in the Guard, and she wondered just how high if he could order the guards of other species around.

"The Council is informed whenever a crime occurs or any time we're forced to kill," he said once everyone was out. He glanced at Marsee. "But you're right. It happens far more often than people are told. Child abuse, murder, and even rape. That information is kept from the general public. I don't have the statistics on the other species, but ours has the added challenge of psychosis. Those who commit crimes often do not survive the psychosis that follows or commit the crime in the first place because of their psychosis, and far too often, those who have been harmed don't survive either, but we do what we can."

"How is it that Jer and Marcus didn't know the punishment for rape?" she asked.

He pursed his lips. "I wondered when that might come up. The Guard stripped it out of the archives millennia ago to protect the families of those who committed that crime, but we apparently missed the copies Councilor Surellis had in his personal archives. We also do everything we can to keep it from going before the Council, including providing new identities for those harmed."

She frowned. "What gives you the right to hide crimes from the Council?"

"We're not hiding crimes. We're protecting the victims. Those who committed the crimes were dealt with."

"Without trial?" she asked.

"Councilor, I don't know what you've been told about psychosis, but it's not rare. We're all susceptible under the right circumstances. Those who commit violent crimes, among our species anyway, have typically done so because they lost control of their instinct or lose control once they're caught. As guards, we have the authority to decide how a violent situation needs to be handled and do so accordingly, without Council approval. Our authority exceeds that of the Council because if the Council is involved in that crime or is trying to suppress the rights of the people, we have the right to remove them from office, at a minimum, or execute without trial if there's just cause. That knowledge prevents most people from even considering violence or crime as an option, and in most cases, our very presence is enough to stop a situation immediately. When Marsee attacked me the other day, I would have been well within my rights to execute her if I felt that there was no other way to handle the situation, and had she not woken up or continued to fight back, I would have, but my first response is not to kill. It's to contain and try to find a peaceful solution to a problem. I train hard every day to ensure that I'm capable of doing so, just like I did with her."

"And what kind of oversight is there to ensure that right is not exceeded or abused?" she demanded.

"We're trained in the law, as well, if not better than the Council before we're authorized for duty, and if I witnessed one of my guards doing such a thing, I would put them down immediately. Any crime committed by a member of the guard, no matter how small, is grounds for execution. Our oath is to protect the rights of the people, not our fellow guards or even the Council, and we take that oath very seriously."

"Apparently, not everyone does," she replied.

"That's a serious charge. Who are you referring to?" he asked with a frown.

She frowned at him in confusion. "Snapper Fish and the other missing guards, of course, not to mention the guards who were watching the monitors of Rip's cell and helped him to escape."

"Snapper Fish is not an Honor Guard and never will be," he replied with venom. "He was only a member of the Sea Patrol. As for the guards watching the monitors, their guilt has not yet been established, but if proof is found that they were involved, they will be executed."

"A police force is still a police force whether you call it Honor Guard or Sea Patrol. Avery, your guard might be honorable as a whole, but ours was not. It was common for districts on our world to be overthrown by our equivalent of the Honor Guard and for individual guards to choose to abuse their power because they had it. It's the whole reason we didn't want a Guard. Our entire justice system was broken, but yours has its flaws, too. How many people were arrested for crimes they didn't commit? Two people were executed for fabricated crimes when they tried to stop Rip, and dozens more were arrested by someone who was given the same level of honor and respect given to the Honor Guard. I wonder how many more were involved. What would you have done in Snapper's situation? If your child had been held hostage, where telling others or not doing what her captor ordered you to do meant her death, would you choose her death over those you were sworn to protect?"

"I would have done everything in my power to find and kill him," he replied without hesitation. "Even if it meant the loss of my daughter, I would have tried to stop him to protect others from harm, and every other honor guard would have been there with me. Trust me, Little Flower, the oath of an honor guard is an oath we take very seriously. Even the slightest hint of impropriety is shut down and severely punished."

"Everyone has their breaking point. I wonder, Honor Guard. What yours would be?"

"I can't claim to be perfect. None of us can. We all make mistakes, and I've certainly made my fair share, but I strive to learn and grow every day to be better than I was before. I do not kill unless I see no other choice. I would end my own life before acting without honor because, without my honor, I would be nothing."

"At yet, you left Marsee and Stormy alone."

He sighed. "I did, and I may very well die for that mistake. Not only did I put their lives at risk, but I put my mentor's life at risk as well. She gave a life oath to your father that I could be trusted, and I broke her trust. Even if I'm not charged with a crime, she has every right to call in that oath, and I would accept that punishment willingly."

She stared at him for several moments. "You really mean that, don't you?"

"With every ounce of my soul," he replied. "I am not above the law. I am a flawed individual trying my best to make amends for the harm my stupidity caused and if at any point Marsee deems me to be guilty of negligence in leaving her and Stormy alone, she needs only say so and I'll end my life. I won't fight it. I put her life at risk with my stupidity and my life is hers to do with as she deems fit."

She looked at him a moment longer, brow raised, and nodded, although she still wasn't entirely convinced. This society was very different from the one she'd grown up in, and she wanted to believe that the Guard could be trusted, but her faith in them had been badly shaken.

"Come, we should let the others return to their practice," he said. "You obviously don't need any more training with the stunner, although you're welcome to practice whenever you want. I'll work with Marsee more tomorrow. We'll head over to the other training arena. Kendra has informed me that she wishes for you to be trained to fight as well if you're still interested. We're aware of your injuries and limitations but we can help you to be strong enough to fight your own kind at least, and I am curious what you can do with that knife of yours."

She nodded and clipped her stunner to her belt as Marsee clipped hers to her harness. Marsee was looking at her funny, though.

"What?"

"Later," Marsee replied and looked at Avery, who was swimming away from them.

Little Flower nodded and followed after.

CHAPTER 46

Little Flower: A Lover's Caress

The entryway was empty, save for Tamarin, Hope, and the guard who manned the counter. Little Flower took Hope back and they followed Avery over to another building. Tamarin again agreed to watch Hope but brought her down into the Arena where a squad of Saber's guards were training. The rest of the arena appeared to be empty.

She took off her flippers and carry sack and was going to take off the stunner, but Avery told her to wear it at all times, even when training, even though he had Marsee take her harness and stunner off. They made their way down into the sandy arena. She didn't have shoes, but the sand appeared to be rock-free, even if it was difficult for her to walk in. He had Marsee put on some protective equipment, which explained why she'd had to take her harness off.

"Five laps around the arena," he ordered.

Marsee sighed and took off, but Little Flower looked up at Avery in surprise.

"Is there a problem, Councilor?" he asked.

"I haven't run since before my coma," she replied. "I have a hard enough time walking on flat surfaces, and once around is a long distance for me."

"I understand. Do your best, and we'll use that as a starting point. If you can't run, walk, but you won't know if you can run if you don't try."

"Have you been hanging out with Ammond?"

He grinned but nodded for her to start.

She rolled her eyes but started off at a careful walk, trying to get used to the uneven dirt. After she felt reasonably comfortable, she decided to try running. She used to be good at it. She took off at a light jog and made it about five or six paces before tripping and falling hard.

"If you keep landing like that, you'll break your arm. Tuck and roll the next time," Avery said, giving her a tail up.

Easier said than done, she muttered under her breath as she brushed the dirt off. She had tried to roll, but her body hadn't cooperated.

"You're angry at me. Why?" he asked, looking honestly confused.

"Because that's what I tried to do," she snapped and then took a deep breath to control her anger. "The last two months have been a constant struggle of being told to do something I couldn't, no matter how much I tried. It was like that when I was in school, too. It felt good being able to shoot earlier, for once not feeling like I'm disabled, and for a brief moment, I thought I could actually run."

"Ahh. My apologies. That was not my intent. I simply do not want you to get hurt."

"I know, and I know I may have to learn to live with these disabilities for the rest of my life, but it doesn't make it any easier."

"I think perhaps not. It may have only been a few steps, but you did run, and in a gravity that is higher than your own. That's something we can build on, but first, let's make sure you can do it safely."

He brought her over to a section of the arena with a large, flat surface rather than sand. "This is a..." he paused and tilted his head, "We use this for practicing how to fall and roll. It's...squishified to protect you from being squishified."

She chuckled at his use of Ammond's new sign. "Appropriate. We called it a crash mat."

He raised a brow, and his tail curled slightly. "Hopefully, there will be less crashing and more rolling by the time we're done. Now. Let's see if we can't figure out where you're having difficulty."

They spent the next fifteen or twenty minutes working through the basics, one small increment at a time, until she was once again able to roll safely. His enthusiasm for her success was no less than her own.

Marsee eventually joined them after finishing her laps. "How is it that I have to run while you get to lay around?"

Little Flower looked over from the starfish position she was currently sprawled in, far too dizzy to stand, and stuck her tongue out at her sister before turning her head to Avery. "I think we need to take a break from this. I'm starting to feel a bit dizzy."

Avery nodded. "Do you feel up to showing me what you can do with that knife?"

"If you give me a minute," she replied.

He gave her exactly one minute.

She glared at him but climbed to her feet anyway and followed him to an area where there was a large wooden wall with various circles drawn on it. *Another universal constant,* she thought, and unclipped her knife. "I was bluffing a bit earlier. I have no idea if I can still throw accurately enough to hit a target, and the balance isn't quite right with this, but it was the best I could find in the warehouse."

He grinned and called something out in Saber. She looked over at Marsee for a translation. "Pay up," Marsee replied.

"You bet on me?"

"We were all fairly certain you were lying. The bet was whether you would admit it before demonstrating."

She glared. "I was not lying. I bluffed. There's a difference. I used to be quite good at hitting a target, but I do not know if I can still hit one, not just because of my injuries but the change in gravity. If I needed to, I would have tried anyway. At that distance, I was fairly certain I could at least hit her if not get the pointy end in the right place."

He tilted his head. "My apologies."

Tamarin called something back. "Five credits, she hits the target within three tries," Marsee translated. Avery took the bet, and the next thing she knew, all of the guards swarmed over to watch and started placing bets of their own. Word of her performance in the shooting gallery must have already reached them because most bet on her.

"No pressure, eh?" she asked.

Avery grinned and motioned to the target. She lined up at what used to be a comfortable distance and heard murmurs from several guards, but she ignored them as she tried to get a feel for the knife. Then, before second-guessing herself, she threw it. The knife landed a few feet short of the target.

One of the guards groaned as he'd bet that she'd hit it on the first try.

She unclipped the second knife she had and threw harder. It hit the board, but the rotation wasn't right, and it bounced off.

She wobbled her way over to collect the knives and returned to her starting position. She closed her eyes, taking several deep breaths, as a memory of her father teaching her to throw resurfaced. She adjusted her grip and stance, remembering the feel of her father's hands as he adjusted her position, then opened her eyes, ignoring the tears of grief that had escaped, sighted the target, and threw.

"Bulls-eye," she whispered. "I did it, Papa. Just like you taught me."

Cheers rang out from the guards, and suddenly, Marsee scooped her up and hugged her tightly. She squeaked in surprise but then laughed as Avery trotted over to the target, went to pull out the knife, and found it thoroughly wedged. Bracing himself and yanking hard, he stared at the blade for a moment and then went to test its sharpness.

"I wouldn't do that," she called out. "lest that knife gets a taste for your blood."

He turned and looked at her and then to Marsee for a translation. He furrowed his brow. "Is that a threat?"

"No," she replied, in Saber, and had Marsee set her down so she could sign easier. "It's something my father used to say. He believed that the only blood a knife should ever taste was the blood of our enemies. I also think it was a way of keeping me from messing around and getting cut. It's really sharp, far more than the knives you're used to."

He nodded and waved everyone else off before walking back over with the knife. She clipped them back to her belt. "Still think I was lying?" she asked.

"No," he replied. "You have more than proven your aim. Now, I think it's time you got back to your laps. Marsee, five more."

She grinned at him as Marsee groaned, but they both took off as ordered. She made it maybe thirty paces before losing her balance and falling again, but she managed to tuck and roll rather than face plant. Pleased with her improvement, she used the wall to help her climb to her feet and took off again. He nodded with approval as he kept pace at a walk beside her.

After about another fifty paces, she was already breathing hard and had to drop down to a walk, but she kept trying.

Marsee had finished her five laps before she finished one, although Marsee was breathing as hard as she was. A few minutes after Marsee completed a cool-down lap, Avery called out something. Marsee groaned and started running again, although not nearly as fast. Little Flower completed her second lap just as Marsee finished her third set.

Avery gave them both a few minutes to rest before starting again.

Her sister was not able to finish running a fourth set without walking.

Little Flower had to take another break after both her third and fourth laps, but Avery had her finish up her last lap at a walk while he started Marsee on the obstacle course. She watched as Marsee ran through the obstacles, surprised that her sister was managing so many of them after the injuries she'd had. She still struggled with many of them, but Avery seemed pleased with her performance.

When he was done with Marsee, he had her try the obstacle course. There were only a few that she could actually do, as they were all built for the bigger species, but some of them turned out to be far easier for her to do than for the others, simply because of how their bodies were designed. Apparently, ladders were hard for them to manage, and their balance beams were wide enough not to be a problem at all, although they were up so high that the height of them was a little unnerving.

Avery informed her that there was a static net below, even though she couldn't see it. Thankfully, she didn't fall. She was exhausted by the time she was through the obstacles she could manage and indicated she needed another break. Avery didn't question it and motioned her over to an area where she could wait and watch while he went and picked on Marsee some more.

When he was done, Marsee crawled over and flopped down beside her to recover, and they both watched while Avery took a run through the course. He was mostly done when someone whistled, and every one replied, including Marsee. Another whistle later, the lights went out.

"What's going on now?" she asked.

"Someone's going through the maze," Marsee replied.

A few minutes later, the lights came back on, and she looked over to see a few guards discussing whatever had happened.

"You want to try it, don't you?" Marsee asked.

"You know me far too well," she signed back. "Every Halloween, a group of people would fix up an old abandoned school across the street from our house and turn it into a haunted house where people in costumes would jump out at you and try to scare you. One year, they had a maze in the pitch-black. It was a lot of fun, as were the corn mazes my grandfathers made every year."

Marsee nodded. "They had a haunted forest in the garden the day you woke up. I wanted to go but ended up not going. I was far too overwhelmed at that point with everything that had happened that day that I didn't dare. I went back and watched you and Hope instead. I hope they do it again next year. I hear it was a lot of fun, and the cubs loved it."

"You want to try the maze in the dark?" Avery asked, walking up to them, having apparently seen their conversation. "Your species doesn't have any way to see or sniff your way through, from what I understand."

"So. I have my brain and my sense of touch. Unless the walls move in there, I'd be able to find my way out. How long depends on how many twists and turns there are. It's not that hard," she replied.

"You seriously think you can find your way out of there without anything but your sense of touch?" he asked with evident disbelief.

"What? You can't?" she replied. "Or are you so used to being able to use your super sniffer that you've never even tried?"

His ears flicked back, and he glared at her challenge. Several of the other guards must have caught their conversation because the next thing she knew, they were all circling around again.

"Five laps says she has a faster time," she caught one of the guards sign to the person next to them.

"Deal," they replied.

Avery saw this as well as he turned his glare on them. "Alright, Councilor. If you think you can do this, I'll bet you a lap for every minute faster through the maze you are than I am and vice-versa."

"That depends. Just how well do you have *this* maze memorized?" she asked.

"Change it up!" he ordered, and the other guards ran to reconfigure the maze.

She stood and grinned at him. "Deal. Shall I go first or you?"

"I'll let you choose," he said.

"Fine, I'll go first. That way, I can sit back and watch you lose," she replied.

Avery rolled his eyes at her, and Marsee snorted. Tamarin, who walked over with Hope at that point, said something to him, and he just glared at the other guard. She turned to Marsee to find out what was said.

"Tamarin just bet him five hundred credits that you'd win," Marsee replied.

Once the maze was reconfigured, everyone returned back to the starting area and he led her inside and shut the door. After the round of whistles, the lights went out. It was even darker in the maze and far darker than she'd ever experienced, which she thought was seriously cool, but she didn't have time to waste.

Sticking her right hand out, she found the wall and started walking forward. Keeping her hand on the wall, she followed it until eventually she found her way out, and the lights flicked on. She guessed it had been about ten minutes. It had been a fairly big maze, as everything on these planets was big, but there hadn't been a lot of twists and turns and certainly nothing as long or as complicated as the corn mazes back home, and no unexpected tricks, outside of a few low platforms she'd had to maneuver around.

"Nine minutes and thirty-two seconds," Tamarin called out.

She walked over to where Marsee was and flopped down on the sand to wait.

Avery took his position. The whistles were called out again, and the lights went off. In the dark, she could now make out the faint light of the clock on the wall of the maze, counting the time. It was like the switch in the Agency that had controlled the covering on the hole of muck. When it neared the ten-minute mark, she started grinning.

At ten minutes, Tamarin whistled, and she heard a growl coming from within the maze that sounded decidedly like one of the swears Ammond had taught her on the trip here. The others around her chuckled, confirming her suspicions.

Every minute after, Tamarin whistled.

Twenty-seven and a half minutes later, give or take a few seconds, Avery finally made his way out of the maze, and the lights flicked on. There was a serious amount of teasing as Avery started his laps, as did the guard who had bet against her. She counted each one out as they ran by. To her surprise, Avery pushed himself with the laps and was panting hard by the time he finished. He did another cool-down lap and stopped for a drink before walking back over to where they were.

"So how did you do it?" he asked.

"You're smart. I'm sure you'll figure it out. Eventually." She stood up from where she had been sitting in the sand, brushed herself off, and turned to Marsee. "I'm tired from all this running around, partner of mine. Shall we head back to the room?"

Marsee's tail spiraled, although she was trying hard to keep a straight face at Avery's evident frustration.

"Seriously. How did you do it?" he asked again.

"I have magic fingers," she signed and wiggled them. "And they know how to find their way around corners in the dark. Right, Marsee?"

Marsee did the closest thing to a blush that the Sabers did and then grinned wickedly as she figured out what she meant. "That you do. Then again, my fingers seemed to be able to find their way around, too."

"Do we have another challenger?" Tamarin asked. "Do you think you can beat Avery's time?"

"Oh sure," Marsee replied. "I could probably beat Little Flower's time, too, since I can walk faster than she can."

"What do you think, Avery, up for a few more laps?" Tamarin teased.

Avery glared at her. "Five laps says you don't beat Little Flower's time," he replied.

"Everyone, we have another challenger!" Tamarin called out and signed.

There were whoops all around.

"I'll be right back," Marsee said and trotted up the ramp, returning with her hearing aid case and tablet. "I haven't figured out how to turn off the echolocation yet. I tried while you were in the maze, and I don't want to cheat even by accident."

Avery nodded at her with approval.

Marsee stuck the hearing aids in and handed her the case before fiddling with the settings on her tablet and handing that to her as well.

One of the guards walked up behind Marsee and roared, which she didn't even notice, proving her ability to hear was completely blocked. She walked over to the entrance. Several whistles later, the lights went out again, and a few minutes later, they flicked back on. "Three minutes and fourteen seconds!" Tamarin crowed.

Avery groaned and started running.

"Well done," Little Flower signed.

Marsee grinned back at her and then wrapped her tail around her as they made their way back across the sands to where they'd left their stuff. By the time Little Flower had wobbled her way back into her flippers and taken Hope back from Tamarin, Marsee had donned her carry harness and cape, and Avery had joined them again.

"How?" Avery asked when he arrived, still breathing hard.

Marsee just grinned at him and swam out.

"There is no way she did it that quickly," he signed.

Little Flower gasped dramatically. "Are you seriously questioning the integrity of an *Honor Guard*?"

Avery growled and flicked his ears back while Tamarin doubled over with laughter, tail spiraling, as they followed out after.

CHAPTER 47

Marsee: Denial

Returning to the suite, Avery deemed it clear of monsters and huffed his way past them to take his post at the door. The moment the door was shut, they both burst out laughing.

"I'll probably pay for that tomorrow, but that was so worth it," Marsee signed. "Thanks for sharing that little tip with me."

"Of course. Besides, they needed to learn not to underestimate us."

"I think you got that point across quite clearly in the shooting range. How did you do that?"

"Lots and lots of practice," her sister replied. "Speaking of the range, what was that look all about?"

"The whole conversation. It's just... The more I learn about your world, the more I learn about my own, and I don't like it. It scares me. Do you really think there are others out there, like Rip, capable of doing what he did to me?"

"Capable? Yes. We're all capable of that if pushed too far. Only some need very little in the way of incentives. We may never know what made Rip the way he was. Maybe his father hurt him as a child. Damon told us why he did what he did. I still haven't decided if I believe him or if he's trying to wiggle his way out of the consequences of his actions, but tell me you didn't enjoy every second of tearing Rip to shreds."

Marsee blanched, feeling sick to her stomach. "You know I did, and I'm horrified by it."

"Do you think he should have lived?" Little Flower asked.

"Moons' no," she replied.

"Do you think he had any chance of turning out to be a decent person if given that chance?"

"Not at all. He was rotten to the core, but that doesn't change what I felt when I killed him."

"Of course it does. He hurt you, hurt people you cared about, and hurt hundreds of others over the course of his lifetime. There's nothing wrong in feeling joy and relief that the person who hurt you can never hurt you again or wanting him to feel some of the pain he caused you. But I know you. You wouldn't walk outside and start attacking someone at random just so you could feel that way again. Rip did, again and again. He probably got off on other people's screams," she said as she started taking Hope's wetsuit off to get her ready for a nap.

"Got off?" Marsee asked.

"Sexually aroused," she replied.

Marsee's stomach flipped over as her memories from her captivity washed over her in a sickening wave. Her skin felt hot, and she started breathing hard to control the urge to throw up. *No. He didn't touch me there. She must be wrong.*

You have such an intoxicating voice. I could listen to you for hours.

"Marsee? Are you alright?" her sister signed.

Little Flower...her heat. Oh, gods! I wasn't reacting to her. He must have... No...no! He didn't touch me there. Mama said he would have to touch me there.

Her stomach flipped again as she realized she'd been unconscious when he took her claws. *If I slept through that...* There was so much she couldn't remember. *But I stopped when Little Flower's heat ended...unless Mama...*

"No," she whispered, shaking her head, then bolted to the waste room and threw up.

Her sister followed her in and hugged her tightly as she continued to gag and throw up. "Shhh. It's okay. He can never hurt you again. I'm sorry I even mentioned that as a possibility. That was stupid and inconsiderate of me."

She sat back on her haunches and wiped at her mouth. "No, I think I needed to know in case that came up at the trial. I... I think you're right. Oh gods..." She looked down as her paws started shaking.

Little Flower hugged her tightly. "Whatever that monster did to you. He's dead and can never hurt you again."

She leaned against her sister as her entire body started shaking. "Water Sprites have a very hard time speaking our languages because they mostly only ever use speech for warning calls until they mature, and then it's a mating call. Many people never learn to speak because it feels obscene to them. Some... Some of the things he said to me make so much more sense now and..."

She blanched and swallowed hard as her stomach flipped again, but it did no good. She threw up again, although little came up this time. She groaned, panting hard, barely able to catch her breath and holding her stomach. "I really don't feel so good," she said as the world darkened around her.

CHAPTER 48

Little Flower: Ripped and Rehydrated

Little Flower watched as her sister slumped to the ground. "Marsee?" She shook her sister hard, but Marsee didn't open her eyes or groan, although she could see that her sister was still breathing. "Marsee, wake up!"

Nothing.

Swearing to herself, she realized her scanner was on the other side of the room, and it would take far too long for her to hobble over there and back. "HELP!" she screamed in Saber. It was one of the few words she knew in all the languages.

Both guards came crashing through her door at a full run.

"Something's wrong with Marsee. She won't wake up!"

Tamarin started to reach for her scanner, but Avery scooped Marsee up, threw her over his shoulder, and bolted towards the door, grabbing her mask off the table on the way out.

She grabbed Hope and their masks and jogged after not even bothering with her flippers. Clearly not fast enough for the other guard, she squeaked in surprise as Tamarin scooped her up and ran after them. Tamarin avoided the lift and slammed her way through a stairway that she didn't even know was there, then leapt over the railing and down several floors. She screamed in surprise with the first leap but recovered quickly and had her and Hope's masks on before they made it to the bottom. Tamarin dove through the outer shield without stopping, grabbed a drone, and took off, somehow managing to pilot the thing while still holding onto her.

Avery was already halfway across the park before they even started.

Sprites flashed with what she assumed was concern as they turned and watched them pass.

A Water Sprite Guard cut Avery off from the direction of the Council Building, grabbed Marsee from him without stopping, and took off faster than Avery's drone could go. It was the first time she'd seen how fast the Sprites could really move, and it made Marsee's capture of Rip all that more astounding. She just prayed that the guard could be trusted but assumed Avery wouldn't have handed Marsee over to anyone he didn't trust.

A minute later, they caught up and swam in through the Trauma Center doors.

The healer at the front stopped them. "Please wait here while they assess the situation."

She growled in frustration but swam over and climbed into an empty seat.

A few minutes later, her father showed up and saw them. "What happened?"

The room was empty save for them and the healer, so she explained. "Marsee and I were talking about what happened to her, and I made a comment that hit a little too close to home. She got sick and started throwing up and then passed out."

"What did you say that made her sick?" he asked, frowning with concern.

"That I thought Rip got off on people's screams, and that's why I thought he went after so many people, or one of the reasons anyway."

"Got off?" he asked for clarification, although she could tell by his hardened expression that he had a pretty good idea of what she was implying.

"Sexually aroused," she replied. "She said some of his comments made a lot more sense in that context. She didn't say what he said though, just threw up again, then said she didn't feel good and passed out."

He looked furious, and the Water Sprite, who had clearly seen what she'd signed, looked positively sick.

"If he wasn't already dead, I'd kill him," her father replied, looking nearly feral with rage. It was something she'd never seen on his expression before but that she fully understood. She felt much the same. But a moment later, he sighed, plastered his mask back on, and reached for Hope. Hope was starting to get cranky from not having had her nap yet. When tickling failed to distract her, he tried snuggling with her, swinging back and forth in the netting. That worked, and she settled and was soon asleep.

A few minutes later, her mother swam out. "She's fine. She passed out from exhaustion and dehydration, nothing more serious. She pushed herself too hard. We're going to give her some fluids, and then she can go back to the suite to rest."

They followed her mother down the hall and into a room where Marsee was floating in a reclined position that looked like she was sitting on a bed, but she couldn't see it. *Must be another one of those static shields that are everywhere.*

Avery floated outside, along with the Water Sprite guard, but Tamarin swapped positions with a nod, and the other guard swam off.

A healer swam in right after them with a bag of fluids that they hooked up to Marsee. *Another universal constant?* she wondered. For all the tech they had, some things were nearly identical. The only difference here was the bag hung from a small drone that hovered above Marsee instead of a hook.

Marsee opened her eyes at the Healer's touch and saw them. "Hey, Papa. I hope I didn't interrupt anything important?"

"Nah. Honestly, as long as you're okay, I'm glad to have an excuse to get away. Your uncle was droning on about some obscure article and section in the Charter. It's enough to make me daydream about requisition meetings."

Marsee grinned, and her tail curled. "You poor thing."

"Indeed." He took a deep breath, and the humor left his face. "Marsee, Little Flower told me what happened. Do you want to talk about it?"

Marsee frowned at the question. Her tail drooped, and she looked like she was going to be sick again. "Honestly, no, but if it will make a difference, I will."

"It would help," he replied. "Most of those who were taken refused to say what happened to them, and nearly two-thirds were female."

Little Flower saw the moment both her mother and the other healer in the room realized what her father was implying before slamming it hard behind their masks.

"Marsee, did he rape you?" her father asked softly.

Marsee was silent for a long time before answering. No one moved as Marsee looked down and rubbed hard at her injured paw. "I...I don't know. I don't really know how Water Sprites mate. He grabbed me by the scruff often, and he did drag me by my tail once, but I can't remember anything else."

Her father reached out and gently grabbed her hands in his to stop her. She looked up at him, looking lost and confused.

"I can't remember, Papa. There's so much I can't remember. It's like trying to grab onto a dream, and it hurts every time I try, almost like he's shocking me again. Why can't I remember?"

He pulled her in for a hug and began purring to comfort her as she cried out large, hiccuping sobs.

Eventually, she pulled away. "Is that why I reacted to Little Flower?"

"No," her mother said quickly and with some force before switching back to sign. "At least, I don't think so. We've been monitoring you closely to make sure you weren't going into heat, and you stopped reacting the moment Little Flower's scent changed."

Marsee sighed with relief, but Little Flower frowned at the look that passed between her parents. "How would Rip raping her cause her to go into heat?" she asked.

"It just does for our species," her mother replied. "Unless you have a hormone blocker."

"Your sister said he said something to you. What was it?" her father asked.

"I don't remember the exact words, but when he shocked me, he'd say things like 'I do so love the way you scream. It's such an intoxicating melody.' I thought he was just enjoying making me suffer. I didn't realize it might be something else until..." Marsee's arms dropped, and she looked away, swallowing hard again.

The Water Sprite Healer swam over and gently touched Marsee's arm to get her attention. "Marsee, did you ever hear any rhythmic thumping, like the fast beat of a drum? Or when you screamed, did it sound like it was echoing back to you but different?"

Marsee nodded. "I heard thumping every time he shocked me, and everything echoed in the cave."

"How did it sound, though?" The Healer pressed.

"Like really bad harmony, off just enough to be grating, out of key," Marsee replied, although she seemed confused by the question.

The Healer frowned and pulled up Marsee's records. The monitor changed to focus on a pattern of jagged lines that crisscrossed over Marsee's entire body but seemed focused on several areas: her scruff, her hands, and two spots on her body, one on either side. The Healer sighed and nodded, pointing to the spots on Marsee's side.

"Sound is very important for a successful mating, and the more harmonious, the better. The female will initiate the song, which the male will respond to. If the female finds the harmony pleasing, they will keep singing. This is very stimulating to both sexes and causes these scales here," she pointed to her sides. "To lift and vibrate. That's the rhythmic thumping you heard. Since joining the Consortium, we've all learned to control that reaction to music and sound when in public. It used to be seen as a sign of great respect for a musician, but now we don't dare because we don't want people to think the wrong thing. In any event, the male will hook their thumb in and under the scales and hold on. There's a gland at the base of the thumb where the male's sperm is released into the open water, which then finds its way through the open scales to fertilize the egg. As long as the female continues to sing, the male will vibrate and eventually release sperm, and the longer the male vibrates, the more likely an egg will be released to be fertilized. I have heard the sound of your screams. Your pitch, even then, is...perfect."

Marsee looked horrified.

"I assure you that none of my healers would be crass enough to respond. If they did, I would shock them myself and drag them before the Council for their lewd and inappropriate behavior."

The Senior Healer turned to Jer. "Councilor, based on what Marsee has said and the locations of the shocks on Marsee's sides, which would be in about the same location as the scales on our species, in combination with the ones on her scruff, which I'm told is part of your mating practice, I believe that Rip Current was sexually assaulting Marsee, even if she didn't realize it at the time. He wasn't partnered, which is unusual for those in our Council since it's typically a hereditary position, but he had picked a cousin as his Junior Councilor, so no one questioned it. More than likely, he wasn't able to find anyone to mate with him, even if they were interested in him because of his position. His lack of ability to harmonize would have been considered *very* unattractive and off-putting."

Jer frowned. "Would he have been able to force a mating or pregnancy with the other females of your species?"

"Yes," she replied. "If he didn't want children, he would only have to stop before he released sperm. Those Sprites we rescued were all collared, so they wouldn't have been able to fight back, and he could have forced them to sing with his shocks, much like he did with Marsee. The scales themselves are easily movable, and a shock to that area would have been far more painful than anywhere else on the body, just as it would be if you were shocked in your most sensitive locations. There are more nerve endings there than anywhere else on our bodies."

Her father flinched at that comment, and having been shocked by the electric fence on the farm before, she could just imagine what it would have felt like if she'd been shocked there instead of on the side of her arm that one time.

"Would you be able to tell if any of the females we rescued were also assaulted?" he asked.

She nodded. "I've already sent my findings. I wasn't able to determine if they were assaulted or not. There was no sign of sperm, but most have so much scarring that it was hard to tell where the shocks originated."

He frowned. "Review the scans again and inform me if there are any scars in or around that area. While Rip is dead, it will affect the level of reparations the Council is preparing to give to his victims."

"I will have that for you in an hour," she replied.

"Thank you."

She nodded and swam off.

"Papa, I wanted to talk to you about reparations, too," Marsee said.

"You said you didn't want anything. Do you want to change it now that you know what happened to you?" he asked.

"No. Not for me, for Rip's other victims. You know how everyone has been donating gifts and credit to me?"

He nodded.

"Have they donated anything to any of the other victims?"

"Not that I'm aware of, but we haven't released the full list of victims to the public yet, either," he replied.

"That's what I thought. My balance has exploded since I showed you that first day. I was talking to Ellie this morning about what to do with it all. It doesn't seem right that so many people gave to me and not to everyone else, and I want to share a lot of it with the other victims. One of the things Ellie suggested was a scholarship that would pay out every year rather than as one lump sum and, if invested in the Guild, would end up paying out more than I could donate. I'm still waiting on the specific information from Nardal, but Little Flower thought that if the

Council is planning on reparations, too, then maybe it could go into the same fund so it could pay out more or last longer."

"That's an excellent idea and very kind of you to think of everyone else. How much were you planning on giving?"

"I haven't decided yet. I have some other things we want to do, and I haven't had time to figure out what that will take. I don't really know what we'll need in the future since I've never had to pay for anything but my craft supplies and books, but I'm reasonably well off now anyway, even if I donated it all. I negotiated Ellie out of a Journeyman's Level Four rank and Master Level One rate this morning," she said with a pleased grin.

"How under the three moons did you manage to do that?" he asked and then looked at her with suspicion. "Did you threaten to demote her again?"

Marsee's tail curled.

"You demoted Ellie?" her mother asked.

"I did, but it was a joke," Marsee told her mother. "No, I reminded her that all of my books are top downloads, that she kept hidden from me for six months."

Her mother snorted. "I always knew that was going to bite her in the tail. I warned her about it."

"You did? She said you were in on it," Marsee replied.

"I agreed to let her tell you when she thought you were ready, but I didn't like it," her mother said. "But then everything happened with your sister, and I forgot about it."

Marsee nodded her understanding. "She also sent me the wrong contract for donating the profits from my translations of the Hue-man books, which didn't include usage rights for my artwork, so I demanded immediate compensation. You should have seen her splutter. It was worth all the credits the Sprites gave me and then some."

Their mother snorted, but their father looked like someone had struck him.

"You didn't know either, did you?" Marsee asked him.

"Do you understand the seriousness of that charge?" he asked. "You'd bankrupt New Hope, and Ellie could be executed for it due to the credit involved."

Marsee rolled her eyes at him. "Of course I do, and thankfully, that won't happen. The only thing I really wanted for compensation was for her to splutter the way I did when I found out about everything. I took care of the issue when I was Acting Senior and filed the updated contract along with my statement that Ellie had a verbal agreement. She didn't, but I wouldn't do that to her or New Hope. It was an honest mistake. That much was obvious from her reaction today, but that was one of the many things Rip brought up that I didn't want on my official statement until I had a chance to look into it. Both Uncle Marcus and Nardal were informed. I'm surprised Marcus didn't tell you. I asked for his input on the contract to make sure I was reading it correctly."

Her father snorted but didn't comment.

"So how much does it cost to maintain or claim a home anyway?" Marsee asked, changing the subject.

"There are a number of factors depending on the size, if it's inherited, or one you claim on your own, and how many people live there. I'll send you the information. Are you thinking of moving out of the tower?" her father asked.

"Not right now, but maybe someday, and I want to be prepared. Plus, if I agree to one of the other ideas Ellie proposed, I might want to have a home on each of the worlds rather than staying in off-world housing like we are now, so we can have some privacy. Then again, we could always live on the ship."

"Ship?" her mother asked.

"Ellie suggested that I use a bunch of the credit towards the Guild's research fund and have me run it. That would mean collaborating with the masters on all of the planets and picking which projects to work on or fund, and she said she'd throw in a ship like hers to allow us to travel whenever or wherever we needed to."

"Just how much did everyone give you?" her mother asked.

"The last I checked, it was over two hundred and fifty-three billion credits," Marsee replied.

"Bright moons!" her mother gasped. "I'm raising your rent."

Marsee snickered since her mother didn't charge them rent.

"No wonder Ellie is making so many suggestions about investing in the Guild and dangling a ship in front of you," her mother continued. "With those numbers, if you cashed out, you'd cripple the economy of all six species, not to mention destroy everything she's worked to build over the last hundred years."

"Yeah, I figured as much. That's why I wanted her suggestions on what to do with it all. There's no way I could spend all of that, and I could literally requisition the biggest public transport ship and not even touch it. I looked. Ellie says that's the annual budget of an entire district."

"Try five," her father said.

"Five?!" Marsee exclaimed.

"The top five major districts, or half the Ice Planet's budget and several times New Hope's budget for decades."

"Why didn't you come talk to me before?"

"Because talking about finances while you're in heat is rather rude." He tried hard to keep a straight face and failed.

Marsee's tail curled in response.

"Plus, we didn't really know what to do about it. We've been in discussion for days on how to handle what would happen if you did decide to turn around and buy your own moon or quit the Guild."

"What do you think I should do?" Marsee asked.

"Honestly, as long as you don't make any major purchases without clearing it with the Council, you can do whatever you want, but if you do keep it all, we're going to have to require you to attend resource allocation meetings and contribute as if you were five major districts."

"Ugh," she replied. "I'd rather stick my paw up a chenzie's butt again. Those meetings are not fun."

He chuckled. "No, they're not, but if you do agree to what Ellie suggested, you would be helping a lot of people. Not just the other victims but everyone else who would benefit from the research you fund. Financially, they have the potential to be very lucrative for you, assuming you pick the right projects. Most are a complete flop, but we learn a lot from those failures."

She nodded. "I'm still waiting on the proposals. Were they unanimous with the Seniors?"

"They were. Some are better than others. Once you've had a chance to read through them, let me know, and we can sit down and discuss the pros and cons of each of them so you're making an informed decision, and I can help you figure out how much should go into each depending on what you decide. It would be highly appreciated if you made a decision before the meeting. I know that doesn't give you a lot of time to decide, but what you choose will affect our budget for the next year at least. We've had to put a lot of projects on hold pending your decision, and it will affect how much we can allocate to the victims fund as well."

Marsee wiggled her claws at her father. "I wonder what Rip would say if he knew just how much power I have in my little paws now, and it's *all* thanks to him."

He nearly choked, laughing so hard. "I'm sure he'd probably explode with rage to know how badly his plans failed."

Marsee smiled wickedly. "Good. That almost makes up for it."

The monitor dinged, and Little Flower looked up to see that it was indicating the fluids were complete.

To her surprise, her mother turned to her and waved her over. "We have one more bag to give her. Tell me what you would do first," her mother ordered.

"Shut off the alarm," she replied, with a bit of snark.

Her mother nodded, not even catching that she'd been joking. She made her talk through each step and then complete the task, supervising each step of the process. She'd only done this once on a simulator that morning. Her mother smiled at her again when she was done, and

Marsee was still very much alive. "Very good. Now, let's go over her original scans so you can check for this in the future. I'm assuming you didn't take the time to scan her."

"No, as soon as she passed out, I yelled for Avery. She'd been heaving so hard I was afraid she'd torn something, and I didn't want to waste any time trying to figure that out on my own."

"That was the correct decision. Every second would have mattered if she'd ruptured something again. Now, it would appear her ability to know when she's thirsty hasn't fully recovered yet, so you're going to have to watch out for that and make sure she drinks enough and doesn't overdo it."

Her mother pulled up the scans and showed her how to tell if Marsee was dehydrated or overexerted herself. When the second bag of fluids was completed, her mother had her decide if Marsee needed another bag or if she had recovered enough to be released.

"She's still a little low, but not enough to warrant another bag. That would be too much," she decided.

"Correct. Now, go ahead and disconnect her. Tell me every step before you do it," her mother ordered. When Marsee was unhooked and again still alive, her mother grinned. "I'll be sure to tell Ammond that you didn't kill your sister. I'm sure that will make him very happy, or at least slightly less grumpy. Take her home and get some rest."

"Yes, Mama," she replied with a matching grin.

Without their own drones, they took their time and swam across the park, checking out the play area, even though Hope wasn't in the mood to play, and decided to have food delivered instead of heading back out to the market for the evening meal.

The moment they made it back to their suite, Marsee climbed into bed, curled up around Hope, and they were both asleep in seconds. She ordered their meal for delivery later that evening, grabbed another piece of the special paper Marsee had given her, and began drawing the scene. She was almost finished when their meal arrived.

Marsee woke with the knock but didn't move since Hope was still sleeping in her arms and using her tail for a pillow. Little Flower answered the door, took the delivery, and then invited the two guards in to join them. After they'd taken theirs, she made up a plate for Marsee and one for herself and brought them over to the bed.

"Are you ever going to tell us how you got through the maze so quickly?" Avery asked.

"Nah, I'm sure you'll be able to figure it out," she replied.

He glared at her and Tamarin laughed, which caused him to growl at Tamarin. "I didn't see you in the maze. You think you could do better?"

"I could certainly beat *your* pathetic time," she stated calmly.

"Five laps for every minute. After our shift," he glared.

"Deal," she replied without hesitation.

Avery glared at Tamarin, but deal made, he dropped the subject. "You both did very well today considering your injuries and I'm pleased you both pushed yourself, even if Marsee did push too hard. I'll increase the water breaks and recovery time, but please let us know if you're feeling sick or dizzy at all."

They agreed, but there was another knock at the door. Avery stood to open it and then let Aris and Thatcher in.

"You're early," he said.

"Kendra sent us over. She wants to see you both in her office."

He nodded and turned back to them. "Thank you for the evening meal. I'll see you in the morning. Have a good night."

"Night," they replied.

Avery turned to walk out, but she called out his name. He glanced back.

"Have fun doing your laps tonight," Little Flower signed with the sweetest smile she could fake.

The three other guards howled with laughter as Avery, normally very calm, stormed out with his tail lashing behind him. Tamarin grinned at them and followed after, her own tail curled tightly.

CHAPTER 49

Jer: Reparations

Jer watched his children swim away, followed by the guards, doing everything he could to remain calm. There was nothing he could do to change what had happened to either of his children, and no way to make it right. When they were out of sight, he turned to face Myra.

Her expression was one of matching rage, but she quickly pulled her emotions back under control and faced him. "Jer, there's something else you need to know, but you can't tell anyone."

"What else did that monster do to her?"

"Not her, Ellie," Myra replied. "Her implant was removed. She doesn't want anyone else to know, not even the rest of the Council. It's her third heat, and it's too late to stop it. I'll be flying back with her, but she's hoping to make it through the trial portion of the meeting."

His emotions spiraled as implication after implication hit him, and it settled on horror for Ellie. "Gods. Why didn't she return home for a new one?"

Myra glared at him. "I think you know why. When were you going to tell me that Marsee tried to kill herself?"

He sighed. "I promised not to. It was the only way I could get her to promise to give us the time you needed to find a cure. I considered it medical confidentiality."

Myra glared at him for a moment longer and then sighed. "Well, it worked. So, I guess I can forgive you. Anyway, Ellie said she was willing to take the risk for a chance at a cub. She's progressing normally, so I'm slightly optimistic that she'll produce a viable embryo, but her second litter was all stillborn, and with all of her additional scarring, she's going to have a hard time bringing even one to term."

"I know. She asked me to advocate for her, but I refused to take the case as I agreed with your decision."

Myra's ears flicked back in surprise. "I didn't know she went to you, too."

He nodded. "I know you well enough to know you would have done anything for her if you thought there was a chance. I think it's an incredible risk she's taking, but I understand her desire, and I know if anyone can bring her through this, it's you. Is she recovered enough to travel back?"

She shrugged. "I honestly don't know. She should be. Most of her injuries were to bones and soft tissue damage, which is mostly healed. Her hands are still recovering, and there's a good chance her left paw will need surgery again, but her chances of survival are better there. Hyacinth is good, but she doesn't have any experience with this. If she doesn't implant, she'll need a massive transfusion, and they're out of her blood type here. It's rare, and they used it all to save her life before. What we brought isn't nearly enough, not for the amount of blood loss likely if she miscarries, and synth blood just doesn't work in this situation. Nerissa is already reaching out to registered donors."

He nodded his understanding. "In light of what happened to Marsee, do you think it was intentional or a consequence of her beating?"

"I have my suspicions," Myra said, "and before you ask, we've found no indications that he used the implant on Marsee. What he was going to do with it is anyone's guess."

He frowned at that thought. "Marsee's heat? You were lying about the cause, weren't you?"

She sighed. "Her mating with Little Flower brought them both joy and healing, and I want to keep it that way."

"But he did rape her?"

She glanced at the scans still displaying on the monitor and let out another heavy sigh before turning the monitor off and swimming out without answering.

He watched her leave and then turned back to the blank monitor and memory of Marsee's scars. He swallowed hard as a thought occurred to him, and he pulled up Marsee's statement.

"He was angry with the entire Senior Council and Ellie, but he hated you most especially," Marsee said. "He was angry because he thought you should have been killed at the Trial or, at the very least, punished. He didn't think you had a right to be on the Senior Council. He believed everything we had done was just an act to gain power. He called it our little coup."

He stopped the recording and had to force his claws from digging into the tablet as he realized what Rip had really been up to. It wasn't just to force him to step down or because Rip was a psychopath who got off on Marsee's screams. Rip had targeted the families of everyone on the Senior Council as punishment for their crimes against Little Flower, but Marsee said he'd been mostly mad at him. Rip had raped Marsee to make him pay for being an accessory in Little Flower's rape. He had followed through on the original precedent.

"It's all my fault," he whispered.

It took him several minutes to force his emotions behind his mask to where he felt safe enough to return to his meeting with the Seniors, even though he had no desire to return to it and the decisions that needed to be made. They had finished their investigation into the Council and Guard that morning and were now trying to decide what to do about what they'd learned, and they were not in any sort of agreement.

Even still, it was all he could do to remain calm on his swim back to the Council Building. By the time he arrived at the Senior's conference room, his control had slipped enough that his tail was lashing, and the people who saw him turned and swam quickly away, although he barely noticed as his thoughts were in a downward spiral of a raging war between his guilt and fury.

Marcus took one look at him and frowned. "How bad was she hurt this time?"

Clear Seas flashed his worry.

He couldn't find the words answer. To speak would be to admit what had really happened to his daughter. He'd been able to deny it before, blame it on her other injuries and Little Flower's heat, or even his attempt to save her, but he couldn't anymore. His jaw shook with the effort to keep from crying.

Clear Seas skin darkened. "Jer, is she...? Is she dead?"

"No," he managed to growl out. "She was exhausted and dehydrated and...and..." His voice broke, and he couldn't say it.

The need to act grew with every breath, but there was no one for him to take it out on and nothing he could do to fix it. He swam over to the dry section of the room where they had begun to review and organize the cases on the pile so he could pace. He needed to do something, anything, but pacing didn't help.

"Jer, what happened?" his brother demanded.

"It's all my fault," he muttered and pulled at his scruff, but didn't help, either.

"What is?"

He couldn't answer.

Marcus left his seat and blocked his path. "Jer, What happened?"

"He raped her." What little control he had vanished with those three words. He spun and hit the nearest wall, leaving a fairly substantial dent in the reinforced wall, then hit it again, not caring that his brother might decide he was out of control and kill him. He felt something snap in his hand, and pain radiated up it, but he didn't care. It was nothing compared to what she'd been through. "Rip raped her to punish me." He hit the wall again, focusing on the pain in his hand. He deserved this. He deserved more than this. He deserved to die, just as Rip believed. "All of this is because I wasn't punished for the crimes he believed I had committed." He hit the wall again and felt another pop.

Marcus grabbed his arm to stop him, but he yanked it away with a growl and hit the wall again. "Jer, stop!" Marcus ordered, then grabbed him by the scruff and spun him around. He didn't fight it this time. His training kicked in almost immediately, recognizing his brother's authority over him, draining him of his rage and leaving him only with his guilt and grief.

"It's all my fault," he whimpered again as Marcus stared at him.

Marcus sighed and pulled him in close. He thought for sure his brother was going to kill him, but instead, Marcus only hugged him. "Shh. It's alright, Little Brother. It's not your fault. She's alive, and he's not. Whatever that monster did to her, she was stronger. She survived, and he's dead. She got her revenge. She tore him to pieces and made him scream to his last breath."

"It should have been me." Tears broke free with a sob, and Marcus held him until he cried himself out. Eventually, he was able to bring himself back under control and turned to face the others. They were all watching with a combination of concern, sympathy, and their own rage. Against him or Rip, he didn't know.

Clear Seas was solid red. "Did Marsee try to hurt herself again?"

He took a deep breath as he shook his head, then took a seat, grabbing the back of his scruff with both hands as he explained what Little Flower, Marsee, and the Senior Healer had told him, along with Myra's implied statement, and his realization of what Marsee's statement had really meant.

The room was silent for a long time after he finished.

Clear Seas eventually brought his skin under control, and he was the first to speak. "Whatever guilt we might hold for the crimes against Little Flower and her people, she chose her reparations, and we have done our best to make amends for our mistakes. It was not his place to enact punishment, even if he disagreed with our decision. It was not his place to target our children and families because he didn't agree with us. There are legal ways to challenge us. He could have called for a vote of no confidence, but he didn't. He chose the coward's way, and he died far too quickly. I don't know how we're going to right this wrong, not just for her but for everyone else he harmed. Did she say anything about wanting additional reparations?"

He snorted. "Well, as you've already determined, she's a far better person than I am. She brought up the topic of reparations on her own, and I asked, expecting as much, but her first thought was to help everyone else. She had the idea of adding what we've been able to scrape together to a scholarship fund. She knows we've been discussing her credits and seems to be on board with our plan, although she's very much aware of how much power she holds over the Consortium right now. I don't think she intends to use it, though. Her only thought was delight in how much Rip's plan had backfired on him. She agreed to give me a call once she's had a chance to rest and look everything over."

Clear Seas flashed his astonishment, although the feeling appeared to be shared by the others. "She didn't ask for anything?"

Jer shook his head. "What could we give her anyway? She already has enough credit to buy a moon, and Rip is dead. I'm just glad she doesn't have to deal with the possibility of being pregnant, too. As much as she wants cubs, I wouldn't wish what Little Flower has been through on anyone. The pregnancy was hard enough, but the last few months have been impossible. Both Myra and the guards watching her have stated that Little Flower has expressed conflicting emotions when it comes to her daughter. She loves Hope, but that doesn't stop the memories or negate the trauma she endured from her rape and from the complications of choosing to go forward with the pregnancy."

"We all knew raising Hope would be a challenge," Wind Rider replied. "Even without her trauma, being a parent is impossible at times. As for Marsee, as much as we hoped it wasn't the case, the evidence was there all along. I don't think it will do Marsee any good to know the truth if she doesn't remember it happening. She's had to suffer enough."

There were nods of agreement all around.

"I suggest that regardless of what the Senior Healer finds, we assume everyone was raped and compensate accordingly," Sammianna added.

"What would even make up for it, though?" Jer replied. "He's already dead."

"I suppose we could offer to let them have at everyone else we execute for being involved in his coup," Sammianna suggested.

"I have family in that pile," Clear Seas said. "It's going to be hard enough to kill them, much less watch someone torture them, too."

"Well, we're going to have to," Wind Rider replied. "Based on the evidence we've found. It's their right."

Apakna sighed. "I'll be honest. I'm having a hard time dealing with the fact that we'll have to kill so many of the people we've worked with over the years. We only have Rip's take on it and what we've been able to confirm. We don't know how many others, like Snapper Fish, were forced into doing Rip's bidding in order to save their families. Shouldn't this go before the entire Council for trial?"

"And if everyone comes forward and says they were being blackmailed, what then?" Marcus asked. "We're not just talking about random crimes. Nearly half of the people on that pile were planning a coup. Blackmail or not, they can't remain in power or be allowed to try again. They were all for taking us out by whatever means possible. What would they do if they were allowed to live? Would there even be a Consortium left? The anger towards my species was far greater than I had any indication of. Who knows how many others feel the same way? If we let them go, how many people will follow suit because the laws no longer apply, or only apply to the people, not to those in power?"

"Are you telling me you'll be able to go in there and kill your friends? People you care about?" Apakna asked Marcus. "I saw you run out of here crying the other day."

Marcus sighed. "I took an oath. It doesn't matter what my feelings are towards anyone. I will do what I have to. Our very way of life is at risk. We've all been suffering in the polls since the Trial. Jer's right. This was as much a reaction to your leniency and our promotion as anything.

If we let our friends and family go a second time, there will be riots in the streets, and not one of us will walk out of that chamber alive."

Clear Seas nodded. "Marcus is right. You've seen what my people did for Marsee. Just imagine what they'll do if they don't feel justice is served to her or the others."

"I know that, but it still bothers me," Apakna replied. "I don't have children, but what would you have done if Rip had kidnapped Stormy?"

"I would have shocked him until he told me where he was and then killed him," Clear Seas replied.

"But you have the right to do that," Apakna stated. "You're a Senior Councilor. For many, Rip could have killed them for disobeying a direct order. If he ordered the Guard or Sea Patrol to arrest someone and they didn't, it could be considered treason."

"Well, what ideas do you have?" Clear Sea's spat back.

Apakna sighed. "I don't know," she said eventually. "But we have to decide soon. We're running out of time."

"We could push the trial back a week or three," Jer suggested.

"No. The Council is already here, and it'll just give them more time to plan something else," Marcus replied. "Right now, the evidence we've released states that Rip was mostly working alone, and most of those people are already dead. If they have a hint we know others are involved, we won't stand a chance, especially with so many in the Guard and Patrol involved."

"You bring up a good point. How are we going to arrest everyone?" Sammianna asked. "Who are we supposed to trust with the Guard compromised? I certainly don't trust Stinger, even if we haven't found anything on him."

"We're going to have to trust someone," Marcus said. "If the Guard does try something, hopefully, the people will retaliate, too. At the very least, we should arrest all of the guards on our list before the meeting."

"Wouldn't that just give it away that something is up and give people time to run?" Apakna asked.

Jer leaned back in his seat as the conversation devolved back over the same points they'd been arguing for hours. He listened but said nothing further. He felt disconnected from the whole conversation. They were in this mess because of how much people hated him. Rip had used that anger, inflamed it, and nearly destroyed his family and people. His mind drifted over everything that had happened this past year, and he wondered if there was anything he could do to protect them."

"I have an idea," he said quietly, stopping his brother mid-sentence. They all turned to look at him, and he explained.

"It might work," Wind Rider replied.

"Or it might give someone we haven't found an opportunity to take control," Apakna replied.

The conversation devolved into another heated argument. Hours later, they were still arguing when Marsee texted to see if he was available. He had never been happier to have a valid reason to leave a meeting. "I think it's time we take a break. Marsee's ready to talk."

"I think I'll join you," his brother said, and they swam out. Marcus, however, pulled him into his office first. "You've been very quiet this afternoon. Are you alright? How's your hand?"

He shrugged and looked down at his swollen paw. "It's probably broken, but the pain helps. It's easier to focus on that than what happened to Marsee."

His brother frowned. "Is it still talking to you?"

He shook his head. "No. I haven't heard it since that day in my office. In fact, it's been far calmer than normal. Not even any pacing. I'm sorry about scaring you earlier. That was all me, not my instinct. I had to let the rage out before it consumed me. I'll pay for the wall."

"The wall doesn't matter," Marcus replied, "and your rage is understandable. Do you think you'll make it through the meeting, or should we go see Kendra?"

They had spoken at length about everything Marcus had learned about the Transition from Kendra and what he had learned from Marsee. Part of him wanted desperately to transition, but he was scared, too. He'd seen the empty hollowness in his daughter's eyes, and he didn't know who he would be without his instinct. The other part, the feral part, reared up for the first time and refused to even let him say it. "After the meeting," he finally managed to say. "If it's still an issue. The safety of my people may depend on how quickly I can react. I don't have the time to train to fight like Kendra, and it could take weeks for my reflexes to return."

His brother frowned again. "You could end up hurting them just as much."

He shook his head. "I don't think so. From my instinct's perspective, they're my children. I love them all, even Damon. If anything is going to put me over the edge, it'll be killing him. Now, either you need to kill me and get it over with, or we need to go see Marsee and figure out how to put the Consortium back together again."

His brother raised a brow. "You know, cub, I'm not sure which would be the easier option. Sadly, I think killing you would only make things worse, as I'd have to clean up the mess *and* still have to figure out how to put the Consortium back together again."

"I love you, too, Big Brother," Jer replied and decided to shift the focus off of him. "So...when were you going to tell me about the contract mixup between Marsee and Ellie?"

Marcus snorted. "Honestly, I completely forgot about it with everything else that happened. Marsee said Ellie had a verbal agreement and that she wasn't pressing charges. Paperwork errors happen fairly regularly, and as far as Lowell was able to determine, Rip was the only one who accessed the contract, so I didn't see any reason to investigate it further."

"According to Marsee today, Ellie didn't have that approval."

Marcus blinked at him with a look that he was sure had been on his own face earlier. "Was that intentional on Ellie's part then?"

"I don't think so. Marsee seemed to be quite amused by Ellie's reaction, although she did manage to negotiate a promotion and rate increase out of Ellie for that and for hiding that her translations were on the top downloads. I'm not sure if that counts as bribery or reparations. Apparently, Myra knew about it, too."

Marcus considered. "Reparations. Marsee had already updated the contract and provided her statement that Ellie had authorization before we found the file Rip had on Ellie. In her place, I probably would have made Ellie squirm a bit, too, just to see her reaction. As she'd given up compensation rights, there was no crime committed in hiding that information from her, even if highly unethical, and her rank and rate have little meaning against her current guild balance and local rank as Translator. I'll need to talk to Ellie to confirm, but if Marsee was willing to give up reparations to protect Ellie and New Hope before all the donations, it would bode well for our meeting with her. We might be able to press for better terms."

"Agreed," Jer replied, although he was very thankful that he didn't have to add Ellie's folder to the pile.

CHAPTER 50

Avery: Dark Passages

Avery dropped the facade of annoyance the moment he was out of Little Flower's room. While he was annoyed with them for not sharing valuable intel, he was far more worried about why Kendra would call him in before his shift was over. She hadn't said anything to him since that first day, which had surprised everyone, including him. Several people had already cashed out from the events of that day, although the betting pool hadn't closed. That she wanted to see Tamarin, too, either meant he was being demoted, or worse, something else entirely was going on. Something big enough to pull him away from protecting Marsee.

Tamarin picked up on his worry and said nothing as they took off across the park at a fast clip, but not fast enough to worry anyone who saw them.

When they arrived, Kendra's door was open. She motioned them in and told them to shut the door. She leaned back in her chair and crossed her arms but didn't say anything for several moments. He couldn't sniff anything off her but the generalized worry he smelled on everyone these days. "I just received a message from Jeran that he has decided to install a permanent guard in New Hope in opposition to his council's continued desire not to have one."

He sighed with relief. "Finally. I was hoping he would."

Her eyes narrowed slightly. "Why?"

"Because they desperately need one," he replied. "That much is obvious. Not just from themselves but from everyone else likely to target them. If there had been a guard present in New Hope, Little Flower wouldn't have been kidnapped. She's starting to trust us, but she doesn't trust the Guard as an institution, and from what she told me today, she has good reason not to. Her Guard was corrupt and not held accountable for their actions, and while her father might have been honorable, it's clear he didn't trust anyone, not if he spent as much time as he did training her to defend herself."

She nodded. "Quinn said much the same after his conversation with GrandFather. Fortunately, it would appear that your gambit has worked. Jer has accepted your squad's offer to transfer and has requested two additional squads on permanent loan."

That shocked him. The transfer would put him and his squad as first squad. "He picked me for his Senior?"

She snorted. "You? No. Of course not. What makes you think you remotely deserve that?"

"I don't," he replied. "That's why I'm so surprised he accepted our offer to transfer." He frowned, considering the implications, and glanced at Tamarin. "If that's not the case, am I being demoted or charged?"

"I couldn't even tell you that for myself. Following the council meeting, *your* orders are to remain here and guard Marsee for as long as she needs, although I expect she may still decide to stay until the end of her watch. The rest of your squad will remain with Quinn in New Hope. As far as the Senior position goes, I will continue to be Senior for both Saber and Little Earth until he decides who he can trust enough for that position."

He nodded, as that made far more sense, and he fully intended to stay until Marsee's watch was up, regardless of his orders. "Yes, ma'am."

She was quiet again for a moment, although her nose flared slightly. "I read your assessment of Marsee this morning," she said, changing the subject. "She did far better than I was expecting with her injuries, but I haven't seen an update on her trip to the Trauma Center. Did she hurt herself?"

"Thankfully, no. It was a combination of dehydration and a trauma response. She did have something to drink after her workout and seemed perfectly fine when we left the arena this afternoon, but I'll make sure she has more water breaks tomorrow. That sense must not be fully back yet."

"I scanned her after her assessment this morning," Tamarin added. "Outside of irritation from the gear and some slight swelling, she was fine. She didn't complain at all after the afternoon session, but I didn't sniff anything concerning. She'll be sore tomorrow, but mostly because of how hard she worked today."

Kendra nodded. "And the trauma response?"

"She realized part of what happened to her and threw up, although whether that was from overexerting herself or her trauma, I don't know," Avery replied. "She says she can't remember what happened to her but now knows she was sexually assaulted. They appear to be sticking with the lie that she was reacting to Little Flower and not in heat from being raped, but they have decided that the shocks to her side and scruff, along with her comments on what Rip said to her, are evidence enough for sexual assault if not rape."

Kendra frowned but nodded. "I suppose that's for the best."

He sniffed a wave of worry off of her and considered her previous comments. "You still think Surellis is going to test her?"

She sighed. "Half the Council has contacted me requesting that I test her as they don't have jurisdiction to call it themselves. They believe Marcus won't because she's family. They obviously don't know him as well as I do. I had orders to prepare for one after she survived her captivity, and those orders haven't been retracted. I expect he'll give her the full six months to recover, but he may be forced into testing her sooner or may test her just to see if we're telling the truth."

He winced. "Gods. After what she's been through…"

"I know." She sighed again, and he sniffed a mix of regret and loathing. "If she can survive what Rip did to her, she can survive the test, and she'll have a better chance than most, but it'll be up to you to get her ready."

He nodded. "If she keeps training as hard as she did today, she will be."

Her eyes narrowed again, this time with mischief. "If she keeps training as hard as she did today, she'll be mentoring you by next week. Or perhaps I should have Little Flower mentor you? Don't think I haven't heard about the maze or the shooting gallery."

He leaned back in his seat with a groan. "Why am I not surprised?"

Her eyes twinkled with amusement momentarily but then became far more serious. "Five laps each for the maze and the shooting gallery. It doubles for every day you fail to meet the standard set by Little Flower and Marsee."

"Yes, ma'am," he replied, expecting no less. It was no less than he intended for himself.

"Two hundred laps for leaving Marsee and Stormy alone in the canyon. Fifty laps for both of you for letting Marsee hurt you in the Trauma Center and another fifty for not scanning her after her training today to ensure she was unhurt. Our senses are good, but they can't tell us everything."

"Yes, ma'am," Tamarin said.

He groaned inwardly, as three hundred laps would take half the night, and he'd be exhausted and hurting for days, especially when added to the laps he'd already done today, but he nodded. "Yes, ma'am." He started to stand, assuming she was done, but she raised a paw. He sat back down.

"Those laps can wait until after the meeting. I need you both at your best. My hackles have been raised since the rest of the Council arrived. Half the Full Council is twanging hard. Something's up, but none of the other guards have been able to sniff out what."

She surprised him by activating his mask and motioning that they should do the same. They did, and she flooded the room. Once it was flooded, she swam over to the waste room and, once inside, motioned that they should follow.

He raised a brow but did as ordered, wondering if there was something she wanted to talk about off-camera as the waste room was off-limits for privacy. Once inside, she shut the door, ordered them to turn their cameras off, and swam up, hitting a spot on the ceiling. A door slid open. "I want to know everywhere these tunnels go," she signed. "There are spy holes. One is above my desk. Watch for sensors and traps. If anyone catches you, say nothing and tell them to talk to me. I want you to make sure you know at least a dozen ways to get Marsee and the Seniors out of the Council Building, unobserved, and off the planet that the other guards won't know or think about. When that's done, expand your focus to the rest of Council Platform."

"You're expecting something?"

"No. The General is."

He raised a brow and glanced at Tamarin before looking back at Kendra. "What are you talking about?"

"Her unusual focus on my desk this morning led to me finding this hidden door, and I've determined that the hearing aids can pick up far more than anyone else realizes yet. Our ability to sub-vocalize is compromised."

He raised the other brow, wondering how the two were related but knowing she would have already told him if she'd wanted them to know.

"No matter what happens to me, follow her lead and protect her at all costs," Kendra continued. "Whether she's the General or not, or whether there's a war coming or not, I'm fairly certain she's already accessing the Knowing. At this stage, it'll be sporadic and likely focused on those she cares about. I want to know immediately if she focuses on something or starts acting out of the ordinary."

"On my life," he promised.

"And mine," Tamarin added.

Kendra nodded and motioned with her to the door. They swam up, and the moment they were both inside, Kendra shut the door behind them, leaving them in pitch black.

"Good thing you have your super sniffer to help," Tamarin teased.

He growled but only halfheartedly as he was examining the floor with his senses to find the way to get back in. "Will you tell me the trick?"

"And spoil all of Little Flower's fun? No. If Marsee won't tell you, I certainly won't. Now, shall we split up?"

"No. It'll be better if we both know every location."

She grunted acknowledgment. "Here," she said a moment later, pointing up higher on the tunnel than he was expecting.

"Good work," he replied. "I'll focus low. You look up."

"Yes, sir," she replied. It wasn't long before she stopped him and pointed out another hidden door leading to the office above them.

"Why do I have a feeling I'm going to wish we were running laps before the night is over?" he asked her.

She chuckled. "Don't worry. *You'll* be doing both."

He growled at her teasing and kept swimming.

CHAPTER 51

Little Flower: Billion Credit Question

Marsee fell asleep almost immediately after the guards left, curled up around Hope. Smiling, Little Flower spent the next hour drawing the scene before returning to her prep for the council meeting. She didn't look up again until there was a groan from Marsee, followed by a muttered swear.

She found her sister rubbing at her nose and looking down at the bed. "Ugh, what a mess. How did you do that? You're wearing a poop sack."

It took everything Little Flower had to keep from laughing as Marsee carried her filthy daughter into the waste room.

"Gah, this is so much worse with my new sense of smell."

Marsee gave both of them a shower while she stripped the sheets and threw them in the sanitizer.

"At least the mattress appears to be waterproof," Little Flower replied and returned to her seat.

Marsee changed Hope into a new set of clothes and grabbed Hope something to eat before returning to the bed and sniffing it with an absolutely disgusted expression. "It may be waterproof, but I can still smell it." Marsee lifted the mattress and peered under it. "Stinky moon cheese," she muttered. "I was hoping I could change the covering."

"I thought you could turn off your sense of smell."

"It's not working," Marsee muttered. "You Hue-man's may smell good, but your poop stinks."

Laughing, she slid the drawing in Marsee's direction. "Well, maybe this will make up for it."

Marsee walked over and stared at it for a long time, not saying anything.

"Do you like it?" she finally asked.

"I...I love it so much more than any picture you've ever drawn before that I can't even begin to express it. We're just sleeping, but... It's like you've captured every last little bit of love and protectiveness I have for her."

"So what's bothering you?" Little Flower asked.

Marsee looked up at her, her expression more confused than anything. "I don't know if I can explain. My instinct saw Hope as ours. After Papa... When you were in your coma, after Papa tested me, I knew I wanted guardianship if you didn't make it. I left with Ellie, hoping to find a mentor, as the added credit would help me take care of her, and I was terrified that your council wouldn't allow the adoption after what happened with Nazari. I knew there was a chance they'd kill Mama, and there was no way I was letting Papa have custody. Walking away from the two of you was the hardest thing I've ever done, but I needed time away from Papa to calm my instinct. It was furious with him, and so was I. Papa came to retrieve me to help care for you when he had to go to Digger, and I told him I wanted guardianship. The moment I came off the watch list, he gave it to me, but the day you woke, he took it away, and I nearly lost control. My instinct's desire to take Hope back was so strong I spent well over an hour pacing on the balcony, trying to keep from going down to your room, but I think I knew if I entered your room in that state, I'd never leave. I was so close to losing control that I decided I needed to go for a run, but it was really late. So, on the spur of the moment, I asked Papa to go with me. I told myself it was because I wanted the added protection from the predators, but really, it was me I was worried about. I was terrified I would hurt you. I was so happy you were awake but also horribly sad at the same time, if that makes any sense. I ran until I couldn't run anymore, and thankfully, that was enough time to bring everything back under control. Kendra or one of her guards must have seen us go out because she followed us. I thought for sure she was going to kill me, and I wouldn't have fought it to protect you, but... but since that day, this..."

Marsee pointed to the drawing.

"This was all my instinct wanted, to curl around Hope and never leave her side. In the cave, this is what kept us alive. The only thing that mattered was stopping him from hurting you both. When I knew I was going to die in that cave, I gave myself over entirely to my instinct for one last chance at killing him. Then, in the canyon, it was thoughts of the two of you that allowed me to break through my instinct and defeat it."

Little Flower smiled at her sister, but Marsee raised a paw to stop her from speaking.

"I don't think I can explain the hollowness of my missing instinct. It's better now, but I felt so very alone, even though Ellie and the guards never left my side. But this...This is all I've ever wanted in my life." She motioned to the room. "A partnership, family, cubs. I had all the credit in the universe, and it didn't matter because I didn't have her, and I couldn't ask you to share. Mama was afraid you'd give up if I offered to be your partner. But you showed up and filled that hollowness with your love and trust. You gave me my life back, and I'll never be able to repay you for that."

"You don't have to. You've already paid it a million times over, and besides, another hour and you'd have found out you were going to make a full recovery." She deflected, feeling overwhelmed by Marsee's comments.

"Physically, maybe. It helped for sure. Don't get me wrong there, but mentally, you're the one who's picking up all the pieces and somehow making them stronger than they ever were before. You're keeping the night terrors at bay. You gave me purpose and a reason to live again, but I'm..."

Marsee turned away for several moments, staring down at her claws before turning back around and sitting down next to her so they were face to face. It took her three tries to even start what she wanted to say.

"I'm scared. Little Flower, before you arrived the other day, I was lost down a hole so deep I thought I'd never get out of it. I...I tried to take my own life. It took Ellie and two guards to stop me. I promised everyone I wouldn't try again if they didn't tell Mama, but I had every intention of trying again the moment I was left alone, right up until the moment you proposed. I'd already hurt Papa. I hurt Avery and Tamarin, too, when they tried to stop me, although they've never mentioned it. Yet you didn't hesitate for a second to trust me with your child, a child so small, I could kill her with a twitch in my sleep. I've come so close to hurting you in the past, yet you threw a ladder down into that deep hole and climbed down there with me, and held my broken pieces together until I had the strength to start climbing out, and never once feared I was going to hurt you. Everyone who knew about my psychosis saw me as a monster, although some did better than others at hiding it, but not you. Not once. Even though I nearly killed you."

She reached out and rubbed the side of Marsee's face. Marsee closed her eyes and purred as she leaned into it.

"I figured you might try to take your own life, and I was terrified I wouldn't make it in time. I recognized the same hopelessness in your messages that I felt at the Agency, and again after I woke from my coma, and again after you left for the Water World. The day after you left, I told Mama I wanted to die. If I could have crawled off the balcony, I would have. I couldn't do it anymore. I saw how hard caring for me was on everyone, especially on you, and I wanted you to be able to live your life free of the burden of caring for me. But, when you were kidnapped, it was like a piece of me was stolen, too. It just took me a while to figure out. I don't fear you because I love you. It was never you trying to hurt me. You've always been my protector. I can't care for Hope alone. I can barely care for myself. I'm a mess, too, but I feel safe around you, and I know you would never hurt us. You protect me from the night terrors, too."

"That's about all I'm good for at the moment," Marsee muttered. "I know you all think I overdid it today, but I promise you I am going to be so fierce and so strong that no one will *ever* dare harm our family again, and if that means running until I drop from exhaustion every day, then so be it."

She grinned at her sister. "I don't doubt for a second that you will be the fiercest Saber these five planets have ever known. You run until you drop. Do whatever you need to do until you feel safe and strong enough, and I'll be right there beside you and stand guard with my stunner while you heal. Because no one is ever going to hurt you or any of my family on my watch ever again. Whatever this universe throws at us, we'll fight it together."

Marsee grabbed her in a fierce hug, nearly too tight, but it wasn't nearly enough for what she needed. She hugged back just as tightly, shook to her very core at how close she'd come to losing her sister.

Marsee pulled back and looked down. While they'd been hugging, Hope had climbed down out of her chair and tugged on Marsee's fur with her sticky, food-covered paws to get her attention.

"Marsee, I done. Pway?"

Marsee reached down, scooped her up, and tossed her into the air, making Hope screech with laughter. "Let's get those sticky paws of yours cleaned up first. Can you say 'Papa'?" Most of it was in English, but 'Papa' was in Saber.

"Papa!" Hope growled out.

"Very good!" Marsee said. Her tail spiraled with joy as she walked over to the sink and started singing a song in Saber as she helped Hope wash her hands.

She'd never heard the Sabers sing or Marsee, and she smiled with appreciation at her sister's deep voice, sweet and pure, yet somehow uniquely feline, with growls and hisses mixed in.

When Marsee was done, she set Hope back down, pulled out a few toys to play with, and laid down on the floor with her.

"What was the song you were singing?" Little Flower asked. "It was beautiful."

"It's part of a really old cub's song. Let me see if I can translate it without losing too much in the process." Marsee thought for a moment and started singing in English.

> *Little kitten, your paws are stick'n everywhere you step.*
> *You're leaving a trail the fleebles will sniff,*
> *and they might just climb up your tail and dance on your neck.*
> *So before they tickle your ears and sit on your nose*
> *You'd better wash those whiskers and sticky ol' toes*
> *or they'll make a nest of your elbows and knees*
> *and you'll find yourself doing nothing for days but itching and sneeze.*

"That's hilarious!" she said, thoroughly impressed at how quickly her sister translated it and even more so that it even came close to rhyming. She wrote it down, already envisioning what she wanted to draw with it. "What's a fleeble?"

"I have no idea. Mama said it must be a crawly we had on our old planet."

"Well, I'm sure I can come up with something. I was trying to figure out what to have in the cub's book to go along with my drawings. That would be perfect. Do you have other little songs like that, or do you think you could come up with something for each of my drawings? Like a lullaby for the two of you sleeping?"

"I could try. Mama and Papa might remember more songs, but shouldn't we include some of yours, too? I can help translate them so they sound good in the other languages."

"That's a great idea!" she said and started jotting down ideas for songs and drawings she wanted to include.

"If it's going to be a songbook, we could work with the techs and make it so you could play the song in each of the languages," Marsee suggested.

"I love it!" Little Flower said. "Maybe we can convince Henry to sing them since everyone can hear his voice, although your voice would be perfect, too."

"Mine?!" Marsee's voice squeaked, and she buried her head under her tail with a groan. "Gods. Not you, too! Ellie was trying to get me to do that with Henry's songs. I don't mind translating them, but my voice is nowhere near as good as his."

"I think your voice is beautiful, and Henry might have difficulty with the other languages," Little Flower replied.

Marsee pinned her ears in a mock scowl before sighing. "I suppose. Well, either way, Ellie's going to drool over this. I, however, am going to go hide in my cave until you're done recording."

She laughed. "Well, if you're that concerned, we don't have to tell her right away. I might change my mind on what I want to do with these drawings anyway."

"That's fair. Speaking of Ellie, I suppose I should probably check to see if Nardal has sent me that information yet." She yawned, stretched with a full-body groan, and walked over to the bedside table where her tablet was. "They're here. I just forwarded them. I'd like you to read through them, too."

She opened the documents and frowned. They were written in Saber. Her grasp of their written language was improving, but it was by no means perfect. Still, it was mostly numbers, which she could figure out. She ran it through the translator, as well, to make sure she was seeing the same information. "Well, it's pretty clear which one they want you to take," she said after a while.

"Option C?" Marsee asked.

"Yup. They want you to invest in those programs rather than doing it on your own. It transfers a lot of that wealth back into the Guild and would mean a lot of work for you, but it would end up being very lucrative long term. The retrofit on the ship can't be cheap."

"What do you think about it?" Marsee asked.

She shrugged. "It still leaves a ridiculous amount of credit to live off of and do whatever else we want."

"Yeah. The only thing I'm not sure about is that it would all go to Ellie's Guild and not any of the others."

"Well, they all ultimately feed into her Guild anyway. If you wanted to invest in research for the Healer's Guild, for example, you could by investing in new tech, like equipment that works underwater."

"True, but I still want to talk to Papa about it. Do you have a number of victims yet?"

She switched over to the council system for that information. "Seventy-eight confirmed so far, with another thirty-five that they're still trying to determine if Rip had actually targeted or was just making plans. Several of those rescued are still sedated in the Trauma Center, so they haven't been able to take a statement. I expect it may be a long time before they figure out who else Rip targeted."

"Alright, I'll round up to two hundred to give plenty of room for anyone else they find," Marsee said and went back to fiddling with numbers. After a while, Marsee looked up. "How much do you think we'll need for your wedding ceremony? Do you know how much the Hallowed Eve party cost?"

She looked that information up, and they spent some time discussing everything involved, with Marsee taking notes. After she detailed everything she could think of that she might want in a wedding, Marsee went back to staring at her tablet.

After a while, Marsee sighed. "I've sent a message to Papa to come over when he's done with his meeting. This is too big for me to wrap my brain around. I'm horrible at math."

"You, Marsee Chenzie Butt Chenzira, are horrible at something?" she teased.

Marsee rolled her eyes. "I can manage, but it takes time, and I rarely have patience for it. I can't see numbers the way I can words."

"What do you mean?" Little Flower asked.

Marsee shrugged. "I don't really know how to explain. When I read, I don't see the words. I see the scene they represent. If you were to write, 'Mama has two chenzies and Papa gave her two more,' I see that scene and Mama now having four chenzies, which I can count up, but if you put two plus two on paper, they mean nothing. I have to give them a context. By the time I figure out what each number represents, I've forgotten what I'm trying to do with them and end up lost in my imagination, with six chenzies strolling through the wilds and Papa chasing after them. In school, I spent so much time trying to see and understand the numbers in front of me that I always missed the rest of the lesson, and then I'd get so stressed I'd want to run and hide."

"You use math with your crafts. I see you writing stuff down all the time," Little Flower said. "And you've been taking all those programming classes."

Marsee shook her head. "Programming's different because it's as much words as it is numbers. I don't have to do the math, and I'm telling the computer to add the chenzies together. With my crafts, I'm mostly recording measurements so I don't forget. Most of the time, I can visualize exactly what I want to build and see every component and angle in my brain, like with my modeling program. For complex projects, like your puzzle boxes, I'll model it on my tablet first, so I don't have to do the math to figure out how long each piece needs to be, but for simpler stuff, I can just match the image in my brain. Ellie's been trying to work with me on understanding the guild reports and the formulas behind them, but it's been impossibly slow. I know what each report is supposed to represent, but I couldn't tell you if any of it was accurate."

Marsee looked back at her tablet but leaned back in her chair a moment later, rubbing the back of her scruff.

"What's bothering you?" she asked.

"I've never considered that my horrible math skills were anything more than a complete lack of ability or interest. I think it might have been another symptom of my illness," she said eventually. "I'm struggling to wrap my brain around all the options and figure out what the best choice is, but for once, this all makes sense. The screen is too bright, which makes everything hard to see, but I understand what they're presenting. I never even considered that I was struggling with math because of my instinct. I suppose it would make sense. What would our instincts need of math? How much of me is me, and how much was my instinct? If I can focus better, that's a welcome improvement, but what if I've lost something important?"

"As far as I can tell, you're still the same slightly less fuzzy Chenzie Butt I've always known, but whatever the challenges, we'll face them together, and it won't stop me from loving you."

"Thanks, Fish Breath," Marsee replied, but she could tell Marsee wasn't entirely convinced.

Their conversation ended, though, as there was a knock on the door. Marsee walked over to open it, and both their father and Marcus walked in. That they both showed up so quickly told Little Flower just how serious this was. Not that she wasn't surprised, although Marsee clearly was.

Marsee shifted to let them both in, but her body was tense, and she didn't shut the door. Both guards outside must have picked up on her nerves as they suddenly went into extra pokey guard mode and turned to watch.

Little Flower hadn't seen her Uncle Marcus since right after she'd woken up from her coma, outside of her brief interaction with him after they arrived on the planet. She knew Marsee had been worried about him, but that was before they'd found out about the Transition, and if the guards were still worried, then she needed to be, too.

"Marsee," he said, tilting his head. "Little Flower. It's good to see you both again."

She nodded.

"I wasn't expecting to see you," Marsee said.

Her uncle clearly picked up on Marsee's unease as he tilted his head again, acknowledging that fact. "I know, but whatever you decide will likely be big enough to require my authorization as your Senior Councilor, and I've yet to have an opportunity to congratulate you on your partnership. You're looking remarkably better than the last time I saw you, although your father says you overdid it today. How are you feeling?"

Marsee didn't respond right away, as if weighing her words. "Physically, I'm recovering, but I imagine I'm going to hurt tomorrow. I'm already feeling it. Mentally, I'm still struggling to work through my trauma. This afternoon was rough."

His face softened into the caring person Little Flower had grown to know, the power of his authority backing off slightly. "I imagine so. Your father informed us of what the Senior Healer said, and I'm infuriated by what Rip did to you. If I could dig him up so you could kill him again, I would. However, sadly, I'm sure whatever was left of him is Leviathan poop by now."

Marsee's tail curled, and some of her tension relaxed. "Good. Although I feel sorry for that poor Leviathan. Rip probably gave the thing a stomach ache from how rotten he was."

Both her father and Marcus chuckled. "I said the same thing when we dumped him in the Trench," her father explained.

"So, what questions did you have for us?" Marcus asked.

Marsee frowned at her uncle and the rapid change in topic but said nothing. She motioned them over to the table and sat on the opposite side of the table from her uncle, as far away as she could get without being impolite. No one shut the door.

Half an hour into it, they called Ellie over as well. They spent the next several hours digging through all of the options, discussing plans, and tweaking them to better fit their goals and the Council's needs.

She remained quiet for most of it, only asking for clarification when she didn't understand something or answering when asked her opinion. It reminded her of the weeks they'd spent reviewing the Charter, but this was a different side of her sister and uncle than she'd seen before. Then, he'd been her advocate. Now, he was advocating for the Consortium, and there was far less trust on Marsee's part. Marsee grilled her uncle hard over every point and detail before making her final decisions and signing the contracts.

After Ellie signed the contracts as well, Marcus set his tablet down on the table.

"Now, before we leave, there's one other question I need to ask you, Marsee," he said. "I've been informed that you lied to me about Ellie having a verbal agreement to use your artwork. Did anyone bribe or force you to change your contract?"

From where Little Flower was sitting, she could see her Uncle's tail curl slightly, so she knew he was mostly teasing, although the others apparently didn't. Both Marsee and Ellie looked like they were going to be executed, and her father slammed his mask down tightly.

"I didn't know about the toys and the other products until I arrived here, not until Stormy swam out of his home wearing a Crawly Man cape," Marsee replied. "I didn't think anything of it until Rip brought it up in the cave. He was going after Papa, though, not Ellie, stating how Papa was taking advantage of me through that gift. After you all left for your investigation, it's one of the first things I looked up. I'll be honest. I never even looked at the contract before signing it, so I had no idea if he was telling the truth, and I wasn't sure if that was implied or not, which is one of the reasons I sent it to you in the first place. What I told Ellie was that I wanted my share of the profit from the translations to go to New Hope, and that's vague enough to be misunderstood. If I'd realized that I could give authorization to use my artwork separately, I would have probably made the same decision. I was teasing Ellie today about it just to get her reaction. I have no need for the credit or the rank, and I certainly wouldn't harm New Hope or Ellie over a misunderstanding. I was completely overwhelmed finding out about how popular my translations were, and I wanted her to splutter a bit like I had when I found out, especially once I realized you hadn't told her about it. I was only upset that she hid their ranking from me, but I understand why she did. I did go practically comatose for several days when my other artwork started selling."

He glared at Marsee for several seconds before turning his glare on Ellie.

"I swear, I sent the wrong contract by accident and gave the orders to begin creating the other products," Ellie said before Marcus could say anything. "I take full responsibility for anyone who moved forward on my orders alone rather than verifying the contract, and I've ordered Nardal to review any contracts I fill out in the future to make sure I don't mess up again. As for hiding the information from Marsee, that didn't happen until after the contract was signed, and I only ordered the best-seller lists to be modified. However, those changes were not specifically targeted to Marsee, even if I might have implied it."

Ellie flipped open her tablet and brought up the page. "I ordered a change to the page with added filters. The default is now designed to show the top one hundred that the person hasn't purchased or that aren't your own works and to maintain whatever filters they last selected. She could have added that back if she'd ever bothered to look at the filter. It's the second option. Also, if she went to either her public page or guild page or looked up the works individually, that information was readily available. Long before Marsee's translations hit the top downloads, we realized that most people were spending a significant amount of time scrolling to find works they hadn't read. I can send you that work order for confirmation or have Nardal send it to you if you prefer. I told Myra about it and asked her not to say anything. I fully intended to surprise Marsee in person with that information, but that was the day Little Flower went into labor. After that, it was never the right time, and eventually, I figured she must have seen it already. I didn't realize she hadn't until we arrived here."

Marcus nodded. "Send me both work orders. As Marsee's not pressing charges, there's no crime, and I wouldn't even ask for it if that wasn't one of the things Rip had on you. We confirmed that Rip was the only one to access the contract, which matches your statement, although I suggest you remind people they should check in the future."

Ellie nodded and pulled up her tablet, and a moment later, Marcus's tablet dinged.

He reviewed it briefly and then looked up at Ellie with a wicked grin. "I hope you realize I intend to tease you about this contract for the rest of your life."

Ellie snorted. "I was wrong. It's not Little Flower that Marsee's been hanging around too much, it's you. But I deserve it, and I'm honestly surprised you haven't already."

Marcus shrugged. "I've been a little busy lately, and it's far more fun teasing people when they're fully recovered. Besides, I can't exactly hold an execution over your head when you're already dead."

Ellie's tail spiraled in amusement. "Well, you'd have been proud of your niece this afternoon. I'm pretty sure I nearly had a heart attack when she brought it up and demanded immediate payment, only to inform me, *after* I spluttered for several minutes trying to find a solution, that she'd already updated the contract."

Marcus chuckled. "I'm honestly sad I missed it, but your reaction a few minutes ago was good enough for me. Now, I have work to do. Come on, Jer, I'm sure the rest of the Seniors are anxiously waiting for our return."

CHAPTER 52

Wind Rider: Worse than a Flyer

Wind Rider yawned as she glanced at the clock. Jer and Marcus had been gone for hours and everyone was starting to get twitchy, well all but Sammianna, who had curled up in her shell to take a nap while they waited. Apakna was tapping a claw on the table as she scowled at something on her tablet, and Clear Seas had been pacing for at least the last ten minutes.

No one had said anything about Jer's outburst earlier, but while she worried about his control, she fully understood his anger and grief. She was still having a hard time processing her own emotions and the harm done to her daughter. Needing a break herself and a distraction from her spiraling thoughts and the impossible decisions she needed to make, she'd pulled a cushion out of dry storage and curled up to read.

She'd been slowly working through a book GrandFather had sent her following a request to know more about the Hue-man mating practices, as that appeared to have far more cultural and legal implications than any of the other species' mating practices did. She supposed that made sense when you had a species that came into heat every fifteen standard days or so. Like the Hue-mans, she could mate whenever she wanted, but every mating produced a clutch. For them, it appeared to be more of a social bonding experience and important enough that it had caused at least two of their males to act out in violence when denied that experience.

The book hadn't been translated yet, which was turning out to be far more of a challenge than she'd expected, but it was good practice, if utterly confusing at times. She was starting to understand why Little Flower hadn't realized 326's intentions, as there appeared to be ritualistic gift-giving involving specific foods that no longer existed.

"Clear, you have a fruit called a jelly egg, do you not?"

He stopped his pacing. "Yes, it's a part of the fire sticks that the Translator apparently likes so much. Why?"

"That's what I thought. I'm reading a book GrandFather shared with me on the mating practices of his species, and they keep mentioning a fruit that roughly translates as 'egg plant'. The passage I just read stated that the male admired the size of the female's melons and the female in turn admired the size of this egg plant that the male had. She then took it, and they began mating. The male's fruit is currently listed as extinct. I recognize that Little Flower's implant was removed, causing her heat, but I'm wondering if Marsee shared some of the jelly eggs with her, and that's why she agreed to mate with Marsee, even though they're not the same species, when she didn't with the male of her species at the Agency. He did offer her food, but maybe it wasn't the right food, or because it was cut up and not big enough. If the other males haven't had access to this fruit to give to the females, that could explain why there haven't been any matings."

"I suppose that's possible," he replied. "I would think if it were that important in their mating practices that they'd be looking for a replacement or even mentioned it at the Trial."

"Unless their hiding it from us or their females are purposely not accepting anything as a valid replacement," Apakna suggested. "Chef Jordan is in charge of ordering food for New Hope."

"It might be worth looking into," Clear Seas said.

"I'll send a message to GrandFather," Wind Rider replied.

Before she could, the door opened, and Jer and Marcus swam in, looking exhausted and defeated. Clear Seas let out a ripple of a sigh and she reached over and tapped on Sammie's shell to wake her. Sammie unwound as the others took their seats.

"Do I even want to know how bad?" Clear Seas asked.

"Probably not," Marcus replied. "Do you want the bad news or the even worst news first?"

"I suppose you should start with the worst," Clear Seas replied.

Marcus rubbed at the back of his scruff. "It's going to be a long night, and you'll need to call an emergency meeting in the morning. Marsee rejected all of our suggestions."

Clear Seas slumped into his seat with a disappointed sigh. "Do I have *any* budget to work with?"

Marcus shrugged. "Some, but I'm not sure what you're going to do with it." He unclipped his tablet and sent Clear Seas the contracts.

Clear Seas pulled them up and began reading, and a moment later, his skin flashed red and orange. "Marcus Rufino Surellis, you are worse than a Flyer!"

Wind Rider glared at Clear Seas for the insult. "What is *that* supposed to mean?"

Marcus grinned at both of them, and Jer's tail curled.

"Marsee agreed to far better terms than we offered," Marcus replied.

"You're serious?" Apakna asked.

"He is," Clear Seas replied, then displayed the contracts on the monitor for everyone to see.

She snorted as she read through the first bit, which detailed Marsee's gift to the other victims. "The Leviathan Fund? Seems to me Marsee has a bit of Flyer in her, too."

Jer chuckled. "It was actually Little Flower's suggestion. She thought that some of the funds should go towards caring for the stomachache we caused the Leviathan by feeding it Rip's rotten corpse, and the name stuck. The conversation devolved at that point into a rather inventive discussion on how to actually administer such treatment. In the end, the best we could come up with was pumping Snapper Fish full of the nano drink Marsee was forced to take and dangling him by a hook off the end of a ship."

She chuckled and bubbles of humor crossed Clear Seas' skin.

"I'm half tempted to award her that for reparations," Marcus replied. "It would save us a lot of effort, but I am concerned it would put others in danger."

"I'm sure we could wrangle up a few volunteers," Clear Seas replied. "Myself included. So, were you also joking about there being bad news, too?"

Marcus shrugged. "That depends on what you call bad. I found out tonight that Ellie did *not* have permission to use Marsee's artwork in the derivative works of her translations."

The humor around the room vanished instantly.

"But she stated on record that it was a contracting error?" Wind Rider replied.

Marcus tilted his head. "So she did."

"She also demanded immediate reparations and repayment from El-lie," Jer added.

Silence again filled the room.

"Did someone force her to give her statement before?" Sammianna asked.

"No," Marcus replied. "That was the first thing I asked."

Clear Seas pinched his nose. "How was this not the worst news?"

"Well, perhaps because about five minutes later, she stated she hadn't given permission but would have if she realized that was a possibility," Marcus replied. "The only thing she actually wanted in reparations was to see Ellie squirm as much as she had when she first learned about the Crawly Man toys."

Clear Seas flashed red again and threw his tablet at Marcus.

Marcus ducked out of the way long before it actually hit, tail curled tightly with laughter.

"I'm beginning to see your point, Clear," Wind Rider said in her own language. "Although I won't go quite so far as calling him Worse than a Flyer. It has taken him nearly two hundred years to get one over on me, but it's a start."

Marcus grinned. "Thank you for the compliment."

"It wasn't a compliment," she replied. "but I understand. You are a bit of a slow learner when it comes to my language."

Jer snorted, and Marcus glared at his brother. "Don't glare at me. She's the one who said it, and you did call her smelly fish."

Marcus snorted, and his glare broke a moment later. "True. I'll save you the effort of reading the rest, as it's late, and a read-through can wait until morning. Marsee matched the amount we were planning on for reparations, as did Ellie on behalf of the Guild. That gives Ellie, Marsee, and a member of the Senior Council equal say in who gets the funds, with a two-thirds majority needed. Ellie will be investing those funds back into the Guild with a guaranteed return to the fund to make it self-sustainable. The deciding vote for the Senior Council will rotate on a fixed schedule that will change following each full council meeting. At Marsee's insistence, to avoid any semblance of bias, the order was pulled at random from a hat by Hope. We have a recording for proof if anyone has an issue with it, as Little Earth is up first. From there, it goes to Flyer, Saber, Digger, The Ice Planet, and the Water World. Should we wish or need to change it, it can be done at any time as long as it's pulled at random in front of the Full Council or the Full Council gives a majority vote for a different order."

"That seems more than fair to me," Clear Seas said, and they all agreed.

"As far as the physical donations that were made to Marsee at the vigil, those were officially donated to New Hope for furnishing the future off-world housing that's planned. Jer has graciously agreed to count those towards the future allocation that was already granted by the Council so as not to skew things further in New Hope's balance."

"I'm hoping this will appease some of the anger that Little Earth is getting more than its fair share," Jer stated. "We would have had to purchase those items anyway, and the benefit will primarily go to the other species."

"That's more than generous, Jer," Wind Rider stated. "Thank you."

"For her own purposes, Marsee only kept an amount ten times what was spent on the Hallowed Eve festival for the Hue-man partnership ceremony Little Flower wants, miscellaneous gifts, expenses, and projects."

"That's it?" Apakna asked. "That's nothing compared to what she had."

"Indeed. The rest she split up between the Research Fund, the Guild, and the Council at far better rates than we proposed. She will be taking over management of the Research Fund in exchange for a ship, equivalent to Ellie's, on a permanent loan from the Ships Guild, with some minor modifications to better suit Little Flower and Hope. Ellie is covering that as a guild expense. Not including any payout from the Research Fund, it puts her at the same annual rate as Ellie. The long and short of it, she essentially gave everything back."

"I honestly can't believe it," Apakna said. "But it's nice to have some good news for a change."

"Agreed," Marcus replied. "So, did you come to a majority decision while we were gone?"

"And there goes the good mood," Clear Seas muttered. "Couldn't you have waited until morning to spoil it?"

"Sorry," Marcus replied. "But we don't exactly have a lot of time, and I imagine you're going to be busy with your council finalizing your agenda in the morning."

It was after midnight before they decided to break. They had agreed that in this, they needed to be unanimous, but still hadn't come to an agreement. She was the hold-out. As exhausted as she was, she didn't return directly to the ship. Her emotions were far too raw to sleep, so she instead swam to the surface and took flight, letting her wings stretch as she enjoyed the warm currents rising from the ocean under the bright light of a nearly full moon.

Night was always her favorite time to fly. It was peaceful and quiet, and the added challenge of flying at night made it exhilarating. It was the first time she'd gone out in several weeks. The last week of a clutch always left her feeling too heavy and awkward to fly, and there hadn't been time since. Every free moment was now spent with her daughter.

She felt guilty about flying now when her daughter wouldn't be able to fly for months, but she knew if she didn't, she wouldn't sleep. She pushed herself hard as she flew towards the islands in the distance, trying to outrun the grief and rage she felt and the impossible weight of the decisions she had to make. It didn't help any more than Jer's attack on the wall.

Legally, she knew that everyone involved in Rip's coup had to die, but far too many of her species were nest mothers. Thankfully, none were close family, like Clear Seas had to deal with, but her species was on the brink of collapse. She didn't know if they would survive the death of that many, but would letting them live be any better? Even without that, how would her people react? Every one of those Nest Mothers had tens of thousands of children. Would they revolt to save them? Would anyone fly with them, even if she let them live to save her species? How many of them had acted with Rip because they felt forced to mate? She'd already made the change to her Charter, and no one had said anything, not even the press.

Eventually, still undecided, she sighed and returned to the platform, landing on the surface near her ship. Shaking the condensation of the warm air from her wings, she greeted the guards who stood at watch outside. "Any issues?"

"No, ma'am," the senior of the two replied. "Did you have a good flight?"

She nodded and made her way inside. She found Petra sprawled in the common area, wings carefully propped on half a dozen large cushions. It was the first time since Petra had left the Trauma Center that she'd seen her daughter's wings extended. Normally, they were carefully bound to her sides. She looked exhausted, angry, and in pain.

Her Senior Healer, who she had dragged with her from Flyer on the slim hope that her daughter was still alive, sat beside her.

"Is everything alright?" Wind Rider asked.

"No," Petra muttered with a glare at Sun Chaser. "I was finally asleep, and your feather-brained Senior Healer had the unmitigated gall to wake me for physical therapy. It's after midnight! Who does physical therapy in the middle of the night?"

"You do," Sun Chaser replied, "if you ever want to fly again. You have to start moving those wings every couple of hours. I know it's painful and exhausting, but it has to be done. If we don't, you're going to have to have surgery to replace all of that new skin when it splits. I waited for as long as I could to let you heal, but you're growing too fast to put it off any longer. Now, come on. Three more sets, and I'll let you sleep."

Petra hissed at Sun Chaser. "I've already been doing this for an hour. I hurt, and I'm tired, and I don't want to do it anymore."

"The more you avoid using your wings, the longer it's going to hurt. Three. More. Times," he insisted.

"I don't care. I don't want to do it anymore."

"Petra, you need to listen to him," Wind Rider said.

"Mama! You're not helping. I said no, and it's my right to refuse treatment."

"You're right. It is," she replied. "But he's telling the truth. I broke my wing when I was first learning how to fly. It was a bad break, and by the time I was allowed to move it again, I couldn't open my wing more than halfway. It took forever to get my range of motion back."

Petra huffed at her.

"Come on. If you can survive what Rip did to you, you can make it through three more reps."

"At least Rip let me sleep," Petra muttered but climbed to her feet and slowly closed her drooping wings.

"A little more," Sun Chaser said.

Petra glared at Sun Chaser but tucked them in tighter, wincing as she did.

Sun Chaser counted to ten, and Petra started extending the wing closest to the healer. When they were about three-quarters of the way extended, Petra's wing began to shake, and she hissed from the pain.

Sun Chaser grabbed the wing to help support it but then slowly pulled it further open.

Petra hissed and grunted and eventually screamed, but Sun Chaser didn't stop until it was fully extended. As much as she hated seeing her daughter in pain, she didn't stop the Healer, either.

Two reps later, Sun Chaser moved to Petra's other wing, and they repeated the process. When they were done, Petra collapsed with her wings on the pillows again, breathing hard, while Sun Chaser injected her with pain meds and began spraying her wing with nanos.

"There. That wasn't so bad, was it?" Sun Chaser asked when she was done.

Petra swore at the Healer.

"Solid effort on creativity, but sadly, I've heard that one before on three separate occasions," Sun Chaser replied. "Now, try to get some rest. I'll be back in four hours."

Petra hissed at Sun Chaser as he walked down to his room, but as soon as the healer was out of sight, she let out a heavy sigh and turned her head away, not quite under her wing, but that was only because there was a pillow in the way.

"I know it's hard now, but you will get better," Wind Rider said.

Her daughter grunted an acknowledgment but otherwise didn't respond.

"I'll let you get some rest," she said and started to leave.

"Mama, will you stay with me? I don't want to be alone out here, and I hurt too much to go back to my room."

"Of course," she replied. "The pain meds aren't helping? Do you want me to call Sun Chaser back?"

"They stopped helping days ago. He said the only thing he could do was sedate me, but I don't want to be sedated. I don't feel safe, even with the guards outside. As exhausted as I am, I don't even want to sleep."

Wind Rider curled up so she could see both her daughter and the door. "You rest. Don't let anything worry you. I'm here, and I'll protect you." She began singing a quiet lullaby. Petra closed her eyes with a sigh of relief, and a moment later, she was snoring.

Wind Rider remained beside her on the uncomfortable floor long after her song was done. She remained awake all night, unable to sleep herself as her thoughts drifted to the decision she had to make in the morning, and her resolve hardened when Sun Chaser returned four hours later, and Petra screamed and swore her way through another session.

When Petra was done, she lifted herself to her feet with a painful groan and trudged back to her room, head hanging low and wings held awkwardly by her side, but it was the look of fear Petra gave her right before entering her room and locking her door that decided her.

Clear Seas had been joking earlier, calling Marcus worse than a Flyer, but there was something so much worse: a monster pretending to be a Nest Mother. They might not have hurt her daughter directly the way Leaf, Willow, and Rip had, but they had sided with Rip, and they had used their rank and influence to commit crimes equally heinous. They might be female, she decided, but they were not worthy of the title of Councilor or Nest Mother, and she did not want anyone capable of what they had done to ever reproduce again, even if it ultimately meant the death of her species.

I'll clutch non-stop for the rest of my life to make up the difference if I have to, she decided, and left to cast her vote.

CHAPTER 53

Little Flower: Mystery Illness

To Little Flower's surprise, Ellie didn't leave with the others but instead, after some light-hearted bantering, she stuck around to discuss the research fund and begin training Marsee on everything she would need to do. It was late, and she was tired, but she was happy to see Marsee so excited.

She started putting Hope to bed as they worked, but when she turned around, she saw Ellie looking at Marsee with an expression that said she was staying here teaching Marsee because there might not be a later. Ellie looked strong and had mostly recovered from her own injuries. Her fur was growing back and was already quite a bit thicker than Marsee's, and aside from some obvious stiffness and pain in her hands, Ellie didn't look sick or injured. *Is she worried about the meeting, or is something else going on?*

Ellie caught her watching, and the expression vanished.

She smiled at Ellie and walked into the bathroom to collect the sheets that were still in the sanitizer.

"We're not keeping you up, are we?" Ellie asked when she was done making the bed and sat on the edge near her scanner.

"No, I have homework from Ammond to do that I've been putting off. I'll be up for a while. You two have fun," she said.

Ellie smiled at her and turned back around to face the monitor that hung on the wall.

Little Flower grabbed the scanner while their backs were both to her. She quickly scanned Ellie, then walked over and made an act of scanning Marsee. Scan complete, she tossed the scanner on the bed, then walked over to the refrigerator and refilled everyone's drinks.

"Marsee, drink. You're dehydrated again."

Marsee didn't hesitate and drank the entire glass in two gulps. She refilled the glass again, put the container of juice away, and then, noticing Ellie rubbing at her hand, she brought over the jar of nano cream.

"Nano's for your paw? I can see it's bothering you."

"Having you in the Healer's guild might actually prove to be a benefit," Ellie signed, then took a large glob, proving it was bothering her. "Your mother would have stuck a scanner in my face and dragged me back to the Trauma Center if she had seen."

"I could grab the scanner again and make a completely uneducated diagnosis if you'd like, as long as you don't tell Ammond. He's holding off on thwacking me with his tail for now, but I imagine the moment he deems me fully healed, he'll make up for it."

Ellie snorted, and her tail spiraled. "I know the feeling." She lifted her tail and flopped the end over kinked as if broken. "My tail is perpetually sore from Guild Masters and proteges who have a nasty habit of thinking they know everything and trying to give me a heart attack on a daily basis."

Marsee chuckled, and Ellie retaliated by thwacking Marsee with her tail hard enough to prove there was nothing wrong with it.

"Still, I don't want you to get in trouble. I know how Ammond is. You're welcome to scan my hand if you like and discuss your findings with Ammond in the morning. If anyone asks, I took the nano cream without asking first."

She grabbed the scanner, but Ellie raised a paw to stop her. "On one condition. When you have the chance, I want you to draw what you find and send me a copy. It'll be good practice for both skills."

She agreed and took the scan. "He really did a number on this hand, didn't he?"

Ellie nodded. "I'm honestly surprised they were able to save it. Hyacinth showed me the scan when they brought me in. It wasn't even recognizable as a hand. Still, it'll be as good as new in another week or two."

Little Flower left the jar on the table in case either of them needed more and then crawled onto the bed, and started examining the scans, trying to figure out what was wrong with Ellie and praying that she'd misread her expression earlier. Her medical knowledge was rudimentary at best, but the scanner was a miracle of technology and quickly identified several areas of concern.

The amount of scarring from Ellie's injuries was astounding, but as far as she could tell, they were mostly healed. A few of the bones in her right paw had not fully healed, but from the looks of things, those bones had been shattered. Several of them had been replaced outright, and the replacement bone was jarringly obvious.

She dismissed them from the scanner's report. Although one bone looked like it might need further treatment, there was nothing there that was life-threatening. Several other items were flagged, but she didn't know what they were. She spent the next hour looking up the terms and symbols and then trying to figure out what they meant. It was slow going, as she had to look up term after term to figure out what they were representing. She hadn't figured it out before Marsee started yawning.

Ellie immediately called it quits and left.

After a trip to the hole of muck, Marsee wrinkled her nose at the bed, clearly still smelling the remnants of Hope's accident.

"Where is it the worst?" Little Flower asked.

Marsee pointed to the spot, so she proceeded to roll all over it.

"Better?" she asked.

"No. Now *you* stink," Marsee said and, with another scrunched nose, turned and walked out of the room. A few minutes later, she returned, with Aris helping to drag in another mattress.

"Did you just take someone's mattress?" Little Flower asked, laughing in surprise. She'd figured Marsee had gone to find some cleaning supplies, not a new mattress.

"No. Of course not. The suite was unoccupied," Marsee replied.

She climbed off the bed so they could swap it out. "You seriously broke into a suite and stole a mattress?" she asked, honestly surprised that the guards had gone along with it.

Marsee huffed, flattened her ears in annoyance, and dropped her end of the mattress to respond in sign. "Do you honestly think I would steal a mattress?"

"No. But you did just imply it."

Marsee frowned. "I did? Sorry. That was not my intention. No, we did not break into a suite and steal a mattress. Aris confirmed that the suite next to us is unoccupied. It's there for them to use if they need it and to provide added protection for us. This mattress smells musty, but it's not as bad as ours. I'll get someone to clean them both tomorrow."

Aris's tail curled tightly. "You're lucky you're not actually in the Guard. We'd normally make you suffer until you learned to deal with it, but I think you've been through enough torture for one week. I know I wouldn't want to sleep on that mattress or next to you, Little Flower. No offense, Councilor, but you stink nearly as bad as your father did earlier this week."

She chuckled as they'd laughed for hours over the picture her mother had shared with them. "None taken. I'll take a shower while you two finish your little not-heist."

For Marsee's sake, she ran the shower twice. When she returned, Aris had left, and Marsee was layering every spare sheet and blanket she could find on top of the new mattress. She grinned but said nothing as Marsee turned her around to make sure she no longer stunk.

"Thank you for humoring me," Marsee said, then curled up on the bed with her own tablet. "So, what are you working on?"

"I'm not sure. I need to figure out what these elevated values mean, but it's slow going since I have to look everything up. The translator is only picking up one in every four words. If that."

"Do you want me to help?" Marsee asked.

"Nah, it helps me learn the words to look them up," she said, not wanting Marsee to figure out she'd scanned Ellie. They hadn't discussed medical ethics yet, but she was sure this was treading on a very fine line between ethical and not, and even if she figured out what was wrong, she couldn't tell Marsee. That much she knew as part of her council training.

Marsee shrugged and started reading.

It took her another half hour to decipher the scans, and it made her brow rise as she read through more on the topic. Ellie was starting her heat. *Does she know?* Little Flower wondered. *She must. Marsee said they were all controlled after the first one since they were so dangerous.* She looked up complications of a second and third pregnancy, and she frowned with concern as she read.

No one would schedule a third pregnancy with the risks so high, and Ellie wouldn't schedule a heat for the middle of a very important Council meeting while she's still recovering from major injuries. So why is she in heat? Ellie was around me, too, right at the beginning of my cycle. Did I trigger it on her somehow, too? Nah, that's unlikely. Mama wasn't affected, and she was here in the room with me in the middle of it. Something else must be going on.

It took her nearly another hour before she figured out why. *Her implant is missing! Why would it be missing?* She stared at the tablet for a long time, looking at the area where the implant should be. There was a lot of fresh scar tissue in that area. *Rip must have damaged it,* she finally decided. *So why didn't they replace it? Maybe they don't have one here. She'd have been cleared to jump days ago, so why didn't she? She went and looked back at the timeline of the heat cycle. If she's at this stage, she would have had to jump before we arrived.*

Marsee shifted in the bed, and Little Flower looked over at her. *Did she stay because of Marsee, to keep her from killing herself? Well, she's stuck without many people to choose from to mate with because of it. I wonder what she's going to do. Walk into the middle of the Council meeting?*

Little Flower nearly snickered at that thought. *That would be a scandal for the history books. I wonder who she has picked out for a mate.*

"Marsee, does Ellie have any family, partner, children?" Little Flower asked.

"No. She had a partner once. She's tried twice to have cubs but wasn't successful. Why?" Marsee asked.

"I just realized I didn't know all that much about her," she replied.

"I didn't find out until last week. I knew she didn't have a partner, but she just told me about the cubs. Something went wrong with her first heat, and she almost died. They fixed it, but then the cubs in her second litter were stillborn. The healers wouldn't let her try a third time. She wanted cubs badly, though. I guess that's why she never came around much after I was born. She said it was too hard."

"I can understand that," Little Flower said, yawned, and tossed her tablet and scanner on the bedside table. "I think I've had enough of this for one night."

She climbed out of bed to use the bathroom and shut the door. She needed a few minutes of privacy to regain her composure. She didn't want Marsee to sniff out her fear, although she was surprised she hadn't already. Ellie was going into her third heat, and that was almost always a death sentence.

Ellie must have chosen not to have it replaced on the slim chance she could survive and have cubs, or she must have had to make a decision between her life and Marsee's and chose Marsee, or perhaps both. I wonder if Mama knows. She must. She didn't come by at all to check on Marsee, and that's not like her. I'll talk to her about it tomorrow.

Splashing water on her face, she walked back out and climbed into bed. Marsee set her tablet aside, and they curled up in their normal sleeping position. As she lay there, she traced Marsee's swirling patterns on her arm and fiddled with the fuzz that was growing back in, her mind in a whirl of implications.

"That tickles," Marsee said with a chuckle.

"Sorry, I'll stop."

"You're quiet tonight. What's bothering you?" Marsee asked. "Are you upset at the decisions I made tonight?"

"No, not at all. I'm relieved, actually."

"Really? Why?" Marsee asked.

"Money changes people. I didn't want it to change you or the people around you, and it was good seeing you so excited this evening and joking with Ellie. Are you meeting up with her tomorrow?"

"For a few hours after my lesson with Avery. She wanted to meet in the afternoon, too, but that's our training session together."

"I'm woefully behind in preparing for the council meeting, and I should really spend the entire afternoon focusing on that. Why don't you spend the day with her? This was supposed to be a fun trip for the two of you, and you've hardly been able to do any of it."

"Are you sure?" Marsee asked.

"Positive. If I finish up in time, Avery can chase us around in the arena in the evening. If he's willing."

Marsee said something in Saber to the Guards and snickered a moment later.

"What?" she asked.

"Aris just said that Avery will likely be too tired to run laps tomorrow. Tamarin beat my time by a full minute."

"Ha! I figured she'd worked out the trick when she agreed to that bet."

"He's going to be grumpy tomorrow," Marsee said.

"Yup. That's another reason I don't want to work out with him tomorrow. Good luck with that."

"What happened to guarding my back?"

"I can shoot Avery with the stunner, but I don't think that's going to help you all that much," she replied.

Marsee chuckled, snuggled back down, and soon fell asleep, but as tired as she was, it was a long time before she fell asleep, too.

CHAPTER 54

Little Flower: Preparation

The next morning, Little Flower's alarm went off way too early, and she contemplated grabbing her stunner and shooting it but decided against it. Reaching for the stunner would take just as much effort as it would to turn off the alarm. Crawling out of bed, she showered and returned to find something to eat but stopped in the doorway and snorted with laughter. Marsee was writhing around on her back, feet up in the air and groaning.

"What's your problem?" she asked. "Did a fleeble crawl up your back in the middle of the night from that stolen mattress?"

"Ha ha," Marsee growled as she continued to writhe on the bed.

Still laughing, Little Flower grabbed her tablet and snapped a few pictures so she could use them for reference to draw later. It was too funny to pass up.

"Laughing at me isn't helping!" Marsee growled. "What kind of healer are you, letting your patient and partner suffer in agony while you stand there and take pictures? I could be having another allergic reaction."

Humoring her sister, she grabbed her scanner. "Nothing's showing on the scanner. It's probably just your fur growing back." She grabbed the nano cream. "Roll over," she told Marsee, and started slathering it on her back, then gave light scratches with her fingernails.

Marsee groaned in relief.

"Was it as good for you as it was for me?" she asked.

"If you stop scratching, I will claw you," Marsee said, flashing her claws as she dug them into the bed for added traction to lean into the scratching, then shifted so her hand was under a different spot.

"Threatening a Councilor, are you?" Little Flower teased in English. *"Oh, Guards..."*

Marsee snorted and squirmed, so a new place was under her hand. "Ugh, this is worse than in the spring when my fur sheds." A few minutes later, Marsee relaxed as the cream took effect. "Thanks. You can stop now."

Chuckling, she returned to her previous task and frowned at the selection in the fridge. They'd decimated their supply the evening before. "Looks like we're going to the market this morning. Hopefully, the vendors are there this early." Still, she grabbed something to drink for each of them. "It's my completely unprofessional opinion that you should be good to go for your workout this morning. Just remember to hydrate."

Marsee downed the drink and started getting Hope ready for the morning while she climbed into her wet suit. Hope was cranky and uncooperative, clearly not ready to wake up either. Yawning, they made their way outside. "Morning," she told the guards, practicing her Saber. She was too tired to even bother teasing Avery about the laps.

"Morning," they replied and followed after, silent shadows of ferocity that made the other platform guests in the common area give them a wide berth. Adding to the whole procession was Marsee, protectively in the lead but matching her slow pace, cape flowing, and scowling at some internal thought. The Darth Vader theme song popped into her head and she started humming it.

Marsee's ears flicked back to listen. "I haven't heard that one before. You're amused, but why does it sound so...ominous?"

Laughing, she explained, but Marsee, who normally ate up everything she shared about her favorite movies and shows from Earth, seemed upset.

"You see me as a villain?"

"No, of course not," she replied. "But you do have as much power and authority, and with the cape and everyone ducking out of the way to get away from that scowl of yours, it reminded me of the scene. I think you should own it. They should remember what happens when people mess with you."

Marsee stopped and sat down to face her eye to eye. "Little Flower, I don't want people to fear me. I don't even want to go home because it'll be even worse there, and I'm not sure I can trust my uncle to protect me. Even after what Kendra has said, he still hasn't made up his mind about me, and if I have to defend myself, it'll be my word against theirs, and I'm the one on a watch."

"I know, but if you think I'm going to let him or anyone else hurt you, you're sadly mistaken."

Her sister flicked an ear back dismissively. "You don't have the jurisdiction to stop him."

"I make my own laws and eat Senior Councilors for breakfast. If I have to start a war to protect you, I will. Now, come on. I'm hungry, and I'll be late for my lesson if we don't hurry."

Marsee snorted and kept walking. "Well, we can't have that. You might like to eat Councilors for breakfast, but I find them a bit gamey and tough."

Laughing at the disgusted face Marsee made, she followed. There were only a few vendors in the market at this hour, but thankfully, they were all food vendors, there for the morning rush. They ate quickly and swam back to the Trauma Center, arriving only a few minutes late for her shift.

"About time you showed up," Ammond grumbled as he took Hope from her.

"She's grumpy," Little Flower warned and sat down to pull off her flippers. "And I'm sorry I'm late. Marsee had a severe case of the itchies and threatened to claw me if I stopped scratching her back."

"Oh sure, blame it on me," Marsee said. "That lasted all of about five minutes."

"And I'm five minutes late," she teased. "Now go on and have fun, and if you're dehydrated when you pick me up later, I'm not scratching your back the next time it itches, threats or otherwise."

Marsee snorted and swam out, tail curled in laughter behind her.

"I'll forgive you this time since you had some extra practice yesterday afternoon, which your mother says you managed to do correctly, but don't make a habit out of it."

"I won't, although I'll need to cut today's lesson short. I'm woefully unprepared for tomorrow's council meeting. Most of last night was spent with Papa, Uncle Marcus, and Ellie trying to figure out a little financial problem."

Her mother snorted from her desk. "Your father didn't get back to the suite until well after midnight and left before I did this morning to deal with the outcome of your little financial problem, but I'm still doubling your rent."

She chuckled and then shut the door. "We need to talk," she signed.

Both Ammond and her mother flicked their ears back at this, but gave her their full attention.

"I'm sure there are all kinds of ethical violations I broke, but last night, after Papa and Marcus left, Ellie stuck around to mentor Marsee. At one point, I caught her looking at Marsee with a look that scared me. For Ellie," she added when she saw their look of confusion. "I'm not even sure I could explain the look, but I knew something was wrong, so I scanned her under the pretext of doing my homework. It took me hours to figure it out, but her implant is missing, and I think she started her heat yesterday or the day before, and from what Marsee said, this would be her third one, too. Also, her right paw needs to be looked at again. The repair on the fourth meta…metatarpal? Failed. The bone fragments shifted, and it was bothering her last night. I gave her some nano cream to help with the pain."

Ammond raised an eyebrow, and her mother sighed.

"It's pronounced metacarpal, and she is," her mother confirmed. "She told us yesterday."

"Why haven't you stopped it? Is it too late?"

"Technically, we could," Ammond said, "But at this point, the risk would be just as high, and she's choosing to go forward with it. Have you told anyone?"

"No, of course not," she replied. "I figured I was in enough trouble by scanning her in the first place."

"You're not in trouble as long as you don't give her a diagnosis without confirming it with a master healer first, but you should have checked with us before giving her the nano cream," he admonished with a scowl. "However, since you Hue-mans seem to require gallons of it just to survive, it's not the worst thing you could have done, but it could mask a problem, and she could end up hurting herself worse by not being in pain and protecting it. When did you give it to her?"

"Around ten."

"Well, it will have worn off before she stops by this morning, and since you already know, it saves me from having to find a way to hide it from you. She should be able to make it through the meeting tomorrow and possibly the next day before she starts releasing pheromones. Hopefully, that will be long enough to make it through the trial."

She frowned. "That's one of the things I didn't understand. If she's in heat, why didn't Papa or Uncle Marcus notice last night? Papa reacted to Marsee the moment he entered the room."

"There's a few reasons," her mother said and then paused as if trying to figure out how to explain it. "Marsee was releasing pheromones in reaction to how you smelled or, more specifically, the change in your scent, much like our males do. If you noticed, Marsee didn't react to your father, even though he did the moment he walked into the room. That's because he wasn't releasing pheromones yet, or at least not at a level she could pick up over your own scent. Our implants counteract our ability to release pheromones, so even if we do find someone desirable, the other person doesn't end up in a situation they don't really want to be in. It's a safety measure. By the time I returned with the pheromone blockers, your father was...very much in the mood, although thankfully, our instincts want the strongest mate, and his instinct fixated on me, not your sister."

She chuckled at the memory of her father's expression that night. "That's why you dragged him out? To make you appear stronger?"

Her mother grinned. "Well, that and I wanted him out of the room as quickly as possible. Besides the obvious reasons, there can be issues if a female in heat believes her chosen mate is being stolen, and I had no idea how Marsee would react if she got a sniff of him."

"And Ellie?"

"In Ellie's case, it has more to do with the fact that she's in a third heat. With every heat, it takes longer to start releasing pheromones, and they're not as strong. The male has to go into heat long enough to get viable eggs for us to get the genetic material we need, but too long, and they're facing the same risks of a failed heat that females do. It's one of the reasons why we have open matings. The stronger a person smells to the female, the more likely they are to produce a viable egg in time and release the right pheromones to start the next stage of pregnancy."

"And if that doesn't happen?"

"That's the risk," Ammond replied. "Much like your species, we have a lining that's shed if there's a failed heat, and when that happens, there's significant blood loss before it can be stopped. It's a side effect of the same changes that caused our growth spurts in the first place. The risks and complications are much the same as what you went through, and Ellie has a rare blood type, which complicates the matter. After the trial, she'll be flying back to a mating center on Saber. There are donors already preparing for her arrival."

"Assuming she makes it through her heat with a viable embryo, she's moving into your room in the tower so I can monitor her through the pregnancy," her mother said. "She'll be on bed rest for the entire time. I figured you wouldn't mind and assumed you were moving back into Marsee's room when she's ready to return home."

"That's fine with me. I don't want to spend another night in that room. Do you think Ellie has a chance?"

"So far, she's progressing normally," her mother replied.

"Now," Ammond said. "Since you've obviously been studying something other than what I sent you home with, let's see what you've learned, and then we'll take a look at Ellie's paw."

"I did my homework, too," she replied.

Ammond raised a brow, but there was just the hint of a smile before he began grilling her and filling in the gaps in her knowledge. They were reviewing the scan of Ellie's hand when Ellie walked in and frowned to see her there.

"She already knows," Ammond said.

Ellie growled at him. "I asked you not to tell her."

"We didn't," Ammond replied. "My impudent apprentice figured it out on her own. You gave it away last night, and she spent hours trying to figure out what was wrong with you. She also found that you've re-broken one of the bones in your hand, but that's not surprising considering how shattered they were. I've already booked an operating room to fix it. It should only take about fifteen minutes or so. If you'll allow it, I would like Little Flower to observe and assist."

Ellie sighed but nodded her agreement and then turned to her. "Please don't tell Marsee. I'm sure by now you've figured out why I didn't jump home when I had the opportunity or one of the reasons anyway. I don't want her to feel responsible if something goes wrong."

"Marsee told me what she tried to do, and for what it's worth, I thank you," Little Flower signed back. "I won't tell her."

Her mother scanned Ellie. "So far, everything is looking normal. You should be clear for the meeting tomorrow, but I'm not sure about the next day anymore. Your hormone levels are higher than I'd expect for a third heat. How bad is the urge to rub?"

"Bad enough that it's likely how I re-broke my hand," Ellie admitted. "I've been using the pain to help control it."

Myra frowned. "I don't like it. You're cutting it far too close. You really should leave now. Jer even recommended that you leave. There's likely little else they can ask you that you haven't already provided."

"I am not leaving Marsee alone through this," Ellie growled. "I promised I would stay here to protect her and I feel bad enough as it is returning to Saber."

"She won't be alone," Little Flower signed. "I'll be there right next to her the whole time. Have Ammond fix up your hand, then spend the rest of the day with Marsee. Make it the best day you've ever had with her, and then leave this evening. If everything goes wrong, she'll remember that far more than you being there at the trial. And...take some toys with you for the trip."

"Toys?" Ellie asked with a blink, clearly not expecting that swerve in the conversation.

"Adult toys. You know, things that go buzz in the night. GrandFather picked up a large bag of them for our unexpected honeymoon. I haven't spoken to him about it, but I'm assuming he picked them up at the Guild, so there must be more to be had. If not, you're welcome to borrow some of ours. Sadly, we didn't get through a fraction of them before my scent changed."

"Things that go buzz in the night?" her mother repeated, barely able to maintain a straight face as her tail spiraled.

Ammond's tail curled as well. "She's got a point. It's going to be a long four days on that ship, and the more stimulated you are, the more likely you'll attract a stronger mate. It could improve your chances of a viable egg. But I also agree with Myra. If you're hurting yourself to stop the urge to rub, you should leave before the council meeting."

Ellie growled and then looked down as she realized she was rubbing her palm. "Fine. We'll leave tonight. *After* dinner. We're all going to Opal's new restaurant. It's her opening night. It's my treat, and I've already confirmed reservations at seven for everyone, including all of Marsee's shadows. Opal sent a message to Marsee, but it was rerouted to the staffers handling her mail. She came and found me this morning since she didn't know where Marsee was staying and hadn't had a reply. As for the toys, I would appreciate the loan. I don't want to raise suspicion with anyone at the Guild should I pick them up. Now, let's deal with this blasted hand so I can spend the rest of the day with my protege trying to thwack a century's worth of knowledge into her brain."

Her mother made quick work of the operation, explaining everything that was happening and having her hand over the various equipment as needed. Ammond ended up being far too busy trying to distract Hope, who had screamed bloody murder the moment he had tried to set her down for a nap.

They performed the operation in the one dry operating room they had, and she had to stand on a chair to be tall enough to see. It was fascinating to watch, although she did have to chuckle when she looked up at one point to see Ammond watching her instead of the operation.

"What is it?" she asked, confused by the look he was giving her.

"You're not bothered by the blood?" he asked.

She snorted. "Why would I be? This is nothing compared to what I've seen, and that includes out of my own body."

"True." He flicked an ear back, although it was more in thought of her question than surprise. "I guess I expected you to have more of a trauma response. Most people have a hard time with their first operation, but you seem fascinated."

"I am. For all our differences, we're very much the same." She held up her hand, fingers splayed. "Bones, tendons, muscles, and nerves. It fascinates me that life has developed in much the same way on six completely different planets, and it makes me wonder if that's another universal constant or if there's sentient life out there that's radically different. Is there a sentient blob somewhere, or a creature made entirely of energy, or does sentience require opposable thumbs?"

He grunted in acknowledgment but refocused on the surgery.

Once her mother was done with the repair, Ammond had her apply the bandage putty and set it, which she managed well enough. Even though she'd had it applied to herself on numerous occasions, the texture was very different than she expected, and it took her a bit of trial and error to get the right thickness. Ellie was patient throughout the whole process and, if anything, seemed amused.

"This brings back memories," Ellie said when she was done and flexed her paw. "Your mother used me for practice regularly. Granted, I was a bit of a klutz then, and it saved me dozens of trips to the trauma center."

Ammond scowled at her mother. "You treated Ellie without another healer present? Even after what happened to her tail?"

Her mother shrugged. "Nothing I did was outside of basic first aid, which anyone is allowed to do, and it was good practice."

Ammond scowled at her for another moment but dropped the subject to examine Ellie's paw for himself. Deeming the patch job marginally satisfactory for her first attempt, Ellie climbed out of her chair, gave Hope a gentle pat on the head, and left.

They began prepping for every possible contingency on the four-day trip back. Once the bags were packed, Ammond remained behind to watch Hope while she and her mother swam back to the suites with the bags of supplies to pack up her spare toys and deliver everything to Ellie's ship.

When they left the Trauma Center, a pair of guards were waiting for them outside. It was nice to know she was being protected, even if they weren't always visible, but it did make her wonder where they were hiding.

Once the guards had checked the suite for villains and monsters, she shut the door on everyone, including her mother, and packed up the toys for Ellie. It might have been her idea, but it was still embarrassing. Still, embarrassment or not, if it gave Ellie a better chance of surviving, she'd do just about anything.

Toys gathered, they followed the guards to Ellie's ship. Ellie had apparently informed the appropriate people that they were expected, as no one stopped them. Granted, the only people they saw were a pair of guards who stood outside the terminal and a rather bored-looking gate attendant who was far more focused on her tablet than them.

After dropping off the bags, she stopped to observe the world from the view-port outside Ellie's ship and found herself enthralled by the diversity of life before her.

"It's beautiful. Isn't it?" her mother asked after tapping her on her shoulder to get her attention.

She smiled up at the giant golden cat beside her. "Beautiful doesn't even begin to describe it. You know, sometimes, back home, I forget that I'm not on Earth. So much of it is like Earth, only bigger and hotter, but here, every tiny detail is alien and strange. My people tame nature to fit our needs, with little care for the creatures around them. You respect them and care for them, but do your part to keep most of them away. Here, there's a harmony I've never seen before. The buildings seem to defy the very laws of nature yet are also designed to allow nature the freedom to co-exist. Imagine what it would be like if we did that in New Hope. You might wake up some morning with a giraffe staring in your window or curled up next to a mountain lion kitten."

Her mother frowned. "That would be incredibly dangerous for your species. We keep most things away because they're deadly."

"Everything is deadly." She looked out at the view again, and it suddenly seemed far less beautiful. "For a few blessed months, I forgot that. I began to believe that the world you showed me was real and that we could change for the better. Now, I doubt that will ever be possible."

"We always knew there was a chance we couldn't save every member of your species, but what happened to our family has never happened before. Those involved will be punished, and we'll recover and move on."

She glanced back at the two female Saber guards, two she'd never met before, standing at calm attention as they guarded them in the otherwise empty hall. "No, Mama. It happens every day. It's been hidden from you and everyone else to give you all the appearance of safety. The only difference now is that we survived."

CHAPTER 55

Marsee: Mentors and Manifests

Avery was in a thoroughly grumpy mood all morning, which Marsee fully expected, but he said nothing as they made their way to the arena, nor did he take it out on her. He was apparently far more annoyed with Tamarin, who couldn't keep a grin off her face or the curl out of her tail.

If anything, he was far more attentive and concerned about her well-being. After yesterday's visit to the Trauma Center, he gave her a five-minute rest between activities instead of two and made her take multiple drinks throughout the session, to the point where she had to start refusing because she was beginning to slosh.

Unlike the day before, they brought her to Saber's personal arena. It was smaller, but only because it didn't have the aerial section used by the Fliers. The obstacles were different and in a different layout, but the ones Avery had her take were all the ones she'd been able to do the day before.

She managed to shave several minutes off her overall time, although that was mostly because she'd overcome her fear of several of the obstacles rather than any specific physical improvement. In reality, she was slower on most of the other obstacles because everything hurt, even with the nano cream Little Flower had slathered on her. When she hissed her way through one obstacle because of the pain in her paw, Avery stopped her and had Tamarin scan it. Tamarin determined the nerve was inflamed but otherwise uninjured, rubbed some nano cream on it, and had her move on to the next obstacle.

She'd expected some form of judgment for her slower times, but they seemed pleased with her effort and determination to plod through her training, regardless of how much it hurt. If someone had told her when she was younger that she'd welcome pain, she'd have laughed in their face. Not only did she revel in the fact that it meant she was recovering and getting stronger, but it was nothing compared to the torment she'd already been through.

After another water break followed by an even longer pee break, Avery worked with her on using her echolocation in the light, which she struggled with, and teaching her how to shut it off in the dark. That she had less difficulty with. When she was sufficiently able to shut her ears off, he made her run through the maze using only her nose to find several objects he'd left for her. That was far easier than before, as she could now easily pick out his scent.

They spent time evaluating her first aid skills, which were apparently far better than either expected, but then she'd spent a good portion of her childhood helping her mother in her clinic after school, and her mother had made sure she could handle triaging and stabilizing the most common injuries. In the South District, where healers were few and far between, it could mean the difference between life and death. When they determined she knew how to use it, they equipped her with a small first aid kit that clipped to her harness.

Avery then had several of the other guards come over and had her sniff them out to work on locating injuries and identifying moods. She had already learned how to pick up on people's moods based on their scent on her own, but he helped her to fine-tune it and understand the more subtle emotions that she'd always struggled to understand, in both herself and other people.

As Ellie had once suspected, she'd been confused by the disconnect between what people wanted her to believe and what they were actually feeling. She'd been working on that on her own, with her instinct's help, but she'd rarely dared use her instinct to sniff people out.

Sniffing out illness and injury fascinated her, even if she had no interest in becoming a healer. Since they could be without medical equipment, being able to identify a serious injury without a scanner was a valuable skill. They had her sniff out the others in the Arena until she started getting a headache. Sadly, it was apparently a skill she couldn't use on herself, at least not very easily, and would probably be something that would take her years, if not decades, to learn due to the way her brain would naturally filter out her own scent.

When she sniffed Avery, she noticed several sore muscles but didn't bring it up. His scent had just the slightest hint of annoyance, but mostly, he was worried, as were all of the guards. When she asked why, they informed her that they expected something to happen at the trial or before, and everyone was on high alert because of it.

They spent time talking with her about what they were expecting and why, along with what had already happened in New Hope. With everything Rip had told her, she expected that others were involved, although she hadn't been thinking about what would happen at the trial or that others besides her family were at risk. Before Little Flower had shown up, she'd not been in a good frame of mind to even care, and after, she'd been rather busy. The incident with Breydhik scared her far more than she wanted to admit as the guards had no idea if Breydhik and his partner had been involved with Rip or if it had been nothing more than misplaced revenge and grief for the loss of their sons, as Kendra's Second had been the target.

Would someone try something to avoid the consequences of being caught up in Rip's scheme, or would they do the honorable thing like her father had done? She had no idea. Her council had all gladly voted against her father to save themselves and their planet from sanctions, so it was entirely possible they would attack to save themselves now.

After another five laps and a drink, they made their way over to the shooting gallery, where she improved significantly, at least from her perspective. She wasn't anywhere near as good as her sister, but she could now reliably hit the stationary targets and even managed to hit about half of the moving targets on the first level. As they left, Avery informed her that she should wear her stunner at the meeting as a precaution, although she already planned to. They would all be there but wouldn't be next to her.

On Little Flower's recommendation, she'd sent Ellie a message saying she could stay for the afternoon if Ellie was still available. Ellie responded with a yes almost immediately. She found Ellie in Agate's office, where Ellie was informing her of the decisions that had been made the night before.

"Good Morning, Marsee. How was your workout?" Ellie asked.

"Pretty good, or at least I don't feel like I need to sleep for three days, so hopefully, I won't end up back at the Trauma Center like I did yesterday."

"Oh? What happened yesterday?" Agate asked with a flash of concern on her skin.

"I pushed myself too hard training with Avery. I was dehydrated and then got sick and passed out when I found out some rather disturbing news. I pretty much scared the pants off Little Flower, thinking I'd torn something again. Avery apparently carried me to the Trauma Center, although I don't remember it. I woke up there."

"Avery's one of your honor guards, right?" Agate asked, nodding in the direction of the door.

"Yeah, the other is Tamarin," she replied.

"Why *are* you training with the Guard?" Agate asked, flashing her confusion. "I would expect the healers to be managing your recovery."

"With our injuries, both Little Flower and I feel unable to defend ourselves right now should anyone else try to attack us. I got lucky with Rip. He underestimated me, but I was far stronger than I am now, and Little Flower can't even run for more than fifty paces without falling down. She's been attacked twice by members of her own species, and there's little she can do to defend herself against one of ours, so Avery has agreed to mentor us both so that we can better defend ourselves in the future. Part of that is building our strength back up, but he's also taught us how to use a stunner. Little Flower is ridiculously good with hers. She beat the simulator on the first try." Marsee beamed with pride for her sister, as she explained.

Ellie's ears pinned back with surprise. "How did she manage that?"

"Her Papa used to be an honor guard and taught her how to shoot to defend herself. She only needed to learn the specifics of how to use the stunner, not how to hit a target."

"Ah, that would make sense. So what upset you so much?" Ellie asked. "You didn't mention anything last night."

Marsee sighed and looked at Agate.

"You don't have to discuss it if you don't want to," Agate said, "Or if you'd like to talk with Ellie alone, I can leave."

"No, it's okay. It'll probably come up tomorrow anyway. I didn't know at the time, but apparently, when Rip was torturing me in the cave, he was also...sexually assaulting me. At least, that's the term the Senior Healer used. He focused many of his shocks on my sides, right about where your scales are. He may have done the same to the others. The Senior Healer was still looking into it when I left. Papa thinks that's why many of the others refused to say what happened to them."

Agate flashed horror and then fury. "That monster!"

Ellie leaned over and hugged her. "I'm so sorry, Marsee. All of this might not have happened if I'd gone out with you."

"And if you had, Rip might have decided to kill us both then and there," Marsee replied and turned to Agate. "I'm okay now. I just wasn't expecting it. I'm not hurt any worse than I was before, although it is kind of embarrassing that my screams resemble your species mating song. Although, from what the Senior Healer said, he was really bad at it. And that thought makes me downright giddy."

"He couldn't harmonize?" Agate asked, with matching bubbles of glee.

"Not even close," Marsee said with a snicker and curl of her tail.

"Good," Agate replied. "If anything, I hope they bring that little tid-bit up at the trial. If not, I might have to start a little rumor. It certainly would explain his lack of a partner. We might not be able to kill him again, but ruining what little is left of his reputation would be very en-tertaining."

Both she and Ellie chuckled at the thought.

"So Ellie was telling me you decided not to buy a moon after all," Agate continued, changing the subject.

"Yeah, it would cost too much to renovate, and I hear the cheese stinks."

Agate looked at her, thoroughly confused. "The cheese stinks? What's cheese?"

Marsee grinned. "Cheese is a Hue-man food made from the milk of some of their creatures. They've come up with a substitute, which I'm told tastes the same. It's very delicious and quite popular. One of our swear words was badly mistranslated into Hue-man as 'stinky moon cheese.'" She explained how the Hue-mans once thought the moon was made out of cheese, which made Agate laugh.

"I can just guess which swear it was, too," Agate replied. "I, for one, am glad you decided to continue to hang around with us, and I think the Research Division is a perfect fit for you."

"Thanks. The idea of buying a copy of every book ever written *had* crossed my mind, though."

Ellie gave her a very focused look and pursed her lips in a frown.

"What?" Marsee asked.

"I clearly missed out on an opportunity. I should have suggested that," Ellie said, with a laugh and a shake of her head. "Well, before you fly away on your new ship, we have a lot of work to do to prepare for the meeting."

The next several hours were spent doing just that. Food was ordered in, and Ellie informed them of their dinner plans, which made Marsee drool in anticipation.

In the afternoon, Marsee and Ellie wandered the Guild Hall for an hour, talking with several of the masters about the ideas they'd submitted. Marsee spent some time reviewing each of the items, but after the third person, she was growling in frustration with her tablet. It was the one her father had given her as a replacement for her missing one, and it was downright awful.

"How does the Council get anything done with these tablets?" Marsee muttered.

Ellie frowned at her. "What do you mean?"

"Papa gave me his when mine went missing, and it's honestly worse than the one I had as a cub," she replied.

Ellie took the tablet from her and snorted a moment later. "It *is* worse than the one you had as a cub." She handed the tablet back and opened her own, flicking through it for some time. A few minutes later, she snorted at something she read. "Come on. Let's get you something better."

They swam off in the direction of the warehouse and found people swarming everywhere. "What's going on?" Marsee asked.

"Either a delivery just came in, or one is being packed to go out," Ellie replied with a shrug and took off in the direction of the tech.

Every warehouse was organized in much the same way. This one was significantly larger than the one in New Hope but not quite as large as the one in Council City. However, when they arrived at the tablet section, the shelves were completely bare.

Ellie blinked in surprise and turned, making her way back to the section of the warehouse where the offices were located.

Iruki and another Sprite she hadn't met were in the office Ellie went to, heads hunched over a tablet they were both looking at.

"Padina, the entire section of tablets is missing. Do you know anything about that?" Ellie didn't even wait for the Sprites to say hello or even acknowledge she was there, making both of them jump and flash white.

"Yes, ma'am," the other Sprite replied, recovering quickly. "We've had a number of recently purchased tablets returned for maintenance and identified a manufacturing problem in the batch we received last month. I had them all pulled this morning to be evaluated."

Ellie nodded. "How long do you expect that to take?"

"A few hours. I take it you were looking for one?"

"Yes, seven, actually. Model 166s. Have them sent to my office as soon as you can."

"Yes, ma'am."

Marsee said nothing but mentally raised an eyebrow. That model was the current top-of-the-line and far better than the drawing tablet Ellie had given her sister.

On the way out, Ellie explained. "Anyone guild master or the equivalent and higher is guaranteed a tablet upgrade every year as part of their rank due to the secure systems they need to access. Neither you or any of the members of the Senior Council are on the appropriate version. In light of what happened to us, I want that rectified. I'm honestly surprised you didn't order a replacement already."

Marsee shrugged. "I wasn't in the mood to care before."

Ellie gave her a look that she couldn't quite decipher, so she sniffed hard and caught a whirlwind of emotions coming off of her mentor: grief, sadness, hope, and even a touch of both fear and desire, which confused her. Her body was riddled with scent, indicating the many still healing wounds, which gave her far more of an idea of how badly Ellie had been beaten than either Ellie or her father had let on.

There was a fresh wound on her paw, covered in bandage putty, but Ellie had already told her that her mother had repaired a break that hadn't healed right that morning, although it was Little Flower's scent she caught on the bandage. She didn't see any of the sickly yellow-green or bright reds indicating a major illness or injury either, so why was Ellie so sad?

When they were back in Ellie's office, Marsee activated the privacy screen. "What's going on?"

"What do you mean?" Ellie asked.

"You and Agate keep flashing me looks like the world is about to end. It's unnerving, and right now, you're a tangled mess of emotions that don't make any sense."

Ellie's ears flicked back. "What do you mean by that?"

Marsee pursed her lips, considering. The Senior Honor Guard said no one outside of the Senior Council should know what she could do, but Ellie was her mentor, and she'd shared many of her challenges over the past few months. She'd only told Ellie that her senses were recovering.

"I'm not supposed to tell you this, and if Kendra finds out, you know, I might get in serious trouble, but apparently, what happened to me with my instinct happens with all of our guards. It's a consequence of them learning how to fight and having to kill. That's the real reason I'm training with them. They're all coming back as strong, if not stronger, than what I could do with my instinct. I'm learning to control it, but it can be overwhelming at times, like with my hearing before, but so much worse. One of the things I can do now is sniff out emotions. I was doing that before without realizing it, which is why I was always so confused by people. In case you're wondering, they can't hear through a privacy screen."

Ellie's ears flicked back in surprise, and then she snorted. "I always wondered how they maintained their control. It's taken everything I had over the years. Does your uncle know?"

She nodded. "Papa said Kendra had a long talk with him, but he hasn't said anything to me about it. If I read him correctly last night, he's still not convinced. I honestly don't know what else to do."

Ellie pinned her ears and gave a low growl. "I should have clawed him when I had the chance."

"When was that?" Marsee asked.

"The first time I met him, I had just moved to Council City, and we were both in the same language studies class. He was an insufferable know-it-all back then. Why do you think Master Yellowtail gave him the wrong pronunciation for greeting a future Nest Mother? Granted, he wasn't a master then, and your uncle was barely a staffer."

Marsee snorted. "That was a prank? My uncle said he'd made a mistake."

"The oldest one in the book. They save that one for people who need to be taken down a peg or two. I honestly don't know if he realizes it yet. Anyway, I'm sorry you still have to deal with that fur-brained uncle of yours. Hopefully, with time, he'll come around. If not, I *will* claw him. That, I promise. As for your question earlier, the trial has me on edge, and I was thinking about how close we came to losing you. It's good to see you excited and back to your old self again. Promise me something, though."

"What?" Marsee asked.

"The next time your life seems hopeless, try to remember the last few days and all the wonderful and amazing experiences you would have never had if you'd ended your life that day. Avery and I are not always going to be around to stop you. Talk to someone. Give yourself time to heal and recover from whatever life throws at you. The one thing I've learned over the years is that the best things in life often happen out of the ashes of the worst."

Marsee thought about everything that had happened since that day. Hope and Little Flower, the outpouring of love from the Sprites, her newfound abilities and growing strength, her very own ship, and access to work on just about anything her heart desired. She still had a long way to go to recover, both physically and mentally, but she was starting to feel confident that it would actually occur. She felt stronger every day. Maybe Little Flower would have proposed anyway, but then again, maybe not. She knew she certainly wouldn't have been able to make a difference in other people's lives like she could now.

Marsee smiled and nodded to her mentor. "I promise. Thanks for slapping me upside the head when I needed it."

"Always," Ellie said, and then practically crushed her in a hug, but it didn't last long. Ellie pulled away and proceeded to glare at her, tail lashing, and then slapped her on the side of her head. Hard. "But don't you *dare* put me through that again! If you do, I promise I'll hit you so hard you'll think Rip was a cub in comparison and keep hitting you until I knock the sense back into you."

"Yes, Senior Guild Master," Marsee replied. She tried to sound contrite, but her tail curled anyway. She deserved that slap, and Ellie had hit her hard enough to know she wasn't treating her like she was broken and injured anymore.

"And don't you ever forget it!" Ellie growled back. "Now come on, we have work to do."

An hour or so later, Iruki appeared with the requested tablets. Marsee took hers and practically drooled over it. It was far superior to the one she'd had before.

"Ma'am, the recycled materials containers are full, and a shipment is leaving for the Ice Planet tomorrow. I'll need a signature to ship.

At that moment, a call came in for Ellie. "Marsee, you handle that," she said and swam off to take the call.

Marsee raised a brow but read through the manifest that Iruki handed her, finding scrap wood, ends of fabric spools, and other craft-related supplies. "Why are you shipping recycled materials to the Ice Planet?" Marsee asked as she kept reading. Her understanding was that most items were tossed in the recycling units and converted into materials for the printers or compost for the gardens, or at least that's what happened in New Hope.

"Their planet has few plant-based resources, so rather than throwing everything into the recycler, we collect and ship it to the Ice Planet when the containers are full. What we see as scrap wood is worth a fortune to them. In exchange, they ship us spools of recycled metals as we don't have the mining operations they do. As there's no charge for any of this, it has to be signed off on to authorize the shipment."

As she'd never signed off on a manifest before, she asked several clarifying questions to ensure she understood everything correctly. She sensed a bit of annoyance from Iruki at the questions, but Iruki never expressed it on her skin and answered all her questions. When she found nothing amiss, she signed off on it, and Iruki swam out.

Ellie paused her conversation for a moment. "Marsee, this is going to take a while. Why don't you swim those tablets up to the Seniors, get them registered to their accounts, and take their old ones to be recycled."

Marsee nodded, grabbed the stack of tablets, and swam out, with her guards shadowing as always, although once they got to the Council Building, she found her father's office empty. Checking his calendar, which she probably should have done in the first place, she noticed he was in meetings with Seniors all day.

"Where's the other entrance to the Senior's Conference room?" she asked.

Avery led her further down the hall. To her surprise, even though the Council wasn't in session, a pair of Water Sprite guards floated outside.

They flashed purple and silver but didn't stop her as she swam up and knocked. Clear Seas opened the door and motioned her in. "It's good to see you again, Translator. What can we do for you?"

"Ellie asked me to bring you these. She says the ones you have now aren't up to code. Once you've logged in, please log out of your old tablets, and I'll have them recycled for you."

She started handing out the tablets to everyone, but her father raised his paw.

"I just picked up a new tablet last week," he replied.

Marsee held out her hand. "May I see it?"

"Do you need me to log in?"

"No, the information I need can be accessed without logging in," she replied and checked once he handed it over. "Did you ask for a specific model?"

"Not by model. I never do. I just asked the person at the desk for a new tablet."

"Ah, I suppose that makes sense. The one you have here is the standard one given to any citizen. Next time, make sure you let them know it's for you. These ones are far more secure, and you're entitled to an up-grade every year, according to Ellie. I suggest putting an alert on the cat-alog for when a new version comes out. I do that just so I can drool over the latest features."

"How do you do that?" Clear Seas asked. "I'm horrible at tech."

"So, Guild Master Agate told me. She says she's tried to convince you to join our QA team on a regular basis."

He chuckled. "Well, I do tend to have techs come up fairly regularly to undo whatever mess I've gotten myself into. Odd that they never mentioned my tablet being out of date."

"They might not know, depending on who was sent up. I didn't un-til today," Marsee replied and showed him how to set the alert.

"While you're here, can you tell me what this is?" Wind Rider asked, sliding a piece of paper over to her.

She took the paper and scanned it. It was another shipping manifest, almost identical to the one she'd signed off on. "It's a shipping manifest. These are all recycled scrap materials. I just signed a very similar one a few minutes ago. The weights are different, but the number of contain-ers is the same."

She frowned as she looked at the one highlighted line. "The only thing odd about this line is that the weight is quite a bit less than the one I signed off on today, but then the code here indicates it's mostly scrap wood, which could vary significantly based on the type of wood included."

She pulled off her tablet and looked up the various weights of the lumber they had in the warehouse. "You'll want to check my math, but based on the volume of our standard shipping containers, it's still rea-sonable if the majority of the shipment was bramble wood. It's fairly popular for both its weight and durability. It's one of my favorite ma-terials to work with, although I rarely do because it's so expensive on Saber."

"Why would the Guild send scrap materials to the Ice Planet with-out a charge?" Wind Rider asked.

Before she could answer, Apakna spoke up. "We rely pretty heavily on those scrap shipments. Everything is expensive on my world. It's one of the most popular trade agreements we have. In exchange, we send scrap metal back."

This seemed to satisfy Wind Rider.

Marsee handed the paper back, and once everyone was done switching out their tablets, she left with the old ones. When she arrived back at the Guild, Iruki was out by the front desk.

"Please see that these are recycled," Marsee said, handing the tablets to her, then swam off, not waiting for a reply.

CHAPTER 56

Marsee: Fire Sticks

Ellie pushed Marsee hard the rest of the afternoon, right up until it was time to collect Little Flower and head to dinner, although Ellie frowned as they left her office and found Aris and Thatcher there. Neither of them had noticed the change in shift. "Where are Avery and Tamarin? I reserved seats for all four of you."

"The hazards of being a Guard," Aris replied. "Kendra needed them for another assignment this evening, but I assure you there will be additional guards both in the restaurant and outside. We're not taking any chances with your safety or the safety of the rest of the Senior Council."

Ellie frowned but nodded. "I'll make sure Opal sends something up to their suite."

"I'm sure they'll appreciate your generosity," Aris said and grinned. "I know I will be."

On the way out, she stopped to pick up a carry sack attachment for her harness that she'd ordered from one of the crafters that afternoon. She wanted to be able to carry Hope around, hands-free, like her sister did. Operating the drones and swimming was a challenge when you had to hold onto something.

When they arrived at the Trauma Center to pick up the others, her mother kicked everyone out, saying she wanted to check on Ellie's paw before they made their way over to dinner. Ammond, Little Flower, and Thatcher started swimming towards the exit, but she pretended to adjust the straps on the carry sack to fit Hope better and remained behind to listen.

"I don't like it. We should leave as soon as we can," her mother said.

She glanced at Aris, who shook her head and smelled of confusion. Aris didn't know what was going on either.

"Understood," Ellie replied.

Nothing more was said, and a minute later, her mother and Ellie exited the room. A fresh bandage covered Ellie's paw.

"Everything alright?" she asked, frowning with worry.

"Ellie's hand is recovering nicely," her mother replied.

Ellie grinned at her and started swimming for the exit. "I'm surprised you're not halfway to the restaurant already. Your stomach has been growling for the last hour."

"I would be, but I don't know where it is. I'm assuming you do?"

"I do. It's just off of Market Square," Ellie replied. "Come on. I'm starving, too."

When they pulled up outside the restaurant a few minutes later, she had to laugh, and her tail spiraled with delight at the sign over the door.

Someone must have been on the lookout for them because Opal appeared before they could hang up their drones. "Welcome to Fire Sticks, Translator, honored guests," she said, flashing the purple and silver and then bowing to everyone. "I'm delighted to welcome you to our opening night. The others have already arrived. If you'll follow me." Opal led them inside to a large booth, where the Seniors, GrandFather, and Henry were all waiting.

Her guards insisted on claiming seats where they had a full view of the restaurant and placing her, Little Flower, and Hope in the most protected areas. One of Opal's staff shifted the child's net that was attached to the table and swapped out the adult dishes for ones better suited for her tiny size. No one said anything as the Seniors shifted to make room for them, but it made her uncomfortable, both to watch members of the Senior Council move for her and to feel so weak and incapable of protecting herself and her family.

That will change, she promised herself.

Even still, it took everything she had not to wrap herself protectively in her cloak. She knew that the others in the restaurant were all watching, although most were trying to be polite and give them a semblance of privacy. She did have to acknowledge the flash of silver and purple from the Water Sprites when she entered, several well-wishes and comments of relief to see her recovering from her injuries as she made her way to her seat, and ignore the murmur of conversation from the other species as they wondered what was going on as they changed seats. Most, she realized, based on the badges they wore, were members of the Council or Seniors from the various guilds.

Her father's and uncle's masks were firmly in place, as were the other Seniors, and her guards were tense, even if they gave the semblance of nothing being wrong. She cautiously examined the room as she waited and found several radiating loathing, contempt, and disgust, even if they were outwardly presenting a mask of friendliness and concern.

How many of them were involved? she wondered, feeling guilty she hadn't spent time investigating.

"Does anyone have any food allergies or restrictions we should be aware of?" Opal asked.

"No fire sticks or anything spicy for Marsee," her mother said. "She's not recovered enough for that yet."

She scowled at her mother, as that was all she'd been drooling about all day.

"I'm sorry, Kitten," her father said.

She sighed dramatically. "My soul is crushed beyond repair, but I suppose I'll survive another week."

"Two," her mother said.

She scowled at her mother again and then glared at Ellie. "Did you really have to invite *her*?"

The entire table laughed, including her mother.

Opal waited, but there were no other allergies. "The Senior Guild Master ordered the chef's sampler for your meal, which consists of five different dishes geared towards each species' preferences. To the best of my knowledge, they are safe for every species should you wish to try them."

"Thank you, Opal," Ellie replied, and a moment later, the dishes started arriving.

"Ellie said Temperate and Petra were invited," Marsee said as she waited for the dishes to appear. "Is everything alright?"

"Temperate's on duty tonight," Clear Seas replied. "Stormy wanted to take his place, but he's currently home and swearing at an overdue homework assignment. Apparently, basket weaving is not in his future. He's been trying to weave a simple basket for days now, and every time he gets close to being done, it falls apart on him."

Marsee chuckled. "Sounds like me when I was learning how to weave. I actually managed to somehow weave my tail into one of my projects, and Mama had to cut me out."

Humor bubbled on his skin. "I remember that picture."

"You've seen it?" she asked.

"Your father showed me. We were having dinner at my house when the picture arrived. I'll have to tell Stormy about that incident. It might help him not feel so bad about his difficulties now."

She grinned and turned to Wind Rider. "And Petra? I keep meaning to find time to come visit."

"She had a hard night and hasn't been sleeping well. She's growing faster than the skin grafts can handle. When I went to pick her up, she was sound asleep, so I decided not to wake her."

She nodded her understanding, although her nose told her more was going on than they were saying. They were taking a risk going out in public as a group before the meeting, and this was as much a show to convince the people that they were safe as it was a celebration of Opal's opening night. "Please let her know I'm thinking of her."

Wind Rider said she would.

"So, tell me, Jer," Ellie said. "Did you ever get your shower fixed?"

Jer growled. "No, and I have no idea what's going on. The shower in Myra's suite still doesn't work. It works fine when the techs are there, but the next time I try, it stops working. Thankfully, the one in my office is working again."

"It works perfectly fine for me," her mother said and popped a piece of food in her mouth. Humor radiated off of her, although her expression was her normal calm mask. "I still think you're using it wrong."

Her father scowled at her mother, but it was Ellie's scent that intrigued her. It was dancing in a way that she'd never seen before.

Ellie made eye contact with her and grinned ever so slightly. It was enough to tell her what was really happening.

"Have you tried resetting it?" Marsee asked, instantly playing along.

"Of course. It was the first thing I tried," he replied. "Personally, I think Wind Rider is behind this somehow."

"I swear I had nothing to do with it," Wind Rider replied. "And the guards can attest I haven't even been near your suite. I'm not even sure where you're staying."

"It would be quite the prank, would it not?" Ellie asked.

Wind Rider shrugged, but based on her scent, she had a pretty good idea what was going on, too. "It does have the markings of a Flyer-worthy prank. You wouldn't happen to know anything about it, would you?"

"I might," Ellie replied and popped another piece of food in her mouth.

Wind Rider grinned, and her father turned on Ellie with a scowl. "You?! You're behind this?"

Ellie shrugged. "Well, how else was I supposed to test all the security updates you requested? Sadly, I keep finding new bugs that Lowell has to squash. She's nearly as frustrated as you are at this point. Her work is not normally quite so sloppy, but then I've been highly motivated to make sure the programming is secure."

"Security updates?" her father asked with a scowl.

Ellie nodded. "Personally, I think you've been overworking her with all your requests. I'm going to have to give her a month off for all the overtime she's put in this week. I, however, have been having a great deal of fun finding new and inventive ways to break into the system and...test it out. I never thought I'd have so much fun programming a shower, but this week has been full of surprises, has it not?"

Laughter followed her statement, mostly prompted by her father's scowl.

"So tell me, Wind Rider? Did I measure up to your challenge?"

WindRider tilted her head in a slight nod. "Eh. It was quite entertaining but rather limited in its scope and target. I think you still have room for improvement."

"So you *were* behind this," her father growled at Wind Rider. "I knew it."

"Not directly," Wind Rider stated. "But if Ellie is going to earn an honorary Flyer status, she'll have to put in the work. I did offer to mentor her in that regard." She turned to Ellie. "How does your shtick go again? Ah yes, Poof. Apprentice Level Two."

"Oh gods," Clear Seas replied. "Can you just imagine Ellie as a Master Flyer? We'd all be doomed."

More laughter followed, but Ellie just grinned and popped another bite of food in her mouth.

Even with the tension, it was by far and away the best meal Marsee had ever had, but it wasn't just the food. She'd never had more than formal interactions with the other Seniors, so this was the first time she'd had to really get to know them.

She'd been nervous at first, but following the teasing of her father, Ellie quickly steered the conversation to some of the research projects they'd reviewed that day and pulled everyone in. They were all very interested to know what she was excited about, which didn't surprise her, as what she decided would have long-lasting impacts on the Consortium. She also discovered that Wind Rider was as much of a fantasy book nerd as she was and had many of the same favorite authors. There was no discussion about what had happened to her or the upcoming trial, just lots of animated discussion and laughter, but the worry and tension never really left the others. Only Hope seemed free of concern.

They were picking over the remains of the last dish when Aris caught her attention as her scent changed to fear. Aris gave a slight nod in Ellie's direction and sniffed.

She turned her attention to Ellie and froze, absolutely terrified as she realized what was wrong with Ellie. She tried to catch Ellie's attention, but she was deep in conversation with Clear Seas.

After some thought on how to inform Ellie without causing a scandal, she pulled off her tablet, which was rude in and of itself, but made a point of wanting to take a picture of the group, which the others humored. Then, she pulled it under the table, appearing to fiddle with the picture. In reality, though, she sent an urgent message to Ellie, with a slight delay, so it wouldn't appear to be coming from her.

A minute later, Ellie's tablet dinged. She frowned and turned to Clear Seas. "Forgive my rudeness. That was my urgent message tone. I need to check this."

"Of course," he replied.

Ellie pulled up the tablet and then flicked her eyes towards Marsee, briefly swallowing hard.

"Is everything okay?" Wind Rider asked, seeing her expression.

"Unfortunately, no. I'm very sorry, everyone, but it looks like I'm going to have to leave early. I've had a...family emergency come up, and I need to head back home immediately. I won't be able to make it to the meeting. Agate, can you cover for me?"

"Of course," Agate said, frowning. "I hope everyone is okay."

"I hope so, too," Ellie replied, frowning with her own worry.

Clear Seas briefly flashed his concern. Marsee could also sniff his confusion, but he said nothing, knowing that others could see him.

"Ellie, you can't jump yet," her mother stated. "It's too soon. You're not healed enough, and you just had surgery this morning."

"I have to, Myra. I'll be fine," Ellie replied.

"Then I'm going with you," her mother insisted.

"That's not necessary," Ellie said.

"Yes, it is. You're not jumping without a healer. The risk is far too high. If you don't want me to go with you, that's fine, but you're either taking a healer, or I'm going to have to ground your ship. Please believe me. It's too soon for you to jump safely."

Ellie frowned but nodded. "Fine. You can come. Everyone, please enjoy the rest of your meal. It's been paid for already. I've really enjoyed tonight, and I thank you for your company."

The others excused her, and Ellie and her mother bolted, only briefly stopping to talk with Opal on their way out.

Marsee watched them go with a solid lump of fear in her throat, wondering if she'd ever see her mentor again. Plastering on a calm face that she didn't remotely feel, she turned back to the table and continued on with the conversation, although at that point, it was clear the meal was pretty much over. They talked for another fifteen or twenty minutes and started making their way out.

While her thoughts were entirely on Ellie, she, too, made a point of swimming over to Opal before they left. "Opal, that was by far the best meal I have ever eaten, absolute perfection. Thank you."

Opal flashed her joy at the words. "You're very welcome, Translator. I hope we'll see you again soon?"

"You're going to be sick of me before I'm able to jump home," Marsee promised.

Opal grinned. "I doubt that's possible. You will always have a seat. I can never thank you enough for what you have done for me."

"That meal was more than thanks enough. Have a wonderful night. Until next time?"

"Until next time," Opal replied with a smile and a flash of happiness.

They swam back to the suite, but she barely listened to the conversation that was happening around her as her fear and grief for her mentor nearly consumed her. She knew it would be days before she knew if Ellie survived or not, but it was her third heat, and she knew in her very soul that her mentor was as good as dead. Still, she prayed to the Ancient Gods to let her mother pull off one more miracle. If anyone could, it would be her.

The moment they were alone in the room and the door shut, Marsee broke down and curled up into a tiny ball on the bed, whimpering with the grief she could no longer contain.

"What's wrong, Marsee?" Little Flower asked, climbing onto the bed to comfort her.

"Ellie's dying. She didn't have a family emergency. She's in heat. How or why, I don't know, but no one survives their third heat!"

Little Flower hugged her but didn't gasp or react in surprise.

Marsee pulled back in fury. "You knew!"

"I figured it out last night. It's what I was working on. I couldn't tell you because of patient confidentiality, and I wasn't sure until I spoke with Mama and Ammond this morning."

"You should have told me!" she yelled. "She's my mentor!"

"I couldn't, Marsee. It's an ethics violation. I would have been in a lot of trouble if I had, but that's why I had you spend the day with her. How did you figure it out?"

Marsee slumped back down, her anger drained and replaced with her fear again. "I knew something was bothering her all day, but I couldn't figure out what. I tried sniffing her out. We worked on that today, like I did with Ammond, but I didn't find anything. Aris told me at dinner to sniff Ellie, and once I did, it was obvious. A few more minutes and every male Saber in that restaurant would have noticed, too. Thank the moons it didn't happen in the middle of the meeting. Could you just imagine the scandal?"

"I wonder who she would have picked," Little Flower mused.

The thought was enough to shake her out of her fear and grief for a moment. "Uncle Marcus," she decided. "Even though she's still angry with him, our instinct gravitates towards strength and power. He's not the biggest or the strongest, the guards in the room would be, but he has the most power."

"That's for sure. He positively reeks of power and confidence. Did I ever show you the drawing I did of him?"

"The one you used in your pictionary?" Marsee asked.

"No, it's one I did of him the day I first met him in person. I walked in on him and our parents talking in Papa's office. He was just sitting in one of the chairs, but he commanded the very air in that room, and our parents are not lightweights in that department either. I gave the drawing to Papa for his office, but I took a picture of it. It's one of my favorites." Little Flower crawled off the bed, walked over to pick up her tablet from the table, and started scrolling. "Here it is," she said and handed it over. "It was all I could do not to run back to the room to grab my sketchbook that instant."

Marsee frowned at the picture. She'd seen that look from her uncle far too many times, and it terrified her every time. She handed the tablet back, unsure what to say, but Little Flower frowned.

"You're shaking," Little Flower said. "Are you alright?"

"No," she replied.

Unable to control her fear or explain further, she climbed off the bed and started pacing, but she stopped a moment later as her tablet dinged with Ellie's tone. Scrambling for it, she opened it up and absently sat down to read.

My dearest Marsee,

I'm so very sorry you had to find out this way. I didn't want you to worry about me before the trial. You have enough to deal with. Thank you for warning me and giving me a way to escape without everyone knowing. Rip Current removed my implant. Why, I have no idea.

I want you to know that it was entirely my decision not to have it replaced. I want cubs. My need for them is so strong that it makes me cry at night, even after a hundred years. I have a feeling you understand. Your mother says everything is progressing normally, and she's hopeful that this will count as my second heat, not my third, since my first one never fully finished. Your mother is one of the best healers on all five planets, and she's pulled off miracles before. If anyone can get me through this, it's her.

Assuming I do make it through my heat, I'm moving into Little Flower's room in the Tower so your mother can monitor my care through the pregnancy. We discussed staying on the Water World, but my only real chance of survival is back on Saber, and I won't be able to leave until after the pregnancy. I know I promised to stay with you and I'm sorry I couldn't keep that promise. I hope you'll understand and forgive me. If something happens, go to Clear Seas and Wind Rider. They'll protect you.

I'm sorry I won't be there for you tomorrow. I really hoped to make it through the trial, at least. I don't want you to worry about me. Keep your eyes open for another attack, remain calm no matter what happens, and focus on Little Flower. She'll need you just as much as you need her.

If you feel safe enough, please join me as soon as you can. I'll be on bed rest, but my tail will be perfectly capable of thwacking you, and there's so much more I want to teach you. If everything goes well, I'll need your help while I'm out on maternity leave. I know that's asking a lot and that you might not feel comfortable or safe returning to Saber, so I'll understand if you don't and will return as soon as I'm cleared to fly.

Know that I have never once regretted taking you on as my protege, even after everything that's happened to us. Time and again, you've proven me right. The decisions you made yesterday changed the universe in ways you may not understand for a very long time, but you did so with compassion and love for billions of people you've never met and without a hint of avarice or greed. Well, except for drooling over that ship, but I can't blame you there. I had a lot of fun designing the retrofit for my ship, too. What's more, you didn't think for a second to use your power over us for your own benefit, outside of teasing us, which we all thoroughly deserved.

You saved the Guild and my life's work and showed me how mature you really are, not that I ever had any doubts. You were a Master long before I met you in person. You excel at everything you put your heart into, but that isn't what makes you a Master. You see the world in a way that no one else does. You fit the pieces of the puzzle together before everyone else even finds the pieces. You are more than ready for your new role, more than anyone I have ever promoted, Guild Master Marsee Bet Chenzira (poof). Of that, I have no doubt.

Whatever happens, live your life to the fullest, and watch your tail around rocking chairs. With all my love and hopes for you to have the most amazing of futures, your incredibly proud mentor, Elliana Reighly Khihar.

The tablet slipped out of her paws and fell to the floor with a clatter, and she just sat there staring at the space where it had been, jaw dropped.

"What is it?" Little Flower asked.

"She has to be pulling my tail," Marsee replied when her brain could finally form words again. She reached down, picked up her tablet, and reread the message. With a shaking paw, she switched over to her guild account and stared at the title on her profile for nearly a minute before pulling up her certificate.

Marsee Bet Chenzira
Guild Master, Research Division Senior

It had been signed and dated the night before, long before Ellie had left, and she hadn't even noticed or realized that a promotion came with the position. She should have, she realized now. Ellie had hinted at it on more than one occasion, but she hadn't realized just how big the Research Fund was. Ellie had made it seem like it was a small side project, a department that Ellie managed on her own, but listed under the certificate were all of the people who now directly reported to her, all of them Guild Masters themselves, heads of research for each planet, one for each of the various disciplines, and they in turn, had staff managing the various sub-disciplines. She was in charge of hundreds, if not thousands, of people now.

"Who, Ellie? What did she do?"

Marsee nodded and handed the tablet over to her sister, mute with panic.

"Guild Master?!" Little Flower squeaked. "She promoted you to Guild Master?"

Marsee sat there for a long time, trying to process it. "She had to," she said eventually with a sigh. "I don't deserve it, but if she doesn't survive, she wants me to take over for her. I'd have to be a Guild Master to be nominated."

"Did she say that?" Little Flower asked.

"Not exactly, but that's in the Guild Charter. The Sprites might still vote for me either way, but the others wouldn't vote for a Journeyman, even if she did publicly state she wanted me to take over. She did say that if she survives, she wants me to fill in for her while she's on maternity leave, and she can't make me the Acting Senior either if I'm not already a Guild Master. We had a long conversation about that after Rip promoted me."

"Can I read what she sent?" Little Flower asked.

Marsee nodded and switched back over to the message.

Her sister sat down on the bed beside her and began to read. When she was done, Little Flower stood up to face her. "Marsee, I need you to trust me and believe me right now. Ellie didn't promote you because of some silly charter. She promoted you because of what you did last night. You gave up a level of wealth and power that these worlds have never seen, but I have. I've seen what that kind of power can do to people. It changes them and the people around them, and *never* for the better. We have a saying. There are no ethically sourced billionaires. The only way someone can obtain that level of wealth is at the expense of others. Even if every credit was a gift, you saw what keeping that gift would have meant, the projects that would have been put on hold, and the amount of suffering the people of this world would have experienced."

Little Flower pointed to the last section. "This. Right here. This is why she promoted you, not because she has to, but because you proved to her last night that you deserved it. You gave up a life of leisure for a job that will come with a *lot* of hard work and many difficult decisions. You could have bought an entire fleet of public transport ships, but you didn't. You picked the smallest ship they dangled in front of you and only made the necessary modifications to make it comfortable for me. The investments you chose were the ones that were financially the best for the Guild and the Consortium, not you. The changes you made weren't to protect your interests. They were to allow you to help a broader range of people, and you only kept what we would need to live comfortably and insisted that it be no more than what Ellie made. You ensured that Rip Current's other victims would be taken care of for the rest of their lives. And if I know you, you'll turn around and reinvest everything you make back into those programs. Your level of skill in any one craft isn't what matters or makes you a Guild Master. This is."

Little Flower whacked her hard in the chest with the tablet. "You. Your heart and your honor."

Marsee grabbed the tablet from her and re-read the message. "Do you really believe that?"

"With every fiber of my being, Guild Master Chenzira. And what's more, you had better swim into that council chamber believing it to your very core because, in another week, you might very well be Senior Guild Master. When she comes out of jump, she needs to see that she's left her life's work in the best possible paws this universe has ever seen so that she can focus on staying alive. She's chosen you to succeed her, not Agate or Nardal or anyone else she's ever worked with, because *you're* the only one she trusts, and she wants everyone else to see that, including you."

Marsee took several deep breaths and watched absently as Little Flower turned and began to get Hope ready for bed. After some thought, she read the message yet again, then fired off a response to Ellie even though she figured she was probably already in jump and out of reach.

"Thank you. I promise I will take good care of your Guild. I love you, and I'll see you in a few weeks."

The thought of going home terrified her, but if Ellie survived her heat, there was no way she was missing out on what could very well be the last few weeks of her mentor's life, even if it put her own life at risk.

Message sent, she fired off another message, and had an almost immediate reply. She stood and clipped her tablet back to her harness, then walked over and helped Little Flower lift Hope into the crib. "I'll be back late. Don't wait up for me."

"Where are you going?"

"To the Guild. Agate and I have work to do. I'll leave one of the guards here," Marsee said as she threw her cloak back on.

Little Flower grinned at her and said nothing, but Marsee could sniff that she was proud of her.

Squaring her shoulders and taking another deep breath, she walked out the door, praying she had the strength to live up to the destiny Ellie had just handed over to her.

Laura Napoli was born and raised in northern Vermont and continues to make the area her home. When not spending her time on the warm clicky box (computer), she is the caregiver to four heating cats who provide her with heat, massage, acu-paw-ture, and purr-therapy in exchange for pets and catnip treaties.

PUBLICATIONS

Book 1: The Tails of Little Flower
Book 2: The Pride of Little Flower
Book 3: The Whiskers of Hope
Book 4: The Paws of Hope
Book 5: Saber's Instinct
Book 6: Saber's Guard

COMING SOON

Book 7: Saber's Guild

IMPORTANT IN-FUR-MATION

CHARACTER PURR-REFERENCE

SENSITIVITY IN-FUR-MATION

HTTPS://HEATINGCATS.COM